Margaret Thomson Davis

HOLD ME FOREVER

A KIND OF IMMORTALITY

arrow books

This edition published by Arrow Books in 2004

Arrow Books
The Random House Group Limited
20 Vauxhall Bridge Road, London SW1V 2SA

Random House Australia (Pty) Limited
20 Alfred Street, Milsons Point, Sydney
New South Wales 2061, Australia

Random House New Zealand Limited
18 Poland Road, Glenfield
Auckland 10, New Zealand

Random House (Pty) Limited
Endulini, 5a Jubilee Road, Parktown 2193, South Africa

The Random House Group Limited Reg. No. 954009

www.randomhouse.co.uk

A CIP catalogue record for this book
is available from the British Library

Papers used by Random House are natural, recyclable products made from wood grown in sustainable forests. The manufacturing processes conform to the environmental regulations of the country of origin

ISBN 0 09 190294 0

Printed and bound in Great Britain by
Cox & Wyman Ltd, Reading, Berkshire

Margaret Thomson Davis

HOLD ME FOREVER

arrow books

Acknowledgements

I'd like to thank all the people who gave so generously their time in helping me with my research. As usual the librarians of the Mitchell Reference Library in Glasgow spared no effort to do what they could for me. Indeed, in any library I've visited I've been equally well-served. It was a librarian who drew my attention to Tony Martin's excellent work on the history of Blackhill.

Other people have allowed me to interview them and as a result I have accumulated a vast number of tapes rich in knowledge and experience that I was privileged to draw on when I was creating this novel.

I thank them all, but especially the following:

One of my most loyal fans, Ina Thomson, who also has taken many strolls down memory lane in order to enrich my research about old Glasgow.

Hughie Healy – an absolute gem and another of my sources for stories about Glasgow life and characters. Then there's Willie MacLean, who has become my expert on life in the Gorbals and quite a 'character' himself.

The ladies and gentlemen who spoke to me in the community centres of various Glasgow housing estates, or 'schemes' as they are known in Glasgow. My apologies to the ladies of Drumchapel if I seem to have done the place less than justice. In this book Drumchapel is seen through the eyes of the awful Sophie character.

Iain Brown, MBE, MA. Med. AFBPsS. Ch. Psychol. who advised me on the psychology.

Mark Hamilton of Rock Steady Security Ltd, a man of courage and integrity.

James Muir, for allowing me to use his poetry.

Robin Lloyd Jones for the title.

My son, Kenneth Davis for advice on the karate scenes.

Chapter One

Andrina didn't understand the reason for her mother's hatred of Bernard, and the intensity with which she fought to prevent her having anything to do with him. It was one thing to dislike someone at first meeting; she could understand that. But such black hatred? That's what it was. From the moment Sophie's flint-like stare fixed on Bernard O'Maley, the intensity of her feelings was obvious. All right. Her daughter was only fifteen and still at school. But Sophie had never prevented Andrina from being friendly with the crowd at the church, which included men even older than Bernard. Although, of course, 'crowd' was the operative word. In the past, Andrina had never been alone with any male person other than her father.

She'd tried to point out to her mother that she was mature for her age. At least, physically mature. This had immediately made everything worse. Sophie had an aversion to anything physical. She became acutely anxious, for instance, the moment Andrina began to develop breasts. She insisted on binding her tightly with a broad stretch bandage to try to flatten her out. She'd bought her girdles and tight elastic knickers in a determined effort to hide the voluptuous swell of Andrina's hips and control the provocative bounce and wiggle of her buttocks. She despaired of what Andrina was coming to, and what she would be like at twenty-one if this was how she was at fifteen.

Flesh, to Sophie, was not only obscene but somehow unchristian. Andrina couldn't help giggling about this with some of her pals at school, although afterwards she was secretly plagued with guilt and anxiety in case her mother would discover her disloyalty. Her mother's extreme views and constant desperation made her seem pathetic and vulnerable as well as frightening. Andrina loved her fearfully.

Sophie was as lean as a greyhound, with prematurely grey hair pinned back so tightly it gave the skin of her face a taut, mask-like appearance. She scorned any kind of decoration and wore only the darkest, the plainest and most severe clothes. Even her glasses were plain steel-rimmed.

'But why are you so much against Bernard?' Andrina asked, all round-eyed and innocent, although by this time she'd begun to suspect why. It wasn't that, according to Sophie, Bernard's family were 'a disgrace', and that his father and brothers had been arrested on occasion for being drunk and disorderly. Or that his mother did the devil's work by reading teacups and cards. It wasn't that they came from Garngad. *Garngad*, of all places – one of the toughest districts in Glasgow. It wasn't that Bernard was four years older than her, or even that he was a Catholic – although his religion, Sophie insisted, was the main reason for her objections.

No. It was because Bernard was too *physical*.

Andrina knew this by the way the thin thread of her mother's mouth warped as she said the words.

'He's too physical.'

The fact that Bernard was so physical was what Andrina found irresistible about him. Already he was a black belt in karate and had shoulders like a prize bull. His eyes were watchful, knowledgeable, and reflected maturity and experience far beyond his nineteen years. He stirred excitement in her. Especially when he smiled and his cleft chin deepened and a wicked glimmer narrowed his eyes. There was no comparison between him and the boys at her school. Bernard was a man.

She remembered thinking on the day they met what a strikingly attractive guy he was, with eyes as dark as his coal-black hair. She had been walking with Mary Gardner and Sheila Preston in Kelvingrove Park. His companions were a couple of gangly youths – she couldn't remember their names now. They had been laughing and kicking a ball about. Bernard spoke first.

Soon they were all talking and laughing together. Then the

girls began kicking the ball and it became quite hilarious. The crowd of them met in the park several times after that and fooled about and had a laugh. Often they went to a café for ice-cream. Andrina became eager to please Bernard. She felt self-conscious about her appearance and hated wearing her gym-slip and her prim, white blouse and navy tie after school hours. They made her look far too young. She pretended to Sophie that she was anxious not to ruin her school clothes but 'keep them good for school'. She pestered her mother to allow her to wear stockings, using a plea that she thought might be the most effective with Sophie: 'It doesn't seem decent to go around with bare legs at my age, Mum. I'll soon be sixteen.' The idea was that because it was summer, wool would be out of the question and so the stockings would have to be silk.

She saved her pocket-money and bought a box of face powder, a tin of mascara with a little brush, and a bright red lipstick. The make-up was applied in secret, safely away from the house, and later rubbed off before returning. She would slip up another close a few yards along the road and around the corner, away from Sophie's watching eyes at the top floor window. There she would fluff sweet scented powder over her face, and while Mary or Sheila held the mirror she'd apply the lipstick. She'd spit on the cake of mascara and rub the brush over it before carefully applying it to her lashes. Then she would take her turn in holding the mirror for Mary and Sheila in between their shared bouts of excited giggling. The girls would shield her with their jackets as she undid the stretch bandage. She'd slip it from beneath her blouse or her dress, then roll it up and stuff it into her pocket. Later, as she became more daring, she even wriggled out of the restricting girdle and knickers.

A couple of times they'd gone with the boys to the local cinema, once to see a Charlie Chaplin film, and another time to see *The Ghost Train*. Andrina had clutched at Bernard during that film and he stretched his arm around her and held her close. The muscle of his arm was hard against her, and the heat of his body made her dissolve into one giant thumping heart.

He'd kissed her for the first time then and it was like rose petals opening up inside her, sweet and beautiful. She couldn't wait for him to kiss her again. His kisses blotted out all her anxieties, her uncertainties, her fears. Everything dissolved and disappeared and she was left floating in mindless ecstasy.

Bernard lost no time in suggesting they go out on their own. He called at the house for her. He dwarfed the kitchen of the small flat in the quiet end of Sauchiehall Street, his muscular body filling the room with a disturbing kind of energy.

Andrina's father, Andrew McPherson, had been pleasant enough. He put aside his newspaper and invited Bernard to sit down.

'And where are the pair of you off to?' he asked.

'Bill Haley and the Comets are in the Regal. We thought we'd go and see what they're like.'

Sophie cut in: 'That dreadful film that's making people riot all over the place and tear up the seats?'

'Oh, I don't think Andrina and I will be rioting or tearing up seats.' Bernard's grin deepened the cleft in his chin and made his eyes narrow. It was then that Andrina saw her mother's hatred.

'She's far too young to be going out at all,' Sophie snapped. 'You've obviously left school.'

'Yes, I'm nineteen.'

'What school did you go to?'

'St Francis.'

Sophie flashed a look at her husband that said CATHOLIC in capital letters.

Anxiously, Andrina tugged at Bernard's arm. She was desperate to escape from the house before her mother spoiled everything. 'We'll miss the start of the big picture.'

Rock Around The Clock was wonderfully exciting with its deafening, pistol-cracking beat. It vibrated an energy that was instantly, wildly infectious. Andrina and Bernard had loudly belted out the words with everyone else, and clapped their hands and wriggled around and bounced about in their seats. Afterwards, they had jived along Sauchiehall Street, not caring what anyone thought. Bernard flung her high in the air, bounced her on his bent knees, down between his legs, high in the air again, then whisked her round and round. She remembered the joyous sense of exhilaration and freedom. Then she'd caught a glimpse of her mother's rigid, disapproving face. The cold stare behind the steel-rimmed glasses watching from the front room window made joy immediately wither away. Fear took its place.

'My mother's at the window. I'll have to go. Thanks Bernard. It was great.'

She flew up the stone stairs into the house, excuses and apologies agitating from her lips before she'd even reached the front room. Then she hurried after Sophie into the kitchen.

'You disgust me,' Sophie said, 'making a disgusting exhibition of yourself for all to see. Get out of my way. I don't want to be contaminated by you.'

The barrier of ice around the older woman was something that never ceased to fill Andrina with panic. The panic had taken root long ago in the nightmare mists of childhood. At primary school it had been tied up with the times she'd come home to find Sophie had gone, and each time she believed it was for ever. So she would huddle down on the stone steps of the close, not knowing what to do. She had been left on her own long before her school days, but these memories were such dangerous pools of terror, her mind's eye shrunk away from them.

Somehow she had developed the conviction that everything was her fault, including the times her mother and father quarrelled – and in the earlier days they quarrelled a great deal. Sometimes her father would say to her mother, 'You ought to be ashamed. It's the talk of the place, the way that child's been treated. It was bad enough finding out that you've been carrying on with every Tom, Dick and Harry while I was away. But to be reported to the NSPCC; to be told that the "cruelty man" was here; to learn that neighbours had found her on her own, shivering and whimpering in the dark, without anything to eat or drink, shut in a room stinking of urine and faeces. I felt horrified and ashamed. But you're obviously incapable of any normal feelings. Especially for her.' Andrina knew and even had some understanding of the neglect she'd suffered, neglect that resulted in what she suffered now. Yet neither the knowledge nor the understanding helped her to cope with her present emotions. Panic overwhelmed her still.

'I've more feelings for Andrina than you, and the chances are she isn't even mine,' her father told her mother.

'You know as well as I do that she's yours,' her mother would rage. 'You're just trying to torment me. It's just your bad mind . . .'

He sadly shook his head. 'You're a fine one to accuse anyone of being bad. I was away fighting for an ideal with the International Brigade in Spain. Then I was fighting against the evil of Hitler. Only to discover I had an evil nearer home to contend with.'

More than once he'd said, 'If I hadn't been a committed Christian, Sophie, I would have flung you out on to the street years ago.'

Then Mother had become 'saved', and joined Father's church – the Church of Jesus. By that time Andrina was about nine or ten, and from then on she saw even less of her mother. Sophie, in her usual extreme way, plunged herself with almost maniac efficiency into doing good works. She was the one who laid out the dead, the one who visited the sick and ran their errands.

When she was in the house she filled the kitchen with people including, ironically enough, any neglected and abused children of the neighbourhood. Tough, snotty-nosed little boys called her mother 'Aunty Sophie'. They were made a fuss of, and sat up on the draining board beside the sink at the kitchen window. They had their noses blown, their faces scrubbed, their hair brushed. They were told what good boys they were. Then they were given a bag of black-striped balls or jelly babies.

Andrina had been darkly jealous of them, and as often as not her feelings were returned. The boys were usually angelic in her mother's presence but outside the house the language even of the youngest could be foul. She remembered one little boy who, if they met on the stairs, used to spit on her. He was one of her mother's special favourites. Andrina hated him, but she was careful to hide her feelings from her mother and from everyone. Just like her mother and father hid theirs.

Sophie and Andrew McPherson still argued in private, although admittedly not so often. Her father had long since forgiven her mother – or so he said. In public, they gave the impression of being almost saintly in their devotion to one another, as well as to the church.

The only time Andrina could remember her mother turning any attention on her, and what she hoped was love, was on the few occasions when Sophie said, 'If you're very good and please Mummy, Mummy will tuck you up and read you a story tonight.' More often than not, despite straining to do her utmost to please, nothing happened. Only occasionally was Andrina rewarded by this much-treasured attention.

She had pleased her mother by promising to have nothing more to do with Bernard, although secretly she couldn't imagine cutting Bernard out of her life. To her he'd become the symbol of life itself. She admired the way he had stuck to his guns about being her friend. He'd spoken first of all to her father. McPherson had listened with that sympathetic concentration he used when dealing with union, or council, or church business. He sat leaning forward, arms resting on knees, hands clasped between them. After hearing Bernard out, he tipped back his portly body and began the ritual of pressing tobacco into the bowl of his pipe, then flaring several matches against it before puffing and drawing on the stem. All this time he appeared to be giving the matter under discussion the serious weight of his attention. Eventually, he removed the pipe from his mouth and gazed sadly at Bernard. He could do this most effectively because he had drooping 'spaniel' eyes set in a loose crêpe skin that looked darkly stained with nicotine.

'Of course I trust you, lad. Despite what some folk think, I believe you come from good stock. Your father and I are both proud members of the Royal Artillery Club.'

'You know my father?' Bernard was pleasantly surprised and suddenly filled with hope.

'We've spoken on occasion at the club.' McPherson smiled between leisurely puffs. 'I remember he was most generous in his congratulations when I received my VC. He insisted on buying me quite a few drinks. He would have spent his last penny on me if I'd let him. I had to explain that I regard my Victoria Cross as representing not only what I did, but as a symbol of the courage of many brave men, like your father himself.'

McPherson enjoyed thinking about the club and it showed in his face. Like most of the gunners and ex-gunners who were members (every Artillery man was a member automatically), he liked a good drink – and Patrick O'Maley wasn't the only man who always insisted on buying him one. 'I don't manage to get to the club so often now,' he said regretfully, 'I'm kept so busy with council business.'

'To get back to what we were talking about,' Bernard prompted. 'If you trust me, does that mean it's OK for me to go with Andrina?'

Councillor McPherson fixed him with another sad stare. 'If it were only up to me lad . . . but . . .'

'I know Mrs McPherson is opposed to our friendship, but can't you talk to her, use your influence?'

'Andrina is very young. I can see my wife's point of view.'

'She's almost sixteen.'

'And still very immature.'

'I'm very fond of her. And I'm determined . . .'

'Yes. I can see you're a strong-minded young man, but I'll have to ask you to leave now.' McPherson pulled a gold watch from his waistcoat pocket and took his time studying it. It was attached to a heavy chain and an amber fob. It had belonged to his late father and he liked to show it off as often as possible. 'I've people coming for advice. I'm on the housing committee and it takes up a lot of my time. Finding a decent home is such a problem for so many people nowadays. I do my best to help but . . .' He rose with a sigh. 'Like most things in life, it is more complicated than people realise.'

Bernard rose too. 'I just want to be friends with Andrina, even if we're just two in a crowd of friends. What's the harm in that? I don't understand what all the fuss is about.'

Although of couse he did. The question about his school, and the look that Sophie McPherson had flashed to her husband, had not escaped him. In Glasgow, the religion you were born into was of prime importance. Even when he was little more than a toddler, he had been faced with the aggressive question of 'Are you a Billy or a Dan?'

'There is no need for any fuss, Bernard. And no need to go on as if Andrina is the only girl in the world.'

But as far as Bernard was concerned, she was. 'I'll speak to Mrs McPherson,' he said desperately. 'But if you could just put in a good word for me first, Councillor McPherson. If you could use your influence . . .'

How many times had McPherson heard that phrase before – especially since he'd become a member of the housing committee. He nodded sagely at the young man. 'I'll certainly do my best on your behalf. That I can promise you.'

'Thank you.'

For a horrible moment McPherson thought Bernard was going to pounce on him and kiss him.

He felt sorry for Bernard. For no apparent reason, Sophie had taken an intense dislike to the young man. Yet he was good-looking, civil spoken, and ambitious to do well. He also thought the world of Andrina.

He was a left-footer, of course, but as McPherson had already pointed out to Sophie, he didn't seem a very devout one. Anyway, what did it matter? Since McPherson had been in the army and fought side by side with Catholics as well as Protestants, he no longer judged a man by what foot he kicked with.

'What does it matter? What does it matter?' Sophie had been outraged. Since her conversion she was much more bigoted than he'd ever been. 'Of course it matters. They're ignorant. They worship idols. They accept everything that man in Rome says as gospel. They blindly follow him, instead of Jesus and the word of God . . .' She had gone on at some length, until he had stopped listening to her. Then she changed tack and said, 'Anyway, that O'Maley creature's disgustingly physical.'

She should talk, McPherson thought. Now he leaned towards Bernard and said, 'She's through in the kitchen, if you'd like a word.'

'No, I'll come back. I'll wait and see what you can do first. Thank you again, Councillor McPherson. It was good of you to hear me out. I know Andrina's young. I know I'd have to wait a year or two before we can be anything more than friends, but I must have a chance. If I'm not allowed to see her at all, she might find someone else and forget about me. That mustn't happen, Councillor McPherson. I want to be friends with her, and then court her, and then eventually marry her.'

McPherson gazed solemnly at the earnest young man and thought with a deep sigh, 'Oh dear, oh dear . . .'

Chapter Two

'She's still seeing him,' Sophie told McPherson.

'You don't know that. I was there when she said . . .'

'I know what she said, and I believed her. But there is something different about her recently. She's lying to me.'

'You've a suspicious mind, Sophie. Always thinking the worst of folk. It's not Christian.'

'Not Christian?' Blotches of colour burned high in Sophie's cheeks. 'How dare you say such a thing? I'm trying to do my Christian duty by her. That's why I'm so worried. It's obvious you don't care. The only people you care about or have any time for are your precious constituents – your all-important voters. You care about them all right . . .'

She could see he'd switched off. Now there was no way she could get through to him. She'd tried often enough in the past. But once that expressionless veil came down over his eyes, once he began leisurely filling his pipe, she was shut out. She was on her own.

His calm self-containment had been one of the things that had attracted her to him at first. His idealism, too . . . and his courage. What a big, fine-looking man he'd been. Not a pick of flesh on him in those days. Not like now, with his heavy jowls and bulging paunch. Of course he'd worked in the building trade then as well as in politics. The job hadn't been a sham then as it was now. He'd really sweated it out on the sites.

She'd been one of his constituents. She'd gone to his surgery for advice. His 'surgery', where he held court once a week, was an empty shop in Dumbarton Road. People came there with their problems and he treated everyone, including herself, with patience and much flattering attention. People liked their young Labour councillor, and they liked him still.

She had gone to see him about her chances of getting a

council house. He hadn't offered her much hope, if any. After all, she was a single woman, and when did the Corporation ever allocate homes to single women? Especially when there were so many married couples on the waiting list.

But he'd been so sympathetic that she found herself telling him more than she'd intended. It had all spilled out about the 'home' she'd been brought up in, run by the sadistic tyrant of a matron, then the string of seedy lodgings and bed-sits. She told him she didn't remember her parents. They'd died when she was very young. Of course, they hadn't died, and she did remember them, and she remembered why she'd been taken away from them and put into what had been euphemistically called 'care'.

She remembered them all right. The filth that they were. She prayed they were dead now. They had ruined her life. They had awakened in her a vile torrent of emotion and erotic desire that had taken many years to repress and control. Even now, saved by the blood of sweet Jesus, she had to be forever vigilant.

In the quiet of the night she'd see them – fumbling with one another, and with her, involving her, abusing her, arousing her. She'd remember how much she once loved them. She'd remember how confused she became. But even in her innocence she had known they were betraying her. The betrayal had been a thousand times worse than any physical pain she'd ever suffered. The betrayal and the contamination of her. Those had been the worst things.

She wasn't even old enough for school when she was caught simulating sex with children in the street. Other parents had complained to the authorities. That's how it had all been found out and she'd been taken away. Taken into 'care'. It made her laugh with bitter sarcasm.

A lot of good that had done her. Nobody had cared for her, and she cared for nobody else. Often her hatred turned on herself, and the thought of being trapped in her own loathsome body nearly drove her crazy.

The church had been – and still was – her lifeline, her saving grace. She couldn't live without it and the high regard with which she was held there. If she had been a demonstrative woman – which she was not – she would have kissed each and every church member's feet with gratitude. She had confessed her sins at the altar and they had forgiven her. All the men she'd fornicated with, all her neglect of Andrina when she was a baby. All wiped out.

It was McPherson who'd told them that her parents had died when she was a child and she'd been brought up in a 'home'. Then she had their pity as well. It was almost like love. She treasured it. And she blessed McPherson for introducing her to the church, and for his part in the saving of her. For all his faults, she'd always be grateful to him for that.

In time, he too had forgiven her. She knew it was the church who had helped him do this. Wonderful, miraculous Church of Jesus and the pure and blessed Christians who belonged to it. She'd rather die than let them down. Andrina would not let them down either. Or her mother. Never. She'd see to it.

'She's only sixteen.' Sophie refused to give up her badgering to get McPherson's attention. 'And that Pape's over twenty. He'll stir up the bad in her. I knew what type he was the moment I set eyes on him.'

McPherson sighed before lifting his newspaper and using it as a barrier between them. 'He seemed a nice enough lad to me.'

'How can you say that, knowing the family he comes from? But it's not only his background.' Sophie hesitated, her mouth twisting. 'It's worse than that.'

She couldn't say any more. Some things were beyond explanation.

Chapter Three

Sometimes Andrina wondered what made her suffer most: the first years of her life, when she had continuously longed for the security of her mother's love and attention, or now, when she had her mother's attention with a vengeance. From the age of sixteen, Andrina was put under a magnifying glass. Sophie was constantly suspicious. She inspected what Andrina wore. Nothing had to be 'provocative to men'. Friends were strictly vetted. Only the offspring of the Church of Jesus were allowed. Even then, Andrina was subjected to a 'third degree'. A Saturday afternoon at the cinema, even on her own, resulted in an ordeal that made a repeat of the outing too exhausting to contemplate. Only the few secret meetings she managed with Bernard made her otherwise unbearably restrictive life worthwhile. On the other hand, she suffered torments of guilt after each occasion. To make up for her wicked deceit she tried extra hard to please her mother. At church for instance, where her mother seemed to gain so much pleasure listening to her and watching her sing in the choir. Sophie always sat in one of the front pews, eyes bright and intense, riveted on her daughter.

She lapped up the praise afterwards too. People would say, 'You must be very proud of Andrina, Sophie. Such a lovely girl, and such a sweet voice. She looks just like an angel, doesn't she?' Sophie's smile would still hover about her thin mouth as she and her husband and daughter walked home. They walked separately. They weren't a touching kind of family. Never in her life had Andrina seen her parents kiss each other.

Sophie had a very straight, stiff back and she was always telling Andrina to straighten up. 'Don't slouch,' she'd say. 'Stand straight in the sight of the Lord.'

Andrina had hoped to widen her horizons after she left school. She had dreamed of going to university. She imagined the freedom this would entail. Now, freedom meant being able to see more of Bernard O'Maley. He could meet her on University Avenue and they could walk over Great Western Road way and along to the Botanic Gardens. All her dreams included Bernard now.

Her father had been quite amenable to the university idea. He was always quite amenable to everything she put to him, of course. So much so that she suspected he was just acting the part of a pleasant, easy-going father. He could wear an earnest and sympathetic expression while she was talking, yet she never felt she was getting through to him. She had the feeling that he wasn't really listening. His mind was occupied with someone else's problem.

Her mother listened all right. 'University? Have you not seen the wild crowd that mill about over there? You just need to look out of our window. Anyway, do you think your daddy's made of money?'

Seeing the so-called wild crowd out of their window was somewhat of an exaggeration, because although the towering grey spire of the university was perfectly visible over on the hill beyond the Art Galleries, the students could not be seen from the tenement window. Unless of course they ventured down Kelvin Way to the Art Galleries across the road, or to the park spreading out and dipping down beside it.

'But I was hoping to try for a degree and eventually become a teacher,' Andrina protested. 'I was speaking to Robert Anderson and he thought it was a good idea.'

The mention of the church, or one of its members, always made her mother more amenable. Sure enough, Sophie's voice immediately lost some of its edge. 'You mean Jean Anderson's son?'

'Yes.'

'He hasn't been to church for a few Sundays. His mother's been coming on her own.'

'He was saying that he runs a club at weekends for deprived children from Blackhill. He teaches in Blackhill.' Andrina almost added, 'and that's near where Bernard lives and went to school,' but caught herself just in the nick of time. 'Robert comes to our painting group on Tuesday nights. He's a great help, with him being an art teacher. I wonder that he can be bothered after working at it all day.'

'He's a nice lad, that's why.' Sophie's voice gathered enthusiasm. 'And a good Christian like his mother, and his late father before him. Jean says he's a gem of a son to her.'

Andrina nearly blurted out that he was hardly a lad. He must have been at least fourteen years older than her. She thought better of it. If there was one thing her mother hated, it was being criticised or corrected. Along with her Christian commitment had come an extremist way of thinking and an obsession to do everything to perfection. She was houseproud, for instance. There wasn't another fireplace in the whole street that sparkled and gleamed as hers did. Every morning she was down on her knees attacking the old range with black lead, and its steel edges with an emery board. Twice a week she had all the rugs down in the back court and whacked them like a wild thing with the carpet beater. Every day (every minute, it seemed to Andrina) she was bumping the carpet sweeper back and forwards. Andrina was allowed to do very little, because apparently she could do nothing right. Even when taking the ashes out to the bin in the back yard, Sophie followed her to make sure no ashes were spilled on the stairs that she'd just scrubbed and decorated with pipe clay.

Sophie began to talk of getting another house. It would be a new house, she prophesied, with a bedroom for herself and McPherson, so that they wouldn't have to sleep in the kitchen as they did there. Andrina could have a proper bedroom too. There would be a bathroom. There would also be a room free to use as a sitting-room. The kitchen would be a place in which to cook, instead of having to live and wash and eat and sleep and do everything else in it.

Sophie was a wonderful cook. Even McPherson gave her credit for that, and not just in front of others. 'That was good,' he'd say, patting his widening girth. 'That's one thing I have to give you credit for, Sophie, you're an excellent cook.'

Sophie wasn't sure at first where the new house should be. She did not know about areas of Glasgow other than the one in which she now lived. Nor did Andrina. Like most Glaswegians she had never gone far outside her own district. She only ventured further along Sauchiehall Street to the centre of town to attend the Church of Jesus, or to visit a cinema, or to gaze at shop windows. Any real shopping was done locally, in the McPherson's case it was along the other end at Dumbarton Road, or in Byres Road which ran up from Dumbarton Road to the West End. It was within walking distance, or a brief tram or bus ride from the house. McPherson's mother lived in Dumbarton Road, across from the foot of Byres Road, and they often visited her there.

Of course, the Art Galleries and the Kelvin Hall nearby were places most Glaswegians knew and had visited at some time in their lives. This gave the area where they lived more of a cosmopolitan feel than the other, more closed districts. The war had widened everyone's horizon to some extent, but people still tended to keep to their own patch where all their friends and relations also lived.

It was therefore a surprise to Andrina when her mother invited Mrs Anderson and her son from Adelphi Street on the other side of the river to visit Sauchiehall Street one Sunday. And they came. Andrina wished it could have been Bernard being accepted into the house, and she told Bernard this on one of their secret assignations. He said, 'It's not so bad if it's Anderson. He's OK.' Robert Anderson was much admired by pupils and ex-pupils alike – more for his prowess at karate and his karate club than his school art classes, Andrina suspected. But he was, as Bernard said, 'OK'. In fact, she was flattered by Robert's obvious interest in her. Sometimes she even suspected that she was the reason he attended the art group at the church. He certainly went out of his way to help her more than anyone else, and more than once he'd said he'd like to paint her portrait.

'You've got such wonderful eyes, Andrina – an unusual kind of turquoise colour,' he'd told her. Touching her hair, he added, 'And that deep rich shade of auburn. I'd love to try and capture it on canvas.'

Another surprise had been when her mother bought her a dress at one of the sales to wear that Sunday. Andrina was so excited that she blurted out about the portrait Robert said he'd like to paint. Immediately the words escaped she violently trembled, fearing the coldness of her mother's disapproval – something to be avoided at all costs.

But no. Miracle of miracles! Her mother looked pleased. Andrina even sensed an aura of triumph. For the first time in her life she felt that her mother was emotionally involved with her – in a pleasant, happy kind of way. They were sharing an excitement. Happy expectation was bouncing between them.

'Stand still,' her mother commanded as she pinned the hem of the dress. Her voice was good-humoured. 'I'll be jagging you if you keep wriggling and bouncing about.'

Gratitude towards her mother for being so unexpectedly close to her gathered like a lump in Andrina's throat. It was as much as she could do to contain her emotions and not burst into tears. Speechless, she gazed at the older woman, the steel spectacles and the piercing eyes behind them, the gleaming hair pulled back so tightly that made her eyes slant a little. At forty-six she had not an ounce of surplus weight, unlike most of the shapeless forms of the other women they knew.

The tiny flat was gleaming and pungent-smelling with furniture wax on the Sunday of the Andersons' first visit. All the work had been done on the Saturday, of course. Sunday was the Lord's day, and whenever possible Sunday was a day of rest. Even the skirting boards were washed and polished. The outside toilet, situated on the landing between the top flats and the next ones down, was thoroughly scrubbed and disinfected. The disinfectant was so strong the smell of it enveloped you as soon as you set foot on the stairs. Andrina had tried to help but her mother shooed her out of the way, insisting, 'I'd only have to go over it all again. I have to make sure of everything myself.' Nevertheless, Andrina had taken a duster and began dreamily smoothing it over everything.

It was when she'd reached the window-sill in the front room and was thinking of Bernard that suddenly she saw him. He was standing at a bus stop across the road, but he wasn't watching for a bus coming. He was staring up at the window. Her pulse immediately quickened and she darted an anxious look behind her in case there was any danger of Sophie seeing him too.

A bus came and went and Bernard was still there. Andrina leaned closer against the window, caught in the hypnotic force of his unsmiling stare.

'Andrina!' Her mother's voice fractured the spell. 'What are you doing through there?'

'Coming, Mummy.' She hurried back to the kitchen. 'I was just doing some dusting.'

'I've already cleaned through there, as you well know. Anyway, they know the front room's your bedroom, more's the pity. It's high time we had a decent house with a proper bedroom each and a proper room to entertain folk in.'

On the Saturday night McPherson was told to go to the Royal Artillery Club to be 'out from under my feet', as Sophie put it. But, 'for pity's sake don't drink too much and let yourself down.'

He went without a murmur. He enjoyed any opportunity of meeting and having a talk with the other ex-servicemen who frequented the place. Old campaigns were relived and argued over with great eagerness and enthusiasm. His visits were most welcome. If trumpets could have been blown they would have heralded his arrival. He was their only VC, and they were touchingly proud of him. He only wished he could go to the club more often.

Unfortunately, the Andersons' visit had increased a hundredfold Sophie's nagging about a new house. 'You've managed to get houses for other people,' she kept saying. 'Why can't you get one for us? It's terrible not to have a decent sitting-room – or any kind of sitting-room. That front room is Andrina's bedroom. And what can I do with it when there's that big wardrobe there? It means we'll have to have the Andersons in the kitchen.'

He'd pointed out, 'We've been having friends and neighbours and folk from the church in the kitchen for years.' But it was no use.

'I know, and I've had enough of it,' Sophie said. 'I'm sick of being so cramped and having to eat and sleep and cook and wash in this one poky wee kitchen. It's not sanitary.'

'There's a lot worse places.'

'I'm not interested in worse places. I want a better place. And not up on a top flat. It's enough to give me a heart attack – climbing all these stairs every day carrying heavy message bags.'

McPherson knew this wasn't the reason. Sophie thrived on buzzing about all the time. Restlessness was a disease with her. It was exhausting to watch. He was glad to get out of the house and away from her fast-moving greyhound body and equally rapid tongue. He sat a lot, often with fellow councillors, in the Corn Exchange Restaurant and Bar in Gordon Street opposite Central Station. There people could approach him, and many a deal was done and favours offered and received. He could get a council house for Sophie, no bother at all, despite the fact that there was a huge waiting list. Every member of the housing committee could be counted on as a friend. He had done them favours in his capacity as a member of the licensing board. He'd used his influence to get more than one licence for Jimmy Barker, for instance, for his new pubs. It was Andrew McPherson that Bill Dodds (also of the housing committee) had to thank for his taxi licences. These were just a few of the people he'd gone out of his way to help. It had always been a case of: 'If you scratch my back, I'll scratch yours'. The housing committee knew better than not to allocate him a house if he wanted one. But he was quite content where he was: this part of Sauchiehall Street was handy for transport and near any amenity, and yet it had the nice peaceful outlook on to the Art Galleries, the trees of the park and the University beyond. But he wasn't going to get any peace now that Sophie was determined to move.

'All right,' he sighed eventually. 'We'll get a council house. I suppose you want Knightswood or Mosspark?'

These were the best and most respectable housing schemes the council owned. Only those, and such as those were honoured by being given the chance of a home there. That was if one became vacant – and vacancies were few and far between.

'No. Drumchapel.'

His stare widened. 'Why Drumchapel?'

'They're brand new houses in Drumchapel, I've heard.'

'Yes . . . but . . .'

'And it's right out in the country.'

'Well, it's still Glasgow but I suppose you could say . . .'

'And it's right next to Bearsden.'

McPherson had never been in Bearsden, but everyone knew it was *the* posh place to live. 'It's not that near.' He suddenly felt exasperated. 'You're city born and bred the same as me, Sophie. What on earth do you want to go and live in the country for? Once Andrina gets married we'll have this place to ourselves. Why can't you settle down and appreciate your nice wee house?'

'I could ask you the same question when you keep leaving it, either to hang about the City Chambers . . .'

'I don't hang about the City Chambers,' he interrupted irritably. 'I sit in at innumerable committee meetings. It's me and people like me who run the city.'

'Or the Corn Exchange Restaurant.' Sophie ignored his interruption. 'Or disappear for weeks at a time on one of your jaunts.'

The jaunts (all expenses paid) she referred to were the times he had visited various parts of England, and even further afield, to study their methods of running their cities, or building their roads, or their bridges, or their housing estates. Or for any reason at all that was thought necessary, or just thought up. His late father, David McPherson, had been a dedicated member of the Labour Party Council before him. He had always refused to go on any jaunts. He had been ruthlessly honest, absolutely incorruptible, and idealistic. He had been so hard-working on behalf of the people of Glasgow that he had, while negotiating one of the first housing schemes and rehousing people out of the slums, even brought a camp bed into his office and collapsed in an exhausted sleep there night after night. 'And what thanks did he get for all his fast-held Socialist principles?' McPherson thought bitterly. 'Where did it get him? To an early grave. That's where it got David McPherson.' Thinking of his father, McPherson was bombarded with the usual mixture of love, admiration, guilt and anger. Once he'd been ready and willing to follow in his father's footsteps and live up to all his father's high ideals. But not any more. You couldn't beat the system. You had to go along with it. You had to do the best you could with it – for everybody, including yourself.

'All right. All right,' he told Sophie. 'We'll get a house in Drumchapel, if that's what you're sure you want. But I'm not a miracle worker. You'll have to wait until a decent one becomes vacant. So content yourself just now and leave me in peace.' More and more, anything for a peaceful life was becoming his motto at home. He went ahead and had a word in a few ears and it was, as he said, 'No bother at all'. He was eventually able to tell Sophie that it had been agreed and she'd have her new house as soon as a suitable one became available.

What he didn't tell her was that he'd come to believe that he could, if he really wanted it, put the pressure on Felderman the builder to have a house specially built for him however and wherever he wanted. He also felt confident they'd sell it to him for a rock-bottom price. But he drew the line at bought houses. The ordinary man in the street couldn't afford to buy a house. It was the duty of the council to make sure there were enough houses to rent. He was supposed to work for Felderman's, but it had been agreed that he would just say he worked for them and they would stamp his cards. It was also agreed that neither of them wanted to do anything illegal – but if McPherson, as a member of the housing committee, could do Felderman's any favours, he would. And he did.

When the construction of all the vast housing schemes had become too much for the council employees, McPherson had been the one who had sung Felderman's praises, who had spoken to this committee member and that committee member on Felderman's behalf. He had been the one who put the pressure on, and reminded the committee of favours done in the past and possibly more favours in the future. He had been the one who had eventually secured Felderman the building contract worth millions. There had been a lower tender, but he had organised that too. The Council was seen to be accepting (as they were supposed to) the lowest tender, only to have that tender withdrawn at the last minute. That left Felderman as the successful applicant.

He was glad that Sophie was not only happy with his promise of a house in Drumchapel but that she kept out of his hair while busying herself with preparations for the Andersons' visit.

She baked two Victoria sponges that were as light as thistledown, sandwiched them together with her home-made raspberry jam and dusted the top with icing sugar. Girdle scones and pancakes and salmon sandwiches also graced the table. Its scrubbed wooden surface had first of all been covered with Sophie's best white damask table cover, and her fluted, rose-patterned wedding china was set out. A pristine white bedspread with a fringed border was spread over the set-in-the-wall bed.

The fire glowed and sparkled redly in the steel edges of the range and in the brightly polished fender.

'Everything looks beautiful, Mummy.' Andrina clapped her hands in excitement, but calmed down immediately her mother snapped, 'Control yourself. You're not a child any more.'

It had been decided now that she'd leave school before the summer holidays started at the end of June. Nothing was certain about what she was going to do after that. Work in one of the posh Sauchiehall Street shops, perhaps? She quite fancied the idea of herself in a smart black frock and pearls, swanning towards a wealthy lady customer with the words, 'Can I help you, modom?'

The Andersons arrived exactly on time, something that Sophie took pleasure in remarking on. She was a stickler for punctuality herself, although Robert grinned and said that in their case it was more by good luck than good habit.

Robert Anderson was only an inch or two off six feet, and of lean build. Not that he was tough in the sense of looking common, as Sophie later remarked. It was just that he kept himself decently healthy with all that karate, or whatever it's called. His face was lantern-jawed, with overhanging brows and blue-grey eyes.

Jean Anderson was smaller and plump and motherly, with sandy hair fading into grey and face and hands blotched with freckles.

Everyone enjoyed their tea, although Andrina couldn't eat much because of nervous excitement. It was all too unusual, too much for her – her mother being so indulgent, so happy. Sophie and Mrs Anderson (just call me Jean, she'd said) and McPherson did most of the talking. But Robert addressed several queries and remarks to Andrina, and they smiled at each other in between eating and drinking tea.

Before they left, Jean invited them all to have tea at her place in Adelphi Street the following week, and Robert addressed Sophie in that confident, aggressive tone that teachers often acquire. 'Perhaps Andrina and I could meet before that. There's an interesting film at the Cosmo I believe she'd enjoy.'

And, miracle of miracles, Sophie smiled and said, 'Yes, I think Andrina would like that. Wouldn't you?'

Andrina was too confused and bewildered to make any response and her mother quickly answered for her.

'Of course she would, Robert.'

Right there and then arrangements were made. Robert Anderson was calling for her on Wednesday evening to take her to the Cosmo Cinema.

The confusion and the bewilderment did not go away. Indeed, these feelings intensified over the weeks and months that followed. But they were private to herself, mixed up with and hidden deep in the same secret place as her feelings for Bernard.

On the surface she was skating along a strange, unreal path; happy in a superficial, unreal way. She was grateful for so unexpectedly being able to please her mother, and she basked in the attention and envy of all the other girls in the church.

'You've all the luck,' they'd say. 'What's it like', they'd ask with barely suppressed longing, 'to go out with a real man?' They too had strict Christian parents. Their parents however were still imposing rigid and inhibiting rules on their lives. Andrina's life had changed completely.

'Wonderful,' Andrina would enthuse, like an actress as soon as a spotlight was turned on. 'He's strong and masterful. He knows his way around too. He takes me to such interesting places. And he's so self-confident. Not show-offy or noisy with it, you understand, not like some of the silly boys we knew at school.'

It was true that she felt proud of Robert and enjoyed going out with him. He was opening new worlds for her. She did admire his relaxed, easy manner, and also the firm air of authority about him. She was impressed by his knowledge of so many things of which until now she had been completely ignorant. But oh, he wasn't Bernard.

When Robert kissed her, the controlled gentleness of his mouth against hers was pleasant enough. But oh, he hadn't Bernard's fire, Bernard's magic touch. Bernard could not only send her blood careering wildly through her veins, but could make her feel that she was part of him – one spirit, one flesh. With Bernard she belonged.

Robert was her bulwark against Sophie. As long as she was with Robert, she was, in a way, free. She had her mother's blessing. Because of this, Robert seemed an incredible good fortune.

Jean, Robert's mother, and Sophie became bosom friends, and they couldn't hide their delight and satisfaction when Robert confided in them that he was going to ask Andrina to marry him.

'I was so happily married,' Jean told Sophie. 'It's my dearest wish that Robert will be settled in the same way before I die.'

'I feel the very same about Andrina,' Sophie replied.

Sophie couldn't wait to rush home and warn Andrina.

'He's perfect,' she enthused. 'A good Christian man. A member of our church. You'd be safe. He'd keep you safe in a respectable home. He'd keep you on the right path.'

'Mummy, what are you talking about?'

'I'm talking about you saying yes to a decent, respectable man when he asks you to marry him.'

'But I've only been going out with him for a few months.'

'You've known him for longer than that at the church.'

'Yes, but . . .' Andrina's mind groped through darkening mists. 'I don't love him,' she wanted to say, 'not the way I love Bernard.' But she hadn't the courage. 'I'm too young,' she said.

'You're near enough eighteen. Anyway, you'd not be married right away. For one thing, we've the move to the new house first.'

Word had come about a house in Drumchapel. A house exactly where Sophie wanted it – at the end nearest to respectable Bearsden.

'But Mummy,' Andrina tried again. 'I like Robert. I know he's a nice man and I've enjoyed going out with him as a friend. But I'm not in love with him.'

'In love.' Sophie spat the words out in disgust. 'You've been reading trashy romance books again. I told you how wicked they were. They fill young girls' heads with stupid, wicked nonsense.'

'No, it's not that . . .' Andrina's face creased with the strain of trying to make her mother understand without alienating her. But how could she express to anyone, far less her mother, how she felt about Bernard? The mere sight of him melted her with warm delight. Oh, how beautiful he was. So tall. His broad chest a warm welcome for her head. His hard features, his soft, sensuous mouth. And oh, those dark, glowing, knowing eyes.

She had only managed to see Bernard once or twice a month, depending on where and when he was working and how successful she was in finding a friend willing to cover for her. Sheila Preston was the only one who would oblige, the only one who even knew about her continuing relationship with

Bernard. Sheila's father was an elder in the church, and her mother was president of the Women's Guild. Sheila was a fellow member of the church choir and taught in Sunday School, but there was more to Sheila than met the eye, and certainly more than any of their respective parents knew about. Sheila was Andrina's loyal alibi. It could also, and often did, work the other way around. Sheila was the one with whom Andrina was supposed to be picnicking in the Campsie Hills. Or visiting the People's Palace Museum. Or attending a performance of Gregorian chants in the cathedral. Instead, Andrina was revelling in a few golden hours with Bernard, cuddling, caressing, sweetly kissing, or being perfectly content to hold hands. Often they didn't even talk.

To be with him was the important thing. Just to see him. To gaze at him. For oh, he was so beautiful. He was the flame that warmed her. There was no need for words. No need even to think.

Looking back, she realised she hadn't thought about anything else that was happening to her, hadn't asked herself any straight questions. What was she doing? How could she have been carried away by the envy of the other girls when they spoke of her relationship with Robert Anderson?

She hardly knew where she was, her life was careering along so rapidly. Sometimes she felt a little frightened. She'd hardly been allowed to abandon her gym-slip, ankle socks and broad stretch bandage for dresses, silk stockings and brassière, before being plunged into talk of wedding dresses and veils, and the booking of the Co-op purvey.

Not that she was afraid of Robert Anderson. But his proposal had such an air of authority about it. The desperate hustling of her mother and the eager expectancy of Robert's mother all conspired to make her agree obediently to the marriage before she'd really thought about what she was saying, or why. She kept telling herself that she'd done the right thing; her mother was so pleased with her, and she was flattered by the admiring attention of all the girls.

'You lucky devil,' they said. 'Fancy being taken out and

around by such a gorgeous man. Even having your portrait painted. And now you're going to be MARRIED!'

Flattery was the key word. Especially in connection with the portrait. Secretly she believed she couldn't, she didn't look as stunningly beautiful as he'd painted her. And did she really have that confused, uncertain but eager-to-please look about her?

Certainly she was confused by the speed and pressure of events, including the change from the tenements of Sauchiehall Street to the incredible space of the three rooms and kitchen and bathroom they moved to in Drumchapel. The space wasn't just inside the house either. There was miles of it outside, and hills in the distance on one side, and on the other, nestling down in the valley, were the villas and gardens of Bearsden.

Andrina had never been out in the country before. None of them had. Her father had fought in the desert during the war. Was that 'country'? She didn't think so. She and her mother wandered about in mutual confusion. Her mother kept saying, 'Isn't this wonderful? Everything looks so green and there's so much space.' Inside the house she never tired of repeating, 'Would you look at all these rooms. And look at the kitchen. And would you believe – a *bathroom!*'

Andrina couldn't. Any more than she could believe that she had allowed herself to agree to marry Robert Anderson. It wasn't just a bit of excitement to giggle about with girlfriends. It wasn't something out of the romantic novels they'd all read in secret. *It was real*. What added to her confusion was that everywhere she went, she kept imagining she saw Bernard O'Maley. She hadn't met him for months now. Not since her engagement. Yet she kept thinking she'd seen him. A dark concentration began to haunt her.

Chapter Four

'I don't know where you get all your energy from,' people often told Sophie. 'You're never at peace. You never seem to get a quiet minute to yourself. No wonder there's not a pick of flesh on you.'

This was how it had to be. She had to keep going. She had to keep lashing herself with work. She could not bear being idle. A quiet minute to herself was an anathema to be avoided at all costs. If no one was in while she was doing housework, she had to have the wireless blaring in the background. Her mind had to be bombarded with sound or occupied with some overwhelming interest, some immediate task or present problem – her own or anyone else's. Often she filled the void with feverish prayers. It was a constant battle to prevent her slipping back and down into the sewer of the past. It wasn't just the furtive fornicating in draughty, evil-smelling back closes with men from far off places, some of which she'd never heard of. All that, she realised now, was bad enough. She had been a slag, a slut, a hairy, an easy lumber. (Her only saving grace was that she had drawn the line at bringing the men into Andrew's house, Andrew's bed.) She'd danced and laughed and had a riotous good time at the Locarno or Green's Playhouse but later, after the giggling and groping had quickened into penetration, she had felt sickened, even while actively enjoying her animal-like coarseness.

Later still, in the house on her own (she never acknowledged the existence of the child crouched in the dark in the hole-in-the-wall bed), Sophie felt even more sickened. She was swamped by the filth that had been her parents. She saw them in her mind's eye, forcing her to watch them having sex, getting a thrill at being watched, forcing her to do things, doing things to her. She had been hardly more than an infant when it had started. She looked back at them with a loathing that had grown and festered over the years instead of diminishing. Even her salvation hadn't cured the poison of her hatred, only driven it deeper so that it didn't show.

When Sophie was a child, her parents' behaviour had been the norm, the only way of life she'd known. That had been the reason for her behaviour with other children. Looking back, one part of her mind recognised the truth and the innocence of her behaviour. At the same time the loathing of her parents spilled over and enveloped the memories of her childhood. Until they were one and the same thing.

Neighbours had complained about their children being in moral danger. Sophie was, in their view, a source of corruption, and was therefore removed to the huge prison-like institution of Moorlands. She'd never seen her parents again – nor did she want to. If they did come back into her life she believed she would take great pleasure in destroying them, as once they'd destroyed her. But probably they were dead. She hoped they were dead. She hoped they had died a slow death of leprosy or cancer. If they were alive, and they could be alive for all she knew, her father would be seventy-six and her mother would be seventy. But the chances were that their filthy flesh would long since have been deservedly consumed by the worms.

Sophie stamped them from her mind. Crushed them out with busy, useful, good, worthwhile things. This had cleansed her. The church was a wonderful saving grace. She enjoyed the fellowship of it, and the rigid framework within which she had learned to function.

Now there was the wonderfully harassing business of moving house. There was the intriguing novelty of the new place, and all the plans she'd formulated of how she was going to decorate it. There was the problem of the extra furniture it would need.

On top of all this, there was all the work and planning for Andrina's wedding. She was doing her very best for Andrina. She had protected her against the sin of casual sexual encounters. She had arranged that Andrina should be safely settled in a good marriage with a decent Christian man. A secret part of herself, a part she refused to recognise, was glad to be getting rid of the girl. That hair, those full lips, that curvaceous body – it was her disgusting mother all over again. From the first moment she'd set eyes on the infant Andrina, as soon as she'd seen the fluffy red down of hair, she'd known.

Nevertheless, Sophie was doing her Christian best for the girl. She had decided that instead of getting the Co-op purvey, she'd do everything herself. Everyone had protested that it would be far too much work for her. McPherson had warned that she'd end up killing herself and there was no need. Admittedly they were having a lot of extra expense with moving house, he said, but they'd manage to pay for a purvey. The Co-op wasn't too dear and they still had a month or two to put a few pounds by.

Andrina too was worried. 'Please Mummy, don't do this. You'll only make yourself ill. I don't want to have you on my conscience on my wedding day. You won't have enough energy left to enjoy it.'

Robert Anderson had told Sophie bluntly that he wasn't going to invite any of his friends or relations to keep down the numbers if she didn't at least come to some sort of compromise.

So in the end she grudgingly agreed to the Co-op providing the steak pies, potatoes and peas, and the trifles. She would bake and decorate the wedding cake. And of course she would make Andrina's wedding dress. It was when she set about gathering all the things she needed that she discovered the first drawback of being in Drumchapel. There were no shops. The Council had apparently not thought of including any amenities whatsoever when they'd built the huge housing scheme. There was no community centre, no school, no church or church hall, no cinemas, no dance hall, no pub or club. There wasn't even a bus service.

It gave her something new to nag McPherson about. 'The crowd of you in City Chambers couldn't run a ménage. You've just flung up these houses and never given a thought to the people's practical day to day living. I've over a mile to walk before I can get a bus to take me to the shops. Then I've all that walk back again, weighed down with messages.'

It was now a terrible business trying to get to church on a Sunday. In Sauchiehall Street they simply had to go out and catch one of the tramcars that passed by their close. On a nice day they sometimes walked along to Rose Street, off Sauchiehall Street, where the Church of Jesus was situated.

'I go down on my knees and thank God,' Sophie kept repeating to McPherson, 'that Andrina is engaged and will soon be safely married. With nothing to occupy them around here, young folk will be bound to get into trouble.'

Special buses collected children early in the morning and took them to schools miles away. By the time they were brought back it was late, which didn't give children much time to do anything once they'd had a meal and done their homework. The trouble would come if they left school at fifteen and no longer had any homework to occupy their time. Already groups of youths were wandering aimlessly about. Lack of discipline didn't help either. So many mothers weren't there to keep a watchful eye on offspring, far less lay down the law and insist that it was kept.

Most people had come from single-ends or one room and kitchen, and hadn't enough furniture to fill their new Drumchapel houses. The result was that many women had to go out to work to make the extra money needed. Then the journeying to and from work made it a long day away from home for them too.

The difficulties at this early stage at least didn't worry Sophie overmuch. Indeed, she thrived on them. They kept her extra busy, hurrying here and there, getting things for the house, painting, decorating, scrubbing, polishing, cooking, baking, planning everything for the wedding.

She helped Andrina with the house she and Robert eventually rented in Monteith Row opposite Glasgow Green. It was a cobbled street of old black tenements, but it was very handy with tramcars nearby and a nice view of the Green from the front room window. They had been very lucky in managing to get two rooms and kitchen with a huge bathroom. Andrina was obviously thrilled at the idea of having her own house and especially such a spacious one.

It wasn't as big as the three rooms and kitchen and bathroom Drumchapel house, of course, although the rooms in the older property were marginally bigger and had high ceilings with carved cornices. However, the kitchen was as cramped as all the tenement kitchens she'd ever seen, with the hole-in-the-wall bed and the big black range, the iron sink, the wooden coal bunker and four-barred clothes pulley dangling from the ceiling. Once a table and chairs were put in, and a sofa against the bed, there wouldn't be enough space to swing the proverbial cat.

The bathroom had more floor-space. They really made the most of having a bathroom. Robert mirrored the walls and laid a lovely black shaggy carpet on the floor – edge to edge. It was really luxurious. Of course, Robert and Andrina were full of bright ideas; Robert was thinking of doing away with the kitchen bed and making the space into a dining area – putting the table and chairs in there, to leave more central floor space.

'Did you ever hear the likes of it?' Sophie asked McPherson. She had been shocked and silent on the subject of the mirror walls in the bathroom, but about the kitchen she was enthusiastic. 'Of course it's with Robert being an art teacher – he makes drawings of everything and plans everything out. He's really very clever and original. Andrina is terribly excited with the idea.' She added in a more accusatory tone, 'Of course Robert takes a real interest. If he had had anything to do with building housing schemes, he wouldn't have made the ridiculous mistakes that you and your crowd at the City Chambers made.'

All the same, she thought Drumchapel was a beautiful place and she was proud of her house. She couldn't have been more busy and happy. And as McPherson said, it was early days. The amenities would come in time.

The wedding plans were going full steam ahead and Sophie had made a lovely job of Andrina's wedding dress. The girl was ecstatic about it. They'd both gone to Copland and Lye's for the veil and white shoes. Andrina got quite a big discount because she was now an employee there. The Co-op florists were going to supply the bouquet of pale pink and white lilies and a deeper shade of pink carnations.

The only annoyance had come when Andrina, bubbling over with eagerness, had asked, 'What kind of wedding did you have, Mummy? Were you married in white? With your slim figure you must have looked lovely. I bet your mother and father were really proud of you.'

'They both died when I was a baby. I don't remember them.'

'Oh?' Andrina looked puzzled. 'I thought you once said . . . I understood that . . .'

'What could you understand about anything?' Sophie snapped, turning away from her, cutting Andrina out, cutting out her red hair and long lashes and shameless curves that she flaunted with every step she took.

The so-called 'Sweater Girl' bra with the pointed cups that Andrina had bought with her first week's wages had been disgusting. Sophie had told her that if she saw her wearing the thing she'd no longer be a daughter of hers. 'As long as you're still under my roof,' she'd said, 'you'll keep some decency and not behave like a shameless slut.'

At least she'd prevented her from buying the tight fitting slacks. Andrina had asked her what she'd thought of the idea. 'All the girls are wearing them now, Mummy, and they're not really tight,' she'd pleaded. 'In fact, they're very comfortable for walking and sports and . . .'

'What kind of sports do you do? And you're too lazy ever to walk to work. You're just wanting to wear these things so that you can flaunt your backside. You're disgusting. You're revoltingly fat. It would suit you better to try and hide your backside as much as you possibly can.'

If Robert didn't put his foot down and watch Andrina like a hawk, God knows what she'd be up to once they were married. Sometimes Sophie wondered if she ought to warn him. Especially now that she'd discovered Robert knew Bernard O'Maley. O'Maley had been a pupil at Robert's school. He also attended Robert's karate class. Now, apparently, he helped Robert to run it.

Sophie worried constantly about Andrina and the O'Maley creature meeting again. Right from the beginning she had seen in his eyes what a filthy beast he was. Surely he couldn't be one of the friends that Robert spoke of inviting to the wedding. If he was, she'd soon score him off the list.

Chapter Five

'Frank's always been too soft. That's his trouble.' Patrick O'Maley made the pronouncement about his youngest son during a family conference at which everyone except twenty-four-year-old Frank was present. 'I've tried everything I could to toughen him up from the moment he began to walk but it's been no use.'

'Och, he's a lovely boy. Leave him be,' Frank's mother pleaded. 'Just because he's not like the rest of you doesn't mean there's anything wrong with him. Far from it. I did his chart the other day and it said great things are going to happen to him. He's got a great future ahead of him, has Frank.'

'You and your bloody fortune-telling,' Patrick said, but in quite a pleasant tone. Then his voice gathered its anger again. 'All that's happened to Frank so far, Maureen, is that he's been regularly duffed up at school. And since he's got himself in a soft job as a pen pusher, that's not likely to increase his popularity with the lads. But the worst thing is, he's shutting himself away all night writing letters to himself. The boy's gone soft in the head now.'

'No, you don't understand, Pat.' Maureen's dramatic eyes bulged. 'He has to address envelopes to himself, see, so that he gets his stuff sent back.'

'What stuff?'

She hesitated uncomfortably, then tossed her wild bush of grey hair. 'His wee verses. Och, he's not doing anybody any harm.'

Michael, a year older than Frank (and Bernard's twin), was incredulous. 'Not doing anybody any harm? What do you think it does for me? Do you think it helps my reputation in the ring having a poof for a brother?'

'What Frank does is nothing to do with you or any of

you,' Maureen cried out. 'And he's not a poof. Stop calling him that.'

Bernard said, 'We're just thinking of his own good, Ma. Frank doesn't seem to have a clue. If he'd come to the karate club with me. Or even let me coach him at home . . .'

'He's just not interested in learning how to handle himself,' Michael shook his cropped head. 'It's not natural.'

'If he was a Ted he'd have to handle himself or he'd be minus a nose or an ear.' Tony, the eldest at twenty-six, worked in a butcher's shop and was a Teddy Boy in his spare time. After shop hours he changed from rolled-up shirt sleeves and striped apron to knee-length draped jacked, drainpipe trousers and thick crêpe-soled shoes that he called brothel creepers. He was fussy about his clothes and his hair. He was forever combing it. (Unlike his brothers, Frank didn't care about his appearance. Frank was a bean-pole topped with lank, straight hair. His clothes, like his hair, never seemed to fit him.)

Michael was a natty dresser in his own way, perhaps a bit on the flash side, with his pin-stripe suits and dark glasses and brightly-coloured ties. At least as a boxer no-one could say he wasn't tough. Already he'd won several amateur trophies and with his iron muscles, his bullet head and his craggy, broken-nosed face, he could boast as pugnacious a manner as any professional fighter. When he wasn't in the ring either training or fighting, he was on building sites doing the same brickie work as his father. He was tough all right, but he had recently come in for almost as much flack from the family as Frank.

Michael's problem was in courting Caroline Stoddart. The Stoddarts lived in Cobden Street, the next street along off Garngad Road. The moment Michael had introduced her to the family they'd been suspicious. His mother had been very pleasant though, and made Caroline a cup of tea and plied her with coconut snowballs. She asked her which street she came from, and of course when Caroline admitted it was Cobden Street she was immediately branded a Protestant.

Not that Maureen or any of the O'Maley family were bigoted. They denied it most hotly. As Maureen said, 'Many a

Protestant from Cobden Street and even as far as Springburn has been made welcome in this house in Bright Street, and has had their teacup or tarot cards read.'

However, Michael knew that the predominance of Protestant clients stemmed from the fact that Father Riley said fortune-telling was wicked. His mother, in her own inimitable way, had interpreted this to mean it was only wicked if she practised it on Catholics.

As far as his courting of Caroline was concerned, his mother warned, 'It can cause so much trouble, son. It's safest to stick to your own kind. Then if you get scratched, it doesn't go septic. What does her family think of you?'

He could have said, 'Not much', but he restrained himself. He and his brothers were all Maureen's 'lovely boys', and no outsider would dare say anything against them without her immediately and indignantly taking up verbal arms. This fire didn't need any fuel.

But the important thing was, as far as he was concerned, he and Caroline got on great. He wasn't planning to marry her family. He didn't think much of them either. Caroline's mother, Big Martha Stoddart, was built like a battleship and was well known for the unusual, the almost unheard-of activity of beating her husband. Jimmy Stoddart made up for his ineffectualness at home by being a loud-mouthed bigot outside of it. He was a grand master of an Orange Lodge. Not in Garngad, which was predominantly Catholic – an Orange Lodge in Garngad wouldn't have lasted very long; it would have lasted an even shorter time in neighbouring Blackhill – but bigger districts like Springburn could accommodate Orange Lodges and the equivalent Catholic establishments.

Michael secretly dreaded the day when the O'Maleys and the Stoddarts got together and Jimmy Stoddart found out that Tony O'Maley, not content with being a Catholic, was also a Republican. It was fortunate that the Stoddarts and the O'Maleys used different pubs, otherwise Jimmy would have found out by now. Tony was a bit of a loudmouth himself. No, that was an understatement. Tony was the world's worst loudmouth. Tony was noisy about everything.

For a time Michael and Caroline had managed to hide the seriousness of their relationship from Martha and Jimmy Stoddart. They had appeared no more than part of a crowd. Occasionally they *had* been part of a crowd, standing at the street corner when the Stoddarts passed by. Even so, Caroline had been warned to 'watch herself' because there were 'a couple of Papes in that lot'.

More recently they had been spotted on their own and the trouble had started. Caroline had been reduced to a nervous wreck. Her face was constantly swollen and blotchy with tears, until Michael braved the lions' den and faced the Stoddarts. He would have preferred to oppose anybody in the ring to confronting Caroline's parents, but he stood his ground. He told them he loved Caroline and Caroline loved him and they were going to be married. Caroline could remain a Protestant if that's what she wanted. Any children they had could be brought up as Protestants if that's what Caroline wanted. All he wanted was to marry Caroline.

What swung the decision in his favour, however (although their pessimistic misgivings remained), was the fact that he had won not only the interclub championships and the Western District championships, but more recently the Scottish middleweight title. As far as Jimmy Stoddart was concerned, even a Catholic Scottish middleweight champion was something to boast about. Big Martha stuck to her prophecies of doom, however, and insisted that a mixed marriage was a recipe for disaster and no good would come of it. A Pape was a Pape – Scottish middleweight champion or not.

Frank was now an added worry for Michael. What the Stoddarts would think of his younger brother he had no idea, but feared it would be much the same as his mates, all of their mates. Frank was a queer fish. Some people believed he thought himself a cut above everyone else. He didn't. It was just that people imagined he did. That was the unfortunate impression Frank gave and it caused a simmering resentment among the locals.

Only a few days previously, when Frank had had a drink with him, there had been an example of this resentment. The beer had definitely been cloudy, and Michael had been going to remark on this to Joe, the barman. If he had, Joe would have been apologetic and pulled another beer. Probably they would have had a friendly and interesting chat about it and Joe would have explained the reason for the cloudiness. Unfortunately, Frank was the one who happened to remark on the beer first. A look of hatred had immediately darkened Joe's face and he spat out, 'Just because you fancy yourself as a know-all writer doesn't mean you know a fuckin' thing about beer.'

Poor Frank couldn't say anything to anybody without having his writing flung in his face. If he'd managed to keep it secret it wouldn't have been so bad, but there had been times when his enthusiasm had got the better of him and he told everybody that he was writing poetry – even, to everyone's acute embarrassment (and the family's shame), he had read some of it out loud. He was only about twelve when it first happened, but tall and lanky even then. He'd also been bug-eyed and eager.

'It's called "What Waits",' he announced. Then, to the stunned crowd in the kitchen of family and friends who had been enjoying a good bevvy, he continued:

> 'What waits,
> When this brilliant burning flame,
> This flame we call life,
> Is done: we finish the unfinished game,
> And cede the futile strife.
> What waits,
> Behind the ever unopened door,
> With breath and body gone;
> We do not know, we wondered before,
> But we shall know – anon!'

What waited for Frank was a clip round the earhole from his father and an exhortation not to be so bloody daft.

But there was a stubbornness about Frank that no clip round the earhole from his father, nor hooting and jeering from his brothers, nor playground beatings, could budge him one inch.

Frank had continued scribbling away at his poems. Maureen was angry when she found out that while she thought he was doing his homework and studying, he had actually been concocting poems. Sometimes he'd been wasting his time making up stories.

'Sweet Jesus,' Maureen cried out, 'would you look what the boy's doing now!' Then to Frank, 'Every penny we can scrape together goes to keeping you and Bernard at school. God gave you and Bernard the brains in this family and it's a sin if you don't make the most of them. Bernard works hard doing his homework, and he's doing a milk round and God knows what else as well. He's a good boy. What are we going to do with you, Frank?'

Neither Tony nor Michael had been offended at the implication that God had dished out less brains to them than to their two brothers, although Michael had no doubts that he was much better endowed in that respect than Tony. He would have flattened anyone who said it, but secretly he accepted the fact that Tony was a bit thick. The mere fact that he kept mouthing off about his support for the IRA was, in Michael's opinion, daft to the point of being dangerous. The truth was that Tony had never had anything whatsoever to do with the Republicans. He'd never been in Ireland. Indeed, none of them had (except their grandads and grandmas on both sides, but they were all dead). He'd been involved in gang fights when he was younger, and more recently the occasional fight with gangs of Teds from other districts. Compared with the IRA, however, Tony's acts of violence were child's play. They couldn't get this through his thick head. But that was nothing to the incomprehension they all felt about Frank.

'What's to be done about Frank?' had been expressed with varying degrees of anguish or anger, or a mixture of both, down through the years.

The whole family had nearly emigrated at one point, such was the mortification Frank caused them. He had actually taken up tennis and was seen going down Bright Street and along Garngad Road in a white shirt, white pullover and white flannels. They had all been vehement in Frank's defence to outsiders, and nobody dared to jeer or laugh or say a word against Frank when Michael or Tony or Bernard were around. Inside the house it was a different story and they did everything but physically abuse him. Patrick had threatened to beat the living daylights out of him and Frank had only been saved by Bernard grabbing his father and struggling like mad to stop him.

Frank didn't seem to care. Or at least, he always stood his ground. He did what he wanted to do and that was that. It was a kind of courage and it aroused in his brothers a grudging admiration. It had to be admitted that to walk the gamut of Bright Street and Garngad Road in white flannels took guts. Either that or it was an act of incredible stupidity, and Frank wasn't stupid. He had passed God knows how many Highers before he left school. Some of the books he read were by names no one could pronounce – like Dostoevsky.

This wasn't the first family conference about Frank. At previous gatherings it had been decided to get the priest to talk to him. That had happened, all to no avail. At this family conference, however, the idea emerged that if Frank could start walking out with a good Catholic girl, that would be sure to do the trick. If they could just get him married and involved in a family (the bigger the better), the responsibilities that would entail wouldn't leave Frank any time for all his nonsense. But what girl would have him? Patrick thought of Bridie Gallacher, one of Scobie Gallacher's daughters. The Gallachers – a monstrous tribe of them – lived in Turner Street, and Bridie's twenty-first birthday party was coming up soon. Frank – as well as Michael, Tony and Bernard – had been invited.

One of Bridie's sisters, Effie Gallacher – Michael remembered her well – had been drowned in the Monklands Canal a year after his brother Sean. The canal claimed several victims every year, but still youngsters ran joyously to it and splashed and bounced about like frogs in its murky waters. It was their only swimming pool, their equivalent of a more affluent person's seaside.

'We can't force him to go out with anybody.' Bernard shook his head. 'How can we even get him to go to the party? You know what Frank's like.'

Maureen interrupted him. 'Leave that to me. I'll tell him how much Bridie's mammy is trying to make this a good do for Bridie, seeing it's her twenty-first, and how much of a comfort the poor wee soul was to me when we lost our Sean, God rest his soul.'

Tony revealed his long, horsy teeth. 'You mean that wee fatty with the specs and the face full of plooks? Only somebody as daft as our Frank would look at her.'

'She doesn't look like that now. At least she's lost her plooks,' Bernard said. 'She's a bit like Frank in a way.'

'A bit daft, you mean?' Tony said.

'A bit of a loner. Maybe because of the mess she looked when she was younger. Neither of them hung about the corners very much.'

The talk of getting Frank paired off with Bridie made Bernard's mind turn yet again to Andrina McPherson. Since he'd first set eyes on her in Kelvingrove Park, she'd never been far from his thoughts. After her mother had laid down the law and forbidden Andrina to see him, they'd met as often as possible in secret, wonderful, exciting, dangerous assignations, as Andrina had made them seem. There was magic in the very air they breathed every moment they were together. His darling. His own beautiful Andrina with her round, childish eyes and sensual body. He wanted to marry her. He had held back from consummating their relationship, something he'd never done with any woman before. But he'd never wanted to marry any woman before.

His ability to keep control of himself sexually with Andrina had been helped in a way by the fact that they had only been able to meet on so few occasions and for such limited amounts of time. But even a moment with her was precious to him and wonderful.

Even after she'd begun seeing Robert Anderson, he'd still tried to talk to her. She'd started work in Copland and Lye in Sauchiehall Street. As often as he could in the evenings he waited outside the shop door, and as soon as she emerged he caught her by the arm and urged her to come with him 'somewhere where we can talk'. On each occasion she had become more and more agitated, and kept looking furtively around as if she was doing something criminal by being seen in his company. He sensed her agony and cursed her bigoted old harridan of a mother for causing it. Even in his dreams he cursed her. It was impossible to communicate with Andrina when she was in such a state. He'd tried everything including anger.

'For God's sake, Andrina. Your mother doesn't live along the road any more. She's away out in Drumchapel. She's not likely to see us, is she? So what are you getting all up tight about? I know what's behind your mother's attitude. It's the Orange and the Green, the Celtic and the Rangers, the Billys and the Dans. Well, I don't care about all that, and I don't believe you do either. We were getting on so well. We were so happy until your mother interfered.'

But no matter how desperately he tried, he could not break through the barrier of her agitation. She seemed completely unable to concentrate on what he was saying. Her expression was miles away, withdrawn, blanked out. Then she started coming from the shop after work surrounded by a tight bunch of other girls. Giggling and chatting, they'd crowd along the street and then all crush on to a tramcar. Sometimes he managed to *will* Andrina to look back in his direction, and he'd see beyond the giggling and chatting to the deep distress in her eyes.

He was convinced that she felt for him as he felt for her, despite all her talk about Robert Anderson and how her mother was encouraging a friendship between them. He made excuses. She was young and impressionable and she was dominated by her evil old hag of a mother. But one day when she was older and stronger, Andrina would break free of that influence. She belonged to him. They belonged to each other. It was impossible to accept that she was never going to be his. All the time he lived in hope. Everything he did he did for her. After he'd graduated from the paper round he'd done while he was at school, he'd worked for all the hours God gave as a bouncer in the Empire, and then for a security firm. He'd gone abroad with them on some highly dangerous jobs. Everything he did to make enough money so that he'd be able to afford to rent a house and furnish it in whatever way she wanted.

Before the McPhersons had moved to Drumchapel, he'd hang about Kelvingrove Park and the Art Galleries, watching for her in every free moment he had. There had been occasions when he'd followed her. Once she'd been with her witch of a mother. The woman even looked like a witch, dressed in black, with dark, piercing eyes glinting behind steel-framed spectacles and skinny body leaning forward as she hurried along. Mother and daughter had gone from their house in Sauchiehall Street along to Dumbarton Road where he knew Andrina's granny lived.

Another time, Andrina had emerged with Robert Anderson and gone in the other direction to the busy shopping part of Sauchiehall Street. They had eventually disappeared inside the La Scala picture house. It tore at his gut to see her with another man. The fact that the other man was Robert Anderson, someone he admired and who had always been his mentor, was a frustrating and confusing element with which Bernard found it impossible to cope.

His pain and confusion grew as time passed and it became obvious that Robert and Andrina were walking out together. It was an agony for him to stand in the shadows and watch them, arms linked, laughing and talking, Andrina glancing up at Robert with a mixture of innocence and teasing flirtatiousness.

It was obvious the way things were going, yet he couldn't believe it when he heard that marriage was on the cards. It had been a proud and happy Robert who had told him. In a daze, he'd shaken hands with the man and murmured his congratulations along with the more voluble ones from the rest of the karate club.

Robert was a great guy. As far as Bernard was concerned no better man walked the face of the earth. He would have done anything for Robert Anderson – died for him if necessary. He wished him well. He wished him everything that his heart desired.

Everything, that is, except Andrina McPherson.

The only clear-cut thing that remained in his mind, in his gut, in his very soul, was the belief that Andrina McPherson belonged to Bernard O'Maley. They belonged to each other. Yet the world kept turning. The wedding day came.

Bernard stood across the road from the church, waiting and watching, his belief overflowing into a kind of madness.

Chapter Six

The only thing that had spoiled the wedding preparations, as far as Andrina was concerned, was her mother's fury when Robert suggested inviting Bernard O'Maley.

'That revolting Pape?' Sophie spat out. 'If you have him at the wedding, you won't have me.'

Robert was astonished. 'What's wrong with Bernard? I've known him for years and I've always thought him a credit to the kind of background he's had. Garngad's a tough area, and not many turn out as well as him. He was working hard even before he left school, and since then he's really used his strength and his expertise at karate to his advantage. I think he'll end up employing people, building up a good business.'

'A good business?' Sophie sneered. 'He's part of the underworld. He's a gangster.'

Robert shook his head. 'He's tough, and perhaps he has to mix with, or deal with some tough people, but he's not a gangster.'

McPherson cut in then. 'I agree with Robert. Bernard always struck me as a decent enough lad, and his father was a good soldier. One of the best.'

'A good drinker, you mean?' sneered Sophie. 'I always know when you've met Patrick O'Maley at the Artillery Club. You come home stupid with drink. A great influence he is on you, or on his son or on anybody else. I will not have Bernard O'Maley at my daughter's wedding. If you have him at the wedding, you'll not have me,' she repeated.

McPherson took a thoughtful puff at his pipe before saying to Robert, 'When Sophie feels so strongly about it, perhaps it would be wiser to think again, Robert. She's never liked him. He used to be friendly with Andrina . . .'

'Yes, he told me he knew her,' Robert interrupted. 'When

they were young, a crowd of them used to meet in Kelvingrove Park.' He sighed. 'What do you think, Andrina? He's a good friend of mine and a valuable help to me at the karate club. I would like him to be at the wedding, but it's supposed to be the bride's big day. I don't want anything to spoil it for you.'

'It would completely spoil it for me if Mummy wasn't there,' Andrina cried out. 'It would be terrible. I couldn't bear it.'

Robert put a soothing hand on her arm. 'All right. All right. I won't ask Bernard.'

It took Andrina some time to calm down, she was shaking so much. Robert had stared curiously at her afterwards when they were on their own.

'Darling, are you all right?'

'Yes, of course.' She tried to laugh. 'Why do you ask?'

'I'm not quite sure . . . You're not afraid of your mother, are you?'

Andrina gave a genuine laugh this time. 'Don't be ridiculous, Robert. Surely you can see she's the best of mothers. She's worked like a slave to have everything perfect for me at the wedding. I adore her.'

'Yes,' Robert agreed. 'She's done everything she can to help us. I'm a very lucky man to have such a mother-in-law. I realise that. I'm just sorry she feels as she does about Bernard, that's all. But not to worry.' He took Andrina into his arms, smoothing his cheek against hers, not saying anything for a time before he let her go. She loved him for making her feel so comforted and secure. Everything would be all right once they were safely married. 'Safely married' was the term her mother always used, and Andrina had acquired the habit of using it. At the same time she was secretly looking forward to the freedom she imagined the marriage would give her. She didn't dare admit it, even to herself, but by freedom she'd come to mean freedom from her mother. She imagined that as a married lady she would be her own boss with her own house to queen it over. She could go in and out when she liked. She could wear whatever she fancied in clothes or in make-up or in jewellery. (Her mother thought anything other than an engagement ring and a wedding ring was wickedly frivolous.)

Oh, how Andrina longed to wear big flashy earrings. Oh, how she longed to be free from guilt and the disapproval that kept chipping away at her self-confidence, and the illogical terrors that had so often plagued her. When she'd still been at primary school, and after her mother had first been saved, her mother had told her about Hell and 'the bad burning fire' that people, especially children, would be cast into if they did bad things. Andrina no longer believed such a threat. Her mind told her there was no such thing as a 'bad burning fire'. At least not in the context of a place called Hell. Indeed, her intelligence told her there wasn't such a place under any name or description. The girls at the shop had often giggled and made a fool of the expression. They too had been on occasion threatened with 'the bad burning fire' and they all, including Andrina, agreed how ridiculous, indeed how hilarious, the expression was. (Although one of them had admitted that what really had scared her was her mother saying that the bad fire into which she could be cast was Dixon Blazes, the Iron Works that was the beacon that reddened the sky over the south side of Glasgow.)

Oh, to be free of all these dark, ridiculous things. Oh, to be free of being constantly watched and warned and questioned. To be married was going to be like having a burden the weight of an elephant lifted clean off her shoulders. It was the instant dispelling of a dense black cloud. She was filled with joy at the mere thought of it.

And, joy of joys, the marriage came with her mother's blessing. Yet over the joy hung a gauze of sadness.

She was a very lucky girl, her mother said, and Andrina was quick to agree with her. The thought skimmed secretly and guiltily across her mind that she was lucky that, by the move to Drumchapel, her mother wouldn't be able to visit her too often. Fleeting as it was she still felt shame at the thought. 'You and Daddy will aways be welcome at Monteith Row, Mummy,' she anxiously assured the older woman. 'I'll arrange for you both to come for your tea as soon as we're settled in.'

What she didn't say was that she and Robert had planned a housewarming party for their friends. She was looking forward to the event so much she just couldn't bear the idea of her mother knowing and probably taking over the organising of the whole thing. She wouldn't attend the event when it was specifically for younger people. (She wouldn't, would she?) But she could insist on coming earlier to do all the cooking and organising. Then perhaps she might stay on with the excuse of helping dish out the food or washing up the dishes afterwards. That would mean the kiss of death to the party. She would watch and criticise what everybody was drinking. She disapproved of women smoking, and so nobody would dare light up. Stolen kisses, even just for a lark, or friendly cuddles, or sitting on boyfriends' knees, would be more than frowned upon. Such behaviour would be publicly denounced.

The housewarming party would have to be kept secret from Sophie, Andrina insisted to Robert, until after the event.

'She'll surely hear about it from some of our friends in the church,' Robert said.

'I'll warn them. They know what mother's like. She does tend to go over the top a bit. They'll keep quiet about it. Anyway, I'm only inviting a few of the young ones that I know enjoy a bit of fun. Our front room won't hold all that many and I want to leave enough space for your friends from work.'

'Some of the teachers at St Francis aren't so young, I'm afraid. But they're a good crowd. You'll like them. Then there's a few lads from the karate club I'd like to invite, including Bernard, of course. I still feel rotten about not inviting him to the wedding. To be honest with you, Andrina, I would have preferred him to be my best man.'

'Oh dear.' Andrina's expression collapsed with distress. She could no longer cope with the reality of Bernard. He had become like a beautiful dream and it was better that way. Nothing could ever have come of this relationship. She'd always known it. 'I'm so sorry, Robert. But you know what Mummy's like about Catholics.'

'She definitely mustn't come to the party then. Most of my colleagues and friends are Catholics.'

'Doesn't your mother mind?'

He shrugged. 'I suppose she's got used to the idea. For a start, when I was offered the job in St Francis there weren't many jobs going around. My father was ill and unemployed and we needed the money.'

'It was unusual for you to be offered it, was it not? I mean with you being a Protestant . . .'

Robert grinned. 'Darling, if you knew how tough a district Blackhill is you wouldn't think it at all unusual that a school there would be glad to get any teacher with enough nerve and optimism to teach in the place.'

Andrina felt a pang of apprehension. 'Is it dangerous?'

Robert's grin widened. 'Not for me it isn't. Or for guys like Bernard. Do you know any of his brothers?'

She shook her head.

'There are four O'Maley boys – Tony, Michael (Bernard's twin), Frank and Bernard. To see them coming along Garngad Road together is an impressive sight. People automatically clear a path for them. That's the kind of charisma you've got to have in places like Garngad and Blackhill.' Robert sighed. 'Sad but true. It's a case of the survival of the fittest. I try to teach them other things as well, of course. But it's a terrible uphill struggle. Especially in my department. So many of them think anything artistic is soft and poncey. You've got to keep proving yourself. God help Frank. I hear he writes poetry.'

'Are Michael and Bernard identical twins?' Andrina asked.

'Well, they're both big, heftily built men, but that's about it. Michael had curly hair like his father, but he keeps it cropped close to the bone now. And his nose has been broken a few times with him being a boxer. He and Bernard have a different look about the eyes too.'

Soon Bernard faded from Andrina's mind again. There were so many exciting thoughts to occupy her. The preparations for the wedding went happily and busily on, as did the more secret plans for the housewarming party. The party was going to take place a week after they returned from their honeymoon (two weeks at the Clyde resort of Dunoon) – just enough time to do a good sized baking. The same sponge mixture could be used in different ways: as small individual iced cakes with a cherry on top; as Victoria sponges stuck together with raspberry jam; as sponge fingers spread on top with ginger jam and nuts. Scones had to be baked as well, and pancakes made. Lots of sandwiches – tinned salmon, corned beef, mashed dates. It was going to be great fun. Andrina was looking forward more to being a busy housewife and entertaining guests in her very own home than to getting married. She hardly gave the wedding a thought. She hardly gave Robert a thought. Except when she was with him, of course. They were good friends. She liked and admired him enormously. She liked being with him.

To her he was awesomely sophisticated. He was not intimidated by posh restaurants. He spoke knowledgeably about art and artists and took her to exhibitions. He introduced her to the world of the theatre. She was grateful. Her hugs and kisses were outward expressions of that gratitude. It was easy to tell him she loved him. She was light-headed with happiness on her wedding day.

'You look like an angel,' her father told her, and kissed her and gave her an affectionate hug.

'What do you think, Mummy?' Andrina turned, shining-eyed, to Sophie.

Sophie was dressed in a black tailored coat, and a black brimmed hat tilted forward over her brow. She jerked on her black leather gloves and thought, 'Her and her red hair, and green eyes, and voluptuous curves.' Hand to mouth, she turned quickly away. 'You'll do,' she managed.

Both Andrina and her father were touched. They thought Sophie had been overcome with emotion.

They were right.

Chapter Seven

'Oh, hello, Mummy.' Andrina opened the door and stood aside. 'What a surprise!' It was her first full day back from her honeymoon. Robert had returned to work, and when the doorbell rang she had been standing in the front room feeling free and happy and proud. The sitting-room was ultra modern and in such good taste. What other house in the street, in the whole area, would have beautiful, original paintings on the walls?

'A pleasant surprise, I hope,' Sophie said, bustling after her daughter into the kitchen.

'Of course. I'll put the kettle on. It won't take long. It's still hot from breakfast.'

Sophie's eyes darted into every corner of the room.

'You haven't dusted, I see.'

'I lit the fire.' Andrina's voice quickened with eagerness, like a child hoping for praise. None came.

'Breakfast dishes still in the sink.' Sophie shook her head.

Andrina hastily explained, 'I was just going to wash them . . .'

'It's past ten o'clock.'

'. . . when my neighbour came to the door . . .'

'You don't want to encourage every Tom, Dick or Harry coming to your door, keeping you off your work. Especially in a place like this. You don't know what kind of people they are. I've heard there's prostitutes often hang about the Green.'

Andrina's mouth fell open and it was a second or two before she could find words. 'I thought you liked the place. You said . . .'

'Yes, yes, you were lucky to get a house with a bathroom and an open outlook on to the Green. But there's a pretty mixed crowd to be found in there, especially if there's a fair on, and there can be a terribly tough crowd. And don't forget there's Bridgeton nearby, and the Calton over the other side of London Road. Not to mention the High Court facing the Monument. There's bound to be a right lot of riff-raff always around there. That's where they used to have public hangings. Facing that monument. Don't you ever go out at night without Robert.'

Andrina laughed. 'Mummy, there's never been any public hangings for donkey's years.' But her euphoria had evaporated. 'Mrs Slater next door seemed all right. She's invited me in for a cup of tea later on. She had to rush out this morning but she said she'd be back after . . .'

'Don't tell me she works, and her a married woman. I can imagine what her house will be like.'

Andrina gave a gasp of disbelief. 'Mummy, lots of women have a job nowadays. Surely you know that. You said yourself that during the war . . .'

'There isn't a war on now. That's half the trouble today. Women going out leaving their children to grow up any old how without discipline or being taught what's right or wrong, or given a good Christian education. Boys getting into fighting and thievery. Girls into pregnancy or prostitution. The world's full of sin and sinners. If God's will's not done there's going to be retribution, you mark my words.'

'But she's divorced and she hasn't got any children.'

'A divorcée!' her mother echoed.

Andrina poured the tea. 'Would you like a biscuit?' She nearly added, 'These are shop ones but I'm going to be doing lots of home baking this week,' but she stopped herself in time, afraid that Sophie might wonder what all the baking was for. Her heart plummeted at the thought. Quite apart from the danger of her mother spoiling all the fun before and during the housewarming party, there was the terrible business of Bernard being there. At least it would be terrible in her mother's eyes.

Her mother startled her by saying, 'When are you going to do some home baking? You don't want to fill your good man with shop stuff like this.'

'I'll probably do some tomorrow.'

'I'll come and give you a hand.'

'Oh no, I've just remembered,' Andrina nearly spilled her tea in her anxiety, 'I've to visit Robert's mother tomorrow. Anyway, Mummy, you can't possibly travel all the way over here from Drumchapel every day. It takes so long. How could you get anything done in your own house? Anyway, there's no need. And I don't want Robert to think I can't bake or do anything by myself. I mean, what would he think of me?'

'I suppose you have a point,' Sophie reluctantly agreed. Then her thin face brightened. 'But I can still keep in touch with you every day.'

'How do you mean?'

'We've got a phone!' Sophie announced triumphantly. 'Andrew should have had one long ago – with all his council business – and we've arranged for you to have one installed as well. As part of our wedding present. Remember we said we had something else for you – a surprise? We thought we'd have it in for you coming back but they couldn't manage it so soon. They've promised to install it for you before the end of this week though.'

Andrina was torn between the thrill of having a telephone to link her to her friends and the fear of the umbilical link it might prove to be with her mother. 'Oh Mummy, it's very kind and generous of you and Daddy, but I don't think you ought to go to all that expense.'

'Nonsense. Your daddy seems to be doing very well just now with one thing and another. I'm sure Robert will be delighted. I'm surprised he didn't think of putting one in himself, a man in his position. That tea's not very strong. You should have let it mask a bit longer.'

Suddenly something occurred to Andrina. 'How could the engineer have got into the house while we were away?'

'Oh, didn't Robert mention it? I asked him for one of your keys in case there was an emergency while you were away and I needed to get into the house.'

Andrina was so appalled she couldn't speak.

'If the place had been burgled, for instance,' Sophie went on, 'and the police needed to check on what was taken. Or needed the place locked up again, I could have come and seen to everything. I'll pour this weak stuff down the sink. Maybe it'll be a bit stronger in the pot now. Just a minute, I'll give it a good stir first.'

'I've never heard about any house-breakings,' Andrina managed. 'Banks, shops in town, bars and bookies' places, but never ordinary tenement houses in working class areas like this, have you?'

'Just because there was never any in Dumbarton Road that we know of doesn't mean there isn't anywhere else. You can't be too careful.'

Anger was trembling inside Andrina, but she tried to sound pleasant enough. 'I'm surprised you didn't use the key today instead of knocking at the door.'

Her mother stopped in the middle of stirring the contents of the teapot. 'Do you actually think I would have walked in here without knocking and risked frightening the life out of you? Is that all you think of me? After all I've done for you?'

'No, no. Of course not. I mean, I really appreciate all you've done, Mummy. You've been really marvellous. A marvellous help.'

'Did you notice I got messages in for you coming back?'

'Oh yes. I really appreciated that. It would have been too late for me to get any milk or bread or anything for Robert's supper. He really enjoyed the meat pie. I did too.' She'd left a key with Mrs Slater next door and had thought it was her that had just been neighbourly.

'I thought it would be nice for you to come home to something in the cupboard,' Sophie said. 'I noticed you hadn't got any messages in before you went away.'

'I know. I'm sorry about that, but what with all the excitement of the wedding and everything, I forgot.'

'That's better,' Sophie said, pouring out another cup of tea. 'Will I fill you up? Oh, you haven't drunk it yet. No, leave it. It's like dishwater. I'll get rid of it and pour you out a fresh cup.'

Andrina could have wept with irritation. She longed to

stamp her feet and cry out, 'It's my home, my key, my kitchen, my teapot, my tea.' But felt ashamed at what she saw as the childishness and pettiness of her feelings. Her mother was only trying to be helpful and caring. (Although she secretly determined, one way or another, to get her key back.) 'Thanks, Mummy,' she said.

'How was your honeymoon? Was Dunoon nice?'

'Lovely. You and Daddy should go there some time. Such a nice clean place. You'd love it, Mummy, and it would do you so much good to get away for a holiday.'

'Oh, your daddy's too busy for me. I hardly ever see him these days. What's that saying? "A shoemaker's bairns are always worst shod." He's too busy seeing to what everyone else needs.'

'You could go with him on some of his trips.'

'And what difference would that make? On the journey in the train he'd have his nose in official papers all the time. Then, when we got to wherever he was going, he'd disappear to meetings and I'd be left on my own in a strange town among strangers. He'd forget all about me. I know your daddy. It's hard enough trying to make him toe the line when he's here.'

Andrina looked at the thin bespectacled face and felt a rush of love and pity. 'Never mind, Mummy. You've always got me.'

'Yes,' Sophie echoed, 'I've always got you.'

Andrina wished she could do something or say something to make her mother relax. There was always such an intense look about her, almost of desperation. It was most unsettling. In a way she couldn't blame her father for withdrawing into himself or into council business. Probably he did it so he could get a bit of peace.

'Your daddy's got an office or some place where he does his council business now,' Sophie continued. 'He never even comes home for his dinner. I don't see him all day.'

'In the City Chambers?'

'He's says it's just a small corner in the chambers. And they've a restaurant for the councillors. I told him – it won't be as good food as you'd get in your own home. He's been staying in the chambers till late as well.' Her mouth tightened. 'I'm beginning to wonder if he's up to something.'

Andrina was shocked. 'Oh no! Not Daddy. Mummy, how could you think such a thing?'

Sophie's nostrils pinched in as she took a deep, firm breath. 'Yes, God forgive me. I must cleanse my mind of bad thoughts. Drumchapel's too far out for most folks to come to the house, apparently. Remember how they all used to come every night after we had our tea? Never a soul now.'

'Oh dear. Are you finding it lonely?'

Sophie shrugged. 'I'll soon settle in and get to know folks. The trouble is so many of the women seem to be out at work. I've said it before and I'll say it again. It's not right.'

'Robert and I will come to visit you at the weekend. Will that be all right?'

'Come to Sunday dinner. I'll get a bit of good steak. I know Robert likes a good bit of steak.' Sophie's eyes brightened. 'And I'll make one of my apple tarts. Remember he said it was the best apple tart he'd ever tasted.' She laughed. 'I don't know what his mother would have thought if she'd heard him. Of course, give Jean her due, she makes very good butter shortbread.'

'I know. I've tasted it.' Andrina couldn't help wondering how long her mother planned to stay.

'I'll rinse these along with your breakfast things.' Sophie snatched up the cups and saucers although in fact Andrina hadn't quite finished her tea.

'I'll do them, Mummy.'

'It won't take a minute. What've you got in for Robert's dinner?'

'We're going to have our dinner at night after he finishes work. I gave him some sandwiches to have in the staffroom at lunchtime.'

Her mother splashed water into the basin and rattled the dishes around. 'Oh, *lunch* now, is it?'

Andrina knew that everyone – or at least everyone she and her mother knew – had their main meal, which they called dinner, in the middle of the day, and a 'high tea' in the early evening – which could consist of scrambled eggs and chips or some sort of fry up, and bread and jam, perhaps scones and pancakes as well. But times were changing.

'It's better this way, Mummy. We can both relax and enjoy our main meal after Robert's finished work.'

'I suppose it's sensible enough when you look at it like that. Yes, it's a good idea. From now on, we could have our dinner at night as well. I must tell Andrew not to stuff himself with a lot of rubbish in the City Chambers restaurant during the day. So what are you making for Robert tonight?'

Andrina felt trapped. She had been looking forward to such a lovely day on her own, doing anything she wanted and in her own time.

'I hadn't made up my mind. I've still to go to the shops.'

'Right.' Sophie put the last of the dishes on to the draining board to dry. 'I'll go and see what I can get while you rake out that fire and set it and polish up the grate. That job causes a lot of dust, remember, so give the whole place a good going over afterwards. Now, where's your message bag? Don't tell me you haven't got one. Never mind, I'll take mine.'

'But I don't know how much money to give you . . .'

'Oh don't be so gormless. I'll tell you how much everything cost when I get back and you can square up with me then. I'll bring a bit of corned beef or a nice slice or two of tongue to make a sandwich for us as well.' She laughed. 'We'll have our first *lunch* together.' She emphasised that word, as happy as a child with a new toy.

The door closed and Andrina was alone again, but no matter how she tried, she could not recapture a single vestige of the joy she'd experienced earlier.

Chapter Eight

The phone rang within minutes of it being installed.

'Hello Mummy.'

'How did you know it was me?'

'I haven't had time to give anyone my number.'

'I asked the exchange. I gave you my number, didn't I? Wasn't it lucky you getting the phone in so soon?'

'Wonderful.'

'What have you been doing today?'

'It's only quarter past nine, Mummy.'

'Don't tell me you've left the breakfast dishes and the fire again.'

'No,' she protested, then flushed guiltily as if her mother could see down the phone and into the kitchen. 'Well, I would have had them done, only the telephone engineer kept me back.'

'Remember to order more coal.'

'Yes, Mummy.'

'Did you see that woman after I left yesterday?'

'What woman?'

'Next door.'

'Oh yes.'

'What was she like?'

'It wasn't that she was working yesterday morning. She had to go and see the factors.'

'Had she got into arrears?'

'I don't know. I never asked her.'

'She doesn't work then?'

Andrina hesitated. 'Well, not in the morning.'

'Well then?'

'At nights.'

'Where?'

Another hesitation. 'In a public house.'

'A barmaid?' Her mother sounded so shocked it was as if Andrina had confessed to being a barmaid herself.

'She seems a very nice person, Mummy.'

'What kind of judge of character are you? Where is this bar?'

'Castle Street.'

'Castle Street? That's near Garngad and Blackhill. I can just imagine what a so-called nice person she is. The next thing will be she'll be tempting you into the rough circle she obviously mixes with. I feel quite ill at the thought. That whole area is a cesspool of sin, Andrina. There's gang fights and prostitution and all sorts of wickedness goes on over that end of town.' She was working herself up into a frenzy.

It frightened Andrina. 'Please, Mummy,' she pleaded, 'there's no need for you to get upset.'

'You've always been a worry to me. You worry me sick. You've always got into bad company. I've always tried to watch you and keep you from the paths of sin. I've tried, God knows I've tried to give you a good Christian upbringing. But all the time I'm fighting a losing battle. You'll be drinking next. That'll be the next thing.'

'Oh, Mummy, honestly!'

'Of course, your daddy's no kind of example.'

'Daddy's a good Christian, surely. He helps so many people, and he hardly ever misses a Sunday at the church.'

'The way he pours the evil stuff down his throat.'

'Oh, I don't think Daddy . . . I mean I've never once seen him the worse for drink.'

'He never staggers about or raises his voice. It would be better if he did. The demon drink transforms your daddy into a stupid, sly, disgusting, revolting beast.'

There were times, and more than one of them, when Andrina had the fleeting suspicion that her mother was mad. 'I don't know why you're talking like this, Mummy. If it's because you're afraid I'll take to drink, please believe me I've no intention of doing any such thing. I don't even like the taste of the stuff. I've never been in a public house in my life and I've no desire or intention of ever setting foot in one. *Not ever!* Please believe me.'

'Promise me you won't have anything to do with that woman.'

'Josie?'

'You see what I mean? You're on first name terms already.'

'But she's my next door neighbour.'

'Promise me, Andrina.' Sophie's voice withered into coldness. The coldness brought the usual spectre of panic to haunt Andrina.

She struggled to cope with it. 'Mummy, honestly, there's absolutely no need for you to worry.'

There was a silence in which Andrina lost the battle with herself and floundered into acute anxiety.

'Mummy, are you still there?'

'There's obviously no point in me saying any more.'

'Mummy?' Andrina hastily clicked the rest up and down. 'Mummy?'

Eventually she replaced the receiver. Wandering about the flat kneading her hands, shoulders hunched up with tension, she tried to remember what it was she had been meaning to do before the phone rang – but couldn't. In the kitchen she stared blankly at the dead embers of the fire.

All she was conscious of was nerves tightening all over her body, impeding the smooth flow of blood to her cheeks, making her heart palpitate, tightening in her neck, making it tenser and tenser until she felt like screaming. A headache gripped her skull like a vice.

The only release, she knew, was to phone her mother and apologise, promise, do or say anything to please her, to bring her closer again, to make everything all right. At the same time she didn't know how she could keep her promise not to have anything to do with Josie Slater, who seemed such a nice open-hearted person.

Josie's mother had recently died after a long illness, and Josie had spent every day nursing her and only went out in the evening after she'd got her mother settled. 'We had to eat, you see, hen. I had to earn a bob or two somewhere.' Josie seemed so eager to be friendly. 'Here, it's great to see somebody young in the close,' she enthused. 'It's awful depressing here with all the neighbours being older. Don't get me wrong, hen. They were all good friends of my mammy and I've nothing against them. All the same, it's great to know I'll have a pal nearer my own age. I'm a wee bit older than you, but not that much. If you run out of anything, hen, or need a helping hand, don't hesitate. Just knock on my door.'

Andrina guessed Josie was a woman of about Robert's age, certainly over thirty, not very tall, but busty and with well-shaped legs precariously balanced in high heeled shoes. She sported large flashy earrings, the kind that Andrina had always longed to wear. They dangled and sparkled and swung about as she talked. The blonde hair that framed her plump cheeks was straight, except for the ends which curled inwards. She looked a bit like Diana Dors. She had been delighted when Andrina had told her this. 'You and I are pals for life, hen. You've made my day, so you have. I needed cheering up. I miss my mammy, so I do.'

Andrina couldn't settle to wash the dishes or clear out the fire or do anything. Torn between her need to dispel the agonising tension caused by any discordant note between herself and her mother, and her inability to see how she could cut Josie dead, she stood helplessly rooted to the one spot in the kitchen. Eventually she couldn't bear it any longer. She phoned her mother. The phone rang for a long time before Sophie's voice intoned the Drumchapel number.

'Mummy, it's me. Please don't hang up. I'm sorry. I know you just want to protect me. To make sure I'm all right. I understand. I won't have anything to do with Josie Slater. I promise.' Even as she spoke she remembered that she had already invited Josie to the housewarming party. Her heart-beats made fluttery echoes in her stomach.

'It's for your own good.' Sophie's voice was still cool but not quite so cool as it had been.

'I know, Mummy.'

'I worry about you.'

'I know.'

'You're my only child.'

'I know, Mummy.'

'Now just you concentrate on your housework and have everything perfect for Robert coming home. Always start with the fire. Get rid of the ashes. Take them down to the back court right away. I hope that barmaid person's going to take her turn of the stairs. You see that she does. Not by talking to her. Don't have any truck with a common trollop like that. Put a note through her door if she misses. Say you'll report her to the factor. I bet she's a Pape. Josie sounds like a Catholic name. Is she?'

'I don't know.'

'I can tell just by looking at them. I can see the map of Ireland on their faces.'

'Gosh.' Andrina affected a spurt of bright surprise. 'Is that the time? And I haven't done a thing yet.'

'Well,' her mother said, 'I'll let you get on.' Her voice warmed. 'It's lovely having the phone, isn't it?'

'Yes, Mummy.'

'Bye bye just now.'

'Bye bye, Mummy.'

Andrina savoured exquisite relief as she put the phone down. There was still the flutter of worry about Josie coming to the housewarming party, but the housewarming party was a secret. Sophie would be none the wiser.

She tied on an apron and hurriedly began raking out the fire. Robert said that one of these days he'd have the big black range with its high mantelshelf taken out. They'd have a gas cooker put in and use an electric fire for heat.

'Think of all the work it'll save you,' Robert said.

He was so thoughtful and she appreciated it. He was even considerate in love-making. The honeymoon had been quite an adventure, especially the first night. The excitement of the unknown, the novelty of being a married lady – it was all very pleasant and enjoyable.

Before the fortnight was over, however, she was beginning to get tired of the sexual act. It was a bit of a nuisance really. Not that she'd let Robert know that she felt this. He seemed to get such a thrill out of it with his little moans and groans of pleasure. She didn't mind him enjoying himself. The sex act was not exactly unpleasant to her. At times it could be quite nice. She decided, however, that they shouldn't do it so often once they got home and had other, more important things to think about and take up their energies. As a result they had settled down to a more sensible level of sexual activity.

She began to sing as she worked. It was lovely having a home of her own. She was so proud of it and it gave her pleasure to see everything sparkling clean and polished. Eventually she gazed around with pride. Her mother couldn't fault the place now.

Andrina went around touching, caressing everything, the round table and spar-backed chairs in the alcove, the lace doily and crystal vase of gypsy gracing the centre of the table, the two occasional chairs, covered with moss-green tweed, one on either side of the range. On the opposite wall a modern kitchen unit in green and white with handy cupboards and drainers for dishes and cutlery gave her special pleasure. From a line of hooks along it hung shiny stainless steel pots and pans. The press over in the corner between the sink and the range was where the food was kept. The floor gleamed with a highly-polished black linoleum. Black linoleum against white woodwork: who had ever heard of such a thing! It was absolutely unique, like the modern geometric rug which lay in front of the fire.

The bathroom of course was a dream. Like something out of a Hollywood film.

Satisfied with everything, she went through to the bedroom and enjoyed the deliciously wicked experience of sitting at her very own dressing-table and putting on make-up. A dusting of powder with a fluffy pink puff, then reddening of lips and a brushing of mascara gave an impressive result. Round, slightly protruding eyes were filled with childish happiness.

Robert said her eyes sparkled like jewels and it was true. He said her hair was glorious. Not red, but a deep rich copper colour.

She enjoyed giving the luxurious, thick, wavy, curly mane a brush before rising, hands on hips, to admire her full reflection. Then she donned her coat, collected her message bag and purse and, singing happily to herself, she left the house. She wasn't yet familiar with the district and felt like an explorer as she strolled along to one end of Monteith Row where stood the impressive archway of the main entrance to the Green. She was tempted to walk along and have a look at the High Court, even go inside. Maybe there was a murder trial in progress. Instead she decided to leave that adventure to another day. Today she had special purchases to make, not only for Robert's dinner but for the baking she planned to do for the party.

Soon she found herself in Bain Street, the end of which was crossed by the London Road. In London Road she had a field day buying everything she needed.

The Calton was bounded by the Gallowgate and London Road, which met at Glasgow Cross at one end, and the equally notorious Bridgeton at the other. She enjoyed her walk exploring the area. She did not find what she'd seen of the Calton either depressing or frightening, despite its dusty broken paintwork, its crumbling black tenements, the men languishing about its street corners, its noisy children kicking tin cans, bouncing balls against walls, shouting and fighting.

Her stride had acquired a bounce to it. She was a married lady. She was a free spirit. Yet a couple of times, as if she was attached to an invisible watcher, she turned, and in vague apprehension looked around.

Chapter Nine

'I would have loaned her plates if she'd asked me,' Maureen said to Patrick. There was no need to lower her voice, indeed quite the reverse because of the racket all around them.

Bridie's twenty-first was going great guns. As well as the Gallacher family, of God only knew how many, plus mother and father Carragh and Scobie, there was Maureen and Patrick, plus all the friends of the Gallachers' offspring. The Gallachers' room and kitchen had never been so chock-a-block.

'Och, what does it matter?' Patrick was already in his cups and didn't care if he had to eat his piece of clouty dumpling off the floor. 'The tablecloth's clean enough.'

'Looks more like a bed sheet to me,' Maureen said. But she felt sorry for Carragh. After all the miscarriages she'd had and such a big family to contend with, God help her, she had more to bother her than finding plates for her clouty dumpling. Anyway, it tasted just as good without a plate. Even the rich, spicy smell of it was mouth-watering.

'Frank and Bridie seem to have hit it off.' Maureen felt really pleased about that. Her prayers looked as if they were going to be answered. Every night she'd prayed to the Holy family, 'Oh Holy Mother, Blessed Mary, ever virgin, Saint Joseph and the Infant Child, please make our Frank more normal. Please stop him making such a silly ass of himself. Please make him take a notion for Bridie Gallacher.'

She and Patrick and Tony and Michael and Bernard had all agreed that no mention of Bridie would be made to Frank before the party. They all knew that Frank was not only peculiar, he was thrawn. If Frank thought you were dead keen for him to do something, or were eager to guide him in one direction, he'd do something else, he'd go the exact opposite way. Or he'd just dig in his heels, put down his head (usually to bury it in a book) and refuse to do anything at all.

If she hadn't seen Frank being born, or at least seconds after he emerged from her body, if she'd had him in hospital instead of her own home, Maureen would have thought there must have been some mix-up and she'd been given the wrong baby. He didn't even look like her or Patrick or any of his brothers.

Patrick was a typical Glasgow working man with his short, stocky, robust appearance and rough-hewn features. Maureen was sonsy in build, 'a good armful', Patrick called her. Tony, Michael and Bernard were all well-made. One look at them told you they were men to be reckoned with. Hard as rocks. Poor Frank, although about the same height as his brothers, couldn't boast a pick of flesh. His clothes hung on him. His hair was lank and greasy. He didn't take a bit of interest in his appearance. And it was true what Patrick said – Frank had a soft nature. Maybe that's why she loved him so much. (They all did really.) Frank was the one who noticed when she was tired and made her sit down while he did the dishes or cooked the meal. He'd even, on one memorable occasion, gone down to the back court and hung out the washing. She'd been laid low with varicose veins at the time. It had been the talk of the place. For a Scotsman to do household chores, any kind of women's work, for any reason, was really beyond the pale. She knew that he would be labelled a Jessy, a Pansy, a Poof, and God knows what else behind their backs. His father and his brothers, in the privacy of their home, had on occasion called him all of these things.

Frank was the one who cut her toenails, a job she found difficult to do herself since she'd put on a bit of weight. ('But all in the right places, hen,' Patrick always assured her.) She could tell Frank her troubles. She was ashamed to admit it, even to herself, but sometimes she felt he was like the daughter she'd never had. She was glad of and grateful for his soft nature. At times like that she'd chastise herself and pray for Frank's sake.

'Dear Sacred Heart of Jesus, help me to be strong and not to take advantage of the lovely boy's soft nature. Don't let me be glad of the comfort of it. Oh, Holy Mother, help me to help him to be hard and strong like Patrick and Tony and Michael and Bernard. Dear God, Dear God, hear my prayers.'

Now she thought to herself, 'God bless Bridie Gallacher'. There the dear girl was, making up to Frank as hard as she could. Listening to him as if he was Jesus Christ delivering the Sermon on the Mount. Occasionally a little sigh would escape and a hand would give Frank's arm a quick touch as if in wondrous disbelief. Probably Frank was boring the pants off the poor girl with one of his poems. Maureen hoped Bridie wouldn't overdo it and make Frank suspicious.

Both Maureen and Carragh had long since suspected that Bridie had a notion of Frank. Although basically a shy girl, she had asked Maureen on more than one occasion how Frank was getting on. Or she'd remark, with forced casualness, 'I didn't see Frank at Mass this morning.'

It worried Maureen that Frank sometimes missed Mass. Admittedly he was forgetful. Even when he was a young child, however, he was beginning to show ominous signs. He was barely more than seven when the most awful thing happened. Frank's teacher and the priest had been going round the class examining the children to see if they knew their catechism in preparation for their first Holy Communion. Each question had an exact answer that had to be learned off by heart.

'Who made you?' the priest had asked Frank.

'God made me,' Frank dutifully answered.

'What did God make you for?'

'God made me to love him and serve him in this world and be happy with him in the next.'

'What is God?'

Apparently at this point Frank had hesitated and the priest had prompted, 'God is a Supreme Spirit.'

'But how do you know?' Frank said, shocking rigid both teacher and priest. And then he'd compounded his crime by adding the phrase he'd often heard from the lips of his Uncle Joseph concerning other questions – mostly relating to the attributes of a greyhound or a race-horse, 'He sounds like a right bummer to me.'

His mother was sent for but too late to save him from the belting he'd already received. Her plea that Frank didn't know what he was talking about and it was all his Uncle Joseph's fault did not absolve him from sin and the warnings of eternal damnation.

She remembered crying all the way home, she'd been so worried about Frank and so afraid of how he'd end up. She was relieved when he'd run around with a gang for a while. He'd got into minor scrapes and trouble like any other normal youngster. He and his pals had tied door handles together, kicked at the doors, then run away. They'd thrown stones at the pupils of the nearest Protestant school. They'd played football in the street, broken windows, been chased, caught and had their ears boxed.

But by the time Frank was twelve, he was already drifting away from normality to become a loner who wrote poems. No belting or ear-boxing could cure him of that. Bridie Gallacher might do the trick. At least she must be interested in books because she'd chosen to work in a second-hand bookshop. Frank loved books.

'If Frank doesn't know he's getting the come-on sign there, and if he doesn't take advantage of it, he's a fool,' Patrick said.

'We don't want him to take advantage of the girl,' Maureen chided. 'Just fall for her and court her and eventually tie the knot with her.'

Patrick shrugged. 'Comes to the same thing. The poor sod doesn't know what she's letting herself in for.'

'Patrick!' Maureen elbowed him in the ribs. 'Our Frank's a lovely boy and well you know it.'

'What are you two fighting about?' Big Bernard came sauntering over and Maureen gazed up at him with pride. 'Och, you know who. Do you reckon they've clicked, son?'

'Frank could do worse than Bridie. Her sister's the one with the looks though.'

'Doris? Ah-ha. Is this another romance brewing then? Och

well, she's a nice enough wee lassie. A bit la-de-da, that's all. She thinks because she works in Daly's she's as posh as the customers.'

'I need somebody to partner me to another do in a few days time over at Monteith Row.'

'Who do you know there?'

'Robert Anderson.'

'The Mr Anderson you help at the karate club?'

'Yes.'

'Aw, a lovely man, so he is.' Maureen remembered with heartfelt gratitude how this teacher had been the saving of Bernard. She'd always worried about Bernard in the opposite way from Frank. Bernard had brains but he had brawn as well, and she'd been afraid of him getting into too much trouble when he was young.

She'd never forget the day he arrived home – he was only a young lad at the time – cut and bruised and battered and with blood soaking through his clothes. He'd insisted he hadn't been involved in a gang fight. He had just been minding his own business when a crowd had surrounded him. He hadn't stood a chance because they had weapons. If it hadn't been for Mr Anderson coming by at the time and rescuing him, he would have been killed. If Mr Anderson hadn't then got Bernard interested in karate, Bernard might have taken the path of so many other boys in the district. He would have joined a rival gang and fought vengeance fights along with them.

The next step would be into crime. Many a lad from a decent family had gone from gang fights to petty crime, and then to the more serious crimes of robbing pubs and bookies and banks and big houses in Newton Mearns. The most hardened cases became real gangsters.

What had saved Tony was first of all getting into a skiffle group. Then he'd gone drum-crazy and bought himself a set of drums. This was a mixed blessing. It nearly drove everyone else into the crime of murder. Murdering Tony.

What had saved Bernard, she believed, was getting involved with Mr Anderson and his karate club. She'd often sent up a prayer for Mr Anderson despite the fact that he was a Protestant.

'It's not Mr Anderson's twenty-first birthday party, is it?' she laughed.

'No. Housewarming. He got married recently.'

'Aw, you should have told me, Bernard. I would have got him a present. I think the world of that man.'

'I got something.'

'Thank God for that. Who did he marry?'

'Bailie McPherson's daughter.'

Patrick joined in the conversation then. 'I'm proud to claim Bailie McPherson as a friend. He won the Victoria Cross during the war,' he announced as if he hadn't told them this a hundred times before. 'A real hero, but you'd never think it to talk to him. Always ready to do anybody a good turn.'

'I thought he was Councillor McPherson,' Maureen said.

'Listen,' Patrick said, 'you can call a councillor a bailie but you can never call a bailie a councillor. He's on the bench now. Gold chain of office and all.'

A sudden flash of hope widened Maureen's eyes. 'Here! He'll have more clout as a bailie. And he's on the housing committee, isn't he?'

'You name the committee,' Patrick said, 'and the chances are he's on it. He works like a slave for the benefit of his fellow man, does Bailie Andrew McPherson. A fine, big man.'

'Well then!'

'What do you mean – well then?'

'Ask him to get us a nice house with a bathroom. Just round about here. I don't want to move away from all my good neighbours.'

'There aren't any nice houses with bathrooms round about here.'

'There are so. In Blackhill or Provanmill for a start.'

Patrick looked uncertain, but he said, 'I suppose I could mention it the next time I see him at the club. But he doesn't manage there so often now. He's a busy man.'

'Go and see him at the City Chambers then, or wherever

folks are supposed to see him about houses. Aw, go on, Patrick. For me, darlin'. It would be heaven, so it would, to have a bathroom.'

Patrick put an arm round her waist and gave her a squeeze. 'What's it worth?'

Maureen squealed with pleasure, making both Patrick and Bernard guffaw.

Bernard thought it was great that his mother and father obviously still enjoyed a good sex life. More than once when friends had been in the house having a drink and a sing-song Patrick had suddenly announced, 'Right, folks, it's been a great night and I've enjoyed your company but I'll have to ask you to leave now. I want to take my wife to bed.'

In his imagination Bernard had taken Andrina to bed and had made love to her many times. He could see her still as she'd looked on her wedding day: so radiant, so sublimely beautiful, her copper-coloured hair shimmering in the sunlight, her veil floating around her like a halo. His mind, his heart, every nerve in his body reached out to her, claimed her irrevocably as his own. He couldn't believe that she was giving herself to someone else. It was some cruel distortion of fate. Had the groom been anyone else but Robert Anderson, he would have rushed across the road to the church, snatched Andrina up in his arms and raced off with her.

As it was, he was paralysed in his agony of love, unable to do anything.

His angel. He would be seeing her again within the week.

'I'd better go and chat Doris up,' he told his mother and father.

Patrick winked at him. 'A big, fine-looking chap like you – it'll be no bother, son. She'll be eating out of your hand in no time, or my name's not Patrick O'Maley.'

Bernard crushed his way through the crowd of revellers towards Doris Gallacher. He regarded her as a bit of a pain, with her pretensions of being a lady. Apart from that she was all right. He'd known her off and on since they went to school together. She'd been in a younger class. He supposed her affectations were her way of trying to get out of her present environment. He didn't blame her.

'How are you doing, Doris?' He smiled down at her. She was drinking a cup of tea with pinky raised.

'Oh, hello, Bernard. Isn't this a terrible rabble? And no plates for the dumpling. Did you ever? I didn't invite any of the girls from Daly's. What would they have thought? Some of them come from Bearsden.'

Bernard kept the smile stuck to his face. 'How would you like to come to a party with me on Saturday?'

She had dark eyes, black lashes, and a bee-hive of cream-coloured hair. Its pale colour made the blush that spread to her cheeks all the more noticeable. 'Thank you. I'm sure that would be very nice.'

'Were you ever in Mr Anderson's class?'

'Was he the one with kind of sunk-in jaws?'

'You make him sound half dead. He's one of the fittest men I know and he's over thirty.'

'He had that kind of face though. But he was a terribly nice man. I remember he told me I drew very nice little pictures.'

Bernard couldn't imagine Robert saying any such thing unless he was being sarcastic, but he let it pass. 'He got married recently and it's his housewarming party.'

'Oh, how terribly nice!'

'I'll call for you about seven-thirty, OK?'

'I'll look forward to it. I really will.' She lowered her heavily mascaraed eyelashes and took another sip of tea. Her pinky annoyed him intensely.

Chapter Ten

Bernard had always worked nights, but he made sure he'd be off on the night of Andrina's housewarming party. It was a bit easier in that respect, now that he was taking on more than one pub at a time and employing Bill Doyle and Jack Rafferty. He would accept a booking for a job, the club or bar owner or manager paid him, and then he paid Doyle and Rafferty, making a profit for himself in the process. He had no regrets about starting to organise work on his own like this.

He had had no regrets about the training or the expertise at the security firm called Bodyguard Incorporated either. He had been barely sixteen at the time, and working in the Empire as a bouncer when he'd first heard about the firm. He had lied to the manager of the Empire when he'd started there because he'd been only fifteen. He looked at least two years older, and husky with it, so there had been no problem, except perhaps to get one of the Empire's red uniform jackets to fit his shoulders. The jackets were padded to make the other guys look broader. He didn't need the padding. He remembered he felt very smart with his black trousers and black bow tie. Even then he'd believed it was important to look well turned out, and he had been right.

A guy that used to come about the place had approached him one day and told him he was from this set-up called Body-guards Incorporated. They were all ex-SAS, and this man said to him, 'I've been watching you. You've got what it takes. Would you like to get involved with my firm?'

Bernard had been doubtful. For one thing he didn't want to give away his age. 'Do you not need to go into the army or anything like that?'

'No, no,' the man said. 'We've got the wherewithal to train you, and the techniques involved.'

So, from the age of sixteen, over a few years, he worked with these people. They trained him in close protection techniques, bodyguarding, evasive driving techniques, and firearms training. He went abroad with them and saw how they worked. He was impressed with what highly-trained professionals they were. The most valuable things he learned from them were self-discipline and one hundred per cent concentration, although he'd also become an expert in judo and a black belt in karate. He'd already had a good grounding in karate from Robert Anderson of course. He survived the close protection or bodyguarding even in the most dangerous situations – with terrorists, for example – because working on the streets of Glasgow had sharpened his instincts.

More and more he'd nursed thoughts of his own business, and he knew the place to start was on the streets. He went back to work in the bars and nightclubs of the city. He still did the occasional jobs for Bodyguards Incorporated, usually protecting a pop star who wanted to relax over a meal and a few drinks at a nightclub after their show in Glasgow or Edinburgh.

He built up a reputation for being able to deal with problems before they began. His mere presence in a bar or a nightclub usually proved a deterrent. He thought a lot about his job and how best he could deal with it. His obsession with his work became almost as strong as his obsession with Andrina. He'd always been single-minded in everything he did, especially in overcoming fear. He remembered as a child how terrified he was to go down the shadowy gaslit stair to the lavatory, especially on winter nights when the wind would be howling and moaning from the close. Inside, the lavatory was total darkness. His mother always told him to climb up and pee in the kitchen sink rather than go down the stairs. But even then, when he was only knee-high to a grasshopper, something in his personality drove him to stubbornly face his terrors head on. He'd stamp, grim-faced, down the stone stairs, then grope determinedly into the black pit of the lavatory.

Sometimes he'd repeat out loud to himself as he did so, 'I don't care about ghosts. I don't care about ghosts.' His ma and da used to laugh at him about that, especially when they were reminiscing about when the family were young.

'Bernard were always a stubborn, determined little devil,' his ma would say. 'Even as a baby.'

His absorption with his work, and the total concentration needed in carrying it out, became reflected in his outward appearance. Even when he laughed, his eyes remained cautious, watchful, ready. More often than not his face was set in a cast-iron mask – hard, expressionless. He was known around the pubs and clubs as 'The Big Man', and for a big man his reactions were astonishingly swift. He was feared for the rapidity of his responses to trouble. Yet he still appeared to keep his calm. He could suddenly bring a man down and make him howl in anguish with a finger to a shoulder nerve or a karate kick, without a flicker of an eye or the slightest change of expression. He had never been known to show anger on the job, never lost the slightest self-control. He was admired for it, even by the gangsters. Quite early on he'd sorted out in his mind his own particular philosophy, his special approach. He'd explained it to Doyle and Rafferty, because it was the lines on which he wanted his business run.

'I believe in showing a modicum of respect for everyone,' he said. 'Even to the worst drunks we have to deal with. That means I cajole them first. And if they've friends around I get them on my side to help. I try to avoid confrontation. With even the worst gangsters I show a bit of respect. You know they're scum; I know they're scum. But I don't let them see that I know. I talk to them as if they're businessmen, because that's what they like to believe they are. Remember, we have to spend night after night standing at the same bar as them. We've got to have some sort of working relationship. They've got to respect us too. That way we keep the trouble we're there to deal with to an absolute minimum.'

Working relationships were very difficult, very difficult indeed. He believed in showing respect to the police too, and in the case of some high-ranking officers, he often showed them more respect than they deserved.

The police were constantly suspicious of him. They saw him talking to criminals and gangsters, and they assumed he must be one of them. It was just as mistaken as the attitude of ordinary punters who, seeing him or his men having a drink at a bar or a meal at a club, thought they were relaxing and having a good time. They thought it was an easy job.

Easy it was not.

For a start, he was forever trying to assure the police that he wasn't running some sort of racket alongside his security work.

One officer had told him to his face, 'We know you're up to something and we'll find out what it is and nail you for it even if it takes us years.'

'Look,' he'd said, 'the only thing you'll ever nail me for is something you've set me up for. No way am I going to work anything on the wrong side of the law. Never.'

He meant it. He knew he was too intelligent for that. Apart from strongly-held principles, he also knew he had the ability to make as much money as the gangsters without joining them. They tried hard enough, of course, to manipulate him and influence him to get him on their side. He kept on apparently friendly speaking terms, but remained his own man. He kept his balance on the dangerous tightrope, the invariable dividing line. It was an art that had taken him years to perfect, and one with which he was still having to practise extreme caution and self-control. Self-control was of vital importance. Only the other night he'd been standing at a bar, to all appearances relaxing and passing the time talking to one of these gangsters. But in fact his guard was not lowered, and he was acutely conscious of everything going on in his surroundings. He was aware that the gangster's girlfriend and her sister were sitting at a table nearby. Gorgeous looking girls, but potential trouble. He had long since decided that women were *the* worst stirrers of trouble and the most difficult to deal with.

While he was talking the gangster's girlfriend got up, came over to him with a pair of nail scissors in her hand and cut his tie in half. He could have killed her with one blow. Instead, he totally ignored her. Her stupid act made not the slightest interruption to what he was saying. After the conversation finished and he had to move away to deal with a drunk who had suddenly decided to pick a fight with another customer, the gangster went over to his girlfriend and gave her a blow across the face that knocked the girl off her chair.

After that, these two girls pursued Bernard, did everything they could to latch on to him. He supposed it was because with their gangster lover no man would dare hook up with them. Any man who did would end up in the Clyde or minus some part of his anatomy. The girls had come to the conclusion that he was tough enough to deal with any trouble. And he was.

But no matter what reason they were throwing themselves at him, he didn't take them on. It was another part of his professional attitude that he didn't mix business with pleasure. To get involved with any woman on the job was strictly taboo. This wasn't easy. He came in contact with quite a few glamorous women, and he was a fit and highly-sexed man. As a result he only had sex with local girls, mostly girls he'd known all his life. Some of them had wanted marriage. They had spoken of a 'nice wee house' and 'settling down'. They seemed to think they could change him; make him into a pipe and slippers man.

A pipe and slippers man he was not. He managed to remain friends with some of the girls. Others had become bitchy and bitter when they realised marriage, or marriage with Bernard at least, was not on the cards.

The only marriage he wanted to make was with Andrina, and that would be an exciting adventure. His adrenalin began pumping at the mere thought of it. At night he had wet dreams thinking about her. Wanting her nearly drove him mad. Even with a girl he didn't love, of course he could have good sex. He was, he realised from what he'd noticed in urinals and by comparison with his brothers, particularly well endowed for sex. Not only in size. One girl had told him adoringly that she'd never known anyone able to 'keep it up for ages like that'.

He wanted sex with Andrina, but it wasn't only lust as it had been with other women. He loved her. Her marriage had been a knife in his heart. With her he was vulnerable. Thoughts of her made his hard shell crumble, his toughness melt away. During the day, he often watched her house, hungry for a glimpse of her. If she emerged he followed her, feeding on the sight of her, every moment obsessing him with desire.

He adored her. Some day, somehow, some way, she would be his. It had to be. He willed it to be. And he was a patient man.

Chapter Eleven

Scobie Gallacher, Bridie and Doris Gallacher's father, couldn't remember Bridie's twenty-first birthday party. These blackouts, the blank periods of his life, secretly frightened Scobie. He'd wake in the morning and see Carragh with a black eye and swollen lip and he'd feel immediate concern and cry out, 'What the hell happened to your face?'

He could never believe it when she told him he'd been the cause. She'd tell other folk she fell or bumped into a door, or she'd refuse to say anything at all. But in private she swore it was him.

There were other occasions when he thought he'd been sleeping on the couch or on the floor after a few drinks. But next day other people told him what he'd done and he didn't believe them either. An army of small, furtive fears was growing in his mind, confusing him. Especially the times when he seemed to have been performing quite normally. He'd apologise for taking the day off work, only to be told that he hadn't taken the day off work at all. He'd been there on the building site working away as usual.

Patrick O'Maley and all the lads would laugh, and he would laugh along with them. But secretly it gave him a hell of a turn.

One day he'd gone in for a pint to his favourite pub in Castle Street. The next thing he knew, he was in Ireland. He'd bought tickets from Glasgow. He'd negotiated a boat ticket to Dublin. Buses in Dublin too. He had the ticket stubs to prove it. Yet he remembered not one thing about either the journey or his sojourn in the capital city.

At first the laughs had kept up. Good old Scobie. Did you hear about his last caper? You'll never believe what old Scobie did the other day. Fellas would say – Aw, you're some man, you. You did this or you did that. And you said this to big Jimmy and you said that to me.

Big Donald McMillan or Hector McLean, the local bobbies, often took him home. They'd have a laugh with him about it the next day. More often now they were having him in and charging him with being drunk and disorderly. But it was still good-humoured. He had some good pals in the local nick. In Barlinnie prison as well. The screws were decent enough fellas. Just doing their job.

More recently, however, Scobie was becoming a Jekyll and Hyde. He apparently was doing things that were completely out of character. One of them was hitting Carragh. Poor wee Carragh, with her long skirts to hide her legs and her wrap-around floral pinnies. Christ, he loved the woman. The fact that he had no recollection of his violent behaviour meant he'd no control over it.

'It's the drink, Scobie,' Carragh would say to try to comfort him. 'It's not you, it's the drink. If you could just stick to one or two pints like your pals . . .'

He always meant to. He'd go into a bar for one pint only. Or perhaps just a half and a whisky. But after one pint or one half he'd feel he'd grown inches taller. He felt more sure of himself. His shoulders swaggered. Just one more, he'd think, no problem. But the more he drank the more difficult it became to leave the bar and go home. He'd make all sorts of excuses to Carragh when he did get back – usually minus most of his wages, or all of the wages, that she was so anxiously waiting for.

He'd say he met Patrick or Tony or Michael and couldn't get away. When he woke up next day and discovered he'd vomited all over Carragh's nice bedspread he'd blame the lemonade somebody had put in his whisky. He'd say he'd been all right in the pub. It was when he came out and the fresh air hit him. It was the fresh air that had got him drunk. The first time he woke up and discovered he'd peed in the bed he was horrified and utterly disgusted with himself. This, he knew, was totally unacceptable.

The first time Scobie got put in jail for being drunk and incapable the horror and degradation had shocked him, and as he'd lain in Barlinnie prison, he vowed to himself, 'Never, ever again. I'm here because of drink, and never, ever, will I take it again!' Yet the first thing he did when he walked down the long road from Barlinnie was to go into an off-sales and get a bottle.

Eventually the unacceptable became the acceptable. Lying in the gutter and getting locked up for the night had become part and parcel of his life.

He could still raise a laugh by saying to the guys on the building site, 'You haven't lived if you haven't gone up the Garngad Road on the ten o'clock bus after the pubs have shut.'

More times than he cared to remember now Scobie had come out of the pub in Castle Street near the Royal Infirmary with a crowd from Garngad and Blackhill. He'd be laughing and singing and staggering along with them, without thinking or caring where he was going, and he'd get on the bus with them. Sometimes he'd doze off into a drunken sleep. At other times he'd bellow out songs at the top of his voice along with the rest.

The conductress never got any money, only a share of the carry-out. 'Hae a slug, hen' was the generous cry as she passed along the aisle. Once he'd offered her the fare and she'd brushed it aside with, 'Why should you be fucking different?'

He remembered one time he'd been sitting upstairs in the smoky atmosphere of the bus in a drunken haze, his *Daily Record* rolled up on his lap. He remembered staring hypnotically at the passing glow of the orange streetlights as the bus swayed round corner after corner. The raucous noise from the front seats washed over him. They were singing, '. . . For freedom comes from God's right hand, and righteous men must make our land a nation once again. A nation once again, a nation once again. And Ireland long a province been – a nation once again . . .'

On the seat next to him sat a fresh-faced youth, his cheeks aglow, his mind no doubt still on his recent passionate fumblings in a handy close. He was softly whistling various melodies as he gazed unseeingly out of the grimy windows.

Then Scobie's drunken reverie was disturbed by a sudden bellowing from the front of the bus. 'Some bastard's whistlin' the Sash! There's a fuckin' Orange bastard taking the piss!'

Oblivious to the concentration of the front row or the deathly silence of the rest of the bus, the boy whistled on tunelessly; but yes, there was a hint of the Sash there.

A drunken tide welled down the passageway, feeding on its own rage, towards the hapless and still oblivious youth. 'Hae you, whit's yer gemme? Can you whistle wi' nae teeth?'

Shocked back to the present by his all too clear impending doom, the boy was obviously at a loss to know what offence he had caused. 'I'm sorry,' he stuttered. 'I don't know what you're talking about.'

This brought a further roar of rage from the incensed rabble. Scobie didn't like the odds. He leaned over. 'Give the boy a break, lads. He's away with it. He didnae mean any harm.'

'Piss off, you drunken old fart,' the leader of the mob yelled. 'Before ah ram yer paper up yer arse.'

Scobie's face went white as if the blood had been siphoned off. To the uninitiated it could be mistaken for fear. It was Scobie's eyes that contradicted this impression. It was said that in a drunken rage Scobie's eyes had the malevolence of a psychotic pit bull terrier.

But the leader of the mob only saw Scobie's pallor and, looking for approval from his mates, he leaned over the back of the seat in front of Scobie and wagged a finger close to Scobie's face. Before he could deliver any more insults, however, Scobie had grabbed the offending wrist, shot his head forward, and slammed his teeth down on the outstretched finger.

The high-pitched scream was abruptly extinguished as Scobie's fist rattled a short, sharp staccato beat around the base of the leader's jaw. This unexpected attack left him slumped forward over the seat with a glazed expression.

For a few seconds the mob behind him were stunned into immobility and Scobie, still not liking the odds, decided it was time for him to leave the bus. This signalled a mad rush towards him. Unfortunately, in their rush the mob trampled and climbed over their now recumbent colleague. Scobie saw the world through a red haze as he lashed out hooks and uppercuts, grabbed lapels, butted noses; he ducked and hooked as he backed off down the bus, dragging a small pool of mayhem with him. His final parting as he went down the steeply spiralled staircase was a full-blooded uppercut into an exposed groin above his head.

He dropped, running, off the back of the bus, having lost his jacket and his false teeth, presumably still attached to the finger on the top deck. And, horror of horrors, he'd lost his *Daily Record* with the day's scores.

Now Scobie couldn't even remember his journeys on the bus. He'd go in to the pub for a pint, and the next thing he'd know was waking up in Patrick's house in Blackhill. Or in the gutter in Blackhill. Or someplace else.

This time he'd been toasting Bridie's health at her twenty-first birthday party, and then suddenly he was lying sprawled all his length in a close in Cobden Street. Big Martha Stoddart was towering over him saying to Jimmy, her man, 'It's that drunken Pape from Turner Street.'

Jimmy Stoddart was a well-known Orangeman and mason, but to give him his due, he bent down and gave Scobie a hand up. Big Martha said, 'Let him get up himself. See you!' she addressed Scobie. 'You dirty drunken wee nyaff? Don't you dare come round here fouling our close. You get back where you belong, do you hear, or you'll get my fist in your face.'

'OK. OK.' Scobie flung up his hands. 'I'm going, hen. There's no need for violence.' He'd felt ashamed. He hurt inside but he managed to dust himself down and walk away as if he wasn't caring a tuppenny toss. He was wondering what he'd done to spoil Bridie's party and give her a showing up. It was usually Doris who accused him of giving her a showing up. Bridie hid herself away, usually in the lavatory with a book, until somebody came battering at the door desperate to get in.

He hoped to God he hadn't hurt anybody. 'Holy Mary, Mother of God, don't let me have battered wee Carragh.' Or Bridie, or Doris, or any of the boys. Or anybody at all, for that matter. 'And don't let me have spewed over anybody. Or insulted anybody.'

Desperately he tried to remember what he had done. But couldn't.

'Hello there, wee man.' Francis O'Donnell, one of his fellow brickies, greeted him in Garngad Road. 'Fancy a pint?'

Just one, Scobie thought. He needed something to pick him up, give him a wee lift, make him feel better. The hair of the dog. 'Aye, OK, son.'

Francis O'Donnell had three pints and then said, 'I'm away, Scobie. I've to get some fish suppers to take home. I promised the wife.'

'I'll just have another one,' Scobie said. 'And then I'm on my way as well.'

He had to ask the barman to put his next drink on the slate. And his next – he lost count of how many. He and Carragh were in debt all over the place but he always made sure when he got his wages, the publican was paid first.

Closing time came eventually, and he had to leave and stagger towards Turner Street. He felt angry – at – he wasn't sure what. It was something to do with the party. Why should he care about the shitting party? But he did fucking care. They'd better not say anything to him when he got back. They'd better not even look at him in the wrong way. He knew Carragh had done a lot of work cleaning the house and making a big dumpling. He knew it meant a lot to her. She was that anxious it would go well. His anger grew until it was unendurable and turned outside of himself. He was a time-bomb of fury, ready to go off.

As he approached his close on Turner Street, his eye fell on Kevin Connelly, the wee upstart that had cat-called his Doris –and when she'd ignored him, he'd made a fool of her, mimicking her polite voice and teetering, mincing walk. He'd heard Doris complain about this to Carragh. 'That horrible Kevin Connelly from downstairs is always pestering me and making a fool of me.'

He'd show Kevin bloody Connelly he couldn't make a fool of any daughter of his. 'See you, you fuckin' bastard,' he yelled. 'You'll no' talk about a Gallacher again!' With that, he lurched towards the suddenly wary and defensive Kevin. Scobie feinted left and lashed out a vicious kick with his steel-toe-capped boot to Kevin's knee. There was an ominous crunch and Kevin's head dropped with a grunt of anguish. Like a striking stoat, the short figure of Scobie bulleted forward. Two chopping short rights to the base of the neck, followed by a flurry of short-range butts into the face, and Kevin dropped to the ground.

Scobie had just started to bury his boot into the young man's ribs when he was forcefully dragged off by a posse of neighbours rushing to Kevin's rescue.

Carragh had seen the attack from the window, and she was crying when Scobie got upstairs, and going on about how Kevin was the son of one of her best neighbours. Doris was saying how Scobie was worse than Kevin Connelly and it was terrible, just terrible. He had to give both of them a belt across the mouth to shut them up.

Next day he woke up in the kitchen hole-in-the-wall bed to the sound of voices. Carragh was saying, 'Oh, that's awful kind of you, Mrs Connelly. I'll really enjoy that, so I will.'

'That's OK, hen. I'll get the bowl later on. No hurry.'

Mrs Connelly had brought Carragh a bowl of soup. Scobie nodded a good morning to the woman but she ignored him.

Afterwards he said to Carragh, 'What the hell's wrong with her? And what's she bringing you soup for? We're surely not that hard up.'

'It's just to show there's no bad feelings against me. She's a good neighbour to me, is Mrs Connelly.'

'Hard feelings against you? What hard feelings?'

'After what you done to her Kevin.'

He had no idea what she was talking about. He struggled out of bed, pulled on his trousers and forced himself to brave the cold and draughty stairs to the lavatory. There he could relieve his bladder.

He did not know how to find relief from his fear.

Chapter Twelve

'In other days I thought I'd never
Find a love to call my own,
That I was meant to walk forever,
My lifelong path alone;
That my lonely heart should never sing
Nor know the joy that love can bring . . .'

Frank chewed happily at his pencil as a vision of Bridie swam before his eyes. He was sitting, hunched protectively over his notebook, at the kitchen table penning his latest poem. Well, to be accurate, he was fiddling about with a poem he'd written some years before. It described walking with an imaginary love on a distant hill and into 'forests hidden ways . . .'. He changed these bits, brought it up to date, but left the ending which seemed so relevant to the wonderful change in his life.

'Now all my loneliness is past,
Now both our dreams are one,
Our hope, our love, shall always last,
Till life itself is done:
Each pledge and promise be ever true,
And love shall live while I have you.'

He felt so inspired he knew he would be capable of writing much better poetry than that. He had even begun thinking about writing a play. He was brimming over with creative energy.

As Tony crushed past him, Frank hunched lower and made a wall with his hand around his notebook. Too often his father or brothers had tried to read over his shoulders, and laugh and jeer or groan and shake their heads. It was difficult to keep going with his creative work in the face of such sustained discouragement. Why did he keep on writing? After all, he'd never had anything published; never made one penny piece from anything he'd produced. He couldn't give a sensible answer to the question. He just had to do it, that was all. It was an obsession, an addiction, a need. It was the only way he was able to communicate his emotions. He couldn't even express his feelings to Bridie – not everything that was in his heart. Except through poetry.

They'd discuss the merits and demerits of a film they'd just seen together. They'd make a plan of reading for the weeks ahead. They'd decide on a list of books they'd borrow from the library, and after studying each one they'd make notes of their critical reactions and discuss them with each other in much enthusiastic detail. But he couldn't find words to fully express how wonderful it was to have someone who shared his interests, who cared about the same things as him, who took him seriously, who accepted him as he was.

Except in poetry.

Then came the most exciting thing in both their lives. He had his first poem published. It all happened because of a nightmare. He had dreamed that Bridie had died; he had lost her forever. Fear haunted him all next day. He couldn't concentrate on his work at the office. His imagination was a dark sea in which he was drowning. He'd gone round to Bridie's house straight after work. She wasn't in and her mother didn't know where she was. What if he never saw her again? He returned home and wrote a poem called 'The Legacy of Love', in which he tried to visualise what his feelings would be if Bridie disappeared forever from his life:

> 'You will not come again, and yet
> I turn my head attentive round,
> Hear voices down the wind, and let
> My hand reach out to touch the sound:
> Or else, in mist's fantastic swarm
> See shaped in shaking line your form.

I go again where we have been,
Revisit each remembered place,
Hold hands on every bridge, and lean
To see in every stream your face:
Laugh laughter that was laughed before
And press each cheek to cheek once more.

Sentience invades insentient things,
The trace of touch outlines the years;
And shapes and sounds where presence clings
Assail receptive eyes and ears:
No more than time can part from tide
Can lover from his love divide.'

It was accepted for publication by a literary magazine and they actually paid him for it. The letter of acceptance and the cheque had been waiting for him one evening. He had met Bridie in town straight from work. They'd gone to Miss Cranston's restaurant for high tea, and then to a concert in St Andrew's Halls. The Glasgow Phoenix Choir had enchanted them both, and Bridie said she'd never enjoyed herself so much in her life. When he'd arrived back home he'd gone into the kitchen to see if there was any tea on the go. His brothers and his father and one or two of their friends were enjoying a noisy game of pontoon round the kitchen table. The small room reverberated with the lusty male voices. It was thick with cigarette smoke and the smell of whisky and beer. His mother was huddled over the fire, enjoying a glass of Guinness and a read of her *Family Star*.

The letter was propped up on the mantelpiece against one of the brass candlesticks. He examined its contents with disbelief, then joyous excitement. 'Here, you'll never guess what's happened!' he suddenly bellowed out. 'A magazine is going to publish one of my poems and they've asked for more. Look, they've sent me a cheque!'

The racket round the table ceased. A silence gripped the room for a few seconds, before one of his brothers looked at his cards and said, 'Fuck! Bust again!', and the game continued as if Frank had never existed.

Frank felt embarrassed, ashamed even. He almost apologised for himself. His mother hissed at him, 'You give that money back, do you hear?'

It occurred to him that there was no use arguing with her, no use expecting any of them to understand. His mother thought there must be some mistake. It smacked of dishonesty. He must have conned the money from the publisher. The others were just embarrassed. They didn't know what to think.

He didn't make a cup of tea. He didn't wash his face at the sink. He left the room as if in disgrace without even daring to bring any more attention to himself by saying goodnight. In the front room he undressed and slipped into one of the inset beds. Alone in the dark the excitement returned, making him shiver and sweat.

If he could get one poem published he could get another poem published. If he could get poems published he could get plays accepted. This was the beginning. This was all he needed. Just one bit of encouragement.

First thing next morning Frank hared round to Bridie's place and told her of the stupendous news. She was over the moon. They hugged each other in secret, furtive joy outside the front door. Bridie's house was always packed to the gunwales and privacy was impossible inside the house.

Poor Bridie had an even worse life at home than Frank had. She was an intelligent, sensitive girl among a right mindless rabble. Except perhaps her sister Doris, who at least had some ambition to get out of the place – albeit for silly, snobbish reasons.

Bridie's father Scobie, in Frank's opinion, wasn't just a heavy drinker like his own dad, but an alcoholic. Scobie was a right Jekyll and Hyde character – a nice enough man when he was sober but a devil when he drank. His wife Carragh was a poor wee soul, only an inch or two over five feet, and with a sparse straggle of hair and bandy legs that she tried to hide under long skirts. Neither Scobie nor Carragh were capable of disciplining or having any control over their innumerable offspring, several of whom were well known and feared local corner-boys.

Feared by all except the O'Maleys. Michael especially was contemptuous of the Gallacher boys. Frank had once heard Michael say to a group of Gallachers and their razor-carrying pals, 'Don't try to tell me how tough you are. I could fight and beat the lot of you with one hand, while I'm doing the crossword in the *Daily Record* with the other.'

Michael said only useless cowards carried weapons. The Gallacher boys were a weedy and unhealthy looking bunch. The saving of them was when they nicked some musical instruments from a shop in town and took a notion to learn how to play them. Already they had started to play as a group in pubs and clubs in Glasgow.

Now there was talk of them travelling further afield. Frank hoped this was true. He couldn't imagine Carragh shedding tears over their departure. Nor could he imagine her shedding any tears when Scobie was locked away in Barlinnie. It was a mystery to think what they saw in each other. Undersized Carragh with her sparse wisps of hair on top and legs like a full moon. Scobie was the same height as his wife. They resembled a pair of bookends. But his sparse wisps of hair were at the back of his skull. He had nothing on top, and his nose looked like a lump of putty squashed on to his face and given a cruel twist for good measure.

How Bridie survived in the Gallacher household, Frank shuddered to think. Half the time it wasn't just a rabble but a drunken rabble. And the place was a tip. The quicker he got her out of there the better. As soon as he made that decision, the urgency of it rapidly increased to unbearable proportions. It was unthinkable that his Bridie should stay in such appalling surroundings for one moment longer than was absolutely necessary. He proposed to her immediately, and vowed he would leave no stone unturned to enable them to get a place of their own as quickly as possible.

He asked his da what was happening with Bailie McPherson.

Patrick had proudly announced that the good bailie had managed to get a Corporation house for the O'Maley family in Blackhill – a two-bedroom, living room, scullery and bathroom in Acrehill Street, just across from the gasworks about a mile the other side of Garngad Road.

Frank had pleaded with Patrick to approach his friend at the City Chambers again, this time on his behalf. Patrick was outraged. 'What do you think I am? For my sake he's taken one hell of a risk of getting himself into hot water. He stuck his neck out for me. There's a waiting list for Corporation houses as long as your arm.'

Then it occurred to Frank that there might be a chance of him getting the rent book of the house in Bright Street changed over to his name when his ma and da and Tony and Michael and Bernard moved to Blackhill. He didn't have to ask Bridie what she thought, although of course he asked anyway. But he knew that her circumstances were so desperate in Turner Street she would have moved with him to a tent on Glasgow Green if he'd asked her.

'Oh Frank.' She was ecstatic. 'It'll be absolutely wonderful. Like a wee palace.'

Frank laughed. 'A room and kitchen with an outside lavatory is not exactly a palace, Bridie. But I promise you, I'll get you a better place one day. One day I'll make a lot of money with my writing. I'll be really successful. I know I will. I'm determined I will.'

'The room and kitchen will do us fine just now,' Bridie assured him. 'Fancy, just the two of us in the whole place. It's like heaven to me just to think of it.'

Even the fact that they didn't have any money to buy furniture and other necessities didn't dampen Bridie's enthusiasm. 'We'll save up, Frank. I'll put every penny by that I can. We both will, won't we, Frank?'

'I've got a few pounds put by already,' Frank confided. 'Enough to get a few basic things. But not much.'

'Och, we'll get other things in time. And we're bound to get some wedding presents, don't forget.'

He loved her all the more for being content with so little. He vowed yet again that one day he would be enormously successful as a writer. He would work like a slave to shower her with every luxury. One day in the future his Bridie would lack for nothing. He felt feverishly excited, as if fame and fortune were just around the corner. He also dreamed of the room and kitchen as it would be after his parents and brothers had gone. A heaven on earth. A place to write in peace. He hugged that dream to himself. It was too precious even to share with Bridie.

Chapter Thirteen

Bernard and Doris got off the tram at the end of Monteith Row. The clangour of its bell rent the air before the tram moaned away into the distance and there was silence.

'Further along,' Bernard said, peering through the fog at the numbers on the dark slits of entrances to the buildings. The closes, like the street, were gaslit. Eerie green circles of light were cast down, deepening the shadows.

Doris linked her arm through Bernard's and gave a dainty shiver. 'My goodness, it's terribly eerie. Just listen to those trees creaking over there.' She wasn't used to trees, and treated all country-type things with the utmost suspicion.

'Haven't you ever been down here before? At the Green?' Bernard asked.

'It was different then. The Shows were there. They made the place all bright and noisy and cheery. I don't go to them now, of course.'

'Why not?'

'Fun-fairs are a teeny-wee bit common. Of course everyone to his own taste.' Her blonde hair was teased and backcombed into an enormous beehive shape, and she'd taken a great deal of trouble with eyelashes and eyeliner. Underneath her short navy coat was a red and white spotted dirndl skirt and scarlet sweater. Underneath that again, a stiff nylon waist slip stuck out and rustled as she walked. Above it, a nylon 'Sweater Girl' bra with wide circle-stitched cups jutted to unnaturally sharp points. Every move was tricky and needed a certain amount of concentration because of the high heels that were necessary to give her much-needed height. She had spent hours dressing up and putting on her make-up in very difficult circumstances with other Gallachers constantly milling and crushing around. In her harassment and frustration she had allowed herself the use of very coarse swearwords, something to which she never stooped outside the Gallacher hell-hole.

She'd managed to make the best of herself eventually. Her hair looked striking and fashionable, and of course she had neat little features and a flawless skin.

'In here.' Bernard indicated Andrina's close. 'One up, I think Robert said.' His feet thumped and echoed up the stairs as he took them two at a time. Doris's heels rapidly click-clicked in an effort to keep up with him. She was thinking how big and powerful he was, charging ahead like a hefty-shouldered bull. He was thinking how wonderful it would be seeing Andrina again, to actually be near her, to be able to talk to her. He'd thought about nothing else for weeks, ever since Robert had invited him.

And suddenly there she was, opening the door to him. Darling Andrina, with her large round eyes sparkling with childish excitement. Yet also their baby shape contained a teasing sexual awareness. No other girl in the world had such eyes. They looked green if she was wearing green, blue if she was wearing blue.

'Andrina, this is Doris Gallacher,' he heard himself say. 'Doris, Andrina Anderson.'

'Come in. Come in.' Andrina welcomed them with breathless delight. 'You're the very first. It's nice to see you again, Bernard. It's been ages, hasn't it? Let me take your coat, Doris, and yours too, Bernard. What a night! I hope everybody manages. There's some free pegs here. Oh, thanks Bernard.'

She relinquished the coats and Bernard hung them on one of the pegs in the hallway. Then Robert appeared wielding a bottle and a corkscrew. 'I was just getting some drinks organised. Come away in.'

They were led into the front room which was furnished as a sitting room in contemporary style. Bernard thought the furniture looked precariously balanced on insubstantial splayed legs. Everything appeared as if it was on tiptoe. He was hesitant about testing his weight on the chairs.

'What a lovely colour scheme,' Doris called out. 'I just love that carpet. Such pretty heather colours. And these soft greys. Such terribly good taste. Of course, your husband's an artist, isn't he?'

Robert laughed. 'Art teacher. What are you having, Doris? I've sherry, port, gin, whisky, beer and soft drinks.'

'Goodness me. What a choice! A teeny glass of sherry will do fine, thanks. I just love your white woodwork. It's *the* latest fashion, of course.'

Bernard wondered how Doris was such an expert on home fashions. The house she came from hadn't even got curtains at the window. He was surprised the paper blinds had survived.

Everything pawnable in the Gallacher house was pawned when Scobie took his drinking bouts. The floors were bare boards, the whitewashed walls weren't white any more, and stained with God knew what missiles Scobie had aimed at Carragh or one of the family and missed. The house was a sordid dump. Compared with the Gallacher house a prison cell would be five-star luxury.

Bernard watched Andrina as he sipped a beer. She flushed under his steady gaze, but seemed pleased and happy to be the target of such a concentration of attention. She fluttered about like an exotic bird with her deep flame of hair and high-necked Chinese-patterned dress. Back and forth she flew to welcome in more and more guests until the front room was thick with bodies, laughter, loud talk and cigarette smoke. Bernard found it difficult to get near Andrina. So near and yet so far. His longing for her increased a thousandfold. It was a knife jammed inside him. He could hardly breathe for the pain of it. He crushed through the crowd towards where she was standing near the door, but just before he reached her she suddenly looked anxious and disappeared into the hall. He went after her only to find her speaking on the phone. Catching sight of him she put her finger to her lips in a warning sign and pointed at the front-room door. Then she said into the mouthpiece, 'It must be the wireless, Mummy.'

Bernard carefully shut the door but remained in the hall, watching her.

'Is that better, Mummy? I've told Robert to turn it down. Yes, of course I'm all right. Why shouldn't I be all right? When did you phone? I'm so sorry we didn't hear you, Mummy. Yes, of course I was in . . . The phone's in the hall, that's the trouble. If the front-room door's shut and the wireless is on . . . Yes, I know we usually sit in the kitchen. I meant the kitchen when I said the front room . . . I don't know why I said it, Mummy. It was just a slip of the tongue. I'm not used to the house yet . . . No, you don't need to phone back . . . Robert and I planned an early night, you see, Mummy . . . No, we're both fine. Honestly, Mummy, I'm fine . . . Yes, I'll be at the church in the morning. Yes, I'll see you then. Yes . . . all right . . . Yes, I will . . . Yes . . . I promise. Goodnight, Mummy.'

She put down the phone and rolled her eys. 'Sorry about that, but you know what Mummy's like.'

'Don't I just,' he said.

Flushing a little, she avoided his eyes. 'Do me a favour, Bernard. Tell everyone it's time to eat. I've already said but they seem to be enjoying talking so much . . .'

Just then the door was flung open and a riotous mob spilled out. Laughing and shouting, they made for the kitchen, sweeping Andrina before them.

She obviously had an artistry of her own. The table in the recess, a tea-trolley, the kitchen unit, the draining board at the side of the sink – every surface was covered with mouth-watering and attractively displayed food. There were golden, mouthwatering meat pies and little tartlets heaped with mashed fish instead of jam. Soda scones, treacle scones and even cheese scones – something Bernard had never tasted before – also delighted the palate. The pancakes and crumpets were as light as a feather, as were all the sponge cakes, whether filled with jam or cream, or decorated with icing sugar.

He thought again how truly wonderful she was. Not only had she looks and brains, she could cook. He knew in his gut she would have a talent for making love as well. People spoke to him, he answered them, but he didn't know what they said or what he said. All the time Andrina riveted his attention. Her slightly protruding eyes, dancing with life and laughter and flirtation, the cheeky tilt of her head, the provocative swing of her hips, the way she crossed and slanted her long legs.

'Is this a serious affair?'

'What?' Bernard looked round in surprise at Robert.

'Doris. You can't keep your eyes off her.'

It was then Bernard noticed Doris speaking to Andrina. He shrugged. 'Doris is all right.'

'Nice figure. She went to St Francis, didn't she?'

'Aye. She lives a couple of streets away from us. Frank's going with her sister. Remember Bridie?'

Robert laughed. 'I hope she's improved in looks.'

'She's still specy, straight hair – and as smart dressed as a Guy on Guy Fawkes night. Frank doesn't seem to notice. Of course, he's no tailor's dummy himself.'

Bernard liked to be smart and was proud of the pin-striped suit and Crombie coat he'd just bought. It was important always to be well-shaved and showered and immaculately dressed. It was one of the things that impressed the punters and the hard men. When they saw you well turned-out, they thought you had your act together and they respected you. He had done a deal with a dance hall and another couple of pubs in town to supply them with bouncers. He was confident more venues would come. It all went by word of mouth. His reputation was steadily growing. He'd roped in more men for the job. He saw that his guys gave a good service and they were glad to get the money. He had recruited them from unemployed young men at the karate club, and thanks to the karate training all were able to handle themselves and were aggressively self-confident. He gave a good service himself. He kept a sharp eye for trouble. Any customer at the pub or the dance hall would simply need to take one step out of line, one flash of a weapon, and they were out on the street before they knew what hit them.

But more often than not he just needed to look at potential trouble-makers for the trouble to die down and disappear. It wasn't just his hefty build. Michael had told him, 'You've got that killer stare, Bernard. You should have been in professional boxing.'

Michael could keep his boxing. It was a mug's game. Michael was riding high at the moment in the amateur scene. When he wasn't humping bricks around he was slugging away in the ring. The next thing would be the ABA championship in London. In the end, though, the chances were he'd be left punch drunk and unable even to hold down his brickie's job. Or just drunk. Michael had always had a special liking for the booze, ever since he used to get a sip of his ma or da's beer when he was a youngster.

Bernard hoped to God Michael wouldn't end up like Scobie Gallacher. The wee sod drank like a shoal of piranhas and regularly duffed up his wife. Father Riley had tried to teach him a lesson and punch some decency into him. All to no avail.

The women in that family had more spunk, including Doris. Even old Carragh could beak up to Scobie on occasion. She'd once knocked him out cold with an iron frying pan.

Everyone except Scobie knew that Scobie was an alcoholic. And a randy one at that.

Thinking of being randy aroused Bernard's own sexuality to an almost unbearable degree. He had to look away from Andrina. Just the sight of her put him in danger of having an erection. Afterwards, going home with Doris, he decided to relieve his sexual tension on her. After all, she was more than willing, so what was the harm? He would be pleasuring her, and getting some pleasure for himself. Too soon he felt sickened, disgusted at himself much more than the woman who gave herself so freely against the wall of the foul-smelling back close.

After all, and much to his surprise, she had been a virgin.

Chapter Fourteen

Jimmy Stoddart was in agony. So for that matter was his wife, Big Martha. For their daughter Caroline's sake they had walked from their home in Cobden Street to the next street along, to visit the O'Maleys. As far as they had always been concerned, Cobden Street was for Protestants, Bright Street was for Catholics, and never the twain shall meet. Now here they were, sitting in the enemy's camp surrounded by holy pictures. The Virgin Mary and the infant Jesus stared over their heads from one wall. Another picture on the same wall was of Jesus with tragic upturned eyes and wearing a crown of thorns. Another wall was decorated with St Francis and a crowd of animals. On one of the bed recess walls (which seemed positively indecent) was a big, gilt-framed picture of the Pope.

Statues of Mary, Joseph and Jesus crowded the mantelpiece beside a rusty-looking alarm clock, two brass candlesticks and an Oxo tin.

To Jimmy Stoddart, being surrounded by so much Popery was almost as bad as being inside a Roman church. He had to keep reminding himself that his future son-in-law was the Scottish middleweight champion, and think of all the reflected glory he could bask in as a result. The next thing Michael was aiming for was the ABA championship in London and he was going to accompany him. This was a chance not to be missed. All the same, brushing shoulders with Popery was a high price to pay. As far as Jimmy Stoddart was concerned, the Vatican and the priesthood were the cause of all the evils in the world. There was no doubt in his mind that the war had been the work of the Pope. Hitler and Mussolini were Catholics, to mention but two Papish bastards.

'Another cup of tea, Mrs Stoddart?' Maureen enquired

politely. They were all being terribly polite to each other. The strain was something cruel.

'No thanks,' Mrs Stoddart replied with a sniff, as if the query had been vaguely insulting. 'I've still got half a cup.'

She was wearing her best black dress and new corsets. The corsets were keeping her in an unnaturally erect position. She was in absolute agony, but would rather die than admit it. All she could think of to relieve her torture was the battering she was going to give Jimmy Stoddart the moment she got him home. It was his fault they were in this terrible position. It was he who agreed to the visit. It was he who had been all for the marriage in the first place. This she knew was an exaggeration, but in her torment she was beyond the niceties of total accuracy.

'A wee fairy cake then?' Maureen was determined, for Michael's sake, to act the perfect hostess.

'Aye, well . . .' Martha grudgingly selected a cake from the proffered plate. 'I hear you're moving to Blackhill.'

'A three apartment, scullery and bathroom,' Maureen beamed.

Martha knew Blackhill was a Catholic stronghold, so she wasn't in the least surprised at the move.

'I'm sure you'll be pleased at Michael and Caroline being promised this place,' Maureen continued. 'Having your girl just the next street along.'

'Aye . . . well . . .'

'You could have knocked me down with a feather after it was promised to Michael – our Frank said he'd wanted it. We knew he was winchin' Bridie Gallacher, but he never said.'

'Well, with Michael getting married first and him being older than Frank . . .'

'That's what we said, and Frank was very decent about it.'

Michael and Caroline smiled at one another. Everything seemed to be going well. The atmosphere was admittedly strained, but that was only to be expected under the circumstances and on a first visit. Michael had recently been in and out of chapel like a yo-yo, praying that everything would go well. Now he thanked God for preventing Tony and Frank from making an appearance. They had been well warned, of course. Indeed, they had been bribed to keep away. The trouble was you never knew with Frank. If his head was full of poetry (and it so often was) he could be dangerously absent-minded. Tony could forget, or renege on his promise out of sheer stupidity. Michael kept having a dreadful vision of Tony bursting into the kitchen, all buck teeth and Teddy Boy glory, yelling 'Up the IRA!', or some such insanity. The mere idea made him sweat. It would mean the end of all his and Caroline's dreams. They could still get married in a registry office without her parents' consent, of course. It wasn't like in England where you had to be twenty-one for that. Here in Scotland it was legal to get married at sixteen whether the parents wanted it or not, and Caroline was nearly twenty. But Martha and Jimmy Stoddart would prove bad enemies. They would make their lives a hell on earth. Michael couldn't see Caroline standing up against her mother. Caroline was sweet and adorable, his little Shirley Temple, and he loved her dearly, but the fact had to be faced that she wasn't the world's strongest character. He didn't blame her for being so easily cowed by her mother. He lost a lot of bottle himself when faced with Big Martha Stoddart.

'I suppose,' Martha said now through a mouthful of fairy cake, 'we'll just have to make the best of it.'

'A drop of the hard stuff in your tea, Jimmy?' Patrick volunteered.

Jimmy put his hand over his cup. 'In my book it's a crime to dilute it.'

'You're that fond of tea?'

'No, whisky.'

Both men laughed, and Patrick poured a generous glass of the amber liquid. 'Have it separate then, and to hell with the tea.'

'As I was saying,' Martha aimed each word like a dagger at the two men, 'before I was so rudely interrupted: we'll just have to make the best of it.'

'You're quite right, Martha,' Maureen soothed. 'It's a

terrible problem, so it is, but the young folks are in love and love conquers all things. I just pray to God that they'll be happy together. With a wee bit of help and good will, I'm sure everything will work out all right. Caroline is a lovely girl, so she is, and Michael's a good boy.'

Both Martha and Jimmy regarded her with suspicion. They didn't trust prayers to a Catholic god. What good could come of that? She'd better not have any ideas of making Caroline 'turn', or having any children brought up as Catholics. If they thought ... Unknown to them Caroline and Michael had already signed a paper promising that any children would be brought up as Catholics. Even Maureen didn't know this, but it was her prayer and fondest hope that one day Caroline would see the light and, of her own free will, become a member of the true church and bring up her children in the faith.

Martha said, 'We've always been good Protestants. Nothing like this has ever happened in our family before.'

Jimmy, like Patrick, had downed his second dram. It was their way of smoothing out the sharpest edge of any problem. 'My father was once a Grand Master of the South Side Orange Lodge.' His eyes were misted with remembrance.

'You must have been hell of a proud,' Patrick said, refilling the glasses. 'When I was wee my ma and da lived for a while in the country. He was sent on a job – building one of these new roads. I remember I followed the Orange Parade on the twelfth of July. I thought it was great listening to the bands and joining in the fun in the park.'

'Good for you!' Jimmy said, warming to the man.

'It seems to be just in Glasgow that there's all this ill will. I wonder why that is.'

Jimmy thought – because there's more bloody Papes in Glasgow insinuating themselves into the police and the Council, and all the positions of power. They'll be taking over the whole city, the whole country if we're not careful. He managed, however, to refrain from expressing his thoughts. 'Beats me,' he said.

That reminded Martha. 'It's time we were getting back to

Cobden Street. It's all settled then. The wedding's to be a quiet affair, but to be blessed in our church, and you and your family are going to be there.' Martha, in fact, had only been twice in the church she claimed her own – once to get married and once to have Caroline christened.

'Well,' Maureen said, 'me and Patrick will certainly attend.' She was able to say this because she'd finally been able to persuade Father Riley (with the help of a bottle of whisky and a large donation to the chapel funds) to give them permission to go to the Protestant church for the wedding ceremony. 'Michael's brothers will have to make up their own minds.'

'The reception will be round in my house so there'll be plenty of room if they do come, and plenty to eat as well.'

'I'm sure,' Maureen agreed. 'It'll be a lovely do, so it will. Caroline's told me you make a marvellous steak pie.'

'Aye, well . . .' Martha was slightly mollified, although her words retained their usual ominous undertones. She rose, and gave a jerk of her head to indicate to her husband that he should rise too. 'We'll see you on the day. Are you coming round with us, Caroline?'

'Can I just wait for a wee while to finish my tea, Mammy?'

'Aye . . . well . . .'

Maureen and Patrick saw the Stoddarts to the door. 'It'll be fine,' Maureen said. 'Don't worry.'

'I hope you're right.' Martha gave a tragic sigh and shook her head. 'As if I hadn't enough to worry me,' she added, referring to Jimmy.

After the door shut, Patrick went back to the kitchen to have another dram and open a screwtop. Maureen went through to the front room window to give the Stoddarts a friendly wave. She stood there for what seemed like ages before they appeared.

Later, in the kitchen, she said to Caroline, 'I was beginning to think your mammy and daddy had got lost, hen. They took that long to come out the close.'

She learned later what had caused the delay. Lizzie Feeney, one of her neighbours, told her that when she had emerged on to the landing en route to go down to the midden to empty her bucket, her path had been unexpectedly blocked. Mountainous Martha had been struggling, with skirts up round her ears, to unhook herself from her corsets.

Lizzie Feeney and Maureen O'Maley laughed so much they nearly split their sides.

Chapter Fifteen

Some Teds weren't so bad, but Tony O'Maley was an eejit. Scobie decided to play a joke on him. Not only because he enjoyed practical jokes, but because what he had in mind would help his pal, Patrick O'Maley, out of a tricky situation.

'As sure as my name's Patrick O'Maley,' Patrick said, 'Tony's going to bugger up Michael's wedding.'

'Can't you tell him he's not to go?' Scobie suggested.

'He's twenty-six years of age. He does what he likes and he likes any excuse to get dressed up. He's already bought a new "drape", as he calls it. It's a black loose thing that doesn't know whether it's a coat or a jacket. And you should see the skinny string of a tie he's got. And his trousers aren't much wider.' Patrick sent a long-suffering look heavenwards. 'Drainpipes, he calls them, and brothel creepers for shoes. The soles are inches thick. And he looks a right cock-a-doodle-do with that quiff stuck on top of his head. Have you seen him done up like that?'

'Aye,' Scobie sympathised.

'It's what's liable to come out of his big mouth that worries me the most, though. To hear him talk anyone would think he was blood brothers with the IRA. What can I do, short of knocking him unconscious? He's determined to be at that wedding – and another thing, he'll want to batter away at those infernal drums of his.'

'Leave Tony to yours truly.' Scobie cupped his hands and rubbed them, then smacked them together in delight. 'I've got one hell of a good idea.'

'I don't want any serious harm to come to him, you understand.'

'Not at all. Trust me, Patrick. It'll just be my wee joke. But Tony won't be at the wedding. He won't put a foot over the door at the weekend, believe me.'

And so it was agreed.

The very next night, Scobie slunk up to Tony in the pub and, tapping him on the elbow to catch his attention (it was a bit of a strain to reach his shoulder – all the O'Maley boys were tall), he looked furtively around. 'A private word, Tony.'

'So? Fire ahead. I'm listening, wee man.'

'You've been honoured, son.'

'Eh? A VC like my da's pal, you mean?'

'Naw, ya bampot.' Scobie darted another furtive look around the half-empty bar. 'You've been chosen, singled out.'

'Who by?'

'Your friends across the water.'

Scobie winked meaningfully and began to sing in a whisper, ' "A nation once again . . ." You've been highly recommended, Tony.'

Tony was beginning to look distinctly worried. 'What for?'

'They will be in touch. They're staying over the weekend.'

'What for?' Tony's long face had now gone a shade paler.

'Tony, you're going to be approached by a brigade commander. If you want to know, I'll tell you. He's from the Belfast Brigade. They don't come any better. He's had a wee word with me, and I've assured him that all he'd heard about you is true. You're a good Republican. A man to be trusted.'

'What for?' Tony's mind and tongue seemed to have got stuck in one groove. Total confusion reigned in his eyes and his mouth hung loosely open.

'Here's what they want you to do,' Scobie confided in hushed, but very clearly formed words. 'You will get two parcels to deliver. Now, don't worry, you will get enough money for a nice month in Spain. Three-star hotel. You'll still have enough money left in the last week. You'll not be counting the pennies. Just two parcels, Tony.' Scobie smacked his hands together, making Tony wince and nearly spill his beer. 'And you won't be in the country when they go off.'

'I'm not planting any fucking bombs,' Tony howled.

'You should have thought of that before, Tony. They think you're willing to be an active member and plant bombs. Now you're telling me you're not. You're just a public house Republican.'

At this point, Tony relinquished his beer as if the glass had suddenly electrocuted him. 'I'll have to go. I just remembered. I've a train to catch.'

Scobie put a detaining hand on his arm. 'Wait a minute, Tony. Did all those people in Ireland die for nothing? For well over eight hundred years we've been ruled by foreigners. Now you're getting a chance to do something about it.'

'Fuck off.' Tony flung aside Scobie's detaining hand and disappeared with the speed of a greyhound.

'What's up with him?' the barman asked.

For a minute or two Scobie couldn't speak for laughter. 'He's discovered he's not such a good Republican as he thought he was.'

'Aye,' the barman said, 'there's a lot like that. Good at the romancing. Singing the Irish songs and buying raffle tickets. But they don't want to have anything to do with active service. They draw the line at getting involved.'

'Aye,' Scobie agreed, wiping the tears of hilarity from his eyes. 'As long as the old Murphy's stout's flowing, and the Guinness, it's hunky-dory. But when they say we've come to collect you, it's hell of a difference. Pull me another pint, son. I'll just have another one before I go.'

Tony was not at Michael's wedding. Nobody knew where he was. He disappeared on Thursday and didn't reappear until Monday night. He'd gone straight to work from wherever he'd been, and wherever he'd been he refused to say. It turned out afterwards that he'd holed up at the house in Blackhill – it was all ready to move into and they all had a key.

The flitting from Bright Street, Garngad to Acrehill Street, Blackhill happened six days after the wedding, just before the happy pair returned from their honeymoon in Rothesay. (They'd had two minds about going away at all because Clyde coast resorts could be pretty nippy in the spring, but in the end the treat of a few days at the seaside could not be resisted.) The flitting had been carried out by the O'Maleys themselves with a little help from Scobie. It wasn't too far to Acrehill Street, maybe a half-hour's leisurely walk. So they managed no bother using a horse and a cart loaned by Spud Tamson, the coal man. This was a lot easier than the handcarts trundled along by other new folk who had been moved to Blackhill by earlier slum clearances. To celebrate the success of the move both Patrick and Scobie had gone on a bender.

'You shouldn't encourage him,' Maureen scolded. 'You can stop, but he can't.'

'Encourage him? How do I encourage him? As for stopping, he's always stopping. Every time he swears he'll never touch another drop. Wait till you see, in a few days, he'll be coming here as sober as a judge and with a terrible hangover and telling us he'll never look at another drop as long as he lives.'

'I wonder if Carragh could get him to go to the AA.'

'Alcoholics Anonymous? No chance. I've told you, he keeps thinking he can stop. He'll never admit he's an alcy.'

Maureen sighed. 'Anyway, I've told Carragh she can come round here any time she's stuck. I think she feels everybody's deserting her, with some of the boys talking about joining the fair and others planning to go down South, and Bridie looking forward to her wedding. Not that any of them are much help to her as it is. Do you think Doris and Bernard will come to anything? She seems daft about him.'

Patrick made a face. 'Bernard doesn't seem very keen as far as I can make out. But then he always plays his cards close to his chest. He deserves better than one of the Gallachers. So does Frank, for that matter. The Gallachers are a right gormless lot. The whole crowd of them put together couldn't even match our Frank.'

'Frank's had no luck yet with a house and Bridie and him are that keen to tie the knot. I know you don't want to take advantage of your pal's good nature, Patrick, but if he's such a nice man, would he not be pleased to give your son a wee helping hand? I read in the paper that Bailie McPherson's had quite a bit to do with these new flats in the Gorbals.'

'Why can't they get their own places?'

'You know Bernard, he'll never ask you to do anything for him. Bernard will always see to himself. And Michael didn't ask you to speak to the factor about Bright Street. He saw to that himself. Tony's not even going with anybody. So it's just Frank. Aw, go on Patrick. Frank's such a good boy.'

'He's put his name on the Corporation list. He'll be allowed a house when his time comes.'

Maureen sent a glance heavenwards. 'Holy Mother of God! Poor Frank could be drawing his old age pension by then!'

'Bailie McPherson went out of his way to get us this house. I couldn't have the cheek to ask him again. Especially so soon. It wouldn't be right.'

'Och, Patrick . . .'

'Look, just think yourself lucky he helped us get this place.'

Maureen sighed, then abandoning any hope for Frank, she gazed around her new home with pleasure. It was her pride and joy, and already many of her old neighbours and friends had come to be shown around. Carragh had been for a bath and said it was the best luxury she'd ever enjoyed in her life. The living room in which Maureen and Patrick were sitting, one either side of a coal fire with a plum-coloured tiled surround, looked out to a back green. Beyond that was the railway line and the gasworks. Already Patrick and Tony had jumped on to some stationary wagons, split them open with axes, and stolen some cartons. But it turned out there was nothing worth selling in them. 'Better luck next time,' they'd said.

Maureen and Patrick slept on a bed settee in the living room. They pulled it out at night. It meant shifting the table and chairs back against the window, and even then it took a bit of manoeuvring to get around. But that was only at night. If the boys wanted a cup of tea or anything to eat after she and Patrick went to bed, there was the beautiful scullery with its gas cooker and wash boiler and slatted shelves for pots and pans.

Tony and Frank shared one bedroom, and Bernard had the other to himself because his work was very irregular, and more often than not he came in during the wee small hours. Sometimes he was out the whole night long and didn't appear until five or six in the morning. Anyway, Bernard could afford to give her more money than the other two, and he insisted that he was entitled to the room. There was never any use arguing with Bernard. He had such a strong will sometimes it frightened her. But he was a lovely boy. Maureen had a secret admiration for him as well as love. If truth be known, he was her favourite. He had always been good to her. But at times, noticing that steely unwavering stare of his, she wondered how he was to other people. Of course it was the nature of his job that he had to be tough. Still, Michael was a boxer and he hadn't the same kind of look. She blamed the difference on the fact that Bernard often missed Mass. She suspected he only went at all to please her, and that was only after she pleaded and cajoled and openly wept for his immortal soul.

Maureen wondered again if he was serious about Doris. All the Gallachers were good Catholics and never missed Mass if they could help it. Even Scobie, while still feeling like death with one of his hangovers, struggled along to the chapel. The priest had tried his best to keep Scobie on the straight and narrow. When he was working and didn't hand over his pay packet to Carragh, Father Riley had come to the house and given him a right doing. That worked for a week or two. Then Scobie would be arrested for being drunk and disorderly and disappear for a spell into the Bar L., as Barlinnie prison was nicknamed. The local bobbies knew Scobie well and it was said that they picked him up every now and again just to give Carragh a breather.

If Bernard was serious about Doris, Maureen couldn't imagine him being married in the chapel. At the same time she couldn't imagine what Bernard could have against the faith he'd been brought up in. As a child he always seemed to go quite happily to Mass and to enjoy the Boys' Guild.

She had noticed his gradual withdrawal into a kind of secrecy. Was it linked with, or caused by his job? she wondered. Had his hard-man image crushed all his finer feelings? Yet he was such a lovely boy, with his smooth black crown of hair. And when he smiled, and that cleft in his chin deepened, he looked so handsome and strong. She loved him dearly. Doris Gallacher was a nice enough wee lassie, but in a different class altogether from Bernard. Bernard was going places. Already he could claim to have his own business. Doris Gallacher wasn't for him. Although it was plain for anyone to see she'd set her sights on him.

Poor Doris, she thought, then wondered why she hadn't thought – poor Bernard.

Chapter Sixteen

'It was you who wanted to come to Drumchapel,' McPherson reminded Sophie. 'I told you Knightswood or Mosspark would be better, but you refused to listen. Anyway, you've barely been here two years. Can't you settle yourself for anywhere for any length of time?'

'If you and your crowd had built the place right, maybe I could have settled here. If you'd thought about what folk needed, like shops and churches and halls . . .' She was polishing the table near where he was sitting, polishing it desperately over and over again as if each mote of dust that landed on it tormented her.

'We've been through all this before,' McPherson groaned. 'What good does it do? You wanted to come here, and now you'll have to stay here whether you like it or not.'

'Don't you dare lay down the law to me about where I've got to spend the rest of my days. You're not sitting on the bench now. I'm the one who's stuck here all the time. I notice you make sure you don't need to spend one hour in the place more than you can avoid.'

McPherson tried to be patient. 'I've my work to go to.'

'Work?' Sophie sneered. 'When did you last lay a brick? Your hands are softer than a woman's.'

'You know perfectly well what I mean.'

'Oh yes, the busy committee man at the City Chambers. Not just a committee man now – chairman of this, chairman of that. The man who can do everything for everybody except his own family.'

'Sophie, if you're now expecting me to get you a house in Knightswood or Mosspark, I'm afraid I'll have to disappoint you. The reason why I said you'll have to stay here whether you like it or not is simply because it's impossible for me to get you a house in Knightswood or Mosspark. People have found that they like it in those schemes. They like living there so much I couldn't get them to move to make a house vacant for you unless I put a bomb under them.'

'Well . . .' She hesitated, outwardly defiant, inwardly shivering at her own outrageousness. 'A house in Bearsden then.'

She had passed many a lonely hour recently walking around the elegant tree-lined streets of Bearsden, imagining how wonderful it would be to live there. There could be no doubt these people had amenities. In the central part, called the village, there was a line of shops with tidy flats above them. There was a town hall, churches and church halls. It was obviously a very busy and Christian community. The halls had notice boards telling of innumerable meetings and social events that no doubt needed conscientious helpers. She longed to be really needed, have something useful to do. She still didn't know any of her immediate neighbours in Drumchapel. They were out at work all day. Some of the others she'd come across she didn't want to know. There were young women who during daylight hours flaunted painted faces and bare feet with scarlet toenails showing through open strapped sandals. She'd told them they ought to be horsewhipped for being such shameless jezebels. After dark she'd caught couples behaving in a shameless and filthy manner in the back close. She'd called God's wrath down on their heads and shone a torch like the light of God on their disgusting wickedness. There isn't a corner dark enough, she'd told them, to hide from the light of the Lord. Filth had poured from the lips of the sinners. They called her obscene names, but she knew she had God on her side and was given strength to survive their hatred. The mothers of these sinners were no better. Lazy sluts who never washed the stairs and couldn't be bothered to discipline even the youngest of their children. Children roamed wild in dangerous looking packs or hung about shouting and laughing. Underaged boys smoked cigarettes. Boys and girls dropped litter and blasphemed. When she chastised them for taking the Lord's name in vain, they jeered and made a fool of her.

Drumchapel was a soulless barren waste of a place. She hated it.

'Bearsden?' McPherson gasped. 'Have you gone completely out of your mind?'

'What's wrong with wanting to live in Bearsden?'

'Houses there cost money. That's what's wrong for a start.'

'We could get a mortgage.'

'You know perfectly well, Sophie, that would go against my principles.'

'Principles, principles. We can't afford those kind of principles. Anyway, just because you support the building of council houses doesn't mean you have to live in one.'

'We can't afford a mortgage.'

'You always seem to find money when you need it for yourself. Anyway, I've seen your bankbook. You're not as hard up as you keep making out. Think about it, Andrew. It would be a step up in the world for you. A man in your position should have a good address. And think how you could relax. You need more time to relax. You could join the golf club and meet decent people you wouldn't be ashamed to invite home.' Her eyes misted, imagining entertaining people to dinner or supper or afternoon tea. 'I've discovered there's a local Church of Jesus there. We could become part of a really nice Christian community.'

McPherson personally didn't think Drumchapel or the people were nearly as bad as Sophie made out. They were always decently behaved and respectful to him.

He began to think, however, maybe she had a point. He rather fancied the idea of being a member of an exclusive golf club. It was true. He didn't give himself time to relax. It might look as if he was relaxed sitting in the Corn Exchange but he was constantly on tap, constantly available for people to approach him for advice or help. And that was over and above his work in the City Chambers committee rooms and his regular stints sitting on the bench of the Licensing Court.

The more he thought of Sophie's idea the more he felt it might have possibilities. Bearsden was the place where the money was and money not only talked – it gave the right answers.

Of course his old mother wouldn't like it. She never tired of reminding him what a good Socialist his father had been. Indeed there could be no denying it. David McPherson had been one of the best. A regular old Keir Hardie of a man, cloth cap and all. Hundreds of Glaswegians had turned up at his funeral.

But his high principles, his brand of Socialism, had meant grim poverty and hardship for his family. A bricklayer by trade like himself, his father had been a great admirer of the Soviet Union and a tireless worker for the Independent Labour Party. He had a strong faith in Marxism but always said he'd defend parliamentary institutions to the death.

McPherson had followed his father's footsteps into local politics but felt his own personal way forward was through the Labour Party, and pledged himself to help the people of Glasgow who lived in appalling housing conditions to be rehoused in suitable flats. He had kept that pledge and had fought for the demolition of slums and the fast rebuilding of houses. He'd fought for the cleaning up of the polluted River Clyde, he'd lobbied for more attention to be paid to the arts and for financial help for the university.

In short, he'd fought and worked tirelessly for his fellow citizens, and it had been said of him that he was a town councillor who saw the advantage of regional planning, new towns and comprehensive redevelopment, and did all in his power to put them into effect. His father would have been proud of him.

Yet sometimes when McPherson gazed at himself in the mirror, looking portly and distinguished in his dark, well-tailored suit and his heavy gold chain of office, he quailed inside as he imagined his father's sharp eyes staring back at him. The truth was the old man *ought* to have been proud of him but wouldn't have been. Yet why not? What good could you do the starving if you starved along with them? In his own way, he did as much as his father ever did for the working class. It wasn't the working man that he made any extra money from. Any gifts, any favours he received, were from businessmen; builders who wanted contracts, taxi owners, and men who wanted to open pubs or restaurants and needed to be sure of getting a licence. Men who could well afford to pay for any influence he used on their behalf. It was worth remembering that any building contract awarded, any restaurant or pub licence given, meant much needed employment for more and more people. He did his best for everybody else. Why shouldn't he do his best for himself? He deserved it.

'We'll see,' he told Sophie, and was taken aback by the immediate and feverish way her face lit up.

'I know it's the right place for us, Andrew. God has called us there. I feel it. I feel it.'

'I just said we'll see,' he repeated uneasily. 'It's as far out as Drumchapel, you know.'

'Oh, but what a different world. A world of God's chosen people.'

Sometimes he wondered if Sophie was mad. She so often went to such extremes. 'I'll have a word with Felderman's and see if they own any property out there. We might come to some arrangement that could be to the advantage of both of us.' He was thinking of the flats in the Gorbals. More and more of the old Gorbals was being demolished. Some new flats had already been built. More were on the cards. The contract for them would be worth millions.

'I'm sure you can do it with God's help, Andrew. We'll both go to Church on Sunday and pray for your success in this.'

He sighed. It was such a difficult trek to get into town from Drumchapel on a Sunday. Public transport was bad enough during the week, but on a Sunday it was practically non-existent. It was high time he had a car. It was ridiculous for a man in his position to have to struggle here, there and everywhere by bus or tram or train. Felderman had a car all right. Felderman had a black Rolls Royce. A wave of bitterness engulfed him. Why shouldn't he have a house in Bearsden and a car and any other of life's comforts? He was a better man than John Felderman. A better man by a long chalk.

'I grant you it would be a lot more sensible and convenient,' he told Sophie, 'to be members of a church on our doorstep, so to speak.'

'Perhaps it's time for us to move on spiritually as well as physically,' Sophie said, thinking of the shabby converted house in the ancient terrace along Rose Street and comparing it in her mind's eye with the noble looking religious edifices in Bearsden.

'Well, yes, I suppose one could make a case for that.' He leaned his elbows down on his knees and thoughtfully made a roof by placing the tips of his fingers together. 'I take your point. Yes, I'll see what I can do.'

Sophie was ecstatic. She couldn't wait to tell Andrina. She phoned her up right away and was taken aback to get no answer. Where could she be? It was only a couple of hours ago that she'd been speaking to her, and Andrina had assured her she would be in for the rest of the evening. All the excitement about living in Bearsden immediately shrank into suspicion. She telephoned again and again. Until eventually Andrina answered.

'Oh, Mummy.' The guilt in her tone was unmistakable.

'Where do you think you've been?'

'It was one of Robert's karate nights.'

'Do you think I'm a fool? You don't go to Robert's karate club.'

'No, I wasn't saying that. I just felt a bit lonely . . .'

'And so you decided . . .' Sophie's voice turned ugly, twisted with disgust. '. . . to seek a little male companionship elsewhere.'

'No! No! I just popped out to have a chat with one of the neighbours.'

'That immoral slut next door. She'd be able to supply you with what you were looking for, all right.'

'No, not Josie, Mummy. She works at night. And honestly, she's a very nice person. She's not what you think at all.'

'Anybody with eyes in their head can see what she's like. That woman's a filthy prostitute.'

'Mummy, please don't speak like that. It upsets me. You don't know what you're saying. You don't know Josie.'

I know you, she thought bitterly, you wicked liar. 'You promised you'd have nothing more to do with that woman and when I arrived unexpectedly to visit you last week, she was in your house.'

'She'd just popped in to borrow some sugar, Mummy. What could I do? I couldn't shut the door in her face.'

'You've always been the same of course. You hadn't left school when you were sneaking off with men. I thought being safely married would change you, but I see it hasn't.'

'If you're meaning Bernard O'Maley, that was years ago and we just met in the park a few times, Mummy. And Mary Gardner and Sheila Preston were there too. And a couple of Bernard's friends. It was all very innocent. You'd no need to worry.'

'Innocent? With a man like Bernard O'Maley?' Sophie spat the words out in disgust. 'You nearly killed me with worry. God forgive you, you nearly killed me and you haven't changed. You lied to me then and you're lying to me now. You met him on your own more than once and you painted your face when you went to meet him. I know all about what you did.'

'Mummy, I didn't mean any harm . . .'

'And you haven't changed. When I caught you with that woman your face was painted like a common harlot. You had as much paint on your face as she had, and you were wearing cheap flashy earrings . . .'

'They were Josie's, Mummy. She was just letting me try them on. It was just a bit of fun.'

'Oh? Was the disgusting bra you were wearing hers as well? Making you stick out – flaunt yourself. I was ashamed for you. You enjoy flaunting yourself and making a vulgar exhibition of yourself. I felt dirtied being in the same room as you.'

Filth.

'Oh Mummy, please don't talk like that.' Andrina had begun to weep.

Sophie banged down the receiver as if it was contaminated.

Chapter Seventeen

Bernard observed Andrina as often as he could, and when he went to karate he tactfully elicited from Robert as much information about her as possible. He learned that every Friday she went into Sauchiehall Street to have a wander about the shops and then enjoy afternoon tea in Miss Cranston's Willow Tearooms.

The tearoom was a Rennie Mackintosh masterpiece. Outside, it sparkled like a little jewel between the darker, more sedate buildings crowding it on either side. It had smart chequered edging and elegant looping ironwork combined with abstracted organic shapes so typical of Mackintosh. Mackintosh also liked symbolism and no doubt that was why he chose the motif of the willow. It came from the name of Sauchiehall Street, which meant alley of willows.

Bernard wished Andrina had been in the habit of frequenting any other restaurant in the city. The Willow seemed a very feminine kind of place, and if he knew anything about Rennie Mackintosh there would be his ladder-backed fragile looking chairs inside. However, there was no question of being put off. He waited and watched across the road from the tearoom. Eventually he saw her arrive, tall and elegant in a grey alpaca dress that fitted snugly over her shapely body in what he'd learned from Doris was the Princess line. The dress had a high horseshoe neck and over it a short white spencer just reached to under Andrina's bust. She wore white gloves and a little straw boater decorated with a broad ribbon to match her dress. She had lost much of her teenage voluptuousness, but she was still a curvaceous and strikingly beautiful woman.

He followed her inside the tearoom. He watched her hesitate under the great flower bowl that marked the transition from the front saloon to the back beyond. Then he watched as she decided to climb the open-screened stairs leading to the tea-gallery above. He too climbed the stairs. The upper tea-room was sumptuously extravagant and sophisticated and it occurred to him that Andrina obviously enjoyed and could appreciate life's luxuries. This gave them something else in common. It was, he believed, linked with sexuality and sensuality, this ability to appreciate, to savour, to enjoy. He felt himself relishing and appreciating the luxury of his surroundings. One wall of long, low, slightly bay windows set with a design in mirror glass looked over the street. The other walls were lined with pale purple silk and had a frieze of leaded panels of mirrors, purple and white glass reflecting light and chairs and customers. A panel set with glass jewels and beads had such a romantic imagery that Bernard now felt that Andrina could not have chosen a better place.

She was sitting facing the window and so she didn't see him approach.

'Hello, Andrina.'

She looked up, startled. 'Bernard.'

For the briefest of seconds he saw pleasure flutter over her eyes.

'May I join you?' he asked, pulling out a chair and sitting down without waiting for an answer.

Already she had become agitated. He could feel the tension in her. 'I don't think you should, Bernard.'

'Why not? We're old friends. And I had to talk to you. I didn't get a chance at the party.'

Her eyes kept agitating anxiously towards the stairs as if she was expecting her mother to suddenly materialise on a witch's broom. She wasn't worried about Robert, or about anybody else seeing them together. Just her mad old mother.

'If my mother saw us,' she said, confirming that he'd guessed correctly, 'I'd die, Bernard. I'm sorry. I know we're just friends and it's perfectly harmless us meeting by accident and having a cup of tea together, but that's not how my mother would see it. I'd just die, Bernard. I'm sorry, but I can't help it. Please go.'

'In a way, your mother's got a point.'

Her sudden, undivided attention fixed on him. 'How do you mean?'

'This meeting isn't an accident. I've been watching you and waiting for you.'

Colour darkened her cheeks. 'You used to do that before.'

'I've never stopped.'

'This is ridiculous. Apart from anything else, I'm a married woman.'

'I'm the one you should have married, Andrina. I know it and you know it.'

She became agitated again. 'This is ridiculous,' she repeated. 'I don't know anything of the kind. I'm perfectly happy with Robert. How dare you spy on me and follow me and say things like that to me?'

'From the moment I first set eyes on you, I loved you and wanted you. Every day I hold you in my thoughts. Every night I hold you in my arms and make passionate love to you in my imagination.'

'This is madness.'

'In a way I suppose it is.'

'You must stop this, Bernard. Stop it at once. I will not have you thinking such things about me, or following me, or spying on me, or upsetting me like this. If you don't leave right now, I will.'

He rose. 'I've no desire to upset you. But I wanted you to be clear about how I feel.'

'It's time you were married with a wife of your own,' she was near to tears of distress, 'instead of pestering another man's wife. Robert of all people too. He thinks you're his best friend.'

'Yes, I'm sorry about Robert.'

'Just go.'

'I'll see you again.'

He'd said all he wanted to say. Out on Sauchiehall Street, despite her words of rejection, he felt animated, energised, inflamed by a love that he knew instinctively was burning in her blood too. Perhaps she hadn't awakened to the fire of it yet.

Perhaps she had not yet found enough courage to face it. But it was there in her exactly the same as it was in him.

The only thing that spoiled this secret union, this promise of wonderful riches to come, was the mention of Robert. The words 'Robert of all people' echoed like a Chinese torture in his mind, tensing every nerve, every muscle.

He had to go to the karate club now. He needed the outlet of karate for his pent-up energies and tensions. On the other hand, he didn't relish facing Robert so soon after making love –albeit only verbal love – to his wife.

Yet at the same time no one really mattered except Andrina. He thought of being with her in no other terms than loving ones. With Doris it was sex – a simple release of nature, like peeing. He tried to behave decently to her in other ways. He gave her a good time. He took her to posh restaurants for meals – something that thrilled her to the core. He gave her presents. He tried not to show his growing irritation with her. It wasn't Doris's fault that he didn't love her.

But Andrina, oh darling Andrina. How he adored everything about her: her baby-shaped eyes, her fiery crown of hair, her creamy complexion, her soft bulging breasts, her neat waist, her delightful wiggle of curvaceous hips, her long shapely legs. She had the mixture of innocence, vulnerability and sensuality of an auburn-haired Marilyn Monroe. He ached to touch her, caress her, stroke her, kiss every inch of her. When he made love to her, and one day he would make love to her, he would take his time and savour every precious moment.

He got off the tram and walked through the grim lines of tenements to the school hall where the karate club was held.

'Hi,' Robert greeted him.

Bernard gave him a nod as he retrieved the white baggy trousers, loose white jacket and black belt that was the traditional karate uniform. He began to undress with Andrina still so livid in his mind it seemed strange that Robert couldn't see her. Robert was already in his karate gear and left the side room to join the boys waiting in the hall, his bare feet slapping on the boards. Bernard followed, the karate discipline banishing Andrina at least temporarily from his mind. Concentrating was important in this martial art. Concentration, and a mixture of relaxation and speed.

Robert took the class through a quick warm-up session. Once loosened, they all lined up. Then with a short bobbing bow Bernard faced Robert. He gave a loud 'Ossu' and slid forward, knees flexed, ankles loose, concentrating on relaxed rhythmic breathing. Suddenly, with a rapid double shuffle, he drove forward off his back leg. A satisfying thud exploded up his extended arm as he scored a solid Yakuzuki into Robert's ribs. He immediately leapt sideways to avoid Robert's counter punch and, on the break, shot a left leg Jodan Mawashigeri into Robert's temple.

He quickly disengaged and continued his circling motion, bouncing lightly, arms and shoulders loose. Robert rushed forward with a loud Kiai and a strong focused series of punches. Bernard continued to spiral away. He knew that, despite his height and the bulk of his shoulders, he was faster, smoother, more in control. He feinted an opening and as Robert leapt into the opening, he dropped his lead hand down across the punch and threw a lightning-fast back fist onto Robert's temple.

With a wry smile Robert called 'Yame' and the class halted. 'You're getting too good at this, Bernard,' Robert said. 'What's your secret?'

Chapter Eighteen

'Andrina?'

'Mm?'

'You were miles away. There's nothing wrong, is there?'

Andrina raised a brow. 'What could be wrong?'

Robert kept his book open on his lap but did not immediately return his attention to it. He peered over his glasses at her. He had taken to wearing glasses for reading. She had never seen him looking more like a school teacher. 'You seem a bit tense and worried.'

'Do I?' She gave a half laugh. 'All I was thinking about was what to have for tomorrow's dinner.'

'Perhaps you should get out and about more. Take up some hobby. Go out with a woman friend instead of being on your own so much during the day. I feel guilty about leaving you on your own on my karate evenings as well.'

'We go out together at the weekend, or we have people in. I'm quite happy with that.'

'Are you sure?'

She smiled. 'Of course I'm sure.'

'As long as you're happy.' He pushed his glasses up to the bridge of his nose again and returned his attention to his book. In the silence she could hear the gas mantle putter and the fire creak. In the peace and safety of their home she felt affection and gratitude towards Robert. It was true what her mother said. She was a very lucky woman.

She struggled to keep her thoughts anchored in the serenity of the kitchen and the comforting familiarity of the man sitting at the other side of the hearth. She gazed at his short brown hair. It was peppered with grey at the temples and beginning to thin a little too. Robert didn't bother so much about the smattering of grey but he was anxious about losing any hair. He tried to pretend otherwise, but he had started to experiment with different shampoos and hair tonics. She worried more about his thin face, the way his cheeks sunk in, pulling his skin tight over his high cheekbones. He laughed at her when she voiced her concern and told her he was proud of the fact that he carried no extra flesh. It was healthier that way. He certainly seemed healthy enough. He had a quick, intelligent mind and a well-shaped and energetic body, despite its leanness.

She flicked through the magazine in her lap but couldn't concentrate on the printed word or the pictures. She felt restless, uneasy, disturbed. No matter how hard she tried to blank him out, she kept seeing Bernard O'Maley. Like Robert he had broad shoulders tapering down to narrower hips. But there was so much *more* of Bernard. He was solid. He had an aggressive self-confidence which, coupled with his straight unwavering stare, could be intimidating. It was impossible to ignore Bernard. He had an almost menacing presence. There was an aura about him. In the restaurant she had felt that presence engulf her to the exclusion of everything else. Even the memory of it made her breath quicken painfully and sweat break over her. Guilty and ashamed of even thinking of another man in the presence of her good husband, especially after all the outrageous things Bernard had said, she went over to the sink, ran cold water over her wrists and dabbed at her temples.

'There *is* something wrong.' Robert laid aside his book.

'No, honestly, Robert. I sometimes take these silly hot flushes, that's all.'

'It can't be the menopause. You're far too young.'

'I know. It's just a kind of nervous thing. Mummy gets the same. I've seen her face go quite scarlet and you know how normally pale she is.'

'Yes, but she probably *is* going through the menopause.'

'She's forty-nine.'

'I believe some women can have symptoms until well into their fifties.'

Andrina shrugged. 'It's nothing. I feel fine. Probably I was sitting too near the fire. I think I'll make a cup of tea. Do you fançy one?'

'Sit down. I'll make it.'

Andrina did as she was told, heart discreetly thumping. The whole thing was ridiculous. She took long, careful breaths.

'Mummy was telling me on the phone today she and Daddy have been looking at houses in Bearsden. *Bearsden* of all places. Can you believe it?'

'That'll cost them.'

'I suppose they'll get a mortgage.'

'Even so.'

'Sometimes I think Mummy's more ambitious than Daddy. She's got that kind of drive that ambitious people have.'

'I don't think she's happy in Drumchapel though.'

'Yes, she misses her old neighbours. Everybody knew each other up her old close. Everybody in the whole building and a few of the other buildings as well. Everybody could leave their key in the door so that the coalman or anybody else with a message could pop in if the person was out. Apparently you wouldn't dare do that in Drumchapel – or so Mummy says.'

'Everybody seems to be moving,' Robert remarked as he poured boiling water into the teapot. 'The O'Maleys – you know, Bernard's family – have moved to Blackhill. Michael's married a Protestant girl, and taken over the house in Garngad.'

Andrina busied herself with poking the fire. 'How's Bernard getting on these days?'

'He seems to be making enough money, by the look of the Crombie coat he was wearing last winter. And obviously he doesn't buy his suits and shirts at the Barras. He's got several other bouncers working for him. Now, *he's* an ambitious type.'

'Does he still go to the karate club?'

'As often as he can. It helps keep him fit. By God, he's good. He nearly floored me the last time.'

Andrina's heart thumped with anger. 'That's terrible. How dare he try to hurt you?'

Robert laughed, but gently. 'Darling.' He leaned over and kissed her. 'It's not like that. Anyway, you've no need to worry. I'm more than able to give as good as I get.'

Nevertheless she felt anxious, apprehensive. 'I love you, Robert,' she said.

'And I love you, darling.'

They drank their tea in silence for a minute, then Robert said, 'I shouldn't have arranged so many outings for the children during the holidays. I should be spending more time with you.'

'Nonsense, you'll be spending plenty of time with me. We don't need to be living in each other's pockets all summer. Anyway,' she laughed, 'their need is greater than mine.'

'Admittedly they're always in danger of getting into trouble with so much time on their hands. The sketching and painting is just an excuse to get them off the streets and out into the country.' He grinned. 'I throw in a bit of biology while we're there. Anything to hold their attention. It's keeping track of them that's the most difficult thing though. You know how thirteen and fourteen-year-old kids can be. Once away from the tenements they're like wild animals let loose.'

'I can imagine.'

'I always have to do a quick count to make sure I don't leave anyone stuck up a tree or wandering about in a cave.'

'A cave?' she echoed incredulously.

'Up the Campsie Hills. I must take you one day. We could have a picnic. You get a panoramic view of Glasgow from the top of the Campsies.'

She nodded. 'I'd like that.'

The telephone rang, making her jerk so violently that hot tea splashed over her hands.

'Andrina!' Robert took the cup from her. 'Your nerves must be bad. Go and run cold water over your hand. I'll answer it.'

She knew it would be her mother. As she stood at the kitchen sink it wasn't only the icy water that made her shiver. Panic swooped and flapped and careered about in her head like a flock of crazy birds. She knew it was crazy, but she was terrified her mother would know she'd been thinking about Bernard.

She could hear Robert chatting on the phone and then saying, 'Yes, she's in the kitchen. I'll fetch her.' Returning from the hall, he said, 'How's the hand?'

'It's fine.'

'It's your mother.'

'Oh, right.' She hurried from the kitchen, then half-way across the hall she remembered to slow her pace and take breath more evenly. 'Hello Mummy.'

'Is there anything wrong?'

'Wrong?'

'You never answered the phone.'

'I'm answering it now.'

'You know what I mean. There's something in your voice. Have you been quarrelling with Robert?'

'Of course not.' Andrina gave a genuine laugh of disbelief. 'What a thing to say.'

'Well, there's something.' A short pause was followed by her mother saying, 'You're hiding something.'

'Mummy, what could I possibly . . .'

'What have you been doing today?'

'Mummy, you've already phoned and I told you.'

'You said you were going to the shops.'

'Yes, that's what I did.'

'What shops?'

'Daly's, Copland's, Pettigrew and Stephen. I saw some lovely things but I didn't buy anything. Everything's so expensive in those big shops. In Sauchiehall Street at least. Argyle Street isn't so bad.' She knew she was chattering, but she couldn't stop. 'There's some shops in Argyle Street, especially along at the Trongate end . . .'

'Who were you with?' her mother interrupted coldly. 'As if I didn't know.'

'Nobody. I just had a wander about on my own. I like doing that. I often do that.'

'You were parading about the streets with that prostitute who lives next door to you.'

'No, no, Mummy. I swear to you. I'll swear on the Bible if you like. I haven't seen Josie all day. I'm a bit tired, that's all. The town can be tiring, you must know that yourself.'

'Robert did say,' her mother's voice acquired a grudging note, 'that he thought your nerves were a bit on edge and you needed a holiday.'

'So does he,' Andrina said eagerly. 'He does far too much for those pupils of his. We might go away somewhere.'

'Remember, Robert's not made of money.'

Andrina thought – neither is Daddy, but it would never have occurred to her to say the words out loud.

'Well, I'll phone you tomorrow and see how you are.'

'I'm fine – really, Mummy.' She had learned not to say, 'There's no need to phone' – This would only open the floodgates to more suspicious questioning. 'All right, Mummy. Sleep well.'

'You too. And don't forget to say your prayers.'

'I won't.'

Her immediate prayer was, 'Please, God, don't let Mummy find out about Bernard.'

Chapter Nineteen

Doris knew that it was the usual and accepted thing to do one's courting in the back close. Everyone she knew did it. Well, perhaps that wasn't totally true. The girls in the shop who lived in Bearsden couldn't do it. As far as she knew there weren't any closes in Bearsden. Anyway, there would be bigger houses there and smaller families. A girl living in a bigger house with less brothers and sisters to get in the way could probably have the use of a front room. Or a sitting room, or lounge, or whatever the best room was called in a place like Bearsden.

Perhaps they did it in the country. That was nice – at least, when the weather was good. She and Bernard had made love in the country. Although it had been a bit of a problem getting the grass out of her hair without bringing it all down. And it had been awfully cold and draughty on her bum. The weather was never all *that* good in Scotland. Surely there could be no nudist camps in this climate. She'd heard there was. She'd had a good giggle with the girls about that. Blue tits wouldn't just refer to the birds of the feathered variety, Betty Campbell had said. That had sent them all into absolute kinks.

Betty was a real scream. She was always doing or saying something to set them off, and make it terribly difficult to approach a customer with a serious face and a polite 'Can I help you, Modom?'

Now winter was here again and it meant a return to the back close. Much as she loved Bernard – perhaps *because* she loved him – she didn't want to stand there any more in the foul-smelling darkness, pinioned against a wall with her clothes up around her ears. She was worried. Bernard was different from the rest of the local men she knew. He was even different from his brothers. He had the look of a man who was going places. He was much better dressed for a start. She admired somebody who took trouble with their appearance. She took great pride in her own appearance. There was the struggle with her bouffant of hair, and the delicate attachment of false eyelashes. There was the careful washing and pressing of clothes. She never trusted Carragh to touch her things.

Despite all her care and all her efforts, physically and otherwise, to please Bernard, he'd never mentioned marriage. All sorts of worries, uncertainties and insecurities had begun to plague her.

Bernard had never said he loved her. Sometimes she became depressed about this and depression brought panic. Sometimes, drooping about the house in her slippers and with her hair down, she'd catch a glimpse of herself in the full-length wardrobe mirror. She'd see herself with all her inadequacies, and be frightened.

She'd think – how could a big handsome man like Bernard O'Maley love a wee smout like her? Was he just after one thing, and she allowed him to have it? And that was that?

She felt ashamed every time she thought of the back close. She'd never allowed such behaviour before. There had been a couple of occasions when a young man had persuaded her, after a night out at the pictures, into the back close for a few kisses. Once his hands had begun to wander, however, she had acted on her dignity and stopped him.

She was saving herself for better things. She had nightmares of being caught in the same trap as her mother and so many other women in the district: marriage; a single end, or at best a room and kitchen; one baby after another; being dragged down in poverty and misery that ruined looks, figure, everything. Especially dreams of a better life – a chance in life.

She was hoping and praying that Bernard was her chance. But even if Bernard wasn't going places, even if he didn't have a job, even if he didn't employ men, even if he didn't wear good class clothes – she would still love him. With Bernard she would be willing to be the breadwinner if he had no job. With Bernard she'd be willing to starve in a single end.

She loved him terribly. Her fear and insecurity about their

relationship made her instinctively gravitate to Bernard's mother. She would drop in to see Maureen after Bernard had gone to work in the evening. She'd take her a box of sweeties, and they'd sit and smoke and talk until Maureen would get tired and say, 'I'll have to get to my bed. I think it must be old age, but I feel so done out some days.'

Often Maureen would tell her about what Bernard had been like as a wee boy. Maureen liked to talk about the past when her boys were young. Doris was greedy for anything about Bernard. It fed her love for him. Knowing everything about him brought him closer, created a deeper intimacy, made bonds that could not be broken.

She and Maureen became closer. One night, Maureen patted Doris's hand and said gently, 'You really do love him, don't you?'

'Oh, yes. Oh, yes, I really do, Mrs O'Maley. Terribly.' Tears blurred her eyes. 'But I don't know how he feels about me.'

'He hasn't said anything?'

Doris shook her head, not trusting herself to speak.

'Why don't you ask him, hen?'

'I'm too frightened,' Doris quavered. 'You know what he's like.'

'Och, he's a lovely boy.' Maureen immediately went on the defensive. 'It's his job makes him seem a bit tough on the outside, but he has a heart as big as a bucket, that boy. He's always slipping me a few pounds to help me out, or buy myself something. "Treat yourself to something nice, Ma," he'll say. "Be good to yourself, you deserve it." A heart as big as a bucket.'

'I know. I know,' Doris hastily assured her. 'He's a wonderful man. There's nobody like him. Nobody in the whole world. He's handsome and strong and brave and generous. I'm just crazy about him.'

'Well,' Maureen relaxed again, 'I'm sure he's very fond of you too, hen.'

'The thing is . . .' Doris plucked up enough courage eventually. 'The thing is, Mrs O'Maley, I'm pregnant.' Immediately the words were out her courage deserted her again and she began to weep. 'And I'm frightened he won't marry me.'

'Now, now,' Maureen hushed and soothed, at the same time trying to give herself time to think. She had grown fond of Doris. She wasn't a bad wee soul. And she loved Bernard, that was the main thing. And if she was having his child (and her grandchild), there was only one thing to do. Bernard could do a lot worse than marry a nice wee girl like Doris Gallacher. And poor Carragh had enough to worry her without having to cope with a pregnant unmarried daughter. No, that was unthinkable. Bernard would have to do the decent thing. 'You'll just have to tell him, hen.'

'How do you think he'll take it? Could you not tell him, Mrs O'Maley?'

'I'll have a quiet word afterwards, if need be, but it's your place to tell him first, Doris. He'll probably be delighted, and ask you to marry him right away.'

A silence followed in which both of them struggled to convince themselves of the truth of this pronouncement.

'Anyway,' Maureen said eventually, 'he'll have to know.'

'What if he chucks me?' Doris's mascara-streaked face was so pitiful in its wretchedness, Maureen felt truly sorry for her.

'He's the father of your child. He'll have to do his duty by you. You come round here tomorrow straight from your work while he's in. You and him can go through to the room. I'll keep Patrick and everybody else out the road.'

Doris nodded. 'OK.'

She couldn't sleep that night for thinking about the ordeal to come. She'd never said so many prayers in her life. She appealed to every member of the Holy family for help. She went round her rosary beads so often it was a wonder that by morning they weren't all worn away.

She nearly took the day off work, she felt so exhausted. But apart from the fact she couldn't afford to take time off, she was dreading spending twelve hours or more at home doing nothing but worrying about what she would say to Bernard and what he would say to her.

By the time she arrived on Maureen's doorstep she not only felt sick, she'd actually vomited twice down the lavatory pan. She felt and looked like a nervous ghost. The thing was, she wasn't only afraid of telling Bernard. She was afraid of Bernard – period.

She hadn't realised it until now.

Maureen opened the door and whispered, 'He's through in the room. I told him you wanted a private word before he left for work.'

'Ta.' She stared saucer-eyed at Maureen, unable to move.

'He won't eat you,' Maureen said. 'Away through.'

'OK.'

Bernard laid aside his newspaper and rose when she entered the room. That was one of the things she loved about him, one of the things that was so different. No other man had ever stood up when she entered a room.

'Hi,' he greeted her.

'I had to talk to you.' Doris plunged immediately to the root of the problem. 'I'm so worried.'

'What's wrong?'

'I'm pregnant.'

'Oh.' It was a flat, expressionless sound.

'I've told your mother. I was so upset and it just came out. But I haven't had the nerve to say anything to my folks yet.'

After keeping her anxiously waiting for a minute or two, Bernard said, 'It'll be all right.'

'Will it?' Her eyes cautiously brightened with hope.

'Of course. I'll look after you.'

'Will you?'

'Yes, I'll pay for an abortion.'

'An abortion?'

'Don't worry,' Bernard said. 'Just leave it to me. I'll arrange everything.'

'But that's a mortal sin.' Doris was so shocked she forgot her fear. 'I'm not having any abortion.'

'No one need know.'

'I'd know. Your Ma would know. She'll be terribly angry at you. She'll not want me to commit murder.'

'It's not murder.'

'It is so.' She was trembling with outrage now. 'I'm not doing it, Bernard. I'd rather keep the baby and face all the shame if you don't want to marry me.' Not knowing what else to say, and suddenly overwhelmed with grief and hopelessness, she ran from the room and the house.

Later, when Maureen found out, she was equally outraged, and the words she subsequently had with Bernard were anything but quiet.

Bernard tried his best to be patient. 'But Ma, I don't love Doris. She's a nice enough girl but I don't love her.'

'You should have thought about that when you were having your way with her.'

'It is possible to have sex without love, Ma.'

Maureen was suddenly exhausted. This was happening to her more and more often recently. For no apparent reason she'd feel drained of all energy. 'Not for a decent wee lassie like Doris Gallacher, it isn't. She loves you. You're breaking her heart, so you are.'

Unexpectedly, she disintegrated into weak tears and, ashamed of her weakness, she tried to louden her voice and rub the tears away with her bunched-up apron. 'And you're breaking mine as well. The shame of it! To the daughter of old friends and neighbours too. If you don't do the decent thing, I'll never be able to look them in the face again.'

'Ma!' Bernard appealed. It shook him to see his mother so distressed. 'It wouldn't work out. Neither of us would be happy. Look, if she feels she must have the baby, I'll pay for its keep. I won't see her or the child want for anything.'

'What a pregnant girl needs is a husband to look after her.' Maureen's sobs had become uncontrollable and were exhausting her so much she could have fainted away. 'And what a baby needs is a father. Money isn't everything. I don't know who you get your hard streak from, Bernard. It's not from Patrick or me. I just don't know.'

'It's not a case of hardness, Ma. I'm just trying to be sensible.'

'Oh, aye. Sensible, is it? Was it sensible to get that poor wee girl in the state she's in today? You just took your pleasure and never bothered about the consequences, Bernard, and now your refusing to take responsibility for your actions. That's the truth of it.' She paused to draw breath and take another wipe at her nose and eyes. 'You've really let me down, Bernard. You're letting the whole family down. You're going to drag the good name of O'Maley through the mud.'

He almost laughed. The good name of O'Maley? His father and Tony were a couple of train robbers to say the least.

Nevertheless, he couldn't see his mother in such a state. She hadn't been looking her old self recently. He was sure she was losing a lot of weight. Her face at times had a drawn appearance as if she was in pain. More than once he'd tried to persuade her to go and see a doctor but she always refused. For his mother's sake he'd do anything – even, he decided, if it meant marrying Doris Gallacher.

The decision brought a weight of hopelessness and depression.

'Come on, Ma, cheer up,' he managed at last. 'I'll tell Doris we can get married. But I'll have to be honest and tell her I don't love her. If she has any sense she'll not have me in those circumstances.'

But he knew in his heavy heart that she would.

Chapter Twenty

The Salvation Army was marching along Garngad Road, blasting out 'What a friend we have in Jesus' with noisy Christian fervour. Some children were dancing and skipping after them. Others in the cobbled corners of side streets were intent on their rhymes and skipping games.

'Gypsy, Gypsy Caroline,
Washed her face in turpentine,
The turpentine will make it shine,
Gypsy, Gypsy Caroline.'

As Frank and Bridie walked round to Turner Street a group of little girls in cheap cotton frocks were chanting counting-out rhymes. The one at the receiving of the last word was O-U-T, and had to leave the game.

'My mother and your mother were hanging out some clothes,
When my mother gave your mother a punch on the nose,
Guess what colour the blood was:
Blue!
B-L-U-E spells blue and that's the colour it was,
And you are O-U-T with a dirty washing clout,
Over your face like THIS!'

Boys were racing, rattling, clanging over the cobbles with iron girds and hoops. Others were hunkered down, intent on a game of chuckies or jorries. Crowds of boys were yelling and jostling and thumping and chasing each other and scattering sedate games of ring-a-ring-a-roses and in-and-out-the-dusty-bluebells.

Outside the black tunnel of Bridie's close (even on a bright summer day the closes into the buildings were black), a crush of ragged little girls were singing:

> 'I'm a little Brownie dressed in brown,
> See my knickers hanging down,
> One, two, three, four,
> Shove the tiger out the door.
> Five, six, seven, eight,
> Here she's coming in the gate.'

Bridie said morosely, 'You could have refused Ma's invitation. Why is she suddenly making such a thing of inviting you to tea anyway?'

'Now, how could I have said no? Your mother would have been hurt and offended. Anyway, having tea at your place isn't all that bad.'

But of course both of them knew that it was. The noisy crush in the kitchen had always been hard enough to bear. But now Scobie had taken to battering Carragh about when he was drunk. Frank was accustomed to a brain-numbing level of noise with Tony's drums, but Patrick had never lifted his hand to Maureen. Bridie's brothers had been bad enough with their habit of boasting about their street fights and who they'd chibbed. 'You ought to have heard the Proddie bastard scream,' they'd reminisce. Thank God they all seemed to be leaving or had left home now. Of course, that kind of violence was common enough in the neighbourhood. Frank had been caught up in fights himself. Not that long ago he'd been walking along on his way home from work, minding his own business – thinking about a wonderful idea for a love poem, in fact – when he heard the shout of 'PAPE'. Suddenly alert to his surroundings and knowing all too well what the shout meant, he saw guys coming at him from all directions. As they attacked him, he backed hard against the tenement wall, intent on keeping his feet. If he fell he would be booted unconscious to the scream of 'Papist Bastard' and chibbed until he could bleed to death.

As he fought like a madman to defend himself, women leaning from windows screeched out, 'Messins. Messin bastards. Polis!', adding to the wild cacophony of screams from the gang, 'Bastard. Fucker. Pape.'

Fortunately the beat bobby had been in one of the shops having a cup of tea and was quick on the scene, brandishing his truncheon. The gang immediately melted away and Frank was left with blood from his nose gushing down over his good suit. Normally he never cared about his appearance. Unlike his brothers he had no interest in clothes. The office of Messrs Goldmayer Ltd, Wholesale Warehousemen, insisted however that their employees should come to work wearing a decent suit, shirt, collar and tie. Not having a decent suit to wear might cost him his job. If that happened, God knows when he and Bridie could get married.

'My suit,' he kept repeating in horror, trying at the same time to stifle the flow of blood with a handkerchief. 'Look at my good suit.'

'Never mind your suit, son,' the bobby said. 'Is there any bones broken?'

Frank was racked with agonising pain. His stomach felt as if it had been punched right through his spine, but all he could think of was how bad luck seemed to be dogging his plans to get married.

'No. I'll be OK, thanks. I'd better get a move on before this blood dries in. If I wipe it with cold water, it might do the trick.'

His mother had run around like a wild thing, calling down curses on everyone who'd laid a finger on him. She'd also bewailed the fact that this was God punishing him for not going to Mass.

He was becoming disillusioned with the Church – and especially with Father Monachan, Father Riley's assistant. Father Monachan had been round at Bridie's mother's, asking her why she hadn't been pregnant for a few years. Poor Carragh, who was like the old woman who lived in a shoe and had so many children she didn't know what to do. Anyway, the silly young fool should have known that Carragh was past the age for childbearing. Not content with berating Carragh, though, when he'd got wind of Bridie's proposed marriage, he started lecturing her about a woman's duty to be fruitful and have children.

'If I had been there,' Frank had told Bridie, 'I would have knocked what little sense he had out of him with this . . .' and he brandished a fist.

Bridie had been terribly upset. So had both mothers. Carragh and Maureen had been horrified, and warned him that if he lifted his hand to a priest, his arm would become petrified.

'Frank, that's not like you,' Bridie wept. 'Please don't get violent like your brothers or my brothers. You've got to stay above the way they think. It's our only chance of a decent life.'

Now she said, 'I don't know how I'm going to stand it much longer, Frank.'

He knew that she meant her life – in what was euphemistically called her home. What upset Frank most was the whole depressing ambience of both Garngad and Blackhill, and the things that dragged so many good people down. Poverty, he believed, caused the drunkenness, the hopelessness, and in many cases the violence of one kind or another. Many youngsters believed that the only way to get out of the poverty trap was literally to fight their way out. The poorest areas of Glasgow had produced boxers like his Scottish Champion brother Michael, and professional boxers like World Champion Benny Lynch. But Benny Lynch, brave man that he was, couldn't conquer the drinking habit, and Frank feared that Michael one day would share the same fate. He'd always secretly thought it a mistake for his father to allow Michael to have sips of his beer when Michael was a child. Patrick had offered him the same 'wee taste', but he had grued at it and spat it out. Right from the start Michael had liked it. Often since adulthood he'd gone out drinking with his father. But Patrick was just a Saturday night drinker. Patrick always maintained, 'There's not two Saturdays in a week, son.' For Michael there was. Not that he got drunk like his father. Patrick would stagger and swing round lamp-posts and fall up the stairs. Admittedly he was never violent like Scobie, but he could make a terrible noise with his shouting and singing.

When he was drunk, he sang the old Irish songs:

> 'God save Ireland! said the heroes,
> God save Ireland! said they all.
> Whether on the scaffold high,
> Or the battlefield we die,
> O, what matter when for Ireland dear we fall!'

Michael could hold his drink. Maybe because he drank more often but not quite so much at a time. Recently though, since his marriage to Caroline, his drinking had increased.

As Maureen said, 'With a mother-in-law like Big Martha Stoddart, who could blame my poor, lovely boy?'

Recently Maureen had been really furious during one of her regular arguments with Martha. In defence of her 'poor, lovely boy', she'd got rather carried away and prophesied that he would show them yet. He would become a professional boxer, and one day be champion of the whole world. He'd make a fortune and be able to move away from Bright Street and buy a big house in Newton Mearns, or Pollokshields, or Bearsden.

Martha had folded her tree-trunk arms and replied, 'Aye, well, you can take the boy out of the bog but you can't take the bog out of the boy.'

On that occasion Maureen had come near to being violent. The overcrowded living conditions were affecting them all. Frank found Blackhill even worse, with its bleak grey tenements like giant gravestones, its lack of shops or any amenities except the karate club at the school. A mobile shop was the only commercial venture that braved Blackhill. There it stood, ready to serve but equally ready to rapidly remove itself.

The bedroom that Frank shared with Tony and his drums looked out on to the gasworks and the railway line. The challenge and adventure in his father and Tony's lives had increased from stealing char from the gasworks for the living room fire to regularly attacking stationary trains with butcher's cleavers. Sometimes the trains weren't stationary, but just slowing down for a few minutes. Then, like something out of an American Western, the two men would run alongside and jump on to the wagons. Sometimes they flung off crates of whisky or other valuable commodities. Sometimes, when they opened the crates, they contained nothing of any interest, like nails or washers, although they always managed to sell whatever it was to the stallholders at the Barras.

If their haul was whisky, or something of value that could buy whisky, there would be a party and much drinking (and wild drum beating) in the house. Patrick and Scobie and Tony and Michael always got stupid drunk. Even Maureen became tipsy and somewhat staggery. Bernard was never there because he worked nights. These parties depressed Frank so much he had to get out and walk the streets, not knowing what else to do or where to go. But walking the streets in Blackhill did nothing to lift his depression. He had once read a description by one of the first journalists who'd gone in to Auschwitz with the liberating army. A heavy silence of death and desolation had hung over the place. No bird sang. Sometimes he was reminded of this description as he walked the streets of Blackhill.

When the place had been built in 1936 it had looked quite neat and tidy. He'd seen pictures in the Mitchell Library. Perhaps, if the tenants who'd escaped from the decaying bug-infested slums to live in Blackhill had also escaped the brutal and harsh economic and social factors which caused their deprivation, things might have been different. As it was, their poverty, their unemployment, their social problems just moved with them.

There were still the good things as well as the bad. There was still the closeness of neighbours, who were ready to help each other and show solidarity in adversity. Frank supposed that the gang warfare that regularly flared up was a kind of tribal and territorial solidarity. At least they contained their violence within the bounds of their gangs. They seldom harmed anyone but themselves.

But this self-destruction depressed him. It seemed such a waste of human resources. And the waste spread like a pall of hopelessness and futility over the area. He didn't want to get sucked in. Once he'd found comfort and a kind of hope in the Catholic church. He'd sat in the church and absorbed the beauty of the architecture and the statues and the priests' robes. The sound of the litanies and prayers had also a kind of beauty that gave nourishment to his soul. The priest taking what could be described as an over-active part in the local community gave him occasional twinges of doubt and unease. Nevertheless, he could understand that when Father Riley's parishioners chose to send for him rather than the police when trouble arose, they had not much choice but to accept his method of dealing with it. As often as not the trouble was a husband spending all his wages on drink instead of handing over housekeeping money to his wife. Father Riley's method of dealing with this problem was to deliver to the miscreant several hefty punches to the nose, eyes and stomach, and a warning of worse punishment to come if the offence happeend again. Father Riley ran the boxing club in the church hall and did his best to keep young lads off the streets and out of trouble.

But Frank was worried by the absolute obedience, the answers to questions being unquestioningly accepted – and the rule by fear. Carragh, poor grey wisp of a woman, exhausted by childbirth and poverty, should not be afraid that she would incur God's wrath by not having any more children.

Visiting Bridie's mother's home was nearly as depressing as walking around the streets of Blackhill. He avoided it as much as he could. But the invitation to tea at the Gallacher home, which he and Bridie were at the moment reluctantly walking towards, had been a formal one. He wondered why. Bridie's arm was linked through his and he pressed it tight against his side to comfort and reassure her as they entered into the dark tunnel of Carragh's close.

Chapter Twenty-One

'I've never mentioned it to Bridie before, Frank.' Carragh creased her grey button face in an effort to produce a pleasing smile. 'I thought it best to speak to you, you see. You being more sensible like. Have another wee cookie, son.' She bent forward over her deformed legs in pathetic supplication.

'No thanks, Mrs Gallacher. Mentioned what?'

'Well, you see, it's like this.' Her voice acquired a 'Once upon a time' confidentiality. 'You know how young Francie, being no right in the head, has been kept in that place? And Tam and Billy and Eamon have gone to England with their group. Geordie and Haggis have got jobs with the Fair folk; they've always hung about the Fair when it came to Glasgow Green – now they're as happy as larks travelling around with it.'

'Yes,' Frank murmured uncertainly.

'What's that got to do with Frank and me?' Bridie wanted to know.

Carragh struggled to keep the smile glued to her face. 'Now Charlie has joined the Merchant Navy.'

'Oh, right. Very good.' Frank's wary uncertainty had developed into downright suspicion.

'I know all that,' Bridie said. 'What's that got to do with Frank and me?'

'Well, you see, I was just thinking. This big place'll be empty with just Scobie and me. And then I thought, there's Bridie and Frank, desperate to get married and needing a place, and what better than them having our big front room?'

'What?' Bridie's voice wobbled between tragedy and astonishment. 'What do you mean empty? There's Doris for a start.'

'Well.' Carragh lowered her voice and looked furtively around as if to make sure no one else was hanging about the kitchen, eager to listen. 'Between you and me and the gatepost, Doris is expecting a happy event.'

'Oh, God,' Bridie groaned. 'That means one extra, not less.'

'No, no, hen. I'm sure Frank's brother's going to do the decent thing and put together some key money for a place. Or a backhander, or whatever he needs to get a house – I'm sure Bernard'll wangle it.'

Frank groaned inwardly. The mass exodus of Gallachers did not surprise him. They had never supported or protected their mother. Now Carragh was pinning her hopes on him. She was afraid of being on her own with an increasingly violent Scobie.

'No way,' said Bridie. 'Big front room?' she added bitterly. 'Call that a big front room?'

'Now, hen, don't be hasty. Talk it over with Frank. It's time you two were married. Don't you think, eh? Once you were here you could still be looking around for a place of your own. But you'd be together. Do you know what I mean, hen?'

'No way,' Bridie repeated, fixing Frank with a tragic gaze.

Frank felt heart sorry for both Bridie and her mother.

'What do you think, son?' Carragh fixed him with a gaze not only tragic, but desperate. 'I'd make you awful welcome. You're like a son to me. Just like my own flesh and blood. It would just be for a wee while, Frank. Just till you got a place of your own, eh?'

Frank said, 'Bridie and I would have to discuss it, Mrs Gallacher.'

'Of course, son. Of course. I'll just run down the stairs and take in my washing. It should be dry by now. That'll give you a chance.' She scuttled across the bare floorboards and picked up a clothes basket from the top of the coal bunker. 'I'd see you lacked for nothing, son. You'd have every comfort here. Every comfort.'

Bridie rolled her eyes after she'd gone. 'Every comfort? Could you beat it? Francie's not the only one that's soft in the head.'

'She's afraid, Bridie.'

'What do you think I am? I'm afraid I'm never going to get away from here.'

'We're bound to get a place soon. Our name should be well up the Corporation list by now.'

Bridie's pale face had become positively sickly. 'Frank, you're not seriously considering living here. You don't know what it's like.'

'It can't be much worse than where I am. I'd rather share a room here in Garngad with you than share a room in Blackhill with Tony any day.'

'I know it's not easy for you either.'

'That's putting it mildly. Tony's one big mindless noise. And I don't just mean when he's battering away at his infernal drums. When he talks, when he coughs, when he sneezes – he lets it all rip-roar out as if noise is something to be proud of. Even when he's asleep that toothy grin of his is hovering over his face as if he's enjoying the racket his snoring makes.

'What I'm afraid of is . . .' Bridie's eyes filled with tears and she removed her glasses to mop at them, '. . . that we just sink into this place, that somehow we'll be trapped, that we'll never get out.'

Frank gathered her into his arms. 'No, no. That won't happen. I promise. Quite the contrary. The way I'm looking at it is I'll have more peace here to write, now that your brothers are away. My writing is our passport out of here, Bridie. I've had quite a few poems published now as you know, but there's no big money in poetry. It's got to be plays, and I need a bit of space and quiet to work on a play. I know I can do it, but not while I'm sharing a room with Tony.' He sighed. 'I love that guy but I hate him as well. Sometimes I feel I could kill him just to shut him up.'

'Oh, Frank, I know how you feel, but do you really think it would be that much better here? There's my father, don't forget, and his drinking.'

'My father drinks as well. All right, he doesn't get violent like Scobie. But he's just as much a pest in his own way. He and Tony are a right pair when they're drunk. Bawling and singing and crashing about. The only peace I've ever managed to get at home, whether in Garngad or Blackhill, was when either of them or both of them were in Barlinnie.'

'If Bernard gets married to Doris and moves out . . .'

'I wouldn't depend on anything Bernard might do. He's a law unto himself. Anyway, if it's his bedroom you're thinking about, what do you bet that my mother and father move into it. It is hell of an inconvenience them sleeping on the bed-settee in the living room.' He cuddled her and stroked her hair and tucked it behind her ear. 'What do you say, pet? Just until I get a play published and make some money.'

'I think I'd rather be a squatter than start my married life here.'

'Now you know you couldn't bear the indignity of squatting in some old army camp with no water or electricity. Or illegally breaking into some unoccupied private house.' Since the war and the shortage of housing, squatting had become a serious problem and was constantly hitting the newspaper headlines.

Bridie sighed and replaced her spectacles. 'I suppose not. That's really the dregs, isn't it? At least here we'd keep our dignity and respectability.' Even as she uttered the words, she suddenly felt so hopeless, so painfully depressed, she didn't even believe Frank would ever write a play, far less sell it. They seemed to be sinking into the morass in which so many couples and their dreams had disappeared before.

'If I just got a run at a play. If I could just get a bit of peace and privacy.' Frank's voice was wistful.

Bridie gazed at his thin sensitive face and loved him for his innocence. 'You really think you could get that here?'

'Well, if we had the room to ourselves, I'd at least have a chance. I've no chance at all in Blackhill.'

Tears welled up in Bridie's eyes again but she struggled to ignore them and make her voice seem bright. 'Well, if it's all right with you, Frank, it's all right with me.'

'Oh, great.' His eyes glowed with optimism, and with a quick, excited movement he flicked back the lock of hair that kept sliding down over his forehead. 'It won't be for long, pet. I promise.'

Bridie noticed his dandruff was getting worse. He neglected himself terribly so perhaps it was just as well they were going to be together sooner than they'd planned. She would see that he washed his hair with an antiseptic shampoo. She'd brush it for him and get it into shining good condition. She would see that he ate properly too. But all the time, the depression and the hopelessness wafted about inside her like a dangerous fog in which she could so easily lose her way.

'It can't be a big wedding,' she told Frank. 'There's no money. It all goes on drink now. And I'm not using my savings. That's for when we get our own house.'

After a moment or two's thought, Frank said, 'I don't mind a registry office, if it's all right with you.'

'Oh no, we have to be blessed in the church, Frank.' Frank didn't have her conscientiousness for attending Mass, and it worried her. It was another thing about him she'd have to work on and change. She could understand his compassion for her mother and her constant pregnancies and miscarriages – Frank was a compassionate kind of person – however, her mother needn't have suffered like that. The church taught abstinence and the safe times for sex. It was Carragh's own fault, or perhaps to be fair, it was more Scobie's fault, that no attention had been paid to the church's teaching on the subject.

'All right, pet. A quiet ceremony in the church.'

'It would have to be just you and me and a couple of witnesses – maybe Bernard from your side and Doris from mine. If we include everybody in our families the church would be packed. Then they'd have to have food and drink afterwards. That could turn out to be a right rammy.'

He smiled. 'Remember your twenty-first?'

'The only good thing about my twenty-first birthday party was that we got together.'

'All right. I'll go ahead with the arrangements and I'll ask Bernard if he'll be my best man.'

Something then occurred to Bridie. 'Perhaps Doris and Bernard will make it a double affair. That would be nice, unusual – really special. Two brothers and two sisters getting married at the same time.' She felt quite cheered by the thought. She had always been drawn to unusual things, like serious music, and paintings, and poetry. That was one of the reasons she'd fallen for Frank.

'Well . . .' Frank's uncertainty returned.

'It'll be all right with Doris,' Bridie assured him.

It wasn't Doris, however, that Frank was seeing in his mind's eye.

Chapter Twenty-Two

Doris hadn't been too upset when Bernard told her he didn't love her. After all, she'd known that all along. Only now she didn't altogether believe it. He was willing to marry her, wasn't he? That was the important thing. The wonderful, exciting, absolutely marvellous thing. It must mean something. She was so happy she persuaded herself that he must have feelings for her. She told herself that once they were married, everything would be all right. No, not just all right – *perfect!*

She was so proud of him. Her head floated light as a balloon and her chest puffed out as she walked along the street arm in arm with him. He was such a big, handsome man, fit and strong in body and character.

She never tired of boasting to her fellow shop assistants in Daly's. 'My Bernard has a very strong character. Very self-controlled. You can tell that, can't you, by that dark unwavering stare of his. He's the strong, silent type.'

Actually, she was having a bit of trouble with that recently – him being silent. He'd never been much of a talker at the best of times. He always seemed quite content to let her chatter on. Now he seldom initiated a conversation, or added to it. The only time she'd seen him animated and talkative recently was when he'd gone on about Uri Gargarin and how he'd gone up in space.

'The greatest thing to happen in our lifetime,' he'd said and she'd made a really big effort to share his enthusiasm.

She couldn't help wishing he'd shown the same enthusiasm for the idea Bridie came up with about a double wedding. Although he did make one contribution to the arrangements. Or rather two: he said he wanted Robert Anderson and his wife to be there; he also insisted that he should pay for a meal for the lot of them after the ceremony.

Everyone in the O'Maley family and the Gallacher family was insulted, offended and upset at the mere idea of such a small affair. They had expected, indeed demanded, that there should be a proper white wedding in the church with not only all the relations on both sides, but all their friends as well. Everybody could have, and should have, gathered at the Co-op hall for the traditional purvey of steak pie, potatoes and peas, followed by sherry trifle. This enjoyable meal would have – should have – been followed first of all by merry speeches and much drinking of whisky, then a noisy knees-up, reels and dashing white sergeants and much screeching and heughing. And more drinking of whisky. Lemonade, Tizer and Irn Bru were always supplied for the youngsters, who increased the general hilarity and confusion by racing around playing tig between the dancers.

Bridie and Doris, even Frank, wavered in the face of family outrage ('Aunt Nellie's never going to speak to you for ages'), pleading ('the wee ones will be that disappointed'), and persuasion ('it'll please poor wee Carragh so much').

But Bernard would have none of it. It was to be a quiet wedding with only Robert and Andrina Anderson – or nothing. That decided Doris, and in turn strengthened the resolution of Bridie and Frank.

The wedding day dawned to disappointment and huff in both houses. Carragh had volunteered to give them a party and make one her cloutie dumplings. And never mind the Co-op.

'It would be no bother, girls,' she assured Bridie and Doris. 'You know how I'm used to cooking for crowds. Remember thon great party I gave you for your twenty-first, Bridie, eh?'

That definitely settled the issue. Doris spent much time back-combing and layering her creamy froth of hair. Great care too was taken on her eye make-up which was thick and black. She was very proud of her long lashes, which, thickened with false ones and several layers of mascara, looked, she believed, really glamorous. She perched a black velvet bow studded with pearls on the back of her monstrous bouffant and blessed the high hairstyle because it helped add to her rather small stature.

This was vitally important when walking with or next to Bernard. She was terribly pleased with her dress too. She'd got it at a genuinely reduced rate from Daly's. It had a terribly smart 'hobble' or 'bubble' or 'puff-ball' line. It had narrow little shoulder straps and a black velvet bodice, and a lime-green taffetta 'puff' that ballooned out from waist to mid-thigh, before changing to a tight velvet band from there to knees.

Round her neck she fastened a pearl choker to match her pearl earrings. (Pearls were in terribly good taste. Jane Dempster from Bearsden always wore pearls with her black dress at Daly's.) Long black gloves and high heeled shoes finished the picture. It had never been easy to walk in such high heels, and the tight velvet band round her knees didn't help, but she managed quite nicely.

Bridie looked plain as usual with her earnest, bespectacled face devoid of all make-up, and straight brown hair caught back on one side with a clasp. With that and her floral print dress she looked like a schoolgirl.

It had to be admitted that Andrina looked rather nice, if you liked tall girls with long auburn hair and green eyes. She was a bit flashy though, in her wide-brimmed straw hat with its cinnamon trimmings, and beige trapeze-line dress with its collar standing away from her neck and the long bow hanging down from it. That dress looked like an Yves St Laurent. But it had to be a cheap copy. After all, how could anyone afford Yves St Laurent on a schoolmaster's wage? Maybe that was why Andrina was wearing hardly any make-up. Make-up was terribly expensive these days.

Frank had forgotten to get his hair cut, but he had managed to have his awful old suit decently cleaned and pressed. He was at least wearing a new white shirt. His black tie, however, didn't go with the brown of his suit and made him look as if he was attending a funeral.

Robert was smart in a grey suit, a paler grey shirt and nicely patterned tie.

But Bernard, oh how wonderful Bernard looked in dark blue, with a waistcoat and a lighter blue shirt over the new style slender-line trousers. His tie was pure silk, Doris was sure. She couldn't believe her luck. Fancy her catching such a big, gorgeous hunk. Unlike Frank, Bernard was interested in clothes and how he looked. And Bernard wasn't dreamy like Frank. No two brothers could be more unlike. Yet . . . sometimes Bernard could give the strange impression that he was somewhere else, thinking about – she knew not what. Of course, his work needed a lot of concentration. It was terribly dangerous. She felt a sudden qualm. What if anything should happen to Bernard? She'd die. *She'd just die.* She wondered if she could persuade him to change his job. Something more nine-to-five, so that he could be home with her at night. Now that he employed quite a few bouncers he could surely let them do most of the rough work. She had to admit to herself however that the toughness of Bernard's job was part of his attraction. She'd once seen him in action and it had both frightened and thrilled her. It had been at Green's Playhouse Dancehall. Some guys had come in and started pestering girls and making a big noise and jostling and threatening and frightening people. All except two had taken to their heels when they saw Bernard striding towards them. The remaining two pulled out knives. The way Bernard disarmed them was so quick she had difficulty bringing the scene to her mind's eye. But what she did remember clearly was the way he pounced on them after he'd disarmed them. He caught them by the neck – one in each of his big hands – then literally ran them out of the door.

After the wedding ceremony they went to a terribly posh hotel that had a restaurant with a little dance-floor in the middle. They sat at a table just on the edge of the dance floor. Doris chatted non stop to Andrina about fashion (Andrina had once worked in Copland & Lye's). The men argued about boxing and football, and the possibility of more men going up in space. Bridie just sat looking uncomfortable. She obviously wasn't used to such a terribly posh place.

'See her over there,' Doris widened her eyes in the direction she wanted Andrina to look. 'That's a Dior if ever I saw one. Did you stock any in Copland's?'

'A few.'

'We had several designer labels in Daly's – Dior, Hartnell, Cardin, the lot. Of course, Daly's is *the* top class shop. I know Copland's is terribly first class too. No offence.'

Andrina smiled. 'None taken.'

Suddenly Bernard said, 'May I have this dance, Andrina?'

Andrina felt flustered. She looked over at Robert but he only smiled and said, 'Go ahead', then turning to Doris, said, 'May I have the pleasure?'

The four of them got up and left Frank and Bridie gazing fondly at each other.

The band was playing 'Always' as Bernard took Andrina in his arms, and as they moved together he whispered, 'Oh, how I wish this was our wedding day. Oh, how I wish it was you, how I wish it was you . . .'

'Stop it! Please don't talk like that.' Andrina began trembling so visibly that Bernard had to tighten his hold to steady her. As they danced, the hard feel of his body against hers thrilled and frightened her. He must be crazy to behave like this on his own wedding day.

After a few minutes she spoke her thoughts out loud. 'On your wedding day of all days, how could you?'

'You said it was time I had a wife and family of my own.'

'All right, but now you have a wife . . .'

'A pregnant wife.'

'All the more reason why you shouldn't speak to me like that.'

'Nothing's going to change the way I feel about you.'

'But what about Doris?'

'She's got what she wanted – a name for her child.'

'I think she'll want more than that.'

'Tough.'

Again Andrina experienced tremors of fear. 'You must promise to put me out of your mind, Bernard.'

'I can't do that.'

'But I'm happily married to Robert. You must.'

'I love your hair. It glows like rubies.'

'Bernard . . .'

'Your eyes sparkle like aquamarines.'

'Bernard, please.'

'Your skin is soft like velvet. My darling velvet. I love every soft smooth inch of you.'

'You're crazy.'

'I'd like to kiss every inch of you from the top of your lovely head to the tip of your toes.'

'You're mad.' She tightly shut her eyes to protect herself from his stare. But there was no way she could ignore the chemistry interacting, the heat generating between their two bodies.

Chapter Twenty-Three

Sophie mentally rubbed her hands together in glee. It had taken her some considerable time to find a place in Bearsden that suited both herself and Andrew and was within the price that he had stipulated.

'Remember,' McPherson kept saying, 'I've still only a brickie's wages plus my expenses from the Council.'

Sophie didn't listen, knowing subconsciously that this could not be true, as indeed it was not. McPherson had been on Felderman's books as a 'consultant' for months now, and was paid considerably more than a brickie. Then, of course, the expenses he claimed from the Council were always inflated. Nobody, as far as he knew, put in a claim for the exact sum for which they had been out of pocket in lost wages, or in money spent on fares or food or anything else. Nobody, that is, except his father, the late Councillor David McPherson, who although outwardly admired for his honesty, had grievously inhibited and frustrated many of his fellow councillors. McPherson had loved and respected his father but he could easily imagine a sigh of relief rising up from the City Chambers after the old man had gone.

The end terrace house in Drymen Road, Bearsden, had lain empty for some time and they had got a marvellous bargain of it. An old man had lived alone in it for years and had never bothered to paint or paper it. 'Or clean it either,' Sophie said. She was just dying to get her hands on it. She couldn't wait to plunge into an orgy of housework. Not to mention the painting and decorating. Bliss, absolute bliss! Her mind raced hysterically ahead, she saw herself like a whirlwind in her imagination. In working, cleaning to the utmost of her ability, she too somehow felt she was cleansing herself of the past and every dark and dirty corner of herself.

Structurally, the house was in very good condition. Drymen Road was the busy main road just next to the line of shops – separated only by a little side street called Kirk Road. There was a church down at the end of the side street and another church across the road. This part of Bearsden was called the village. It was the heart of the place, the oldest and busiest part and, as far as Sophie was concerned, it just couldn't be bettered. She would never have a dull or idle moment here. Even sitting and looking out of the front-room window would be bliss – or even the side window. The sitting room and dining room had side windows looking out on to Kirk Road. From there she could get a side view of the shops and people going down Kirk Road to the field to exercise their dogs. Good, smiling, well-dressed, solid people.

There were no gasworks, no brickworks, no factories, no sawmills here to pollute the air or discolour the beautiful silvery walls of the buildings. The lovely trees that rustled in the streets were fresh, pure green, as if God himself had washed each leaf until it glistened. No litter, no old newspapers, no smelly chip papers would dare flap about these pavements. The streets of Bearsden were kept pristine clean.

Sophie adored the house. She had enough imagination to see how the dark brown inside walls and floors could be transformed by light paint and attractive wallpaper and carpets. In a daze of admiration she walked through the high-ceilinged hall into the spacious sitting room, then into the dining room, then further along into the kitchen and the scullery beyond and the back door that led into her very own garden. Upstairs was a bathroom on a half landing and a bedroom. Then upstairs again there were three other bedrooms. A veritable palace of a place.

To go back to Drumchapel was like descending into hell. Even the inhabitants looked drab and seedy and neglected. There were people in the streets, yet the people had no substance. The streets seemed empty – a vast concrete desert of a place with neither heart nor soul. She hated it. She couldn't wait to be free of it. Over and over again she thanked God for her release. She had been sinking into the hopelessness of the place herself but God in his infinite mercy had saved her before depression had irrevocably weighed her down.

On her knees she thanked Him.

Several times a day she phoned Andrina to eulogise about the house, the shops, the churches, the people. She organised the removal with a hymn in her heart. Getting the house in Bearsden was her salvation. She didn't care that McPherson did very little to help. She enjoyed being given a free hand. He wouldn't have done anything to her complete satisfaction. He was too easygoing. Sometimes he nearly drove her mad with his attitude.

'What do you need to do that for?' he'd say. 'It's perfectly clean as it is. Sit down and relax.'

But to sit down and relax and do nothing was impossible. The sight of a picture not quite straight could trap her into deep anxiety. Even if she didn't see anything she would have a nameless fear of something being wrong, of something being unclean.

She worried about Andrina's house, and meticulously questioned her each time she phoned about what housework she'd done and how thoroughly she'd done it. She worried about Andrina's neighbour, the filthy Slater woman, coming into the house and contaminating the chairs with her fat thighs. Once Sophie had been visiting Andrina and on reaching Andrina's landing, she'd noticed the Slater woman's door open. The windowless lobby was a dark tunnel, but she could make out a chair with clothes flung carelessly over it. Underclothes too, shameless black satin. Some magazines lay on the floor and the whole place had an immoral, dirty look.

The woman had come hurrying breathlessly up the stairs clutching an oversized basket. 'Oh, hello, hen,' she called out. 'I just ran down to the back to hang out some washing. I don't get that much time with me being out working. Is Andrina not in?'

Sophie had stabbed at the bell. She was glad to turn away from the woman. The dyed hair, the painted face, the flashy earrings, the obscene cleavage. The smell of cheap perfume made her feel sick.

The moment Andrina opened the door she'd pushed inside and shut it behind her. 'That woman's out there.'

'Josie? She's harmless, Mummy.' Then Andrina had laughed. 'She's not going to bite you.'

She'd hated Andrina then. Hated her for her stupidity, her lack of understanding, and her laughter. 'I can still smell the dirt from her house. That woman is a bad influence on you in more ways than one. I got a glimpse of her hall just now. She'd left her door wide open. I shudder to think what her rooms are like if that's the way she keeps her hall. An untidy house is a sign of an untidy mind. A dirty house is a sign of a dirty mind.'

Andrina was wearing a modest black dress with a neat white collar high at her neck. No make-up was visible on her face, which was startlingly pale and creamy against her deep flame of hair.

'You ought to tie that hair of yours back,' Sophie told her. 'It looks positively indecent hanging loose about your shoulders like that. Pin it back like mine.'

'It's difficult to keep it back, Mummy, with it being so thick and wavy and curly. It's easier with your hair. Yours is straight and smooth as glass.'

'Get it cut short then.'

'Remember I did that once and it curled up more than ever?'

'Well, give it a good hard brush and pin it back as tight as you can.'

'Yes, Mummy.'

Sophie was suspicious of Andrina and her 'Yes, Mummy's', and her evasive eyes when she uttered the words. There was an aura of wicked sensuality about the girl. She couldn't hide it by averting her gaze or by fixing Sophie with one of those wide-eyed innocent looks. The way she was dressed and her unmade-up face didn't fool her either. Sophie thought, 'This is for my benefit. What does she wear when I'm not here? That's what I'd like to know.'

The intensity of her worry about Andrina however was

swamped by the excitement and the amount of time and attention she needed to devote to the house in Bearsden.

Oh, happy removal day. She'd arranged that McPherson would drive her over so that they would be in Drumchapel to check that all their belongings were safely packed on to the removal van. Then they would be at the house in Bearsden to see that everything was properly unpacked and the furniture placed exactly where she wanted it.

McPherson had bought his first car, a modest little Mini. It didn't compare with the Corporation limousine in which he was in the habit of travelling when attending to council business. Nevertheless, Minis were very popular and fashionable. She was perfectly happy with their smart little car. Perhaps one day she would learn to drive. Although McPherson jokingly said that a public safety warning would have to be given each time she went on the road.

'You don't have the nature to be a good driver, Sophie,' he explained. 'You're too quick and impatient. You function on too short a fuse.'

She had become what McPherson called 'a back seat driver' instead. Although in fact she sat in the front beside him, she'd keep a running commentary while he sat in heavy silence, leather gloved hands loose on the wheel, staring determinedly ahead.

'Watch that child. He might dash out . . . Remember it's left turn here. Talk about me being quick. You're racing along, Andrew. Watch these lights, they're going to change. What's he doing in front?'

Sometimes she'd thump at the horn. This at least elicited a response from McPherson.

'*Don't do that, Sophie!* If you touch the horn again I'm stopping the car and putting you out. You can wait for a bus.'

Of course, he wouldn't dare. Oh, happy, happy removal day.

She took a last look around the Drumchapel house. She had scrubbed every inch of it, of course. Nobody would be able to accuse her of leaving a dirty house. But it looked so small, so seedy, so pathetic. The word formed like a sneer in her mind.

Pathetic. Outside, some shabby looking youths were hanging about at the street corner. Waiting to see what trouble they could get up to, no doubt. It wouldn't matter what kind of houses, what size of houses, they built here, the people who lived in them would bring the place down to their level, making a slum of it.

Goodbye, Drumchapel. Good riddance to you all.

As the van and the car moved away, her heart and head were reverberating joyously with the song, 'Onward Christian soldiers, going as to war, with the cross of Jesus, going on before . . .'

Once in the house in Bearsden, she bustled about giving orders and making cups of tea for the men. McPherson said, 'Do you need me to stay any longer, Sophie? I've a couple of people to see at the Chambers.'

'No, no, on you go.' She hardly noticed him.

'Right, I'll see you later.'

'No, no.' She rushed after one of the removal men. 'Not in there. Upstairs. That's to go upstairs.'

'But you said . . .'

'I've changed my mind. Put it in the big bedroom, the one at the front. I'll show you *exactly* where it's to go.'

She hurried upstairs in front of the man. McPherson escaped. He hadn't to see anyone in particular but he thought it best to get out of the way and leave Sophie to it. She was in her element. As happy as a dog with two tails. At first he thought he'd go to the club. Then he remembered he hadn't had a decent meal all day. Instead of his usual cooked breakfast, Sophie had put a few slices of toast and a pot of marmalade on the table and he'd had to make do with that. A cup of tea and a sandwich had passed for lunch. He decided to make for the Corn Exchange. He could relax there, have a good meal, enjoy a brandy and a cigar.

He had barely settled at his favourite table, hadn't even given his order, when a voice said, 'Do you mind if I join you, Bailie McPherson?'

It was Bernard O'Maley.

'Bernard! Sit down. I haven't seen you in here before. How are you getting on? You certainly look prosperous enough.'

'I come here now and again. I've been doing fine – building up a good-going business and a reputation along with it.'

'Splendid. Still in the same line, are you?'

The waiter came to take their order. After he'd gone, Bernard said, 'I've got some good men working for me and I'm making contacts for more work.'

'Oh yes, I believe Robert mentioned you had quite a few pubs and clubs on your books now.'

'I'm ambitious, Bailie McPherson. I intend my business to keep expanding. I was thinking of going into other areas. Crowd control at outdoor or indoor events for sport or entertainment. Personal security for visiting dignitaries, pop groups, you name it.'

They finished their prawn cocktail, then Bernard continued, 'The Corporation organises quite a few events or gives licences for events as well as premises.'

'Yes.' McPherson was beginning to get the drift. 'That's true. There's always something going on in Glasgow, and indeed, in the City Chambers.'

'Here's my card,' Bernard said.

McPherson studied it. 'The Trongate?'

'Yes, I've rented a small office there. It suits me for the moment. If you put any work my way I would, of course, show my appreciation with a commission for your trouble – a generous percentage of the fee.'

McPherson tapped the card against the tips of his fingers. He was a good man, Bernard. He'd always liked him.

They talked in more detail until the Entrecôte Steak Belgrade arrived. It looked delicious. 'Let's have a bottle of their best wine,' Bernard said. 'This is on me,' he added with a careless wave of the hand to indicate whatever was on the table. They ordered a Châteauneuf-du-pape. Bailie McPherson leaned back in his seat and hooked his thumbs in his waistcoat. He felt pleased with himself, and the world, and Bernard O'Maley.

A decent big man, Bernard. One of the best.

Chapter Twenty-Four

Frank could hardly believe his eyes. Although why he should be so surprised he didn't know. There was surely a naïvety about him. Like a child, he always expected the best in people; he seldom foresaw the worst scenario. As a result he kept being surprised, disappointed, let down – although he valued, indeed treasured in retrospect, the process of learning about life and people. People were endlessly interesting to him.

His brother Michael was sitting on the pavement outside his boxing club in Garngad Road, cropped bullet of a head thrown back, drinking a bottle of beer. He knew Michael liked a drink but surely never during training.

'Michael, I thought you were training.'

'So?'

'You won't get fit with drinking in the middle of it.'

'If I'm lucky I'll get blotto.' Michael's bruised and broken-nosed face was a picture of misery.

'What's wrong? I thought you were doing so well. You're making a steady wage and a good bit extra with your boxing. And you've your nice wee house to yourself and your lovely wife.'

'The trouble is, Frank, I've got a not so lovely mother-in-law.'

'Och, ignore her.'

'Easy enough for you to say that. She's not your mother-in-law. I'm living in the next street to the Stoddarts. Caroline runs to Big Martha with the slightest complaint about me or a problem in our marriage, and round Big Martha comes to sort me out. She even barged into the pub the other night and laid one on me. See this black eye? That was her. Then she punched and pummelled me all the way out on to the street. What could I do, Frank? If it had been a man, I would have felled him with one blow. But I can't hit a woman. Especially a woman old enough to be my mother. But, by Christ, she can throw a hammer of a punch.'

Frank didn't know what to say. It seemed an insoluble problem. There was no use suggesting Michael tried to stop Caroline from running to her mother every time she had some complaint or grudge. Everyone knew that Caroline, as an only child, had been spoiled and babied all her life. In Frank's opinion, however, any baby would have more brains. Talk about a dumb blonde! He had always thought that Bridie's sister, Doris, came into that category (although according to Bridie, Doris's hair was dyed and Caroline's was not), but Caroline was ridiculous. It always fascinated him to observe people – what made them tick, and he mulled endlessly over both his brothers' choice of wives. There was Bernard, so tough no one would ever dare say 'boo' to him, so hard-eyed and to all appearances completely insensitive that one would have thought he wouldn't have cared less about any woman becoming pregnant by him. Frank wouldn't have been surprised if Bernard had told Doris to go to hell. Yet he'd married her. Hard-faced intelligent Bernard – there could be no denying that Bernard had brains – had chosen a silly, empty-headed wee snob like Doris Gallacher for his life's partner. Admittedly, once you got to know Doris and looked past her surface silliness, she was harmless enough. Frank wasn't so sure about Bernard.

Then there was Michael. Another tough guy in his own way – and he had married a silly, empty-headed wee girl as well.

There was nothing so strange as folk. They fascinated Frank so much he was finding more and more that only through drama could he fully explore the relationships and conflicts they sparked off. Although poetry was still his first step in exploration and communication. But it had become only a first step.

He had started on a play as soon as he'd moved into Bridie's house – or rather, Scobie and Carragh's house. Everything seemed to be working out quite well at first. He and Bridie had everything in common. It was wonderful to be so close to her, lying with his arm around her in the recessed bed in the Gallachers' front room. After they made love, they'd lie like that, discussing the latest book they'd read or play they'd seen. More and more they were spending their precious savings on theatre tickets, but as Frank said, 'It's really an investment, Bridie. An investment in my career and our future. I've got to study drama – and as you know, I read as much as I can about it – but there's nothing to beat seeing plays brought to life on the stage.'

Bridie agreed. The only thing they had disagreed about was his decision to come and live with her in Turner Street. Of course, as it turned out, she had been right. It had been fine at first. In fact, it had been sheer heaven compared with sharing a room with Tony. He much preferred Garngad to Blackhill too. This might seem strange to some people because Garngad was made up of old cobbled streets, ancient black tenements, and constant crowds of people milling about, especially on the busy Garngad Road. Women having a 'hing' leaning, arms folded on the sills of open windows, and watching the teeming life underneath them: the children playing; the men going in and out of the pub; the street buskers; women shouting across to each other and enjoying a gossip; children racketing around on the cobbles that lead off Garngad Road; the streets that Frank and Bridie were so familiar with – Turner Street, Villiers Street, Bright Street, Cobden Street.

In comparison, Blackhill had relatively new houses. Many of them had patches of earth at the front that had once been tidy gardens. They boasted bathrooms and sculleries and gas cookers and tiled fireplaces. When his mother and father had got their house in Blackhill, their old friends and neighbours had come to visit and be proudly shown round the house. Many of them came especially to enjoy a bath as well.

Yet to Frank – despite all the disadvantages of outside lavatories and unhygienic kitchens, coal bunkers spreading coal dust over everything including kitchen beds, and pots of food simmering on old black ranges – he preferred Garngad.

Of course, as Bridie said, the reason everything went well at first was due to the fact that Scobie had disappeared for one of his sojourns in Barlinnie. He had been caught breaking into a pub and stealing bottles of whisky. He had actually been caught in the pub drinking the whisky. Moreover, he had refused to leave. Indeed, he had become violent and hit the beat constable over the head with one of the bottles. The bottle broke, the constable continued his struggle with Scobie, and he ended up having his face lacerated with the jagged glass of the bottle.

Scobie, when sober, was perfectly good-humoured with the police, and they with him. Scobie always greeted the local bobbies by their first names and wished them a friendly good morning. When drunk, he cared about nobody and he had no friends. When drunk, he was a different person altogether. The scarring of the local bobby meant Scobie had lost the benefit of any good humour any members of the Glasgow police force ever had towards him.

The house in Turner Street without Scobie was quite bearable. There were no physical comforts, not even a rug or a piece of linoleum to cover the floor, but at least there was peace and quiet. A rhythm or pattern became established. After work, Frank and Bridie and Carragh would have their tea. Then he would go through to the room and write for at least a couple of hours. Bridie stayed in the kitchen with Carragh. She didn't mind. The quicker he got on with his writing and made some money the better, as far as she was concerned. He wouldn't get much chance once Scobie came out again, she warned.

On Sundays, the three of them went to Mass. Usually they met Maureen and Patrick and Doris there. Sometimes they went over to Blackhill to have what Doris called 'lunch' with the O'Maleys. Sometimes Michael appeared in the chapel. At first, Caroline had come with him. Her father and mother had soon put a stop to that. Apparently there was a running battle with the priest over this. According to Michael, Father Riley and Father Monachan had been giving him hell on one side, and Big Martha Stoddart and Orangeman Jimmy Stoddart had been giving him hell on the other.

Then one day, on his way home from work, Frank met Michael again and found him in a worse state than ever. He had obviously been at the pub and was still clutching a bottle of beer.

'Don't you start on me, Frank,' Michael warned. 'I've had it up to here with the lot of them.'

'I don't know what to say, Michael.' Frank felt upset on behalf of his brother. 'I wish I could help in some way. Do you think if I had a word with Martha . . . ?'

'What?' Michael gave a mirthless laugh. 'Thanks, pal, but no thanks. I've enough on my plate without worrying about you being flattened.'

Frank sighed. 'Well, try and keep off the drink, Michael. You don't want to become like Scobie.'

'That reminds me,' Michael said. 'Scobie's out.'

'He can't be. He has months to go yet.'

'He'll have had his sentence reduced for good behaviour. How's that for a laugh?'

'I hope to goodness he behaves himself in the house.'

'Forever an optimist, that's you, Frank. He was roaring drunk the last I saw of him. Challenging all comers to a fight, silly wee nyaff.'

'Oh God,' Frank groaned. 'I'd better run in case he's in the house.'

'He was making in that direction.'

'Oh God. Be seeing you, Michael.'

'The best of luck, pal.' Michael raised his bottle of beer.

By the time Frank reached Turner Street and climbed the stairs of the Gallacher close, he was gasping for breath. He'd never had much time for exercise and he was definitely out of condition. In his haste the key stuck in the door and it took him a long minute to get it to turn properly. He could hear Carragh screaming and he thanked God that Bridie had said she would be calling in at the library on her way home from work.

'Scobie!' he shouted when he burst into the kitchen. 'What do you think you're doing, man?'

'None of your fuckin' business,' Scobie sneered round at him.

Frank had never before realised how revolting Scobie could look. It wasn't the bald head with its collar of grey hair. It wasn't the nose like a misshapen potato or the pocked skin. It was the bleary, sneery, ugly expression.

'Leave her alone.'

'Piss off.'

'Get your hands off Carragh right now or I'll call the police and get you put away for another stretch.'

'This is what the busies call "a domestic",' Scobie sneered. 'They don't care a fuck about domestics.'

'Then, if need be, I'll deal with you myself.'

Scobie let out a roar of laughter. 'You? You big leek. You couldn't deal a pack of cards.' And with that he gave Carragh such a blow in the face it sent her reeling back to crash against a chair and clatter with it on to the floor.

Frank was horrified and sick to his soul. He hated any kind of violence at any time, but witnessing brutal violence against a frail elderly woman was too much to bear. He rushed at Scobie, but before he could even aim a punch, Scobie had thumped him below the belt and he'd doubled up, breathless with pain.

The pain made him lose his temper and he quickly made another lunge at the smaller man, only to be felled again. Once on the floor Scobie put the boot in to Frank's head and body, making Carragh scream again.

As Frank lay huddled on the floor in a haze of pain, he realised that Scobie was capable of kicking him to death in his drunken rage. Frank's fingers fumbled round the heavy poker, and with a desperate lunge he swung it in a scything arc across Scobie's legs. As Scobie crashed forward on to his hands and knees bawling murderous obscenities at him, Frank wielded the poker in a clumsy back-handed swipe across the older man's head.

Chapter Twenty-Five

'Is that Bernard's car down there?' Robert's voice held a note of surprise.

Andrina's spine hardened into a stiff icicle. She kept her back to Robert. 'I didn't know he had a car.'

'Yes, a Ford Anglia.'

'Well, if it is his car, either he and Doris are about to pay us a visit, or they're having a day out in the Green. It's Fair Friday, don't forget.'

'The car's across the road. I can't see who's in it for the trees. Or if anybody's in it.'

'We'll be late for Mummy, if we don't get a move on. You know what a stickler she is for everyone keeping exact time.'

'Right.' Robert moved away from the window. 'If the O'Maleys had been coming here, they would have parked at the close.'

'So it can't be them. There's a tram due at the end of the road in five minutes, Robert. If we run we'll just make it.'

They caught the tram by the skin of their teeth. It took them to near where they'd get a bus for Bearsden. Robert said, 'This is your mum's big day. Showing off her new house for the first time. She'll be in her element.'

Andrina barely murmured a reply. Her mind was filled with Bernard. And the fear of him. She didn't know if he *had* been in the car, yet all the time, in her heart, in her bones, she did know. Earlier in the day, she had been out doing some local shopping. Had he been there then – watching her, following her? She trembled inside at the thought. It was something impossible to cope with. Beyond understanding. Crazy.

'I offered to help, you know,' Robert continued. 'In any way I could. Painting, decorating. But she would have none of it.'

'She never trusts anyone to do anything properly,' Andrina

managed. 'She's obsessional about getting everything perfect – or what's perfect in her eyes.'

'She'll wear herself into an early grave if she doesn't slow down a bit.'

'There's no telling her. I've tried. Dad's tried. Sometimes I think she's getting worse as she gets older. It's just her nature, I suppose.'

'Obsessive behaviour can be a symptom of something serious, some hidden problem.'

Andrina smiled, but she felt far from happy. 'When are you going to put up your shingle? Doctor Anderson, psychiatrist, specialist in obsessional behaviour?'

'Just something I was reading the other day. An article in the *Sunday Times*. Didn't you see it?'

'It takes me a week to read that paper, plus the daily *Glasgow Herald*.'

'Your mother came into my mind while I was reading it. I felt quite worried about her.'

She touched his hand. 'That was kind of you. But she probably just needs a few tranquillisers. Something to slow her down.'

To Andrina, obsessional behaviour didn't have anything to do with the speed and thoroughness with which her mother worked. Obsessional behaviour was the slow determination, the patient pursuit of her by Bernard O'Maley. She wished now she'd read the article. Although she suspected it might only have made her more frightened.

Sometimes she wondered if she ought to tell Robert about Bernard. Each time she immediately shrank from the terrible consequences such a revelation might bring. Bernard was Robert's best friend. It would ruin not only their friendship, but their helpful association at the club. Worse, Robert might attack Bernard, and Bernard would be likely to seriously hurt him. It would cause bad feeling and terrible distress all round, including distress for Doris. And at the end of it all, would Bernard change his obsessional behaviour towards her? Andrina doubted it. There was also more to it than all these considerations: deep down she was rather flattered and excited by having such an ardent (and attractive) pursuer. The danger of it had an edge of excitement, a secret thrill. It was just her over-active imagination, of course, like how she used to feel when she read romantic novels in secret. (Her mother banned them as wicked.) She suffered with the heroine. She fell in love with the handsome, brooding and often brutal hero. Of course, the books always had a happy ending and the hero always turned out to be a really nice man after all. And safe.

Drymen Road was tree-lined and quiet. The terraced houses were tall and imposing, in good quality silver-grey stone.

'Nice place,' Robert said. 'Though the danger of being here too long might be that you'd forget how the other half lives.'

'Sometimes I wonder how Daddy can afford to live the way he does.'

'He got a real bargain of this place.'

Robert rang the bell and the door was immediately opened by Sophie, who must have been watching for them coming off the bus. Her silver hair was pulled so tightly back, it seemed to pull her eyes wide. It looked painful. She was wearing a dark wool dress with a cameo at her throat.

'Come in. Come in. I've put another mat just inside the door here so that you can give your feet an extra wipe. That's the worst of light coloured tiles and self-coloured carpets. They show every spot of dirt or dust. What do you think of it?' She waved an arm around the hall.

'Beautiful, Mummy, absolutely beautiful.' Andrina was genuinely amazed and overcome with admiration for the sparkling white woodwork, the outsize royal blue and cream tiles on the hall floor and the royal blue carpet on the stairs. The royal blue carpet also covered the floors in the sitting room and dining room. The kitchen and scullery had cream linoleum.

'You'll have a terrible job keeping all this linoleum clean,' Andrina said. 'Especially in a kitchen and scullery.'

'Oh, I'll manage,' Sophie said happily, although her sharp eyes and thin face betrayed a feverish flush.

'Where's Andrew?' Robert asked.

'Come on through to the sitting room.' Sophie hustled them before her.

Not a thing was out of place and, as Robert and Andrina admitted to each other and laughed about afterwards, they wondered if Sophie had tidied McPherson away. However, he'd just been upstairs at the bathroom.

'Him and his filthy old pipe,' Sophie had complained after they'd enjoyed a wonderful meal of poached fresh salmon with cucumber sauce, followed by Scotch trifle.

McPherson calmly ignored his wife and continued to puff away. Sophie watched him in agony. As soon as he knocked some ash into the ashtray, she grabbed it and dashed to the kitchen to empty it and wash it.

After coffee they were shown the back garden which consisted of a drying green and a patch of earth at either side of the path the length of the green.

'It was an overgrown mess,' Sophie told them. 'A right jungle. I dug up the side and planted some flowers.'

'I had the job of mowing the lawn,' McPherson said. 'One of these days, I must get a new mower. All we've got just now is an old rusty thing left by the previous owner.'

'We've joined the local branch of the Church of Jesus. The minister's very nice, isn't he Andrew? Very gentlemanly. The manse is a beautiful big villa. Most of the houses here are big villas of course. There's a really good class of people here.'

Robert couldn't help smiling at this. 'What does it feel like to be a Labour man in a Tory stronghold, Andrew?'

'Oh, I don't hold their politics against them. Anyway, it's not them I represent. I do my best for the ordinary working man. They're the ones who voted me into office. That's where my first loyalties lie.'

'But for health reasons,' Sophie interrupted, 'he needed to live as far away from his work as possible. He needed a bit of peace. Remember how people were never off our doorstep, Andrina?'

Andrina began to say 'Yes, but that was when you lived in Dumbarton Road, not Drumchapel', but her mother rushed on, ignoring her.

'All the time, every minute of the day and night, they were after your daddy for help and advice. He was being completely drained. I was too. We both needed a bit of peace and relaxation.'

'It's certainly a lovely place,' Andrina said.

'Yes. And it's so easy to get out into the country from here. Especially now that we've got our wee car. Isn't it, Andrew?'

'When I can manage to persuade her to lay down her duster or scrubbing brush and take off her apron and come with me.'

Sophie ignored him too. 'Now that we've got the place more or less organised I thought I'd invite a couple of the neighbours in for tea one day soon. Get to know them. Next door have a grown-up daughter. I peeped out the back bedroom window the other day and saw them – mother and daughter – sunbathing on deck-chairs. They looked very relaxed and elegant in good quality cotton sundresses and dark sunglasses. I went to the local library to find out the husband's profession. He's a headmaster.'

'Oh?' Robert was interested. 'What's his name?'

'Maurice Pemberton.'

'Pemberton? Unusual name. I think I met him at a conference last year. I believe he was about due for retirement.' He turned to Andrina. 'Remember that thing I went to on Standards in Modern Education?'

'Good.' Sophie clasped her hands together and shook them with pleasurable anticipation. 'That'll give me another point of contact, something to talk to them about.'

'Do you think that's a good idea, Sophie?' Robert gave one of his amused little smiles. 'As headmaster of an exclusive private school in Bearsden, he might not be all that impressed with a teacher in Blackhill Secondary.'

'Maybe not.' Sophie had obviously taken him seriously. 'Yes, you're quite right, Robert. Safer not to mention it.'

Robert and Andrina had laughed about this on the way home, and later, over their evening cup of Ovaltine, Andrina said, 'Poor Mummy, she's so excited about living in Bearsden. It's almost as if she's been blessed and arrived in heaven. I hope it lasts. I mean, I hope the people of Bearsden don't disillusion her. I don't think she could bear it.'

'I suppose once she finds her niche she'll be all right. No doubt she'll join the Women's Guild at the church and become involved in all sorts of good works and local events.'

'Did you hear Daddy talking about joining the golf club?'

'I heard what it cost. I was a bit surprised your mother didn't draw the line at that.'

'I know. But what puzzles me is where is he getting all the money? They've bought all that extra furniture as well.'

Robert shrugged. 'God knows what these big firms pay for consultants. And he's got more than one consultancy now, hasn't he?'

'I've no idea.'

'I hope . . .' Robert hesitated, worriedly.

'What?'

Robert shook his head. 'Nothing. Let's go to bed. I'm very fond of Sophie, but I must confess she exhausts me more than a class full of kids. And, believe me, coming from where I teach, that's saying something!'

'She has the same effect on me. I'm sorry for Daddy. At least we can get away on our own.'

'Oh, I think he manages that too.'

In bed, she cuddled towards him and he made love to her, gently, as usual, and with his usual restraint. He was a most self-disciplined and considerate man. She'd never seen him lose his temper although he could express anger at injustices.

She could imagine him controlling a class full of Blackhill rowdies with good humour, as well as his authoritative voice and manner. His reputation as a karate black belt would help, of course.

She loved and admired and trusted him. She kept assuring herself of this as she lay, long after he'd fallen into a deep sleep, and she was left, round-eyed in the darkness, in a strange, disturbing limbo.

Chapter Twenty-Six

The Gallacher kitchen looked even more like a tip than usual. Wooden chairs with spars missing wobbled on their sides on the uneven floor. The table had also been knocked over. A milk bottle had gushed out a white river. Sugar crunched underfoot and mixed with mince and mashed potatoes. It was a late summer evening and sunshine, beginning to fade, abandoned the room in dusty shadow. There was a smell of onion and cabbage, sour sweat, and blood.

Bridie had arrived home while Frank was out phoning for an ambulance. Carragh was whimpering in the corner between the sink and the press. Scobie was lying on the floor with his head near the metal fender. There was blood on the fender and on the floor. It looked as if he'd fallen and struck his head on the fender's sharp metal edge.

Before Bridie noticed the bloodstained poker, she knew instinctively that there had been a fight and Frank was in danger. She felt no concern for her father. He'd been asking to be cut down for years.

'Where's Frank?' she yelled at her mother.

'Away phoning for an ambulance, hen,' Carragh sobbed. 'Is your da all right?'

'Fuck him,' Bridie shouted with uncharacteristic coarseness. 'If the police see this they'll think Frank done it and they'll arrest him.' She rushed at the poker, snatched it up and, pushing her mother away from the sink, proceeded to scrub at the poker and wash off the blood.

'Frank didn't mean it, hen. He was trying to protect me. But your da didn't mean it either. It was the drink. See if he's all right. Please, hen. I don't feel able. I'm in such a state. I think I need an ambulance myself.'

Bridie thoroughly dried the poker and laid it in the

fireplace. Only then did she kneel down beside her father.

'Da?'

A groan and a mumble told her at least he wasn't dead.

'Da, you listen to me. My Frank never touched you. Never touched you. You were steaming drunk and you staggered about and tripped and fell and knocked your head against the fender. You did this to yourself, do you hear? My Frank never touched you.'

Another groan seemed to indicate compliance.

'Right,' said Bridie, struggling to her feet. She rushed around putting the room to rights. The table was lifted. Chairs were tidied around it. Milk was mopped up, mince and potatoes scraped off the floor. She was in the middle of doing this when an ashen-faced Frank appeared.

'The ambulance is on its way. Christ, I'm sorry, Bridie. I haven't killed him, have I?'

'Now, you listen to me.' Bridie came over to him and stared close as if her glasses weren't functioning properly. 'Whether he lives or dies, you never touched him. He was drunk and he fell and hit his head against the fender.'

'But . . .'

'Damn it, Frank,' she shouted at him, 'there's no buts about it. If he lives you could get a long jail sentence. If he dies they could hang you. Our lives would be ruined, finished. I'm not going to allow that, Frank. I'm not going to allow that drunken bum to finish us, Frank.'

'Good God.' Frank pushed back his hair. 'The man must be in pain. He could be dying. How can you just stand there calling him names? Get out of my way.' He knocked her aside and went over to kneel beside Scobie. 'Are you all right, Scobie?'

'Of course I'm not fuckin' all right,' Scobie managed. 'You've bashed my fuckin' skull in.'

'You heard me, da,' Bridie warned. 'You heard what I said. If the doctors or the police ask what happened, Frank never touched you. If you say anything against Frank, I'll be the next one to bash your skull in. I'm telling you, da. I mean it.'

'Aye, aye,' Scobie groaned.

'Right. How about you, ma?'

'Anything you say, hen.'

'How do you feel?' Bridie asked Carragh, still in an uncharacteristically aggressive voice. 'Are you in pain? Do you need to go in the ambulance?'

'I'll have to go with your da, hen. It's my place.'

As it turned out, nothing was needed to be said – not to the ambulance men, at least. They had collected Scobie before – from street pavements, from pubs, from closes, even from railway lines.

'At it again, was he?' they greeted the family. Then to the patient, 'See you, old man, one of these days we'll not be able to patch you up.'

As they lifted him on to the stretcher, Scobie mumbled something that the others couldn't catch. One of the ambulance men obviously heard, because he replied, 'Up yours as well!'

Afterwards, alone in the house, all Bridie's aggression suddenly evaporated. She began to sob and moan. Frank grabbed her into his arms and they clung tightly to each other.

'I warned you, Frank. I warned you what it was like and what it would do to us.'

'He's not always been as violent as this, surely?'

'Maybe he's got worse, but he's always been violent. If it wasn't to my ma, it was to the boys or to me and Doris, or to someone outside – some local gangster. I suppose he's got worse because the drinking's got worse. It's the drink, right enough. Da's good natured when he's sober. He likes a laugh. Sometimes he plays practical jokes. I don't go along with that kind of thing, but you've got to laugh at him sometimes. You've just got to laugh.' She was still helplessly weeping as she spoke, and Frank had to keep hushing her and comforting her.

'The thing is,' Frank said later as they were both drinking a cup of tea, one on each side of the fire, 'he'll have to stop drinking.'

'And pigs'll have to learn to fly.'

'No, I mean it, Bridie.'

'So do I. He's over sixty and he's been drinking all his days.'

'It's never too late.'

'How do you know, Frank? I don't suppose you've ever been drunk in your life. One or two pints of beer and you're quite happy. You don't want to, you don't need to drink more than that. Once my da starts he can't stop.'

'He's an alcoholic.'

'Of course he's an alcoholic. We've known that for years.'

'Alcoholics have been known to stop drinking,' Frank said thoughtfully. 'If I can get him to Alcoholics Anonymous.'

'If you can get him to AA, you're a worker of miracles, Frank.'

'It's worth a try.'

Bridie sighed but said nothing. Frank visibly stiffened with resolve.

'When Scobie comes out of hospital, I'm going to do it, Bridie. I'll get your da to AA or die in the attempt.'

'Don't say things like that even in a joke, Frank.'

'I'll have to get him there, Bridie.'

For a long minute Bridie stared across at her husband.

'What are you thinking,' he asked eventually.

'I was just remembering how you persevered all these years – ever since you were a wee boy – to get a poem published. And how, against all odds, you succeeded. And I was just thinking, if anyone can persevere and get my da to change his ways, you can, Frank. You just never give up, do you?'

'I'll get my play accepted next. You wait and see.'

'I believe you.'

'And I'll get your da to go on the wagon.'

Bridie sighed. 'Oh, he's always doing that. He never stays on it, that's the problem.'

'This time, he will. I promise you.'

'Try not to be too optimistic, Frank. I don't want you to be hurt and let down.'

'Trust me.'

She smiled. Her glasses were steaming up with the heat of her tea, but she could still make out his thin, eager face and the clothes that hung on him so inelegantly.

'I trust you. I love you as well.'

'One of these days . . .' Frank began, and she knew and loved what was coming, 'I'm going to take you out of all this. You're going to have a lovely roomy house with high carved ceilings and deep-pile luxurious carpets on the floor. The fireplace will be tiled, and there'll be beautiful paintings on the walls. The furniture will be solid and elegant and carved from beautiful wood. In the kitchen you'll have every modern gadget. The cupboard will be full of the best linen. The wardrobe will be packed with expensive and fashionable clothes. Everything your heart desires, Bridie, you will have. I promise you.'

'I know, Frank.'

'It'll be wonderful.'

'I know.'

His eyes had dreamed over. 'And I'll be a famous playwright. And you'll be proud of me.'

'I'm proud of you now.' She took off her glasses and rubbed at them with the corner of her skirt. 'And I know you know best about writing and what you want to say, only . . .' Her words hung in the air, held up with worry and uncertainty.

'Only what?'

'I can recognise people in what you've written of the play so far, and I'm a bit worried . . .'

'Oh, I don't think anybody will recognise themselves. People seldom do. As Rabbie said, "O Wad the Power the Gift tae gie us, to see ourselves as others see us." '

'Still, do you not think . . .'

'And when a friend of D. H. Lawrence expressed her concern about how Lawrence was using things about her, he said he was not falsifying her "truth", he was erecting a work of fiction on a frame of actual experience. The thing that matters, you see, Bridie, is that it should be my presentation of what I see as the truth – and it should also, if possible, be a work of art.'

'The scenes with the priest especially,' Bridie persisted. 'I'm afraid the Church isn't going to like that.'

'No,' Frank admitted, 'I don't expect it will. But an inhibited writer goes nowhere, Bridie, unless his very inhibitions are his subject matter. I believe that to write is to indulge in an intentionally promiscuous communication.'

She loved him when he talked like this. He was the dearest, the cleverest, the most talented man in the world. And to think he'd developed his talents and his brain and his decent nature against a background of places like Garngad and Blackhill. To her, he was a walking, talking miracle and every day she thanked God for him. But it was because she believed in God and His goodness and mercy towards both her and Frank that she wanted to protect Frank from the wrath of the Church, and maybe even the turning of God against them.

'I know that, dear,' she agreed gently and replaced her spectacles. 'It's just that our church and priests have their good side, don't you think? They do quite a lot of good around here. I mean there are two sides to everything, don't you think?'

Frank sighed. 'I know. I know. But they go about so many things in the wrong way. Beating up Scobie for instance. That's never helped or cured him. And they've no right to do it. I'd no right to touch Scobie either, but at least I've the excuse of self-defence.'

'Well, I suppose they probably look on themselves like an ordinary father chastising a son.'

Frank shook his head. 'In too many areas of life they go too far. So often they're wrong, Bridie. So terribly wrong!'

'Maybe it's the way you feel just now, dear. Just the way you're seeing things at the moment. Things haven't been easy for you.'

He'd written a poem about how he felt at the moment:

> 'I did not doubt before, but now
> I feel unsure of all my past
> Of self and faith; I know somehow
> I must be free,
> I must be me,
> To find a surer way at last.'

He didn't tell Bridie about the poem. Instead he said, 'It's my duty as a writer to express things as I see them as honestly as I can.'

'Yes, but to take on the Church, Frank. I'm afraid . . .'

'Exactly! That's one of the things that's wrong with it. So much of their teaching is based on fear. For instance, you're afraid I'll be damned and burn in Hell for questioning and making other people question, aren't you?'

'No, no, dear,' she said. But she was. Apprehension was tightening its grip on her. She tried to tell herself that the recent violence in the house, and the terrible business of Frank's involvement, was what had really unnerved her.

She didn't know. She couldn't think. She had been talking to Frank about his play in her usual quiet and gentle voice, as if Frank hadn't nearly committed murder. Maybe only now the shock of it was catching up on her. She was shaking, collapsing inside.

She smiled and blinked over at Frank. 'I wonder if Da's got any whisky hidden in the house. I wouldn't mind a wee drop in my tea.'

Chapter Twenty-Seven

'You can't go out and leave me like this. Where are you going? Why are you getting all done up? What's going on, Bernard? For pity's sake, tell me.' Doris had to shout because of Tony's drums racketing through from the next room.

Bernard was going out again without her. He had told her he was going out on a job and it was true that he worked most nights, but he was taking far too much care about his appearance to be just going to work. He looked like a hundred dollars in his smart, lightweight suit and fashionable silk shirt. He was bending a little at the knees so that he could see in the mirror to smooth a palm over his hair. She felt a real mess in comparison. Her dark hair was showing at the roots. Her belly bulged. Her skirt drooped. She was tormented with a varicose vein, and she was wearing horrible flat-heeled shoes.

'Bernard!' She tugged at his sleeve. 'Don't just ignore me.'

He flicked at his jacket as if she'd contaminated it. 'I'm going to work. And my work needs total concentration, Doris. I've explained all this to you before.'

She immediately began to howl and cry and swear. She howled and cried and swore a lot these days. 'You bloody selfish pig. You don't care about anybody but yourself.'

'You're just getting yourself into a state.'

'Is it any wonder? If you're not out at work, you're in bed asleep and if you're not asleep, you ignore me.'

'What is there to say?'

'It's not fuckin' good enough,' she shouted broken-heartedly.

He looked at her then – a cold, distasteful look that made her weep all the more. She knew he didn't like coarseness in a woman. He never swore himself. At least, she'd never heard him. She would rather he had shouted and sworn at her, even hit her, like her da used to hit her ma. At least it would have shown some emotion, some feelings towards her.

She felt helpless, childlike. She wanted him to hold her and comfort her and love her. She knew she was doing everything all wrong. She didn't know what to do to make things right. She kept making things worse. Shouting at him, swearing at him, trying to force him to stay in with her, pay attention to her – nothing was any good.

He was polite, always so bloody polite, never an unkind word. She bloody hated him. If she'd been a man, she would have battered him with her bare fists. 'I'm going to tell your mammy on you,' she sobbed.

After he'd gone without another word, she trailed miserably through to the living room to find Maureen wasn't in. She had just dried her eyes on her smock when Tony came clomping and whistling through from his room.

'Jesus, Doris, you look like something the cat dragged in.'

It was too much. Howling louder than ever she ran past him and out of the house. She had a vague idea of going to Garngad to be with her own mother. She was so upset she didn't pay attention to where she was putting her feet. She remembered an initial feeling of surprise when she suddenly lost her balance and went hurtling down the stone stairs, bouncing, crashing, crunching against them. She lay at the bottom for what seemed like forever. She felt in pain literally from head to toe. Her head had cracked against one of the stairs and she'd twisted her foot under her when she landed.

'Tony.' She tried to call out but her chest hurt and the word came out as a faint moan. She tried the names of some of the neighbours. Nobody came. Most of them would be in their living rooms at the back watching television. Or they'd be out. She tried to help herself and had just managed to crawl on all fours up a few steps when Tony came whistling and clattering into view.

He gave one of his big, buck-toothed laughs. 'What's the game?'

'Help me up to the house,' she managed. 'I've hurt myself.'

None too gently, he heaved her up and she howled with pain.

'I told you I've hurt myself, you eejit. I fell down all these stairs.'

'I'll carry you if you like.' He was still grinning.

'OK. But take it easy. I'm in agony.'

Once in the house he propped her into a chair.

'Will I get Bernard? I know where he'll be.'

She hesitated. She needed her husband more than she'd ever needed him before, but she knew he would be scant comfort – if any comfort at all. He would do his duty by her but there would be no love with it. That was the terrible thing. The ultimate loneliness. There could be no hiding the fact any more. Bernard didn't care about her. She began to moan and weep.

'Stay there,' Tony said. 'I'll get him.'

After Tony had gone, she tried not to faint or be sick. She couldn't move out of the chair. Never in her whole life had she experienced such pain, had felt so ill. When she heard the key turn in the outside door, she prayed that it would be Maureen. From her, at least, she would get some love and sympathy. But it was Bernard who strode into the room. He was saying, 'I hope this isn't just another of your . . .' Seeing her, he stopped.

She didn't say anything. What was the use?

'What happened? Tony just called out something was wrong with you and disappeared before I could ask him anything.'

'I fell down the stairs.'

He took a few steps towards her. 'It'll be all right.' He'd said that before but it hadn't been all right. 'I'll go and phone for an ambulance. That's what Tony should have done right away. I'll tell one of the neighbours to come in and wait with you. I'll be lucky if I get a phone box working within a mile of here. Can I get you anything first? A brandy or something?'

She shook her head.

'I'll be back as soon as I can.'

In a few minutes Mrs Hennessy appeared. 'Is this no terrible, hen? And you carrying the wean. It was with you being so heavy at the front. It would knock you off balance. Poor wee soul. Is it awful sore, hen? Will I make you a wee cup of tea?'

'Ta,' Doris managed, and Mrs Hennessy bustled away through to the scullery.

Years seemed to pass before Bernard returned, quickly followed by the ambulance men.

Bernard came with her in the ambulance. He sat talking to the ambulance men. It was the ambulance man who patted her and held her hand. She desperately clung to him as the pain increased.

Andrina went to see Doris in the hospital and was shocked at the sight of the grey face and lank hair. There was a look of Carragh about her – except that Carragh never had the bitter look that Doris had now.

'I was so sorry to hear about the baby.' Andrina took Doris's limp hand and squeezed it sympathetically.

'It was a wee girl. I called her Carragh after my mammy.'

Andrina didn't know what to say. At last she managed, 'You'll have lots more children, Doris.'

'Do you think so?'

'Of course. Why not?'

Doris's lips twisted. 'Oh aye. Why not?'

'Has Bernard been in to see you?'

'He came with Maureen last night.'

'Is he coming again tonight?'

'I hope not.'

Andrina was shocked. 'Doris! I'm sure Bernard must be very upset.'

'What? Him?'

'He won't be able to show his feelings. You know what men are like.'

'I know what he's like. A right cold-hearted bastard.'

Andrina patted Doris's hand. 'He's got a very tough, stressful job. That probably has a lot to do with what he's like. It won't have anything to do with you, Doris.'

'No?'

'No.'

'As soon as I get out of here, I'm going to try to get my old job back.'

'What will Bernard think about that?'

'I don't care a f . . .' she caught herself in time and struggled to find some of her old ladylike restraint. 'I don't care a fig what Bernard will think. Anyway, knowing him, he won't be in the slightest interested in what I do. All he's interested in is himself, and his business. I've never known anyone in my whole life so single-minded.'

'I know how you feel about going back to Daly's. I often miss Copland's: the company of the other girls, some of the laughs we used to have.'

'I know.' Doris's eyes saddened, remembering. 'I miss it terribly.'

'And the interest of all the different customers, and the smart clothes. I asked Robert only the other day what he would think if I went back to work. I've never seen him look so offended. He's a bit touchy and old-fashioned about that sort of thing. "I'm perfectly capable of keeping my wife," he said. "If you're short of anything all you have to do is tell me." I couldn't make him understand it wasn't the money. He clammed up. Didn't want to know anything about it.'

'Why don't you just do it?' Doris said. 'Like I'm going to do it, and to hell with him.'

'Well, Robert's really very good to me. I don't want to hurt or upset him. And of course, there's my mother. She would hit the roof.'

'What's it got to do with her?'

Andrina gave a dazed little laugh. 'Well, I . . . Mummy's very fond of Robert, and she'd think I was neglecting him by going out to work. You don't know her, Doris. She can make me feel so guilty. It really upsets me.'

'I know enough about her. She hates Bernard, doesn't she? That's why Robert didn't invite him to your wedding. I wondered at the time what she had against him. Mr Wonderful, I thought he was at the time. Your mother obviously was better at judging him than me.' Doris's mouth twisted. 'A very clever woman, your mother.'

Andrina felt uneasy in the silence that fell between them. To break the awkwardness of it she said, 'As soon as you're better we must meet and have a nice meal together somewhere. And we could call in at Daly's and Copland's and see all the girls. You won't be starting work right away, will you?'

'As soon as I can fix it up.'

'You'll have to get your strength back first, Doris.'

Doris smiled and her hand tightened on to Andrina's. 'You're a good friend, Andrina. I'm terribly grateful. Yes, we'll have our day out. I'll look forward to it. What I'm not looking forward to is going back to live in that house in Blackhill. I used to think it would be so much better than Garngad and my da. But you know Patrick is just as awful in his own way. He's a right thieving git, so he is. You'll pardon the expression. And there's never a bit of peace inside the house, what with him and Tony. Nobody seems to mind except me. They switch the wireless on for music at mealtimes and Tony batters away at the rhythm on the table with his big paws and makes all the dishes rattle about. They just laugh. Maureen thinks he's a lovely boy. Can you beat it? Him with his mouth always hanging open in a silly grin showing those big horsy teeth of his. Our Francie wasn't right in the head, but at least he was quiet and harmless. I never thought they should have put Francie away. I was terribly upset about poor wee Francie.'

Andrina patted her hand. 'We'll meet regularly. Have a good time. Forget all our troubles.'

Doris nodded. 'Ta.'

'Is there anything else you need brought in? How about some peroxide for your hair? You'd feel better if you got it back to normal.'

'Would you, Andrina?'

'Of course.'

'You're a real pal.'

'I'll bring in some make-up as well. It can do wonders for the morale.'

Doris nodded, but tears had sprung to her eyes.

'Oh, Doris, please don't cry.'

'I thought there might just be a chance . . .' The tears overflowed and poured unchecked down Doris's cheeks. '. . . that the baby would bring Bernard and me closer together. It was a wee girl. I called her Carragh after my mammy.'

'I know. You told me.'

Doris looked so lost and helpless in her misery that Andrina stretched over and pulled her into her arms. Patting her back as she would have comforted a child, she tried to hush the distraught woman.

'Sh . . . Doris . . . Sh. Will I call the nurse? Maybe she could give you something to calm you.'

'I'm a terrible nuisance.'

'No, you're not. Of course you're not. You just lie back. I'll fetch the nurse. It's no trouble.'

'Ta.'

The nurse gave Doris something that soon made her appear not only calm but sleepy. Her eyes kept closing and the hand that clung to Andrina's became limp again.

'I'd better go and let you have a good sleep,' Andrina whispered close to the colourless face. 'I'll come again tomorrow with all the things I promised.'

Doris didn't answer and Andrina slipped her hand gently away. Outside, she caught a tram back to Monteith Row. She hardly dared think, she felt so upset. Words kept chasing each other round and round in her mind.

'Oh God, poor Doris. Oh God, poor Doris. Oh, dear God!'

Once home she made herself a cup of tea and sat nursing it beside the empty fireplace.

It was nothing to do with her, she assured herself. Bernard was mad. She had told him he was mad. She had done nothing to encourage Bernard's attention. She had refused to listen to him. She was happily married to a dear, good man. She had made that perfectly clear to Bernard. It was really shocking the way he had treated Doris.

'Oh God, poor Doris. Oh God, poor Doris. Oh, dear God!'

She was still sitting nursing her cup when Robert arrived

home from taking his class for a sketching lesson in the Campsies.

'Darling, what's wrong? You look like a ghost sitting there. Your tea's stone cold. I'll put a match to the fire, then I'll make you a fresh cup.'

'I was in visiting Doris.'

'I see. How is she?'

'In an awful state.'

'No wonder. But she'd be glad to see you, I'm sure.'

'Yes, she was. But I wished I could have done more to help her.'

'Losing a child must be the worst thing in the world. I don't suppose there's anything that can be done to make anyone feel better in such circumstances.'

'I suppose not.'

'You're doing your best, Andrina. Try not to get too upset. Once Doris is on her feet again, we must have her and Bernard over for a meal.'

'I've promised we'll meet in town and have a meal. Just her and me.'

'You can do that too. But it would be nice for the four of us to get together more often.'

Andrina made no comment. Robert soon had the fire creaking and crackling in the hearth. They'd had the old range and high mantelpiece taken out, and a modern tiled fireplace and gas cooker put in place. The coal bunker had been removed and hidden in a cupboard in the hall. With the dining recess where normally a bed would have been, the room was now a kitchen cum dining room, and a very cosy and pleasant place either to work or to relax in.

More often than not, they used it as a living room, especially in the winter. They only used the front sitting room when they'd company, or on a nice summer evening they'd sit at the window and look out at the Green in between reading or listening to the wireless. They had two wirelesses (or what were now called transistor radios) – one in the front room and one in the kitchen. One had been a wedding present from the girls in

Copland's. The other had been from Robert's uncle Jimmy, who had since died.

This evening the summer sun had cooled and the kitchen had turned chilly and dull.

'I'm sorry, I forgot the time.' Andrina roused herself, got up and rinsed out her cup at the sink. 'I've some of that pie left that I made yesterday. Will that do with chips? It won't take me long to peel the potatoes. And I can soon make some custard.'

'Let's go out,' Robert said. 'You need cheering up. Come on, get your coat. It's not often we treat ourselves. Bernard was telling me about a new place that's got the best food in town – and he should know.'

'Should he?'

'Of course. It's his job. It takes him to all sorts of places. He's become quite a connoisseur. He's a strange mixture, isn't he?'

'Yes,' she said, avoiding his eyes. 'Very strange.'

Chapter Twenty-Eight

Sophie was thrilled at being invited next door to Mrs Pemberton's for afternoon tea. As she said to McPherson, 'Fancy! I didn't need to make the first approach. She did. She put a little card through the door. On one side there was their name and address and telephone number. On the other was the invitation to afternoon tea.' (She'd learned afterwards that Mrs Pemberton hadn't telephoned because she didn't know if their phone had yet been installed.) 'Andrew! Andrew, are you listening?'

'Yes, dear.' McPherson was sucking absently at his pipe, his eyes above their pouches of dark lizard skin were dreamy. He was thinking of a very lucrative deal he'd managed to put Bernard's way. He also would gain much benefit from it. One of these new pop groups was coming to Glasgow. Youngsters went mad about them apparently. Bodyguards and also very strict crowd control were needed. It was to be an outdoor event on the Green. Television cameras were going to be there. It was going to put Glasgow on the map – hopefully in a good way for a change. There mustn't be any trouble. For too long Glasgow had suffered from a bad reputation, especially for violence, although nowadays at events like this a lot of what was called flower people turned up and drug taking was the problem with them. He'd said to Bernard that drug-taking hippies and Glasgow neds didn't seem a good mix. Bernard had assured him that everything would go well. Security and crowd control would be – to use Bernard's words – as tight as a badger's arse.

'You'll notice,' Sophie was saying, 'that she didn't come knocking at the door. They don't do that here like they do in the tenements. There's no running in and out of each other's houses. They show a bit of respect for privacy. I'm really looking forward to it. Andrew! Andrew!'

'Yes, dear.'

'I wonder what I should wear.'

'Your brown dress with your cameo. That's a good cameo. A real family heirloom.'

'I know.'

'There you are then.'

'Yes, and my brown dress is plain but good quality. Yes, you're quite right, Andrew. I'll look perfectly respectable in that.'

She couldn't sleep the night before the visit, and the next morning she took a bath and put on clean underwear and brushed her hair and pinned it so tightly back her eyes took on an oriental look. She had already polished her shoes until she could see her face in them. She pressed her dress. She even washed her cameo and polished it up with a soft duster, and did the same with her spectacles. She worried about whether or not to take a gift to Mrs Pemberton. It was the custom in working class districts always to take a gift if it was the first visit to anyone's house. Indeed, it was quite usual to take a packet of biscuits or a cake or some small offering any time you visited anyone. But would that be proper in Bearsden? She didn't want to appear common or insult the woman by taking something. On the other hand she did not want to risk looking ignorant or mean. Eventually she decided on her home-baked butter shortbread, packed prettily in tissue paper, in a little cardboard gift box in a discreet fawn colour, and neatly tied with a gold-coloured ribbon.

Mrs Pemberton seemed delighted. 'We must exchange recipes, my dear. I've never quite mastered shortbread. I have quite a good Madeira cake recipe you might like to try. I never divulge any of my recipes as a rule. One gets known for one's special little treats. Each one to his own, I always say. But as a little gesture of good will to a new neighbour, I'll make an exception with my Madeira cake.'

Already Sophie was enjoying herself. As Mrs Pemberton went to fetch the tea tray her eyes rapidly took in the comfortable room, the white Adam fireplace, the heavy lined curtains, the chintz chair covers. There was a trolley nicely set with fine china cups and saucers and tea plates and a three tiered cake stand. The cake stand boasted a plate of tiny scones, a plate of buttered fruit bread, and a plate of dainty sponge cakes. Then, to top all these delights, Mrs Pemberton returned with a silver tray on which sat a silver teapot, sugar bowl and milk jug.

Sophie couldn't contain herself. 'A silver tea service! Mrs Pemberton!'

'It is beautiful, isn't it? It's a family heirloom. It belonged to my husband's mother.'

'Like my cameo.' Sophie fingered it with pride. 'It belonged to my husband's mother too.'

'I noticed it right away, Mrs McPherson. I always recognise and appreciate quality.'

'Yes, so do I. Your tea service is so . . . so elegant.'

'Yes, isn't it?'

Mrs Pemberton too was elegant in a matronly kind of way. Sophie guessed she could be anywhere between fifty and sixty. Her hair was light brown and beautifully permed. Not one grey hair was to be seen. She went into town every week to have it shampooed and set. She also had a special rinse to cover the odd grey hair or two.

But that was another of her little secrets. Her dress was well cut and in pretty shades of turquoise. Sophie was fascinated to learn that Mrs Pemberton had made the dress herself.

'I'm interested in dressmaking too,' she confessed in between delicious sips of Earl Grey tea, 'but altering is about my stretch. You know – taking up hems, letting out or taking in a tuck here and there.'

'Oh, you must allow me to help you make something for yourself.'

'I couldn't put you to all that trouble, Mrs Pemberton.'

'No trouble at all. It'll be a pleasure. Now, can I be honest with you, my dear?'

'Yes, of course.'

'Well, I don't think brown is your colour. I can see the

material is good quality. But brown doesn't flatter you, Mrs McPherson. You need something to brighten you up.'

Sophie began to feel uncomfortable, began to shrink protectively inside. 'Oh, I'm not one for bright colours. Not for myself.'

'Something just a *little* softer – lavender perhaps?'

'Well, I don't know.'

'You have such a lovely fair skin and slim figure, my dear. I envy you. I'm afraid I'm too fond of these.' She offered Sophie a sponge cake and selected one herself. 'Your husband's a Glasgow bailie, I believe.'

'Yes.'

'We must make a four for bridge some evening.'

'I'm afraid I've never played bridge.'

'Oh, my dear, you must learn. *Everybody* plays bridge. We go to *so* many bridge parties. My husband is a *very* accomplished player. We'll get together as a foursome first to break you in, so to speak. You'll soon pick it up.'

Sophie began to relax again with the prospect of many happy evenings with new friends and neighbours. Church membership was discussed next. The Women's Guild and the flower arranging club were recommended. Golf was another must.

'For me?' Sophie had to laugh. The idea of her out on a golf course was too much. 'I can't imagine playing golf. I've never been one for sports of any kind. My husband is keen, though. He's already applied for membership of your local club. I must admit I was rather shaken at the cost of the subscription.'

'Oh, my dear, it's worth it. You meet so many important people. People who would be a help to you and your husband in so many ways. And why shouldn't you play golf? Lots of ladies do. I do. It's also good for helping to keep fit. By the way, there's a very good keep fit class in the town hall.'

It was all working out beautifully. Better even than Sophie had ever dared hope. Perhaps some of the ways of keeping busy weren't exactly as she'd expected – she'd been thinking more in terms of 'good works', but no doubt she'd learn about that too in time. After all, she'd hardly settled in the place yet.

She could hardly wait to tell McPherson all about the visit. 'She already knew you were a bailie. She never mentioned you being Labour, of course. She was too well-bred.'

'I'm not ashamed of being a Labour man,' McPherson protested. Although in fact he had been wondering recently if he wasn't developing more towards Liberalism. There was something so well-balanced about the Liberal Party. There was nothing too extreme about it. It had a proud history. He had been reading quite a bit about it recently. Of course he couldn't rush into anything like that. Glasgow was a red-hot Labour place, and it was Glaswegians who had elected him. He wasn't a fool. He knew that it paid him to remember that.

He had no doubts about his move to Bearsden. He liked the house. There was space to move, to breathe in it. Room to get away from Sophie. He had commandeered the bedroom on the half landing next to the bathroom as his study. In it he had a desk and swivel chair, bookshelves, a carpet and a comfortable easy chair beside the fire. There he could sit enjoying a pipe and a bit of peace after telling Sophie that he'd paperwork to attend to.

Although, in actual fact, he and Sophie had been getting on surprisingly well since the move to Bearsden. She was so much happier for one thing, which made life a lot easier. Quite often they went for a walk together in the evening, he with his black walking umbrella and she with her coat and pull-on hat and brogues – the proper thing for week-day walking. Although it was September the air was still balmy and pleasant. They explored around, getting to know the place, absorbing the solid, prosperous, secure atmosphere.

Sophie walked apart from him as usual, but he could sense her happy excitement. 'It's magic, isn't it, Andrew? You feel it too, don't you?'

He had to agree with her. He had never felt so happy and content in years. 'Will you never learn to relax?' But he laughed as he said it. He knew that would be expecting too much. Sophie was like an overwound alarm clock or a time-bomb waiting to go off. She was – always had been – a hysterical type. At least now she was hysterical with happiness.

She looked better too. The first time they'd been to Bearsden church she had worn a new, very smart costume in navy blue, instead of her usual shapeless muddy brown things. With it she teamed a white blouse which tied with a bow at the neck. This, for Sophie, seemed outrageously frivolous. Not as frivolous, however, as the tiny pearl stud earrings she'd taken to wearing. He'd never in all the years he'd known her seen her wear any jewellery whatsoever, except the cameo he'd given her.

He said to her, 'You look very nice.'

She'd flushed with pleasure and looked quite pretty. He felt proud of her too when the next week they'd attended church. He wore his trilby hat and best pinstripe suit with his heavy gold watch and chain over his ample girth, Sophie wore a dress in soft lavender shades she'd made herself. Her hat and gloves and shoes and handbag were navy blue. They went with Mr and Mrs Pemberton and their daughter, Samantha. He and Sophie didn't of course walk arm in arm like Mr and Mrs Pemberton. Sophie never touched him in public.

Samantha was a charming girl whose hobbies were riding and skiing. She was in her late twenties and unmarried. There was no hurry, Mr and Mrs Pemberton explained. It was so important to find the *right* partner. He and Sophie had been in no doubt that the Pembertons meant somebody with money.

'And why not?' Sophie had said.

Why not indeed? They were both beginning to regret their own daughter's hasty choice of a husband. Robert was a nice enough man but – a schoolmaster in Blackhill of all places! And to make matters worse he showed no signs of having any ambition whatsoever. McPherson often thought that Andrina would have been far better off married to Bernard O'Maley, Catholic or not. But of course that was something he knew better never to even hint at to Sophie. Sophie had been thinking of the respectable young men in the Bearsden church. Professional men from good homes (large villas), like Doctor James Honeyman, who was building up a very lucrative private practice, Mrs Pemberton said. Or the lawyer Blair Matheson, who was in partnership with his father – a very lucrative partnership, Mrs Pemberton said.

'What elegant young gentlemen,' Sophie remarked. 'Isn't it a pity Andrina didn't meet someone like them?' Not, of course, that I've got anything against poor Robert,' she added hastily. 'Poor Robert is a good Christian man.'

It was the 'poor' that was the trouble.

Sophie discovered that it was *the* thing to have an 'At Home', and so she invited several of the neighbours and one or two of the other ladies from the church. For days beforehand she cleaned and baked and polished until she was in a near frenzy. But everything went superbly. She was complimented on the lightness of her French Fancies and the crispness of her almond biscuits. Mrs Hawthorn from further along the terrace (her husband was a bank manager) said they were all so glad to have such a *suitable* newcomer to the terrace. One never knew these days. With young people taking over so much and standards being not only eroded but tossed to the winds. My dear, have you seen those Beatle young men's long hair? They had all seen even worse. There had been pictures and stories of Elvis Presley and the disgustingly sexual gyration of his hips while he sang. There were scenes of nakedness and debauchery when hordes of so-called flower people got together. There were Mods and Rockers and motorbikes and drug taking. There were pictures of young people dressed like absolute tramps on CND marches. What was the world coming to?

It was all most enjoyable.

Andrew was pleased to hear that Sophie's 'At Home' had been such a success. He was able to share the pleasures he had experienced at the golf club. Sophie was always keenly interested in who he had met and always asked, 'What does he do?' He was pleased to be able to tell her that he'd got on so well with old Hawthorn, the bank manager, or Sanderson of Sanderson and Galbraith, the well known firm of architects, or the Reverend Dinwoodie, who lived in such a beautiful manse surrounded by trees beside the loch.

It was a great source of pride when he and Sophie were invited to a dinner party at the manse.

'Dinwoodie and I have been getting on really well at the club. Did I tell you I showed him round the City Chambers the other day and gave him lunch there? He was impressed, I could see.'

'Yes, dear.'

Sophie was thrilled at the invitation. She had, so far, only admired Bearsden's beautifully proportioned villas from a distance. It would be fascinating to see what one of them was like inside. Mrs Pemberton was delighted for her, and accompanied her into town to help choose a new outfit for the occasion. Mrs Pemberton was already a dear friend; a wonderfully kind woman, a perfect lady. They had tea in the Willow Tearoom; Mrs Pemberton said it was *the* place to go. They chose a spotted shantung dress with a black velvet belt and back fastening. It was, as Mrs Pemberton said, smart, sophisticated, but discreet. It was also rather expensive but as McPherson said, it was important to make a good impression, and anyway he could afford it. He said he was making quite a bit of extra money these days, and who better to spend it on than his wife? McPherson was a different man since he'd come to Bearsden. He spent much more time at home. They'd never, in all the years they'd been married, got on so well.

Just before they left for the manse he said, 'Just a minute, Sophie. I've a present for you.' And, to her surprise and delight, he fastened a strand of pearls round her neck. They were such a good match for her pearl studs.

'Oh Andrew! Thank you. They're just perfect. In such good taste. You're really a very generous man.'

He could sense that if she had been a demonstrative, affectionate type of woman, she would have thrown her arms around him and kissed him. She was teetering very near to it. But of course she didn't. Instead she turned away, fingering the pearls with that strange, furtive sensuality of hers.

There was another couple at the dinner party, a Professor Brodie and his wife. Charming fellow. Of course, the university was hoping for a higher grant from the council. A lot of people tried to be as charming as possible to influential men like Andrew McPherson from the City Chambers. Everyone knew that he was in the running to be Senior Bailie next year, and from there the natural progression was Lord Provost.

The Reverend Dinwoodie was talking about his elderly parishioners and a concert that he was organising for their entertainment. Some of the elderly ladies and gentlemen would need transport to bring them from their homes to the church hall on the evening of the concert, although most of them were still able to drive their own cars.

'I was just talking to old Noble the other day – he must be nearly eighty now – and I offered to pick him and his good lady up myself – but no, he's a game old bird, he would have none of it.'

Andrew said, 'Noble? An unusual name. It was my wife's maiden name.'

The Reverend Dinwoodie smiled over at Sophie. 'Really? Do you think our Nobles would be any relation, my dear?'

'No. I have no living relations.'

McPherson said, 'Sophie was an only child and her parents died when she was young. I never met them.'

All in all it was a delightful evening. McPherson remarked on this to Sophie on the way home in the car. 'A most successful evening,' he said with satisfaction. 'An evening to remember.'

Sophie didn't answer. She seemed lost in thought, miles away. It wasn't like her to be so quiet. She must be exhausted. She tried so hard. She always flung her heart and soul into everything. He retreated into his own pleasurable thoughts.

Chapter Twenty-Nine

'Are you sure you're doing the right thing, Michael?' Frank asked worriedly. He'd sought his brother out at the boxing club in Garngad Road as soon as he'd heard.

'Sure, I'm sure. And I'll tell you why. It's not just the money. It's the chance of getting away as often as I can from Big Martha Stoddart. But there's quite good money to be made fighting at the booths all the same. And there's plenty of them –there's booths in Edinburgh and Falkirk, nearly every town of any size. Then there's all the travelling with the fairs in the summer time. I'm told you can get a fight a day there, if you're game. And I'm game, Frank. I'm game for anything that'll give me a wee break away from here.'

'Some wee break,' Frank said. 'A fight a day at travelling booths. You'll be punch drunk before you're thirty.'

'But there's always the chance of a real improver. I could hit the big time, Frank. Then, if I'm good enough, I could make hundreds, maybe thousands, just for one fight. I'd better get back up. Be a pal and stay and watch. It won't take too long. Then you can tell me what you think.'

'OK, OK.'

Frank regarded it as a measure of Michael's desperation that he would in the least value his opinion. Michael had been one of those who had seen Frank's practice of writing poetry as being 'weak' and 'pouffie'. Michael knew that Frank had an equally low opinion of boxing. However, to please his brother, he stayed in the club and watched as Michael climbed back into the ring and continued with his training.

It wasn't in any way a pleasant place, as far as Frank was concerned. It was bleak and grimy and cold. Broken windows were boarded up. Knots of gangsters crouched around the ring playing pontoon and smoking. Smoke continuously thickened the air, new smoke adding to ancient smoke. Smoke that had stained the ceiling and walls a muddy brown. Smoke that mixed with the stale odour of sweat and sickness in Frank's nostrils. And there was a coarse yet empty echo about the place that saddened him.

Michael was shadow boxing, head down, his dark crop of hair glistening with sweat: southpawing forward, upper-cutting, jabbing, counter punching, weaving and swaying, checking and reaching, giving fist flurries at an imaginary opponent. Despite the cold air, sweat was beginning to steam off him. Eventually he dropped his hands to his sides and did a shuffle on the spot, shaking his head from side to side, before climbing out of the ring and returning to Frank.

'How did I look, Frank?'

'You looked great, Michael. First class.'

'Thanks, Frank. How're you doing yourself?'

Frank glanced at his watch. 'I'll tell you after I've been to the hospital.'

'Och aye, the word's been going around that you were collecting old Scobie today.'

'They've promised to hang on to him till five. Even if it hadn't been my half day off work, I would have taken the time off.'

Michael laughed. 'To stop him doing a pub crawl? I wouldn't bet on it.'

'I'm aiming to do more than stop him doing a pub crawl today. I'm going to stop him drinking altogether.'

'Poor old Scobie.'

'What do you mean – poor old Scobie?'

'Well, I know how it feels to *need* a drink. *And* how it feels when you get one.'

'I know how it feels when Scobie gets more than one. He nearly kicked the stuffing out of me. Not to mention Carragh's black eye and other bruises.'

Michael shrugged. 'Oh well, best of luck to you, pal.'

Scobie was waiting for Frank in a shabby, baggy-trousered suit and big cloth cap jerked to one side of his head.

'By Christ, son,' he greeted Frank, 'I'll never look at another drink as long as I live. I swear to you. I've had my last drink. I'll never touch another drop as long as I live, so help me.'

'I'll help you all right, wee man,' Frank said, gripping Scobie by the elbow and manoeuvring him outside. 'As soon as we get back to Turner Street, you and I are going to have a long talk.'

'Aye, right you are, son. Anything you say.'

They took a tram to Garngad Road and after they got off, Frank took a grip of Scobie's elbow again as they passed the pub at the corner of Garngad Road and Turner Street. Already the gas-lamps were lit, softening the grimy black tenements, sparkling the cobbles.

'You don't need to worry, son,' Scobie assured him as they turned into their close. 'I'm a reformed man.'

'I wonder how many times you've said that, Scobie.'

'A few, son. A few. But this time I mean it.'

Carragh had the door open for them when they got up the stairs.

'Hello there, hen,' Scobie greeted her. 'How's my favourite wee woman?'

'Fine, fine.' Carragh stirred a pot on the range. 'I've a nice plate of mince and tatties for you.' She dished Scobie's up first.

He smacked his hands together and gave them a vigorous rub. 'My favourite! You're a wee stoater, so you are. And how's my other wee girl?' He turned to Bridie who was sitting at the table, her head bowed over a book. Bridie was depressed about Scobie's return, and when Bridie was depressed she always retreated into a book. Both she and Frank ate their meal in silence. Scobie and Carragh chatted away quite happily. It was as if nothing had happened. After the mince and potatoes, Carragh proudly produced some apple tarts from the City Bakeries.

'My favourite again,' Scobie cried. 'By God, it's good to be home.'

'Right then,' Frank said, once the apple tarts had been demolished and they were on their second cup of tea, 'can I talk to you, Scobie? Can we have a serious talk? It's important to both of us, all of us.'

'Fire away, son. Fire away.'

Carragh hastily began clearing the table. Then, as she washed the dishes at the sink, she tried to be as small as possible and pretend she wasn't there. Bridie took her book through to the room.

'Is this the way you want to go on with your life?' Frank asked. 'You're losing your self-respect and the respect of your family and friends. You're ruining not only your own life but all of our lives. Is this how you want to go on?'

'No, son, I do not. I know it's like wee Carragh says – it's the drink, and I've given it up.'

'Yes, you've told all of us that – over and over and over again. But you never give it up, Scobie. Look at you, man. Look at you!'

'OK, OK. I'm fed up fuckin' looking at myself. But what else can I do?'

'You could try the League of the Cross. You can sign the pledge there and Father Shannon is very supportive, I've heard. He has a lot going on. There's card schools – solo and pontoon – you'd enjoy that . . .'

'I can enjoy a card school or a game of pitch and toss at any street corner. I don't need to join the League of the Cross.'

'Well, I've heard that the AA can work wonders.'

'For fuck's sake . . .'

'No, for your good wee wife's sake. You regularly batter her silly. Last time you would have killed her if I hadn't stopped you. You nearly killed me. You're getting worse, Scobie. You know you are.' Frank leaned eagerly forward, one hand pushing back his hair. 'Now listen, there's a man in my office who's an alcoholic. He doesn't make any secret of the fact that he's a member of Alcoholics Anonymous. It's worked for him. Maybe it could work for you, Scobie.'

Scobie sighed. 'I know you mean well, son, and I know I should give up and I will give up. I promise you.'

Frank banged back on his chair again. 'Oh shut up, Scobie. We're all sick of your stupid promises.'

'No. This time I mean it, Frank.'

'OK. It's up to you, Scobie. But as I say, I hope you realise you're not only harming yourself but your family. *And* you're losing friends. *And* things are going to get tougher. After what you did to Constable MacLean's face the police are more likely to kick you down the stairs, down the whole length of Turner Street and Garngad Road, the next time they come to arrest you.'

'This is one hell of a way to speak to a man when he's just come out of hospital. It's not Christian.'

'And don't get it into your head,' Frank went on, 'that Father Riley will believe you either. You've had a beating from him before, Scobie, and you're very likely to get one again.'

'OK. OK. First thing after Mass tomorrow I'll go and see Father Shannon. Just to see what he has to say about the League of the Cross. I'm not promising any more than that.'

'How about the AA? I could go with you.'

'Let me sleep on that, son. I mean – it's such a terrible disgrace.'

'What?' Frank rolled his eyes and smacked a palm to his brow. 'You that's beaten your wife? You that's fought with all your friends? You that's vomited all over the place, been scraped up from the gutter – you think going to the AA is a disgrace?'

'Well, you know what I mean.'

'No, I don't know what you mean, Scobie.'

After a few seconds Scobie half-laughed and said, 'A lot of us used to think – I mean, not just me, even your own da – that you were a bit of a weak-kneed jessy with all that poetry and stuff. But you're not, are you, son?'

'Scobie, you can be tough inside without looking tough on the outside, or by taking part in violence. Anyway, toughness of any kind isn't the be-all and end-all of everything.'

'It is in Glasgow, son.'

'You only know one part of the city, Scobie.'

'It's where I live.'

'Your life could change – but it's up to you.'

Scobie sighed. 'OK. We'll give it a whirl.'

'The AA. Good man!' Then, seeing the worried apprehension in Scobie's eyes, Frank added, 'Don't worry, I'll come with you. We'll just look in and see what goes on. As I say, it's entirely up to you.'

Bridie's curiosity had got the better of her feelings of hopelessness. She'd been listening at the kitchen door. Frank found her when he was on his way through to the room. Once they'd shut the door behind them, she said, 'Oh Frank, do you think it'll work this time?'

Frank flung himself on to the bed and shielded his eyes with one hand for a few seconds. 'I don't know. I can't be by his side watching him all the time. If I can just get him to the AA, I think that's his best chance. This man in my office says it worked for him. Of course it's alcoholics helping one another. They know what it can be like. No doubt they'll keep an eye on him when I can't. I've my work to go to.'

'You've done wonders already. By the way, did you see Michael?'

'Yes, it's true enough. He's packed in his job. He's going to do the rounds of the booths. He reckons that way he'll make some money and escape from You-Know-Who.'

'Talking about jobs – Doris has gone back to work in Daly's. You wouldn't have thought she needed to, would you? I mean they're not like us. I need to go out for the money because we're saving up.'

'I expect she couldn't stand being cooped up in Blackhill all day and every day. I don't blame her.'

'Come to think of it, Frank, I wouldn't like to be cooped up here all day and every day. Especially if you weren't with me. I could stand anything just as long as we're together.'

He smiled over at her, his eyes becoming dreamy. 'I love you. And one day I'm going to take you out of all this. You're going to have a lovely roomy house with high carved ceilings and deep pile luxurious carpets on the floor.'

She'd heard it all before so many times – word for word.

'Everything your heart desires, Bridie, you will have. I promise you.'

'Yes, dear,' Bridie said, but her heart was heavy. Frank had little enough time for his writing after he came home from a hard day's work. Now some of that precious time was going to be taken up by struggling to keep Scobie on the straight and narrow. If anyone could sort Scobie out, Frank could. But even so, she feared it was a hopeless task. They were on a slippery slope, her and Frank. They were being dragged down. Frank wasn't getting the chance he deserved. More and more she feared nothing but a black pit awaited them. Frank couldn't see it. Part of his life, part of his mind, was separate from her – lost in the images of his fiction. He had another world in his head to which he could withdraw, escape. It was a world that gave him enormous pleasure and satisfaction, despite the hard work involved. In his world he could give life a unity, a meaning, a shape to suit the purpose of his fiction.

Maybe the getting away from Turner Street, maybe the dream house, the carpets, the furniture, the clothes – maybe all of that was no more than fiction.

She picked up her book, adjusted her spectacles, and began reading.

Chapter Thirty

They were sitting, one on either side of the kitchen fire. The fire was burning cheerily, but its brightness was not reflected in the faces of either Doris or Andrina.

'Talk about golf widows,' Andrina said. 'We're karate widows.'

Doris sighed. 'When it's not karate it's work with Bernard.'

'Robert's the same.'

'He doesn't work at nights, does he? Teaching's a day job.'

'It's supposed to be. But he's always bringing work home at night – to mark things, give assessments, write lectures, prepare future projects, things like that. Then there's Parent- Teacher Association nights at the school. At weekends he often takes pupils for painting and sketching trips. He says his workload is nothing compared with the English and Maths teachers. Like a lot of people, I used to think teachers had a right cushy job with such short hours, nine to four. I thought, what a walk-over. Nothing of the kind. It's the most stressful, demanding occupation. They need all the holidays they can get. Especially a conscientious teacher like Robert. He really cares about his pupils, worries about them.' It was her turn to sigh. 'They take up more of Robert's time and thoughts than I do.'

'Knowing how you feel makes me feel a wee bit better. I keep wondering if there's something terribly wrong with me.' Doris patted her lacquered confection of hair and tried to give a light-hearted laugh. 'I can't think what, but there you are.'

'There's nothing wrong with you, Doris. You're a very pretty girl.'

'Right enough he still wants me for love-making.' Despite her efforts to keep her voice light, it dropped into bitterness. 'If you can call it that.'

'It's different with men. They don't understand.'

'You're only a year older than me. What makes you an expert on men?' Immediately the words were out, Doris's face crumpled with distress. 'I'm terribly sorry, Andrina. I didn't mean to be nasty.'

'It's all right. It's just that Scotsmen are supposed to be notoriously bad at showing their emotions. They think it's being soft; they have to have this "hard man" image. But I suppose I was meaning how it is with Robert and me. I've no other personal experience. All I had before was romantic stories, and we shouldn't go by them. They're just a big con.'

'Definitely. Not one of them that I've ever read described the quick in-out-and-Bob's-your-uncle that Scotsmen call love-making.'

Both women suddenly hunched forward, overcome by a fit of the giggles. At last Doris managed, 'Sorry for being so terribly coarse and unladylike, Andrina. But some men drive you to it, don't they?' She lit up a Woodbine. 'I take it you still don't smoke.'

'My mother would have a fit.'

'She certainly knows how to lay down the law. A terribly strong character, is she?'

Andrina hesitated. 'She has very strong views.'

'Same thing.'

'I don't know. I worry about her a lot. She's so . . . so intense, so highly strung. She cares too much, I think. Especially about me. She phones me a couple of times every day. And I see her at least a couple of times a week.'

'You're an only child. I suppose that explains it. My ma always had too much on her plate – too many problems with my da, for a start – to have any time to bother about me. Or any of us, for that matter.'

'She would care about you just the same.'

Doris shrugged. 'God alone knows. It's the same with Bernard.' She avoided Andrina's eyes. Pride wouldn't allow her to admit to being totally unloved. 'I don't know if he cares much about me.' She blew smoke out and tossed her head back as if it didn't really matter.

'Oh Doris,' Andrina murmured, 'I'm sure he does.'

'You don't know him. He's Mister Charming when he's here. The perfect gent.'

Andrina didn't know what to say. The last time they'd all been having dinner together, Bernard had indeed been the perfect gentleman, although she'd found his reaction to certain innocent things she said a bit confusing and disturbing. When, for instance, she'd been trying her best to be a good hostess and asking each of them if they wanted second portions of anything or more wine, she'd said to Bernard, 'What can I do for you, Bernard?' His only reply was to raise an eyebrow and slide her one of his slightly amused sideways looks. Doris and Robert had been chatting to each other and hadn't noticed. It was nothing really. Yet it made her flush and quickly divert her attention away from him.

There had been one or two other little incidents like that – subtle, fleeting, and dangerous. She had not been able to relax until he and Doris had left.

Tonight, the four of them would be having dinner together again, after the men returned from the karate club.

'Did he mind you starting work again?' Andrina asked.

Doris puffed at her cigarette and shook her head as if not trusting herself to speak.

Andrina rose. 'They'll be back soon. I'd better put the potatoes on. How about an aperitif?'

'That would be terribly nice, I'm sure.'

They were still in the kitchen sipping their Martinis when the men returned, filling the small room, dominating it with bouncy swaggers, as if barely able to contain their enormous energy.

'What's for dinner?' Robert asked, rubbing his hands together. 'We're starving.'

Andrina went over to peer into pots and examine the contents of the oven. 'Robert, give Bernard a drink. Oh, and open the wine, please. I'll just get all this organised and on to the table. I've got baked ham with pineapple to start with, and apple pie with custard.'

'Sounds good. What'll you have, Bernard?'

'If you're opening the wine, a glass of that'll do.'

'Just plonk by your standards, Bernard. I can't afford champagne on a teacher's wages.'

'I've told you. You can get a job with me any day.'

Robert laughed. 'I've certainly got plenty of experience with crowd control for a start. When the kids get out at so-called playtime, it's like releasing a crowd of wild animals. My mother tells me it was never like that in her day. According to her they were too afraid of the teachers even to make a noise in the playground. Not that I believe her. At least not to that extent.'

'I was afraid of you when I was a kid,' Bernard said.

'Never! You've never been afraid of anybody in your life, Bernard. You were a right tearaway when you were a kid. I'm not that old, mate. I remember.'

Bernard grinned. 'Well, let's say all the kids, myself included, respected you.'

'That's better.' Robert raised his glass. 'Here's to your continuing success.'

Bernard took a sip of wine. 'Thanks. It's not all plain sailing, but I'm getting there.'

'Where?' Doris suddenly butted into the conversation. 'Getting where?'

'Where I want to go.'

'Oh? And where's that, Bernard? I'd be terribly interested to know.'

'Soup's out,' Andrina announced. 'Sit in, everyone. Have a glass of wine, Doris. Doris and I were having a lovely chat while we were on our own, weren't we, Doris?' She hastily filled Doris's glass, knowing from past experience that drink put Doris into a more happy and relaxed mood.

'This is delicious,' Bernard said. 'I know I've told you before but you really are an excellent cook, Andrina.'

'Thank you.' Andrina felt pleased. She was proud of her talent in the kitchen. She had her mother to thank for that. Sophie was up to cordon bleu standard, really first class. She'd never formally taught Andrina, but Andrina had watched her mother's culinary efforts with great interest. She had picked up a lot of tips just by watching and admiring.

The sweet (one of Robert's favourites) was another triumph for which everyone congratulated her. By the time it was consumed much wine had flowed. Robert had very quickly had to open another bottle. And then another. Everyone was getting very merry.

They had brandy with the coffee. Robert and Bernard had two brandies. Eventually Bernard said, 'My God, Robert. I forgot I was driving. I hope there's no cops about. I can't afford to lose my licence or get into any trouble with the police in my line of business.'

'What the hell,' Robert said with a somewhat drunken wave of his hand. 'Stay overnight. We've a spare room.'

Doris giggled. 'Great. But there's only one teeny wee problem. I haven't brought a nightie.'

'Andrina can lend you one, can't you, darling?'

'Yes, of course,' Andrina murmured. She suddenly felt stone cold sober.

Doris said, 'I'd have to leave here not later than eight-thirty in the morning. Daly's like their young ladies to be ready to start work a wee bit before nine.'

'I'll give you a lift in,' Robert said. 'We'll let Bernard have a long lie, seeing he's a night bird. Unless you've any early jobs on tomorrow, have you, Bernard?'

'I'll stay on one condition.' Bernard winked at Robert. 'And that's if Andrina gives me breakfast in bed.'

'Sure, sure,' Robert laughed. 'Nothing but the best of service in this house.'

Andrina felt herself flush. She desperately fought to appear calm. 'I'll do nothing of the kind. What do you think I am?'

'Darling, we were only joking.' Robert was obviously enjoying the joke. He was drunk. She felt annoyed with him for being so stupid.

Doris too – equally blind, equally stupid – was laughing. 'Quite right, Andrina. Don't encourage him.'

'Encourage him?' Caution smoothed out Andrina's voice.

Doris said, 'He doesn't need any encouragement to be the typical Scotsman who thinks the little woman is just there for his convenience – to serve him hand and foot, to use when and as he pleases. Just part of his goods and chattels. It's terribly old-fashioned, but there you are . . .'

'Andrina doesn't know anything about that type of man, Doris,' Robert said. 'She's married to me, remember?'

'Ooh.' Doris widened her mascaraed eyes. 'Modest with it, isn't he?'

'I'd better start the washing up.' Andrina began stacking the dishes.

'Oh, leave those till the morning,' Robert said. 'You'll have all day tomorrow to wash them. It's late. Let's all get to bed.'

Andrina rolled her eyes. 'I've nothing else to do all day tomorrow, of course.'

'I'll give you a hand with them tomorrow before I leave,' Bernard said.

Robert put his arm around her waist. 'Go on. Take Doris through and fix her up with a nightie and whatever else she needs. I'll lock up and be through in a minute.'

In the spare room with Doris, Andrina could hear the two men laughing together in the kitchen. Deep, rumbling male sounds. She imagined she detected a coarseness. She wondered if they were telling each other vulgar jokes. The mood Robert was in, she wouldn't put it past him. He was always different in Bernard's company – rougher, tougher – not the quiet, artistic, sensitive Robert she knew. She experienced a violent spasm of hatred towards Bernard. Then fear at the thought of being alone in the house with him next day. It seemed impossible to face such a prospect. Utterly impossible. Doris was chatting away to her but she wasn't listening. Her mind was darting desperately about. At last a solution occurred to her. First thing in the morning she'd slip next door and ask Josie to come in and stay with her until Bernard left.

She was so relieved at the thought, as soon as she went to bed and her head hit the pillow, she sank into a deep sleep. Too deep.

When she woke up, Robert had gone from her side. She lay listening, totally alert now, and apprehensive. She heard Doris and Robert call out to Bernard, 'See you later'. She heard the outside door close. She was alone in the house with Bernard. The realisation made her heart race in alarm. The whole bed seemed to reverberate with the beat of her pulse.

She heard his footsteps cross the hall and fade. Into the other bedroom? Or the kitchen? She strained to listen. The footsteps grew nearer again. The bedroom door opened and Bernard came in. He stood over her, holding a cup of tea. 'Morning, sleepy-head. I've brought you some tea.' He wore nothing but a pair of white cotton underpants. His tanned, muscular body was acutely disconcerting and frightening.

She was suddenly aware too of how she must look – her tousled hair, her lack of make-up. Embarrassment added to her other emotions. As she pushed herself further up on her pillow in order to drink the tea, he sat down on top of the covers. She shivered, unsure whether it was caused by the cold air on her bare shoulders and arms, or if it was her apprehension.

'Cold?' He reached out to rub her arms and shoulders.

'I'm all right.' She shrank back into the pillows and tried to concentrate on finishing the cup of tea. But she couldn't stop herself from babbling in between sips. 'I don't usually bother with tea. I'm an early riser, as a rule. I don't know what went wrong this morning . . . I'm usually up and making Robert's breakfast long before he's up. He should have wakened me. It's most unlike him to rush out like this without any breakfast . . . He must have slept in too. Of course, we were very late last night and we all had more than the usual to drink . . .' She couldn't stop.

Eventually he took the cup and saucer from her and laid it on the bedside table. Then he just sat staring silently down at her until her skin prickled with heat under his careful scrutiny. Then, with one easy movement, his mouth was on her with a tender passion she had never experienced before. Through his lips she called out, 'No . . . no, this is wrong . . .'

All she could picture in her mind's eye was her mother's face looking down at her in horror.

Her mother and God.

Chapter Thirty-One

As Bernard eased back from her, she saw that his face had changed. His features, normally hard-edged, had softened. His eyes had lost their cold menace. Instead, from them waves of tenderness washed over her. She knew then, despite her protestations, that she already belonged to him. Nevertheless, as soon as his lips covered hers again, she struggled and tried to move away. But suddenly, without any apparent fumbling or movement, his big frame engulfed her. He was pushing inside her. She was stunned, yet at the same time physically aroused. Mind and body became a mad merry-go-round of conflicting, confusing thoughts, emotions and sensations. She was horrified and panic-stricken. At the same time her body opened and revelled in hysterical ecstasy. As his thrustings grew faster and deeper, she heard herself make coarse, uninhibited animal noises.

Eventually they both cried out in unison. Then he withdrew and began gently kissing her eyes, her cheeks, her nose, her neck, while whispering over and over again, 'I love you . . . I love you . . . I've always loved you . . . You're so soft and feminine and adorable . . . You hold me like a velvet vice . . . My adorable little velvet . . .'

Shock and horror returned and she began to struggle to free herself of him. 'Please let me go. Please go away. This is so wrong.'

'No. We love each other. That can't be wrong.'

Somehow she got out of the bed, fled to the bathroom and locked herself in. She slumped against the door. Unable to bear the guilt, she tried to pretend to herself, despite the ecstasy still pulsing inside her, that nothing had happened. Eventually she persuaded herself that what had happened hadn't been her fault. She had nothing to blame herself for. She would not be the recipient of God's wrath for condoning the sin of adultery. She had been raped. Admittedly it had been a loving rape, but a rape nevertheless.

'Andrina, darling, are you all right?' Bernard shook the door handle.

'Please go away, Bernard.' Then, to make sure he'd go, she lied with feeling, 'My mother said she was coming for coffee this morning. I'd die if she arrived and found you here. Even the thought makes me feel sick. But I'll be all right as long as you go away.'

She heard him sigh through the door. 'All right, for your sake. But I'll be in touch soon.'

She listened to his heavy tread across the hall. Then the outside door shut. Still she felt apprehensive. Very gently she creaked the bathroom door open. The silence in the shadowy hall reassured her. She hurried across to the kitchen, praying as she passed the phone that it wouldn't ring. She made herself a cup of strong coffee and sat hunched over it, nursing it, trying to sort out her thoughts. But her thoughts had become a dark whirlpool of guilt and fear.

She was illogically certain that her mother would know. The certainty tightened her into a tense ball, waiting for the phone to ring. When it did suddenly jangle into life, it sent her rushing to the sink to violently retch and vomit. At the same time the phone kept exploding in harsh bursts of sound, filling the house with its relentless insistence.

She went to answer it eventually but had to lean against the wall, she felt so weak and faint.

'Darling, are you all right? I'm phoning from the box in Garngad Road. I was worried.'

'Just leave me alone.'

'Darling Andrina, I love you.'

She replaced the receiver as if it was burning her fingers.

Hurrying through to the bathroom she ran a bath and threw in plenty of perfumed bath salts. Her mother might arrive at any moment and smell sex on her. She realised she was being ridiculous. It was Friday, her mother's turn of having the daily coffee morning shared by the ladies of the Guild in Bearsden.

Her mother couldn't possibly arrive on the doorstep this morning. It didn't matter.

Perfume rose with clouds of steam from the bath, thickening and sickening the air. Andrina lay in the hot water, trying to purify herself physically and mentally.

Beginning to relax, despite herself, she remembered the smooth flowing, then quick ecstasy of Bernard inside her, and marvelled at it. It was something she had never felt with Robert. She closed her eyes, remembering Robert and Doris, but they were only a passing thought. Her mother was by far the most overpowering concern. It was as if her mother was there in the flesh, her flinty eyes narrow with disgust and hatred. And behind her, a dark ominous shadow of a vengeful God. Nothing could blot out that face, those eyes. After bathing and dressing, Andrina tried to keep herself as busy as possible, to concentrate on other things. She was grateful for the debris of the night before: the dirty dishes cluttering the round table in the dining alcove in the kitchen; the pots and oven dishes lying on top of the cooker and on the draining-board at the side of the sink, food hardening round the edges; the crushed table napkins; the crumbs on the floor.

She set about clearing up and washing the dishes at breathless speed. Instead of just sweeping and mopping the floor, she got down on her knees as a sort of penance and thoroughly scrubbed every corner of it. Then she went through to the two bedrooms and forced herself to strip off the beds and remake them with clean sheets and pillow-cases. She stuffed the other sheets into the washing machine, convinced that they smelled of sex.

By lunchtime the house was immaculate, the sheets were folded over the clothes horse in front of the fire, and she couldn't think what else to do. She didn't feel like anything to eat, but forced herself to heat some soup left over from the night before. While she was absent-mindedly eating it the phone rang, making her nerves jangle into life again. She went through to the hall and stood staring in anguish at the instrument before gingerly lifting the receiver to her ear.

'Hello?'

'You took your time answering.'

'Oh, it's you, Mummy.'

'Who did you think it would be? Were you expecting someone else to call?'

'No, I wasn't thinking. I've been doing a bit of spring cleaning.'

'It'll soon be Christmas.'

'You know what I mean.'

'You and Robert will be coming here for Christmas lunch, I hope.'

'Oh yes, thanks, Mummy.'

'I'm inviting Robert's mother as well.'

'That's kind of you.'

'She'd be on her own otherwise.'

'Yes.'

'Are you all right?'

'Of course.'

'You sound as if you're not all there.'

Andrina affected a laugh. 'What a thing to say.'

'How did last night go?'

'Last night?' Her voice tightened warily.

'You had people to dinner – you said.'

'Oh, but I told you when you phoned last night. They enjoyed the meal, everything went well. I told you what I made. For starters we had . . .'

'Who were these people?'

'Mummy, I told you – a friend of Robert's from the school, and his wife.' In a way it wasn't a lie and so she could say the words with some conviction. 'How are you, Mummy? How did your coffee morning go?'

'Fine. Fine.'

It was Andrina's turn to detect something wrong, something subtle she couldn't place. 'Are you all right, Mummy?'

'Why shouldn't I be all right?'

'You always go to such extremes. I hope you aren't overdoing things. Did you bake for the coffee morning ladies?'

'I certainly wouldn't dream of offering anyone shop cakes and I hope you never do either. You never know what's in bought stuff.'

A silence followed. Unusual for her mother. 'Are you still there, Mummy?'

'Yes.'

'Are you sure you're all right?'

'A bit over-strained, that's all. There are very high standards to live up to in a place like Bearsden. I have to be extra careful.'

'Nobody could have higher standards than you, Mummy. You've nothing whatsoever to worry about on that score. You're a wonderful housekeeper, a superb cook, a conscientious Christian . . .' Andrina gave a short laugh. 'If anyone needed character references for the place, yours would be absolutely impeccable.'

'I've always done my best,' her mother said, and there was another silence.

'Do you want me to come over and see you today?' Andrina asked.

'No. I'll see you and Robert on Monday. I'll have to go now. I'll phone again tonight.'

'Take care, Mummy.'

'Why do you say that?' The usual edge of suspicion returned to Sophie's voice.

Andrina sighed. 'Just because I love you and want you to keep safe and well.'

'Come straight after you've been to church. Our church here is just along the road, so I'll be home long before you get here and have everything ready before you and Robert arrive.'

'I'll look forward to it, Mummy.'

The phone clicked. For a few seconds, Andrina stood looking at it. There was this almost psychic thing between her mother and herself. Usually it only worked the one way. That is, Sophie seemed to immediately tune in to the worried wavelengths of her daughter. This time it was the other way around. Something was worrying her mother and, Andrina felt certain, it wasn't just about her.

In a way she was glad of the distraction, to take her mind off herself and the enormity of what had happened. It helped too to pay a visit to Josie next door and have a cup of tea and a chat before going out to buy something for Robert's tea. At least she could feel safe for half an hour or so in Josie's, knowing that her mother couldn't burst in and discover her, although it occurred to her that her life – certainly her relationship with her mother –was becoming more and more based on deceit. Deceit had taken root, and was growing like a pernicious weed, more and more out of her control.

She longed to confide in Josie about Bernard, but she felt sick at the thought. Later, when she was travelling into town, or while she was strolling around the shops, there were times when her spirits lightened and she began to forget about what had happened. For brief moments she actually felt happy. Then the memory would suddenly flood back and she would feel sick again. It hadn't been a dream. Yet it was impossible to believe. And all the time her body betrayed her by aching for Bernard to hold her, to engulf her again.

'Oh God, please forgive me,' she kept thinking. 'Oh God, don't let my mother find out.'

She had a meal of the best fillet steak waiting for Robert, and she greeted him with unusual warmth. They had never been all that demonstrative with each other.

He laughed. 'To what do I owe this special treatment?'

'What do you mean? Can't I just make you a nice meal and kiss you hello without being questioned?'

'Calm down. I was only joking.'

'Sorry. For a minute I thought you sounded like my mother.'

'Your mother?' Robert echoed incredulously.

'Suspicious – you know how she's always questioning me.'

'She cares about you. Dotes on you. I suppose you could say we have that in common.'

'She phoned earlier. I thought she sounded . . . I don't know . . . a bit worried.'

'Tell me something new. Your mother's a worrier, especially about you.'

'No, this time I thought it wasn't just me.'

'What made you think that? What did she say?'

Andrina shrugged. 'Probably it was just my imagination.'

She was glad of the diversion. Glad that Robert enjoyed the steak and had two helpings of chocolate mousse.

Later, in bed, they made love and she tried to be as affectionate as possible. Making love with Robert had never been in any way unpleasant. On the contrary, she had always believed it to be perfectly adequate. She realised now that this was only because she'd had no other experience to compare it with. She kept thinking about the other experience as Robert made love to her, kept struggling to purge the image of Bernard from her mind.

'I must never, never, allow such a thing to happen again.' She repeated the words to herself like a mantra. 'Never, never, never.' She would never even wear that nightdress again. It was made of green silk, low cut to show her cleavage, and trimmed with lace. It had a split up each side to the top of her thighs, the slits also trimmed with lace. She loved beautiful, sensual underwear. It was something her mother no longer could see and in which she felt free to indulge. She always kept her underwear in a locked drawer just in case her mother ever decided to poke about in the bedroom. If her mother found a locked drawer Andrina could always pretend that it contained Robert's papers for the school.

Lies. Lies. Lies. They were the eggs she had to continually walk on.

'I love you,' she said to Robert. But he was already sound asleep.

Chapter Thirty-Two

Even going along the few yards to the shops, the respectable Bearsden shops where she met respectable Bearsden people, was spoiled. Sophie hurried along like a criminal, eyes furtively, apprehensively darting around. In the shops she was absent-minded, forgot what she'd come for, didn't hear the assistant speaking to her, jumped when someone said hello.

She kept struggling to quell her panic, kept telling herself that her filth of parents weren't the only ones in the world with Noble for a second name. How ironic the name was, how totally inept. Noble. Noble, of all things! Of all things, noble they were not. She was afraid to make any enquiries. Afraid of what she might find. Yet she was obsessed with finding, ferreting out. She had to know. She couldn't live with the fear, the disgrace, of suddenly being confronted, being claimed by them in public. She had to know from where to hide.

She kept urging herself to have some common sense. Her fears were illogical. They had last set eyes on each other when she was a small child, a lifetime ago. How could they recognise her? How could she recognise them?

Oh, she would recognise them all right. Their disgusting behaviour had been carved with a red hot poker on her mind. She burned with hate at the thought of them. The fire of her hatred had never been quenched.

She had prayed a thousand times that they were dead, and now she prayed for their death with even more fervour. Going to church had become an agony almost beyond endurance, in case she would suddenly come upon them in the congregation. Especially the service on Christmas Day.

'Are you feeling all right, Sophie?' McPherson asked. As usual they were walking along a little apart, he with a leather-gloved hand holding his bible, she clutching her handbag.

Sophie was so abstracted she didn't hear him. He did not speak louder, but injected his voice with more urgency.

'Sophie!'

'What?'

'Is there something wrong? You look so tense and anxious.'

'Do I?'

'I thought you were looking forward to Andrina and Robert and Jean coming for Christmas lunch.'

Christmas had gone right out of her head. Spoiled. Forgotten. Irrelevant. Oh, she'd prepared the lunch. The Christmas pudding and the cake had been made ages ago, in another, happier world. The soup, the turkey and all the trimmings she'd prepared yesterday. It all had been done automatically, as if in a dream.

'I am looking forward to them coming. Everything's ready. I told them to come after church.'

'You haven't seemed well for some time. I think you should see Doctor Manders. He seems a nice chap. Remember we met him at the Allisons' bridge party?'

Doctor. Doctor. Take a few minutes from your bridge party with the Reverend Dinwoodie and his genteel little wife, and cure me of my putrid, perverted parents. 'It's my nerves,' she said. 'I haven't been sleeping too well recently. Once all the excitement of Christmas and New Year's over, I'll be able to relax.'

'Old Manders might be able to give you something.'

A couple of doses of Belladonna poison to help Duncan and Agnes Noble die in the agony they deserve? 'I'll see. But I'll have to wait until after the holidays now. I expect his surgery will be closed over Christmas and New Year.'

'Phone and ask.'

'On Christmas Day?'

'Well, as soon as you can. You look like death, Sophie, and you seemed absolutely radiant with good health for a while. Something's gone wrong.'

'All right. All right,' she hissed at him. They were approaching the church now and she was obsessed with her private agony. People were streaming through the gates from all directions, stylishly dressed, carefully coiffured, dignified, smiling people. People content with their lot. The sound of car doors shutting made an orchestra with the chiming of the church bells. From inside the church the organ added its richer, deeper notes.

Happy, happy day, the whole orchestra proclaimed.

God, oh God, don't let it be them, Sophie kept praying. Have mercy. Help me. Let them be dead.

The church was packed; the pews in the middle, at the sides, up on the balcony were all full. They sat downstairs near the back. The front pews were all private, booked and paid for. Sophie's eyes scannned all the heads. She couldn't see them. Unless they were upstairs. Unless it wasn't them at all. All during the service she prayed it wasn't them at all.

Later, after she'd arrived safely home, she was able to relax with relief. Putting the last touches to the lunch kept her busy. She was able to greet Andrina and Robert and Robert's mother in a bright and cheerful manner.

'Happy Christmas, Mummy.'

'Happy Christmas, Andrina. Happy Christmas, Robert. Happy Christmas, Jean. Come away in.'

She hurried her greetings. McPherson was the one to do the kissing and back-slapping on such occasions, not her. Any physical display in public she regarded as embarrassingly indecent, worryingly unchristian.

Once coats and hats had been put away and the guests settled beside the fire, McPherson offered them what they had both come to call 'a little refreshment'. Sophie had always been against drink and had often in the past nagged McPherson about his indulgence in it. In Bearsden, however, it seemed one of the civilised things to do: to have 'a little refreshment'. After all, it said in the bible, 'a little wine for the stomach's sake'. An aperitif was the thing before lunch or dinner, wine with a main meal, a brandy or a liqueur afterwards. At least, when one had guests.

Andrina and Robert had a Martini. McPherson had a

whisky and lemonade and Sophie and Jean sipped at sherries. There were two bottles of wine to have with the meal, a claret and a chardonnay. The white was chilling in the fridge. The red had been opened to breathe at room temperature.

There were crimson and gold crackers and yellow and orange and green and blue paper hats. It was a merry and enjoyable meal. Everyone complimented Sophie on it. The only complaint was that they'd eaten too much. Afterwards, they opened all the presents.

Robert gave McPherson a box of cigars which he much appreciated. He had acquired a taste for a good cigar, although he still smoked his pipe when relaxing at home. The cigars were normally kept for special occasions, either when visiting in Bearsden or after business meals in the city or elsewhere.

Sophie gave Andrina a leather-bound, gilt-edged copy of *A Life of Christian Self-Denial* by Lady Jessica Ford-Smythe.

Robert, Andrina and Jean Anderson stayed for a late-afternoon tea – Earl Grey tea, turkey sandwiches, Chistmas cake and chocolate peppermint creams. A lovely time was had by all.

'You must all come to me at New Year,' Jean Anderson said.

'No, no. Please come to me,' Andrina pleaded. 'We had New Year lunch at Adelphi Street last time. It's our turn, isn't it Robert?'

'Definitely,' Robert agreed. 'We insist. New Year's lunch at Monteith Row.' They always made it lunch rather than an evening meal for Sophie and Jean's sake. They didn't like to be out late.

The invitation was accepted and goodbyes were said. Another kissing, back-slapping, hand-shaking performance from McPherson, and another hasty wave and shrinking away from Sophie. She waved again from the window as Robert and Andrina and Jean walked along Drymen Road to the bus stop.

'I should have run them home,' McPherson said.

'You did offer.'

'I know, but I should have insisted.'

'Too late now. There's the bus.'

'You'd think Robert could afford a car by now. Even a second-hand one.'

'You know how poor a teacher's wages are. He dresses well, thank goodness. Both of them do.'

'Yes, he's a decent chap. But Andrina could have done better. She's a fine-looking girl.'

Except for the Noble red hair and green eyes. The words were a bitter sneer in Sophie's mind. 'Yes, she could have been the wife of Doctor James Honeyman. Such an elegant gentleman with that carnation he always wears in his lapel. Or the wife of that wealthy lawyer, Blair Matheson. Think of it. She could have been mistress of one of those lovely big villas on Roman Road.'

McPherson sighed his regret along with hers. 'Pity. Yes, a great pity. Such a lovely girl, she could have had the very best.'

Before she'd left, Jean had insisted on washing up all the lunch and tea dishes. Andrina had dried them while Sophie put everything away in its proper place.

After they left, however, and McPherson had settled himself in front of the television (a new acquisition and much enjoyed), Sophie went through to the kitchen and washed all the dishes over again. She trusted no one to clean anything really thoroughly and conscientiously but herself. Then she hoovered the dining room carpet, examining under the table and chairs and sideboard and in every corner for any stray crumbs.

McPherson felt like calling out, 'Do you need to do that today – Christmas Day – a holiday?' But he saved his breath. He knew Sophie well enough to realise she *did* need to do it. No, she had more than a need to scour and clean and scrub and wash and hoover. It was an obsession. She was the same with her personal hygiene. He often said, if she could have steeped herself in bleach or disinfectant and boiled herself to sterilise herself, she would. She bathed and washed her hair every day – more than once a day, he suspected. And she had developed an absolute compulsion to keep scrubbing at her nails and hands.

He decided just to relax and enjoy a pipe and watch the Christmas variety programme. Sophie would come through and sit down when she felt she could. Even then, of course, her fingers would be busy, knitting or sewing or darning or mending. This time she came through and, much to his chagrin, seemed to want to talk.

'Remember the Reverend Dinwoodie mentioned the Nobles?'

'Yes.'

'Did he say anything else to you?'

'You were there.'

'You've played golf with him since then.'

'Yes, but . . .'

'Well, did he mention them then?'

'I don't think so.'

'Think, think, think now.'

'For goodness sake, Sophie, there's surely no need to get so worked up.'

'Did he mention their first names?'

'Why do you want to know? You don't believe they could be relations of yours, do you? You told me . . .'

'Never mind what I told you. Did he mention their first names?'

McPherson puffed at his pipe in silence for a few seconds. Then he said, 'No. The Nobles have never been mentioned since that night of the dinner.'

'I wonder how I could find out. I've *got* to find out. I can't stand it any longer.'

'Can't stand what any longer? Sophie, is there something I ought to know?' He felt suddenly uneasy, apprehensive.

She hesitated, wringing at her hands, her eyes twitching vaguely about.

'Sophie!' He had known there was something wrong. He could only hope it was nothing that might affect his good reputation.

'All right. All right. Maybe I should have told you. But I never thought there would be any need. As far as I was concerned, my parents were dead. But in fact they might not be.'

'What the hell is that supposed to mean? They're either dead or they're alive – there can't be any "might" about it.'

'I was taken from them because they . . . they were not fit to be parents. I was taken into care, put in an institution. I never saw them again. I never wanted to see them again. They're dreadful people. Cruel, vulgar, common, wicked . . .'

'Good God! And you've not only lied to me – you've told the Pembertons, the Brodies, the Dinwoodies, and God knows who else in Bearsden, that your parents were dead.'

'Maybe they are,' she cried out wretchedly. 'I don't know.'

'But you think the Nobles. . . ? Good God, Sophie.'

'How can I find out? You'll have to help me, Andrew.'

'Calm down. I'll find out.'

'How? What will you do?'

'There's the electoral roll for a start. That'll give their full names.'

'Duncan and Agnes Noble.'

'Duncan and Agnes Noble,' he repeated after her. 'I'll find out. But what we're going to do if it is them, Sophie – God alone knows.'

Chapter Thirty-Three

The Alcoholics Anonymous office was up a dark and dirty stair in West Nile Street. Scobie promised he'd meet Frank there straight from work – straight from Frank's work, that is. Scobie finished work earlier than Frank.

Frank had to do a tax return or some sort of extra work this week, and he didn't get out of his office until after seven. He would just be able to grab a sandwich somewhere and reach Scobie in West Nile Street in time for quarter to eight.

The AA meeting started at eight, but when Frank had phoned they'd told him to come at about quarter to, so that he could have a cup of tea and meet everyone.

The AA office was round the corner from the Bay Horse pub, and Scobie decided he'd nip in for a pint before Frank arrived. He hadn't let on to Frank but he was up to high doh about the meeting. He really needed a drink. At first, arriving at the close in West Nile Street, he'd paced back and forth trying to work up courage. He'd cursed Frank for putting him into this agonising situation. At the same time he knew it wasn't Frank. Frank had left it to him.

Frank had said, 'Look at you, man. Look at you.' And that was enough. He knew how he looked. He knew what he was doing to himself. It hadn't mattered enough when he thought of what he was doing to Frank or to Carragh or to his family. It had been bad enough to know that he was hurting them physically, but it was his personal hurt that was really getting to him. He was hurting deep inside. He was lost. He was lonely. Even in a crowd, he was lonely. Even in bed with his wife he was lost and alone.

For the first time he could see, and he could accept in his own mind, that he needed help. He wanted help. But first of all he needed just one pint to give him the courage to go and get it.

He was still in the pub when Frank arrived.

'I thought I'd find you in here,' Frank said. 'OK, what's it to be, Scobie? Are you coming with me to the AA, or do I leave you here and let you end up in that gutter outside? It's up to you, wee man.'

Scobie nodded. For once the drink wasn't making him feel a big man with a swagger. He was still a wee man, and he was hell of a frightened one. He hadn't a clue why. But he growled, 'What the fuck are we standing here for? I said I was going, didn't I?'

They went along West Nile Street, in the close and up the stairs in silence. Both of them were afraid to say a wrong word.

In the office – which consisted of a biggish room with brown linoleum on the floor and some folding chairs – men and women were standing or sitting around in groups drinking tea and talking. A man at a small side table was pouring mugs of tea, only half filling them out of consideration for the recipients, so that they wouldn't spill the tea and draw attention to their shaking hands.

The man said to Frank as he handed him the mug, 'Hello there, my name's Jimmy. Have I met you? Have you been here before?'

'No, I'm Frank. I'm with Scobie, my father-in-law here.'

'Right, Scobie, havin' trouble with your bevvy, eh?'

'I suppose you could say that.'

'Well, you're in the right place. There's none of us will tell you you're an alcoholic. That's something you'll need to decide for yourself, but if you hang about with us, hear what we've got to say, and if you want what we've got to offer, it's there for you.'

'Fair enough.'

'I'm an alcoholic, but we'll see. You can come to this decision yourself. The meeting will be starting in ten or fifteen minutes. Do you want a cup of tea?'

'Aye, thanks, Jimmy.'

'Sit down, the pair of you.' Whilst pouring the tea, Jimmy turned his head and called across to a group nearby. 'Peter, do you want to come and talk? Here's Scobie. It's his first time.'

And as Peter came towards them he added, 'He's having a lot of trouble with the old booze.'

'It's sore, isn't it?' Peter said, sitting down beside Scobie. 'Well, up here you'll hear talk about it like you've never heard before in the pub. I suppose you've tried to stop drinking yourself, Scobie?'

'Aye,' Scobie said. 'Thousands of times.'

'I know, I know. You get up in the morning and you've made a right arse of it and you say – never again.'

Scobie shook his head. 'Oh, the times I've said that. Never again. I'll never touch another drop for the rest of my life.'

'We don't say that here, Scobie. We just stop drinking for a day at a time. You just say – I'm not going to take a drink today. I'm not going to ask you to stay away from a bottle of whisky, or a barrel of beer. I'm going to ask you to stay away from one drink for one day. It's as simple as that.' He looked round at Frank. 'Is this your boy?'

'No, it's Frank, my son-in-law.'

'Are you all right, Frank?'

'Yes, I can take it or leave it.'

'That's fine. Well, we're not interested in people who can take it or leave it. We're not even interested in people that should be stopping the drink. We're only interested in people that *want* to. You've got to *want* to stop.'

'I want to,' Scobie said. 'Christ, I want to. And that's the truth.'

'OK. But another thing to keep in mind, Scobie. It's no use stopping for the wife, or the boss, or for anybody else. You have to stop drinking for yourself. But don't worry, the wife'll benefit. Here, the meeting's going to start. We'll just turn our chairs round and face the front. That's Sam at the table. He's the chair. The man next to him is Tommy, he's tonight's speaker.'

Sam rose and gazed at the audience. He was a mild looking man in a well-cut suit and a waistcoat with a gold watch chain strung across it. He looked as though he'd never taken a drink in his life.

'Good evening, friends. My name's Sam and I'm an alcoholic. I want to welcome you all to this Monday night group of Alcoholics Anonymous, here in West Nile Street. I'd like to welcome anybody that's new, anybody that's struggling, anybody that's just come back. I don't want to take up much time because Tommy here is going to share his experience, strength and hope with us.' He picked up a piece of paper from the table. 'I want to read the preamble first. It tells us what Alcoholics Anonymous is and, just as important, it tells us what it isn't.'

Frank was impressed by the man's sincerity and the directness.

'The preamble goes like this,' Sam went on. 'Alcoholics Anonymous is a fellowship of men and women who share their experience, strength and hope with each other that they may solve their common problem. There are no dues or fees for AA. We are self-supporting through our own contributions. AA is not allied with any sect, denomination, political organisation or institution. It does not wish to engage in any controversy. Our primary purpose is to stay sober and help other alcoholics to achieve sobriety.'

Sam replaced the paper and waited for a few seconds to allow everyone to digest it. Then he said, 'Now, when you listen to Tommy's story, it is advisable to look for the similarities, not the differences. If Tommy was in the jail and you weren't, don't be saying to yourself – oh I'm not an alcoholic because I wasn't in the jail. If Tommy's *not* been in the jail, don't you be saying – oh I've been in the jail so I'm different from him.' Sam leaned forward, palms down on the table. 'Where you drink, what you drink, how much you drink isn't important. *It's alcohol*. This is the last card in the pack for us. We've tried the churches, psychiatrists, hospitals, signing the pledge, not signing the pledge, going to the pub half an hour before shutting time, going out with only a pound in our pocket. We've tried the lot. Nothing works. Nothing works except what you'll learn here. One last thing before I hand you over to Tommy – sit back and relax. Any worries you've got, lay them at the door. Any religious concepts or any bigotries you've got, just lay them at the door – pick them up on your way out. All right, Tommy?'

Tommy lumbered to his feet. He must have been at least eighteen stones with an orange peel skin and a liberal sprinkling of dandruff on his navy blue duffle jacket.

'My name's Tommy and I'm an alcoholic . . .'

Afterwards, when Scobie and Frank were going down the stairs, Scobie said, 'You marked my card there, Frank.'

'How do you mean?'

'You told that Tommy bloke all the things that I've said and done. Don't try to deny it. That bloke wasn't talking about himself, he was talking about me.'

'But I didn't, Scobie. I swear it. I've never spoken to Tommy in my life. All I did was phone the AA number and ask what time the meeting was and if we could go along. That was all.'

'Aye, sure.'

'Scobie, as soon as we get home, I'll swear on the Holy Bible, on my Granny's grave – anything you like.'

Scobie lapsed into a worried silence. He was still silent and somewhat subdued when they arrived home. His mind was in turmoil. He was amazed. He had believed he was the only person in the world that said and did the things Tommy had admitted to. But there had been other things Tommy had been speaking about that Frank couldn't have known of – the hidden fears. Being afraid and not knowing what you're afraid of. Being lonely in a crowd. The hopelessness and despair.

Carragh was hovering about offering cups of tea, her eyes anxious yet hopeful. It was pathetic. He had no hope. He had stopped drinking before, for a day, for a week, even for as long as a month. A lot of good it had done him.

'How did you get on, Da?' Bridie asked.

Frank answered for Scobie. 'He's promised to go back tomorrow night. Haven't you, Scobie?'

'A lot of shit,' Scobie said.

Frank sighed. 'So you're not going to go. OK. Nobody's going to twist your arm.'

But he did go. Just to see how he'd get on without Frank at his elbow. Jimmy and Peter greeted him like old pals.

'There you are, Scobie. Just in time for a cup of tea. On your own tonight?'

'Aye. Just thought I'd drop in.'

'You're always welcome, Scobie.'

'I thought Frank had marked my card yesterday. There was that much Tommy was saying . . .'

'It sounded as if he was talking about you?' Jimmy interrupted.

'Aye.'

'And me,' Jimmy said.

Peter added, 'And me. And, Scobie, if you do hear anything that hasn't happened to you, add the wee word – "yet".'

Jimmy passed him a steaming mug of tea. 'You'll often find, Scobie, we all go down more or less the same road. The slide down into alcohol is like being on a bus. You can go to the terminus – and the terminus is premature death and a wet brain. But you can get off the bus whenever you choose.'

'That's right,' Peter agreed. 'You can sit here and listen to all the horror stories and say to yourself, I've never done that, but just add that wee word – "yet". That's *the* most important word to remember.'

Scobie took a slurp of tea. 'I don't remember what I've done half the time.'

'I used to be the very same,' Peter said. 'Many a night I went to bed with a Rita Hayworth and woke up beside an old witch. I've never gone to bed with an ugly woman, Scobie, but by Christ I've woken up with a few.'

Scobie couldn't contain a cackle of laughter, and Jimmy and Peter laughed along with him.

Then Peter turned serious again. 'But all the same, it's humiliating, Scobie, and it's even worse for a woman alcoholic. A woman was telling me at the meeting the other night how she used to wake up and have to search for her knickers and bra while a man lay snoring in the bed – a man she didn't know. As far as she was concerned, she'd never seen him in her life before.

Didn't even know where she was. Terrible for a woman, that. A terrible humiliation.'

'Aye,' Scobie agreed.

Then the meeting began and Scobie heard more stories. This time, after he got home, he told Carragh something about it.

'There was one man,' he said, 'told some story. My God, Carragh, you should have heard him. He's been in jail fifty-six times for drunkenness. I'm not as bad as that.'

'Aye, Scobie, but there's many a time you should've been in the jail and you weren't.'

It was then he remembered the times that Doris or Bridie wanted to send for the police and Carragh wouldn't let them.

He also remembered the wee word he'd been told that was so important. He should have said, 'I'm not as bad as that – *yet*.'

Chapter Thirty-Four

Bernard and Doris had come for a game of Scrabble and a bite of supper. They'd been enjoying the game. Bernard kept trying to get away with rude swear words that triggered off noisy but hilarious arguments and had them all checking the dictionary. Andrina kept trying not to blush. She marvelled at the nerve of Bernard accepting Robert's invitation to come again. It was awful to think what he'd done, and yet there he was – Robert's best friend, Doris's normal husband – just as if nothing had happened. Every time she looked at him, she felt truly shocked, absolutely appalled.

Despite this, she found herself being coquettish, giving him arch sideways glances. She was ultra-conscious of herself every time she moved. Walking over to the fridge to get Robert another beer, or to fill up the bowl of crisps, became an art form, a symphony of sensuality. Fear made her heart falter, yet still the sensuality remained. It was the way she turned her head, the slow movement of her fingers, the inward, caressing attention she gave to her breasts and hips when she walked, the leisurely way she crossed her long legs. Every part of her told him, told her, she had been awakened again.

They had their game of Scrabble at the table in the dining alcove in the kitchen. Then after the game, when they were clearing it away in readiness for supper, she went over to the cupboard for cups and saucers. Bernard followed her.

'Let me help you,' he said as she reached for the dishes. As he lifted them from the shelf he pressed his body against hers. She immediately drew away, shocked, frightened, heart thumping with the danger of it. And the excitement. They were all helping to set the table, laughing and bumping into one another, but when Bernard's body came against hers, there was a slowness to the movement. Every touch was a caress. Even passing the salt during supper when his fingers brushed against hers – it was flesh to flesh, warm and suggestive. She tried not to look at him, to avoid him, head held high to purposely ignore him. Doris became the centre of her bright, polite attention. She laughed encouragingly at Doris's chatter about all the so-called amusing happenings in Daly's.

Doris would precede her stories with a flap of her scarlet-nailed hand and, 'I had to laugh. It was so terribly amusing . . .'

Andrina laughed, not knowing or caring what she was laughing about. She was amazed that neither Doris nor Robert seemed to be aware of the electricity sizzling in the space between her and Bernard.

Just before he and Doris left, Doris announced, 'Must pop into the little girls' room.' Robert went through to the bedroom to fetch the coats.

'We've got to meet,' Bernard said, coming towards Andrina.

She pushed him away. 'Don't, please. This is awful. You mustn't.'

Yet only a few minutes previously, when she had been putting pots away in the cupboard under the sink, she had not kneeled down as she normally would. She had kept her legs straight and bent over, knowing that she was revealing herself up to her thighs, and lingering that second or two longer than was necessary.

Even when she was pushing him away and hissing at him in shocked tones, her body was still moving with sensual provocation.

'I'll call here tomorrow,' he said. 'Ten-thirty in the morning.'

She just managed an anguished 'No' before Robert appeared with the coats.

That night she was in a fever of restlessness and apprehension. Previously she had gained some comfort from assuring herself that she hadn't really committed the sin of adultery. She had said no. She had struggled. She had fought to resist giving in to any feelings of pleasure.

She said her prayers, pleading yet again for God to forgive her.

Next morning, after Robert left, she bathed and perfumed her body. She brushed out all the tangles from her curls and applied her make-up with extra care because her hands were shaking so much.

Bernard arrived exactly on time, and for a few seconds of panic she thought she couldn't go and open the door. She simply wanted him to go away. She couldn't cope with such a dreadful situation. He knocked again, loudly, insistently. He wasn't going to go away. Somehow her legs carried her through the hall.

Every time she saw him now, she experienced a shock. It was like plugging into the electricity of life. Sharing her heightened sense of urgency, he led her straight to the bedroom, laid her across the bed and immediately lay on top of her. He kept repeating 'I love you, I love you', as he plunged inside her over and over again. She tried to remain passive, unmoved. In some strange twisted sense of morality, she didn't feel so guilty if she was denying herself pleasure from him.

He had reached a climax and was still on top of her when the doorbell jangled through the house.

'Dear God. Don't let it be my mother!'

Panic-stricken, she punched at him and fought herself free of his smothering weight. The bell jangled again as she jerked and tidied at her clothes. She ran out to the hall, then stopped to take a deep breath before opening the door.

'Hello, hen.' It was Josie. 'Can I come in a wee minute?' Josie always preceded her visits with this request. It heralded a normally enjoyable gossip about Josie's bar customers of the night before over a cup of tea or coffee and an Ayton Sandwich. Sometimes Josie appeared with a pot of tea or coffee. Today she was proffering a bag of biscuits.

'Oh, Josie, it's you.' Andrina nearly burst into tears of relief and, taking Andrina's pleasure at seeing her as an invitation, Josie came in and made straight for the kitchen.

'Here, you've slipped up today, hen.'

'How do you mean?'

'You haven't even the kettle on.'

Andrina's tremors of panic had not quite died away. She was confused. 'Did we arrange for this morning?'

'Did we arrange for this morning . . .' Josie echoed in disbelief. 'What's up? Lost your marbles or something? Last night, when you were seeing your visitors out and I came home from work, I said, "Tomorrow morning?" And you said, "Yes".'

Probably she did. Although she had no recollection of it. When Bernard was anywhere near her, she couldn't concentrate on anything or anyone else.

'Could you put the kettle on, Josie? I won't be a minute.' She shut the kitchen door behind her and hurried back to the bedroom. Bernard was standing staring out of the window.

'You'd better go,' Andrina whispered. 'It's my neighbour.'

Turning towards her he said, 'I'm going to move heaven and earth to snatch every moment I can to be alone with you.'

'Please, just go. And as quietly as you can.' Hastily she retreated back to the kitchen and shut the door again. Josie was putting the Ayton Sandwiches out on a plate. Ayton Sandwiches were their favourite biscuits.

'What happened then?' Josie asked. 'How did it go?'

'What do you mean?'

'No need to snap my nose off. What's up with you today?'

'Nothing. I don't know why, but I thought it was my mother at the door.' She had to laugh. 'It quite unnerved me.'

'Oh aye. With me due as well. That would have been a turn-up for the book, right enough. See them born-again Christians!'

'I'm afraid my mother thinks everyone who isn't is destined for hell – is half-way there already, in fact. If you decided to be saved, she'd probably accept you with open arms.'

'No thanks, hen. That would be like being pals with a piranha. I'll just take my chances and keep on my job at the pub.'

'How did you get on last night?'

'I didnae meet the man of my dreams, if that's what you mean. I wouldn't mind the Big Man, him that was visiting you last night.'

'Bernard?' Andrina feigned innocent unconcern. 'I told you, he's a friend of Robert's.'

'I know him and his brothers. Well, when I say I know them I mean they sometimes come into the pub. Occasionally he's come in with them. I haven't seen the Big Man for a while, though. I suppose with him being married and going up in the world as well. Although I haven't seen Frank or Michael or Tony either for a wee while. And Michael – that's the boxer one, Bernard's twin – he certainly likes his tipple.' She gave a hoot of laughter. 'His mother-in-law's Big Martha Stoddart. The last time he was enjoying a few drinks at the bar, she marched in and hauled him out. He's terrified of her. And him a champion boxer as well, and every bit as big as Martha. See us behind the bar, we nearly had a fit, we laughed that much!'

Andrina thought she heard the front door click shut. It helped her to relax. She made a pot of tea and put out the cups. 'I've never met any of Bernard's family, except his young brother Frank. I've heard about all of them from Robert. Bernard mentioned last night that Michael was fighting in fairground booths. Loves it, apparently. Can you imagine?'

'No. Getting punched about every day is no my idea of making a living. Funny both him and Michael being in violent kind of jobs. They don't look much like each other, but obviously they've some things in common.'

'I suppose. Help yourself to milk and sugar, Josie.' Andrina kept her eyes averted.

'Thanks, hen. That's a nice looking wee wife Bernard has. A bit too wee for him, I'd have said. But everybody to their own taste, I suppose.'

'Her sister Bridie married Bernard's young brother, Frank. It was quite an unusual wedding. Robert and I were the only other ones there.'

'Fancy! They're Papes as well. That's what Big Martha's got against Michael, I suppose. Poor sod. No wonder he loves travelling about with the booths. Gets him away from here. See mothers and mother-in-laws. A right torment, so they are!'

'My mother-in-law's really nice.' As she said the words,

Andrina's heart suddenly gave a flutter of fear. Jean Anderson lived just over the other side of the Green and the river. It didn't take her long to come across the bridge and along Monteith Row. It could have been her at the door this morning. 'She doesn't visit me very often.' She said the words out loud, trying to gain extra comfort from the sound of them. 'Even though she's just across in Adelphi Street.'

No extra comfort came. Guilt, fear, danger did a mad dance inside her.

The feverish heat of excitement was also awakened.

Chapter Thirty-Five

The age of miracles was not past. Scobie had not had a drink for over six months.

Every night he'd gone to the AA meetings. 'Ah've never missed one night,' was his regular boast now. The AA had become the most important thing in his life.

Patrick O'Maley had once said, 'You don't need to go to the AA, Scobie. Can you not use a bit of will-power?'

Scobie's reply to that was, 'Have you ever tried stopping diarrhoea with will-power?'

He had thought a lot about his drinking, and talked a lot about it at the AA. He'd come to the conclusion that he'd been obsessed with drink before he started drinking. He didn't know why.

His father took a drink, but only a few pints on a Saturday night. He had been a labourer in the gasworks. A muscly wee man he'd been, with a big walrus moustache and a laugh to match. Scobie remembered his father enjoying the parties they used to have in the house. His father's party piece, which he boomed out with great gusto, was a song about a model lodging-house. Why these doss-houses for down-and-outs were called models, no-one knew.

'When it's springtime in the model,
The model in Carrick Street,
The bugs begin to yodel and
Ye cannae get to sleep.
You get up to read the paper,
Or wash your dirty feet,
When it's springtime in the model,
The model in Carrick Street.'

Scobie remembered being loved by both parents. He looked back on his childhood as a happy one. They were poor, but then so was everybody else. He had never felt deprived.

But right from the start he'd had this obsession with the drink. He'd started at about fifteen. From then until his late twenties had been a honeymoon time. He could take it and hold it. Of course, during that time, he'd never taken too much. Not compared with his more recent years. Or at least, as far as he could remember. The trouble was, he could remember very little. He couldn't even remember the year he got married.

Nowadays, he could go into his old haunts, mostly the pub in Castle Street. He felt more at home there because it was the favourite of both his Garngad and his Blackhill pals. He could go in now and drink a glass of Irn Bru or any kind of ginger. He knew he had to keep off that first alcoholic drink, that one drink for just that one day. That was all he had to worry about.

Patrick was now saying to Michael, 'Can you no use a bit of will-power? Why can't you just take a few pints of beer or a few whiskies and leave it at that?'

Michael was in danger of careering down the same slippery slope that Scobie knew so well. He was going to end up punch drunk into the bargain if he went on with so many fights. Scobie had gone with Patrick on the road for a few days to watch Michael fight at the booths. He had been surprised at the size of the crowds that were always attracted by the barker's 'Hurrah, hurrah, hurrah . . . Who's going to challenge these great men?'

On the platform stood the line-up of pugs, including Michael, arms folded across his chest. In their colourful dressing-gowns they stood, crooked noses, torn and misshapen ears, daring anyone to challenge them.

'What Michael needs,' Patrick said, 'is a good manager and a really hard training session to get him fit enough for the big time.'

'What Michael needs,' Scobie said, 'is to get off the drink.'

'I keep telling him . . .'

'And I keep telling you, Patrick. Michael's like me. He can't just take a few pints or a few halfs. He mustn't touch it at all.'

Patrick sighed. 'Oh, I don't know. Would it do any good if you had a word with him, Scobie?'

Scobie thought this a bit of a joke. He could do damn-all with his own sons. Admittedly, thank God, they weren't all alcoholics. 'Sure, sure, no harm in trying.'

'The thing I can't understand,' Patrick scratched his thick bush of curly hair, 'why is he like that? I can take a good drink and leave it. So can Frank. So can Tony. So can Bernard. All good, sensible boys.'

Scobie thought that to include Tony, and even Frank, into this description was somewhat of an exaggeration. But Patrick was prone to get carried away at times. Out loud Scobie said, 'Did you know Frank's had another book of poems published and another story in some high-brow magazine.'

'Don't embarrass me. I've enough on my plate with Michael without worrying about Frank.'

'I'd better go.' Scobie rose in an energetic bouncing movement that matched the swagger of his walk. Since he'd stopped drinking he was aggressively fit. Even at his sixty years he could have taken on any of the pugs at the booths and given them a good go for their money. 'I'll see Michael as soon as I can.'

Out in Acrehill Street he took a deep breath of spring air – a somewhat risky thing to do in Blackhill with the gasworks, the railway, the dust and the litter floating about the place, to mention but a few hazards.

As it happened, Frank was coming in the opposite direction, thinking along similar lines. He'd heard his mother wasn't keeping well and had come over to pay a quick visit. He and Scobie met in the lane that cut in to the far end of Acrehill Street near the distillery. This was the way into Blackhill from Garngad.

'Hello there, son,' Scobie greeted him.

'Did you see Ma?' Frank's thin face was anxious.

'Naw. She was having a wee lie down. Your da and me were having a blether about Michael.'

'I'd better go and see how she is.'

'Aye, OK son. See you later.'

Frank raised a hand in agreement, turned off the lane and went loping along Acrehill Street. The place had got worse. He wondered if the changes were affecting his mother's health. Usually good-humoured if somewhat melodramatic, she had become tense and anxious and her voluptuous plumpness had melted away. She now had a slim figure. It wasn't normal for her. Even her thick mop of grey hair had thinned and hung limp and straggly about her face. Only her big, dramatic eyes were still the same.

She worried about Michael, who was making a real cock-up of his life. Big Martha had developed phlebitis and could no longer get out and around, so she wasn't the main problem in Michael's marriage now – as far as coming round to Bright Street or the pub and bullying Michael was concerned. Caroline and Michael had twins, a boy and a girl, Sean and Sally. Michael was apparently leading Caroline a terrible life – at least when he was the worse of drink, which according to Caroline was happening more and more often.

But Frank felt sure it wasn't just worry about Michael that was affecting his mother so much. After all, she'd had her share of worries with Bernard and Tony and indeed with himself. She'd come through all that, to all appearances unscathed. He believed that the biggest part of his mother's problem was her present environment. Blackhill had always depressed him, but at least at first it had been comparatively peaceful. Now all tranquillity that had ever been there had gone. Aggression had taken its place. The first post-war generation were in their teens now and sweeping aside all the old accepted values. Pop groups like the Beatles and, more aggressively, the Rolling Stones epitomised the radical changes in outlook of this new generation.

People now 'did their own thing'. They wore outlandish clothes, they did things and said things hoping to shock. They joined extremist cults in their efforts to find their 'inner selves'.

In Glasgow, gang warfare, violence and vandalism were becoming rife. And nowhere more so than in Blackhill. In the 1920s and 1930s the razor gangs fought one another. They were never really a threat to the general public. Hard-core slum dwellers of that time, of which these gangs were a part, were the product of unhealthy, overcrowded houses, unemployment and undernourishment. As a result, they included debilitated people, low in energy and initiative. The problem since the fifties had become centred round youths who at least were reasonably well-fed. They had become vigorous, and were able to express their alienation and frustration at their bleak future through violence and vandalism, although they didn't consciously realise why they acted as they did. They had become a threat to a wider society.

Cars were stolen, brought into Blackhill, stripped of their valuables and set on fire. The streets were littered with burnt-out shells. Or they were driven into back courts off Acrehill Street and left to burn or rust away.

Despair and ruination hadn't been helped by the Glasgow Corporation, who'd crowded the area by building even more houses in Blackhill, using up any green spaces with no thought to the quality of life of the inhabitants. Also, no decent maintenance or repairs had been done to the older houses.

Frank wasn't sure who or what was most to blame. New houses fell into disrepair and neglect as soon as they were built. Gardens were left as pieces of dirt ground. Children dug holes in them. An old lady in the bottom flat had allowed Patrick to have her bit of garden and Patrick had managed to grow a few roses. He'd been really proud of them, but had thrown in the towel in disgust the day he'd found somebody had broken all their heads off. Now dogs urinated on every piece of ground fronting the tenements. Stairhead windows were smashed and left unrepaired. Wind howled through them and sent rain battering over landings and against doors. Closes were daubed with graffiti, a new phenomenon that was desecrating walls, bus shelters and even the walls of schools, and becoming more and more aggressive, more obscene. Stairhead coal cellar doors were smashed through and used as toilets by young delinquents. Back court middens were smashed into piles of rubble. The houses themselves had broken windows and flaking paint.

His mother had done her best to keep her house clean and decent but surrounded by such neglect in such a depressing desert of a place, was it any wonder that her health and her spirits had become affected?

His father opened the door to him. 'Scobie's not long away, son.'

'Yes, I met him in the lane. How's Ma?'

'A bit tired. She's having a lie down.'

'Is that you, Frank?' His mother's voice agitated through from the bedroom. 'I'm just coming, son.'

'Don't get up, Ma. I'll come through.'

'No, it's all right.' Panting for breath, she appeared in the doorway. 'I was just lying on top of the covers.' She was fully clothed, but her clothes hung loosely on her and looked crushed and shabby. At one time she'd had quite a flair for clothes. She never settled for dark colours, as so many women did, to give a slimmer silhouette. The vivid colours she favoured shouted to the world, 'To hell with it!'

'How are you, son? I'll make you a nice wee cup of tea.'

'Sit down, Ma. I'm fine.' He put his arm round her shoulders and led her through to the living room. 'More to the point, how are you?'

'I get a bit tired these days. Old age creeping on, I suppose.'

'Don't be daft. You're not old. You're in your prime. Isn't she, Da?'

'I keep telling her. There's not a finer looking woman in the whole of Blackhill and Garngad put together than my Maureen O'Maley.'

'Away with you,' Maureen laughed. 'I know you're dying to meet up with your pals. I'll be all right now Frank's here.'

'And Doris'll soon be in from the shop,' Frank added.

'Away you go, I said.'

Patrick did as he was told and left.

'He worries about me,' she explained after he had gone, 'but there's no need. I just get a bit of a headache now and again.'

'I worry about you, Ma. I wish you could get out of this place.'

'Where to, son? No use thinking of going back to Garngad. They're knocking it down. Anyway, I'd miss having a scullery and a bathroom. Although, mind you, I had many a happy day in my wee house in Garngad. Which is more than Michael and Caroline are having, it seems. Not that Caroline ever complains to me, but your da tells me Michael's drinking too much.'

'Any place would be better than here,' Frank said, his mind still haunted by the bleak surroundings. 'Even taxi drivers are refusing to take fares to Blackhill. And I'm sorry for the train drivers at the back there.'

It must have been a nerve-racking journey for the drivers passing along the back of Acrehill Street. They were under constant attack by all sorts of missiles and obstacles. Sometimes the track was blocked altogether and of course the cargoes were never safe.

'I keep telling your da,' Maureen sighed, 'but there's no stopping him and Tony when they get together. They gallop along like cowboys after these trains. The other night it was a whole crate of whisky they came back with. Your da never used to be like that. Honest as the day is long, my Patrick used to be.'

'Is Tony at home?'

'No, he's off again. To Newcastle, I think he said. He's with this new group.'

'I hope to God he doesn't still bang away at his drums when he's here. It's enough to give anybody a headache.'

'Och, there's no harm in him, Frank. He's a lovely boy. And so is Bernard. Only, I'm awful worried about how Doris and him are getting on.'

'How do you mean?'

'Most of the time he seems to ignore the poor lassie. I can't help feeling sorry for her. I worry in case it was all my fault.'

'Don't be daft, Ma. How could Bernard's marriage problems be your fault?'

'Well, I . . . I was the one that persuaded him to marry Doris. She was expecting his wean and I thought it was the right thing to do. That's what I thought at the time.'

'It was the right thing to do. If Bernard was responsible for getting Doris pregnant, then he had to face up to his responsibilities.'

'I suppose so, son. But the awful thing is neither of them is happy. I thought they'd settle down. Doris thought that too, poor wee lassie. She had visions of her and Bernard settling down eventually like a right old Derby and Joan.'

There was a moment's silence as both of them tried, and failed, to visualise the picture.

'Well,' Frank said eventually, 'they'll just have to make the best of it.'

'There's such a cloud of misery over the place when they're both in the house. Bernard has never blamed me. He's never once cast anything up to me. He seems to love me just the same. In a way that makes me feel worse, he's that good to me. Always bringing me things to tempt my appetite. He even has flowers delivered to the door for me, all done up fancy in cellophane and ribbons. And not even on my birthday. He says it's just to cheer me up. But Holy Mother of God, I wish he'd do something to cheer Doris up. She's the one that needs it.'

'Surely Bernard could afford to get a place of his own. It's not fair on Doris or you, especially when Tony keeps coming home. It's too much of a crush here.'

Maureen sighed. 'I doubt if it would make any difference, son. He's up to something, though. I know Bernard.'

'How do you mean?'

'Remember when he used to go after something he wanted? He always used to clam up. Remember even that first paper-round? We didn't find out about that until he started getting up earlier in the morning and disappearing. It was the same with that SAS thing. We would never have known about that if it hadn't been for Gordon Dougalston getting into the same line of business and *his* mother knowing about it.'

'He's working for Bernard now.'

'I know. Mrs Dougalston told me. She's got a mouth the size of Loch Lomond, that woman.'

'What's all this got to do with Bernard and Doris?'

'I'm not sure. I just feel it in my bones that Bernard's up to something. I've tried to get it out of him. But as I say, he's always been good at clamming up and shutting people out when he wants to. I'm that sorry for poor wee Doris. But don't get me wrong, Frank,' she added hastily, 'Bernard's a lovely boy.'

Chapter Thirty-Six

Duncan and Agnes Noble. It was them. Duncan and Agnes Noble, The Cottages, Bearsden Lane, off Drymen Road.

'What age were you,' McPherson asked, 'when you were taken from them?'

Sophie was wringing her hands, clinging to herself, shivering. 'I don't know. Four, I think. Four or five. Or maybe six. I can't remember.'

'The chances are they won't recognise you. I mean, how *could* they recognise you?'

Just when everything was going so well. Everything was so wonderful.

'Sophie, are you listening to me?'

'Look at Andrina.' Her voice was monotonous, inward looking. 'We've got photographs of her at that age. Look at her now. If we'd never seen her in between, we'd recognise her. I'd recognise her.' Her with her round baby eyes and red hair.

'That's different.' McPherson didn't sound too sure.

'If *they* ever saw Andrina that would banish any doubt. She's the image of my so-called mother as I remember her. Red hair. Chubby face. Cupid's bow mouth. Curved body that she flaunted, just like Andrina flaunts hers.'

'She'll be an old woman now.'

'What's that got to do with anything?'

'Don't pick on me, Sophie. This is all your fault.'

'All my fault?'

'You know what I mean. You shouldn't have lied.'

'What was I supposed to say?'

'If you'd told me the truth in the first place, we could have discussed the situation and thought of something that would have prevented this complication from arising.'

'I never thought there would be any need.'

'So you keep saying. The only way I can think of is for one of us, or both of us, to have a private word with the Reverend Dinwoodie, and probably everyone else you've lied to.'

'Tell them?'

'As diplomatically as possible.'

'We're not talking about one of your political deals.'

'No, this is more important. It's about our credibility and our reputation and standing in this community.'

'I know. I know.'

'All we need to say is that you were taken into care as a young child and you'd assumed your parents were dead.'

'No details?'

'What *are* the details?'

'No details,' she repeated, half to herself. 'I suppose it's the only way?'

'Who have you told? About them being dead, I mean.'

'At the Dinwoodies' dinner party, somebody asked me about my parents.'

'So that's the Dinwoodies and Professor Brodie and his wife, for a start.'

'It was the same at my At Home.'

McPherson groaned. 'You'd better have a coffee morning or something and mention it there. I'll be meeting Dinwoodie and Brodie at the Golf Club this afternoon. I'll have a quiet word with them. Nobody might ever find out. The Nobles, even if they did recognise you, might never say anything. But just to be on the safe side . . .'

'They'll recognise me,' Sophie interrupted. 'They'll know me. They'll make no secret of it. They won't be ashamed. They were never ashamed. Absolutely shameless.'

'All right. All right. We'll prepare the ground. Don't worry. Handled properly, people will sympathise with you. Just calm down. Yes, they're bound to sympathise.' He was assuring himself as well as her. 'Yes, it'll be all right, don't worry.'

Afterwards Sophie phoned Andrina. 'Are you all right?'

'Of course I'm all right, Mummy.'

'Have you been to church?'

'I told you when you phoned this morning.'

'That was the morning service. It's time for the evening service now. Are you going?'

'Yes.'

Sophie's tormented mind detected the minutest hesitation. 'You're lying.'

'No, Mummy.' Andrina's voice heightened with anxiety. She had arranged for Bernard to visit her while Robert was at evening service. 'It's just that I've a bit of a headache. I was just thinking how nice it would be to take a rest.'

'What have you been doing to give yourself a headache?'

'I don't know. Nothing.'

'You must have been doing something.'

'I haven't been doing anything.'

'You're singing in the choir. How can you not go to church? How can you let people down? What will they think?'

'I never said I wasn't going to church, Mummy.'

'What will people think?'

'I will go to church, Mummy. I promise.'

'What will you wear?'

'I don't know.'

'What did you wear this morning?'

'I . . . I can't remember.'

'You don't change on Sundays for evening service. What are you wearing now?'

'My black suit,' she lied.

'You told me yesterday that suit was at the cleaner's. You've been tarting yourself up, giving yourself a showing up at the church. Giving us all a showing up. What'll people think? Have you no shame?'

Now Andrina really did have a headache, and the enormity of what she'd planned with Bernard was draining all strength from her legs. They could no longer support her. She groped for the hall chair. To commit adultery was sinful enough. To commit it with Bernard was a thousand times worse. To commit it while she should be in God's house was unforgivable.

'I'm sorry, Mummy. I got mixed up. It's my headache. I forget. I meant to wear my black suit.'

'You didn't wear that disgustingly short green dress to provoke men?' Sophie's voice dropped to quiet menace. 'Not in the church. Not that disgusting dress that shows your thighs and your breasts. Not in the church. If you wore that disgusting dress in God's house, I'll never speak to you again.'

'No, Mummy. Honestly I didn't. I swear I didn't. I wore my ... I wore my ...' The fact she was wearing the green dress now unnerved her, but she hadn't worn it to church that morning; '... new navy coat and cream straw hat with navy ribbons,' she babbled with relief, remembering.

Then she started worrying about how to get word to Bernard if she did go to church now. She was so distracted with the idea of Bernard coming to the door and finding she had gone, she hardly heard the rest of what her mother said.

She replaced the receiver and sat staring at the door.

Robert had already gone to collect his mother who always accompanied them to morning and evening service. She had promised him she would take a couple of painkillers and have a quiet rest. She couldn't just turn up at the church now, she told herself. Surely Robert would think it odd after the act she'd put on for his benefit less than half an hour ago. Anyway, by the time she'd changed back to more 'churchy' clothes, she would be far too late for the service.

All the time in the back of her mind was a tremor of fear. She was afraid of what Bernard might think or say or do if she wasn't waiting for him. She could never feel sure about Bernard. He could do such strange, unusual, sometimes delightful, often dangerous things. He could tell her exactly what she'd been wearing, down to the last detail, on exact days, years before they'd got together. It was unnerving and a little frightening to realise she had been under such close scrutiny yet had been completely unaware of it at the time.

He was so different from Robert in this respect. Although physically tough, there was an old-fashioned gentlemanliness about Robert, and at times he could be absent-minded.

Sometimes, Robert forgot her birthday or their anniversary. Bernard forgot nothing. Recently he'd sent a beautiful bunch of long-stemmed red roses – one rose for each year that they'd known each other, right back from when they'd both been at school. She'd had to pretend to Robert that she'd bought them herself because they'd been going so cheap in a sale in a flower shop in town. It never seemed to occur to Robert that a sale in a flower shop was highly improbable. She'd certainly never heard of such a thing.

Bernard had fingered them and smelled them and admired them that evening when he and Doris had come for supper. He and Doris visited quite often, and the visits were fraught with danger. Indeed, each minute was a knife-edge of potential insanity, crazed excitement. If they were left alone together for even a few minutes – when perhaps Robert had to answer the telephone in the hall and Doris had to go to the bathroom – Bernard would come rapidly over to her, plunge into her, have sex with her while she was nearly fainting with the physical thrill, mixed with the terror of being discovered.

But they never were discovered. When Doris or Robert returned to the room it was always to find Andrina and Bernard sitting, calmly chatting, exactly as they'd been before.

Every time they made love she tried not to respond, to lessen the pleasure and with it the guilt. Every time, in her imagination, she felt her mother's eyes upon her, heard her mother calling her 'filthy adulteress'. Every time, she shrank back at the thought.

She was still sitting in the hall when the doorbell shrilled through the quietness. Weak with anxiety she went to open it.

Bernard was wearing a light grey Armani suit and a dark blue shirt the colour of his eyes. He came in without a word. Then after the door closed, he said, 'No one has ever made love to you. Your husband has had sex with you many times, no doubt – but tonight I'm going to love you.'

The bathroom was large and had mirrored walls and a thick, deep carpet. With casual ease Bernard picked her up and carried her through the doorway, kicking the door shut behind him. Then he laid her gently down on the floor. Swiftly he unbuttoned her clothing until her entire body was naked before him as he crouched over her. Then he began at the tips of her fingers and kissed, rubbed, sucked, stroked and made his way into the palm of her hand. She was amazed at how highly erogenous her palms were. He continued up her arms, shoulders, neck, face, eyebrows, earlobes – not one inch of her was neglected. He continued down the entire length of her body, down each leg to the tips of her toes. An hour passed without a word being exchanged. The still summer evening was silent except for her tiny moans and sighs. Finally his mouth rested on her private mound, by this time swollen with desire. Once again she felt about him the odd juxtaposition of power and gentleness, and it sent pleasure burning into the core of her being. It was then, as usual, she became aware of her mother, aware of God, aware of the seventh commandment.

Bernard, sensing her withdrawal, said softly but with authority, 'Not this time. Lie back. Switch off. Let the physical overtake the emotional. Enjoy my love. Come, my velvet. Let yourself come.'

She relaxed, forgot everything except him and the ecstasy he was creating inside her.

She cried out his name.

Afterwards she knew she would never be the same again. After that evening she made up for lost time. She realised the highly sensual side of herself that she had suppressed to some degree or another for all of her adult life. Now she really became aware of her body, aware of the pert shape of her breasts, the fullness of her nipples, the voluptuous curves of her hips, the long slim shapeliness of her legs.

She became aware of men – their eyes, their mouths, their broad shoulders, their male mannerisms. But she desired only one. His approval, his opinions, became the yardstick for dressing, for shopping for clothes and underwear. He was fastidious. Nothing but the best pleased him. Lingerie, night-wear, everything had to be luxurious, sensual, but never crude or tacky. Hands obsessed him. Every female who came his way was first judged on her hands. As a result, she became fastidious about manicuring her nails and giving her hands a massage with cream. It became a nightly ritual that she never failed to perform. Red varnish was not permitted. He only liked soft colours on long, elegantly shaped nails. She had to wear gloves and take great care while doing housework.

She became as obsessed with him as he was with her. It seemed as they became more and more daring a miracle that neither Robert nor Doris had ever found out.

Although Doris knew that something was wrong. Or, to be more accurate – that everything was wrong.

Often she'd come to Monteith Row on her own when Bernard and Robert were at the karate club. She'd sit neatly on the edge of a chair in her short, tight skirt and sip a G & T. She thought it terribly smart and upper-class to call gin and tonics 'G & Ts'.

'I'm sure there's another woman. He doesn't want me any more, he doesn't need me any more, not even for sex.' Suddenly tears flooded from her eyes. 'The terrible thing is I still love him. Oh Andrina, I'm so terribly unhappy. What am I going to do?'

And Andrina hushed her and patted her and then went to make her a comforting cup of tea.

Chapter Thirty-Seven

Frank whispered to Patrick, 'I'll sit with her now. You'd better go home and get some rest.'

Maureen had been brought into hospital, and was now drifting in and out of sleep. She looked more relaxed and peaceful than she'd done for years. Happier too, yet apparently she was dying of cancer. Tony had been sent for; Michael too. Bernard had looked in earlier on his way to work, and had promised to come back first thing in the morning.

The next day, true to his word, Bernard arrived exactly on the hour he'd promised, filling the screened-off area with vibrant health. It made Frank exhausted and depressed just to look at him.

Patrick came trailing in behind Bernard. 'How is she?'

'Much the same. Heavily sedated.'

'I might as well have sat here all night along with you, Frank. I've just tossed and turned at home. I'll take over now, son. You'd better go and have a wash to freshen yourself up and then get off to your work.'

Bernard was standing at the foot of the bed staring at his mother. He said, 'Did the doctor see her again last night?'

Frank nodded.

'What did he say?'

'It's just a matter of time.' Frank turned to Patrick. 'I can't go to work today, Da. I can't leave her. I promised I'd stay. Anyway, I'm not fit to work. I couldn't concentrate. And I'd never forgive myself if she . . . if it happened . . . They said it could . . .'

Patrick sank down on to the chair and buried his head in his hands. 'What am I going to do? I'm no use without her.'

Bernard said, 'Pull yourself together, Da. You're no use to anyone if you let yourself go to pieces.'

'You don't understand,' Patrick began to sob. 'I love her.'

'You think I don't?' Bernard said.

'It's different for you. It's a different kind of feeling altogether. We've been together since we were younger than you. Before any of you came on the scene.'

Frank patted his father's shoulder. 'I know. I know, Da. But you don't want her to see you like this. If she wakens and sees you like this, she'll be upset.'

Bernard said, 'I'll go and have another word with the doctor or whoever is on duty. Then I'd better phone Tony and Michael again. They might not have realised how urgent it is that they get here right away.'

'OK, son.' Patrick wiped his eyes with a grubby-looking handkerchief. 'And thanks.'

Michael had already left the booth where he'd been working and was on his way to Glasgow when Bernard phoned, but Tony was still in Newcastle. After a late gig he was sprawled in bed, completely given up to sleep. His thunderous snoring filled the house and seemed to shake it to its foundations. His landlady battered wildly at the door, even kicked it in her desperation not only to get him up, but also to shut him up. Eventually, scratching and yawning and showing every one of his tombstone teeth, he reached the phone in the lobby. He wore nothing but a vest and Y-fronts, neither of which was all that clean.

'An absolute disgrace,' the landlady called him, and not for the first time.

'Oh it's you, Bernard. Yeah, I was coming today. How is Ma? Jesus, as bad as that? Aye, right Bernard. Pronto.'

It was a terrible carry-on. Poor old Ma. Pity he'd miss tonight's gig. But if the old girl wasn't going to last out . . . Anyway, Bernard would kill him. Scratching and yawning again, he wandered back to his room to pull on a pair of frayed denims and a T-shirt, then left to catch the first train back to Glasgow.

It was just as well the train didn't go any further than Glasgow's Central Station because he'd fallen asleep again. A cleaner had to punch him awake. 'Here you, ur ye gonnae get aff here, or ur ye no?'

'I had a rough night, hen. Didnae stop till three o'clock this mornin'.'

'You'll have a rough mornin' as well if you don't get oot ma way.'

'Keep your hair on, hen.' He picked up his case and plodded off to find a taxi.

'Where to?' the driver asked.

'Acrehill Road, Blackhill.'

'Just ma luck,' the driver groaned. 'Ah felt in ma bones it was gonnae be wan o' them days.'

'Here wait a minute, Jimmy. I've no tae go home. I've to go straight to the hospital. The Western. It's ma Ma. She's dyin'. My brother Bernard says I'll be lucky if I see her before she goes.'

'Oh, I'm sorry, son.' The driver was immediately contrite. 'I'll put the foot down.'

They'd only gone a few yards when Tony spotted a couple of his mother's old neighbours.

'Here, stop a minute, Jimmy.'

He opened the door and called out, 'Hey, Mrs Donnelly, Mrs O'Hearn.'

'Oh, hello son. Is this you going to see your mammy?' Mrs O'Hearn spoke in a hushed tone instead of her usual bellow.

'Aye. Can I drop you off anywhere?'

'Well, it's on your way right enough. Our Jessy's. You know Jessy? Our other sister.'

'Oh aye. Hop in then.'

'How is she, son?' Mrs Donnelly enquired in an equally low, respectful tone.

'Bernard sent for Father O'Rourke.'

'It's any minute then?'

'That's what Bernard said.'

They commiserated at some length, and when they reached their sister Jessy's corner they waved Tony a sad farewell. The taxi continued on its way to the Western Infirmary but just before it reached its destination, Tony suddenly leaned forward.

'Here Jimmy, stop here will you?'

The driver gazed in the direction indicated. He could not believe that his passenger was meaning either the Caledonian pub or Harry Tate's, the bookies.

'Here?'

'Aye,' Tony said, 'I just want to have a wee half and put on a line first.'

The driver was dumbfounded. But of course he hadn't been on the job for very long.

When Tony eventually did arrive at the infirmary, his mother had, the nurse informed him, quietly passed away. He was stunned. He had never really believed that his mother would ever go away anywhere. He was the one who went away. She was always there waiting for him when he came back. She always had been there. He had taken it for granted she always would be.

Bernard had to lead him home like a child. Bernard took them all home. Bernard saw to everything – the funeral arrangements, including booking a restaurant for the funeral tea. Doris wept as if it had been her own mother who'd gone. She told Andrina later, 'I feel I've nobody now. At least nobody in that house who understands or cares about me. She was Bernard's mother and she loved him, but she knew what I was going through. She was kind to me. I'll miss her terribly.' She gazed at Andrina with tragic, mascara-smeared eyes. 'Thank God I've still got you.'

After the funeral Bernard had called for Robert and they both went to the club and did a hard session of karate. Doris told Andrina, 'The sweat was pouring off him when he got back. He had a bath and went straight to bed without a word. It's terribly hurtful when he does that – ignores me. I mean I'd rather he hit me. Much rather. I could just die when he ignores me like that. It's just terrible, Andrina.'

Doris was in a pitiful state. She had obviously lost weight. She looked scraggy and miserable. Robert said she looked as if she might go the same way as Maureen. Andrina felt furtive and fearful with guilt. And the guilt about Doris sharpened the fearful guilt about Sophie. When she was with Bernard, she said, 'I'm so sorry about your mother,' and she put her arms around him, wanting to comfort him. But soon everything was forgotten in the insanity of their passion. They had both become insatiable; their behaviour was nothing short of madness. It brought her out in a cold sweat just to think about some of the things they'd done. They were simply asking to be found out.

They physically linked at every possible opportunity, however short a time, however awkward a spot or position. If they had only two or three minutes they climaxed with incredible speed and urgency. No corner of her home was left undiscovered. They made love squeezed in cupboards, in the bath, over the kitchen table. Her particular penchant was for making love in unusual and risky places. And they took incredible risks – out on the landing, over the bannister, in the back close.

Her heart was constantly racing with the danger of it all.

She phoned Bernard at his office and told him it would have to stop. Doris was not only incredibly unhappy, Doris was suspicious. Doris had become convinced there was another woman. It was surely only a matter of time until Doris found out who the other woman was.

Bernard said maybe that was the best thing that could happen – bring everything out into the open, once and for all. Let Doris know. Let Robert know. Let everybody know. Then they could both get a divorce. 'We could get married, Andrina. We must get married. I've wanted to marry you from the first moment I saw you.'

'Everybody' meant her mother. Even the thought made Andrina panic. 'No. Doris trusts me. It would be terrible. I couldn't bear it. I couldn't do that to her. I feel bad enough as it is.'

'I'll see that I get a divorce then. It'll be a first step.'

'I don't want her to know about me. I'll never speak to you again if you tell her about us. I'll never forgive you.'

If Doris knew, Doris would stop at nothing to reek spiteful revenge. Doris would broadcast it from the rooftops. *Sophie would be sure to find out.*

'The rotten two-faced shite,' Doris had once thrown all ladylike pretensions to the wind and yelled in anger and disgust about a colleague at work who had once let her down. Andrina could imagine Doris adding, if she ever found out about her, 'and her supposed to be a goody-goody Christian. She even sings in the bloody choir!'

'She won't know about you,' Bernard assured her. 'Leave it to me.'

'It's no use. I can't see you again, Bernard. I mean it this time. It's all getting far too complicated.'

'Then I'll uncomplicate things. One step at a time. Leave it to me.'

'You don't understand. I can't marry you and it's not only because of Doris and Robert. There's my mother. It would kill her, Bernard. I just couldn't do it to her.' She couldn't explain to him how her mother needed the image of perfection in her daughter. It had become worse since Sophie had moved to Bearsden. She'd never stopped boasting to everybody about her. It was 'my Andrina can do this', and 'my Andrina can do that'. The extremes of her mother's behaviour, the apparent desperation and anxiety behind everything she said or did, locked Andrina into her mother's neurosis. There was nothing more infectious than anxiety.

'You're not a child,' Bernard said. 'You can do what you like.'

'If only it was that simple.'

'It can be that simple.'

'Not for me. Never.' She was bound to her mother by invisible chains that grew ever tighter and more painful. She would never be free as long as her mother was alive.

'One step at a time,' Bernard repeated. He was a dreadfully obsessive man. It frightened her that he did not understand about her mother.

'I'll always love you,' she told him, 'but I can't go on this way.

We've both been acting crazy. It's impossible to go on like that. Please don't phone me again. Don't be alone with me again.'

She hung up. Then she stood, shivering with relief that it was finished – all the madness, all the wickedness, all the guilt. It had been getting so much worse. Absolute madness. She couldn't stop shivering. She'd made such a narrow escape.

Chapter Thirty-Eight

'Why can't you just face the truth?' Bernard said. 'It isn't working out. It never will work out. We've no child to consider. The only sensible thing is for you to divorce me.'

Doris smoked in silence.

'I'll be straight with you, Doris . . .'

She gave a sarcastic hoot at that but Bernard continued.

'There's someone else.'

Doris's mouth twisted. 'I knew it.'

'Look, we've been friends for most of our lives. Why don't we part on good terms?'

'We've never been friends.'

'All right, have it your own way. We've known each other for . . .'

'We haven't even known each other.'

'I'm trying to be civilised about this.'

Doris made another sarcastic, derisive sound.

'OK,' Bernard said. 'If you don't want it the easy way, you can have it the hard way. I've never loved you. Never for one second, and I never will. I don't just love this other woman, I adore her. Now I may never be able to marry her but whatever happens, we'll keep on loving each other.'

Doris looked away so that he could not see the pain in her eyes.

'As far as our divorce is concerned,' Bernard went on, 'I can arrange to be caught and photographed with a woman who won't mind her name or her picture being used. It's the quickest way out for both of us. You'll be free to get somebody else as well.'

But she only wanted him. 'You're forgetting one important thing.'

'What?'

'We're Catholics.'

'So?'

'I don't need to spell it out.'

'Look, Doris, I wouldn't care if I was the Pope and you were Mother Theresa. Has it not sunk in what I've just said?'

It had sunk in all right. She had known from the beginning that he'd never loved her. But still, she'd hoped against hope. Now, with him actually saying the words. And worse, telling her that he loved someone else . . .

'Who is the lucky lady then?' she sneered. 'Have you broken your golden rule of not mixing business with pleasure after all? I knew you didn't get all dressed up like a tailor's dummy every night just to deal with drunks and trouble-makers. Not the kind of trouble-maker you were trying to make out.'

'Are you or are you not going to divorce me?'

'Why should I?'

'Why shouldn't you? Our marriage, such as it is, is well and truly over – finished, Doris. Caput. Understand? Now, either you walk out that door, or I do. If you co-operate, I'll see that you never go short of money. If you don't, you'll find that one way or another, and to put it mildly, your life will grow more difficult by the day. Depend on it.'

Her heart had started to thump. She suddenly feared all her vague suspicions about Bernard could become a reality.

'All right,' she said, puffing at her cigarette and sending a jet of smoke towards his face. 'Have your fuckin' divorce. I'll be a lot better without you.'

'A lot better,' he agreed.

But she was broken-hearted. She couldn't rest in peace. She ran to Andrina for comfort.

'I'm just pole-axed, Andrina. Absolutely gutted. I knew he just married me to give the baby a name but still . . . to toss me aside and be so cold and dead-pan. It was terrible.'

'You'll be better without a marriage like that,' Andrina soothed. 'You hadn't been happy for ages. You're a very pretty girl. You'll easily find somebody else.'

'I can't think of anybody else. He's like a dark shadow over my life. I'll never feel free of him.'

'Now you're just being melodramatic – letting morbid feelings get the better of you.'

'I've felt so depressed . . .'

'It's only natural.'

'Such a failure . . .'

'Well, when a marriage breaks up, I suppose . . .'

'So terribly inadequate, any self-confidence I ever had has gone.'

'It'll come back if you give it a chance. You'll build a new life, you'll see. You have your job at Daly's. You're an excellent saleswoman. The floor manager once remarked on that to me.'

'Did he?' Doris brightened slightly.

'Yes, I just came in to have a word with you about our lunch arrangement, remember, and you showed me some new stock that had just come in and I ended up buying that lovely little black dress with the deep, plunging neckline.'

'Oh yes!'

'On my way out of the department I mentioned to the manager that I hadn't really come in to buy anything. And he said, "Ah, but our Mrs O'Maley is an excellent saleswoman. We value her services very highly." '

'Did he?'

'Honestly.'

'I like my job right enough.'

'And everybody there likes you. Including all your customers.'

Doris gave a helpless laugh. 'You certainly work hard at trying to cheer me up.'

'Well, you deserve to be happy.'

'Oh, Andrina, what would I do without you? I feel better already.'

And so she did. But much later, when she was back in her mother and father's house in Garngad, and lying on the 'hurley bed' that was now dragged out from under the kitchen bed, the shadow returned to haunt her. She listened in the darkness to the snores of her mother and father and felt lonely and bitter. She determined to find out who Bernard's fancy woman was.

She'd find out even if it was the last thing she did. What good it would do her she didn't know. But the mountain of hatred and resentment growing inside her had to have a focus. They might have worked out, her and Bernard, if this rotten, scheming bitch hadn't wormed her way between them. The rotten bitch had lured Bernard away. This happened often in the serial stories in the Red Star Weekly, Secrets, and Family Star. Doris was an avid reader of melodramatic serials and it was easy for her, especially now in her unhappy state, to get fact and fiction confused.

It turned out that Vera Thomson who worked in Haberdashery had a boyfriend who worked for Bernard, and in the canteen over every meal or tea break Doris sought Vera's friendship, co-operation and advice. Vera enjoyed being a part of a conspiracy and promised she'd use all her wiles to try and get any information she could out of George, her boyfriend, about any woman in Bernard's life.

'Mind you, it won't be easy,' Vera warned. 'Impossible, in fact, if George thinks I'm trying in any way to be critical of his boss. He admires your Bernard, he really does. I think they all do.'

'Oh, he's a great tough guy, you see,' Doris said. 'Men like that. That's the be-all and end-all for most men.'

'I must admit I go for tough guys myself,' Vera giggled. 'That's why I go for George in a big way.'

'If you're fly about it,' Doris urged, 'you know – use a bit of tact, be real crafty, do you think you can do it?'

'I can but try.' Then something suddenly occurred to Vera. 'Oh but here, why do you want to know? I mean, you're not going to do anything to her, are you? That would give the game away, put me right in it. I want none of that.'

'No, no. I swear it's just curiosity. I just can't rest until I know. Wouldn't you feel the same yourself? I'm just dying to know, that's all. What's she got that I haven't got? That's all I want to know.'

Vera giggled again. 'OK, then.'

It turned out to be money – which was a comfort in a way.

This was something that George admired about Bernard as well. Bernard knew how to get on in life. Bernard always had an eye on the main chance. A man – Mungo Ford – who owned God knows how many dance-halls all over the country, was putting a lucrative amount of jobs Bernard's way. So much so that Bernard had to take on more men. Part of the reason Bernard was the chosen one out of all the other security firms was the fact, according to George, that Mr Ford's daughter, Jane, had fallen hook, line and sinker for Bernard. They'd met when her father had invited Bernard home to dinner one evening.

Apparently Jane and Bernard had a lot in common.

'She does karate, would you believe?' Vera giggled. 'A right keep fit fanatic. A great gymnast, apparently. She's even picked up prizes for that. And of course she's got oodles of money. Or at least her father has, and she's an only child. A late one as well. George says it's common knowledge her mother was middle-aged and her father quite elderly when they had her. Now her mother's dead and she'll inherit everything when the old guy snuffs it. She was married but it didn't work out. She's divorced now.'

Doris treated Vera to sausage and mash in the canteen and two caramel wafers for her tea. She also gave her a present of a Max Factor foundation. Vera was delighted.

Jane Ford. Jane Ford. The name kept going round and round in Doris's head. Sometimes, in bed at night, she'd imagine herself tracking Jane Ford down, confronting her, scratching her eyes out. Sometimes she thought – to hell with both her and Bernard – she didn't care.

Sometimes she just hid her head under the blankets and wept until she was exhausted.

Chapter Thirty-Nine

Scobie felt sorry for Patrick. His family was breaking up around him. Michael had been in hospital with delirium tremems and was a wreck of the man he'd once been. Despite this, he still could put up a decent show at the booths and he'd never stopped saying (without being asked) that he could control his drinking. Patrick said he didn't know how Caroline put up with him. Because of shortages of money they'd moved from their two apartment to a one apartment, or 'single end' as it was known in Glasgow.

Scobie could imagine what Caroline was suffering, cramped in that tiny room with not only Michael and the two children, but as often as not Michael's drunken pals as well. Carragh had put up with the very same when he'd been drunk.

The O'Maley single end was upstairs from Scobie and Carragh's room and kitchen, and they could often hear the rabble of fighting and singing. The kind of songs bawled out depended who had brought the bevvy. If the bringers of the booze happened to be Catholic, they'd all bellow out Catholic songs:

'Take it down from the mast, Irish traitors,
'Tis the flag we Republicans claim,
It can never be owned by Free Staters
Who shed nothing on it but shame . . .'

If the ones who'd brought the bevvy another night happened to be Protestants, the shout was 'Fuck the Pope' and 'The Old Orange Flute'.

'A married a Fenian, her name was McGuire,
She picked up my flute and she flung it in the fire

But as it was burning she heard a strange noise,
Twas the Old Orange Flute playing The Protestant Boys . . .'

Michael joined in no matter what the song happened to be. The important thing was getting the alcohol. That was what had once ruled Scobie's life, and now it ruled Michael's. Scobie had spoken to Michael as he'd promised Patrick, but the boy didn't want to know.

'There's no problem, Scobie,' he'd insisted. 'I can control my drinking.'

Michael hadn't yet reached his rock bottom, the level at which enough shame, humiliation and fear took over and made you accept the fact that you were an alcoholic and that you wanted help.

Scobie had managed to help others, though. At first he'd gone round with another guy from AA to visit alcoholics in their homes. The other guy, Scott Manderson from Bearsden, had insisted he'd do the talking. Scott was a nice chap in his own way but when it came down to brass tacks, he wasn't the best one to talk to hard men (or women) from places like Garngad, the Gorbals or Blackhill. He very soon saw this for himself and agreed that Scobie was the man for these areas. So Scobie spent much of his time in dangerous excursions into the toughest areas of Glasgow talking to some of the dregs of humanity who had hit rock bottom. To a lesser man, this could have been overwhelmingly depressing, but Scobie could usually manage to see a funny side to even the worst situation.

'Sometimes ah've got to laugh . . .' he'd confide to Scott, or Jimmy, or Alec at the AA. 'No to their faces, but afterwards. Ah cannae help it.'

Only a few days previously he'd visited a single end in the Gorbals. It was the pits. Every penny had long since gone on drink. Everything pawnable had been pawned. Not even a piece of linoleum covered the floor. There was evidence of much violence. Whitewashed walls were streaked with missiles of food and drink that had missed their intended target. The backs were broken off wooden spar chairs. No coal warmed the rusty grate. The window was broken and covered by a piece of old cardboard. In the hole-in-the-wall bed lay a pathetic specimen of a man covered by an old coat instead of blankets. His equally afflicted looking wife hovered helplessly at Scobie's elbow. Her hair hung in lank strands around a sunken-cheeked face. A cardigan with holes in the sleeves drooped over her skinny body and she was wearing a pair of men's socks. Scobie found it difficult to judge by appearance who was the alcoholic in such a situation, because the partners of an alcoholic had also gone through hell.

'What's your name, hen?' he asked the wife.

'Nellie,' she quavered.

'Right, Nellie. You make us a cup of tea, hen.'

'Aye. OK.'

'Now then, Tommy.' He turned his attention to the twitching, unshaven, red-eyed figure on the bed. 'You're having a wee bit of a problem with the drink, eh?'

'Aye,' Tommy agreed, 'you could say that.'

'Right.' Scobie launched into his usual spiel. 'Now I'm no going to ask you to give up a bottle of whisky or a barrel of beer, Tommy. And I'm no going to ask you to give up drinking for the rest of your life. All I'm asking you to do is to keep off the drink for one day . . .'

At first Tommy seemed to be listening, but soon his eyes glazed; his attention had wandered. Scobie knew he'd lost him.

'Tommy!' He raised his voice. 'Tommy, where are you? What are you thinking about?'

Slowly Tommy returned. 'Ah was just thinking, Scobie – if I stopped drinking, what would happen to ma social life?'

Scobie's eyes rolled around the pit of a room. 'What bloody social life?'

'Well.' Tommy thought for a minute. 'For instance, when I take Nellie out for a meal for a wee treat.'

Nellie had been shuffling towards Scobie clutching a lidless teapot and a cracked cup. She suddenly let out a howl of derision. 'Whit? Oot for a meal? We've never been ower that door thegither for twenty bloody years!'

Scobie knew that Tommy was only trying to find excuses for not stopping drinking. It was the same with Michael. Caroline would become another Nellie. She should leave Michael – but of course, where would she go except back to Big Martha? And she'd vowed she'd never do that.

But Doris had left Bernard. Apparently Bernard had been having it off with some woman whose father owned a string of dance-halls. Bernard's firm did regular work for the father. Jane Ford, her name was. Worth quite a bit of money, apparently. She owned a big villa in Pollokshields.

'I can't understand it,' Patrick said. 'I've given these boys such a good example. I was happily married to my Maureen for all these years. Yet would you look at the mess they're making of their lives. Michael's made a right cock-up of everything. Bernard's wife's divorced him. No lassy'll have Tony. And Frank writes poetry.'

Scobie shook his head in sympathy. Secretly he was glad his Doris was shot of Bernard, although it had upset Carragh from a religious point of view. It upset him as well that Doris had been excommunicated. Poor Doris was pole-axed about it. Shattered to the core. Nevertheless, she'd never been happy since the day she'd married Bernard. Bridie had got a far better deal with Frank, poetry or not. And wee Carragh thought the world of him. It was a bit awkward though since Doris had moved back to Turner Street. Now Frank and Bridie were never away from the Corporation Offices, pestering everybody in sight about getting a council house allocated to them. The latest development was Frank thinking of going to plead his case to Bailie McPherson.

'Use Bernard's name,' Bridie urged. 'Doris says McPherson often does business with Bernard.' In her desperation, she had been all for asking Bernard to make the approach to the Bailie, but Frank said that Bernard had plenty on his plate with his business, which seemed to take up more and more of his time – not to mention Jane Ford. Then they learned that Bernard was moving away from Acrehill Street and Blackhill. No Corporation house for him, however. He'd acquired a flat in Sauchiehall Mansions. A beautiful place it was, a spacious two-room and kitchen and bathroom with a square hall you could have a dance in.

Bridie was quite bitter about it, and could hardly bring herself to be polite when Bernard showed them round.

'What's he needing a big house like that for now that he's on his own? It would have fitted him better to have provided a place like that for his wife.'

Frank had to agree.

Bridie said, 'What does he think he's playing at?'

Frank didn't know. He often had a vague feeling that there was something shady, not quite above-board in what Bernard did.

Nevertheless, he'd been surprised when Bernard said, 'If you're expecting Bailie McPherson to do you any favours you'd better be ready to give him a good bung.'

'Bailie McPherson takes bribes?'

Bernard laughed. 'You always tended to live in cloud-cuckoo land, Frank. But I wouldn't use the word "bribe". Have a bit of tact. Slip him a hundred quid in a large brown envelope, and say you'd like to treat him and his wife to a nice night out – for any trouble he might go to on your behalf.'

'A hundred quid!' Frank echoed.

'I'll lend you the money.'

Bridie said stiffly, 'We don't want anything from you, Bernard. We've got all we need.'

Bernard shrugged. 'Suit yourself.'

Afterwards Frank repeated incredulously to Bridie, 'A hundred pounds. A fortune! And him sitting up there on the bench like a saint dealing out justice to other people. Could you beat it?'

'Nothing surprises me any more, Frank. Or shocks me. Bernard's no saint either. I know he's your brother, but the less we have to do with him the better.'

'Oh, hang on Bridie . . .' Frank began worriedly.

'He's going to end up in serious trouble and we don't want to get involved.'

'He seems to be doing very well. You just need to look at the way he dresses. And that flat . . .'

'He's violent – and so far he's got away with it.'

'But that's his job – to deal with violent situations, I mean.'

'That's the kind of man who gets on in the world and gets a house in Sauchiehall Mansions.' Bitterly she added, 'It's not fair.'

'Don't worry, we'll have a nice house too, Bridie.'

Bridie sighed. 'I know we vowed we wouldn't be affected by anything around us, we'd keep our own standards, we wouldn't be dragged down, but I'm so desperate to get a place of our own, Frank . . .'

'You think we should offer the bribe?'

'We've got over a hundred saved, and if it's the only way, Frank . . . Even with my da being sober, it's terrible in that wee dump of a place. Never any peace or privacy inside the house. Always a queue for the lavatory outside. The whole building's a cesspool. It's depressing me so much I can't stand it any longer. Remember I've had to suffer it longer than you. I've been stuck in that place ever since I was born.'

The thought of offering a bribe went completely against Frank's grain, but he felt for Bridie's sake he had to do it. Resentment and hatred flared inside him. He hated the saintly, socialist, Christian Bailie more than he'd ever hated anyone in his life. One day he'd show him up. He'd write a play about the Glasgow Corporation and all the graft and corruption involved. Already he'd had plays published by Samuel French which were being performed here and there by amateur companies. The one about the priests hadn't been accepted yet though, and he was planning to have another go at rewriting it. He could understand why local companies wouldn't have the nerve for that one. But one day a television or a film company would. He was determined they would. One day they would also snap up the one he was going to write about a bent Bailie.

Feeling even more bitter than his wife now, he kept thinking, 'One day . . . one day.'

Chapter Forty

'It's like something out of a book,' Mrs Pemberton said. Although in fact she'd read very few books.

'Why were you taken into care?' asked Mrs Hawthorn.

Sophie shook her head. 'It's such a long time ago. A lifetime ago. I was only a small child. I really don't know.'

Mrs Jones from the other end of the terrace leaned forward and dramatically lowered her voice. 'And you're sure it's them?'

'Duncan and Agnes Noble,' Sophie said. 'It would be too much of a coincidence for both to have the same name. And I gather from Mrs Dinwoodie that they're the right age.'

'How fascinating!' Mrs Jones was a dedicated member of the local drama group. She thoroughly enjoyed any 'heightened life experience', to quote her own words. As a rule, however, not many heightened life experiences came her way. 'What are you going to do?'

'I don't know,' Sophie answered honestly. 'But I feel very strongly that I don't want anything to do with them. They must have neglected me or done something wrong to warrant me being taken from them. They can't be very nice people.'

Mrs Pemberton said, 'People grow older and wiser, my dear. They've always seemed a charming, elderly couple to me.'

'Yes,' Mrs Dinwoodie said, 'the Christian thing is to forgive them, Mrs McPherson. They're in their twilight years. Perhaps this is God's way of giving them a chance to make up for any unkindness they might have done to you when they were young and foolish.'

Mrs Hawthorn agreed. 'Yes, after all these years it would be such a happy reunion.'

Mrs Jones was ecstatic. She clasped her hands and gazed

heavenwards. 'How lovely! I can just see it. Child and parents re-united after a lifetime of being lost to each other . . .'

Sophie was thinking behind her tight, polite expression. What did they know about anything? Everything had been lovely for them, all right. 'I'm afraid I don't have your generous, forgiving hearts . . .' she said.

Mrs Pemberton smiled. 'You've a very nice nature, dear.'

'And you're a good Christian,' Mrs Dinwoodie said. 'That is why you will be able to forgive your mother and father.'

'Forgive and forget, they say.' Mrs Jones pronounced the words with a dramatically raised hand as if she was reciting 'To be or not to be'. 'But you have already forgotten. So all that remains is for you to forgive.'

'Yes, you must get together as soon as possible,' Mrs Dinwoodie decided. 'And I think the manse would be an appropriate place, with the Minister and myself at hand, to make sure the reunion is smooth and happy, and has God's blessing.'

Sophie was beginning to feel sick. 'I really don't think . . .'

'Mrs McPherson.' Mrs Dinwoodie was determined. 'You'll have to meet them sometime. It's a wonder you haven't come face to face already. Far better a proper Christian reunion in the manse than an unexpected confrontation in the street where you might be flustered enough to say the wrong thing. Do remember that they are an elderly couple and the Minister is responsible for their welfare as well as yours.'

Sophie was so choked with hatred at the mere thought of the 'elderly couple' that she couldn't speak.

Mrs Dinwoodie took the silence as capitulation, and proceeded to arrange the exact day and time of the meeting.

Afterwards Sophie told McPherson that she didn't know how she could possibly go.

'You'll have to go. We don't want to get on the wrong side of people like the Dinwoodies. Their friends are our friends now. You don't want to alienate yourself from some of the most influential people in the district.'

She didn't.

The meeting was set for the next day. The minister had arranged for the couple to arrive at the manse earlier than Sophie so that he 'could gently prepare them . . .'

'If we're not very careful,' Mrs Dinwoodie said, 'the shock could kill the old souls.'

It was the only cheering thought Sophie had to cling to. She couldn't eat any breakfast, and because she felt faint by lunchtime she forced herself to eat a sandwich. It turned to acid in her stomach and churned and burned with her hatred.

McPherson said he'd take the afternoon off and go with her. She was grateful for this. He could, as he said, divert some of the attention away from her.

They drove to the manse in silence, along the tree-lined main road, down the leafy side-street towards the loch, up the winding drive to the imposing villa with its peaceful view over the dark mirror of water. McPherson stopped the car and sat for a moment, leather-gloved hand on the wheel.

'Now remember, we've to go on living here. The best you can do at the moment is to force yourself to be polite.'

'All right. All right.'

'You don't look all right. You look demented. For pity's sake try and relax.'

She took a deep breath.

Mrs Dinwoodie opened the door. Smiling, eyes shining, obviously enjoying herself. 'Come in. Come in. Mr and Mrs Noble are so looking forward to meeting you.' She laughed. 'That sounds strange – as if they've never met you before. Seeing you again, I mean.'

In the drawing room sat an old woman with a dried-up, wrinkled face and wispy grey hair. But the eyes were still round and slightly protruding, like a child's. Like Andrina's. They were strained with anxiety and apprehension. The old man stood up, brazening it out. She remembered the slight, rocking swagger, the shoulders twitched back. Still the cocky bastard.

'Well, could you beat it?' he said.

She couldn't.

'After all these years. It's great to see you. Isn't it, mother?'

'I've thought about you so often,' the old woman quavered.

And oh, how often I've thought about you.

'Well,' Mrs Dinwoodie said archly, 'aren't you going to give your old mum and dad a nice kiss?'

'I'm not a kissing kind of person.'

McPherson said, 'That's right. The more emotion Sophie feels, the less she's able to show it. I'm Andrew, Sophie's husband.' He strode across the room and gave both Duncan and Agnes Noble a hearty handshake. 'Fancy us all ending up living in the same place. Nice area, isn't it? Sophie and I are very happy here.'

Mrs Dinwoodie said to Sophie, 'Do sit down, Mrs McPherson. I was just about to pour the tea. Now isn't this nice?'

Somehow the afternoon passed. McPherson dominated most of the conversation, except when the Reverend Dinwoodie solemnly spoke about the wonderful reunion, which he blessed as if he was performing a marriage ceremony. Sophie hardly uttered a word, but when she was forced to speak she managed to be polite. Even to bring a small, cold smile to her lips.

Eventually, the Reverend Dinwoodie said, 'I collected Mr and Mrs Noble in my car and brought them here, but I'm sure you'll want to give them a lift back home . . .'

'Of course, of course,' McPherson immediately agreed.

The Dinwoodies came to stand at the front door of the house to wave them off. McPherson packed the Nobles into the back seat. Sophie sat stiffly beside her husband at the front. She managed a smile and a wave for the minister and his wife.

The car crunched over the gravel of the drive, then out on to the street.

'It was so nice to see you again,' Agnes Noble said.

'Well, it wasn't nice to see you,' Sophie replied.

'Sophie!' McPherson sounded shocked.

Sophie ignored him and went on, 'And I hope I don't see you again. I suppose it's bound to happen in passing because we live in the same place. Or some other well-meaning person like Mrs Dinwoodie will try and get us together socially. But I just want you to know that I don't want anything to do with either of you. I hate the sight of you.'

'Sophie!' McPherson really was shocked.

In the back seat Agnes Noble began to cry. Her husband put a comforting arm around her.

'It's one thing,' Sophie continued, addressing McPherson now, 'pretending to our friends, but I see no point in pretending to that pair. It'll save a lot of complication and difficulties if they know exactly where they stand. As far as I'm concerned, that's nowhere near me.'

McPherson said, 'Sophie, we're supposed to be committed Christians, and because of that if nothing else . . .'

'I'm just being honest. If I'm forced to meet them again socially as I was today, it's better that they're under no illusions about me wanting to see them. I'll never come near them of my own free will.'

McPherson didn't say any more. The car was filled with the old woman's heartbroken sobs and the misery of the old man's silence.

As soon as they reached the cottages, McPherson opened the car door and assisted the couple out. The old man and woman were tottering, clinging to one another for support. McPherson saw them to their cottage, helped them find their key and opened the door for them. 'Will you be all right? Do you want me to come in with you?'

Duncan Noble shook his head.

Back in the car, McPherson said, 'That was shockingly cruel, Sophie. Especially to two old people.'

'What's being old got to do with it?'

'Being old like that means being helpless.'

'I was helpless as a child. They didn't care about being cruel to me.'

'So you do remember what happened, then?'

'Yes, but I don't want to talk about it. I can't.'

'Don't worry. I'm not going to force you.'

By the time she got home she was absolutely drained of energy. She collapsed back in a chair and closed her eyes.

'I'll make you a cup of tea,' McPherson said.

After sipping the tea she felt a little better, happier, safer. The Nobles would avoid her now. There would be no repetition of today's afternoon tea party. She could begin to pick up the threads of her life. Everything was going to be all right. She tried to keep assuring herself of this. Everything would go back to normal. Life in Bearsden, the good life, would return to being exactly as it was. She had been enjoying it so much. Yet now, no matter how she tried to cheer herself, the joy had gone. A thousand uncertainties, a thousand fears, gnawed at the dark edges of her mind.

The Dinwoodies wouldn't let the matter rest. They would keep visiting the Nobles. It had always been considered part of both the minister's and his wife's duties to visit the elderly of the parish. They would question the Nobles. When would they be seeing their daughter again? They were not seeing their daughter again? Why not? Would the Nobles be eventually pressed into confessing? Surely not. Yet she could no longer be sure of anything. Except the fact that if they did confess the truth, that would be where the interest, all the sympathy, would end. All the influential, solid citizens they knew in this most decent and respectable of places would draw their skirts away from the dirty puddle of such a truth. They would avert their faces in disgust from the Nobles, and from her.

She could only be really safe if Duncan and Agnes Noble were wiped from the face of the earth. If she could think of any way of doing it without being found out, she would do it. That was one thing she was *absolutely* sure of.

Chapter Forty-One

Bernard didn't phone very often because he was away so much. When he did phone, however, sometimes from England, once from Ireland, Andrina hung up on him. She missed him, yet at the same time there was the enormous relief from worry and anxiety. She might have succumbed to temptation again when Bernard returned to Scotland, however – but she was saved by the fact that she became pregnant with Robert's child. For a panic-stricken few minutes she'd wondered if it could be Bernard's, but in quickly counting back she realised it couldn't. It made the relief, the escape from worry and anxiety, all the more wonderful. She thanked God for it. She couldn't bear to think of what might have happened if the child had been Bernard's. Horrifying scenarios of her mother looking at the child as soon as it was born and seeing a resemblance to Bernard kept rearing up in her mind to make her sweat with fear. She had to keep reminding herself, reassuring herself. It was all right. She was safe. The next time Bernard phoned she briefly told him about her pregnancy before hanging up again.

Gradually she relaxed. She enjoyed being fussed over by everyone. Needless to say, Robert was especially delighted. So was Josie, and they had lots of chats over the coffee cups about knitting patterns and names. She couldn't bring herself to tell her mother, and so sent a brief little note instead. Sophie never mentioned it. Attending the church with Robert either in Bearsden or Rose Street, Andrina felt good and pure. And safe. In the choir she sang like an angel.

Josie said, 'Pregnancy suits you. You look not only beautiful, but serene.'

'I feel so well. I suppose I'm lucky I'm so healthy.'

Quite often, especially as the birth drew near, Sophie insisted that Andrina stayed at Bearsden for a few days at a time, so that she could look after her. It was wonderful to lie back and have her mother put cushions behind her to make sure she was properly supported. Sophie would also put a footstool under her feet. She would ply her with her favourite chocolates, and cups of tea and tasty meals. Surely her mother must love her?

The actual pregnancy or birth was not discussed. Her mother had never spoken about such things. It was just as if Andrina had some sort of debilitating illness and had to be properly looked after. And properly looked after she was.

McPherson always maintained that Sophie was at her best when someone was ill. She never spared herself. 'She'd keep going all night and all day; she'd run herself into the ground looking after any of us,' he would say.

And he was right.

Andrina had the baby at home in Monteith Row. The midwife and doctor were there with a gas-and-air machine, and all went well. She gave birth to a little girl. Robert had been anxiously waiting in the kitchen and when he was called through, Andrina was propped up in bed, washed and powdered and in her white satin nightdress, her auburn hair brushed out over the pillow. The midwife was holding the baby. Robert rushed over and gazed at his new daughter admiringly, incredulously, before turning to Andrina.

'She looks beautiful, darling, absolutely perfect.'

Trust him, Andrina thought with an inward pout, to do the wrong thing: it should have been her he looked at first, her he admired first; and he should have congratulated her. However, he sat on the bed and held her hand and asked her how she was feeling. Then the midwife placed the baby in her arms and he went into raptures again, gently touching and tracing its sleeping face with his finger, holding and kissing its tiny hand.

Andrina was thinking how strange it was that here they were with their child, her and her husband, and she had no love for him. She had thought she loved him once – so long ago, it seemed – now she knew that love was being with Bernard. Love was the stirring passion that could fill her heart and mind to the exclusion of everything else. Too late she realised how little

Robert meant to her. She lay back on her pillows and closed her eyes. She hadn't really anything against him. He was a good husband. He was kind, he cared about her, he could be depended on to provide for her. She just didn't feel anything for him. Nothing at all.

'You must be exhausted,' he said. 'I'll leave you to have a good sleep.'

She smiled without opening her eyes. She felt the midwife lift the baby from her.

After a few days, once she got up and around, she was happy showing off the baby to Josie and Doris and Robert's mother, and anyone else who cared to come. Some of the girls she used to work with in Copland's arrived one night, all bringing presents. They had a real fun night. They congratulated her on producing such a beautiful, placid baby. They also enthused about what a wonderful supper she produced. She was a marvellously creative person, they said.

She kept the baby beautifully too. She took pride in that. She carefully, conscientiously, bathed her every day, and powdered her and dressed and fed her. She enjoyed putting her to the breast. It gave her a thrill that was almost sexual. When Doris visited her they'd both take the pram out for a walk around the Green. Doris would get a turn of pushing the pram; she'd keep gazing longingly at it.

'You're so terribly lucky, Andrina,' she'd sigh. 'A good husband, a nice home, a lovely baby. God's even blessed you with looks. You've got everything.'

'Do you ever hear from Bernard these days?' Andrina asked casually.

'Not *from* him,' Doris replied. 'I hear *about* him from Bridie because of course Frank's in touch. Not all that often because Bernard's away so much, but they do get together occasionally.'

'Has he married again?'

'Bernard? No. That woman – Jane Ford – probably chucked him because of his work. He turns night into day. It's not natural.'

Andrina couldn't help feeling glad that Bernard was not with anyone else. Although she daren't see him again it helped to imagine him still carrying a torch for her. 'Have you got over all that now?' she asked Doris. 'You were so bitter for a while, especially about the woman, weren't you?'

Doris shrugged. 'I suppose so. Although what I'd feel or do if we ever came face to face, I don't know. I still think if it hadn't been for her . . .' She shrugged again. 'Oh well, that's life.' Then something occurred to her. 'Robert used to be friendly with Bernard. Doesn't he ever see him now? Bernard used to help Robert in his karate club, didn't he?'

'Robert used to be his teacher in the school as well as the karate club,' Andrina said, 'so they've known each other for ages. But with Bernard being away, I suppose – I don't know – Robert hasn't mentioned him for a while.'

Then one day, out of the blue, Robert said, 'Oh, by the way, Bernard was at the club last night. I forgot to tell you. We had a good session. I've invited him to come for a bite of supper tomorrow night and to see Jennifer.' Robert laughed. 'He told me she just cannot be as beautiful and as perfect as I was making out.'

She had to go and make a cup of tea and potter about with her back to Robert in case he detected her confused and heightened emotions. Or saw the violent pulsing of her heart. Suddenly, from drifting pleasantly along on a calm surface, she was plunged into a highly dangerous, totally exciting, wild current of life again. She struggled to hold on to the safety of the calm shore.

'I might go over to Mummy's tomorrow night.'

'What?' Robert was incredulous.

'I'd leave Jennifer with you.'

'Don't be daft. We've not seen Bernard for ages. How do you think it would look if your purposely went out? You can see your mother at any time. He'd know that.'

She couldn't think of anything else to say without arousing suspicion. 'Oh, all right.'

She couldn't sleep. Next day her mind and emotions were in

a turmoil as she cleaned every corner of the house. She forgot to feed Jennifer, and was only reminded by the child's indignant crying.

'Darling, I'm sorry. I'm sorry.' She soothed and kissed the child's warm head as she suckled her. It occurred to her that it was time Jennifer was off the breast altogether. Her mother had long since presented her with a couple of bottles and teats and tins of powdered baby milk. Although she'd never actually mentioned the word breast-feeding, Andrina suspected her mother thought it was too disgusting for words.

She took a long time bathing and dressing, then making the supper. Robert said he and Bernard were having a karate session then coming home together. The moment her eyes met Bernard's, she knew nothing had changed. The electricity between them frightened her. She knew only too well all the complications and difficulties it could lead to in her life.

Bernard said, 'As beautiful as ever, Andrina. I've told you before, Robert, and I don't mind repeating it, you're a lucky man. I'd change places with you any day.'

Robert laughed. 'Just you keep your eyes off my wife. You're here to admire the baby, not her.'

'OK, OK,' Bernard said. 'I'll come back when you're not in.'

'Not if you value your life, mate.'

They had always joked like that. Bernard seemed to enjoy tempting fate. He had the most wicked, devilish, nerve-racking courage. It terrified and exhausted her. She never knew what he'd say or do next.

He'd brought a bottle of wine to have with the supper and a solid silver teething-ring with a little silver bell on it for Jennifer. Jennifer grabbed it in her tiny fist and shook it about and giggled with delight.

'She's absolutely gorgeous,' Bernard said. 'Just like her mother.' And he put an arm round Andrina's waist and squeezed her. Andrina pushed him away. Fool that he was, Robert laughed.

For supper she'd made shepherd's pie, with treacle sponge to follow. Fortunately she and Bernard were never alone, and eventually Robert saw Bernard to the door. When he returned to the kitchen to begin helping Andrina clear the table and do the dishes, Robert said, 'It's good to see Bernard again. I'm glad to hear he's doing so well. I always knew he would be successful, of course. I always said, didn't I?'

Andrina kept her head averted as she worked. 'Yes.'

'I've never understood what your mother had against him.'

'He's a Catholic.'

'Well, OK, he's a Catholic. But the strength of her dislike seemed to go far beyond the religious thing. It was downright hatred. I expect if she saw him today she'd still be the same despite the fact he's done so well for himself.' He shook his head. 'I'm very fond of your mother. She's been good to us. But she is a woman of rather worrying extremes.'

Oh, didn't she know it. Didn't she know it.

Leaning over the sink, conscientiously, religiously cleaning the dishes, Andrina began to sweat.

Chapter Forty-Two

'Will you marry me?' Bernard persisted on the phone next day. It was as if her original conversation with Bernard, far less her relationship with him, had never been interrupted.

'I've told you – no. I can't.'

'I love you and you love me.'

'Yes,' she agreed. Her feelings for him had not changed. They had only retreated into her dream world. She made love to him in her mind while she was suckling her baby. He plunged inside her as she lay in bed with Robert. Sometimes she longed so much for the reality of him that she wept, but quietly so that Robert wouldn't hear. Never a day, never a night passed that she didn't think of him and long for him.

Jennifer kept her busy, of course. Her mother adored the child. Sometimes she thought the baby was Sophie's saving. Sophie had been heading for a nervous breakdown. Her father confided to her that it all stemmed from the terrible childhood she'd had. Apparently her parents weren't dead as she'd always pretended, they were actually living in Bearsden. Seeing them again had stirred up all the trauma of Sophie's childhood, McPherson said, and he had to force her to go to the doctor and get tranquillisers. She'd worked herself into a dreadful state.

What a strange world it was, Andrina thought, that could repeat patterns like that. She couldn't bear to look back at her own childhood. Sometimes though, when she felt overtired or stressed, memories would come unbidden. She would feel helpless, terrified, alone in the darkness listening to strange menacing sounds. Sometimes she'd see fearsome shapes and shadows on the walls, not knowing then that it was the flickering reflection of the fire. Then the fire would die and there would be stillness. And pitch blackness. And freezing cold. Oh, the terror of those long hours. The indescribable relief on seeing her mother again. The desperate clinging to her.

She didn't want to know what childish traumas her mother had suffered. It was enough to try to cope with her own, and yet their unspoken terrors bound them together. Not that her mother ever gave any demonstration of affection – even to baby Jennifer. Andrina felt inhibited, almost ashamed to show any affection for the child herself when her mother was there. While her mother was under the same roof, Andrina gave Jennifer furtive, secret kisses. But Sophie showed a keen interest in Jennifer. She bought her clothes. When she visited Monteith Row she insisted on bumping the pram down the stairs and going outside for a brisk walk with the baby in the Green. She changed her nappy and bathed her and tucked her into her cot. She encouraged visits to Bearsden. She insisted that Andrina and Robert had nights out. She'd attend to Jennifer. She was terribly efficient with the child. It was as if she didn't trust Andrina to do anything properly for the baby. Just as years ago, she'd never trusted her to scrub the floor clean enough, or empty the bin without spilling ash.

'Try and come as often as you can,' McPherson said. 'It keeps her busy. Keeps her mind off other things.'

And of course Sophie never tired of showing the baby off to all her Bearsden neighbours and friends.

She'd become a regular sight now – earnestly, busily pushing the pram down Drymen Road, spectacles glinting in the sun, hands locked over the handle. Andrina spent nearly every weekend at Bearsden. Sometimes Robert couldn't come because he had a karate class or he was away on some outing he'd promised his pupils. On these occasions she'd sit around the house fantasising about Bernard, or walk alone around Bearsden dreaming about him. Or she'd just feel resentment against her mother for taking over yet another part of her life. Her mother always pounced on Jennifer the minute she saw her and did everything for her. It left an empty ache in Andrina's heart.

If she dared to object, her mother withdrew into that dark silence that she feared so much.

When she spoke to Bernard about it, he laughed and said, 'Why the hell are you so afraid of her? What can she do to you? You're a grown woman. Do you think she'll strike you or something? It's ridiculous.'

She didn't care what Bernard thought about her relationship with her mother. In encouraging or threatening confrontation with her mother, he triggered off blind panic. That was all that mattered.

'Well then,' Bernard insisted, 'why can't we get married?'

'We've been through all this before. Nothing's changed.'

'Of course things have changed. I'm divorced, for one thing.'

'Yes, I heard all about that.' She couldn't keep a note of bitterness from her voice at the thought of Jane Ford.

He ignored the hurt tone. 'And for another thing, I've got a flat. Look, it's no use trying to talk over the phone. Why don't you come to the flat and we can talk properly? There's a few things I want to explain. And I'd like you to see the place. You could advise me about decoration and furnishings. Whatever way you'd like the flat to be – that's how I want it to be.'

He told her the address and she couldn't resist the temptation to meet him there the following afternoon. She threw all caution to the winds. Now she was feverish with excitement. She had no difficulty in persuading herself that as long as the relationship was kept secret, everything would be all right. Now that Bernard had a place of his own, it would be more than all right – it would be perfect. It would be so much safer, more discreet – their secret love nest. She'd have to take Jennifer, of course, but that wouldn't matter. The child could be put in another room with a toy or something. She began dreaming and planning about how she would furnish the flat, exactly to her taste. She was so excited she had an orgasm just thinking about Bernard making love to her again. She knew perfectly well that once alone in the privacy of his flat they wouldn't just talk. Previously, apart from anything else, it had become difficult to be alone – especially during the long school holidays when Robert was at home so much. More importantly, there was always the danger of her mother arriving. Doris had always kept in touch, of course. Hungry for any news of Bernard's private life, Andrina had encouraged these visits. From time to time, she also heard snippets from Robert. He had told her that Bernard was getting more and more caught up with work. He'd had several jobs not only in different parts of Scotland, but in England as well. Well-known groups were employing him and his men to accompany them on tours of clubs and theatres, which kept him away from home often for months at a time.

Robert blamed Bernard's job for the divorce – being away so much, and also meeting so many glamorous women. Andrina had suffered at the thought of the glamorous women, but long ago Bernard had assured her that no one could match her in looks and other women meant nothing to him. His thoughts of love were for no one else but her.

The next day she bathed and shampooed her hair and brushed it until it gleamed like burnished metal. She slipped into the silky sensual underwear that Bernard admired. On top she wore a strapless white cotton dress with golden polka dots. It fitted closely at the bust and waist but had a wide circular skirt. On her feet she wore soft white leather pumps.

She used very little make-up, just mascara and pink lip-gloss. Happy with herself she did a twirl of admiration in front of the wardrobe mirror. She looked healthy and full of life – eyes, hair, teeth, lips shining.

Then she went to put on the baby's coat. Jennifer sat sucking a dummy teat, looking very pretty with her sky-blue eyes and silvery blonde coxcomb of hair. Andrina felt a wavering, an uncertainty. She had a sudden disturbing vision of Bernard's attention and admiration fixing on the child, as so many people's did. She felt ashamed of the thought and the feeling of jealousy that accompanied it. She quickly kissed the child's forehead. 'Mummy's darling little girl,' she said.

Yet she was unable to shake off the shameful jealousy. She didn't want to take Jennifer with her. She wanted Bernard's flat to be a special place only for Bernard and herself. She wondered about leaving the baby behind. It wouldn't be in any way like when Sophie had left her. It wouldn't be cold and dark. She wouldn't be neglected and hungry. It was a beautiful summer's day. Jennifer was dry, adequately dressed and well fed. Andrina hesitated, wanting to leave her, unsure if she could cope with the guilt. Eventually she ran next door to Josie.

'Josie, could you do me a really big favour?'

'If I can, hen.'

'Could you look after Jennifer for a couple of hours? I'll be back in plenty of time for you to get to work, I promise.'

'As a matter of fact, I'm not working tonight. A pal and me have got tickets for a show in the Pavilion. As long as you're back in plenty of time for letting me away for that.'

'Oh thanks, Josie.'

She ran back to fetch Jennifer. She hugged her and showered her with kisses. 'You're going to be all right, darling. Everything's going to be all right, I promise.' Then, feeling free as the wind, she joyously hurried to Sauchiehall Mansions.

He opened the door to her and, without a word of greeting, moved aside to allow her to enter. In the hall, he stood gazing at her in silence for a time, before taking her hand and leading her into the bedroom. He laid her on the bed, spread out the circular skirt of her dress, extending it from one side of the bed to the other. Then he stood watching her. Long ago she had come to accept this habit of his, and could now relax under his long silent scrutiny. She knew he was admiring the sight of her, eating her with his eyes, and as the sun streaming in through the bay window warmed her skin, she almost purred with pleasure. She felt sensuous under his gaze. To her it was a kind of foreplay and it had just as powerful an effect. Eventually he fell on top of her, just as she was, complete with dress and stockings and shoes. She cried out in delight and soon they were both groaning and moaning and making uninhibited animal sounds of pleasure.

Afterwards his hands gently caressed her breasts and her abdomen and he said, 'You're so soft and feminine, Andrina, and when we make love, you hold me like a velvet vice. I love you and I want to marry you.'

Talk of marriage agitated her again. She struggled away from him into a sitting position. 'Why can't we just go on like this? It'll be perfect now that you've got a place of your own.'

He sighed. 'My darling velvet. You have a husband and a child to go home to when you leave here. You forget I'll be on my own.'

'I can't imagine you living like a monk, Bernard.'

'Darling, I swear to you, you are the one love of my life.'

'All right, I'll come as often as I can. But no more talk of marriage. We'll have wonderful times here together.' She swung her legs off the bed. 'Now, *please* show me your flat.'

He took her hand again and led her around while she suggested colours and furnishings and furniture with all the excited eagerness of a child.

'You'll notice,' he said, 'that I already have a few basic essentials.'

'Yes,' she laughed, 'the bed.'

'First things first.'

Time flew as they made their plans. Bernard gave her a credit card so that she could order whatever was needed for the flat. It seemed to her that it was just like getting married. In fact, Bernard's flat was far more 'hers' than the one in Monteith Row. In Monteith Row many things were to Robert's taste. There had been the presents too, from Robert's mother and her mother and other friends and relations, so that in fact the place reflected a mixtures of tastes. In Sauchiehall Mansions Bernard gave her an absolutely free hand. Everything, down to the style of the last teaspoon, was exactly what she liked. She had chosen the ornaments, the furniture, the carpets. It felt more like her flat than Bernard's. She loved the place (as he did too), but she also felt keenly possessive towards it.

When she went shopping for the flat, she took Jennifer with her. When she visited Bernard at the flat, she left Jennifer with Josie. Or, more and more often, she managed to leave her in Bearsden with her mother on some trumped-up excuse. It had always to have some kind of twisted truth to it, because her mother was like a bloodhound in sniffing out lies. For instance she told Sophie, 'I'm helping a friend settle in to a new flat. I've already helped choose the colour scheme . . .' She chattered on, making sure first of all that her mother's attention was mostly taken up with Jennifer. She'd always plop the child on to Sophie's lap before she began to reel off her excuses. It helped of course that Sophie was always so eager for the chance of being left with Jennifer. Andrina escaped gleefully from these encounters, shivering with success and excitement but also with fear and vastly-increased guilt.

She also felt the fear, to a lesser degree, when Bernard phoned her. Often he'd phone and she'd be standing in the hall listening to his words of love and sexual passion, while in the kitchen her mother and father and husband would be sitting talking, or enjoying a meal.

Robert never asked who was on the phone, but her mother always did. It was her mother's habit to pry into everything. Eyes would narrow to hard slits behind steel-rimmed glasses. Her voice would sharpen.

'Who was that?'

Andrina went over to the cupboard so that her face could be hidden. 'That friend I told you about – you know, the one who's got a new flat. Who wants pudding and who wants cheese and biscuits? Or you can have both if you want.' Then she popped her head round the cupboard door, all wide-eyed and innocent. 'What about you, Mummy? It's bread and butter pudding – your favourite.'

Or she'd just say, 'Is that Jennifer crying?' And her mother would forget about the phone call and rush through to the bedroom to see if there was something wrong or if Jennifer needed anything.

One evening, not long after the work on the flat was finished, Bernard called her from work and asked her to be in the flat waiting for him dressed in the lingerie, the wedding dress – everything that she'd worn on her wedding day. She agreed, but with a fast-beating heart and a feeling of danger of a different kind than usual. Surely this request was very strange. But then, Bernard was a strange person – quite different from anyone else she'd ever known. It was Josie's day off, and she was going on a trip to Rothesay with one of the other girls from the pub. Andrina persuaded her to pretend to Robert that she was going along too.

'I'll explain later,' she told Josie.

Josie was mystified, but agreed. And so it was that Robert was left to look after Jennifer for the whole day and most of the evening.

Andrina spent hours in the Sauchiehall Mansions bath, perfuming her body in preparation, then paying great attention to her hair and make-up just as she'd done on her wedding day.

She had bought a record of classical music. She watched out of the window, and put the record on as soon as she saw Bernard's car come into view down the street. Then she stood waiting for him, in her silvery white crinoline dress and her sparkling tiara and veil. But he went first of all into the other room to change into a morning suit – striped trousers, morning coat, and starched shirt complete with grey silk tie. When he entered the bedroom he stood staring at her for what seemed like hours. Tears began trickling down his features and blurred their hardness. He took her arm and led her over to the mirrored wall. On the fourth finger of her left hand, after discarding her original wedding ring, he placed a gold band.

'I love you, Andrina, and now I feel you're really mine.'

Then he lifted the skirt of the dress and hooped crinoline undergarments and entered her with a force that was quite frightening. His erection was throbbing with power inside her. His thrusts were perfectly timed, long and gentle at first, then building until eventually he seemed to plunge his wonderful, muscular body, his entire being, into her. Their love-making went on for most of the evening. He climaxed again and again but could not content himself. Time and again he entered her, remaining hard for hours. She thought him a truly remarkable man.

And he was hers.

Chapter Forty-Three

'I'd rather give key money to a private factor than encourage that two-faced bastard,' Frank said. He had thought he could approach Bailie McPherson – now *Senior* Bailie of the City of Glasgow, no less. In his desperation for a decent house for Bridie and himself, he had said he would do it. In the end, though, it went too much against the grain. At least it was well known about key money. One could almost say it was honest and above board. It had become so common it was accepted as the normal channel and practice to go through in order to get a house in the private sector – if and when there was one available.

'I'm past caring about how we get a place,' Bridie said. 'Just so long as we get out of here. I'd even go to Blackhill if it meant being on our own.'

The Council were knocking down the old Garngad bit by bit and rehousing people in Blackhill.

'No way,' said Frank, 'anywhere but Blackhill.'

They were both speaking in undertones in case anyone heard them. They had got into the habit of this desperate whisper. It had been bad enough with Scobie and Carragh always moving about in the kitchen (which was within hearing distance), or in the tiny windowless space between the kitchen and the front room, or one of them coming into the room for something, like using the pail in the cupboard. (If there was a queue waiting for the lavatory on the downstairs landing, or if it was during the night and it was too cold and dark for Carragh to go out to the lavatory, she would creep through to the room and use the pail.) She was always awfully apologetic about these disturbances but, as she said, 'When you get older, son, ye cannae wait.' The smell of urine constantly pervaded the room, even though Carragh religiously emptied the pail every day.

Now, to add to Frank and Bridie's miseries, Doris was mooning about all the time. It was beginning to seem as if she'd never get over Bernard.

'To think,' she kept saying, 'that he kept me stuck in that dump in Blackhill, and then as soon as we're divorced he gets a posh flat in Sauchiehall Mansions for his fancy woman.'

'Oh, I don't think he's living with anybody, Doris,' Frank tried to comfort.

'What's he needing a big flat like that for, then?'

'You know Bernard. He's always had big ideas.'

'I know Bernard all right,' Doris said bitterly. 'There'll be another woman. There's always a woman with him.'

'I'm not so sure about that . . . He spends so much time in physical training. And then with his job . . .'

Doris's mouth twisted. 'Aye, well, now we all know what he was training for.'

'I'm sorry it didn't work out for you and Bernard, Doris. If there was anything I could do . . .'

'Thanks, Frank. It's over now. It's just . . .' Tears welled up and messed mascara down her face. 'I don't seem to be able to forget . . . I mean, he hurt me something terrible, Frank.'

Frank felt even more sorry for Doris than Bridie did. Perhaps because he had lived under the same roof as Bernard, he had more of an idea what Bernard might be capable of.

Bridie tried to be patient and sympathetic to Doris, but alone in the front room, she whispered to Frank, 'She's driving me up the wall with going on about Bernard so much. Why doesn't she at least make some effort to forget him and get on with her life? Honestly, Frank, if we don't get out of here we'll both go mad. You're not getting any peace to do your writing. I can't even get a minute's quiet to read. If it's not Doris, it's Carragh, and if it's not them, it's Scobie. Sometimes I think it's worse living with him now that he's sober.'

Scobie liked to have a blether. Or a game of cards. Or dominoes. During the day while Frank and Bridie and Doris were at work, and as often as not Carragh was out for her messages, or at the steamie, or just blethering with a neighbour,

Scobie joined the corner boys. They weren't all boys of course. Some were elderly like himself. Some were too old to work. Some were young but couldn't find any work. Some were ex-servicemen who had fought for their country and had once again been let down. They'd returned to nothing else but signing on at the 'broo', as the labour exchange was called. Some of them had come back to bombed shells that had once been their homes.

Young or old, employed or unemployed, they met and hung about the street corner and talked about football and female conquests and the state of the nation. Sometimes they'd hunker down and have a game of pitch and toss. At other times, especially in the evenings, Scobie was glad of a change of company and welcomed a blether or a game of dominoes with Frank. Or he'd pester Frank and Bridie and Doris to make a foursome in a game of cards. Scobie had always to be either talking or doing something, or both. And he enjoyed a good laugh. Bridie couldn't stand it when he either told jokes or played jokes on anyone – especially on her or Frank. Bridie had not inherited her father's sense of humour.

In the end, Frank went to a factor's office in town, paid him key money, and eventually was informed that he could have a flat that had become vacant. It was in the Gorbals; not a place they would have chosen. However, they were assured that much redevelopment was planned there too – indeed was already in progress – and they would be rehoused into one of the brand new houses in the area as soon as they were built. The new Waddell Court in the Gorbals had been opened by the Queen in 1959. A high-rise block of flats was already being built and was due to be ready for the first occupants in just over a year, in 1965. Each of the new flats had every modern convenience – beautifully equipped kitchen, bathroom, central heating throughout.

Frank and Bridie were in seventh heaven at the thought of eventually having such a place. 'It's worth putting up with an old house for a wee while in order to qualify for a place like that,' Bridie said. Frank agreed. 'And we'd be on our own,' Bridie said. 'We'd have privacy.'

Shangri-La.

Bridle warmed to the subject. 'I bet you're just meant to be there, Frank. The Gorbals has produced lots of famous people. Thomas Lipton became the world's richest grocer. Allan Pinkerton, the founder of the world's biggest private detection agency.'

Frank caught her enthusiasm. 'John Buchan, novelist and Governor General of Canada.'

'Isaac Wolfsen, founder of one of the biggest store groups in the country.'

Frank laughed with excitement. 'Michael would include Benny Lynch, world Champion boxer, on the list.'

'One day everyone will include Frank O'Maley, world famous writer.'

'Oh Bridie,' Frank sighed, and they clung to each other in happiness and hope.

The house was a room and kitchen, with an outside lavatory, in Cumberland Street, one of the main shopping areas of the Gorbals. It was just under half a mile long and had a continuous row of shops on both sides of the street. As well as the shops there were traders with barrows selling fish and fruit and coal briquettes. It was a crowded, bustling, noisy street, but it had a warmth and friendliness. Frank enjoyed studying it from the quiet privacy of his own room window.

'After all,' as he told Bridie, 'people are my raw material.'

They made the room and kitchen as nice as they could afford. Helped by an upstairs neighbour, Mr Menzies, they took down the long high shelf in the kitchen and put in a free-standing kitchen cabinet. The cabinet was Bridie's pride and joy. It had frosted stained-glass doors in a sunburst pattern on the top part, and cream doors, then a pull-out enamel work surface, two drawers, and then two more doors.

'Wonderful amount of shelf space for everything,' Bridie boasted to everybody.

They had a kitchen table with an enamel top ('So easy to keep clean – just a wipe over'). The floor was covered with linoleum tiles the same colour as the sunburst glass of the cabinet, and there was a pretty autumn coloured rug in front of the fire. They hadn't been able to afford the old range being taken out.

Frank said, 'It's not worth the bother if we'll be moving to a new place soon.'

They hadn't got rid of the high hole-in-the-wall bed either, preferring to sleep in the cosy kitchen, keeping the front room as their best place and always looking nice to receive visitors. Despite this, it actually worked out that when any of the family came to visit, they automatically walked into the kitchen. The front room was seldom used except by Frank who enjoyed watching the world go by from the window.

'I'll have to move that wee table from the window,' he told Bridie eventually. 'I'm so interested in watching everybody down on the street I'm not getting on with my writing.'

The Gorbals had a fascinating mixture of people. Down through the years it had welcomed the Irish, the Jews, the Poles, the Lithuanians, the Highlanders, and the Lowland Scots from rural areas. From this international mix a new type of Scottish character had emerged. It had the devil-may-care of the Irish, the shrewdness of the Jewish people, the solidarity of the Eastern Europeans, plus the natural wit and industry of the Scot. Wonderful people – just asking to be written about!

As often as not now, Frank wrote at the kitchen table while Bridie was washing dishes at the sink, or preparing a pot of soup for the next day's dinner, or just sitting by the fire and reading. Sometimes he found himself nodding off to sleep over his papers. After a hard day's work and a good meal of Bridie's soup and mince and potatoes, or toad-in-the-hole, it wasn't easy to work for another few hours – even if it was at his writing.

Frank and Bridie talked about it, and it was decided that he'd get up at five-thirty every morning and write for a couple of hours before he went to the office. So that's what he did. After doing his writing stint he insisted on giving Bridie a cup of tea in bed and then, while she was drinking it, he made the breakfast.

'You've a day's work ahead of you too, Bridie,' he told her. 'Why should you do all the cooking and housework as well as your ordinary job? No, it's only fair that we share it.'

Nevertheless Bridie always hurried home from the bookshop and did as much as she could before Frank arrived. 'You're already doing two jobs with the office and your writing,' she said.

With both of them working so hard, they didn't have much energy left for entertaining, apart from the family who visited sometimes – more often than Bridie and Frank might have wished. Scobie especially liked to drop in. Doris and Carragh too.

Their immediate neighbours in Cumberland Street were cheery and friendly, and said they'd 'fairly enjoyed the wee night' when Bridie and Frank had invited them in for supper – 'so that we can all get to know each other,' as Frank had explained.

Nevertheless, despite all the eager preparation Bridie and Frank had made to ensure the evening's success (their first formal supper party), a slight reserve had developed among their guests. There had even been a few awkward periods of silence, especially after Frank had spoken about his writing. Everybody had been very nice and polite when saying goodnight. But Frank, ever sensitive to nuances of mood, caught in their voices and their lack of lingering an element of relief.

Later, lying cuddled together in the kitchen bed, he and Bridie discussed the evening. 'Let's face it, Bridie. It's always been the same – I embarrass people.'

'I wouldn't put it as strongly as that, Frank. I think they had a good night. I mean, they enjoyed the meal and everything. And I'm sure they liked us. It's just that we haven't much in common with them.'

'It's not you, Bridie. It's me. It's me and my writing. But I don't care. One day they'll boast about knowing me.' They laughed together and cuddled each other closer. 'One day they'll say, "Here, I used to live up the same close as that famous guy. Believe it or not, he once had me into his house for supper." '

They clung to each other, feeling blessed that they had each other, and truly grateful for their love. Bridie thanked the Blessed Mary, Mother of God, every night for her good fortune in having Frank, and their wee room and kitchen in the Gorbals. As they made tender love to each other they were oblivious to the sounds of drunken songs outside on the stairs, or the cats howling in unison in the back yard, or the faint echoes of a domestic battle in one of the other flats, or the weeping and wailing of a baby.

It was a cold night outside. A bitter wind was raging down through the black caverns of the tenements and sending gusts of rain battering against the kitchen window. Every now and again the window rattled and the cream paper blind puffed out. But the kitchen fire filled the small room with a rosy glow, and the storm outside only made Bridie and Frank feel more grateful for the warmth of their love and the safe haven of their own home.

Bridie no longer felt envious of Bernard's flat; Frank never had. He was truly sorry for 'poor wee Doris', as he was now in the habit of referring to her. After he and Bridie made love they lay in each other's arms in the cosy hole-in-the-wall bed and chatted about this and that – including Doris and Bernard.

'I never thought she seemed right for him,' Bridie said.

Frank agreed. 'It's funny, though,' he said. 'As far as I know, he's never been all that much of a womanizer. But of course he never used to speak about that side of his life – still doesn't.'

'There's definitely been that woman – Jane Ford.'

'The thing is, with Doris being a good Catholic, I suppose she still feels married to him. In the eyes of the church she still *is* married to him.'

'I know.'

'Poor wee Doris. I saw her the other day. I was up near the Charing Cross end of Sauchiehall Street in my lunch hour to buy some typing paper. It must have been her lunch hour too. She was standing across from the Sauchiehall Mansions gazing up at Bernard's flat.'

'That's pathetic,' Bridie said. 'No good can come of her doing things like that.'

Frank agreed.

Chapter Forty-Four

The strain was tying Sophie in knots. But the more she felt over-strained, the harder she worked. As well as attending church services three times on Sunday, she rushed out to every other service that was held during the week. She was a member of the Women's Guild, and helped run whist drives and jumble sales and coffee mornings for various church charities. She was forever beavering away in the church kitchen or hall. Her total commitment and her capacity for hard work made her a natural choice for innumerable committees. The only area she firmly declined to have anything to do with was the care of the aged in the community.

'I'm sorry, Mrs Dinwoodie,' she told the minister's wife, 'but it would upset me if I had to have contact with the Nobles again. I did try, as you know. But it was no use. I just feel now that I don't want to take part in anything that might bring me into contact with them.'

'I understand, my dear. I and all your friends feel for you. One would think at their age they would know better. They don't even come to church now. They say they're not able to get out and about, but several people have offered them a lift. I'm sure you must have done so yourself.'

'They just don't want anything to do with me. They never have. It upsets me even to talk about them, Mrs Dinwoodie. I would be grateful if you would try not to mention them in my presence.'

'Of course, my dear. I'm sorry if I've upset you.'

McPherson expressed the view to Sophie that she might regret not making it up with her parents while she still had the chance. 'After all,' he reminded her, 'they might not last much longer.'

'What do you know about how I'd feel?' she raged at him. 'It would fit you better to attend to your relationship with your own mother. How often do you go and see her? She's a widow living on her own in that wee dump of a place, and you hardly ever go near her.'

McPherson went stiff with annoyance. 'I'm a busy man. I visit her when I can.'

'I'm a busy woman but I visit her more often than you do. And I keep in close touch with Andrina both by phone and by visiting her. When did you last speak to your daughter or go to see her? And you work in the City Chambers, not ten minutes in the car from her place. Don't you dare lecture me about how to treat family.'

'You go to extremes, that's your trouble,' he accused. 'You're never off that phone to Andrina – and it's not just for a motherly chat. You give her the third degree. You've missed your vocation. You should have been in Hitler's Gestapo. Don't imagine she'll enjoy hearing from you or seeing you. All you'll do for her, if you go on the way you're doing, is make her as bad a nervous wreck as yourself.'

'You don't know what you're talking about,' Sophie said. 'No mother could be more attentive and caring, and she knows it. That girl couldn't do without me. Look at how she depends on me to help her with Jennifer.'

'By God, you weren't always caring or attentive, Sophie. As I said, it's always one extreme to another with you. And if you ask me, it doesn't seem right that Andrina's always so keen to dump that child on you.'

'What a way to talk! She doesn't *dump* her. She knows that Jennifer will be well looked after while she does her shopping or cleaning or sees to her friend.'

'It would fit her better to see to her child. Maybe it's like mother, like daughter with her and you. Is that why you're always giving her the third degree? You're afraid of her becoming like you used to be?'

'Don't talk rubbish. Andrina's had a good Christian upbringing, which was more than I ever had.' She felt worried and suspicious. Andrina *was* leaving Jennifer with her rather often.

Not that she personally objected to having the child. She would happily keep her all the time – forever, if it were possible. The child meant so much to her, was so necessary to her. She felt she could devour her; she felt fiercely possessive towards Jennifer.

But why was Andrina leaving the child with her so often? She made plenty of excuses. Too many excuses. Was Andrina trying to avoid responsibility for Jennifer? Or was there some other reason? Suspicion and fear became worms in her brain, poisoning it, rotting it. She couldn't bear any thoughts of Andrina bringing disgrace or shame of any kind on her good name in Bearsden. She'd worked hard to make a place for herself in the community. She was accepted as one of them now. No one knew the whole truth about her background, and she prayed that no one ever would. The Nobles had not tainted her reputation here after all.

Life had been going on the way she wanted it to – needed it to – frenetically busy, with gratitude and praise being showered on her for all her good works. Now she kept taking off her spectacles, vigorously polishing them, hooking them back on again and peering through them as if to catch and pin down anything suspicious.

She dialled Andrina's number. There was no reply.

Andrina hadn't seen her neighbour for some time – not since the day Josie had looked after Jennifer and she'd gone to see Bernard's flat. There had been a friend of Josie's in when she'd arrived (much later than she'd promised) to collect her daughter. Josie had been waiting to go out. They'd tickets booked for a show and they rushed from the house the moment Andrina arrived. Andrina called her apologies after them as they clattered away down the stairs, but she wasn't really bothered. She was too happy, too elated.

Since then she'd managed to persuade her mother to have Jennifer – sometimes for a whole day at a time – and as a result she'd not needed Josie as a babysitter again, until Josie's day out to Rothesay, when she agreed to pretend that Andrina had gone with her. On that occasion Robert had looked after

Jennifer. She promised to explain to Josie later, but again it was some time before she'd seen her neighbour or at least had the opportunity to speak alone with her. Either Josie wasn't in, or had somebody in with her, or was at work, or on her holidays. She'd gone for two weeks to Dunoon. Apparently, the place was packed with American sailors – and Josie liked sailors.

Eventually they did get together for a cup of coffee. Andrina had decided to confide in her friend. She felt so happy, she had to tell someone. Anyway Josie, she felt sure, was unshockable – working in a pub, and such a rough one at that, and going out with sailors . . . She listened with some impatience to Josie's giggling stories about her dates with an American called Dwain from the deep South. Eventually she got her turn.

'Oh, Josie, I've got the most wonderful lover. You know who I mean. He used to go into your pub with his brothers. Bernard – one of the O'Maleys. Remember he and his wife visited here? I've known him off and on since I was about fifteen – but we didn't really get together until comparatively recently. He's really tough and very ambitious. He's getting on so well and he's got a flat of his own now.' Her large round eyes shone with joy, remembering. 'It's a beautiful place. That's where I was that day of your outing to Rothesay. Bernard and I spent the whole day together, and I dressed up in my wedding dress, and I did my hair in the special way I had on my wedding day, and I took extra care with my make-up, and I wore my wedding tiara and veil, and he made love to me like that . . .'

'That's bloody obscene!'

'What?' For a moment Andrina was confused. She had been so happily carried away with her memories of the day. She stared at Josie with blank eyes and sagging mouth.

'Do you mean to tell me,' Josie's voice climbed a ladder of incredulity, 'that you got me to lie for you? You got your husband to look after your baby, while you dressed up in the clothes you married Robert in, and allowed some other guy to fuck you?'

Andrina began to tremble like a frightened child. 'It wasn't like that.'

'What do you mean it wasn't like that? You've just told me it *was* like that. It's bloody obscene,' Josie repeated. 'And here was me thinking you were such a lady, and a goody-goody one at that. Here was me thinking – God, I've got to laugh – here was me looking up to you. Such a great one for cleaning the house, such a great cook and baker, such a great church-goer. You even sing in the bloody church choir!'

'You don't understand – Bernard and I love each other. And he's so romantic. There was nothing obscene or vulgar about it. There never is with him. Everything is so romantic. So . . . so perfect.'

'My God,' Josie groaned. 'Well, it's really none of my business, hen. And I don't want it to have anything to do with me. So don't you ever again ask me to look after that innocent wee wean again. Because, much as I like having her, the answer'll be no way – no chance.' She shook her head. 'And to think I'd been wondering if I should confess to you about my giggle and slap and tickle with Dwain. And him and I free agents, not married or anything. God, I feel a right fool.'

Andrina was upset for the rest of the morning, but after preparing lunch for Jennifer and having a glass of sherry and a light but nourishing meal herself, she began to feel better. After all, what did Josie know about love? Love changed everything. Love was the most important thing in life. It even said so in the Bible.

Thinking of the Bible made her remember the filthy word 'adultery'. It made her stomach cave in. But she quickly turned her mind to what it said in Proverbs: '. . . love covereth all sins', and gradually she felt better again. She did love him – totally, passionately. At the beginning she had been shy, easily shocked, inhibited by guilt. As time passed, she became more aware of the strength of her own sensuality. Her pouting mouth, her full up-tilted breasts, her softly rounded hips. She became more and more aware of Bernard's sexuality. But he was romantic too. He made everything different and beautiful. They had been spending a great deal of time together, but the poignancy of the situation was that the times they specially wanted to be together, they had to be with their families. Now that his mother was dead, Bernard felt his father needed his family, and him more than ever, at Christmas and New Year. They spent Christmas Day at Frank's place. On Boxing Day, they all gathered together with Bridie's mother and father and the rest of the Gallacher family in Blackhill.

However, at times like Christmas and New Year and birthdays and Valentine's Day, Andrina and Bernard coped by celebrating these occasions on special dates of their own.

Their Christmas Day, for instance, was on 22 December. The planning began in their minds weeks before, however. Much consideration was given to what she would wear. After trailing round Argyle Street and Sauchiehall Street and Buchanan Street many times she settled on a burgundy velvet dress. She knew Bernard loved the soft sensuousness of velvet and she always thrilled when he called her 'my beautiful velvet'. The dress had a sweetheart plunging neckline. The sleeves were very narrow taffeta of the same dark colour, and a ruffled tail at the bottom of the skirt was in a matching fabric. She thought it classic because of the cut and shape and the richness of the fabric. Admiring herself in the mirror, turning this way and that, she also decided it was terrifically sensual because of its figure-hugging fit and the way it accentuated every curve. Also, to make the most of her curves, she wore underneath the dress a black satin basque which laced up the front and had black suspenders. To add to the effect her legs were provokingly sexy in sheer black lace-topped stockings. Black satin court shoes completed the alluring picture.

On the more mundane side she had shopped in plenty of time for a small frozen turkey, cranberries and all the trimmings. She carefully stored them at the back of her freezer. If Robert saw the turkey he would just take it for granted that she would be going to cook it for him and Jennifer and herself. If he asked her about it – after all, they were all going to her mother's for Christmas again this year – she would be ready with some lie or other. It had become quite easy to lie to Robert.

The most exciting purchase was a magnificent spruce Christmas tree, and she enjoyed searching around for all-white decorations with which to adorn it. Gradually, during the month of December, all these things were sneaked out and taken to Bernard's flat in preparation for their Christmas on the twenty-second.

The night before the big day she took Jennifer to Bearsden and asked her mother to keep her overnight and all next day on the pretext of doing the Christmas shopping.

On the morning of the twenty-second, she let herself into Bernard's flat with her key and set to work decorating the place and doing all the cooking. Then she set a small table at the bottom of the bed and draped it in a white damask cloth trailing down on to the carpet. The centrepiece was an extravagant display of red roses and fresh holly, finished with three red candles. Two fine-stemmed crystal glasses and silver cutlery completed the picture. A beautiful Christmas music record was ready to play on the machine. After everything was under control in the kitchen, she set to work on the tree. It stood in the corner of the bedroom shimmering with the white baubles, angel hair and white lights.

Finally, she showered and carefully dressed and made up in time for Bernard arriving home from work. He also showered and, still in the bathroom, changed into a smart suit and white wing-collared shirt she'd left ready for him.

On entering the bedroom he stood, quite mystified. The only light came from the tree and the candles on the table. Wafting in the warm air was the heartwarming smell of turkey and bread sauce. In the background the old familiar carols chimed out. He took her in his arms and they danced wordlessly round the room, round the Christmas tree and the Christmas table. They seemed to be silently floating in a sea of love. Then, standing by the tree, they gently made love as they gazed and feasted on each other.

Eventually she managed to pry herself away to serve dinner. They chatted happily over the various courses, and sipped champagne and laughed with the sheer delight of it all. Then, after exchanging gifts, they lay down in front of the tree and made passionate love under the twinkling lights.

Three days later, she went through the motions of a family Christmas.

Chapter Forty-Five

Michael was ashamed. He was ashamed of being beaten in one booth too many. He was ashamed of his flattened nose and cauliflower ear. He was ashamed of losing the sight in one eye and not being allowed to box again. But most of all he was ashamed of his fears. He didn't know why he was filled with fear. He'd open the door, meaning to go out, and he'd hear Mrs McAllister on the stairs and he'd feel afraid and hastily shut the door again. Why was he afraid of Mrs McAllister? He didn't know. There was no sense to it. Nothing in his life made sense any more. He loved his wife, but when he was sober he'd look at her and be shocked at the difference in her appearance from when they were first married.

Caroline had been such a pretty girl with her fair Shirley Temple curls and rosy cheeks. Now she looked like a bent old woman. Her face was grey and gaunt, her hair a dry frizz, and there was a frightened, apprehensive look in her eyes. What Caroline was afraid of was him.

Time and time again he tried to make it up to her. He'd swear he'd stop drinking. He'd get his old job back as a brickie. He'd give her most of his wages. He'd keep away from the pub – he kept trying. He played snooker. Or he went on Sunday to watch the street team from Garngad playing the Blackhill boys on the football pitch between Barlinnie and Hogganfield Loch. Football, especially in Garngad, was more than a sport – it was a disease. Locals or pals could forgive a man for committing adultery, but they couldn't forgive him for not playing football. They'd say, 'Och, she must have been a slag anyway'. Sunday kick-abouts could reach a really high standard. The teams were often made up with young men waiting to go to Celtic, Rangers, Partick Thistle, etc. Or else it was guys who were finished with the senior teams and had stepped down to juniors. So you often had guys playing football who were juniors, but they were bald and fat and maybe thirty.

Sometimes violence erupted among the spectators. Players were knifed and the referee had to be very tough not to be intimidated. Michael felt the sport was a poor second-best to boxing. At first he'd gone to the boxing clubs and hung about watching young up-and-coming fighters in training. But he'd had to take a few drinks to get him there. It hurt him so much to know that he was no longer part of what he regarded as 'The Noble Art'. He'd been flung out of the clubs on several occasions because he'd been so drunk he'd tried to climb into the ring and show the boys how it should be done. Now the clubs had banned him.

Men who used to ask for his autograph when he was champion of Scotland had looked at him as if he was dirt and sneered, 'I wouldn't give you a job if you were the last brickie on earth.'

He'd got a job eventually with a firm over on the north side of the city. The boss who engaged him didn't know about his drinking, or didn't care. After all, most building site workers took a drink, needed and deserved a drink after running up and down ramps all day carrying heavy hods of bricks.

He'd told Caroline, 'This is our new start, pet. We'll be able to buy some nice things for the kids and a few comforts for the house. Not to mention something for yourself. You deserve a wee treat.'

That first pay-day he'd hurried straight home, avoiding his workmates who were all hanging about the corner waiting for the pub to open. He handed over most of his pay to Caroline, and she was so pleased and hopeful. The kids were delighted too with the sweeties he'd bought for them.

They'd all enjoyed a good tea, and then he said he was just going out for a game of dominoes. The happiness and the hope once more died in Caroline's face. Dominoes were played in the pub.

'I'll just have one pint while I'm having a game.'

'Oh Michael, how many times have you said that? You must

have said it about as many times now as you've promised to give up the drink altogether.'

'No, but this time I mean it, pet.'

The fact was he always meant it.

'You always say that too.' Suddenly Caroline began to sob and weep broken-heartedly. This had set the kids off as well. He couldn't bear it. After a struggle with himself he said, 'All right, all right, I won't go. I'll stay in.'

And he did. And he stayed sober all week.

The next week he meant to do the same. But on pay-day he thought he'd just have one pint before going home. Instead of hanging about with the lads waiting for the pub to open, however, he hid in the Co-op. Why did he do that? He didn't know. He had the same furtiveness when buying a bottle of whisky to take home. He slipped it into his jacket pocket and slunk out as if he was stealing the thing. At home he hid it under the bed.

After that he went into the pub every pay-night. He stood at the bar or sat in his corner drinking and feeling guilty and listening to all the lads talk the most awful shit. They talked about Celtic and Rangers and he had no interest in Celtic or Rangers. (He often went to Celtic Park, but that was because there was always plenty of booze on the bus.) They talked about horse-racing and he'd no interest in horse-racing. He knew every fight they'd been in, every woman they'd made love to, or every woman they claimed to have made love to. Until he was bored out of his skull.

He got to the stage beyond guilt. He *wanted* to be in his own house. He *wanted* to be home. And he couldn't go. It was a terrible dilemma. For an unknown reason he couldn't go. It was inexplicable.

Time after time, knowing that Caroline was waiting, desperate for his wages, he spent them all. Long ago he'd sold his Crombie coat to get money for drink. All successful boxers wore Crombie coats – it was like what a fur coat meant to a woman. In his case it had hidden cigarette burns on his suit. He smoked when he drank and fell asleep. He used to say, 'I only smoke when I have a wee refreshment.'

Sometimes, as well as drinking in the pub near his work, he'd go on to the pub in Castle Street where he'd meet the Garngad and Blackhill crowd. There he was liable to get into serious trouble. Men like the coalman he owed money to would be there. They'd say to their pals if they had to leave, 'Watch him – and if he goes on to the whisky, nail him.'

Going on to the whisky from beer meant he must have more money than he'd been letting on. He was ashamed of the fact that on more than one occasion he – the ex-champion of Scotland – had been beaten up by some small-time gangster.

Caroline had wept on these occasions too. It was an added worry that some of the regulars at the Castle Street pub weren't just small-time gangsters. Some of the bigger boys had guns. All of the men, gangsters or not, took their sport and their hobbies very seriously. One of these hobbies was pigeon-keeping. He'd seen one of the gangsters put a gun to the back of a man's head and say, 'Are you going to give our Bobby back his fuckin' hen?'

He'd seen the day when, guns or not, he would have seen any gangster off, such was his contempt for them. Because he was drunk, however, he'd done nothing. He never had fought when he was drunk.

'That's one thing about Michael,' people would say, 'he never fights when he's drunk.'

What they didn't know was that he *couldn't* fight when he was drunk.

His father used to say he made a virtue out of necessity. That was the truth. Now his father would have little if anything to do with him. 'It's a disgrace how you treat your wife,' Patrick would rage. 'You're a disgrace to the whole family and to yourself. Pull yourself together, man. Have a bit of will power. Take a leaf out of Bernard's book. Look how well he's doing. He's never come snivelling to me for money for drink, or anything else. He gives *me* money. He's a good lad, our Bernard.'

Bernard, who had never stuck to any rules of the Noble Art. Bernard, who was as quick to use his feet as his fists. He could call it karate or whatever he liked, there was nothing noble nor even fair about it. What Bernard did was fast and sharp and jerky and vicious. There was nothing graceful about it. To Michael, boxing had always contained an element of dance. To him it was like ballet. Not the latter-day slugging in the booths, but the real art in the ring he'd once been so proud to take part in.

He was ashamed that, after trying everyone else, he had been forced to go to Bernard for a loan of money. His wages had gone on drink. There was no food in the house and the children were both ill with asthma. It was terrible to see them and Caroline suffer. He felt shattered by the sight of them. So much so he could have killed for a drink as he made his way up Sauchiehall Street to the Sauchiehall Mansions. He hated the prospect of asking Bernard for help. He knew Bernard thought no better of him than Patrick did. Everybody seemed to have turned against him. He felt he was dying with thirst inside. Surely Bernard would help him. Bernard was his twin.

His brother's close was tiled and clean and quiet. In fact, unlike the closes in Garngad and Blackhill, it had a cathedral-like hush. Michael's legs – once able to spring up the Campsie Hills – trembled weakly on each stair.

Bernard took a long time in coming to the door. Once inside, Michael had a good idea why. The smell of sex was thick and hot in the air. Bernard showed him into the kitchen, but as they passed the bedroom Michael sensed someone else's presence. An aura of waiting, of suspended animation, hung about the place.

'You're sober, I see,' Bernard said. 'I suppose that means you're skint.'

'I really need your help, Bernard.'

'No way,' Bernard interrupted. 'You're even more stupid than I thought you were if you actually believe I'd give you money for booze.'

'No, not for booze. It's for Caroline. She's worried sick about the kids. They're both ill and there's nothing in the house . . .' He had never before felt so ashamed as he did under Bernard's look of disgust.

'Who's to blame for that? You've got a job. You get wages.'

'I swear,' Michael said, 'I'll never again spend a penny on booze. I've had my last drink . . .'

'Aw, shut up,' Bernard said. 'I can't even give Caroline any money because you'd get it out of her. You'd even steal money off your own kids to get a drink.'

To his eternal shame, Michael began to weep. 'Bernard, I swear . . .'

'Get out, you drunken bum.'

He had no alternative but to shuffle miserably back along the hall. He hadn't even his bus fare back to Garngad. It was a long walk, and waiting for him was not only a distraught Caroline and two ill children in a fireless room, but an outraged Father Riley.

'Talking and preaching's obviously no good to you,' the priest shouted, taking off his black jacket and dog collar. 'You rotten, selfish bastard. This'll maybe teach you to think of your poor wife and children in future.'

Michael took the beating gratefully. He knew he deserved it. And nothing could hurt him more than he was already hurting inside.

Chapter Forty-Six

Michael shuffled fearfully, furtively back and forward past the close in West Nile Street for what seemed hours, but still couldn't muster enough courage to go in. Eventually he gave up and returned to Garngad. But on his way upstairs he stopped at Scobie's door.

'Jesus, Mary and Joseph,' Scobie cried out. 'What a state you're in, man!' He stood aside to allow Michael to shamble into the house. 'You get worse looking every time I see you.'

Carragh and Doris were in the kitchen drinking tea. It was Saturday afternoon and Doris, who'd had a dose of flu, wasn't due to restart work until Monday.

'Holy Mother of God,' Carragh said. 'Sit down, son. I'll pour another cup.'

Michael's good eye was swollen and half-shut. His lips were contorted with bruising. His whole face was so puffy and discoloured he was unrecognisable.

Nobody asked what had happened.

'I'll pour his tea,' Scobie said. 'You sit where you are, Carragh.'

He passed Michael a half-filled cup. Even so, Michael had to concentrate very hard and use both of his hands to lift the cup without allowing its contents to slop wildly over the top.

Carragh said, 'I took a bowl of soup up for Caroline and the weans. They were all wiring into it before I came back down. It'll put some strength into them. I made it with good beef stock.'

'Thanks Carragh,' Michael mumbled. 'You know I drank all my wages last night.'

'Many a time I've done the same,' Scobie said.

'Aye, many a time,' Carragh echoed.

'I tried to get a loan from Bernard but he sent me packing.'

Doris stiffened. 'Hard-hearted bastard. To his own brother too. I'll give you a loan, Michael.'

Michael shook his head. 'No. He was right. I'd only have spent it on drink. Caroline or the weans wouldn't have seen a penny of it.' Tears welled up from his grotesque face and lost their way back down it. 'He said I'd steal from my own weans if they had any money, and he was right.' He turned to Scobie. 'I went to West Nile Street this morning.'

'You did the right thing, Michael. You'll get help at the AA. Look how they helped me.'

'But I didn't go in the close. I didn't have the courage. Me!' The words 'Champion of Scotland' hung in the air.

'Don't worry, son. Drink up your tea. I'll go back with you. I would never have got there in the first place if it hadn't been for Frank.'

Michael was visibly trembling all over. Even his head was nodding out of control, making it all the more difficult to bring his cup to his mouth. 'Aye, Frank's OK. But I can understand how Doris feels. Our Bernard's a hard-hearted bastard. He's always got his own way. He could twist Ma round his little finger. It didn't matter what he did, he was always Ma's "lovely boy", her favourite. She used to stick up for Frank, but underneath Bernard was the one she admired. He was always her "lovely boy". I didn't stand a look in, of course.'

There was a bitter ring to his voice and Carragh said, 'Och, don't be such a self-pitying slob, Michael. You're talking nonsense and you know it. Your ma loved all of her boys. She loved each of you in a different way, that's all.'

'Drink up your tea, son,' Scobie said, 'and we'll be away.'

'Aye, OK Scobie.'

The bitterness about Bernard still hung about his mind like a fog on the way back to town. It was as if all the frustration, guilt, shame and hurt he had previously been suffering had found a focus.

'He *is* a rotten bastard.'

'Who?' Scobie asked.

'Bernard.'

'Well, I have to admit, son, he didn't do right by my Doris. And she didn't want to divorce him, you know. She's a good Catholic, our Doris. But he persuaded her or talked her into it. I don't know how he managed it, but he did. It was him that wanted the divorce.'

'And he always gets what he wants, just as I said. And he doesn't care how he manages it, or who gets hurt in the process.'

'Well, it does look as if you're right there, son.'

'All my life I've fought fair and square, and look where it's got me.'

'Aw, now haud on there, Michael, haud on. You've nobody to blame but yourself for what's happened to you. Make no mistake about that. You've literally drunk yourself into the gutter. I know what it's like. I've been there myself. Take it from me, it's no use blaming anybody else. Who's fault was it that I nearly drank myself to death, eh?' Helplessly Michael shook his head and Scobie went on, 'I had a mother and father that showed me more love than most. I had a sister and two brothers – all dead now, God rest their souls – and none of them were alcoholics. God forbid that I should blame Carrràgh. Her that's stuck by me all these years. Or my two wee lassies.' He grinned. 'Mind you, sometimes I think my boys would drive anybody to drink. But they got off their mark as quick as they could and I don't blame them. I was making their life a misery. I was making everybody's life a misery – just like you are, son. It's got nothing to do with Bernard.'

They were nearing the AA close, and Michael's steps began to falter.

'You'll remember,' Scobie said, 'how I used to treat poor wee Carragh. God, I was so ashamed but I went on and on. If I hadn't eventually admitted to myself that I had a drink problem and gone with your Frank to the AA, I would have been the death of Carragh – and I love my wife, always have loved her.'

'I love Caroline.' Michael made an effort to straighten his

shoulders. 'I'll do it for her. I'll go up there and I'll take the pledge. For Caroline's sake . . .'

'No, no, son,' Scobie interrupted. 'It's nothing like that. You've got the wrong idea. In the first place you've not to do it for your wife, or your da, or your boss, or your pal, or anybody else. You've just to do it for yourself.'

Michael felt frightened again and he suffered another humiliating attack of the shakes. He felt like an old man, older than Scobie who had taken his arm and was helping him up the dark, quiet stairs. He needed a drink more than he'd ever needed one in his life. Just one drink.

Bernard could down drinks whenever it took his fancy, and he never needed to face the humiliation of God knows what in a place like this.

Michael wanted to run away. Yet to turn and run now would be an even greater humiliation. He despised himself enough as it was. Yet at the same time he believed he was a better man than Bernard. Hadn't he been champion of Scotland? Bernard was probably no better than a gangster.

And Bernard had not been faithful to Doris. Bernard never spoke about his conquests, but he had a look of sexual self-confidence and experience about him that spoke volumes. It was in the relaxed, open-legged way he sat, in the easy swagger of his walk, in the narrow knowing look in his eyes.

'I've always been faithful to Caroline,' Michael told himself. Yet even as he thought this, he knew that physically it was not true. When he was sober he had been faithful, and always in his head he had been faithful. But there had been times after a night of boozing when he'd wakened up in a strange bed beside a dirty wee scrubber.

He groaned in anguish at the memory. He felt ill with the shame of it.

'You're going to be OK, son,' Scobie comforted. 'You're just going to go up here and have a wee cup of tea and a blether with other guys like yourself and like me. We're all in the same boat.'

'Aw Scobie,' Michael managed brokenly, 'you don't know some of the things I've done. You don't understand.'

'Try me,' Scobie said.

'I love Caroline. Yet when I've been drunk, I've gone to bed with other women.'

'Same here,' Scobie said.

'You're not just saying that?'

'Why should I lie, Michael?'

Michael's head twitched about helplessly, the floodgate of memory draining him. 'I've given Caroline a terrible life. I've brought the scum of the neighbourhood into her house. And still I've turned on her, blamed her. I remember once blaming her for a crowd of drinking buddies going away early. I said they'd gone home because they were too embarrassed to ask her for the lavvy key. They'd just gone home because the booze had run out, of course. And anyway, one of them was big Danny Malloy and if he was game enough to shoot a policeman and axe a police dog, he was game enough to ask for a lavvy key. But that's how ridiculous and stupid I've been, Scobie. Fancy blaming Caroline . . .'

'OK. OK. So you were bloody stupid and ridiculous. But that's all in the past. Just like all the stupid, ridiculous and downright wicked things I've done are in the past. Oh aye, son. I could top any of your stories any day. I've been a right wicked bugger in drink and that's the truth. You just ask Carragh for a start. But first you'll hear plenty stories from guys in this AA office that'll match yours. Believe me, son.' He opened the door and ushered Michael into the windowless hall. Through another door was a biggish room with brown linoleum on the floor, some folding chairs stacked against the wall, and men and women standing or sitting around in groups talking. A man at a small side-table was pouring mugs of tea.

The man said to Michael as he handed him a mug, 'Hello there, my name's Jimmy. Have I met you? Have you been here before?'

Scobie said, 'This is Michael. He's a pal of mine.'

'Right, Michael,' said Jimmy. 'So you're having a wee bit of trouble with your bevvy, son?'

Chapter Forty-Seven

'Bridie! Bridie!' Frank was beside himself, frantic, gone mad, dancing, leaping about the kitchen waving a piece of paper high in the air.

Bridie scrambled up in bed. 'What's wrong? Frank, what is it?'

'Nothing's wrong. Everything's wonderful. Wonderful! They've accepted my play. Television! Hallelujah!'

Bridie paled. 'The one about the priests?'

'No, the bent Bailie. Don't look so worried. This is the answer to all our prayers. People kept telling me there was this "Magic Circle" – a few writers got all the work. A newcomer like me didn't stand a chance.' His thin face was feverish, his eyes protruding. 'But I've done it, Bridie. I've done it!'

Bridie climbed down from the hole-in-the-wall bed and searched about for spectacles and slippers.

'Aren't you going to congratulate me?' Frank yelled.

'Of course, dear. You've worked hard and you deserve every success. I just hope this doesn't get you into any trouble, that's all. Cause any unpleasantness for us. We've been so happy here in our nice wee house. I don't even care any more about getting one of the new flats. And the neighbours are really kind. Mrs Gormley offered to take my washing with hers to the steamie the other day . . .'

'Bridie, what on earth's Mrs Gormley and the steamie got to do with me getting a play accepted for television?'

Bridie found her spectacles and pushed them up the bridge of her nose. 'Now, Frank, don't act the innocent. You know perfectly well what I mean. Some of the things you write are liable to offend people. The bailie in your play is based on Senior Bailie McPherson, and he's a friend of your father's. And Bernard's got a lot of work through Bailie McPherson. That's enough potential trouble for a start.'

'I'm sure Bernard is well able to handle any trouble that comes his way.'

'And so soon as the newspapers get a whiff of scandal, or any suspicion of graft and corruption – and that's what your play's all about – it's going to hit the headlines. You know what the papers are like, the tabloids especially.'

'Great publicity.' Frank's eyes misted with joy. 'With that kind of publicity it's bound to be a success.'

'But Frank, success isn't everything. Think of the repercussions for everybody. Think what it might do to Bailie McPherson and his family. *They* won't think publicity like that's very great, will they?'

'I don't care what he thinks. He deserves all he gets. But you're forgetting something, Bridie. My play's a work of fiction, not a documentary. Only you and I know that I based the main character on Bailie McPherson.'

'It's about a Glasgow Bailie.'

'There's more than one Glasgow Bailie, and none of them are called John Munroe.'

'But Frank . . .'

Frank laughed. Nothing could spoil this wondrous moment for him. 'Stop worrying. John Munroe is younger than Bailie McPherson. He lives in Newton Mearns, not Bearsden. He has a handsome son, not a beautiful daughter.'

'All the same . . .'

'Be happy for me, Bridie. *Please.*'

Bridie blinked and tried to smile.

'They want me to go to the BBC to discuss it. Look! Read the letter. They're most impressed, they say. Most impressed.' He savoured the words. 'The BBC.'

'And so they should be,' Bridie said. 'You're a wonderful, talented man. I'll put the kettle on.' She couldn't altogether understand why she wasn't as joyously happy as Frank. She struggled valiantly to hide the fact, but the truth was she felt inexplicably depressed. She tried to tell herself she was just worried about what Frank's play might stir up, the uncertainty, not knowing what effect it might have. At the same time, she knew it was more than that. A different fear had taken root. 'Do you think you should warn your da and Bernard about it?'

'Oh, I expect it'll be ages before it actually reaches the screen. I'll tell them about the acceptance, of course. My God, I feel like running around the Gorbals and Garngad and Blackhill broadcasting the news through a megaphone.'

Bridie managed to feebly laugh along with him. Frank was such a child at times with his high hopes, his optimistic dreams, his wild enthusiasms. He had such an open-faced guilelessness too. She loved that about him. She loved his pale, pinched face and lank hair that he kept forgetting to get cut. She loved the way he never looked tidy and she had to keep straightening his tie and flicking dandruff from the shoulders of his jacket.

Frank didn't forget to get his hair cut before he went to the BBC, though. He laboriously pressed his suit. She starched his shirt. (Shirts always looked so crumpled on him.) He bought a new tie in Woolworths. He was feverish with excitement when the great day came, so much so that Bridie thought he was actually coming down with flu. He couldn't eat any lunch.

'Wish me luck,' he said before he set off. And she did. He'd wanted her to go with him but she was much too shy. Even in the shop she preferred working in the back rather than out front, dealing with the public.

Frank was walking on air when he returned. Everything had gone well. She became confused with all the people he'd met and what their jobs were. But as far as Frank was concerned, it had been no trouble. No trouble at all. He'd enjoyed it. He'd got on well with everybody. Everybody had been excited about the play. There had to be other meetings. Lots of meetings.

He ate a huge dinner. Afterwards he was much too restless to settle down to write, or even just to watch TV.

Despite her protests about it being too late and him having to get up early for his work in the morning, he insisted on going to visit his father to tell him the good news. He would have gone the day he'd first received the letter, but Patrick had not been in. He'd phoned Bernard but there was no reply. He'd gone to Michael's house in Garngad and never managed to find him either.

'I told you you were wasting your time there,' Bridie said. 'Michael's as bad as Da now. He's never out of the AA offices. Anyway, you know what your family's like.'

But of course Frank, forever the optimist, imagined they'd all be delighted for him. She reminded him about how his father had received his first poem.

'Och, that was years ago and the poem was rotten. Da loves his telly. He'll be thrilled about this.'

She groaned inwardly. No way could she see Patrick O'Maley being thrilled about anything Frank did, especially anything he'd written. However, she said no more and went quietly along with her husband.

'Da,' Frank cried out immediately he burst into the house in Blackhill. 'You'll never guess. The BBC has accepted one of my plays. They're going to put it on television.'

Patrick's eyes narrowed suspiciously beneath their bushy grey brows. 'You're pulling my leg.'

'No, Da. Honestly.'

'How did you con them into that?'

'They liked the play. They're really excited about it. They think it'll cause quite a stir.'

'What've you been saying? I hope you haven't been saying anything about Blackhill.'

'No,' Frank's face lit up. 'But what a good idea!' He suddenly saw a scene in which his father and Tony were galloping along beside a moving train armed with meat-axes, ready to hack open stolen crates. 'That's a great idea,' he enthused.

'You just watch it,' his father warned. 'Watch it, do you hear?'

'It's so much more atmospheric than the City Chambers,' Frank said out loud to himself.

'What've you been saying about the City Chambers? Here . . .' Patrick heaved up from his chair with a sudden rise of indignation. 'You haven't been saying anything about Bailie McPherson, have you?'

'Not as such,' Frank murmured absently. He had already written the first page of his Blackhill play in his mind.

'What do you mean – not as such?' Patrick's bloodshot, bulging eyes demanded an answer. He was skint and hadn't been able to go to the pub. He was in no mood for Frank. He never was in the mood for Frank, at the best of times.

'What Frank means,' Bridie blurted out, 'is that it's about a *type* of Bailie. A fictitious character. It's not about any *real* person.'

'It's one thing making a bloody fool of yourself,' Patrick shouted. 'It's another thing altogether making a fool of other folk.'

The sudden loudness of his father's voice snatched back Frank's attention. 'What's up with you?' he asked in astonishment. 'All I said was I've had a play accepted by the BBC. I thought you'd be pleased.'

'Well, I'm not fuckin' pleased.'

'OK, OK,' Frank said. 'There's no need to bawl your head off, Da.'

'We'd better go.' Bridie tugged at Frank's arm, adding apologetically to Patrick, 'We just popped in for a minute.'

'Aye, well, you can just pop out again.'

After they left the house, and were walking down the dark dusty street with its old newspapers and tin cans careening aimlessly about in the wind, Frank said, 'Could you beat that? He's getting worse in his old age. But here, Bridie, he set me thinking. Blackhill could be a very dramatic setting for a play. So would Garngad. I've been using other districts as backgrounds but why should I? Write about what you know. I read that somewhere. It's good advice.'

Bridie now felt not only worried but ashamed. It would be dreadful if Frank started writing about good friends and neighbours. It was going to be bad enough when the play about the Bailie and the City Chambers came out. If Frank started writing about people nearer home, how could she face them? She imagined herself slinking about, avoiding people. Patrick's fury would be multiplied a thousandfold. She began to sweat.

Frank hugged her arm through his as they passed the dark corners of closes and ghostly walls desecrated by graffiti. 'Come to think of it, Bridie, Garngad and Blackhill and the Gorbals are hotching with characters – real characters.' He was happy and excited again. 'My God, I don't need to look any further than our own families. That's where real originality lies.'

Bridie, far from being original, was thinking entirely in clichés. She was thinking of hornets' nests being stirred up, and cats among pigeons, and thorns in sides. She felt quite distracted and wished Frank had never had anything accepted. She had always been proud of him being a writer. It made him different from the rest, different amd special. Now for the first time she wished he'd just stick to his safe nine-to-five job in the office of Messrs Goldmayer Ltd – Wholesale Warehousemen, and forget about all his other carry-on. It was different enough being a 'collar and tie man', as Carragh proudly referred to her son-in-law. The more she thought about it the more she became convinced that Frank was being selfish and insensitive. Another thing, she disliked the sound of the television people and the actors and actresses. They seemed to inhabit a different world altogether from the one to which she and Frank belonged. She didn't want Frank to have anything to do with these people. No good would come of it.

All the time she struggled to be happy for him. 'I'm really proud of you, Frank. I really am,' she kept assuring him and herself. She felt furtive, guilty and disloyal about her thoughts. She also felt apprehensive, insecure. She had a sudden vision of Frank mixing with glamorous strangers. Normally she never gave her appearance a thought, but now she became conscious of her plain, bespectacled face, her straight mousy hair, her dowdy clothes. For days afterwards, alone in the kitchen or in the lavatory, she nursed her rosary beads for comfort. Over and over again, she rapidly repeated, 'Hail Mary full of grace, the Lord is with thee, Blessed art thou among woman and blessed is the fruit of thy womb, Jesus. Holy Mary Mother of God, pray for us sinners now and at the hour of our death. Amen.'

Chapter Forty-Eight

There were times of tenderness, romantic music in the background, gentle words of endearment. At other times there would be shouts and screams and groans and grunts of utter abandonment, and the smells of sex and sweat. All self-consciousness had long since been thrown to the winds. Bernard and Andrina had invented their own Kama Sutra. Everything was in the merciless pursuit of orgasm.

They made it their business to take every opportunity to be physically linked together, he inside her, she enveloping him.

He called her his velvet vice. There was nothing she wouldn't do to please him and therefore please herself. He would telephone and tell her what to wear the next time she came to him, and what he wanted her to do. Even the call excited her. He liked her to look very smart and sophisticated, and especially to wear hats. He had a 'thing' about hats.

He called her and told her he'd bought her this fuchsia-pink wide-brimmed straw hat to match a dress she had of that colour. He'd been fantasising about her in high heels and wearing this hat. He wanted her to be sitting on the edge of the bed wearing it that evening. As usual, she looked forward to carrying out his directions. She made an excuse to Robert about going to some extra-mural class, and in a shopping bag carried out everything she needed for Bernard's flat. There she bathed and made up extra carefully. She washed her hair and styled it to perfection. She donned her fuchsia pink silk taffeta cross-over dress and wore nothing underneath it. She slipped her feet into elegant high-heeled shoes of matching soft leather. Then she placed the huge-brimmed hat to sit low over her eyes to create that mysterious smouldering look she knew he loved. Previously she'd prepared a supper of tiger prawns in a champagne sauce over wild rice. She'd set a small round table at the foot of the bed with pretty glasses and pink candles. Strawberries with a hot chocolate dip were to follow. Even the food had to match the colour theme of the evening. They always paid scrupulous attention to detail.

At his estimated time of arrival she perched herself, perfectly prepared, on the edge of the bed. She crossed her legs, revealing a long seductive stretch of smooth golden-brown skin, lotioned, glistening. Her heart raced wildly as she heard Bernard's key in the door, then his slow deliberate tread across the hall.

Once inside the bedroom he closed the door behind him and stood for a long time staring at her in silence. He always obtained great pleasure just by looking at her, knowing she was prepared for him. She found his stare highly flattering, and it spurred her to desire him with an even greater longing. But first he asked her to walk around the room for him. At one time, she'd found this embarrassing. He'd persisted, however, with gentle words, assuring her it was his love for her that created his desire to watch her move before him. Eventually, after many occasions, she had become skilled at parading provocatively around and enjoyed the sensation of his eyes boring holes in her ankles, her legs, her hands, her breasts.

She always looked forward to what he had in store for her next. The next time, in fact, he had instructed her to be in the shower on his return. She didn't hear him come home or lock the front door behind him. She didn't hear his footsteps cross the hall or enter the bedroom. It startled her when the shower door was opened. Then his tall muscular body towered behind her. Already the warm, steamy atmosphere was mildly sensual. His hands held her shoulders, then slid caressingly down over her back as the warm drops of water soaked their hair and skin. Taking the soap, he picked up each of her feet in turn and pulled the soap between every toe, then round the sole, then with gentle rubbing motion up the calves of her legs, stopping short of her bottom. From the ankles again, he went up the front and the insides of her calves and thighs, just leaving off before he reached her most secret, exciting place.

Again he turned her round. He reached down, and taking

each buttock firmly in each hand, soaped them, rotating them together. Lust and heat fevered her. She felt light-headed with excitement and desire as he eased her round to face him. Regardless of the water cascading down over them both, he kept her at arm's length, staring at her, before beginning to sculpt her breasts in lather. As he moved the breasts together, a beating, a madness, an exquisite shuddering desire took possession of her. He drew her closer and pressed himself against her breasts. By this time she was frenzied with the need to feel him inside her. Tantalisingly, he pressed his penis against her, rubbed it softly against her groin, teasing her to distraction until she begged him to enter her. As he did, he gripped her tightly and she cried out his name, over and over again.

More and more now, when they made love, it was a kind of madness. It was something they craved all the time, like an addiction. But they were not able to get together nearly as often as they wanted. Sometimes Bernard would be away on business, but more often than not it would be because Andrina, for one reason or another, couldn't get away. There was no longer any use asking Josie to babysit, and Sophie was becoming too suspicious and difficult.

Weeks, sometimes months, would pass without them seeing each other. When they did, it was like going home. She loved the flat as well as Bernard, and she was proud of it. Although her name was not on the door, she felt it belonged to her. Just as Bernard belonged to her. It gave her a wonderful, luxurious, supremely satisfied feeling – like a cat with a bowl of delicious cream.

Lying in the comfortable bed in the flat, happily exhausted after making love for an hour, she was unprepared for Bernard spoiling her euphoria by talking about marriage – although she should have known that Bernard's obsessiveness meant he would never give up trying to completely possess her.

'Darling velvet, we can't go on like this. I know we've gone over it all before, but you must try to think from my point of view. It's not natural for me to remain celibate for most of the time – for weeks and months when you say you can't see me. I love you. I'm proud of you. I want you to be constantly by my side. I want you to accompany me when I go on tours. I want to show you off as my beautiful wife. I want everybody to know you're mine. No, please don't run away,' he added hastily as she stiffened from him and made to rise. 'Why do you always panic like this? What is there to be afraid of?'

She shook her head, hugging herself. 'I don't know. Please, don't make me think about it. I'm happy going on just as we are.'

'Well, damn it, I'm not!'

She was shocked at the venom in his voice. Suddenly, for a second or two, she caught a glimpse of another person, a stranger. She began to weep and immediately he was Bernard again, gathering her gently into his arms, whispering tender endearments.

'My darling, my dearest beautiful Andrina. I love you, but I'm only human. It's not natural for a normal healthy man to be such a loner.'

'Well.' Her large, childish eyes desperately searched for an escape from the immediate situation. 'Don't be a loner. Get a girlfriend to go around with you. Live a normal life.'

'Without you?'

'We could go on seeing each other like we do now – just as often as we can. I've got Robert, so why shouldn't you have somebody for when we can't be together?'

He sighed. 'Nobody can compare with you. How could any woman match the perfection of my lovely little velvet?'

She laughed with relief, gave him a quick kiss and swung her legs off the bed. 'I'll have to run.'

The truth was she'd left Jennifer alone in the house and sleeping. Love-making with Bernard had blotted out all thoughts of anybody else, but now she'd begun to feel agitated and apprehensive. What if Jennifer woke up and began to cry? What if she'd hurt herself? What if one of the neighbours heard Jennifer? What if one of the neighbours had seen Jennifer's mother going out? What if they sent for the police? What if it got into the papers? ***What if Sophie found out?***

Once outside she began to run and, far too agitated and impatient to wait for a bus, she hailed a taxi. She sat on the edge of the seat, bent forward, tense, hands twisting together. In her posture at least she looked exactly like her mother.

'My God.' Her thoughts flayed her with anguish and regret. 'How could I have done this? How could I have left my little girl on her own?'

Josie met her in the hall. She was nursing a tear-stained Jennifer. 'It's a bloody good job I had your spare set of keys.' She was pale-faced and bug-eyed with anger. 'You're a bloody disgrace.'

'Oh Josie, I'm so sorry.' Andrina grabbed Jennifer from her neighbour, and showered the child with kisses. 'Darling, I'm sorry. Mummy's sorry. It's all right. You're all right now.' To Josie she cried out, 'It'll never happen again. I promise. Please don't tell anybody, oh, *please!*'

'That wean could have choked, or anything could have happened. I just don't know how you could have left her like that.'

'I shouldn't have left her. I realise that now, but she was sound asleep and I only meant to be a few minutes.'

'You're a bloody liar. You've been away well over an hour.'

'I didn't think I'd be away all that time.'

'He took longer than usual, did he?' Josie sneered. 'You made sure you were back in time for Robert, though. That'll be him coming up the stairs now. Timed exactly.'

'Oh Josie,' Andrina began to weep. '*Please. Please!*'

'Don't worry, I won't say anything to anybody. If I ever find out you've left that wean again though . . .'

'Never again. Never again.' Hastily she wiped at her eyes. By the time Robert reached the door she was quite composed.

'Hello Josie,' he greeted her. 'Are you coming or going?'

'Just going.' Josie passed him at the door. 'Time I was getting ready for my work. No rest for the wicked.'

'Darling,' Andrina said to Robert after Josie had left. 'Take Jennifer for a minute, will you? I made a steak pie earlier. I've just to pop it in the oven and do the potatoes.'

'Sure. Come to daddy, love. Have you been crying, pet? What's the matter, eh?'

Jennifer clung close to him, still hiccoughing with sobs.

'I think she fell or banged herself,' Andrina said. 'You know how she's beginning to get into everything.'

'Och, poor wee pet,' Robert soothed. 'Show Daddy the sore bit and I'll kiss it better.'

Andrina busied herself at the oven and the sink. She felt shaken with relief. No harm had been done. No harm at all. Josie wouldn't say anything. It was as if nothing had happened. Nothing had happened. She kept trying to reassure herself, but every now and again a wave of horror would engulf her. She must have been mad to leave Jennifer. What had she been thinking of to do such a dreadful thing? Yet all the time she knew.

She made a bread and butter pudding for Robert. He liked solid, unimaginative things like bread and butter pudding. There was delicious home-baked apple pie afterwards to enjoy with his coffee. Andrina was a good wife – Robert was always saying so.

So was his mother. 'You're a wonderful cook and baker,' Jean Anderson often said admiringly. 'And you keep this wee house beautiful – absolutely spotless.'

And she was a good mother. Robert and Jean said that too. Dear little Jennifer. Andrina didn't want to do anything that would put her at risk. She wondered if she dared ask Robert's mother to babysit. But Jean was now troubled with arthritis and hadn't been keeping well for some time; her hands had become quite deformed and swollen. She'd probably say she wasn't able to look after the baby.

Andrina sighed over her apple pie and Robert said, 'Anything wrong?'

'Wrong?' Eyes wide and innocent, she smiled across the table at him. 'Of course not!'

Chapter Forty-Nine

'But why?' Bridie was near to tears. 'We've got a lovely wee house here, and anyway we're liable to get allocated one of the new flats any time now. And we both *like* the Gorbals. It's such a *friendly* place.'

She thought of all the times that Mrs McLachlan next door had let the coalman in when she and Frank were at work. Or the gas man. All the keys fitted all the doors in the building, and as often as not people just left their keys in their doors.

Everything was moving too fast. Even the screening of Frank's play had been quicker than either of them expected. It had slotted, all too conveniently as far as she was concerned, into a series already in production.

'The West End is where the BBC is.' Frank struggled to be patient. 'It would be so much more convenient. And it's where they all stay. The BBC people and the actors and actresses, everybody. It's a wonderful district, Bridie. It's so *interesting*. There are so many different types of people.'

'You said there were interesting people here. You're always watching them out the front room window. You said a fascinating panorama of life passed by that window.'

'I know. I know. The whole of Glasgow is a fascinating panorama of life.'

'We're perfectly happy here.'

'And we'll be perfectly happy in the West End. At least come and look at the place, Bridie. It means so much to me. Steve Martin's got a job with Grampian and he's moving up to Aberdeen. He and his wife want somebody to buy their marvellous flat in Botanic Crescent. They're really sorry to leave it.'

'Anyway, Frank, we can't afford to buy a flat.'

'I can get a mortgage. I've been making enquiries. One of

these days I'm going to give up my job in the office – and write full time.'

'Oh, Frank . . .

'I didn't tell them that. Apparently, they're not so keen on giving mortgages to full-time writers. Unless you're making a fortune, I suppose. I would never have had the nerve even to ask about such a thing before. But now I have real prospects, Bridie. I'm going places, and I don't mean just to live in the West End. I was just waiting to see how the play was received and look at the reviews.' He tossed a pile of papers into the air. 'Look at them!'

'I've seen them, Frank.' She had read each review several times. So had Frank. Astonishingly flattering words leapt from the page of each newspaper: 'wonderful . . . gripping . . . hard-hitting . . . honest . . . revealing . . . brilliant.'

'Well?' Frank said.

'They're very good.'

'They're rave reviews. *Rave* reviews. That's what the producer said on the phone.'

'But we can't plunge ourselves into a huge amount of debt – thousands of pounds, Frank, we'd have to get a mortgage for all that money – just on the strength of one play. It's madness. I think you should try to calm down. Calm right down, Frank. Get back down to earth.'

'But they've accepted my other play. That's the piece of good news I was keeping till last. I knew you'd be worried about the mortgage but there's no need, pet. They've taken *another* play. They want more hard-hitting stuff, they say. Apparently they can't get enough of it. I could give up the office now. It would give me so much more time to write.'

'Oh Frank . . .' Bridie wailed.

'But I won't. I won't. I'll stay for a wee while yet. Just to please you. Just to set your mind at rest. But oh, Bridie, Bridie, please come and see the flat in Botanic Crescent. It's so beautiful, overlooking the park – you'll love it. And it's so handy for the BBC. And the BBC Club is where everybody from the BBC meets for a drink and a talk. It's in Botanic Crescent, just a few doors along from the flat.'

Bridie's heart sank.

'Say you'll come, Bridie, for my sake, pet. Please!'

Reluctantly she nodded. 'If you're that keen.'

'Aren't you going to congratulate me?'

'What about?'

He laughed. 'You get more dozy every day. The play, of course. They've accepted another play.'

'The one you've been working on? I thought you weren't going to be finished with that one before Christmas.'

'No, no. The one about the priest.'

'Oh, Frank . . .'

'Don't worry.' He laughed again. 'What can they do? Except excommunicate me.'

'Holy Mother of God. It was bad enough with Doris . . .'

'Just joking. Just joking. All it will do is raise a bit of controversy. That's a healthy thing, Bridie. Nothing for anyone to be afraid of.'

That was what decided her about moving to the West End. At least no one there knew her, and there wouldn't be such a concentration of chapels and priests. It would be impossible to hold up her head on the Gorbals, impossible to go to Mass there, after Frank's play about the priest came out. She hardly spoke a word on the way over to see the house, she was so devastated. Frank didn't notice. He talked excitedly and non-stop until they reached Botanic Crescent.

'Look at it! Didn't I tell you it was a lovely place? Just look at it, Bridie.'

A low road ran off Queen Margaret Drive (where the BBC was situated) and alongside the leafy, tree-lined Botanic Gardens. Arching up to the right of this road, and separated by a grassy belt and more trees, was Botanic Crescent. As they walked up the Crescent, they passed large three-storeyed terraced houses, one of which housed the BBC Club. Then there were four-storeyed red sandstone buildings with big bay windows and gardens in front.

'Aren't they beautiful? Isn't everything absolutely beautiful?' Frank enthused.

Bridie couldn't deny it. Yet even before she entered the beautiful tiled close and climbed the quiet stairs, and saw the beautiful stained glass door of the flat, she felt homesick for her own wee house in the Gorbals. Her first impression, when Steve Martin opened the door and ushered them into the house, was of a cavernous space filled with rows of doors. A huge cheeseplant, lit from beneath, cast a giant jigsaw shadow over the walls and roof. Bridie and Frank walked forward, feet sinking deep into the soft mulberry carpet. Bold, colourful paintings sat with quiet authority on the walls, softly picked out in the glow of brass downlighters.

'I think Samantha's in the kitchen. Come on through,' Steve said.

The kitchen was huge, bigger than their front room in the Gorbals. Terracotta tiles gave a warm but practical flooring. Mellow timber units contrasted with the Mediterranean lilac blue of the walls. A collection of Majollica plates clustered in a friendly huddle on one wall. Their bright colours made a vivid splash against the subtle background.

There was no Samantha.

'Through here, darling,' a voice called.

Steve laughed. 'Through to the sitting room, folks. Sorry about that. I was in the study when the doorbell went.'

They followed him across the hall and into an even more impressive room. Bridie was first stunned by the imposing bay window, carefully stripped back to its original wood, the soft honeyed oak. The curtains were pale cream as was the carpet. The whole room seemed a symphony of ivory and cream except for the huge scarlet abstract painting above the fire. Like a splash of carmine blood it brought strength to the subtlety of the room.

There was nothing subtle, however, about the woman who rose, arms outstretched, to greet them. 'Darlings!'

Samantha made Bridie feel like a colourless mouse. Blonde hair was pinned haphazardly on top of her head with tendrils hanging like rivulets of pure gold. Mexican shell earrings dangled noisily from her ears as she spoke. A dramatic scarlet and turquoise kaftan billowed around her. She swooped towards Bridie on bare feet flashing scarlet toenails that matched fingernails so long that Bridie marvelled at anyone being able to function with them. How did Samantha manage to peel potatoes or do any normal household chores?

It turned out Samantha had a 'treasure', in the form of Mrs Hennessy who lived in Maryhill. Mrs Hennessy came every morning to 'do' for Samantha. It was Mrs Hennessy who peeled the potatoes and did all the normal household chores.

'You can inherit her, darling,' Samantha said, gaily flicking cigarette ash all over the place, 'unless of course you have your own staff.'

Bridie stared down at her feet and murmured something incoherent.

Frank laughed. 'We come from a room and kitchen in the Gorbals. Your Mrs Hennessy has probably been used to more than us.'

'Frank!' Bridie muttered, glaring furtively round at him.

Steve joined in the laughter. 'Samantha hasn't a clue. Her daddy's in merchant banking. She thinks this . . .' he flung his hand around, 'is poverty and hardship.'

'You have a beautiful home,' Bridie forced the words out, hating Samantha for her careless self-confidence.

'Thank you, darling.'

Afterwards Bridie told Frank, 'If she'd called me darling one more time, I would have throttled her with her own beads.'

'Och, Samantha's all right. It's just the way they talk.' Frank hadn't been a bit shy. He'd taken everything happily in his stride. He never ceased to amaze Bridie. 'What do you think? About the house – wasn't it wonderful? Did you see the view from the window – a sea of green – did you ever see so much lush greenery?'

'I'm surprised at you, Frank. I really am.'

'How do you mean?'

'I thought it was people you liked to see from your window. You've never been in the slightest interested in trees or any kind of greenery before. You've never been interested in going for holidays or even a day out in the country.'

'This is different. We'd have the best of both worlds – all worlds – there. There's the lovely view, there's the park. But two minutes away, there's the BBC Club – always packed with creative people.' He sighed with pleasure. 'I could enjoy talking shop to them to my heart's content. Then, less than two minutes beyond that, there's Queen Margaret Drive and the BBC. Five minutes from the flat, at the end of Queen Margaret Drive, there's the main Great Western Road, and off that there's Byres Road.' He hugged Bridie in his enthusiasm. 'You'll love Byres Road, Bridie. There's a library and all sorts of interesting shops there. Lots of fascinating people. The West End's the university area too, so there are students and academics as well as BBC people. What do you think, Bridie? About the house?'

She thought of Mrs McLachlan next door, and the Gordons and the Menzies upstairs. Mr Menzies was a godsend – a more eager-to-help neighbour you couldn't meet. He'd fixed their rattling windows. He'd replaced a doorknob that had fallen off. He'd even fixed the television. Frank was absolutely useless with his hands. As he admitted himself he wouldn't know one end of a screwdriver from another.

Mrs McLachlan had always insisted on taking Bridie's turn to wash the stairs. 'Och, you're out working every day, hen. I'm at home all the time. And I've time on my hands now that the weans are at school.'

When both Bridie and Frank had gone down with the flu, all the neighbours rallied round. Their key would turn in the door, and there would be a shout of, 'It's only me, hen.' And in would come Mrs Gordon or Mrs Menzies or Mrs McLachlan, or Mrs Sinclair, or Mrs Webster from downstairs. They would bring a bowl of soup or pudding. They'd make pots of tea and hot lemon drinks and straighten up the bed.

Bridie's throat tightened at the thought of all her good neighbours. She'd never appreciated them more than she did now.

'Bridie, what do you think?' Frank repeated.

'If it's what you want, Frank.'

'But I want you to want it too.'

She felt a stab of bitterness and resentment. She fought to ignore it. 'Whatever makes you happy makes me happy, Frank. But I'll miss the Gorbals and my neighbours here. They've been good to us.'

'We're not going to the other end of the world, pet. You can still come back here and visit them.'

But visiting wouldn't be the same.

She smiled. 'Yes, all right, dear.'

'Oh, Bridie, Bridie.' Frank's eyes gazed rapturously beyond her into the future. 'Didn't I always say that one day all our dreams would come true?'

Yes, she thought sadly. But when did our dreams separate and become different?

Chapter Fifty

Michael and Caroline were delighted to get Frank and Bridie's flat in the Gorbals. Garngad was becoming a derelict area. Buildings were being torn down all around them.

Dereliction was going on in the Gorbals too, of course. Plaster dust thickened the air, and everywhere mud squelched underfoot. But the flat in the Gorbals was a room and kitchen. Michael and Caroline's single end had become chaotic with the twins and the new baby.

'What with the pram, and the twins' bed, and the table and chairs, there wasn't an inch of space for us to move in that room,' Caroline said. 'It was driving us mad.'

Nevertheless, Caroline looked a changed woman. Her fair hair had a healthy bounce. Her eyes were bright and happy. She looked comfortably plump. She and Michael were having a housewarming party and all the family were crowding in to what had once been Frank and Bridie's front room.

'We hadn't to do a thing to this place,' Caroline enthused. 'Frank and Bridie had it so nice.'

Hearing her, Bridie felt like weeping. It was an agony to see someone else lay proud claim to her room. The Gorbals flat still felt like home to her. This was where she belonged. Already she hated the West End.

'Oh, there you are, Bridie,' Caroline greeted her. 'I was just saying to everybody how nice you and Frank had kept this place.'

Drowning in a sea of misery, Bridie's gaze dropped. 'Thanks.'

'How you doing, Michael?' Frank said cheerily. 'Still keeping off the booze?'

'Of course. But we've got beer for anybody that wants it. And gin for the girls.'

'Just a soft drink for me,' Bridie murmured.

Doris, trying not to totter on her stilts of heels, joined them. She was on her second gin and tonic. Alcohol was proving no comfort. She wished she'd never come. She had known Bernard would be there, and she'd bought a new scarlet minidress to make sure he noticed her. She'd hoped against hope that a miracle would happen and he'd turn to her again. She'd picked over every minute of their relationship a thousand times, trying to understand it, trying to find out where she'd gone wrong. In moments of terrible despair she'd stare at herself in the mirror and tell herself it was simply because she looked too small, too fat and too common. The whole family, including Bridie, were too small. It was terrible. The only consolation was she and Bridie hadn't inherited Carragh's bandy legs. She'd moan and sob broken-heartedly against the mirror, and feel that no amount of back-combing and piled-up hair, no amount of make-up or false eyelashes, would change what she was. It didn't matter how tight her pantie girdle was, or how high her heels – nothing made any difference.

Yet Bernard had wanted her once. He had made love to her. He had asked her to marry him. How had it all gone wrong?

At other times she'd assure herself that maybe she was a bit on the small side, but actually she wasn't a bad looker. Other men had told her so. (Eddy McGuire in despatch was always trying to get off with her and telling her what a smasher she was.) She was definitely better looking than Bridie. Bridie had always been plain and had never been in the slightest interested in making the best of herself. Yet she'd got (and kept) Frank. All the same, Bridie had better watch out – Frank was mixing with glamorous actresses now. How long would it be before some bitch got her claws into Frank? And Bridie would be left in the same boat as her.

Because that's what it came down to in the end: some cruel, selfish bitch had taken Bernard away from her. She'd been afraid that he'd bring Jane Ford with him to Michael and Caroline's housewarming party, though she had no idea if he was still seeing her. She'd hyped herself up, ready to scratch the bitch's eyes out. But there he was – as cool, as self-confident, as uncaring as ever. He'd given her a nod of recognition that didn't disturb the flow of his conversation with Scobie. She felt a stab of hurt and resentment at her father for having anything to do with Bernard. She'd expected him to show more loyalty, and she said so under her breath to Bridie.

'Och, what is he supposed to do?' Bridie asked, somewhat impatiently Doris thought – making her even more hurt. 'He's Michael's best friend, so he had to come. And Bernard's family, so he had to come.'

'Nobody *had* to come!' Doris said.

'Why did *you* come then?' Bridie snapped.

'Charming!' Doris downed her gin and tonic. 'That's all I need, you to bite my nose off.'

Bridie sighed. 'I'm sorry, Doris. I just wish I was back here, that's all. I hate where I am now.'

'How can you hate a place like Botanic Crescent? It's terribly posh. I'd give my eye teeth to live there, so I would.'

'I've got a horrible neighbour. Every time I go out or come in, her door opens a crack. Either she or her husband watches me all the time. It's really horrible.'

'Just shout, "Mind your own business, you nosey old bag." '

'I wish I had the nerve.'

'Next time I come to see you, I'll do it. Now that you mention it, the last time I visited you somebody opened that door and pretended they were polishing the door knob.'

'That would be her husband. He seems to do all the housework, while she just floats about with a frilly gauze cap over her curlers and a frilly négligé.'

'Don't let a couple of arseholes like that get you down, Bridie. Just think yourself lucky you've got a good man and a lovely house.'

'I suppose I am.'

'Of course you are. But Holy Mother of God, Bridie, try to do something with yourself.'

'What do you mean?'

'Well, look at you – not a scrap of make-up, and you never

put a curler near your hair, and your clothes just hang on you. It's bad enough being short-sighted and stuck with glasses, but there's lots you could do. Buy more fashionably-shaped glasses for a start.'

'Och, Doris, you know me . . .'

'More important, Bridie, I know men. They're suckers for a pretty face and an offer of a good shag, and Frank's a man, and now he's mixing with . . .'

'I know. I know,' Bridie interrupted miserably. 'But I can't possibly compete with actresses. It's not just actresses either – he meets all sorts of women, including women writers. I can't do anything about them. He just loves to talk about writing. He always has. He's in his element meeting other writers. He's joined a writers' society now and goes to their meetings. Oh Doris, what am I going to do?'

'I told you, you'll have to make a bit more effort with yourself.'

Bridie blinked and pushed at her glasses. She was blinking a lot these days. It had become a nervous habit. 'People would just laugh at me if I suddenly started painting my face and curling my hair. I'm sure Frank would. It's just not me.'

Doris reluctantly agreed. She couldn't honestly see make-up or curling performing any miracles for Bridie. 'Well, treat yourself to some sexy black underwear and a black lacy nighty.' She didn't have much hope for sexy underwear making Bridie attractive either. What Frank had ever seen in her, God alone knew.

She went over to the sideboard to get herself another drink but Carragh stopped her with a hand on her arm. 'I think you've had enough, hen. You don't want the big man,' she jerked her head in Bernard's direction, 'to see you making a fool of yourself.'

'Bastard,' Doris said brokenly.

'Now, now.'

'I'll never get over the way he humiliated me, Ma. He was terribly cruel to me, so he was.'

Carragh tutted. 'Your da's been cruel to me in his day, by

God he has. And well you know it. Bernard was never as bad to you as your da was to me.'

Doris sighed. 'I don't know how you stood it.'

'I didn't see I'd much choice, hen. I couldn't have done what you did.'

'Oh, Ma, don't start.'

'I don't know what the world's coming to,' Carragh said. Her face, under her squashed black felt hat, acquired an aggrieved expression. She kept her hat on when out visiting because she had become self-conscious about the fuzz barely covering her scalp. It was one thing for Scobie to have gone bald on top, but for her to go the same was a hard cross to bear. 'What with you divorcing your man. And Bridie's man writing a play about a priest. That's the next one that's to come on the telly, Bridie told me. Talk about being upset – and no wonder, by all accounts. That's why she agreed to move. What Father Riley will say, I dread to think. And what's possessed Frank to make an attack on the church – because that's what Bridie thinks it is – I just don't know. He's such a nice chap, you know how fond of him I am. And he's always gone to Mass, and the church has never done him any harm. I just can't understand young folks any more.'

'Attacking the church?' Doris squealed. 'That's terrible, so it is. What next? I'll feel humiliated all over again. We'll probably *all* have to move.'

Carragh sighed. 'We will all be moving again, hen, by the looks of things. I'll be sorry to leave Garngad.'

'We'll get a nice new house.' A flicker of hope widened Doris's eyes for a second or two. 'With a bathroom.'

'Aye, they look nice enough,' Carragh said without much enthusiasm. 'But I've heard folks in the new flats have been complaining about dampness. I just wonder how long these places will last. Our building in Garngad must be over a hundred years old. I wonder if them new flats'll still be standing in a hundred years' time.'

'They'll surely see us out,' Doris said.

But no optimism could raise Carragh's spirits. She was

seeing not only the old familiar buildings being torn down, but the break up of the close-knit communities within them.

Michael came across then. 'What are you drinking, Carragh? Can I get you something?'

'No, I'm fine, son. I'm surprised you have any hard stuff in your house.'

Michael grinned. 'I'm hoping you lot'll finish it all off so's I won't be left with any temptation. My da's doing his best at the moment. Him and Tony.'

'Aye, I can see that. Any moment now Patrick's going to give us a song.'

Sure enough, minutes later, Patrick suddenly threw back his head and belted out:

'In Mountjoy Jail one Monday morning,
High upon the Gallows Tree,
Kevin Barry gave his young life for the cause of liberty.
Just a lad of 18 summers and there's no-one can deny,
As he walked to death that morning,
Barry held his head on high.
"Won't you shoot me like a soldier,
Do not hang me like a dog,
For I fought to free old Ireland,
On a still September morn . . ." '

Laughing, Frank came over to Bridie's side. 'Da's well away.'

Doris suddenly looked as if she was about to burst into tears. 'Holy Mother of God, it's supposed to be a happy occasion. What's he singing a sad song like that for and depressing everybody? Your da's about as bad as Bernard. He doesn't care a damn about other folks' feelings.'

Bridie stiffened as Frank put an arm around her shoulders. He was happy all right. He didn't care a damn about *her* feelings. All the O'Maleys were the same.

Chapter Fifty-One

'Bailie McPherson?'

McPherson nodded, then accepted the outstretched hand.

'I'm Tom Gordon of Gordon Construction. I've been told through a mutual friend, Bailie McPherson, that I could approach you. You're a man I could speak to.' In other words, he knew Bailie McPherson was a man who would take a bung. 'John Douglas . . .' Gordon went on, 'from the Church of Jesus in Rose Street.'

'A good man, John,' McPherson said. 'Gives a lot of support to the church.'

'As you do yourself, Bailie, as you do yourself.' In other words, friends that pray together stay together. 'What are you drinking?'

'Whisky.'

Gordon ordered a good malt. 'I'd like to tender for the Northern Road flats. Any chance, do you think?'

Bailie McPherson took his time, savouring the whisky before answering. 'I could use my considerable influence with the planning department.'

'I would be grateful if you could, Bailie McPherson.'

'After all, you are an old established construction firm.'

'We are indeed, and if we got this contract . . .'

'I will certainly argue your case to the best of my ability . . .'

'You won't regret it, Bailie McPherson.' In other words, it was going to be a really good bung.

McPherson felt pleased with himself. He enjoyed several more whiskies and a splendid meal at Tom Gordon's expense. On the way home in his silver grey Mercedes, he savoured a Havana cigar. The Merc was a new acquisition of which McPherson was extremely proud. A real bargain from someone for whom he'd done a few favours. A present of Havanas had been given to him at Christmas by a hotelier who had been grateful for receiving yet another licence. Pub owners too had showered him with bottles of Glenmorangie or Famous Grouse. He'd had gifts of vintage port and 'sherry for your good wife'.

He leaned well back in the driving seat, mostly because he felt so pleasantly relaxed, but also because he had grown more portly. Sophie had begun to nag at him about losing weight. His cheeks and nose had become mottled with fine red veins, giving his skin a brightly coloured hue. Sophie warned, 'If you don't cut down on all this rich food and drink, and lose a bit of weight, you're going to take a stroke or a heart attack.'

It was all very well for her. She'd always been built like a greyhound. Her nature helped keep her thin. Always worrying and ferreting suspiciously about. He just wasn't like her. He was generously built, and it was good that it was so. It made him look more imposing – a man of substance. He no longer worried about what his father would think or what his father would do. His father had lived in a different world. His father was one of the old school of socialists. His father had been willing to die for the working man that he represented. Andrew McPherson had decided to *live* for them, and live as well as he could into the bargain. This meant learning a thing or two from what went on in big business and among Tory colleagues. He knew about quite a few businessmen's tax fiddles and ruthless practices, some of which were on a criminal scale that was breathtaking in their scope and audacity. He often suspected they only got away with it because they made enormous donations to the Tory party. He felt saintly in comparison. He helped ordinary folks get houses. He helped small guys with wee corner pubs get licences. He listened sympathetically to problems of all kinds from the poorest section of society – and he did what he could for them. He'd even done a few police officers a good turn when it was needed.

He was a very popular man.

He'd phoned Sophie to tell her he was working very late and would snatch something to eat in town. This was in case she'd kept a meal hot for him as she often did. Sophie was a good wife

– too good sometimes. He just wished she could relax a bit. Tonight she'd be waiting for him in a house in which never a speck of dust would dare descend. His slippers would be waiting for him inside the front door. The back door was only for tradespeople. She always gave him his place. The cushions on his favourite armchair by the fire facing the television would be plumped, ready for him to sink thankfully into. His pipe and tobacco pouch (the soft leather one she'd given him at Christmas) would be lying on the small table beside his elbow. He still enjoyed a pipe in the privacy and comfort of his own home.

When he did arrive in time for dinner, Sophie would present him with a wonderful meal. Indeed, more and more he was insisting on business lunches instead of later meals. Not even the best cordon bleu chef in town could compete with Sophie's dinners. He had never been tempted with other women. He was a strict believer in the sanctity of marriage and was genuinely shocked to learn of the extra marital adventures of colleagues or friends. A committed Christian, as he always had been, and Sophie now was, could not and certainly should not ever contemplate anything that might endanger the marriage vows.

When he had said 'Until death do us part,' he had meant it.

'You know the latest news?' Sophie asked once he had donned his slippers, loosened his tie and settled in his chair to concentrate on the business of filling a pipe.

'No. What?'

'Agnes and Duncan Noble have committed suicide. They were both prescribed sleeping pills and tranquillisers, and apparently they saved them up and took them all at once.'

'My God, Sophie,' he cried out, his pipe forgotten in the shock of such a revelation. 'That's terrible. I'm so sorry.'

'Why? I'm not.'

It was then he noticed how feverish her face was, and how unnaturally bright were her eyes. She looked quite demented. Insane almost.

'My dear, they were your mother and father. Whatever happened in the past, they were still your own flesh and blood.

Here, let me pour you a glass of whisky. It'll help calm you down.'

'They robbed me of my childhood. They made a nightmare of most of my life.'

'Sophie, that was all years ago. You've been harming yourself ever since – harbouring such black emotions, being so bitter and unforgiving.'

'You don't know. You don't know about them or about the so-called "home" they caused me to put into. For years I couldn't bear to think about them – it was too painful. I still can't think about the institution and what I suffered there.' She put her hands to her head. 'My mind blacks out.'

'My dear . . .' was all he could say. He felt for her. He wanted to put his arms around her to comfort her, to show her some loving tenderness. But he knew sadly it would be no use. They didn't have that sort of relationship. In the silent darkness of their bedroom she would cling to him with furtive passion and she'd have rapid, desperate sex with him before turning away into her cold, closed world once more.

'We'll have to go to the funeral,' he said. 'Everybody will expect it. It would look bad if we didn't.'

'One more ordeal,' Sophie said, half to herself. 'One more ordeal, and then it'll be finished for good. I'll be free of them.'

'That's right. Just cling to that thought. Everything's going to be all right.' But secretly he doubted it. Sophie was Sophie. He couldn't see anything ever making her any different. Who was it who said, 'Give me a child for his first five years and you can do what you like with him afterwards'? Sophie's character had been long since formed. It wouldn't matter what happened now. He suspected the only way Sophie could change, if she changed at all, would be to get worse. No matter what she was trying to make out, she must feel the most awful guilt.

Suddenly he felt anxious. 'It's just occurred to me. There'll be an inquest. I hope to God nothing is dug up that will damage our reputation.'

Sophie began agitatedly pacing about the room. 'Even

beyond the grave they won't leave me in peace. Even beyond the grave they'll try to ruin my life.'

'Now wait a minute,' McPherson said. 'Let me think . . .'

Sophie was wringing her hands. 'If the newspapers got a hold of the story behind this . . .'

'No, wait a minute, Sophie. A lot of people owe me favours. I should be able to use my influence to hush anything up. Leave it to me. Try not to worry. I'll make a few phone calls. I'll see a few people tomorrow.'

'The phone's hardly stopped all afternoon. I've had to leave it off the hook. You'd wonder how the news got around so quickly. They were only found this morning when their home help went in.'

'I hope to God they didn't leave a note.'

'Apparently it just said they were sorry.'

'Oh God!' Surely Sophie *must* feel guilty. After all, most people even felt guilty at any normal death of people they loved.

'Sorry!' Sophie laughed bitterly. 'I hope they burn in hell.'

'Sophie, you're upset. You don't mean that.'

She laughed again. 'What would you know? Brought up by a mother who always thought you were marvellous. No doubt your father doted on you as well.'

Now *he* felt guilty. He hadn't visited his mother for some time. They'd had her for Christmas dinner, but he'd only popped in to see her a couple of times since then and it was now June. Certainly Sophie had visited on separate occasions and had had her over to Bearsden for afternoon tea. But he seldom managed any spare time during the day and so he hadn't seen her then. Andrina visited her too, although the old girl must be getting senile because she denied ever seeing Andrina for months.

'She's been to see you several times, Mother,' he'd patiently persisted. 'Robert told me.'

'Well, if she's been telling Robert she's been coming to see me, she must be up to something. She must be sneaking off to see a fancy man because she certainly hasn't come to see me.'

'Mother!' He was horrified that there should be such ideas in her head. 'You mustn't ever think such things. Our Andrina's a good girl and a perfect wife to Robert. Indeed, Sophie and I often say she's too good for him. He's not as committed a Christian as we once thought he was. Andrina never misses a service, and to see and hear that girl sing in the choir is like watching and listening to an angel. Sophie and I are really proud of her. But we know from friends who still go to Rose Street that Robert is a very poor attender. Andrina is too loyal, of course, to ever say a word against her husband.'

'That may be so,' Mrs McPherson insisted, 'but she never comes to see me.'

McPherson sighed. That was one of the reasons he avoided going to see his mother too often. Her mind was beginning to go and it saddened him.

'She's still never appeared on that doorstep,' she'd said, as if simply carrying on their previous conversation from where it left off.

'Mother,' he had said gently, 'Andrina said she saw you only a couple of nights ago. She tucked Jennifer up in bed and left Robert to babysit while she came and checked that you were all right. She worries about you being lonely since we've moved away to Bearsden.'

'Think I'm daft?' his mother jeered.

In actual fact he did. After all, she was in her eighties and had acquired some disgusting habits, like taking out her false teeth to eat – something she would never have done ten years before when she was in her right senses.

'They hurt my gums when I eat,' she explained, but it was no excuse.

'Think I'm daft?' she repeated. 'Well, think again. I'm telling you, there's more to that girl than meets the eye.'

Chapter Fifty-Two

Andrina had been admiring the new négligé she'd bought when she heard the doorbell ring. It was eleven in the morning; coffee time. But she knew it wasn't likely to be Josie popping in. They were on speaking terms, but no longer as close as they had once been. Andrina wished she'd lied to Josie. It had been a mistake to tell her about Bernard. She hoped Josie wouldn't see him coming up the stairs this lunch time. Bernard was due to arrive within the hour.

The doorbell gave a longer, more aggressive buzz. It was definitely too early for him. He always came exactly on time. She felt apprehensive as she hurried to answer the door.

'Mummy!'

'Well,' Sophie snapped, 'aren't you going to ask me in?'

Mind and heart racing in panic, Andrina opened the door wider and stood aside. She followed the older woman into the kitchen. 'Is there anything wrong?'

'I had to come to town to buy a black coat and hat. There's a funeral I've to attend in Bearsden.'

'Is it anyone I know?'

'No.'

'A cup of coffee?'

'Yes.'

'Would you put the kettle on, Mummy? I was just on my way to the toilet when you rang the bell. I won't be a minute.' She shut the kitchen door behind her and flew across to the bedroom. The négligé must be hidden in case her mother came through. She stuffed the froth of satin and black lace under the mattress, then with shaking hands tried to smooth the coverlet back down. The thought of Bernard coming to the door while her mother was in made her sweat. There was nowhere she could hide him. By the time she returned to the kitchen she felt sick and faint.

Her mother said, 'I never heard the chain being pulled.'

'Gosh,' Andrina turned back into the hall. 'I get more forgetful every day.' In the bathroom she pulled the chain, then returned to the kitchen, anxiously glancing at her watch. 'I thought you had a black coat, Mummy.'

'An ancient, shabby old thing. Your daddy insisted I get something really smart.'

'So this is you on your way to Sauchiehall Street, is it?'

'Your daddy said I should pay you a visit.'

'Oh? I tell you what. Why don't you have a very quick coffee just now, go and do your shopping, then come back here – say about four o'clock – for a nice leisurely afternoon tea, and you can show me what you've bought?'

'Where's Jennifer?'

'She's through in her room having a little nap.'

'At eleven o'clock in the morning?'

'She was up very early. She gets tired running about. She's a very active two-year-old.' Two years, five months. Another one year, seven months before she could be accepted into the local day nursery. It would be good for Jennifer. Everyone said how the little ones loved the nursery and how it made them so clever. Actually Jennifer wasn't all that active but now that she could get around (and she could talk), she could pose problems when Bernard came to the house. If she were kept up late, however, and awakened early, and kept amused to keep her awake, she was usually ready for a nap at about midday. Although at the moment she was simply lying, clutching her teddy and sucking her thumb. She was really a very good little girl. But maybe she was bored at times, not having any other children to play with. She'd enjoy the nursery, Andrina kept assuring herself.

For no apparent reason, she remembered how, when she was much older than Jennifer and she'd been naughty, her mother made her lie across the bed. Then she'd slapped her legs, slap, slap, slap, until her skin burned, and there seemed more hatred in every blow. It was the only physical punishment her mother had ever meted out to her.

All of the other children were going to the swimming baths,

and she was desperate to go too. Instinctively – knowing her mother would never allow this – she'd not told a lie but omitted part of the truth. She said she was going to Mary Ferguson's house and they were going to do their homework together. But before the homework, Mary loaned Andrina her sister's bathing costume and they'd joined a crowd of girls and boys in a noisy splash and a lot of laughs in the local baths.

Her mother (she should have known) had checked up on her and found out the whole truth.

'Half naked, and with boys!' she quietly accused. 'You wicked, wicked girl.'

She had never smacked Andrina again after that, maybe because she was getting too big a girl to be smacked. She had simply shut her out in icy disgust – completely ignored her. This was a thousand times worse than any physical attack. It had taken a long time of desperately trying to please her mother, and being perfect enough in every way, before Andrina regained the slightest attention.

'It's a disgrace. You ought to be ashamed of yourself.'

Andrina's eyes flew wide. 'Disgrace?'

'You should be out with that child in the Green. She should be getting some sunshine and fresh air. A park right across the road and you've got that poor child shut up in her room.'

Andrina sank down on to the chair. Her legs had literally given way. 'I've pulled a back muscle. I'm not able to get the push-chair up and down the stair. I'm sorry, Mummy. I know she needs to get out, but my back hurts even when I lift her. She hasn't been out for ages.' This was true. All she'd omitted to say was how she had strained her back. She prayed her mother wouldn't ask.

'Forget the coffee,' Sophie fussed to her feet. 'I'll take Jennifer for a walk right now.'

'Will she need her coat?' Andrina's voice was anxious. She was still unable to relax.

'No. It's lovely and warm outside. I'll take it just in case though.'

In a matter of minutes Sophie had the child in the push-chair and was bumping her down the stairs. Andrina ran through to watch out of the front room window.

'Don't let Bernard appear. Dear God, don't let her see Bernard.' She felt she'd have a nervous breakdown, completely collapse, if her mother saw him coming to the house. If her mother saw Bernard, she'd immediately know everything. It was at times like this that she didn't want to see Bernard ever again. No one or nothing else mattered but the anguish she was in.

I can't stand this, she thought, running to the phone to dial the number of Bernard's flat.

'Bernard?' She thanked God he was still there.

'Darling, what's wrong?'

'Don't come. Mummy is here.'

'How long before she leaves?'

'For pity's sake, don't come.'

'Darling, I hardly ever see you when it's Robert's school holidays. Taking his class out sketching today is our only chance. Then there's my tour. I'll be away for over a month. Where is she now?'

'Across in the Green with Jennifer.'

'Persuade her to take Jennifer for the rest of the day. Overnight if possible.'

'She's supposed to be going shopping.'

'Your mother is a very capable woman. She'll manage. And you know how possessive she is with Jennifer. She'll be easily persuaded.'

'I couldn't relax here with you now. Not today. I'm too shaken. I don't think I could even make it over to your flat.'

'Phone me once you've made the arrangements with your mother. Then I'll call for you and take you to Loch Lomond for a picnic. That'll help you to relax. I'll bring the champagne if you can put some food together. And darling . . .'

'What?'

'Wear something accessible.'

As Bernard had predicted, there were no problems persuading Sophie to take Jennifer back with her to Bearsden, although there had been a few unexpected questions about Granny McPherson.

'Granny McPherson says you've never been to see her.'

'Oh, Mummy, you know how forgetful she is.'

'I know she forgets where she puts her purse and her doorkeys and her spectacles, but she always remembers when I've been to see her.'

'She complained to me about you and Daddy not going to see her.' The one occasion when Andrina had visited Granny McPherson in the past year the old woman had indeed made this complaint.

Sophie stared hard at her daughter and then, apparently deciding she was telling the truth, she busied herself with manoeuvring the push-chair out of the door. 'You don't need to come for her tonight. I can manage for a few days.'

'No, I'd better. Robert misses her. I'll come at about seven.' That would give her plenty of time to get home before Robert. Or to phone him from Bearsden.

As soon as her mother was safely away, she phoned Bernard. Then she rushed out to the shops to buy the necessary food. Family picnics meant sandwiches of corned beef, sausage rolls, iced cookies (Robert's favourite), and chocolate biscuits (Jennifer's favourite). Picnics with Bernard were always sumptuous affairs, with smoked salmon, half chickens, strawberries, Belgian chocolates, and a bottle of champagne. Andrina took care to pack a white damask starched cloth to spread out, and two fine crystal glasses. After the meal they would savour sex. It always seemed even more thrilling out of doors, and as usual she looked forward to it with breathless excitement.

The drive to Loch Lomond was picturesque. It never ceased to amaze strangers to Glasgow how easily and quickly such beauty spots could be reached from the city. They stopped at the quaint little hamlet of Luss, right on the shores of the Loch. It had become Andrina's favourite place in the whole world. On a grassy spot they set out the picnic. They both loved to eat alfresco and take in the sights and sounds and smells of the natural surroundings. They fed each other erotically and sipped champagne from each other's glasses. They lazed and chatted. Entwined in each other's arms, they strolled along the shingle. Then they stopped to lean against a huge old tree. Bernard lifted her up in his arms and, supported by the tree trunk at her back, she wrapped her legs around his waist. Each time he plunged inside her he called out, louder and louder, how much he loved her, adored her, as if he wanted the whole world to hear.

And all the time she groaned and moaned in abandonment and delight. The breeze caressed her face and hair. She felt its coolness on her bare legs and bottom. Waves softly lapped against the shore. The pungent aroma of pine tantalised her nostrils. She opened herself to her lover, relishing him and the wondrous sensuousness of nature. Beyond caring about anything or anyone, she wanted the flame inside her to burn forever.

Chapter Fifty-Three

McPherson had not seen the play. He had been far too taken up with the council and other business. At home, the trauma of the funeral engulfed his attention. He only became aware of the impact of the play when newspapermen began sniffing around. Soon he realised that a dangerous situation could arise if care was not taken.

Fortunately, he'd always been a careful man. He had always been a calm, easygoing man as well. This play by Frank O'Maley, however, made him angry. He phoned Bernard O'Maley's office, only to be told he was away on a tour with some famous pop singer and his group. He wouldn't be back for another week or two. This inconvenience gave fuel to McPherson's anger. How dare an O'Maley, of all people, stir up trouble like this? Through a contact in the BBC, he managed to get a copy of the script of the play. Reading it, fear overshadowed his anger. No wonder the newspapermen were on the hunt. Here was a dramatised account of his political and Council experience. He realised of course that what happened to the man in the play and how he functioned could apply to other politicians, local or national – and councillors and bailies. He believed it was how the system worked. It was just the way of the world; it was life. It was simply being practical and realistic. It was being mutually helpful and co-operative.

This play, however, was taking a different view of it, using ugly, unacceptable words like 'graft' and 'corruption'. Frank O'Maley seemed to have an uncanny knowledge of exactly what went on. How could this be? He was only a clerk in the office of some back-street warehouse. Emotions chased around inside McPherson: confusion, uncertainty, suspicion, fear. Surely Bernard hadn't been the source of his brother's information? Bernard wasn't a stupid man. Nor was he indiscreet. At least, McPherson had never thought of him as an untrustworthy, indiscreet man. Anyway, Bernard had slipped him many a long brown envelope – if there were to be accusations of guilt flung around, Bernard would be as guilty as anybody.

On the other hand, Bernard or anyone else in a similar position could argue that they had been forced into offering 'sweeteners'. They could claim, quite wrongly of course, that they had been held to ransom and had no choice. But why should Bernard put him on a spot like this? Anyone else in a similar position, who had experience of giving so-called 'sweeteners', wasn't Frank O'Maley's brother. It had to be Bernard who'd spoken to Frank and, purposely or not, given him the idea for such a dangerous and scurrilous piece of work.

He could hardly wait until Bernard came back. The waiting was an agony.

Sophie's sharp eyes noticed the change in him, the barely concealed anxiety. 'Is there something wrong?'

McPherson hesitated, puffing at his pipe in a futile effort to draw comfort from it. 'You remember the O'Maleys?'

Sophie's eyes narrowed and her sleek grey head pushed forward, suspiciously, aggressively. 'What about them?'

'You only met Bernard. But there's four brothers. One of them, Frank, does a bit of writing. He's recently had a play put on the BBC about graft and corruption in the City Chambers. A tissue of lies, of course, but a lot of people – especially newspaper people – are thinking where there's smoke there's fire.'

Sophie sat down. 'Surely they're not believing a silly play? It was a story, wasn't it? It wasn't put over as a documentary.'

'No. It was supposed to be fiction. Unfortunately, there's a widespread belief that most writers get their ideas from real life, and base their characters on real life people.' Worries scurried about his brain like ants. Who else in the City Chambers had as many 'consultancies' – especially on the payroll of building firms – as he had? Who else had done as much work over the years in persuading fellow committee members that such and such a firm most deserved their vote? (Some of the firms he now had shares in.) Who else had as much influence and used it on so many occasions, indeed at every opportunity, and in so many ways? Once the lid was lifted on the day-to-day workings in the committee rooms and boardrooms, once questions began to be asked, there was no telling what picture might emerge. He suddenly saw the intricate web of people involved, the paid officials and civil servants who put people his way, and who also received gifts. He had learned that everyone had his price. But he was at the top of the pile; the buck stopped with him.

He felt shaken to the very foundations of his being. He was in terror of losing his good reputation, his respected place on the bench, his trusted position as a representative of the people of Glasgow, his Christian character in the church, his respectable standing in Bearsden. Even his marriage could be in jeopardy. His chest tightened. It was all so damned unfair.

'I always knew that family were trouble makers,' Sophie said.

'I've heard a rumour that one of the papers is thinking of running a series on what they claim goes on – how people get contracts, etc. Once these things start . . .' He puffed resolutely at his pipe. He mustn't allow his imagination to run away with him. Keep calm, that was the thing. He'd have a word with Bernard as soon as possible.

'And no doubt,' Sophie said, 'that Bernard has never forgiven us for stopping him having anything to do with Andrina. This could be a way of getting back at us – of blackening your character.'

'It's not Bernard who's written the play. It was his brother.'

'Comes to the same thing. They were as thick as thieves, that crowd. They *were* thieves. I heard all about them. They've all been in jail . . .'

'Not Bernard.'

'Why do you always stick up for that Pape?'

'I don't always stick up for him. I've never even mentioned his name to you for years.'

'He'll do us harm, Andrew. I know it.' She twisted her hands in her lap. 'Have I never to have any peace? Every time I think everything's all right, and I can relax, something else blows up.'

He nearly said, 'You've never relaxed in your life. You wouldn't know how,' but he contained himself. Instead he murmured, 'It might not come to anything. Even the newspaper thing – even if the rumour was true, it would just be another story to them. They would soon lose interest and find something else.'

He didn't sound convincing. Nor did he convince her.

'No good will come of this. I know it. I just know it.'

'Now calm yourself, Sophie. It'll certainly be no good to anyone if you get yourself into a state.'

'All these expensive gifts at Christmas from all these firms.' She spoke worriedly out loud to herself. 'And that huge donation to the church – just because I mentioned that we needed money for the restoration fund. It'll look bad.'

'We'll just have to wait and see what happens.'

'Just wait and see? Just wait and see? Can't you do better than that?'

'It wouldn't be wise for me to contact Frank O'Maley direct. But I'll go and see Bernard. He might be able to influence his brother – perhaps into making a public statement that the play had no connection whatever with any real character or situation. Bernard has influence in other directions as well, and plenty of useful contacts. He might have people in the newspaper world . . .'

'How do you know where he is?'

'I heard he has a flat in Sauchiehall Mansions. He sometimes does work for the Council – protecting visiting dignitaries, etc.'

Sophie's eyes darkened murderously. Her mouth set with hatred. 'That filthy Pape's the one to blame for all this. He'll have put his brother up to it.'

'I'll have to think,' McPherson said. 'Just let me think.' His thoughts soon turned bitter. It was all very well for aspiring local Tory politicians. They were practically all businessmen; monied men in the first place. Most Labour councillors were ordinary working men with only their pay packet at the end of the week. Colleagues like Will Chalmers was employed as a labourer. Tommy Hayes was a plumber. Joe Donnelly was a brickie like himself. All of these men and more, including himself, had been brought up on conditions of scarcity. Was it any wonder that in dealing with, and having unheard amounts of money under their control, they became somewhat overwhelmed? That they accepted a few gifts to smooth their path along the way? Although, of course, monied Tories or not, he knew of a few of them who were into more than taking gifts. But he, and most of his colleagues on the Council, including the Tories, had done their best for the people they represented. He had also fought for his country. Surely his countrymen could not throw him to the wolves?

He and Sophie hardly spoke at all for the rest of the night, but the atmosphere in the house was taut with anxiety. She made them both a hot toddy with plenty of honey in it to help make them sleep. They knelt side by side by the bed and silently said their prayers, knowing that both were desperately praying for the same thing. Except that Sophie was also praying that Bernard O'Maley would be banished to hell to burn there forever.

After they both climbed into bed they lay side by side, minds busily ferreting away for answers and escape routes.

McPherson thought again about tackling Bernard – not in his office, that would be too public, too risky. No, he'd go to the flat as soon as he confirmed that Bernard had returned. Despite what Sophie had said, he still didn't think that Bernard had purposely set out to do him any harm. Why should he? They had been getting along so well. Many a good meal they'd had together. Many a gift Sophie had enjoyed without knowing where it had come from.

Sophie had always been a woman of extremes, and her feelings for Bernard were only a symptom of her own nature. Bernard had been in love with Andrina in his youth but he'd taken defeat with good grace. Perhaps he'd married Doris Gallacher in a kind of extended rebound, who knows. That and the pressure of a doting mother whom Bernard adored.

No wonder the marriage hadn't worked out.

One comfort out of all McPherson's present problems, he assured himself, was the fact that his marriage would stand firm through anything that life might fling at him. Sophie had faults aplenty but she knew that he had always stood by her in her darkest hours. She would do the same for him.

A tremor went through him as he thought of how his darkest hour might soon be approaching.

'Oh God,' he prayed again, 'please help me.'

Then he resolved again to go and see Bernard.

Chapter Fifty-Four

'My dearest, darling velvet,' Bernard wrote, 'I have just put down the telephone and your voice is still in my ears, your vision is still in my mind, reinforced by your picture; and my love for you fills my heart.

'There are other parts of my body that show signs of love for you but poets don't write about those much. These past few months without you have been bad enough, but when I look back at earlier times, it is terrible to think there have been not only weeks and months, but years between our kisses and caresses – even our sight of each other. But the flame of love, passion and devotion never flickered. Something fed it and kept it burning.

'I look at your picture now and I want so much to touch your face with my fingertips, trace your lips with my tongue, bury my face in your neck and whisper my love for you as I gently kiss you. To feel your wonderful body in my arms, to smell and taste you, but above all, to be near you.

'To hear you talk is one of the great luxuries of my life, and to see you is a prize I value so highly. To kiss and caress you makes me as rich as kings, and when our bodies smooth and fuse and thrill together, I am in the realm of the gods.

'I long for you so much. You are my last thought at night and the first in the morning and my day-long delight. We shall enjoy each other's company for days – yes – even longer than we've had before. We shall love, laugh and live together for longer periods. We shall walk, eat and listen to music together. We shall hold hands in a quiet peace. We shall move our naked bodies together in a beautiful exciting fashion, and our lips will linger long over every part of each other.

'We shall enjoy making love and find even greater thrills with each other too. I love the way you dress for love – but if you had no perfume, no make-up, and were even in dull clothes, I would adore you just as much.

'I love *you*, Andrina. All you are and all you want to be. I want to be with you, in you, all around you, and somehow, when we talk I can feel almost in that state.

'Give me a sight of you soon.

I am,

Yours forever,

Bernard.'

Andrina wept after reading the letter, she thought it was so beautiful. She wept again that night in bed after Robert was asleep. The school holidays were over again and Robert was out during weekdays until after four o'clock. He was out a couple of evenings too at his karate club. But it still would be difficult to get a chance to be alone with Bernard. It always had been. She'd reminded him of this over the phone. Arranging to see him was like planning to walk through a minefield. Apart from the danger of people finding out, there was the problem of what to do with Jennifer. In a few months she would be three. Already she had met Bernard when he'd come home with Robert for a drink. She called him Uncle Benad, climbed up on his knee and showered him with kisses. Watching the scene, Andrina was consumed with jealousy. As quickly as she could she'd packed Jennifer off to bed. Then she'd felt ashamed and hurried back to the bedroom to kiss Jennifer goodnight again and tell her that she loved her.

But still she knew in her heart of hearts that it was a different kind of love from the obsessive, all-consuming passion she had for Bernard. Bernard possessed not only her body, not only her every emotion, but her mind. Hardly a moment passed without her thinking of him.

Over two agonising months passed before she and Bernard managed to get together. Her mother had been even more of a nuisance than usual. She had taken to coming to town more often and unexpectedly dropping in to see her.

'Mummy, you were on the phone this morning,' she would say. 'Why didn't you mention you were coming into town this afternoon? I might have been out.'

'You were going to do your shopping in the morning,' her mother would reply. 'Where could you have gone?' Or, 'You didn't mention to me that you were going out.' Once she'd nearly fainted when her mother had suddenly said, 'What about that big Pape?'

'Big Pape? Who do you mean?'

'You know who I mean. Bernard O'Maley.'

'What about him?'

'Have you heard anything about him? Or his brother?'

'His brother?'

'Don't keep repeating everything I say, Andrina.'

'But I don't know what else to say, Mummy. I don't know what you're talking about. Which brother? He's got three brothers. I've only met one of them – Frank.'

'I hope God strikes both of them down,' Sophie said. 'I hope both of them burn in hell.'

Bernard often called Sophie an old witch and she was certainly becoming more like one, at least in the way she talked and behaved. There had been such venom in Sophie's words, such an almost manic strength of feeling, Andrina was shocked and frightened. She desperately wanted to know why her mother suddenly brought up the subject of the O'Maleys but felt it was much too dangerous to ask.

Fortunately her mother was diverted by Jennifer who always demanded her 'nanna's' full attention and got it.

Later, after Sophie had gone, Andrina was left with fierce thoughts and longings for Bernard. It was as if the danger of her mother's curiosity about him had acted as a charge of electricity, of excitement.

That night in bed, while Robert was through at the kitchen table doing some school marking, she wrote to Bernard.

'My dearest one,

'I love you so very much – yearn to be engulfed in your strong hold, ready, willing – no, EAGER – to succumb to your manly charms and feel your love. No potion or elixir is necessary to arouse my deep feelings for you; the sight of you, to hear you speak my name, is aphrodisiac enough. Sensing your desire for me releases my soul to cry out in glad response to you – to pursue your searching lips and find them on my face and neck and breasts and desperately await them travelling all over my body to arouse me to even greater heights. What creates that overwhelming desire? The essence of you – everything you are. My raison d'être. Is it such a crime to fall in love?

'I am alone, in bed, pouring out my love and desire to you in this letter. Having just showered and brushed my hair and teeth, I have slithered between the crisp, white sheets, naked and deliciously lotioned, experiencing the tortuous sensations of the cool bedlinen as I stretch out languorously and imagine you standing in the room.

'Silently, slowly, you approach the bed. Your eyes never leave me. You note the warm gloss of my hair brushed over the soft pillows, my arms outstretched awaiting you, the hint of pert nipples peeking from above the top sheet.

'Pulling back the covers you reveal my nakedness in its entirety and your arousal becomes apparent, inflaming my already surging desire. Body to body – skin on skin – my softness, your hardness. Your probing, my yielding, our own sexual rhythm, our own natural ebb and flow. Caressing, tingling, pulsating, stroking, sucking, nibbling, swallowing – a gourmet extravaganza.

'Gentle tender beginnings progress to a faster pace. A quickening of breathing, a desperation of purpose, bringing each other to the very brink of our climax. Now hot, now throbbing, plunging faster, deeper, stronger, pumping, thrusting.

'Simultaneous soft moans herald the ultimate moment. The juices flow – we are one.

'Oh, the deep, deep need to be yours again. I will arrange a time soon, my love.

'Yours forever,

Andrina.'

But it had been nearly Christmas before there was an opportunity. Robert's mother had become quite crippled with arthritis and her sister on the Isle of Skye said if Robert could manage to bring her in the car, she would look after Jean over the Christmas and New Year period. They seldom saw each other now and it was agreed it would be a great treat for them both. Robert wanted to take Andrina and Jennifer too.

'We would all stay with Aunt Betty over the festive season. Jennifer would love the beach.'

'The beach in the middle of December?' Andrina had laughed. 'No, I don't think so. Skye's a bleak place at the best of times. Anyway, my mother hasn't been at all well recently. My father doesn't seem so good either. I think I'd better spend Christmas and New Year with them. I'll go and stay in Bearsden for the few days that you're away.'

'I could take her up and come back here for Christmas, and go back up for her at New Year.'

'What? Make that dreadful journey four times in a week? It'll be difficult enough doing it twice.'

'I don't like leaving you and Jennifer,' Robert said unhappily. 'Christmas is a family time. And I was looking forward to seeing Jennifer's excitement when she wakes up and finds all her presents.'

'She'll have plenty of other Christmases with you, Robert. This time you can keep your presents until you get back. That way she'll have them to look forward to.'

Andrina could barely conceal her joy. At last she'd be with Bernard again. She'd make some excuse to get away from Bearsden on her own. She'd go to Bernard's flat – that enchanted place.

Everything there was magic to her – so much to her own taste and nature. And everything that she had chosen, Bernard found desirable. He had added touches of his own, of course: the erotic paintings, the jungle of lush plants, the black silk sheets and pillowcases, the tall scarlet candles burning at the altar of their love.

After Robert left, Andrina's father and mother collected her in their car and took her and Jennifer to Bearsden, but all the time Andrina's heart was singing through the flat in Sauchiehall Mansions. In her imagination she was swirling around each room in sheer uninhibited joy. She was preparing herself for her lover. Bathing, perfuming, powdering her body.

Inside, in secret, she was shivering with excited anticipation. She could not look at her mother, dared not meet her eyes. Passion and desire were burning from her with such intensity she was terrified her mother might see it.

'Bernard, Bernard,' every part of her moaned out to him. 'My love.'

Chapter Fifty-Five

Bridie wept when she read the poem. To her it confirmed and reflected what she had begun to fear. It was the first subtle hint of a separation to come. It was called 'Islands', and that was what she and Frank had become. They still loved each other but they were different, and the gulf of that difference would widen until they would not be able to reach each other across the divide. She had thought that only she had been aware of it, but the poem indicated that Frank had begun to feel the sadness too. She could hardly read the verses through her tears.

'There will always be you and I,
However we pretend that there's a 'we',
For when that word is used it must imply
That there's a single you and single me.

And though we try to bridge that gap each day,
In all the different ways that we can find –
In all the things we do, and all we say –
A trace of isolation haunts the mind.

We try each time we smile, each time we meet,
Stand together, play a game or walk
Hand-in-hand, or wave across the street;
And, most of all perhaps, when we just talk.

Or maybe most of all, when we two lie
With bodies intertwined in love's embrace,
And share each tender touch, each kiss and sigh,
We come the closest to excising space.

Yet even then a hint of self lies deep,
And final joy is felt to be one's own.
And when our minds are wrapped in separate sleep
They take their separate ways, and dream alone.'

She felt that Frank was taking his separate way. The Frank she had known in Garngad was no more. The serious, sensitive, devout youth taking Mass and attending the Boys' Guild. The pathetically optimistic young man who was always brimming over with impossible dreams and hopes. The scraggy man in his loose, ill-fitting suits over which his lank hair showered dandruff.

The make-up girl at the BBC had cured his dandruff. His hair was still straight. It still flopped forward over his face, but it was glossy and healthy looking. He now wore tight-fitting denims and blue open-necked shirts that brought out the blue of his eyes. He was no longer pathetic skin and bone. He was lean and fit. He had such confident vigour he seemed almost to swagger with energy. He had given up his job in the office. The insecurity of the future terrified her. She had an equally frightening feeling that he would succeed. In his continuing success, she believed, lay the seeds of their separation.

Parties they had now (and they had quite a few because Frank revelled in company) did not comprise of family. The family didn't feel any more comfortable or at home in the house in Botanic Crescent than she did. Occasionally Carragh and Scobie paid a visit. Sometimes Doris came on her own. But more often than not Bridie visited them.

At the parties Frank had – because they were all for Frank's friends – Bridie cowered in a corner of the noisy, smoke-filled room clutching at a glass of lemonade. (Her father had long since put her off any thought of alcohol.) She tried to keep smiling and looking intelligent, but it was always a relief to slip away to the kitchen to wash some glasses or make another pot of coffee. Or, if she could get away with it, to settle down at the kitchen table with a book. Frank's 'arty-farty friends', as her father called them, loved to talk. They talked very loudly and laughed even louder. They drank a great deal. Bridie worried at the amount of money Frank spent in the off-licence for these gatherings. They smoked continuously. They called each other darling and kissed when they met as if they'd not seen each other for years.

One man, a producer, kept calling her 'Dear heart'. She detested his hypocrisy. She felt hurt and insulted by it. She felt painfuly different, the proverbial square peg in a round hole.

Doris kept trying to help. Bridie was closer to her sister now than she'd ever been in her life. They would huddle together in the kitchen drinking tea and sympathising with one another while Frank was away in the other world of his imagination in his study. It was a four room and kitchen house, and Frank used one of the bedrooms as a study (as Steve Martin had done before him).

He quite often worked at night now – especially if he'd been at the BBC during the day. He'd shut himself in his study supposedly for half an hour. Invariably he would forget the time and never surface again until bedtime. Sometimes Bridie went to bed without him. Then he'd come hurrying through full of apologies, and he'd put her book aside and cuddle her and kiss her, as if she was a child and he was kissing the hurt better.

He was working hard at short stories and journalism now to try to keep a regular flow of money coming in. This was as well as the play writing. She had begun to hate his writing. Sometimes when, full of eagerness and enthusiasm, he gave her one of his stories to read in manuscript, her feelings showed and he'd cry out, 'You don't like it? What's wrong with it, Bridie? Be honest. Please tell me the truth. It's important to me to get it right.' In this respect – as far as his writing was concerned – he was as sensitive as he'd always been.

'No, no. It's fine. Honestly, Frank,' she'd manage. But even though she resisted the temptation to undermine him with critical words, he would still look worried, uncertain. His enthusiasm frittered away. He'd wander back to his study again, clutching the manuscript, wondering where he'd gone wrong.

His writing, like his friends, was something she couldn't cope with. His writing always won. It held him in an iron grip. She knew it would never let him go. No matter what she said or didn't say, he'd still beaver away alone in his sanctum, lost in a world of his own creation.

Doris said for the next party she should make a real effort. She still loved Frank, didn't she?

'Of course I love him,' Bridie muttered, lowering her gaze, afraid to meet Doris's eyes in case the agony of her love would be revealed. 'He's my husband.'

'OK,' Doris said. 'Why don't you borrow one of my outfits – we're both the same size – and let me make you up and do your hair.'

Bridie's eyes miserably twitched and flickered about. 'I don't know.'

'Oh, come on Bridie. You'll never get anywhere if you don't try. Give Frank a treat. Let him see how you can be. All his friends – women friends anyway – wear make-up, don't they? I wouldn't be surprised if some of those arty-farty men do as well.'

'Oh, all right then,' Bridie reluctantly agreed.

'Great.' Doris became quite excited and found she really enjoyed making Bridie's transformation. First she helped her into a short, tight fitting, low-necked dress. 'That shows a nice bit of cleavage,' she assured Bridie. 'Men like that.' Then she got to work on Bridie's colourless face. 'You know,' she chatted happily, 'I think I've got a talent for make-up. Maybe I should go in for the beauty business. Beauty salons are terribly popular these days. I think I'd quite enjoy it.'

She took great care, tongue absently peeking out, as she concentrated on applying rouge and lipstick and eye liner and eye colour and mascara to Bridie's anxious, upturned face. Then she energetically back-combed Bridie's hair and with many kirby grips and hairgrips and much hair lacquer, managed to keep it up in some sort of bouffant.

'Your hair's not really long enough to do it right,' Doris said, 'but at least I've managed to give it a bit of a lift.'

They both gazed in the mirror, Doris with pride at her handiwork, Bridie with shock and horror.

'Oh Doris, do you really think . . .'

'Great,' Doris enthused. 'Though I say it myself, I've done a terribly good job. Now I'd better go before Frank comes in. Time I went home anyway. Mammy'll be keeping my tea hot.'

'You could have had something here with me and Frank. You could stay for the party. Or come back for it if you'd rather. They usually start arriving between eight and nine.'

'No thanks, Bridie. Some of them are a bit weird for my taste. I don't know what they're talking about half the time. They make me feel uncomfortable.'

'I know what you mean,' Bridie said miserably.

'Never mind. You'll be a hit tonight. Frank'll be terribly proud of you.'

'Do you really think so?'

'He's got eyes in his head, hasn't he?'

After Doris left, Bridie put a pot of soup on to heat that she'd made earlier. She tried to remember what else she'd meant to have for the evening meal. After dinner Frank would help with the preparation of the party food. He enjoyed every aspect of entertaining. He'd happily fry cocktail sausages and spread sandwiches and sing to himself while arranging everything on the dining room table and admiring how the spread looked.

He used to help with the washing up, and Bridie had enjoyed sharing the task with him. She always washed and he dried and they'd chat together while they worked.

But he'd bought her a dishwasher. 'Every labour saving device,' he'd enthused. 'Every luxury, Bridie, just like I always said.'

She heard his key in the door and stood, with fast-beating, hopeful heart, waiting for his entry into the kitchen. She'd purposely not put on her apron so that he could see the full effect of the dress.

'Good God!' Frank gasped as soon as he saw her. 'For a minute I thought you were Doris.'

'She was here earlier and made me up for the party. Do I look all right?'

Frank closed his eyes for a minute. Then he opened them and said kindly, 'Bridie, please wash your face and brush your hair. And put on one of your own dresses,' he added.

'I look awful!' Tears gushed up and trickled down Bridie's cheeks. She had to grope off her spectacles to wipe at her eys.

Frank came over and took her into his arms. 'I just want my beautiful Bridie, that's all, not a look-alike Doris or anybody else.'

'But I'm not beautiful, Frank.'

'You're beautiful to me.'

He cuddled her close and kissed away her tears. She tried to feel better. She assured him she was all right now and hastened to scrub every vestige of paint from her face and tug a brush through her hair. They had dinner and Frank told her all that had happened at the BBC and the latest fuss over the play about the bailie. He told her the plot of his next story.

Frank loved to talk, especially about his writing. He had always been the same. Eyes down, Bridie went on eating the food on her plate. For no apparent reason she felt resentment building up inside her.

'Damn him and his bloody writing!' she thought.

Chapter Fifty-Six

For the first time since he'd known Bernard, McPherson detected a sliver of vulnerability in the big man's eyes. It only lasted a second. McPherson took it for guilt.

'I want to talk to you. Can I come in?'

'You've picked a hell of an awkward time, McPherson.'

It was then it occurred to McPherson that Bernard probably had a woman in the house. 'It won't take long. I just have to get something straight.'

Bernard stood aside. 'Come through to the kitchen.'

'Funny time of day to be in your dressing-gown,' McPherson remarked.

'What I wear and when is my business.'

'Fair enough.' McPherson's anger began to show. 'But what about the play? Whose business is that?'

'Play? What the hell are you talking about?'

'You know what I'm talking about. The play your brother wrote.'

'My . . . oh, Frank? I thought he just wrote poetry.' He hesitated, remembering. 'You're right, he did go around trumpeting about a play he'd had accepted some time back. Must be over a year ago. Maybe two. What's it got to do with me?'

'That's what I'd like to know.'

'I'm still not with you.'

'You mean you haven't seen it?'

'I've been away on a job for months.'

McPherson was taken aback. 'I didn't think of that.'

'Are you going to tell me what all this is about?'

'I'll tell you what the play is about. It's about a Glasgow bailie who takes bribes, who gets involved, and gets other people involved, in graft and corruption.'

'Shit!'

'Exactly.'

'Listen. What do you think I am? Stupid? I hardly ever see Frank. Even if I saw him every day I wouldn't have said City Chambers to him, far less mention your name.'

McPherson calmed down. 'To be honest, Bernard, I didn't think it could be you. I just didn't know what to think. Who *could* it be?'

'How should I know? It's probably just Frank – his overworked imagination, or writer's intuition as he calls it. He used to always be rabbiting on about writer's instinct or intuition. He's my brother and I love the guy, but he's a nutcase. Always was. But I'll have a word with him if you like.'

'Thanks, Bernard. You never know, it might help. I've been hoping and praying it'll die down.'

Bernard grinned. 'Will I put a Catholic prayer up for you?'

McPherson took him seriously. 'It wouldn't go wrong. I've been on radio and television praising the way local government in Glasgow is run and making it plain how offended and insulted I and all my colleagues in the Chambers feel, and how I hope God will forgive these gutter-press journalists who care nothing for the truth or for the feelings of hard-working and honest representatives of the people.'

Bernard gave him a wink. 'That's the ticket, Bailie. You tell them.'

'Maybe it *will* all die down.' McPherson was beginning to feel much better and more confident. Cheerful even. Bernard had that effect on him. He liked the big man. Admired him too.

'Would you like a dram?' Bernard asked.

'No, I've interrupted you enough. I'll let you get on with enjoying yourself. You'll be good at that.'

'You're right there, Bailie.'

'A man of many talents.'

'Right again.'

McPherson laughed and made for the door. 'You must come to lunch soon. At the Chambers, I mean.'

'I didn't think you meant Bearsden.'

'I'll give you a ring.'

They had reached the front door.

'Take it easy,' Bernard said. 'Stay loose.'

McPherson laughed again and gave a wave before Bernard shut the door. He felt as if a ton weight had been lifted from his shoulders. Earlier, he'd slowly puffed up the stairs like a tired old walrus. Now, although he still kept a hand on the banister for support, he'd regained his proud and portly bearing. It had been foolish of him to get into such a state. It never did any good to panic. Bernard would never say a bad word about him. He should have known he could trust Bernard. He could trust all the contractors who employed him as a consultant too. Why should they bad-mouth him? He was too valuable to them and to many others. Why should he worry about an upstart scribbler like Frank O'Maley? Bernard would soon put him straight.

He wondered if he should tell Sophie that he'd been to see Bernard. He doubted, however, that his visit would be of comfort and reassurance to her as it had been to him. Sophie had a very twisted view of some things and people, and nothing could ever untwist her. Any time he'd tried it just made her worse.

No, better leave well alone. Let things take their course. God worked in mysterious ways, he'd tell her. Their faith would be rewarded. God would protect them. He would make everything all right. They went to church on Sunday morning and stood side by side and sang the hymns and listened earnestly to the sermon, and felt comforted. Andrina was staying over the weekend and sang a solo, standing like an angel in her white dress in front of the pulpit.

Both McPherson and Sophie felt proud, and pure, and uplifted. It was a special kind of happiness.

Afterwards he said to Sophie, 'We're very lucky, you know. We've a good daughter. Not only a good Christian but a really lovely girl. She suits white, don't you think?'

Sophie agreed. 'And a lovely grandchild.'

'Yes, dear wee Jennifer,' McPherson said. He was very fond

of the child. The church had started a crèche in the small hall and it was proving extremely popular. Sophie had helped collect funds to supply it with toys, and often took a turn of staffing it. Sophie was a wonderful worker for the church. Both the Reverend and Mrs Dinwoodie often said they didn't know how they'd ever managed without her. He too was a veritable pillar of the place and never spared himself to do whatever he could.

'You know,' Sophie said some days later, 'you were right, Andrew. We should always cling to the rock of our faith and trust the Lord to look after us. Things seem to have died down. There's been nothing more in the papers.'

He believed he had been right in saying this. God had looked after His own. No doubt, of course, this had meant allowing Bernard to oil a few palms and twist a few arms. This is what he meant when he told Sophie that God worked in mysterious ways.

He was also grateful to God that he was on good terms with the police. It helped being Chairman of the Police Committee.

Yes, God had been good to him. He in turn had been good to his family – to Andrina and little Jennifer. He had also tried to help Robert. More than once he'd told him, 'Look, Robert, I can easily use my influence to get you a better job. Or if you're still determined to remain in teaching, I could at least have you moved to a better school.'

Robert, however, was a very stubborn and foolish man. He not only wanted to remain in teaching, he insisted on remaining in Blackhill. Blackhill of all places!

'You'll never get promotion in a Catholic school, Robert,' he'd reminded him. 'Never as long as you're a Protestant.'

Apparently Robert didn't care. 'I believe in doing a worthwhile job where I'm most needed,' he insisted. 'And I'm most needed in Blackhill.'

McPherson had remarked to Sophie, 'He's a bit of a masochist, if you ask me.'

Sophie agreed.

'And he doesn't look too happy with it,' he added. 'Have you noticed that look about him recently?'

Sophie nodded. 'He'll be worried about his mother. I don't think she's long for this world. That trip up north last Christmas was far too much for her. She's never been right since. The last time I saw her she told me she has angina now as well as her arthritis.'

McPherson looked suitably solemn. 'Robert's always been very fond of his mother.'

'I've never said he wasn't a good enough son. He's just not a good enough husband for our Andrina.'

McPherson agreed.

Sophie said, 'Even for his daughter's sake he should be looking more to his own future. Has Jennifer to grow up in that tenement in that rough part of town? I know it used to be a good enough area but there's so many awful types hang about the Green now, especially during the fair.'

'I've told him,' McPherson spread out his hands, 'I could lend him the deposit for a decent house out here. Something with a garden for Jennifer to play in. I'd give him a present of the money.'

'I know. It's very selfish of him to refuse. He can't even see that it would be far better for him as well as Andrina and Jennifer if he worked in a better school and lived in an area like this. He's always been gaunt-faced and lantern-jawed, but he's become quite grey-looking recently. It's all the tension of working in that awful place as well as the worry about his mother. But maybe once his mother goes, it'll be different.'

'I never thought of that.'

They both felt suddenly pleased with themselves. Everything would work out all right in the end. In time they would have Andrina and Jennifer living nearby. They would enjoy the pleasure of watching their granddaughter grow up among a good class of people, go to a good school, have the best chance in life.

McPherson experienced a pang of guilt when he found himself thinking in terms of class. He had nothing against ordinary working folk, most of whom were perfectly decent and good living. There were still people like his father, committed

Socialists, union leaders, still fighting their corner with all the old idealism and fervour. The world was changing, however. Power and profit were the things most sought after and admired.

Another new element had arisen, and with it a different outlook, a social transformation. Youth had taken over. A new generation was intent on defying and mocking the existing order of things and doing everything they could to shock and disgust. They dressed in a freakish, ridiculous manner. They stripped naked at festivals. They squatted in other people's property. If it wasn't hippies, it was so-called Mods and Rockers. Teenage vandalism was spreading like a rash. As were cases of arson and incendiarism. Telephones were being smashed by the thousand. Young boys were derailing trains and causing people to be killed. Addiction to heroin and cocaine had risen by a frightening amount. It was even worse with addiction to semi-addictive drugs. And of course the illegitimate birth rate had almost doubled.

What shocked McPherson more than anything was the different social attitudes, the different set of values nowadays: the Kray brothers had been included in David Bailey's 'Box of Pin-Ups' as the most glamorous figures of 'swinging' London; the 'Great' train robbery was being portrayed as some heroic wartime exploit; long-haired, arrogant youths like the Beatles were given MBEs by the Queen. Too many people in authority were paying too much attention to stars of pop and television and giving them a sort of status, even reverence. Society was in a very dangerous condition.

Yet there were still good living Christian folk around, and young people with a sense of decency and self-discipline. Once again he thanked God for his good wife, and his lovely daughter and grandchild.

He felt pleased with himself again.

And safe.

Chapter Fifty-Seven

The Orange Walk had a special trot, a jaunty swagger. It was held to commemorate the Battle of the Boyne in which King William of Orange – King Billy to Glaswegians – had defeated the Feenians.

It was a crush of orange sashes and rippling banners and flags and tootling flutes and banging drums. Fancy uniforms for men and women of blue and orange with big tammies, cocked to one side with long stiff feathers, rainbowed the streets. Hordes of men, women and children followed the bands. They wore their best clothes and proudly displayed their orange sashes. They came from all over the city and were aiming for Queens Park where they'd have a picnic, women would drink tea, children would play games and men would get steaming drunk. There had been a time, according to park officials, when everybody had cleared up afterwards. Paper cups and bags, lemonade and beer bottles, were gathered up and put in waste baskets or taken home. The Orange Walk left the park as they found it. But not now. The park attendants and the local residents dreaded their coming. The green and pleasant slopes of the park were awash with debris.

Ominous looking groups of people came to the doors of local residents wanting to troop in to use the toilet. Or they made what seemed equally suspicious and dangerous requests for drinks of water. The residents now locked their storm doors and hid silently inside, only allowing themselves the occasional peep from behind lace curtains as their normally peaceful area reverberated with reckless sound.

There was nothing silent about the residents of Garngad and Blackhill when the Orange Walk swaggered down Castle Street, past the town entrance leading to both these districts.

The Catholic residents turned out in force and shouted and

bawled at the Protestant marchers, 'Come on up here, you bastards! Come on, march down Garngad Road!'

Other abusive and provocative remarks were hurled at the 'Walk', but its marchers wisely never took up the challenge. Garngad was sometimes called 'little Ireland'. To trot through there carrying a King Billy banner was asking for it to be knotted round your neck. In Blackhill they'd be liable to shoot holes in it, and you as well. Jimmy and Martha Stoddart had been glad when they'd been rehoused in Castlemilk and were now well away from 'little Ireland'.

Jimmy Stoddart marched along, shoulders aggressively forward like a miniature John Wayne. Men like himself who belonged to Orange Lodges followed the bands proudly wearing black suits, black bowler hats and white gloves. An orange and blue velvet shoulder cape edged with gold fringes made a vivid contrast to some of the men's black suit jackets.

'Hey, Michael,' he heard Scobie Gallacher shout, 'there's your Proddie father-in-law.'

Keeping his eyes riveted on the man in front Jimmy Stoddart ignored Scobie, and Michael O'Maley, his big ugly-looking one-eyed son-in-law. He kept up the swaggering tempo of the trot.

'Ignorant rabble,' he told himself. Martha had been quite right. What had Caroline been thinking of, marrying a Green Grape? That one especially. He'd meant nothing but grief to her. She seemed, by all accounts, to be getting on better now that Michael had gone off the drink. But how long would that last?

The whole O'Maley family were no-users. To see Tony galloping and howling about the stage like a buck-toothed idiot was downright embarrassing. And that Bernard – some reputation he had, frightening the life out of folk.

As for Frank, he'd always acted like a right pouff – him and his stupid poetry. It was the luck of the Irish that had obviously protected Patrick O'Maley from serving half his life in prison. Everybody knew he made quite a business on the side selling things he'd nicked off trains. He was always boasting about his old army mate Bailie McPherson and how they both belonged to the Artillery Club. So he knew a bailie. So what?

It reminded him of the story of the carter who stopped at a pub and asked an amiable-looking man if he'd watch his load for a minute. The response to this request was, 'My man, do you realise I'm a bailie of the City of Glasgow?'

'Aye, OK,' the carter said, 'but surely to God I can trust you with my horse.'

It was a long walk to the Park and the temperature seemed to have crept up to boiling point. The air shimmered before Stoddart's eyes and his bowler was cutting into his head like a red-hot wire. Sweat oozed from every pore. It was purgatory wearing a suit, a stiff collar and a tie on a sweltering day like this. His new shoes hurt. His proud trot became a somewhat undignified hirple. In front, the bandsmen, equally sweating, abandoned their flutes for a time. The march depended on the monotonous, funereal beat of the drums.

Women began to straggle. Children whined. The bands, sensing the flagging enthusiasm, started up again and blasted out 'The Sash My Father Wore' with renewed vigour. Some folks were inspired to burst into song,

'Sure it's old but it's beautiful,
And its colours they are fine.
It was worn at Derry, Aughrim,
Inneskillin and the Boyne,
My father wore it as a youth,
In the bygone days of yore,
And it's on the twelfth I love to wear
The Sash My Father Wore.'

Stoddart struggled valiantly to keep pace. Singing was beyond him now. Not only his feet hurt – a tight pain gripped his chest. He began to have difficulty in breathing. He tried to tell the man marching next to him.

'Aye,' the man said, 'I'm parched as well. To hell with the

picnic. I'm attacking the first beer crate I see as soon as we get to that fuckin' park.'

The pain in his chest grew worse. It took complete possession of him. The tramp of feet, the babble of voices, the cheeky tootle of flutes, the tum-tiddely-um-tum of drums, shrank to nothing. He hardly felt the crack on his head as he hit the ground.

'We'll have to go,' Caroline said. 'It's either that or Mammy coming to live here, and where would we put her?'

Michael groaned. The thought of living under the same roof as his mother-in-law, either in the Gorbals or out in Castlemilk, was enough to put him back on the drink.

His one eye squinted down at his wife. 'Just when we were getting on so well in our nice wee house.'

'I know,' Caroline sighed. 'But what can I do, Michael? She depended on Daddy and now that he's gone . . .'

'What worries me, Caroline, is she'll try and put you against me. She's always hated my guts. She could ruin our marriage.'

'No, never.' Caroline put a hand on his arm and squeezed it. 'I've stuck by you through thick and thin so far, haven't I?'

The anxious look still clung to his mis-shapen face. 'And that house'll be in her name now.'

'Maybe we could persuade her to let you go to the Corporation and ask them to transfer it into your name.'

'I can't see Big Martha doing me any favours, can you?'

'We could try. She's older now and practically helpless.'

'You're going to have a lot of extra work, and you've already got more than enough with three kids.'

'I'll manage. What else can I do?' she repeated helplessly. 'She's my mammy. I'm all she's got now.'

'OK, OK. We'll give up this place and go to Castlemilk.' His heart was heavy. He could hardly credit that such a nightmare could become a reality. Actually live in the same house as Big Martha Stoddart! As he told Scobie later, 'God knows how it'll all work out. That woman's enough to drive anybody to drink.'

Scobie laughed. 'You cannae drink in Castlemilk, son. There's no pubs.'

'A desert of a place. There's absolutely nothing for anybody.'

'Now, don't cross your bridges before you come to them, Michael. It might not be as bad as you think.'

'No pictures. No billiards.'

'Nice houses, I've heard though. Caroline'll be pleased you'll have a bathroom.'

'Oh aye, that's all we needed to make our life perfect. A bathroom in Castlemilk.'

'Well, you could look at it this way. You'll spend more time away from the place, what with travelling back and forth. You'll be longer with your mates on the building site in the Gorbals than with Big Martha in Castlemilk.'

'I hope to God the houses out there are made of better stuff than the new ones we're helping to put up in the Gorbals.'

'Aye, there's some cheap rubbish there and no mistake.'

'I've felt like telling my da to get his bailie pal to come and have a good look around, and speak to folk that are suffering dampness and God knows what else in the houses already put up. But I thought better of it. Nobody dare say a word to Da against Bailie McPherson.'

'I don't think it's so much the likes of him, son. It's the planners and architects – they've got it all wrong. They're not thinking of the Glasgow climate, for a start.'

Michael scratched his head. 'It makes you wonder, doesn't it? Guys like that with degrees and God knows what, and they design places with long corridors like prisons, and lifts that can't take folk's furniture, or stretchers or coffins.'

'Well, just be thankful for small mercies, son. Just imagine if Big Martha had one of the high flats. Think of trying to carry her coffin down from the fifteenth floor!'

Michael could have coped with carrying her coffin anywhere. The trouble was, Big Martha was alive. He hadn't seen her for ages. Even Caroline only visited her very occasionally because her mother criticised him so much.

'She's all right with Daddy,' Caroline always said. 'He does everything for her so I don't need to worry.'

Now they were both worried. But, as Caroline said, what could they do?

The night before they moved to Castlemilk, Michael lay in the kitchen bed watching Caroline sitting by the fire in her nightie, brushing her fair curly hair. When he'd first known her she'd had a sweet round face. Now it was plump with a hint of a double chin. Her body was soft and plump. She'd gained quite a lot of weight, but he still thought her a lovely woman.

She laughed, making her loose, unbrassiered and uncorseted flesh wobble. 'What do you think you're staring at?'

'My beautiful wife,' he said, but sadly. And after she put out the light and climbed into bed, he clutched her tightly against him. He felt ashamed of his fears but was suddenly at the mercy of them. 'I'm sorry, Caroline.'

'What for?' she sounded puzzled.

'All the awful things I did when I was on the booze. The way I treated you.' He couldn't understand what she saw in him, especially now when he was as ugly as sin.

'For goodness sake, that's all over and done with ages ago.' She cosied happily into his arms. 'You're my own good man. You always will be.'

'Blessed Mary, ever virgin,' he prayed, 'Saint Joseph and the infant child – let it be true.'

Chapter Fifty-Eight

'Oh, it's you, Doris! Come on in.' Andrina kissed her unexpected visitor. 'Nice to see you. Let me take your coat. It's an awful night, isn't it?'

'I know, I hate November. It's terribly depressing.'

'Hello Doris,' Robert greeted her when they arrived in the kitchen. 'How are you doing?'

'Fine, thanks.'

'Still working at Daly's?'

'Uh-huh. I'm in ladies underwear at the moment. We stock terribly good class garments.'

'Can I get you a drink? I was just going to pour one for myself and take it through to watch a programme on television. Unless you two want the use of the front room?'

'No,' Andrina said. 'We'll be cosier in the kitchen. You go ahead. I'll attend to our drinks.'

'OK. See you later, Doris.'

Doris smiled and coyly fluttered her Sandie Shaw eyelashes at him. She thought Robert was terribly sexy. There was something about his lean, hard body and the sensation of suppressed energy about him. A time-bomb ready to explode.

'Sherry or gin or vodka?' Andrina asked.

Doris settled herself in one of the chairs near the fire and giggled. 'You know me . . . Do you mind if I pull my boots off? They're absolutely killing me, so they are.'

'No wonder, with the size of those heels. I don't know how you manage to find boots and shoes with such high heels.'

'It's terribly difficult right enough. These white ones are really smart though, aren't they?'

'Is that enough gin?'

'Ta. I hope I'm not keeping you off your favourite programme.'

'No. I hardly ever watch TV. It's not often Robert watches it either, but there's this Japanese thing tonight and he's interested in anything Eastern. How's the family, Doris?'

Doris crossed her legs, revealing a large expanse of thigh beneath her black and white plastic skirt. 'Oh, Mammy's found the Bingo . . .'

'Bingo? What's that?'

'A numbers game. When Da goes out with his pals now, she goes out with hers. It's good to see her enjoying life for a change. I'm terribly worried about Bridie, though.'

'Your sister?'

'Uh-huh. I've been doing my best to help her, but nothing seems to work.'

'What's the problem? I thought you said her husband was doing great and they had a gorgeous flat in the West End.'

'So they have. That's the problem, I think. He's doing too well. He's got all these arty friends. Terribly glamorous, some of them. And poor wee Bridie so plain.' Doris lit a cigarette. 'Life's funny, isn't it?'

Andrina agreed.

After a couple of thoughtful puffs at her cigarette, Doris went on. 'There she is in that lovely flat with a successful husband who just showers her with everything. She's got a dishwasher, a washing machine and God knows what else. And she's as miserable as sin. She does nothing but moan and complain about Frank any time I go to see her. The last time, I told her – think yourself lucky you're not like me, I said, on my bloody tod – if you'll pardon the French. Bernard's not on his tod, of course!'

The last bitter remark was so unexpected, it nearly took Andrina off her guard. She nearly said, 'I know, he's off to Paris on a job with some of his men.' She jerked herself back just in time.

'I always said – he'll never be without a woman, him,' Doris continued. 'I didn't know at first if it was that Jane Ford or not. I just saw him come into the shop with this slimmer than slim creature looking as if she'd just stepped off the catwalk. I could have rushed at her and scratched her eyes out. Then I thought –what the hell? What good would it have done me? It wouldn't have got him back. I would only have lost my job and been worse off. So I just served her, sweet as pie, after he went off. He didn't see me there. There were quite a few girls and customers there at the time and of course he wouldn't even remember I worked there. He was never interested in anything I did. I heard him saying he'd meet her in the restaurant. One of the other girls went forward first of all but I elbowed in and took over.'

Andrina said nothing.

'I was curious, you see. I've always been dead nosy. She bought *terribly* expensive pure silk camiknickers and bra and suspender sets, and the most glamorous nightie we had in the department. I said to her, all innocent like – Is Madame purchasing for a special occasion? And she purred like a cat full of cream and said – I'm off to Paris tomorrow afternoon.'

'When was this?' Andrina asked quietly.

'Just today. And it *was* Jane Ford. She paid by cheque so I saw her name. You should have seen the clothes she was wearing. She's obviously loaded with money. Her father's one of Bernard's best customers, you know. Gives Bernard a lot of work. Are you feeling OK, Andrina?'

'What? Yes, I'm just upset for you. You must have felt dreadful.'

Doris sighed. 'I still do actually. That's why I came here straight from work. You're a terribly good friend, Andrina. My very best friend really. I know I can always talk to you and you'll understand. I always feel better after I've been to see you.'

'You must be starving.' Andrina got up and began fussing about in cupboards with her back to Doris. 'If I'd known you were coming I'd have had something really nice ready, but I'll soon rustle something up.'

'I should have phoned but my head was so full of what happened I couldn't think of anything else. I know me and Bernard's ancient news now. But it still hurts, Andrina . . . I still feel humiliated when I think of the way he treated me, the things he said.'

Andrina didn't turn round. 'What things?'

'About this other woman. And how he'd never loved me. Never for one second.' Doris began to weep and Andrina went over to nurse her head tightly against her shoulder.

'Don't worry, Doris,' she said. 'He'll get what's coming to him. Dry your eyes now and have another gin while I make a pot of tea and something to eat. You've made a right mess of your mascara now. You'd better go through to the bathroom and clean up your face before Robert sees you.'

'Aye OK.' Doris hiccoughed weakly.

By the time she came back, Andrina had made a mushroom omelette and plenty of chips. Doris was very fond of chips (liberally sprinkled with H.P. sauce and vinegar).

'The thing is,' Doris said in between mouthfuls, 'I haven't been able to have anybody since. I've lost my nerve, so I have. I just can't bring myself to trust a man any more.'

Andrina was sitting opposite her at the table nursing a cup of tea. 'I can understand it.'

'Between you and me, Andrina, my confidence in myself is just terrible. I mean, I try not to let it show. I can still be quite chirpy and cheeky at times, but underneath I could just die. I feel so terrible about myself.'

'It's not you,' Andrina said, 'you're all right.'

'But Holy Mother of God, Andrina. He had sex with me. He made me feel like a prostitute. He must have been just using me,' she chewed and blinked rapidly, 'if he never loved me.'

'Try to forget all about it. It's all in the past.'

Still blinking, Doris nodded. She even tried to smile. 'Sorry to go on about this.'

'It's all right.'

'But you're the only one I feel I can talk to.'

Robert appeared in the kitchen then. 'Any tea going?'

'Sorry,' Andrina said, 'we got talking and I forgot to take you a cup through.'

He winked at Doris. 'She neglects me dreadfully, you know.'

'I don't believe it,' Doris said. 'You've a woman in a million there, Robert Anderson.'

Robert dropped a kiss on top of Andrina's head. 'I know.'

'I wish I could make an omelette like this,' Doris said. 'It's as light as a feather. How does she do it?'

Robert spread out his hands. 'What more could any man want? A beautiful woman who can cook like an angel.'

Doris laughed. She felt more relaxed. Some of her self-confidence returned. The tea was putting some strength into her. She felt grateful to have such good friends.

'Give me a shout when you're ready to go home,' Robert said before disappearing away to the sitting room with his mug of tea. 'I'll give you a lift.'

'That's terribly kind of you, Robert,' Doris called after him. 'It's such an awful night. I'll really appreciate it.'

'See you later,' Robert said.

'More tea?' Andrina asked after he'd gone.

'Yes, please. What a nice man he is!'

'Yes.'

'And he obviously adores you.'

Andrina filled both of their cups then concentrated on sipping at hers.

Doris said, 'He's worth ten of that bastard. I'm sorry, Andrina, but I can't just put him out of my mind like that. When I think of what he's done to me – and as for that bitch – I should have bloody scratched her eyes out. Scarred her for life so that he would have got rid of her. He wouldn't have come back to me but he would have dumped her. Everything has to be just perfect for him. It would have been worth losing my job to spoil things between them. To get my own back on them both. Revenge is sweet, they say. I bet it is. Bastard, so he is. When I think of that big bastard . . . enjoying himself fucking that woman in Paris just now – excuse the language.'

'Drink up your tea, Doris.'

'Aye, OK hen.'

Will she never go? Andrina kept thinking. God have mercy on me. Make her stop talking. Make her go. But after she had gone it was shocking to be left on her own in the silence. It was terrifying to be alone with such rage, such anguish. She couldn't believe it of Bernard. She *wouldn't* believe it. He couldn't do this. Not to *her*. She couldn't bear it for him to be making love to another woman, to be taking her away to that beautiful love capital of the world.

She needed proof. She was going mad. She didn't dare let Robert see her. She crept through to bed and hid under the blankets and pretended to be asleep.

Tomorrow afternoon she'd go to the airport. She'd wait and watch. She tried not to shiver. She hugged herself, and dug her long nails into her arms until she drew blood.

Chapter Fifty-Nine

First thing next morning, after Robert had left for work, Andrina hastily dressed Jennifer and herself and dashed over to Bearsden. She didn't even take time to phone her mother.

'Andrina!' Sophie had an iron-grey dutch apron knotted round her lean waist. One hand clutched a washing up cloth. Behind steel-rimmed spectacles, her slate coloured eyes narrowed. 'What's wrong? You've never been this early before.'

'Aren't you going to let me in?'

The door was opened wider and as Andrina trundled Jennifer's push-chair into the hall, Sophie followed her.

'You never phoned.'

'I'm sorry, Mummy. I've had the most dreadful migraine. I've got an appointment with the doctor. I'll have to rush right back.'

'What's given you that? What have you been doing?'

For a moment Andrina lost control and snapped at her mother, 'This is bloody ridiculous! I've even to make excuses to you and give you reasons for feeling ill.'

Jennifer cried out 'Nanna' and held up her arms. Sophie lifted the child and carried her through to the kitchen. She gave her a biscuit and said, 'Who's Nanna's good girl?' Then she went on with wiping the table. She ignored Andrina.

The silence, the coldness, the shutting out nearly drove Andrina demented. She couldn't cope with it today. She wanted to weep. 'Mummy, I'm sorry,' she managed at last in a low tremble of a voice. 'I don't feel well, I didn't mean to snap at you. And I never usually swear. Honestly, I never swear, Mummy. Please forgive me.'

'If you're going, you'd better go,' her mother said coldly. Forgiveness was not so easily won.

Andrina left, weeping without tears. She had never felt so desolate, so distraught. She couldn't remember in all of her life her mother ever putting a comforting arm around her, or kissing her, or showing her the slightest demonstration of affection. Bernard made up for this lack of love. His love had encompassed everything she needed – including security and trust. She was in such a state she didn't know how she got to the airport and found the appropriate gate. In a daze she merged with the milling crowd.

Eventually she saw him. Tall, dark-eyed, always aware, always on the look-out. Not a hair out of place. Immaculate in his Armani suit and Gucci shoes. That slight swagger of his broad shoulders. And the woman. Blonde. Tanned. Expensively dressed in beige. They looked right together. A perfect pair. He put his arm around her as they passed through the ticket barrier. They were laughing.

Suddenly he was a stranger. Andrina didn't know him. She felt alone in the world. Terrified. She began running away through the crowd, away from the babble of people, the hollow echo of the tannoy, the deafening roar of the planes. Outside she took a taxi to Bernard's flat. She had a key and she opened the door and raced straight through to the kitchen. She grabbed the biggest, sharpest knife she could find. She began slashing at everything in sight: the kitchen curtains, the chairs, the dishes. She flew through to the hall wielding the knife crazily above her head. She ripped it through paintings in the hall, and in the sitting room. She tugged it through settee and chairs, all the time grunting and growling and snarling like a wild animal. With all her strength she scraped it down the wallpaper. She swiped at ornaments sending them crashing to pieces on the ground. She stumbled through to the bedroom and slashed and tore and ripped the black silk sheets and pillowslips to shreds.

Then she fumbled for her lipstick and wrote as large as she could on the wall, 'Welcome home, you bastard. I hope she was worth it.'

Rage protected her against hurt. Somehow she returned to Monteith Row and let herself into the silent flat. Already it was getting dark. Rain was tapping at the kitchen window. The fire had gone out. The place had never looked so gloomy. She didn't want to be here. Nor did she want to go to Bearsden. She collapsed into a chair beside the table and sobbed broken-heartedly into the green and cream checked teacloth.

Soon Robert would be home and expecting his meal to be ready and she'd still got to go back to Bearsden and collect Jennifer. She dried her eyes and took deep breaths before starting to prepare her husband's meal. But still emotion was careering out of control. She felt resentment at the thought of Robert. She didn't love Robert. She'd never loved him. She realised that now. She'd married him to please her mother. Resentment immediately ballooned at the thought of her mother. She hated her. She wished her mother was dead. As long as her mother was alive, she'd never be free to live, to love, to be herself. If it hadn't been for her mother, everything would have been different. She would have been married to Bernard. He would have been all hers. They could have had a proper home together. Oh, how she hated her mother. As usual, however, guilt wormed its way in. Guilt frightened her. Fear diminished her. She locked doors inside herself for protection. But when Robert arrived she was able to greet him with a bright-eyed smile and a steak and kidney pie which he downed with relish and said it was the best thing he'd ever tasted.

He was sympathetic about the migraine she told him she'd suffered earlier, and offered to go and collect Jennifer while she relaxed and watched television. She agreed, and was soon left alone in the house again. It was then the memory sneaked back into her mind of how she had told Bernard to have a girlfriend, to lead a normal life. 'I've got a home and a husband and a child. You have nothing,' she'd said. 'I don't mind if you have somebody else too.'

But she *did* mind. That was the problem. She couldn't bear to share him. She loved him too much. She wanted him to be hers and hers alone. How could he love her and not want the same? But he did, of course. At least that's what he'd said. He'd wanted to marry her. Blind rage grew up inside her again. She didn't care what she'd said, or what he'd said in the past. He was away in Paris right now making love to another woman. That was all that mattered. The thought caused her so much pain she nursed herself and rocked from side to side, witless with the agony of it.

'Bastard. Bastard,' she cried out loud. 'Don't you ever come near me again.'

By the time Robert returned she had washed the dishes and tidied up. She put Jennifer to bed and tucked her up with her dummy and teddy and left a nightlight burning. Jennifer was afraid of the dark. Unable to settle to watch television, Andrina busied herself baking some scones, a Victoria sponge cake, an apple pie and a batch of shortbread biscuits.

'Andrina,' Robert protested. 'Why on earth are you slaving away like this at this time of night? I thought you weren't feeling well.'

She gave him one of her perky smiles, eyes round and bright and sparkling. 'No, I'm fine. Absolutely fine.'

Robert stared at her. 'Sometimes I don't know what to make of you.'

'Don't make anything of me.' She fussed about with brittle cheerfulness. 'I enjoy baking and cooking. What's strange about that?'

'Come to bed. Leave all this and come to bed.'

Jesus Christ, she thought, don't let him touch me. 'You go,' she said. 'I can't leave the kitchen in a mess like this. My mother would have a fit.'

'Your mother's not here,' Robert said quietly. 'And what you do or do not do in your own kitchen is your own business. It has nothing to do with your mother.'

She almost laughed out loud. How little he knew about her, about anything. She could no more leave her kitchen in a mess than stop the world whirling round. It was an agony she couldn't possibly contemplate. Everything in her house, especially everything she had, everything she did, had to be perfect.

Like her mother she bathed every day, religiously manicured

her nails every evening, feet and hands, brushed her hair every evening until her scalp tingled, laid out clean underwear and clothes for the next morning. After every meal she meticulously brushed her teeth until they gleamed.

Everything in the house gleamed. Like her mother, she was always straightening things and plumping up cushions. She had to be the last to go to bed at night so that she could conscientiously check the perfection of everything before shutting each room door. If Robert was last, she had to creep up again after he was asleep and go around checking everything. It was impossible to rest, to sleep until she had done so.

'Your mother's not here,' Robert had said. But she *was* here. She was everywhere. Always. She was at her side, at her back, inside her head.

Then suddenly all the things she'd been doing over the years with Bernard hit her like a physical blow. It almost felled her. She felt sick with terror at the risks she'd taken. It was a miracle that her mother hadn't found out. How could she have taken such risks? A million times worse than leaving a kitchen in an untidy mess. Sweat poured from her and she paled at the thought. She must have been mad.

'Andrina, what the hell's wrong?' Robert strode across to her and gripped her arm. Shakily, she sat down. She was safe. She was safe. Her mother had *not* found out. She knew she would die if her mother found out.

'Oh, thank you God,' she kept thinking. 'Oh, thank you God.'

Robert shook her. 'Andrina what's wrong with you?'

Somehow she gathered her wits together. 'This headache,' she said. 'I told you. It just comes over me. For a minute or two I can't see . . .'

'I'll phone the doctor.'

'No, no. It's all right now. It was just a minute or two. It's just migraine. Rest and take a couple of painkillers until it passes, that's what the doctor said. I'll be all right. Don't worry.'

He helped her, half-supported her, through to the bedroom.

'You're trembling,' he said. He lowered her on to the bed. She sat like a child, allowed him to undress her and pull on her nightie. He tucked her in and undressed himself. He came into bed beside her and tried to gather her into his arms. She stiffened away.

'Please, Robert,' she said. 'Not tonight.'

'I only wanted to hold you.'

'I just want to be left alone to go to sleep.' But she didn't. She waited until his breathing became deep and even. Then, assured that he was sound asleep, she crept from the bed and the room.

Through in the kitchen she began to wash up the baking tins and stack them neatly away in their proper place.

Chapter Sixty

'Nobody would ever do this in the West End.' Bridie's mouth had taken an almost permanent droop and her eyes were dark with misery.

'Do what?' Carragh asked.

'Have a hing.'

Both women were at the open window of Patrick's house in Acrehill Street. Their folded arms were leaning on the sill. At the next window Doris had taken up the same position. They were watching Patrick and Tony and Michael and Frank and some other men of various ages, most of them unemployed, having a street race. This was one of the diversions the local corner boys had for passing the time and providing themselves some sort of challenge. It was obvious by the wild look in their eyes, the way their heads were thrown back, and their arms and legs going like pistons at full speed, they were giving the race their all.

'I thought you meant the race,' Carragh said.

'They wouldn't do that either.'

Carragh sighed. 'What's come over you, Bridie? You'd think Garngad and Blackhill were bits of paradise to hear you talk now. Look at your da.' Her attention was caught again by the race, which had been won by a shabby-looking man who was now trembling and choking and laughing in triumph. Scobie was staggering about as if he was going to have a heart attack. 'They're mad, the lot of them, but especially men of your da's and Patrick's age.' Carragh raised her voice to bawl, 'Scobie! Are you coming in for your tea?' In a quieter tone she added, 'Daft wee gowk!'

The three women withdrew into the room and shut the windows.

Doris said, 'I'm surprised at Frank.'

'Nothing surprises me about Frank any more.' The corners of Bridie's mouth drooped down.

'What about Frank?' Carragh asked.

Doris said, 'I thought with all his posh friends – you know – he'd be above carrying on with the likes of them out there.'

'Here you,' Carragh said. 'Watch your tongue, Miss High and Mighty. Your da's one of them out there, remember.'

'You have to laugh though, Ma.'

'Oh? What about?'

'Well, Da's wee legs whirring along and Tony galloping beside him with every buck tooth in his head showing, and Patrick taking the whole width of the road. What a pantomime!'

'Och well, they enjoy it.'

'I bet Michael let Francis Maloney win. I mean, Michael used to sprint up the Campsie Hills.'

'Maybe so, maybe so,' Carragh said. 'But don't let Francis hear you say that. Come on, you two, help me set this table.'

'Patrick should get married again. He's obviously hopeless without a woman. Look at this place. It's like a tip. Did I tell you I saw Bernard with that woman, Jane Ford? They came into the shop and . . .'

'Aye, aye, you told us, hen. At least half a dozen times. I don't think Patrick'll ever forget Maureen.' Carragh sighed. 'I miss her as well. She was a good pal. Many a good laugh we had – her reading my teacup. She asked me to keep an eye on Patrick. She knew he'd be a pour soul without her.'

'He's just too damned lazy to clean his house,' Doris said.

'Watch your tongue,' Carragh repeated. 'Honestly, you're a right miserable pair. I don't get many laughs with you, that's for sure.'

'At least I've a right to be miserable.'

'You should never have divorced your man.'

'He made me, Ma.'

'How could he make you?'

Doris shrugged and creaked lethargically over to the table in her PVC boots and skirt. 'He just did.'

'And as for you,' Carragh turned to Bridie, 'it's time you did something with your miserable face or you'll be losing your man as well. You were never a raving beauty, Bridie, and that dour huffy look does nothing to improve you.'

'It's just that Frank's changed, Ma.'

'Frank?' Carragh said. 'Him that was racing out there with the lads? Him that was kicking a football about the streets with them earlier? If you ask me, hen, it's you that's changed, not your man.' Of course, Carragh didn't realise what a traitor Frank was. To Carragh and Scobie, Frank could do no wrong. Bridie said as much to Frank later, after they'd returned to Botanic Crescent.

'I know what you were doing there today.'

'Visiting my father?' Frank suggested.

'More than that, and you know it. You were putting Blackhill under a microscope. You were just using everybody there. You're going to write about them, aren't you?'

'What's wrong with that? I'm a writer.'

'You'll betray them – your own kind. You'll make them out to be rotten.'

Frank's face turned grey with anger. 'Is that how little you know me or what I'm trying to do?'

'What are you trying to do, Frank? You tell me.'

'I'm trying to tell the truth. I'm trying to show what it's like to be brought up in an environment like Blackhill. What the place, what the system, can do to people. How it can affect their lives for good and for bad. I'm trying to show the whole picture so that people outside that environment can at least have some sort of understanding and compassion.'

'Oh yes? Is that what you were doing with your last play and the one before that?'

'I'm trying to tell the truth, as I see it. That applies to all of my work.'

'And of course it doesn't matter to you who gets hurt in the process.'

'What the hell's wrong with you, Bridie? You used to be all for my writing.'

'Was I?' she said sarcastically. 'Fancy that!'

He had reluctantly suspected for some time and now he was sure that Bridie was jealous of his work and the success it had brought. In his secret heart too, he knew that Bridie was floundering out of her depth. His anger melted away at the thought. Pity mixed with his love for her. He didn't know what to do. He couldn't stop writing any more than he could give up his new lifestyle and go back and live in Blackhill or Garngad or the Gorbals. He had experienced the hard life. He'd done his share of roughing it. Enough was enough.

He compromised by trying not to talk so much to Bridie about his writing, or to expect her to be the first to read his manuscripts. It was a terrible effort for him because he was always bubbling over with such enthusiasm and eagerness to share the joy of creation with her.

He forced himself not to invite people to so many parties in the flat. This went so much against his grain it was a real agony to him. People, all sorts of people, were eternally fascinating to him. But it was a special joy to be with creative people who had this God-given talent in common with him. One of his favourite quotations was by Robert Louis Stevenson, who said, 'If any man loves the labour of any trade, the Gods have called him'.

A sadness touched him. Because of the restraints and cautions he had to put on himself because of Bridie, or when he was with Bridie, the closeness they'd once had together was diminished. They had periods of silence that were awkward and strained, unlike the peaceful, loving, sharing quiet they'd once enjoyed together. When a silence stretched between them now, his mind frantically searched for something to say that had nothing to do with his work, or his colleagues in the Society of Authors, or the PEN Club, or the BBC.

He tried to build up her confidence by playing himself down. But when she took a lead from this, he felt resentment. She began reading his work again – the bread-and-butter short story manuscripts, a few poems he'd been commissioned to do for a literary magazine. Sometimes she'd do a serious criticism of which some points were valid and on which he acted. But there were a growing number of niggles and nit-picks. She began to sound as if she was only searching for faults. When she did manage to find any, she pounced on them and was maliciously pleased if she wounded him.

He locked his play in a drawer in his desk. It was the only locked drawer and he was thankful for it.

Yet they still had loving moments. They would still walk hand in hand through the park. They would still laugh together. They could still treasure moments of tenderness and physical closeness in bed.

It was the other closeness that was gradually disappearing, as if some terrible creeping paralysis had infected both Bridie and himself. He didn't know how to stop it. He didn't know what to say that wouldn't make her harder and more defensive and shrink further and further away from him. Words had become dangerous weapons between them. It occurred to him that this disintegration of a marriage would be a good theme for a play. He was shocked – not by thinking about using the theme – but that his marriage might, in fact, be disintegrating. His mind, his whole being, became torn between distress and the creative process. Gradually, the one form of suffering merged with the other until they became confused, and the dividing lines softened. It hardly mattered which was which.

He became withdrawn, absent-minded. Sometimes he didn't hear Bridie when she spoke to him. He shut himself away in his study for longer and longer periods. He was living partly in a dream world. He was gaining sustenance from it. Excitement was quivering in his loins, in his heart, in his head, in his very soul.

It didn't matter now about parties, or colleagues, or talking, or entertaining, or visiting, or thinking about or doing anything that would divert him or take him away from his desk. He had all the company he needed now. People were crowding together in his head. He could see them moving, hear them talking. He knew them better than anyone else on earth because he knew their innermost thoughts, their most intimate and truest feelings. They were creating a new world. He loved them like a father loves his children. A fearful urgency grew inside him. He mustn't die before they finished telling their story; or the house mustn't go up in flames. Burglars mustn't get their hands on the precious pages or destroy them. At the same time the excitement grew and grew. And the joy.

It was working. It was good. It was coming alive. *Really alive.* The characters were taking off on their own.

Hallelujah! Hallelujah!

He was a happy man.

Chapter Sixty-One

'Welcome home you bastard. I hope she was worth it.'

Bernard stared at the scarlet-smeared words, read them over and over again. He'd already wandered around the house. He felt not only devastated, he felt sad. The thought that he had caused Andrina to wreak such violence and destruction depressed him beyond words. His Velvet, soft and sweetly feminine, was not like this. He had driven her to behave completely out of character.

Her distress must have been unendurable. He was sorry. But what could he say that would change anything now? The truth would be no use. The truth was that he was so randy he had to have a woman much more often than every few weeks or few months. Yet at the same time, it made no difference to his loving Andrina. He had sex with other women, but he loved her and her alone. He had loved her from the first moment he saw her when she was only fifteen, and he would love her till the day he died.

He remembered her in all her stages, in all her moods, in all her styles. One day her dark auburn hair had been parted in the middle and plaited. It hung over each shoulder in long, thick pigtails. He remembered the time her full pouting mouth boasted its first bright coat of lipstick. He recalled the demure skirts and blouses that could not hide her provocative curves. When she had been pregnant he had watched her and followed her. She had worn a navy cord velvet coat with leg o' mutton sleeves, a swing back and edge-to-edge at the front. On a hot day she wore a navy and white striped dress with a white collar and navy and white shoes.

She'd long ago forgotten all about these outfits. She always marvelled at how he remembered every tiny detail about everything she'd ever worn.

The white tailored shorts she'd sported one hot summer's evening had been topped with a sleeveless white blouse. Her accessories were a broad gold belt, gold earrings and bangles. White and gold against the deep burnished gloss of her hair was striking.

The black satin basque, the lace-edged knickers, the black lace-topped stockings, the high-heeled black sandals.

The way she stretched and eased her arms high and piled her long hair on top of her head, her eyes innocent and inviting.

He loved the soft vulnerable curve at the nape of her neck.

How could he explain that he loved her now? She would never believe him. The strength and finality of her disbelief was all around him. Yet he had to try. He phoned her.

'Darling Andrina,' he began, but before he could say any more she hissed at him.

'Bastard! Don't you dare ever try to contact me again.'

He'd never heard any voice so charged with hate. He sat down on the wreck of the bed and supported his head in his hands. Depression weighed heavy on him, and for the first time in his life, he was attacked by a plague of indecision. He didn't know which way to turn, what to do, where to go. He couldn't stay here. Not tonight. Even the mattress on the bed had been slashed. He couldn't have a drink. He couldn't even make himself a cup of coffee. Every dish in the kitchen had been broken, his decanter of whisky had been smashed, every bottle of wine in the wine rack had been poured over every floor.

A sense of failure hit him with a wave of panic. He was a failure in personal relationships. He already had one failed marriage behind him, but the woman he wanted to marry wouldn't have him. He'd gone through a string of sexual partners. His latest one, Jane, was definitely angling for marriage and although he admired her in many ways, he didn't love her. Not as he loved Andrina.

A worry bell rang in his head. If he didn't get a grip on his personal life, the time might come when he'd fail in his business too. He couldn't afford to be indecisive in his business. He couldn't afford to panic. Indecision and panic could spell death, either for a client or himself. Or both.

He tried to banish Andrina from his mind but, surrounded by the wreck of the flat, the symbol of their wrecked relationship, he could not. The outer devastation was worming its way back inside him.

He suddenly strode out of the house and locked the door behind him. The click of the latch closed over with a sense of finality. It brought home the feeling of the end of an era. He leant forward, pressing his forehead against the hard wall of the landing. The deep coldness of the stone seemed to draw the heat and anguish from his soul like a leech. He straightened his neck and slowly closed his eyes. His jaw relaxed and he concentrated on his breathing. In through the nose for four slow seconds, the cool air trickled down to his throat, sucked down deep into his stomach. He held the air inside for another four seconds, before allowing it to dribble slowly, slowly out of slack lips. His chest empty, totally, he remained airless for the same time again. Then he repeated the cycle, kept repeating it.

Gradually his being cleared. His feelings marshalled themselves into a patina of normality. With a last deep sigh, he clattered down the darkened stairwell into his life once more.

He decided it was wiser to delay going to any of the pubs or clubs. Straight away he'd be on duty. He couldn't guarantee total alertness, not yet. Cobwebs of distraction still clung. He went to Pollokshields where Jane lived, cocooned in her big villa. Walking up the curving tree-lined drive, it occurred to him that he hadn't phoned. It would seem strange that, having put her in a taxi and said goodbye to her only a few hours ago, he should suddenly turn up on her doorstep. Again he struggled with indecision. What the hell was he doing? Just then he heard a rapping on glass and saw Jane waving to him in the lighted window of her sitting room. She hurried to open the door to him.

'Darling, I heard your step on the gravel.' She was flushed with pleasure. There was also what looked like a beacon of triumph in her eyes. His depression took another turn when he remembered her earlier hints of marriage. She was a determined girl and, he later found, a recklessly impulsive one. She started saying things like, 'It seems a pity for me to be on my own in this big house and you on your own in that flat.' Soon she'd become more pointed. 'If we promised to endow each other with all our worldly goods, darling, you'd get a very good deal, don't you think?'

She was certainly loaded. Sometimes he asked himself, 'Why shouldn't I take this million-dollar chance of setting myself up?' The truth was he didn't care much one way or the other. If he couldn't have Andrina as his wife, no other woman mattered – except for regular sex. Entering the lofty hall with the chandelier sparkling down from the ceiling, he suddenly thought of his mother having to cope with a husband and four sons in a wee room and kitchen. It would have fitted twice into this hall and still have room to spare. He shook his head.

'What's wrong, darling?' Jane linked arms with him and walked with him into a room the size of a Hilton lounge.

'I felt bad,' he said truthfully.

'Oh darling, I felt the same. And it's so unnecessary separating like that when we'd been so happy together.' She wound herself around him. 'Move in with me.'

'Live together?' He knew perfectly well she meant marriage.

'Now, you mustn't tease.' She kissed the tip of his nose. 'You know I'm not that kind of a girl.'

He felt like saying, 'You could have fooled me!' They had been going at it hammer and tongs every night in Paris. And she'd enjoyed it. To the point of embarrassment, in fact. Every morning she'd rush out and buy him presents, gold cuff-links, gold wristwatch. She had been about to lash out on a gift of a Jaguar car. He'd just managed to stop her in time.

'Darling,' she enthused. 'You're worth it. You're a wonderful lover. I adore you. I'd do anything for you, give you anything.'

'Calm down,' he'd told her. 'What do you think I am? A gigolo?'

She'd thought that hilarious. 'You a gigolo? Darling, anything but. You're your own man. I know that. Anybody would know that just to look at you. I just admire you, that's all. I want to be with you all the time. For always.'

What the hell! he thought.

He took her quickly that night, almost brutally. Afterwards she lay in his arms and kept whispering over and over again, 'I love you, I love you, Bernard. We will get married, won't we? You want to marry me, don't you?'

Eventually he thought – why not? She was beautiful, she was wealthy, and most important, she was unattached.

'All right,' he told her, 'we'll get married.'

'Soon, darling?' she'd cried out in delight.

'As soon as you like,' he said.

Why not? After all, he too was unattached.

In the morning Jane wakened him with a kiss, then presented him with a tray the housekeeper had brought up. She was already showered and made-up and dressed for outdoors.

'Where are you going?' he asked.

She kissed him again. 'Take your time and enjoy your breakfast, darling. Then do your exercise routine. My trampet's under the bed. There's no need for you to worry. I want to do everything right and I'm so excited, I just can't wait. There's so much to see to: shopping for clothes, bookings to make. Absolutely everything to do with weddings has to be booked *ages* in advance these days. But don't worry. I'll organise the whole thing. See you later.'

He nearly said, 'Forget it!' But it was too late. The bird had flown, taking no chances, giving him no time to change his mind. Again he thought, What the hell! Life had to go on and, as far as he was concerned, it couldn't go on without a woman. It had crossed his mind more than once to ask himself why women found him so attractive. He'd stare at himself in the mirror and feel certain that innumerable men were far better looking than him. Yet he'd never once stood at the bar of a pub or club without a woman trying to get off with him. He had come to the conclusion that it was power, or the aura of power. Women seemed to find this irresistible.

It seldom worked the other way around. Jane's wealth had

given her a brick wall of self-confidence. She had always got her own way and was pushy with it. He would have to do something about that if they were going to have any sort of harmonious life together.

He struggled to concentrate on a future with Jane. What was the use of feeling suicidal about life without Andrina? He'd never actually had a life *with* Andrina. But those occasional snatched minutes, or hours, had been his lifeline. Those were the times when he had lived with every braincell in his head and every nerve in his body, every fibre of his being. They had kept his adrenalin pumping.

The twilight world of work was another world in which he walked a tightrope, existed on a dangerous knife-edge. He had always lived to the hilt, forcing himself to the utmost limits, no matter what he did.

After knocking back a glass of orange juice he pushed the tray aside, then padded through to the bathroom. Once shaved and showered, he returned to the bedroom. He pulled the trampet out and switched on the stereo. The throbbing beat of Deep Purple filled the room. He jumped on the trampet, bobbing up and down, side to side, shadow boxing, dancing, using imaginary skipping ropes, deliberately getting high on energy. After twenty minutes he was covered in a sheen of sweat as if oiled from head to toe. Drips coalesced on his eyebrows and pooled under his nose.

He lay on the floor and flung his legs over the bed. Hands on head, he began to crunch his stomach muscles into a tight hard wedge, lifting his upper body up to his knees. He managed four sets of sixty before collapsing back to the floor with a climactic grunt of release. Next he went over to two low stools and placed his hands on either stool. Then, breathing regularly, he began pumping out deep, stretched press-ups. He forced out the hundredth rep before slumping forward on to his towel. Slowly he stood up and shook his head, arms down, gently, before a final cool shower and rub down.

He thought, 'One of the first things I'll do in this house is get a top-class gym set up. He could see it now. Not just free weights and a lat pulley. No, he would indulge in high tech as well. Pec dec, definitely, and he'd investigate some nautilus equipment.

Positive action. Positive thinking. The absolute necessity. The survival kit. Downstairs he leafed through the phone book, found a firm of office cleaners and arranged for them to clean up the flat. He told them to call at his office for the key.

So far, so good. Back to work. Calling in at the pubs and clubs. Talking to his men. Scanning crowds with dark, sharp eyes. Supervising.

Pub owners, club owners anxiously waiting for him. 'Thank God you're here, Bernard. It was a bit dicey to tell you over the phone but . . .'

'Stay cool.' Dark eyes steady and piercing. 'What's your problem?'

Chapter Sixty-Two

They were married quietly at the Registry Office in town. Jane was Protestant, but didn't care one way or another. Nor did he. She hadn't been inside a church since her Sunday School days. He hadn't taken Mass since his divorce. Sometimes, thinking of his mother, he felt guilty. But guilt, like fear, was something he'd learned to cope with.

Jane wanted to go on a honeymoon abroad. It was their first test of wills. He couldn't take time off work after having been so recently on holiday in Paris. She had actually booked tickets for the Bahamas. She was in her element organising things and pushing ahead with her plans without any consultation. She was a regular and enthusiastic announcer of *faits accomplis*. He could imagine her in a few years time doing sterling work for charity on innumerable committees, bullying people to part with money.

'Cancel the tickets,' he said. 'Or cancel the wedding.'

She cancelled the tickets. There was no argument. He saw the fear in her eyes . Pushy or not, self-confident or not, she loved him too much to take any risks.

'Next year,' he said, 'we'll discuss a holiday together, and in plenty of time so that I can make the necessary work arrangements.'

He only mentioned the gym. Next day she had everything installed.

'Shit!' he said when he saw it.

'Darling, don't you like it? I thought you'd be so pleased.' Again the vulnerability filled her eyes. The bewilderment.

'Of course I like it. But when will you learn to discuss things with me first? We're supposed to be a pair – partners. Stop dashing off on your own bat.'

Nevertheless, they shared some satisfying times in the gym.

It was good that they had this interest in common. She was terrifically fit. And a real trier. Sometimes he had to laugh at her determined struggle with the weights. In some things she was as extreme and as determined as him. She was impulsive, however – he was not.

It was good to be seen with her too. Eyes turned to admire her glossy cap of blonde hair, her deep tan, her lean, long-legged figure. She was always immaculately dressed. It demoralised her when he refused to take her to nightclubs. 'Are you ashamed of me or something?' she'd ask, the defiance in her voice contradicted by the dark anxiety in her eyes.

He saw the desperation of her love for him. He realised how, without the slightest effort on his part (or even the slightest interest), he could shatter her confident façade. 'Don't be stupid,' he told her. 'I don't want to put you at risk, that's all.'

He had dozens of clubs on his books now, in Glasgow and in Edinburgh. He tried to explain the risks involved in accompanying him, but her hurt remained. She had no understanding of the dangerous waters, the treacherous undercurrents, in these places. She had no idea of the kind of situation that could suddenly erupt that he would have to calm down. He had to be ready to deal with anything and everything in whatever way was appropriate.

He took her out for the occasional meal to a hotel or a restaurant instead, and each time she was as eager and excited as a child at Christmas. It was on one of these occasions, on a lovely spring day, that he and Jane bumped into Robert and Andrina. Andrina's hair was piled up on top of her head with wisps teasing down at each side of her face at the nape of her neck. She was wearing a white silk blouse with a high mandarin collar and high puffed chiffon sleeves with tiny buttons. Her shapely waist and curvaceous hips were flattered by a high-waisted, long and straight black skirt. On her feet were high-heeled black suede court shoes.

She looked stunning. It took every vestige of his control to calmly make the necessary introductions. Jane invited Andrina and Robert to join them. On the surface the evening went splendidly. Bernard was irritated by Jane's all-too-obvious pride in him. 'My husband did this; my husband did that.' It was embarrassing. He wished she'd shut up. It was as if he and Andrina had been together only yesterday. Nothing had changed. It seemed miraculous that their two partners never saw the electricity that fizzled across the table every time their eyes met. Everyone else in the world shrank into insignificance. There was only the anguish of love in his heart, the hot throb of passion in his loins.

His wonderful, sensual Velvet.

The next day he sent a bouquet of long-stemmed roses, one for each year he'd known her. The accompanying card said, 'To Velvet'.

Then he phoned her. And even the sound of her voice sent the adrenalin pumping. He said, 'Where can we meet?'

'Robert's on his spring break.'

'My house then?'

'What about your dear wife?'

The bitter twist in her voice made him shout down the receiver, 'The same as your dear husband. Jane or any other woman means nothing to me compared with you. Life goes on, Andrina, but so does our love for one another. I wanted *you* to marry me, remember?'

'Will she be out?'

'She goes to her Health and Beauty class tomorrow evening at seven-thirty. You know the house?'

She said, 'I know it.'

'Christ, Andrina, how I've missed you. I'm only half alive without you. I can't wait to hold you in my arms again.'

The phone clicked and went dead. Andrina had hung up. He knew however that she would come. He had felt the vibes of her passion winging over the telephone lines to him. He was excited. He was fully, vibrantly, electrifyingly alive once again.

For days and nights after she wrecked Bernard's flat, Andrina had wept and grieved, hated him and longed for him. When she'd read the notice of his marriage in the Glasgow Herald, she'd gone through the same gamut of emotion again. Gradually she'd settled down to a half-life – the kind of life, as far as she could see, that everyone else had. A normal, routine, ordinary, day-to-day kind of existence. Only, she was a better wife than normal. She was obsessively conscientious, a perfect housewife, a devoted mother, a cordon bleu cook. She went to church three times every Sunday and choir practice twice a week. Her mind bitterly discarded Bernard O'Maley. She was finished with him.

Yet, oh, in the stillness of the night, how she'd lain awake dreaming of her love. How she'd posed for him. How his eyes had devoured her. How his hands had caressed her. How his mouth had moved and licked and nibbled and sucked at every inch of her. How he'd entered her, and entered her, and entered her. And wetness had waited for him. And breasts had ached for him. Now the dream had become reality again.

She buried her face in the roses. She danced around the house. Only with feverish difficulty did she hide her rapture from Robert. He thought she was going to her usual choir practice and so no questions were asked. He only saw her leave with her coat on. He did not see how unsuitably dressed she was underneath for any kind of church attendance.

Next to her skin she wore a black satin basque above which the white of her soft breasts bulged. Black lace-topped stockings, a turquoise satin crossover dress that startlingly reflected the colour of her eyes, its tulip shaped skirt accentuating the sensuous bulge of her hips. In the secrecy of the hall she slipped on high-heeled shoes of the same vivid turquoise colour.

She travelled by taxi to the villa, got out at the gates, then walked up the drive with racing heart. What if Jane was still there?

He opened the door to her. The wicked thrill of being in another woman's home. What if Jane came back unexpectedly – suddenly appeared while she was parading and posing around the marital bedroom? While she was obeying Bernard's every carnal instruction?

They took their time. They pushed danger to its limits in the bed in which Bernard slept with his wife, and, as Andrina knew, in which they would lie together many times. As they would live and love in Robert's bed. As they would make love when Jane and Robert were in the house. As they had made love before, for snatched minutes, for dangerous indulgent hours.

She knew it was wicked. And it was the wickedness that drove her crazy with excitement.

Bernard confessed to her afterwards that since that night and their passionate reunion he hadn't been able to make love to Jane. 'I get so far,' he said, 'then I think of you and I can't go on.'

They made a foursome many times, met for meals in restaurants, entertained each other at home. Jane had become quieter, almost timid. She kept staring at Bernard with adoring yet apprehensive eyes. Often Jane and Andrina waited and talked while Robert and Bernard were at the karate club. Then they all had dinner when the men returned.

Jane and Andrina became friends.

Jane confided in Andrina. 'I don't know if it's my fault . . . if it's something I've done. Or something I've not done. It used to be so wonderful but . . . Bernard isn't the same any more. Half the time it's as if I didn't exist. Probably he doesn't mean it, Andrina, but . . . there's other times when he can be quite cruel. He makes it so obvious that he doesn't love me. He . . .' Miserably she hesitated. 'He's become impotent.'

So Bernard hadn't lied to her. Andrina felt grateful. At the same time, a knot of misery for the other woman twisted in her heart, making her shoulders hunch forward with the pain of it.

'It won't be you,' she tried to assure Jane. 'It'll have nothing to do with you. You're a beautiful, desirable woman.'

'Thanks, Andrina,' Jane said gratefully. 'The old self-confidence was beginning to sink. But I always feel better after I've been to see you. You're a good friend.' Suddenly tears filled her eyes. 'My best friend, really. I know I can always talk to you and you'll understand.'

God forgive me, Andrina thought, as she hushed her weeping

friend, and soothed her and patted her. But despite her misery, despite her sympathy, despite her guilt, despite everything, the strength of her feelings for Bernard remained. My wonderful, passionate lover, she prayed, hold me forever.

Then she hurried away to make Bernard's wife a comforting cup of tea.

Margaret Thomson Davis

A KIND OF IMMORTALITY

arrow books

To my son and my adopted son,
the two men I most admire

The loneliness which we rightly dread is not the absence of human forces or voices – it is the absence of love . . . Our wisdom therefore must lie in learning not to shrink from anything that may lie in store for us, but so to grasp the master key of life as to be able to turn everything to good and fruitful account.

Caroline E. Stephen, *Christian faith and practice in the experience of the Society of Friends*

Art was given for that;
God uses us to help each other so,
Lending our minds out . . .

Fra Lippo Lippi
Robert Browning

LOVE

Love endures through all our years, and ties
Us fast together, though with silken ropes;
Love need not shout, nor look with jealous eyes,
But seals in quiet trust our faiths and hopes,
And when surrounded by our darkest shades
Love is the guiding light that never fades.

But more than this, when we are gone
Our love will live in memoried care,
And others in their loving dawn
May feel its presence in the air.

James Muir

I

BESSIE ALEXANDER KNEW she was a disgrace. She sat in the Quaker Meeting House with head lowered, listening to the reverent tick of the clock on the wall high above her. To all outward appearances she was a decent, pious woman of forty years, loyal wife of Peter, devoted mother of Daisy. Instead of praying, however, she was thinking randy thoughts about Gregory Seymour. The awful thing was, he was married as well. Her thoughts became so lewd and indecent that her cheeks began to burn and she surreptitiously glanced around, afraid that some of her fellow worshippers could see into her heart. But everyone except her seemed perfectly at peace in the deep silence in the Meeting House.

It was a spartan place of plain painted walls, with no curtains at the window. Everyone sat on wooden benches arranged in a three-sided square with a table at the fourth side. At the table two elders, a man and a woman, sat, sometimes with closed eyes, sometimes just staring blankly out at their fellow Quakers. Their inward eye, Bessie felt sure, was concentrating on higher things. On the table lay a copy of the Bible, a copy of *Christian faith and practice in the experience of the Society of Friends*, and a copy of *Advices and Queries*. The latter was the nearest thing Quakers, or members of the Society of Friends, to give it its proper name, had to dogma. Except it was nothing like dogma. It didn't lay down any law. It didn't answer any questions.

Her question at the moment was: should she or shouldn't she? Gregory was doing everything he could to persuade her. She didn't need any persuading, really. She wanted to. Indeed, in her mind, she'd had wild, passionate sex with him a thousand times. She was doing it again!

Hastily she picked up her copy of *Advices and Queries* and opened it at random.

'Are you patient and considerate,' she read, 'even towards those whom you find it hard to like and those who seem to you unloving and ungrateful?'

Sometimes she felt she'd been too damned patient and considerate with Peter. That was half her trouble. And he was certainly unloving and ungrateful. Not that she wanted any gratitude. But a little loving now and again wouldn't have gone amiss. Of course it could be argued that it was all her own fault right from the beginning.

She began to sweat again. Fool! Fool! And a wicked one at that. She stole a glance at the person sitting next to her. It was Mary Harvey, looking serene in a khaki anorak and striped woolly hat and apparently unaware of the proximity of such wickedness. Of course what had happened when she'd first met Peter was before she'd joined the Society of Friends. Peter had been, and still was, her father's accountant. He 'did' her father's books. Or at least one set of them. She knew perfectly well that her father kept two sets of books for the shop: one for Peter and the taxman, another truer account for himself. Mother and Father were devout members of the Church of Jesus and worshipped in that imposing building with its spire reaching high into the heavens. But it was the stained-glass windows that had fascinated her when she was a child.

Oh dear, oh dear. Bessie mentally shook her head. The hypocrisy of it all. It surely wasn't necessary to defraud the income tax in order to succeed in business. There were many Quaker firms to prove that honesty could be the best policy. Cadbury's, Fry's, Rowntree, Horniman's Tea, Clark's Shoes, to mention but a few. Indeed, she sometimes thought that Quakers seemed to have an embarrassing knack of making a great deal of money if they went into business.

She'd met Peter when he'd come to the house to see her father.

It had happened one New Year's Eve when her sister Moira was spending New Year with a colleague in Dundee. Mother and Father were away at a friend's ruby wedding party which coincided with New Year. They were staying in a hotel and couldn't take the dog, so she was detailed to be dog-sitter. She had been surprised when they'd trusted her with old Towzer. They had never believed she was good enough for anything else. Of course they were probably quite right. Peter, not knowing they were away (or so he said), had arrived on the doorstep on Hogmanay to 'first foot' them. He had brought the traditional bottle of whisky and piece of coal for good luck. Some good luck he'd brought her!

But then she shouldn't have drunk so much. Well, she didn't really. Not that much. She just wasn't used to the stuff. She didn't even like the taste of whisky.

But there you are. The next thing was she'd woken up feeling hung over and awful cramped in bed. Then, swivelling a bloodshot gaze sideways, she'd been astounded to see this baldy-headed wee man lying in bed beside her. Shock! Horror! He wasn't quite old enough to be her father. But almost. She'd never liked him. Then the guilt set in. She could almost see her mother rearing up at the foot of the bed pointing an accusing finger.

'You have sinned!' Again! Bessie was always doing something wrong. Admittedly this was a new low.

Even yet, after twenty years of marriage, she still squirmed. She still suffered mental anguish at the thought.

She should never have married him. Especially when it meant taking on his old devil of a father as well. But there it was. Her mother, her father, the Sunday School, her sister Moira, the Bible class, the Church, God Himself, had all seemed to gang up against her at the time and force her to assuage her guilt and make an honest woman of herself by entering holy matrimony.

How could she have done such a thing? Of course, this was an all too familiar cry about everything. Every member of her family flung the question at her at some time or other.

Not only about marrying Peter. As if it wasn't enough that she had never fitted into her parents' home. Now she didn't fit into her husband's. Nor had she ever fitted into their church. On the occasions when her father was in a jolly mood, like in the shop on a good day, he'd say, 'I think there's been a mistake with Bessie. Either there was a mix-up in the maternity hospital, or she's a changeling.'

She'd grown up with their reluctance to lay claim to her. Even her granny, when she'd been alive, and a kinder woman you couldn't meet, often used to say, 'I don't know where she's come from.'

It wasn't her appearance. Or maybe it was? She could never be sure about anything. Nowadays she tended to slouch about in trousers, baggy tops and comfortable sandals. And she was always getting her clothes and her hair smudged with paint. Her mother and Peter and even Daisy were always lecturing her about what she ought to wear. And why she should give up this filthy hobby she had of painting awful pictures. Her mother, in a gentle way; Peter with his own almost permanent sneer. It infuriated Peter how she spent so much of his 'good money' on canvases and paints and 'all that rubbish'. He had tried every way he could to cure her of this 'ridiculous habit' down through the years. All to no avail. She could be too soft and easily put down in other ways but as far as fighting to keep on painting was concerned, she was like a tiger.

'It's an obsession with you,' Peter accused. 'It's not natural.'

There was a floored loft area in the flat with a ceiling that sloped almost down to the floor at one side. It had big dormer windows that let in lots of light. Bessie had immediately commandeered it as her studio and kept her easel and all her canvases up there. She had spotlights fixed up so that she could, if necessary, work late at night. Often that was her only chance, because during the day Granda always needed so much attention. And of course there was all the cooking, housework and shopping to do. Often when Peter commanded her to come down from her loft retreat she responded by desperate singing to drown out his voice, or shouted out, 'I'm not listening. I'm not listening.' Sometimes she took the radio up and turned it on full blast to drown him out. Or she'd belt out Beethoven's Ninth Symphony on the record player.

Daisy was embarrassed and ashamed of her. Daisy was a younger version of her Aunt Moira, whereas Bessie was as different from them both as chalk and cheese. Old photos showed her with a riot of fair curly hair. Her mother said it was a terrible job to keep that hair tidy. She had serious eyes and a gentle, timid expression, almost as if she was expecting someone to hit her. Nobody did, of course. At least, not at home. She'd got the belt a few times at school but then, who hadn't?

Moira had straight, dark hair like in youthful photos of their mother and father. Right from an early age Moira had to wear glasses (also like Mother and Father). Moira had always been the favourite. Moira had been brainy, of course, and always correct and conventional, even as a child. Now she was a senior librarian. She had never married and was still at home in Bearsden with Mother and Father.

Bessie couldn't imagine Moira getting drunk and sinning with a man. Or being dreamy and forgetting things she'd been asked to do. Or not being able to hold down a 'decent' job. Or – horror of horrors – wanting to go to Art School and mix with all the hippie riff-raff in the country.

The 'decent' job had been helping Dad in his small but select menswear shop in Bearsden. She was never allowed to measure an inside leg, although once she had while Dad had slipped through to the back shop to the lavatory. She'd protested later in her own defence that he'd never told her that that particular part of the job, or the anatomy, was taboo.

'If you'd any common sense or decency you wouldn't need to be told,' her father had said. 'You just can't be trusted for a minute on your own.' The later incident at New Year proved this to be only too true.

Now her senses were in danger of deserting her again. Mother and Father had always tried to stop her 'wasting time' with drawing or painting pictures. It had been all right at first when she'd been small. Well, not *perfectly* all right, because they never understood her pictures. Nobody did. Least of all Peter who made such a fool of them. Peter's old father, who was the Neil Alexander half of the accounting firm, Alexander & Son, was the same. She was sure he had Alzheimer's disease but Peter wouldn't hear of it. Peter's talent was to close his mind and shut his eye to anything he didn't want to acknowledge, and he had become a hundred times worse since the time not so long ago when she'd put one of her pictures into the Shawlands church bazaar. Gregory Seymour, who had come along with the people he'd been visiting, had not only bought it but had tracked her down to tell her how original and talented she was.

He was an art dealer and owned a couple of art galleries. Surely he must know what he was talking about. He certainly seemed a very intelligent and knowledgeable man. Oh joy of joys! Oh warm glow of gratitude! Oh golden mesh of delight! She would have done anything for him: fallen at his feet, kissed the ground he walked on.

When he asked to see more of her work she dug out canvases from under the stairs, from up in the loft, from under the bed. He was astonished and undeniably impressed. He stood, stroking his beard and staring at her pictures. He'd suggested an exhibition of her works at one of his galleries. It was a very small gallery and the exhibition had only been on for a few days, so no more than a handful of people had seen the paintings. Nevertheless, Peter had been furious as well as shocked. So had her parents. Admittedly some of the pictures contained nude, rude parts. That reminded her of one of her earliest sins. Her mother and father had never to this day got over it. She had been hardly more than a child herself when she'd persuaded a boy to strip off so that she could make an accurate drawing of his body. Such a thing had never happened in the history of Bearsden.

She could defend herself in one thought – if only to herself. After all, they hadn't allowed her access to books on anatomy, and had subsequently forbidden her to go to Art School. They had threatened God's wrath and her rapid descent into hell if she went to evening classes on the subject. They had heard that there were nude models there as well as in the Art School. They sincerely believed, because they were fundamentally sincere, good people, that this strange side of her nature, this peculiarity, was something that, for her own sake, her own protection, had to be rooted out, purged and purified.

It wasn't as if she drew nice flowers or fruit and just as a wee hobby. She seemed to have this shameful obsession with naked bodies. There was something, it seemed to them, unnatural and obscene about her pictures that truly upset them. She was really sorry. Over and over again she tried to stop, tried to please them, but failed. Now her thoughts were scattered by the sudden creak of the bench as someone got up to speak – or 'give ministry', as they called it in the Society of Friends. It was Penelope Braithwaite (a right old Quaker name, that). She had chosen to read from the *Advices and Queries*. What was said in ministry often spoke to someone's 'condition', to use another Quaker phrase. In this case it was Bessie's.

'Do any of your interests, important though they may appear to you, unduly absorb your time and energy to the hindrance of your growth in grace and of your service to God?'

Could this mean her interest in art? Or the art gallery owner, Bessie wondered. Probably both. Remembering Gregory – big, barrel-chested, very masculine Gregory – started her thinking of sex again. And could anyone blame her? She'd never had any for about fifteen years. Not since Peter had become impotent. Or, as he said, 'gone off' her. He'd only married her in the first place because he had to, he said. Out of respect for her parents, not her. She'd missed a period. Fancy, just after that one time at New Year.

But there you are. Everyone would blame her. She blamed herself. Especially for what she was thinking right now. She lowered her head again.

She wished there was music at Meeting for Worship. It would have been a welcome diversion. However, although there were other occasions devoted to music, Meeting for Worship concentrated on just that. No music, no clergy, no rituals – nothing was supposed to come between each individual and their direct communication with God. Normally she enjoyed the silence and the idea of communication, but today she was too busy tussling with herself.

'Oh to hell!' she thought eventually, knowing at the same time that that was exactly where she was heading.

II

WHEN JENNIFER ANDERSON was small she absolutely adored Andrina. She had never looked like anyone else's mother, with her beautiful turquoise eyes, her warm ruby-coloured hair and her curvaceous body. Jennifer remembered desperately wanting to stay with her when the marriage broke up and her father walked out. As a little girl at primary school, it had been Robert she'd hated for taking her away from Andrina. Her hatred had been a powerful force that could visibly shake her whole body. Yet she still loved him. It was funny how such strong emotions could alternate or even exist side by side at the same time.

No one had explained why the marriage had come to an end. Her mother had been bitter and said that Daddy had left them because he didn't love them any more. Every time she'd had access to Jennifer, Andrina had bitterly complained about Robert. After he remarried, Jennifer had been sent back to her mother.

Now, at sixteen years of age, Jennifer had grown to resent her mother for many reasons, but most of all for putting her against her father. As a young child she had been insecure enough without being devastated, utterly destroyed, by her mother's bitterness. In one way, her mother telling her about all the things she'd suffered with Robert and what a bore he'd been seemed to bring them closer together. After all, Andrina had never spoken much to her before and she'd always longed for her mother's attention. So often she'd been ignored by her, told to go away and be quiet, banished to her granny's, been forgotten and left at school. She'd learned to come home on her own, despite the intimidation of the busy roads between school and the flat. Then if her mother wasn't there, she'd either sit on the stone steps outside the building, or she'd go across to Glasgow Green. Their building was practically *in* the Green, it was so close. She'd wander about the Green for a while trying not to feel hungry. Or worse – frightened. Not because of the tramps and old winos who sometimes hung about the place. Her terrors were always that her mother would not return. She always did return, though. Usually looking flushed and out of breath and looking more beautiful than ever. She'd hug Jennifer and hurry her inside saying, 'Don't tell Daddy I was late, will you, darling? It wasn't Mummy's fault. Mummy needed to do so much shopping in town and the traffic was horrendous on the way back.'

Jennifer had always been so relieved and happy to see her again, so surrounded by the warm glow of the hug that she'd never noticed the lack of shopping. Never one package or parcel. Never one shopping bag. Now she remembered with a bitter twist of her mouth the glamorous dresses, the tight skirts and sweaters, the sheer stockings, the high-heeled shoes.

She'd been with a lover. Jennifer wondered who the man had been. Or men. Knowing her mother now, there would have been more than one. Oh yes, there had been quite a string of 'uncles'. Sometimes, instead of being sent to her granny's, she would be cajoled into going to bed early. She'd lie and listen to her current uncle's throaty laughter and her mother's giggles. Then there would be other, stranger sounds that would make her cover her ears with the blankets, or burrow deep underneath them and weep helpless tears.

Her father had tried to keep in touch after his marriage to Laura. Every week he'd collect her and take her to the zoo or the cinema or to a toy shop to buy her a dolly or a teddy. Whatever she wanted, in fact. Later, he'd tried to interest her in clothes.

'How would you like Daddy to buy you a new dress?' he'd say.

She'd thought it pathetic. She'd hung back, moody, resentful and depressed. It was him and his love she'd wanted. Her father and her mother together, an ordinary family, like the families of the other children she knew. Mothers used to come to the school gate every playtime with flasks of Bovril or juice for their children in case they became cold or thirsty. Never once had her mother been among that eager, loving group. Nor had she ever turned up at open days when the pupils' work was proudly displayed. She remembered a picture she'd drawn that had been pinned up on the class wall. It was of her mother and father holding hands. Sheer imagination. She'd never seen them holding hands. Or kissing. As far as she could remember they either ignored one another or argued.

She remembered how furious her father had been when he'd discovered Andrina had not gone to the teacher-parents' night at the school. She'd told him she had gone and had made up a pack of lies about Jennifer's progress.

The primary school teacher had eventually got in touch with Robert at the secondary school where he taught and told him how worried she was about his daughter. How withdrawn she was. How she wasn't able to concentrate on her lessons. How she seemed unable or unwilling to mix freely with the other children, even in the playground. Always hanging back on her own in some corner or other, watching but never taking part.

'I had a headache and couldn't go,' her mother protested. 'Why should it always be me, anyway? Why can't you take some responsibility for your own daughter?'

'You know perfectly well why I couldn't go,' her father shouted back. 'I had to be at Sinnieglen talking to the parents of my pupils on the same night. As head of the Art Department, it's my job to organise everything and to show a good example. I *had* to be there.'

'Show a good example?' her mother echoed sarcastically. 'That'll be the day . . .'

And so it went on.

Headache, was it? Jennifer remembered being alone in the house. Walking with fast beating heart through the heavy silence of each room, then standing in the windowless hall, paralysed.

She didn't know what she felt about her father now but she knew what she felt about her mother. Her father's new wife was also a teacher. They had no children and were obviously devoted to one another. There was no place for her there. Oh,

Laura was always nice to her when she went to visit. A lovely tea was provided. Polite conversation was maintained. Her father pushed plates of sandwiches and cakes towards her. Then before she left to return to her Granny Sophie's house along the road, he'd slip a pound into her pocket.

Once a week she visited her granny just along the road from where her father now lived. She stayed overnight at her Granny's house. Grandpa McPherson was dead now and Granny was always glad of her company. Granny gave Andrina short shrift. For years she hadn't even spoken to her daughter. Granny was a very enthusiastic churchwoman. Even now in her late sixties, she was still on innumerable committees and was always doing something for either the Church of Jesus to which she belonged, or for some charity or other. Sophie had kept on speaking terms with her son-in-law after the break-up of the marriage, but not with her daughter. Jennifer had often wondered why. Now she knew.

Her mother's present lover was called Paul Fisher. He was married and that was why, her mother explained, they couldn't become man and wife at the moment. He was going to get a divorce, however, and as soon as it came through, they planned to marry. He was a slim man with cream-coloured hair, pale eyes and a neat blond moustache. He always wore bow-ties and immaculately pressed clothes. He frightened Jennifer. Not, of course, that her mother noticed. Her mother was up on cloud nine, all sparkly-eyed and ridiculously flirtatious for a woman of forty-two years of age. She ought to be ashamed, but Jennifer had long since come to the conclusion that her mother was incapable of such an emotion.

Paul Fisher appeared to have plenty of money, which figured. That's why Andrina never had any respect or time for Robert Anderson, a dedicated teacher with next to nothing as a wage and apparently quite satisfied to continue in such an unrewarding profession. As far as her mother could see, that is.

Jennifer suspected that Andrina had married Robert in the first place to please Granny McPherson. Or that she'd been under pressure from her. Sophie McPherson was still a very strong character. In the many long conversations Jennifer had had over the years with her granny, Sophie had confided in her. Especially since she'd been a teenager and almost a grown-up. Although, as her granny said, there had always been a serious part about her that was far beyond her years.

Granny said that her mother had this boyfriend – oh, from way back.

'From your age. Can you imagine? A hard-faced, wicked young man. I just knew by the look of him. But of course he came from a rough family. A Catholic family too. Unfortunately, your poor grandpa wasn't such a good judge of character. Your grandpa thought he was all right. But that was before we found out.'

'Found out what?' Jennifer asked although, knowing her mother only too well by this time, there was really no need to ask.

Her granny sadly shook her head. 'I always knew in my heart of hearts she was up to something. But I tried my best, my very best, Jennifer, to keep her on the straight and narrow. To protect her. I gave her, your grandpa and I gave her, a good Christian upbringing. But it was all to no avail. I'm sorry to say this, Jennifer, but Andrina has bad blood in her.'

She shook her head again.

'Oh, the awful deceit of her. When I think of all the lies . . . Anyway, we found out eventually when that awful man actually came to my door to tell me. When I wouldn't let him in – to be honest Jennifer I was afraid of the man – when I slammed the door in his face he shouted through the door what they'd been doing for years behind our backs. Your grandpa, me, Robert's mother, God rest her soul, and of course poor Robert. Oh, and what vulgar, obscene language that man used, Jennifer. I couldn't repeat it. *And* he accused me of preventing him from marrying Andrina in the first place. I was the one who was to blame for everything, according to him. Do you know, Jennifer, I thought he was going to kill me. I really was petrified of that man. I remember at the time the papers had been full of the murders of respectable women of my age. And of course I got it into my head – I know it sounds daft now but there were other reasons for me thinking that he was the murderer.'

Jennifer found these stories fascinating. She had seen the cuttings her granny kept in a leatherbound scrapbook all about the 'Glasgow murderer' and how her granny had been attacked one dark night as she walked home from her flower-arranging class. How she'd fought her attacker, scratched his face and neck and had finally been rescued by Robert, who had been babysitting at her granny's house while her grandpa was away in England on some council business or other. It was after the break-up of her parents' marriage, and God alone knew where her mother was that night. Probably with another lover.

Anyway, when her granny hadn't returned as early as she'd promised, Robert had got a neighbour in and gone to look for her. That was when he'd rescued Granny. The murderer hadn't been the man Granny had thought at all.

Jennifer loved her granny more than anyone else in the world. Her granny was always the same, and always there for her. It was her granny who'd said, 'Bring any of your friends home here and I'll give them a really good tea. Or you could both stay overnight. You know how I enjoy your company. And I know what your mother's like. Your friends would get scant attention from her.'

She didn't tell Granny that she would be ashamed to take any friend home. And she had a special friend now. A best friend. Her very first. She loved her almost as much as Granny. When she did take Daisy Alexander for tea to Granny's, Granny really liked her – which was a great relief. Granny could be very strong in her beliefs and opinions. But then Daisy looked very serious and respectable with her straight hair and horn-rimmed glasses. She had an Aunty Moira who worked in the library, which was also a help. Nevertheless, Granny had checked all Daisy's credentials.

'What church do your folks belong to?' Granny asked and Jennifer had been worried about that because Daisy's mum was not a member of the Church of Jesus. Worse, she was a Quaker, which seemed odd. But of course, Daisy's mum was a very odd person altogether.

Surprisingly, Granny had been intrigued, even impressed.

'Quakers? They're very good-living people, I've heard. I'd like to meet your mother some time.'

Afterwards Daisy and Jennifer discussed how they could

manage to persuade Daisy's mother to clean herself up and at least *look* respectable.

'All that stinky paint!' Daisy rolled her eyes. 'If I don't do something, she's liable to turn up with green and purple hands. She even gets the stuff in her hair.'

Daisy suffered terribly with her mother.

III

SUNSHINE FILTERED THROUGH the window of the cottage, ambered the dark red flagstones of the kitchen floor and cast a lazy haze over everything else.

'I've baked an apple pie.' Caroline squeezed her plump body past her husband to admire the table and straighten the cutlery and serviettes. 'It's one of Bernard's favourites, isn't it?'

Michael O'Maley rolled his one eye ceilingwards. His other eye had been put out during a boxing match. For years he'd worn a black eyepatch. What with that and his flattened nose he was 'no beauty', as Big Martha, his mother-in-law, never tired of telling him. He was Bernard's twin brother but as Martha also observed more than once, 'You're as different to look at as chalk and cheese. He's a handsome big fella, our Bernard.' He noted the *our* with a secret sarcasm that bordered on bitterness. Both his mother-in-law and his wife made such a goddam fuss of his brother.

OK, Bernard had done them all a big favour by letting them rent this cottage and at next to nothing. He had saved them from a rotten miserable life in a high flat in Castlemilk. That damp hell-hole had been slowly killing the kids with asthma, and Martha with arthritis.

The cottage had originally been Bernard's love nest. He'd seen Bernard with a woman in a car one day when he was working on a country building site. Then on another occasion, just a day or two after the first, he saw him going into the cottage with the same woman. In a rash moment he'd mentioned it to Caroline, and later she confessed to him that she'd let it slip to Bernard's wife. That was something she now felt guilty about. In those days Caroline had never liked Bernard. Bernard had refused to help him out with money and called him a drunken bum. Caroline couldn't forgive him for that. At least not then – even though he'd told her a thousand times after the incident that Bernard had been quite right not to give him a handout. He'd only have spent it on booze. He was an alcoholic and Bernard knew it, but he was off the drink now, thank God. And Alcoholics Anonymous. He still went to the meetings as often as he could.

Neither Jane, Bernard's wife, nor anyone else, had discovered who Bernard's fancy woman was, but Jane had flung Bernard out and the marriage had broken up. He'd bought a flat in the city because, he said, he needed to be nearer his office. Then he'd offered them the cottage.

Since then, Bernard could do no wrong as far as Big Martha and Caroline were concerned. Michael was grateful too but there was a limit to anything.

After all, he'd always worked hard to provide for Caroline and the family. In his boxing days, he'd made a fair bit of money. Immediately, he felt guilty. He always did when he remembered that time in his life. He was only kidding himself when he said he had always provided for his family. When he'd been drinking he spent every penny he had. Often there had been no food in the house. But that was a long time ago. Since he'd been working on the building sites he'd done OK by the family. More than OK. He'd done his damndest to make up for all the bad times. He'd even put up with Caroline's old harridan of a mother for years. Not that Big Martha had been quite so bad since coming to live at the cottage. She'd mellowed a bit, but not much.

Of the four O'Maley brothers it could be said that Michael O'Maley was at the bottom of the pile. Bernard employed God knew how many men now in his security business and he travelled all over the world. He regularly bodyguarded famous film stars and pop stars and organised crowd control at big events. He moved in a different world from the rest of his family now, but as Caroline said, 'He's still the same old Bernard.'

He had to agree. Bernard had always been cool and laid back yet with a subtle swagger of self-confidence. His iron-hard muscular body certainly hadn't softened now that he was in his forty-sixth year. If anything, he looked tougher. Caroline said it was something to do with his eyes. Always had been.

'Those dark eyes of his are so sexy,' Caroline enthused. 'I know there's an awful hard glitter there at times as well. But a kinder man no one could meet. Look how good he's always been with the children. And with Mammy.'

That really got to Michael. He was the one that had been saddled with 'Mammy' for donkey's years. He was the one who'd been daft enough to buy her a wheelchair and condemn himself to pushing her about in it every day. After a hard slog at work he had to heave the mountainous ould sod around and listen to her rabbiting on non-stop. He even had the job of cutting her hair and her toenails. Once she'd got stuck in the bath and Caroline had to shout for his help to heave her out. Christ, what a sight! It was enough to put a man off women for the rest of his life. Fortunately, Caroline was nothing like her mother – except in her adoration of Bernard. To her credit, though, Caroline never compared him to Bernard, never pointed out how Bernard had done so much better financially. Or Frank. Even Tony had gone up in the world. Martha often said, 'I don't know what the world's coming to when that idiot brother of yours can make so much money. All he does is bang away like a madman at those drums of his. At least you do a decent day's work for what you earn.'

It wasn't often that his mother-in-law paid him a compliment, and he appreciated it. It wasn't easy to cope with three successful brothers. Frank was famous as a television playwright. Michael could never quite get over that. He'd never believed for a minute that Frank would come to anything. None of them had. Many a time he or Bernard, or even Tony, had rescued Frank from some playground bully. Later there had been street corner thugs. The O'Maley family had been brought up in Blackhill, real gangster land. You had to be tough to survive that place. Frank had been a skinny sensitive child and a lanky, dreamy young man. The only thing he'd shown any toughness about was in his determination to become a writer. There never had been any budging him from that. They'd all had a go at him about the daft wee poems he used to scribble in his Woolworth's jotters. Many a clip on the ear he'd got from their da, God rest his soul. But Frank had stuck to his guns, and look at him now. At least he had more brains than Tony.

'Are you going to get yourself washed and changed?' Martha said now. 'Or are you going to look like a one-eyed down-and-out when Bernard arrives?'

'Aye, OK. OK.'

'Put on your good navy suit, dear,' Caroline urged.

'What?' he cried out in protest. 'It's a Sunday forenoon in the height of summer and I'm going to do a bit of gardening.'

'No, you're not, dear.' Caroline dropped a kiss on the top of his head. 'At least not until after Bernard's visit.'

'He'll not be wearing a bloody suit. I'll just look ridiculous.'

'Yes, he will,' Caroline said, 'Bernard is always perfectly turned out.'

Martha shouted from the other side of the room, 'You'll look ridiculous anyway, you ugly one-eyed monster.'

'Mammy!' Caroline chided, and then to him, 'You know fine how smart Bernard always is. But you can put on as good a show if you try.'

'I don't want to put on a show. I just want to relax in my own house.'

That was a mistake, and Big Martha of the big mouth, as well as the big bulk, immediately pounced on it.

'It's not your house. It's his house and don't you forget it. If it wasn't for our Bernard we'd still be living in misery in that dump in Castlemilk.'

'Aye, OK. OK. I'll go and get ready to receive Saint Bernard.'

'I'd probably be dead by now,' Martha said, 'if it wasn't for him.'

Curses on his head, Michael thought, but managed to keep his mouth shut. Through in the bedroom he shared with Caroline he could hear Maureen on the garden swing. It creaked lazily backwards and forwards. He didn't need to peer out of the small bedroom window in its perfumed frame of roses. He made a mental note to cut back the wild profusion of green and pink before it completely darkened the whole room. He could see clearly in his mind's eye his youngest child outside in the garden, kicking up her heels. At fifteen and a half Maureen, their youngest, alternated between resentful, rebellious adult and loving, vulnerable child, depending on her mood of the day. The twins, eighteen-year-old Sean and Sally, were in their rooms dolling themselves up for Bernard's visit. Annoyance needled Michael again. Sean seemed to think more of his Uncle Bernard than his own dad. Sally had actually begun to flirt with him.

Caroline had laughed when he'd told her this.

'You're just jealous.'

'What? Of Bernard?'

'You know fine all the children adore you. It's just that Bernard is so glamorous . . .'

'Glamorous?' he'd echoed incredulously although he knew exactly what she meant. They didn't see Bernard all that often and when they did he could tell them all sorts of tales about glamorous places and famous stars. Then there was the danger element that the children found so exciting. This had become a real worry. Sean wanted Bernard to give him a job.

'After all the sacrifices we've made to keep you and Sally at school, you'd throw away all that good education to be a glorified bouncer!' he'd roared at them. 'Over my dead body!'

It was this aspect of the job that worried Michael the most. Bernard had been shot at more than once and nearly killed when he'd been bodyguarding some politician or industrialist or other.

But Bernard always survived. He had the luck of the Irish. Sean might not be so fortunate. Now even Sally was thinking of asking Bernard if he could take her on.

'After all,' she'd pointed out, 'Uncle Bernard has lots of women as well as men working for him.'

She, like Sean, had been taking lessons in karate and God knew how many keep-fit classes to toughen themselves up and impress their uncle. Both of them were forever jogging about in their T-shirts and shorts, up hill and down dale. They had weights that they trained conscientiously with, sometimes in their rooms, sometimes out in the garden.

Michael loved his children and was already losing sleep worrying about their safety. It seemed to him that Bernard, who had once been the family's saviour, was about to be the cause of their destruction. He tried to keep a sensible balance in his mind but despite his struggle, he'd never been nearer to hating his brother.

'Here's his car. Here he is!' The excited cry rang out.

Michael remained rooted in front of the wardrobe mirror staring, unable to go and look at his handsome brother's face.

IV

AFTERNOON TEA IN Bearsden. Bessie sighed. For Daisy's sake she had agreed to put in an appearance. Not only that, she had promised to have a bath beforehand, wash her hair and wear something that had never been anywhere near her loft studio. She had to be absolutely paint-free, in other words. There was something funny about the invitation because it was not from Jennifer, or Daisy's best friend's mum, but her granny. Jennifer's mum lived beside (almost inside) Glasgow Green, a much more interesting place, in Bessie's opinion, than Bearsden. Glasgow Green was the most important historic site in the country. It was one of the great battlefields of Scotland and a place of meetings and demonstrations. The fight for political freedom – one man one vote, then one woman one vote – had been fought there, for instance. From her reading of its history and from her imagination, Bessie had painted many of the turbulent scenes that had taken place there. She still had an ambition to paint James Watt as he strolled on the Green one Sunday afternoon in 1765 and thought of the idea of a separate condenser. The application of this idea in the development of the steam engine had changed the whole course of industrial and human history. The mere thought of the place excited her.

Bearsden didn't excite her at all.

'Jennifer's granny's awful nice, Mum,' Daisy assured her for the sixth or seventh time, which made Bessie suspicious. Daisy had already warned her not to mention her painting but added, 'She's interested in you being a Quaker so that's all right.'

Bessie had set off with her daughter from their flat at Shawlands Cross, in the southern part of the city, with a heavy heart. Although she'd been brought up there herself, and her parents before her, Bearsden was not her scene. It was, she had come to believe, death to an artist. It was too conventional, too comfortable.

Peter had wanted to buy a house there when they'd got married. It was the one thing she'd fought against. Well, not fought exactly. She'd pointed out how much more expensive it would be and enthused at how beautiful the warm, red sandstone building was at Shawlands Cross, how classy the tiled close and the stained-glass windows on the landings. How reasonably priced the flat was, how handy it would be for Peter to get to his office in the centre of town. It was all perfectly true, of course. It was just she hadn't mentioned how wonderful she thought the loft would be as a studio. Nor had she realised the power of the financial side of her argument. She'd learned over the years how mean Peter was. He was practically a miser. It was soul destroying. According to him, if she treated herself to a cup of tea in town, she was a lunatic spendthrift whose reckless extravagance would be the death of him yet. At first he'd tried to teach her how to keep housekeeping books in which she had to detail every penny she spent, down to the last toilet roll. He had questioned the amount she spent on that, even asking her how many pieces of paper she was in the habit of using. Two pieces was quite sufficient, he'd said; any more was sheer extravagance. And the money she spent on sketchbooks and the like nearly drove him to distraction. But Bessie had made such a mess of the accounts he had been forced to give up in the end. Or, as he said, go mad. She forgot to record purchases, or she lied verbally and on paper about the price of things. Especially things for herself. She always knocked a few pounds off everything. If Peter had his way, she would be going about minus make-up and knickers. All in the cause of saving money. In fact, she would rather have gone without make-up and knickers than paints and canvases.

He was more indulgent with Daisy, but not that much. Peter liked the good things in life, like tasty food washed down with a glass or two of wine. He enjoyed his evening tipple of whisky as well. He needed it to relax him and help him to sleep, he said. Where did he think she could get the money to pay for luxuries like that?

He didn't want to know. She was supposed to work some kind of miracle: to be frugal and save him money yet make it possible for him to live the life of Riley. At first she'd done it by getting into debt. Then robbing Peter to pay Paul, as the saying went. Only she'd never robbed the real Peter. Far from it. If anyone robbed anyone it was the other way around. As often as not, she borrowed money from her mother. Occasionally she sold a painting; if in desperation for money she was able to force herself to copy a photo of some friend of her mother's or customer of her father's.

Not that she minded putting any money she earned into the kitty. If only Peter would at least recognise that she did her best to contribute to the home and its occupants. The fact was he did his best to stop her painting.

Peter hated Gregory yet any time they'd met he'd been perfectly nice and polite to him. It really sickened Bessie. She'd come to the sad conclusion that Peter was a weak man as well as a two-faced one. Probably he was two-faced *because* he was weak. He bullied and browbeat and made a fool of her in the privacy of their home. In public, or to outsiders, he was a right little charmer.

The address she and Daisy were going to was one of the terraced houses along from the shops in Drymen Road. The end terrace, it turned out, a big corner site with a lane running along the back. This part of Bearsden had always been known as 'the village'. Drymen Road, although a main thoroughfare, rustled with trees and in summer the sun dappled through the branches and made intricate patterns on the clean warm pavements. Most of the houses were large villas set back from the road fronted by velvety lawns and silvery grey stone walls.

Bessie's mother and father lived at the other end, the not nearly so posh part, of Bearsden. Their flat was above another line of shops, which included the menswear shop. Her father had recently retired and his place of business, as he called it, had been taken over by a Pakistani who sold papers and groceries, and everything else on earth by the look of the place.

'They take no pride in their windows,' her father complained. 'Everything's just stuffed in there any old way. It really lowers the tone of the place.'

As far as Bessie knew, Mr Akhtar was the first Pakistani to scale the heights of Bearsden. He seemed a nice friendly man of about her father's age. He and his wife and their daughter and a son lived in Great Western Road in Glasgow. Of course, mother and father would be polite to the Akhtars. Father was a bit like Peter in the two-faced stakes but Mother was generally kindly and would never have the heart to snub anybody. Still, she often sighed and shook her grey head in the privacy of her home or the home of one of her friends, and wondered what the world, and Bearsden in particular, was coming to.

'McPherson?' Bessie peered at the nameplate as they waited for Jennifer's granny to open the door. 'That name sounds familiar.'

'It's a common enough Scottish name,' Daisy said.

'I know but . . .'

Just then an elderly woman as thin as a greyhound, with steely grey hair and eyes to match, opened the door. Her welcome was warm and enthusiastic.

'Come away in, come away in. Jennifer has told me so much about you. I feel I know you already.'

She had a tea trolley set with the most mouth-watering home-baked cakes Bessie had ever seen – fairy cakes with cream bulging up between sponge wings. Tiny iced cakes topped with a scarlet cherry. Wicked-looking chocolate gâteau. Crisp fingers of sugar-dusted shortbread. Sandwiches, too: cucumber, tomato, date and banana, chicken mayonnaise.

Bessie tucked in with great enjoyment. She was so accustomed to serving other people, indeed being at everyone's beck and call, that it was enormously enjoyable a treat to be made a fuss of by someone else.

'Just call me Sophie,' Mrs McPherson urged as she poured out Bessie's third cup of tea. The older woman seemed to be genuinely happy to make a fuss of her and the girls. Bessie was having an unexpectedly lovely time.

'Here,' she suddenly cried out, 'are you the woman who once fought off the Glasgow murderer?'

Sophie laughed.

'Goodness me, that was a long time ago.'

'I knew the name McPherson rang a bell. But when you said Sophie, it all came back to me. My mother and father are members of your church. I know it's a big congregation and you probably won't have met them . . .'

Sophie looked thoughtful.

'Alexander . . .'

'No, that's my married name.'

'Oh, of course.'

'McVinney. Mamie and Guy McVinney.'

'No,' Sophie shook her head. 'I can't say I know the name. But as you say, it is a big congregation. I'd maybe know them by sight. Do they belong to Bearsden?'

'Down Emerston Road.'

'That's where a Pakistani family have moved in.'

'Well, they've opened a grocer's shop where my father's menswear place used to be.'

Sophie shook her head again.

'Isn't it awful. I haven't anything personally against coloured people, you understand,' she added hastily, 'but they're not Christian. We must remember that.'

Bessie wanted to say 'Why?' She was tempted to recite number 22 of the *Advices and Queries* out loud: 'Do you behave with brotherly love to all men, whatever their race, background or opinion? Do you try to make the stranger feel at home among you?'

For Sophie's sake as well as for Daisy's, she managed to keep her mouth shut. After all, according to Daisy, Sophie was very highly strung and on medication for her blood pressure.

'You're a member of the Society of Friends, I hear,' Sophie said, her stiff, lean frame tipping forward with interest and curiosity. 'That's a very narrow sect, I believe. Very strict.'

'Oh no,' Bessie laughed. 'Not at all.'

'But I heard that even music isn't allowed.'

'That's just at Meeting for Worship. Other than that we believe that music, and drama, and painting and sculpture and books all help develop our perception and enjoyment of life and the search for truth and fulfilment.'

'Oh.' Sophie didn't look too sure about all that. A glint of suspicion entered her eyes. Maybe it was the word enjoyment. Bessie thought it wiser to change the subject.

'Fancy you being the woman in all the papers. You were headline news at the time, I remember. Very courageous, they said you were, and no wonder. I'm sure I would have died of fright.'

'My son-in-law was the brave one. I'd never have survived had it not been for him coming to my rescue. He's married again and lives just along the road in the bungalows. I'm always encouraging Jennifer to visit him when she comes to see me but she's not keen on his wife. I don't know why. Laura is a very nice woman.'

Bessie decided not to pursue this subject in case she put her foot in it, but it seemed an interesting situation. Several times Sophie mentioned her son-in-law and even his wife with affection, but never a word about her daughter. Jennifer didn't mention her mother either.

Later when they were back home, Bessie remarked on this to Daisy.

'Oh, Andrina's awful.' Daisy screwed up her face. 'Jennifer hates her.'

'Oh dear, surely not? Her own mother?'

'There's this man comes to the house and Jennifer says he's not the first one. She hates him as well. She tries to keep out of the house when he's around.'

'Oh dear,' Bessie repeated. 'The poor girl doesn't appear very happy, right enough. She's got a kind of haunted look about her.'

'Mum!' Daisy groaned. 'You're beginning to sound like your pictures look.'

Bessie laughed at this but in an absent-minded way. A ıeeling of unease hung about at the back of her mind. It wasn't just about Jennifer either.

She'd enjoyed the visit to Bearsden yet now, looking back and thinking of Sophie, she felt worried. There was something disconcerting about the woman. She tried to pinpoint exactly what it was. She kept wishing she could have the opportunity to capture the strong essence of Sophie on canvas. There was certainly an unusual intensity about her. It seemed to be burning somewhere within her outer shell. No matter what perfectly ordinary comment Sophie had made or question she had asked, the intensity flamed in her eyes.

She's like two people, Bessie decided. The outside person is the middle-class, conventional grandmother with her etiquette book and her immaculate house. No doubt every house in the terrace served afternoon tea on a trolley, used bone china and offered crustless sandwiches and dainty home-made cakes.

The inside person was the one who intrigued Bessie. Inside Sophie she suspected there hid a can of worms. She had a sudden colourful vision of a can of worms but immediately banished it. No wonder the family thought her paintings so weird. She did get some awful ideas that too often she transposed on to canvas.

'How about Sophie and Jennifer's mother, then?' she asked Daisy.

'Oh, Sophie thinks Andrina's awful as well. She's disowned her.'

'Surely this Andrina can't be as bad as all that. And even if she is, it's very sad to think of so much hatred in a family.'

Daisy shrugged. 'I suppose. But that's how it is.'

It occurred to Bessie that that's how it was with her as well. She hated Peter and Granda. She felt so guilty and ashamed of this sudden insight she made a special effort to cook them a really good dinner.

V

USUALLY BERNARD HAD no problem concentrating one hundred per cent on his principal, as the person being looked after was called. What distracted him in this case – and it was very dangerous to be distracted – was the fact that the pop singer, Eve Page, reminded him so much of Andrina McPherson, or Anderson as she'd become. He hadn't thought of her for years. Not seriously. Now, his mind kept sinking in a morass of lust and anger. No woman he'd known since could match her for uninhibited passion and sexual fulfilment. He'd lived for her then; but later he had realised what a bitch she was. She'd kept him dangling for years – half a lifetime – in the hope that she'd leave her husband and marry him. He groaned every time he thought of all the deceit the affair involved. Her husband, Robert, had taught him at school, then coached him in karate. Robert Anderson had been his mentor, the man who had saved him and so many other youngsters from the streets and a life of crime. Robert had trusted him, but he had been so obsessed with Andrina that he'd betrayed his best friend.

He'd betrayed his wife too. Jane had had everything – beauty, and fitness that would have rivalled any of the women security officers he now employed. She had also inherited that huge villa in the Pollokshields from her father, not to mention a very large sum of money. They'd had fitness training in common: every day they'd worked out together in the gym she'd had installed in the villa, and he'd started giving her karate lessons. Many a good laugh they'd had as well. The truth was, Jane had much more in common with him than Andrina. He was glad that, during the past ten or eleven years since the divorce, she seemed to have lost most of her anger and bitterness. They'd at least become friends.

Why had he never felt for her as he had for Andrina? Why had Jane's lean body never excited him, drowned him in passion, like Andrina's soft voluptuous curves? He told himself that Andrina would now, in her early forties, look fat and matronly compared with Jane.

Even after all these years his anger could still flare up. It was anger directed at himself as well as Andrina. He, as much as Andrina, had been the cause of her marriage to Robert breaking up, and his own marriage to Jane.

He succeeded in banishing Andrina from his mind at last. At first he managed this feat of willpower by throwing himself into his work. In a way, his obsession with Andrina had taught him a lesson connected with his work. Or rather, reinforced something he'd always known. In his job, to do it properly, he needed to focus completely on what he was doing. He could never afford to be seen to be too close to anyone, because they would become his Achilles' heel. It was for that reason that he never employed any of his family. They might have distracted his attention when he was looking after a principal.

That was why he was angry now for allowing himself to think of Andrina. Eve Page was so like the Andrina he remembered. She had the same coppery glints in her hair, the same creamy skin, the same curvaceous shape. Only the eyes were different. Andrina had such unusual aquamarine-coloured eyes. Those eyes could change from childish innocence to impish mischief, to smouldering passion. He remembered her in every mood. They had both revelled in the danger and the excitement of their lovemaking. They'd had sex on many crazy occasions practically under the noses of Robert and Jane. They'd made love while Andrina and Robert were visiting the villa. Or while he and Jane were visiting Andrina and Robert's place at Glasgow Green. Every moment they found themselves alone in a room, they had these crazy hurried sessions. At other times they had long indulgent hours in Robert's bed while he was at work. Or in Jane's bed while she was out at one of her yoga or keep-fit classes. Robert had found out eventually that Bernard was Andrina's lover but Jane had never found out. Jane often spoke about Andrina: they were still the best of friends. It was obvious from these conversations that Andrina was not only the deceitful bitch she always had been, but that she was still after sexual excitement. Apparently she was now involved with another married man. God knew what was happening to that daughter of hers. He recalled Jennifer as a serious, gawky child, anything but happy looking. He'd been perfectly willing to accept Jennifer along with her mother. If they'd just been able to get married it would all have worked out happily enough, he'd thought at the time. At least he'd no children of his own to worry about.

He had been the one who had finished the affair. Enough was enough. His life was being ruined. He was being made a fool of by her – and he was making a fool of himself. He'd told her to fuck off, and that was that.

He was taken by surprise at how quickly the old wound opened up again when he'd met Eve Page. It wasn't, strangely enough, that he felt any attraction towards her. Maybe because he had been a professional too long to allow himself to become in the slightest involved in any personal way with a principal. His reputation was high in the business. The highest, in fact. He prided himself on that. He always kept things under control. He didn't have to make an effort to prove anything. His reputation, and people's perception of him, was enough.

His next job was to organise Eve's visit, along with her backing group, to America. She and the group were performing in a film that Paramount Pictures were making. She was only in a few scenes, so her stay in Hollywood wouldn't be for long. But she and the others would no doubt want to visit restaurants or clubs in Los Angeles and God knew what else. All the work it entailed for him and his men was onerous, even for a short visit.

He'd to fly over to the States in a couple of weeks. First he'd promised to visit Michael and the family at the cottage. This time he wasn't looking forward to his visit as much as usual. The cottage had been the love nest he'd shared with Andrina on so many passionate occasions. Now, with memories of her stirred up, it was painful to see the place. Again the pain took him by surprise. The cottage was sparkling white in the sun with its small windows glinting like diamonds. It sat back from the road in a colourful profusion of flowers. Close behind it rose a velvety green hill.

As usual, Caroline, Big Martha and the children made him almost embarrassingly welcome. Michael, when he finally appeared, was slightly more restrained in his greeting. No wonder, with everybody making such a fuss. Poor old Michael, slogging away as a brickie, still lumbered with his monstrous mother-in-law. He couldn't offer him a job. What use would a one-eyed ex-alcoholic boxer be in his business? Anyway, Caroline had long ago made it plain that she couldn't stand the thought of Michael being in such a risky occupation. She'd suffered enough worry when he'd been boxing. In the past he'd tried to slip Michael a few pounds but Michael had been adamant that he didn't need handouts. 'You've done more than enough letting us have this cottage,' he insisted.

Bernard was taken aback – indeed they all were – when, after a good lunch in the kitchen with its low oak-beamed ceiling, the twins said they wanted a job in the business. He'd always been fond of Sean and Sally. They were the nearest he had to children of his own. He'd always spoiled them, bringing them gifts, indulging their eagerness to hear all about his adventures.

Now his stories were coming home to roost. He was horrified, although he managed to keep his usual cool on the outside. Before he could say anything, Caroline cried out,

'Are you mad, the pair of you? Your Uncle Bernard has a very dangerous job but he's used to it. You two would get yourselves killed.'

'No, we've been training.' The twins were starry-eyed with enthusiasm. 'We've both got our black belts in karate. We're fighting fit and ready to go.'

Michael looked across at Bernard. 'Thanks very much,' he said.

'Look,' Bernard protested, 'I started them in karate as a sport, something for them to enjoy and to keep them fit. That was all.'

He realised for the first time, admitted it to himself, that he'd enjoyed the love and admiration of his niece and nephew and had done everything in his power to encourage it. Even now he couldn't bring himself to disappoint them or to risk losing any of that affection.

'Oh please, Uncle Bernard.' Sally was fluttering her eyelashes at him. She moved nearer and looked as if she might even slip on to his knee and entwine her arm around his neck as she'd done so often when she was small. For the first time it occurred to him that she was no longer a little girl. Yet at the same time she was so innocent. Especially as far as the security business was concerned. She hadn't a clue.

'Sally, Sean,' he managed, 'you might think you're trained but you're not. I have to be honest with you about that. There's a lot more to it than a black belt in karate.'

They had been brought up in this gently idyllic place. Could they learn what being streetwise meant for a start? He had learned it from the moment he could walk: his training had been in the streets of Blackhill, Glasgow's gangster land. There he had developed an instinct for survival that they'd never have.

But they were pleading now and ignoring their mother and father and grandmother's objections. Eventually he said, 'I'll make a bargain with you. I'll see that you get the training you do need. If the pair of you survive that, and still want a job, you'll get one.'

On the face of it, it seemed a risky line to take. But he hadn't known ex-SAS men for nothing.

VI

BESSIE STRUGGLED ALONG Kilmarnock Road towards Shawlands Cross, arms gorilla-length with the weight of two shopping bags. She was developing round shoulders with being such a beast of burden. Peter didn't believe it was manly to go shopping. 'It's a woman's job,' he maintained. Daisy was usually either at school or away somewhere with her friend, Jennifer. The two girls had become like Siamese twins. Granda was too old to help, even if she'd wanted his help – which she didn't. He always put a price on everything and she knew only too well what kind of repayment he'd try to elicit from her. Dirty old codger. He'd once offered to help her by paying the gas bill when she hadn't known how she was going to pay it. She'd been sitting staring at it in horror and despair when he made the offer. Thankfully, she had accepted. What a load off her mind it had been and, after all, Granda used most of the gas. He had that big gas fire of his going full blast morning, noon and night.

As soon as she'd accepted his kind offer, he had made a pass at her. Immediately she'd shrunk away from him, her horror returning a thousandfold at the feel of the gnarled old hands trying to grope her. He looked huffed and disappointed.

'Old-fashioned type, are you?' he'd sneered.

'I obviously must be.' She'd got up and was backing away from him, nearly knocking the chair over in her agitation.

He flung the gas bill back at her.

'You can forget that then.'

Meaning his offer to pay. She should have let her anger rip then.

Dirty, rotten old swine! she'd wanted to shout. You're as mean as your miserable pig of a son.

She didn't, though. She'd long since found that losing her head or arguing with Peter or Granda didn't get her anywhere except into a state of exhaustion and depression. It was usually Peter she argued with. Granda tried to argue with her but nowadays she just agreed with him, tried to pacify him no matter what crazy thing he said. He was always accusing her of not giving him his meals, for instance. Sometimes she gave him two breakfasts or dinners or teas rather than get into a pointless argument. She often wondered how he'd been as a husband when his wife was alive. He was a right whining, complaining, argumentative old sod as a father-in-law. He was also far from clean in either his person or his habits. It was a devil of a job to force him to have a bath. He had a dirty mind as well. She was sure he was angling for her to give him his bath. But she'd get a nurse in first, even if it meant going round the doors trying to sell her paintings to get enough money. Or maybe she'd get a man. That would maybe stop the dirty old devil.

He'd made several advances and propositions over the years. The first time she'd been really shocked and upset. She had told Peter as soon as he'd arrived home, but Peter had just laughed and said at first she must be imagining things. Then when, still trembling with distress, she'd insisted, he'd become impatient and dismissive and said: 'For God's sake stop making such a stupid fuss about nothing.' He'd said that the old man must be in his second childhood, and in one way he certainly had returned to childhood. He regularly peed the bed. Bessie was sick, sick, oh so sick, of stripping his stinking bed and washing his stinking sheets. Sometimes she wondered if he did it on purpose. He wasn't that daft. He could appear perfectly sane and sensible, usually when Peter was around. It was when Peter wasn't there, or during the night when Peter was dead to the world, that the old man went to pieces. She'd smell burning and hurry out of bed to see what he was doing. Sometimes she'd find he'd tried to light a paper at the fire in his bedroom and let it drop on to the carpet. Sometimes he'd dropped his pipe and it lay smouldering. She'd never dared to take a sleeping tablet but remained apprehensively awake for long hours every night.

Sometimes he raved a lot of nonsense at her in the wee small hours. She could see then that the poor man was senile. She had tried to get the doctor but Peter insisted that there was nothing wrong with his father. The old man, in his lucid times when Peter was there, would insist exactly the same thing.

'You're not going to get me put away,' he'd say. 'I'm not daft.'

She'd feel sorry for him then. It was understandable he didn't want to end up in some institution. Not that she had any intention of banishing him to one, even if she'd been allowed to. Although she had once, on the point of collapse, pleaded with Peter to arrange – or allow her to arrange – for his father to go somewhere, anywhere, for just a week or two to give her a break.

'What?' Peter had been outraged. 'Turf my father out on to the street . . .?'

'No, of course not. That's not what I said.'

'I'll see you on the street first!'

She'd hidden herself away upstairs in her loft studio as soon as she could after that. She clambered up the ladder and crashed the hatch down. She scrabbled the bolt into its catch, effectively imprisoning herself. The back of her mind registered the ranting shouts from below as a background buzzing as she looked round for sanctuary. The pungent smells of turps and linseed oil wafted over her. She picked up her palate and a handful of brushes and attacked her canvas with savage brushstrokes. She worked furiously, stabbing and sweeping her brush over the large surface. New marks and splashes spattered the old timber flooring, mingling with the layers of dust. She kept working till the pale slanting sunlight that filtered in through the dormer window cast a massive and gloomy shadow across her canvas. Then she slowly sank to her knees, rocking to and fro, her hands, smeared with paint, clasped round her legs as she quietly wept. Gregory later said that painting was an astonishing statement of passion and anger. She had never sold it, though. People couldn't face it on their walls. Too disturbing, apparently. Her brushstrokes had slashed at the canvas. Glaring purples and throbbing reds streaked across it, sombre greys and blacks oppressively crushing, overwhelming anyone who looked at it. Her anguish was a tangible thing pulsating over the surfaces of every picture. Especially this one.

'You appear such a gentle little soul,' Gregory said. 'It just goes to show that one can't go by appearances. No one has any idea what goes on inside someone's head.'

True. True.

She remembered the incident with Granda and the gas bill for another reason which was even more shameful. In desperation she'd sneaked into the old man's room that night when he was in the bathroom and pinched ten pounds out of the Oxo tin he kept stashed with notes under the bed. She could never justify that act of dishonesty to herself. Although often and often she'd tried. She always ended up cringing with guilt and thinking: Some Quaker!

Over and over again since, in an effort to prevent a repeat of the crime, because it had to be said she was tempted, she read *Advices and Queries*.

'Are you honest and truthful in word and deed? Do you maintain strict integrity in your business transactions and in your relations with individuals and organisations? Are you personally scrupulous and responsible in the use of money entrusted to you, and are you careful not to defraud the public revenue?'

It was really dreadfully difficult being a Quaker and she often wondered why on earth they had accepted her into the fold. She lived in constant expectation of being drummed out in disgrace. Or at least for being totally inadequate. All the others in meeting seemed so morally and spiritually strong. They all took their turn at sharing in the responsibility of running the meeting and the meeting house. There were elders and members of committees that did good works, in 'Meetings for Sufferings', 'Meetings for Church Affairs', 'Eldership and Oversight', and 'The Peace Testament'.

All she'd ever done was scrub the floors in Meeting House when it had been decided to convert the basement into a multi-racial nursery. They had praised her for doing that as if the menial task had been important. Her heart had warmed towards them and she'd felt like scrubbing the whole building from top to bottom in gratitude. After that she'd eagerly volunteered for any cleaning jobs or for dish-washing or any shopping that was necessary. Shopping was something she had years of experience at, but carrying heavy loads so often didn't do her back any favours.

She was having such a struggle getting along Kilmarnock Road with her two shopping bags that she hadn't even enough spare energy to think of Gregory Seymour.

'Just another few yards,' she kept urging herself onwards. Dammit, she wasn't going to let half a stone of potatoes, a few vegetables and a dozen assorted tins of beans, spaghetti and processed peas get the better of her. She gritted her teeth and staggered on until it seemed that the shopping bags were dragging her along on her knees. But, as usual, she made it to the close. It was cool there, a dark tunnel out of the sun where she was able to rest for a few minutes leaning against one of the maroon-tiled walls. There, she could gaze up the well of the stairs and gain some comfort from the beauty of the stained-glass windows. The dancing pattern of coloured light shimmered like a spiritual being encouraging her on. Then there was the next leg of the endurance test: the stairs to the flat.

'Daisy,' she called out once she'd unlocked and pushed open the front door. The long empty corridor stretched dark and gloomy.

No reply. It was the school holidays. Daisy would be away somewhere with Jennifer. Peter would be at work. She didn't want to know where Granda was. She dumped the bags on the kitchen table, filled the kettle and lit the gas. A cup of tea would soon put her right. She slumped into a chair.

It was then, half comatose with fatigue, that thoughts of Gregory came drifting back into her mind. What a fine-looking big man he was – maybe a bit on the hefty side but she'd always thought a man should be bigger and stronger than a woman. In her romantic dreams her perfect man had been big and strong, but gentle and tender at the same time. Did such a paragon exist? In her dreams now Gregory was like that. He was gentle and tender and promised to protect and look after her and keep her safe.

In reality he had asked to have sex. Did that mean love? He'd never said he loved her. Neither had Peter. Neither had Mother. Neither had Father. None of them were demonstrative people. They shrank from any display of emotion as if it was a sin. It occurred to her that Sophie McPherson was like that. All tight and held in. Sophie hadn't even shaken hands with her. Instead she'd given a brief nod when introduced. It was the same when she and Daisy had left after that afternoon tea in Bearsden. Sophie had visibly shrunk back. A brief nod again and, a minute or two later, a wave from her window. She'd been very kind and hospitable all the same. Bessie still nursed happy memories of those home-baked cakes. Sophie had invited her to return and Bessie had every intention of returning.

We're all victims of victims, she often thought. A child shows love innocently, generously. But so often that expression of love is rejected, ridiculed, betrayed, until it becomes a source of vulnerability, even danger, that has to be hidden or hardened away. She had been rejected and betrayed in a thousand ways she could not bear to think about.

Probably so had Sophie. But Sophie McPherson had created a hard shell with which to protect herself. Bessie Alexander had not yet managed it.

'Have you not got the tea made yet?' Granda came shuffling into the kitchen. 'What are you lazing about there for? Peter'll be in in a minute.'

He was a small man like Peter and age had shrunk him even further. His long cardigan hung over a bundle of bones. So did his trousers. Both, especially the trousers, were disgustingly stained. Peter was always going on about how she neglected his father.

'I got you a washing machine,' he'd say although in fact she'd got it for herself from the sale of a painting of an old man. 'There's absolutely no excuse for neglecting Granda and not keeping his clothes clean.'

She was always washing the bloody things. It was impossible to keep up with the dirty old devil.

'OK. OK, Granda.' She got up and started putting the shopping away in cupboards. 'I was just going to make it.' Bang goes my quiet cup of tea, she thought, as Granda settled down at the table.

'I bet you've forgotten my paper.'

She had.

'I'll run back out and get it.'

Anything to escape the catalogue of moans and endless lists of her faults and foibles that would inevitably follow.

'Oh don't bother for my sake.' The old man's mouth drooped and slavered. 'I'm just a poor old man. No use to anyone. Just a nuisance, a burden . . .'

It was self-pity day.

'Won't be long,' she called out, already flying along the lobby.

Peter was slowly climbing the stairs as she was descending. He had the same drooping, bitter mouth as his father.

'Where do you think you're going?'

'I forgot Granda's paper.'

'Trust you.'

Oh, if only someone would.

'The kettle's boiling and I won't be a minute.'

The kettle could boil its head off. It would never occur to Peter or Granda, or even Daisy, to make the tea. She must have spoiled them, done something wrong. Everything, probably.

She phoned Gregory while she was out. He might have been somewhat fierce-looking with his thick mane of hair and bushy beard, had it not been for his soft brown eyes. He had a gentle voice too. Very serious, though. He was an earnest man.

'How could I possibly get away,' she spoke half to herself. 'I mean, what excuse could I have? I'm losing sleep over this, Gregory. I can't just . . . not just for that. In the first place, I'm a hopeless liar.'

Silence for a long minute. Then Gregory said, 'I tell you what. There's a summer school down south. I'm going to be talking at it. I'm also going to see what potential talent there is.'

'Talent?'

'New talent.'

'Oh . . .' For a minute she'd taken the wrong meaning of the word. Sometimes she thought she had a one-track mind.

'Work to display in one of the galleries. I like to encourage young people. Why don't you come along?'

'I'm not young.'

Unfortunately.

'You know what I mean. Tell Peter you feel you've a lot to learn.'

Hadn't she just!

'Tell him this summer school is just what you need. Bring your paints and canvases. There'll be plenty of easels there.'

'They'd never manage on their own.'

'It's time they learned.'

She supposed it was, really.

'Peter would never let me go.'

Gregory sighed.

'Bessie, you're a mature woman living in a free country. You're not his slave. It's time you had a life of your own. Just say you're going, that's all.'

Only, that wouldn't be all.

VII

'ARE YOU GOING to be in this evening, darling?' Andrina asked.

'You mean, get out of the way because Mr Fisher's coming,' Jennifer said.

Andrina rolled her eyes. Eyes made even more vivid and sparkling with a dusting of green shadow, and mascara separating each long curly lash. She was elegant in a beige dress and high-heeled sandals. She never wore slippers or anything unglamorous, even when alone in the house.

'I meant no such thing. You're always snapping my head off these days. I only wondered if you were going to visit Granny. And it's Uncle Paul, Jennifer. We both want you to call him Uncle or at least Paul, if it makes you feel more grown-up.' She pouted full, rosy lips. 'Mr Fisher sounds so formal and unfriendly.'

'He's not my uncle. And I don't want to be friendly with him. He's a creep. I hate him.'

Andrina sighed and turned away, glancing appreciatively at her reflection in the glass door of the kitchen cupboard. Already her cheeks were showing the first flush of excitement. She wondered if she had been so extreme and emotional when she was sixteen. She had not been in love with Robert. It seemed ridiculous now but she'd actually married him to please her mother; also, of course, to escape from her. She remembered how eagerly she'd looked forward to queening it in a house of her own. Doing what she liked, dressing in whatever way she fancied. She had always to dress so primly to suit her mother while all the time she longed for low-cut dresses, high heels, dangly earrings, bracelets. Robert had scarcely featured at all in her hopes and dreams. To be fair, though, she had kept the house shining clean, his clothes were always laundered and pressed and no one could fault her cooking.

As it turned out, she hadn't escaped from her mother. Far from it. Even now her blood boiled at the memory of how Sophie had pestered her with phone calls and unexpected visits in order to spy on her and check on her every move.

If it hadn't been for her mother laying down the law, she would have married Bernard right at the start. But Bernard had committed three unforgiveable sins. First, he was too 'physical'. By that her mother meant sexy but could never bring herself to utter the word. Secondly, he was a Catholic. And thirdly, he not only came from a Catholic family but a 'tough crowd' from Blackhill. Blackhill was another name for hell. His father and his brother Tony had been in Barlinnie Prison. As far as Andrina remembered, their crime had been nothing more serious than breach of the peace. They'd been drunk at the time. That carried no weight whatsoever with her mother. Indeed her mother had always had such a passionate hatred for Bernard, Andrina often wondered if there was some other deeper reason for the emotion that even the mention of Bernard's name could trigger off. Andrina suspected that, even more than his religion and his rough background, it was Bernard's strong aura of sexuality that upset Sophie so much. Her mother had a phobia about sex: she was terrified at the mere mention of the word. Now she had dangerously high blood pressure, so Jennifer said. No wonder, the way she carried on. She'd always had a neurotic need to fit in, to keep up with the Bearsden Joneses. Most importantly, a spotless Christian reputation was the be-all and end-all of her life. Her daughter had to be a clone of her, reflect even more glory in her direction. She had always enjoyed it when her church friends called her daughter a 'little angel' when, dressed in virgin white, Andrina used to sing solo in the choir.

Andrina realised what a shock it must have been to her mother to discover the affair with Bernard. She had been shocked to the core herself by Bernard's betrayal of her and had strenuously fought to deny any intimacy with him. All to no avail. She could now at last look back on their passionate lovemaking with erotic pleasure. She had enjoyed other lovers since. How wonderful it felt to be herself, to know herself. She had no false modesty. She was a beautiful, sensual and loving woman and could see nothing but good in loving a man. She still stood up and sang with heartfelt sincerity in the choir of the Church of Jesus. Only now she never visited the church in Bearsden. The Rose Street church in town was the one she attended. She went regularly, although not three times every Sunday, as she had been forced to do as a child.

Paul laughed the first time he saw her pray. She was so surprised and upset that he'd apologised and never laughed at her again. Often now, he accompanied her to church. He lived in Edinburgh but stayed with her when he worked late at his Glasgow casino. No one at the Rose Street church knew that he was married. They thought he was her fiancé, and so he was. As soon as his divorce was through, they were going to be married.

Paul was not a wonderful lover like Bernard, but he had infected her with his own brand of excitement. He had introduced her to the world of gambling and many a thrill she'd experienced standing by his side in the plush glamour of casinos.

Paul was different. He was a dapper man, fastidious about his appearance. He kept his fair hair slicked back with haircream and his moustache was always neatly trimmed. He went for a regular manicure. He was not as tall or as well made or as handsome as Bernard. But Paul was wealthy, which could make up for a bit. He owned a large casino in Glasgow. Not only could he give her a good and secure life, but he could shower her with whatever her heart desired. That's what he wanted to do. Already he'd offered to buy her a decent house.

'I don't like you living so near the Green on your own,' he'd said. 'It's becoming very seedy and run down.'

'I won't be alone once we're married,' she told him. She was determined that they should set up house respectably together. She had no intention of being shuttled into the position of a mistress; Paul could become satisfied with that. As it was, she could still keep him guessing. She was the one who called the shots. If she so wished, she could invite someone else to her own home, and sometimes she did. She could refuse Paul sex. She had never been able to refuse Bernard. Sometimes she even fantasised that it was Bernard she was having sex with while Paul was making love to her. Nevertheless she and Paul had some great times together, especially at casinos. One of these days he was going to take her to Las Vegas. As it was, he'd flown her to Paris for the weekend. Another time to Amsterdam. Always he took her to the best hotels and restaurants. And of course they visited all the casinos and gambling clubs everywhere they went. Paul often laughed at the keenness of her appreciation.

'You almost purr with pleasure,' he told her. 'Like a cat enjoying a bowl of cream.'

His wife was a semi-invalid, crippled with arthritis. That was the problem. It wouldn't be easy to walk out on her. Then of course he had three grown-up children. Andrina had pointed out to him that it wasn't as if he'd be leaving his wife on her own with no one to care for her. Not when there were three daughters. She was sorry for Linda of course but, after all, arthritis wasn't a life-threatening disease. Lots of people had it. Money was a great comforter too and Paul would not leave Linda penniless.

He was putting his daughters through university. 'I want them to have the chance that I never had,' he told her.

She had laughed at him then, 'Darling, you've done very well without a university education and I'm sure they could too.'

But he had a real 'thing' about education and his lack of it. Come what may, his daughters were going to get the best education money could buy. He'd even offered to pay for Jennifer to go to university as well. He was very generous. She loved him for that – although she doubted that Jennifer would thank Paul for anything.

VIII

As it happened, Jennifer had planned to go to Daisy's anyway. First she washed and brushed her hair, glad its glossy brown colour had none of her mother's red in it. Daisy's hair was straight like Jennifer's but black, and without Jennifer's fringe. In fact, Daisy was a younger-looking version of her Aunty Moira. Glasses and all. She wasn't as prim and proper, though. Daisy had bought tickets for the Who Dunnits' open-air concert in the Kelvingrove Park. The Who Dunnits weren't her favourite group but they were all right. They had originated from Glasgow – Old Garngad of all places. Hardly the stuff that excitement was made of yet Jennifer was soon caught up in the tide of emotion all around her. She was jumping up and down and screaming with everybody else. Only her screams were more an expression of despair than appreciation. She was adding her racket to the huge tide of hysteria careering out of control as a kind of release as the Who Dunnits belted out their hit numbers in a determined fight to be heard. At the end of the concert when they tried to leave, the crowd swelled forward. Daisy and Jennifer, near the front, were swept along, their feet hardly touching the ground. A row of security men and women formed a barrier round the stage. Two or three of them leapt up on to the platform and hustled the performers bodily and none too gently away out of sight. The other security men and women held their ground and kept roaring out that it was all over. Time to go home.

Jennifer thought of her mother in bed with Paul Fisher and felt sick at heart. She longed for her own bed, her own room, her own home. But no chance. Not while *he* was there. Tears came near to welling up. At the same time she felt angry at the way she was being knocked and pushed about – behind by others in the audience, in front by one of the security women. More of a girl she looked, hardly much older than herself. Suddenly the woman put a hand on her shoulder – barely touched it, it seemed, yet the pain was excruciating. It brought Jennifer to her knees, screaming in agony.

'Hey you!' Daisy was struggling towards her and shouting at the woman. 'What the hell do you think you're doing?'

But before Daisy could reach her Daisy was brought down as well. Then a bunch of security men closed in – huge gorilla-like guys. Suddenly the crowd caught a glimpse of the Who Dunnits' limousine bumping across the grass towards the road. The yell arose: 'There they are!' – and everyone sped after the vehicle.

Daisy and Jennifer were helped to their feet. The physical pain had been the last straw for Jennifer and the tears were spilling out, blurring her vision. All she could see was a vague shimmer of a face bending over her. It belonged to one of the security men.

'Here, take this.' He offered her his handkerchief. After she mopped at her eyes, she was able to get a better look at him. He seemed familiar. He grinned at her. 'Come on, cheer up. It's not the end of the world. I'll tell you what. I'll arrange for you to meet the Who Dunnits. That should cure the pain, eh?'

Daisy let out a squeal of delight.

'Me too? She hurt me too.'

'Yeah, yeah. You too.'

It was the wink that brought it all back to Jennifer. He was one of her earliest 'uncles'. One that she'd really liked. Her Uncle Bernard. He used to visit the house when her dad was there. He was a friend of her dad's. So he must be different. He was all right.

'Uncle Bernard,' she said, unexpectedly pleased and happy.

He stared at her, puzzlement darkening his eyes. Then in astonishment, he said, 'Jennifer?'

'Yes.'

'My God, you've changed!'

'Well, I should hope so. I was only about six or seven the last time you saw me.'

'Yet in a way you haven't,' he mused. 'I should have recognised you.' He smiled down at her. 'You were always a very serious little girl.'

'You once brought me a teddy with a bow-tie round its neck and looking very smart in a tartan waistcoat.'

'Did I?'

'You don't remember? I've still got that teddy. I've always loved it. I used to sit on your knee when you came to visit.'

'Oh yes, I remember that.' He gave another wink. 'We must do it again some time.'

Daisy piped up then, 'Excuse me if I interrupt your stroll down memory lane, but when are we going to meet the Who Dunnits?'.

'You know the Central Hotel?'

'Of course.'

'Well, be there tomorrow morning around 10.30, 11a.m. I'll arrange for you to have a cup of coffee with them and get their autograph.'

'Oh great,' Daisy enthused. 'Come on, Jennifer. We'd better get our beauty sleep tonight and look our best for tomorrow.'

'You're sure you're all right?' Bernard asked Jennifer.

'Yes, fine, thanks. I've forgotten about the pain in my shoulder with the surprise of seeing you.'

'I still have to attend to some things here but I could arrange for a taxi to take you home.'

Daisy answered for her.

'That would be great. Thanks a million.'

Later, in the darkness of Daisy's bedroom, Daisy still couldn't stop talking about the night's events and the wonderful, incredible date they had the next day.

'I'm glad the holidays are nearly over. I can't wait to get back to school and tell everyone. Can you imagine how jealous they'll all be? And we'll have the autograph to prove what we're saying is true.'

'I don't want to go back to school. In fact, I've made up my mind. I'm not going.'

'You're kidding,' Daisy squealed in astonishment.

'No, I'm not.'

'But what about university?'

'I don't care about university.'

'But you must.'

'You're beginning to sound like my mother. I can just imagine my father being the very same when I tell him.'

'But . . . but . . . what else can you do?'

'Get a job of course. I'm sixteen, not six.'

'But surely you'd get a far better job if you had a uni degree?'

'I just can't wait that long, Daisy. I've got to get away from home. I've been thinking – if I got a job, any kind of job, I don't care as long as I make some money. Then I could get a place of my own – even just a room in digs.'

'Is it that awful?'

'I can't stand it any longer. Not with that man there, and he's there every week now.'

'Gosh. I don't know what to say. My mum has her faults. She can be real dippy. You should see some of her crazy paintings. But at least she's not a tart. She'd never cheat on Dad. Do you think your mum takes money for it?'

'She's not a prostitute,' Jennifer shouted.

'OK. OK. Keep your voice down. There's no need to fly off the handle or blame me. It was you who told me your mother kept bringing guys to the house. What am I supposed to think?'

Jennifer was glad of the cover of darkness. She was trembling violently with distress.

'I'm sorry,' she managed, 'it's just all the excitement of tonight. And thinking about tomorrow . . .'

'I know. It's driving me bananas as well . . .' Daisy was off again but Jennifer was no longer listening. She wanted to weep but didn't know why. One moment she felt grown-up, determined to find a job and make a life for herself on her own. The next minute she was afraid and wanted to cling to her mother and feel safe. But safety, like love, was an illusion. She was on her own, always had been and always would be. Her aloneness was deeply rooted inside her.

Her fear increased a thousandfold. Lying in the now silent darkness in one of the single beds in Daisy's room, she wished with all her heart she'd remembered to bring her teddy. Thinking of it brought Bernard into her mind. She remembered the dark eyes, the tight jaw, the bulky muscles. She'd touched his upper arm as she'd passed him to climb into the taxi. It had been a spontaneous gesture of affection and thanks for his kindness. She was surprised at how iron-hard his muscles were. His eyes had smiled into hers as the taxi moved away.

He had been a friend of her father's. She supposed he must be old enough to be her father. She recalled the affection she'd always had for him.

Uncle Bernard. Bernard. A new confusion added to all the others in her life that she was trying to cope with.

She closed her eyes. But Bernard's face was still there.

IX

'Aye ok, Sally. So you're tougher than I thought. But listen to me. In my outfit you avoid violence as much as you can. Whether it's a karate strike or a head butt, you don't use it unless as a last resort. Violence is mainly used – when you have to – to defend a principal. Are you taking this in?'

Her eyes were bright stars in a round baby face.

'Yes, yes. But did you see how easy I brought those two girls down, Uncle Bernard? And I could have done the same with a man.'

Bernard pinned her with one of his hard stares.

'If that's what you're in the job for, if that's all you can be proud of, you can chuck it right now.'

Her joy wilted with uncertainty.

'I thought you'd be pleased.'

'You've hardly been in the job thirty minutes and you use a pressure point on two schoolkids. I've been in the job for the best part of thirty years and I've only used that particular one on a single occasion. That was on a man who kept challenging me to a fight. A huge gorilla he was. An aggressive and determined guy too. There was no other way to stop him. Five times I had to put him down before he called it a day.'

There was admiration in Sean's voice.

'I can just see you do that, Uncle Bernard. Cool as a cucumber you'd be. I don't believe you've an ounce of fear in your body.'

'Don't be stupid. It's important to feel fear in dangerous situations because it's natural. It helps the adrenalin flow, and channelled into the right places, that's what makes you tick.'

'I felt the adrenalin tonight. I really felt *alive*,' said Sally.

Sean enthusiastically agreed.

Bernard sighed.

'And here was me thinking after a few jobs you'd go off the idea.'

'No way!' Sean said. 'Just you tell us what the next job is and we'll be there.'

'No, you won't. I'm going over to Hollywood with Eve Page and the Page Boys.'

'Hollywood!' the twins yelled in unison. 'Oh please, *please*, Uncle Bernard.'

'No way. It's a close protection job – bodyguarding – and that's very different from crowd control at a pop concert. You put your life on the line with bodyguarding.'

Sally was bouncing up and down on her chair with enthusiasm. She was so childish in her eagerness it was ridiculous.

'You've seen how tough I can be, Uncle Bernard. I could stand and fight. I could fight any man who tried to attack – '

'Sally, have you not heard a word I said?'

He regretted allowing Sean and Sally to have had any training, or allowed them to come on a job.

'If you're a bodyguard, the *last* thing you want to do is stand and fight. You want to extract your principal from the area. If someone pulls a gun, all you can do is block the bullet, and if you've got a gun yourself, fire back.' He had a sudden horrible vision of Sally being in such a situation. It made him experience a deeper fear than he'd ever felt before. He forced himself to continue in a calm, even tone. 'If it's someone with a knife, what you aim to do is disarm that person, or keep the person at length, away from the principal. It's not easy.'

'We could learn, Uncle Bernard,' Sally assured him. 'Couldn't we, Sean?'

'Definitely,' Sean agreed. 'No problem.'

'No problem?' Bernard echoed. 'Christ, Sean, you don't know what you're talking about. There's problems all right and plenty of them. If you're a bodyguard, you have to defend because that's your job – you're defending the principal, and yourself second. You have to think of the principal first at all times.'

'Be fair, Uncle Bernard. You've admitted you've been doing

all this a long time. You've learned by experience. We have to learn by experience as well. You've got to give us a chance to get that experience.'

Sally joined in.

'And you *promised*, Uncle Bernard. And we *trusted* you. We took you at your word. The job would be ours if we survived the training, you said. We'd be on the permanent staff of your firm.'

'Hang on. I didn't go as far as that.'

'Oh, Uncle Bernard.' Sally moved closer to him. '*Hollywood*! It would be a dream come true. Oh please! *Please*!'

'Sally, you're forgetting something. You're only eighteen. I'd feel responsible if anything happened to either of you. Your mother and your granny'd be worried sick. Your dad's mad at me already and I don't blame him.'

Christ, he thought. Jennifer was even younger than eighteen. Just a schoolkid. And some of these pop stars could be bastards. He'd better check that everything was all right. He'd never forgive himself if anything had happened to her.

'Oh, please, please, Uncle Bernard.'

He really was distracted now.

'Oh all right,' he said impulsively. His immediate concern had shifted to Jennifer. 'But crowd control, remember. You just deal with the fans.'

His thoughts turned to Jennifer again. He couldn't get her serious, vulnerable little face out of his head. The Who Dunnits would be well away from Glasgow by this time, otherwise he would have gone to the hotel and had a word with them. He decided, for his own peace of mind, to go to Monteith Row and check with Jennifer.

It was years since he'd been near Glasgow Green. The sight of Monteith Row and Andrina's close brought memories crowding back. He'd come here on visits with his first wife and his second. He'd also come alone. He'd fucked Andrina in every part of the house, including on top of the kitchen table. He'd never been with such a passionate, such a sex-hungry woman, before or since.

His blood began to heat at the thought of seeing her again and he fought to control the spasms of excitement he felt as he entered the familiar building. By the time he'd reached her door, he was breathless with sexual tension.

'Damn the woman,' he kept thinking. 'Damn her!'

He rattled noisily at the letterbox.

Jennifer answered the door. It was as if a light switched on inside her head at the sight of him. Her eyes brightened.

'Bernard!'

'Just came to see how you got on at the hotel the other day.'

'Come in. Mum's out just now but she won't be long. She said she'd be home in time to make the evening meal.'

He followed her into the kitchen and watched as she began filling the kettle at the tap.

'Meantime I'll make you a cup of tea.' Her eyes filled with anxiety. 'Or maybe you'd prefer something stronger?'

'No, tea'll be fine. So, tell me. What happened? How did you get on?'

'It was great. Daisy went on about it for hours. She's the fan, you see. Their music's all right but I don't go overboard for them like Daisy does. Still, it was quite an experience meeting them like that and getting their autographs. They gave us lovely chocolate gâteau with the coffee. I really enjoyed that.'

Bernard laughed, more with relief than anything else.

'I'm glad it went well. I know quite a few celebrities. Maybe I can arrange for you to meet someone you really admire.' Although not a male someone, he told himself.

She was a nice kid. He was drinking the tea and chatting to her when the kitchen door opened and Andrina came in. For a moment she looked as if she was going to faint. Bernard rose, surprised that Jennifer had obviously not told her mother about meeting him. Yet not surprised. It was then that he noticed the man behind her.

'Well, this is a turn-up for the book,' the man guffawed. 'Our Jennifer caught entertaining a secret lover.'

What a fool the man was. Bernard stared him down and his laughter petered away foolishly.

'Paul,' Andrina said, recovering. 'This is Bernard O'Maley, an old friend of my ex-husband. Bernard, this is my fiancé, Paul Fisher.'

'Pleased to meet you,' Fisher said.

She was as beautiful and as sexy as ever. Amazing woman. All the time since he'd last been with her melted away. The chemistry between them sparked across the room.

Jennifer looked sullen and withdrawn now. Obviously there was no love lost between her and Fisher. He didn't blame the child. He didn't like the look of the man himself. A right shifty-eyed git.

'I bumped into Jennifer the other day and arranged for her and her friend to meet some pop stars I know. I called to see if she'd enjoyed herself.' He glanced at his watch. 'But I'd better be going. I've an American tour coming up and still some organising to do.'

'I'll see you to the door,' Jennifer said.

He looked at Andrina as he passed her. Looked into her eyes and recognised the same hungry passion he'd known so long ago.

They didn't say a word to each other, never touched, but he had an erection before he reached the darkness of the street outside.

X

BESSIE MIGHT AS well have announced 'I plan to commit a gruesome murder and cause my whole family as much pain and scandal as possible.' Everyone could not have been more shocked and against the idea.

'Anyone would think,' she tried to laugh, 'that I'd announced I was going to commit some heinous crime. I only said I was going away for a week's course in watercolours.'

'To England!' Peter said. As if that compounded the crime.

Peter had always gone to Millport every year as a child, then as an adult. He had Millport on the brain. Not that she had anything against the place. It was a lovely little island. But as far as she was concerned, once was enough. There were so many lovely places to see – in Scotland, in England, all over the world. Each year she'd tried to persuade Peter to go somewhere else but he had the solid and enthusiastic support of his dad and his daughter. She was always howled down. She'd hoped – no, felt sure – that once Daisy had reached her teen years she would be an ally and rebel at such boring repetition: year after year, the same place. But not a bit of it. Daisy was building up her own precious stores of fond and happy memories of dear old Millport. Just like her old dad and granda.

'Live adventurously' had been one of the *Advices and Queries* that had most attracted Bessie to join. She daren't, of course, mention Quakers to Daisy. 'Trust you, Mum. It's just the kind of thing you *would* go for.'

In every other way Daisy seemed a normal teenager. She went ga-ga over the most repulsive-looking pop groups and played their music loudly on her record player.

The fact that she rebelled against her mother and everything her mother stood for didn't worry Bessie. Or, at least, she suffered it as best she could. It was very hard at times, though. Especially when Daisy criticised the clothes she wore, and the way she did, or didn't do, her unruly hair. And of course the heinous crime of getting paint under her fingernails. Obviously what Daisy wanted was a normal middle-class, middle-aged mum. She was always lecturing her about looking her age and dressing her age and behaving like a woman of her age should.

'You really embarrass me, Mum,' was Daisy's usual heartfelt cry. As if denim trousers, Indian shirts and curly hair was somehow the sole and sacred prerogative of the young.

But apart from how she looked and her love of painting, had she done anything so terrible? OK, she did disappear up to the loft at every opportunity. Nevertheless, she had been their 'normal' skivvy – no, absolute slave – for years. Lifting and laying for them, cooking and scrubbing for them, always being at their beck and call. All right, she didn't wear hats and carry handbags. So what? Thank God nobody bothered about such things at Quaker meetings. She had immediately felt at home among the motley crowd in the Meeting House. No fashion plates, no fashion rules and regulations there.

'Trust you,' Daisy cried, 'to get in with a crowd of cranks and eccentrics.'

'They're no such thing.' Bessie tried to defend the faith and the faithful but her words fell on deaf ears. (There were one or two eccentrics of course but what was the harm in that?) Daisy, she often thought rather sadly, was far more Peter's daughter than hers. She always echoed what Peter said, even what Granda said. They all backed each other up, a solid, impenetrable wall against her. Always had been.

But this time, although they didn't know it, she had Gregory on her side.

'Don't ask them,' he'd advised. 'Just tell them you're going and no argument about it. You're entitled to your own time.'

She'd known that there *would* be an argument. And that wasn't the worst of it. It was the continuous carping that always got to her. The way she was mocked and made a fool of and undermined. It had become like a Chinese torture. Often it confused her to such a degree she didn't know who she was any more. It depressed her so much she became paralysed. Hidden away in her bedroom she'd feel too weighed down to do anything but stare at the walls. At other times she'd feel like committing murder and then the only pleasure she got out of her existence was thoughts of murdering Granda. Granda had met a horrible death in all sorts of ingenious ways. Only Granda didn't die. In despair, she believed he never would. At other times, she felt full of guilt and remorse at having such wicked thoughts. She'd even on occasion harboured them in the peaceful silence of Meeting. To make up for her thoughts she'd cook Granda one of his favourite meals and let him beat her at dominoes. Then she had to struggle valiantly against a resurgence of murderous plans when he gloated over his victory, or laughed at how stupid she'd been. Or when he gleefully suggested a game of strip-poker.

Peter always thought this hilarious.

'Granda's a right card.'

Often she nursed murderous thoughts against Peter as well. But she seldom if ever spoke up, certainly never argued. Oh, once she had, long, long ago. And even then, she had been far too reasonable. She'd always tried to see the other point of view.

Gregory said, 'You know your problem?'

'No.'

'You're such a gentle soul.'

'Me?' She enjoyed a genuine laugh at that. Her with the murderous intentions?

'Yes, you. Try to be firmer with them. Harder, Bessie. Speak up clearly. Tell them what you want to do and then just *do* it.'

So she'd stood up in front of Granda and Peter and Daisy and said, 'I've booked to go on a week's course for watercolours at a college in York. I leave on Saturday. I've bought my train ticket and everything's organised. I'm really looking forward to it.'

'What?' they'd screeched in unison.

'Don't be silly, Mum,' Daisy said. 'College at your age? You're just making a fool of yourself again.'

Peter and Granda said, 'What about us? Who's going to look after us? Who's going to cook our meals?'

'I told you,' she said, 'I've everything organised. The fridge and freezer are packed with things I've already cooked. All you have to do is defrost them as you need them, and heat them up.'

She'd worked herself nearly into the ground with shopping and cooking and getting everything ready for them in advance. She felt absolutely knackered. It would be a miracle if she'd enough energy left to pack her case. It was always the same. Even when they went to Millport. She never had any time to herself for seeing to other people. It was just as well on this occasion that she'd been too busy to think, otherwise she would never have got as far as buying the train ticket. Now, with the house hoovered, the kitchen scrubbed and even the meals made for them, there was just her bag to pack. Now, she was beginning to worry. Not about Granda and Peter and Daisy. She was beginning to worry – no, panic – about having an affair with Gregory. That's what it would be, wouldn't it? Her heart swelled up to her throat with the fearful, sinful enormity of what she was planning to do. After all, whether you were the Church of Jesus, the Society of Friends or the Salvation Army, it said quite categorically in the Bible: 'Thou shalt not commit adultery.'

She hadn't been able to face going to Meeting the previous Sunday, as if God would be there in person to accuse her. It was bad enough to think of facing other Quakers. She felt she was letting the side down. That was the least of it, though. She was panicking on a far more urgent and practical level. She kept examining herself naked in the long mirror on the back of the bathroom door. What a humbling sight! She was pear-shaped. Boobs too small, hips too big. Her ankles weren't as slim as she'd like them to be either. She stood on tiptoe to simulate high heels. That helped, but she seldom if ever wore high heels.

She was about to get herself into a vulnerable situation where all her faults and weaknesses would be on public display. That's what it felt like. She'd known Gregory for only a few weeks. He was a stranger. How could she do it? If she had the appearance of a Marilyn Monroe it would have been entirely different. But look at her! She even had stretch marks on her belly.

In desperation she covered herself in Johnson's baby oil. Then she didn't have time to massage it in before Granda started banging on the bathroom door. He took these terrible urgencies to get to the lavatory pan and always, it seemed, while she was in the bathroom. She had to slither rapidly into her clothes. She was lucky to have been able to snatch the time to have a bath.

Usually she wore tights and white cotton panties and bra, and in the winter found comfort in her thermals. For the York trip she'd bought a black lacy bra, a narrow strip of frilly lace that purported to be a suspender belt, and black stockings. Feeling like a cross between a thief and a Jezebel, she'd secreted them at the bottom of her case inside a pair of bed-socks. (She had awful poor circulation and was afraid a strange bed would be too cold.) At the last minute she'd splashed out on a new nightie and négligé. Black too, both flimsy and free flowing from the wickedly low-cut neck. Not that she believed that she and Gregory would actually sleep together. The college brochure had contained pictures of small, spartan-looking single rooms with narrow single-sized beds. Anyway, she'd never sleep a wink in such nerve-racking circumstances. She had a vision of him perhaps visiting her on a respectable business pretext. She hadn't imagined the details of what exactly that might be. She would let him into the room, in all the glamorous glory of the black nightie and négligé. Her riot of fair curls would be a shining frame to her modestly blushing face and he would tell her how beautiful, how gorgeous, how desirable she looked.

The vision crumpled and dissolved into dust. In her heart of hearts, she couldn't believe it. Brainwashed into thinking the exact opposite for too long, she was left wishing she could dissolve into dust as well. Disappear into nothing. How could she have ever thought for one moment that she could put herself into such a vulnerable position – *again*? That's what had happened with Peter and she was still suffering the trauma and degradation of it. She couldn't possibly take any more. She'd rather die.

Yet she'd bought the ticket to York. She'd told the family. She'd packed her case and now it was Saturday and she was setting off despite the heavy gloom behind her. She had left the family sitting as if in mourning at a wake. Not her wake, though. The way things were they'd be more likely to cheer if anything happened to her. Cries of 'Serves you right. Good riddance to bad rubbish' would follow her to the grave.

Nobody had helped her to carry her case to the waiting taxi and it weighed like an elephant. What on earth had she crammed in there? Her packing had been done so quickly she couldn't remember. She hurried down the stone stairs jerking awkwardly from one side to the other like a man with a wooden leg. Inside she was in terrible turmoil. It was as if she was leaving her family for ever, shamefully deserting them, letting them down. She wished with all her heart that she wasn't going. She wished she'd never heard of York, or Gregory Seymour.

The devil, along with the crowd at the station, jostled her onwards and before she knew it, she was aboard the train and it was hastening her on to perdition.

XI

JENNIFER TURNED HER key in the door as quietly as possible. She had returned early from another overnight visit to Daisy's house. It hadn't been much fun at Daisy's this time. There was a terrible atmosphere in the house. Daisy's mother was away somewhere enjoying herself on her own, without a thought for Daisy and her family, it seemed. This surprised Jennifer, as it had astonished and outraged Daisy. Jennifer envied Daisy for having such a calm, motherly kind of woman who was always there to look after everybody and listen sympathetically to their problems. But to Daisy her mother was a source of constant irritation.

'All right,' she'd argued with Daisy more than once, 'your mum's hair is a bit wild, and she buys her clothes secondhand from Oxfam, but at least she doesn't grudge you anything and she doesn't put every horrible Tom, Dick and Harry before you. You come first with your mum. You really *matter* to her.'

Admittedly she couldn't at this moment add her usual 'Your mum's always *there* for you.' But after all, Daisy's mum had only gone for a week's painting holiday. It was the first time in Bessie Alexander's whole life she'd been away anywhere on her own. She'd said that in Jennifer's hearing. Bessie had never even gone anywhere on her own before she was married. Surely she deserved a break.

'I don't know what you're moaning about,' Jennifer had told Daisy. 'My mum's always disappearing. And not just to do something harmless like painting a picture either. You should think yourself lucky, Daisy.'

But Daisy didn't. It occurred to Jennifer that Daisy was a bit spoiled. More than a bit, really. She'd been glad to escape from Daisy's selfish, self-pitying complaints. The house at

Shawlands Cross was horrible and depressing. For the first time, Jennifer realised that its warm and welcoming atmosphere had been solely generated by Bessie Alexander.

The door opened with a creak and Jennifer tiptoed into the silent hall. She couldn't be sure if she was alone in an empty house or if her mother was still asleep. Her mother had never been an early riser. Then she was startled by the appearance in the bedroom doorway of Paul Fisher, clad only in a pair of Y-fronts. Jennifer averted her eyes and went into the kitchen. She'd left Daisy's place before they'd got breakfast organised and hadn't even had a cup of tea.

To her apprehension, Paul Fisher appeared behind her. He looked obscene. She fixed her attention on the kettle.

'I'll make Mummy's tea,' she said. 'There's no need for you to do it.'

'Mummy has run out to the grocer's to buy some milk.' His sneery tone of voice frightened her.

'Then I'll just leave her to do it herself.'

Jennifer's priority now was to reach her own room. Head lowered, she hurried past him. Sensing as well as hearing the pad of his steps following her, terror spiked her. She reached her bedroom and tried to shut the door but his foot was in it. Then he was in the room.

'Get out of my room.'

Her voice sounded childish and trembling. 'I'm going to tell Mum on you.'

He mimicked her. 'I'm going to tell Mum on you. Yes, you like trying to come between your mother and me, don't you? Always putting me down. I'll give you something to complain about, my girl.'

The speed with which he roughly grabbed her and knocked her on to the bed made her gasp and choke. Before she could scream his hand clamped over her mouth. Beads of sweat suddenly glistened on his forehead. His other hand fumbled with her clothes. She punched and kicked and struggled with all her strength but couldn't get free of him: she remained pinned underneath his body. The horrible hard thing he began bumping between her legs sickened her beyond all sickness.

Suddenly, he scrabbled away from her and rushed from the room. Her mother's voice now, calling from the hall:

'Sorry I've taken so long, darling. The man in the grocer's had slept in, would you believe? He was at a friend's "stag do" last night. I got some rolls as well. Would you like one with bacon and eggs?'

Fisher's voice. Calm. As if nothing had happened.

'Wonderful, darling. I'll come through and make a cup of tea while you're seeing to the fry-up. Won't be a tick. Just getting dressed. By the way, have I ever told you that I love you?'

Soon Jennifer could hear giggling. Then she caught the sound of her mother's little moans of pleasure. She felt ill. She was shivering violently.

'Mummy,' she called out. 'Mummy, please . . .' She could hardly talk for nausea, and the way her body was jerking and shaking.

'I didn't know you were home, dear.' Her mother came smiling into the room. The smile vanished at the sight of Jennifer and she rushed over to take her daughter in her arms. Jennifer clung gratefully to the soft, perfumed flesh.

'Jennifer, what's the matter, dear? Have you caught a chill or something? Shall I send for the doctor?'

From the corner of her tear-filled eye, Jennifer saw Fisher standing in the doorway. Dapper in flannel trousers, pinstriped shirt, and bow-tie.

'Don't let him come near me, Mummy,' she wept. 'Please keep him away.'

'Ssh, ssh, darling. You've just been having one of your nasty dreams. Mummy's here now. Everything's all right.'

Jennifer's sobs sharpened with anger and frustration. 'I haven't been dreaming. I've been over at Daisy's. I've just come in. How could I have been dreaming? It's him. He tried to have sex with me.'

'Who, dear?'

'You're the dreamer. Who do you think?'

For a moment her mother looked genuinely puzzled and Jennifer felt that, despite her warm perfumed nearness, Andrina was as far away and as alien to her as she'd always been.

Her mother turned her gaze towards Fisher.

'God.' He shook his head. 'I've always known that she hated me, Andrina.' He sounded as if he too was about to weep. 'But this is too much. I can't cope with lies like this.'

Andrina swivelled her attention back to Jennifer, at the same time shrinking away from her.

'This is what comes of you going over to my mother's so often. It's her that's put you against me. She did the same with your daddy. She's always hated me and tried to prevent me from having a little happiness. You're not to go over there again, do you hear?'

Jennifer fumbled for a handkerchief and rubbed at her eyes. 'That's so typical of you,' she said. 'You're incapable of thinking of anyone but yourself. You've never cared about me!'

'What nonsense. I've not only given you a good home and provided for you all these years, I've been the one to put up with your moods and your troublemaking and your constant criticism of me. You get more like your father every day.'

As usual, at the mention of Robert her voice acquired a bitterness tinged with petulance.

Fisher said, 'Well, you might have to put up with her, Andrina, but I don't. I'm not going to stay here and have her make accusations like that against me. For whatever reason, she's always been hell bent on ruining our relationship. Well, this time she's succeeded. I'm off and I won't be back.'

'No, wait!' Andrina cried out. 'Darling, don't go. She's young. I'll speak to her. It'll be all right. She won't act like this again. I promise.' She got up and followed him hastily out of the room, turning at the door for a brief moment with anger flashing in her eyes.

'How could you do this to me, you wicked, ungrateful girl. You'd better apologise to Paul, do you hear?'

Jennifer heard the kitchen door shutting. The shivering and shaking was now deep inside her. There was no way she could defend herself, no way she could cope. She grabbed the backpack containing the overnight things she'd had at Daisy's. She crept from the bedroom and house, hardly daring to breathe until she reached the street. Then she began to run and didn't stop until her legs gave way. She had to hide in a close in one of the streets: she collapsed and crouched there, hugging her knees, rocking backwards and forwards, staring at the large billowing masses of cloud in the sky. Seeking comfort but finding none.

Eventually she gathered enough thoughts together to decide to go to Bearsden to Laura's house. She could never think of it as her daddy's place because it had always been Laura's house. Her daddy had just gone there to be with Laura.

At first Jennifer thought of going to her father as a solution. Once she got off the Bearsden bus, however, and was only a few yards away from Laura's bungalow, she began to tremble with uncertainty. Her father was happy and settled with Laura. They were perfect partners with everything in common. Both were art teachers, both liked the same kind of music and theatre. A runaway daughter suddenly turning up on their doorstep would surely upset their happy lifestyle, and cause unwelcome problems. She would be a nuisance here with her father just as she'd been a nuisance at home with her mother. Still in a state of shock, however, and the need for her father's protection outweighing every other consideration, she knocked at Laura's door. No one came to open it. She knocked again. And again. Still no reply. Then, like a physical blow to her heart, Jennifer suddenly remembered that her father and Laura had gone off to Florence with a group of their pupils. She had been too distraught to remember. She was still distraught, and thirsty and hungry too, as well as needing the toilet. Helplessly she looked around. She wandered back to Drymen Road. It was then that she saw her granny's house just along the road. Of course, she would go there. She almost wept with relief. She didn't know why she'd thought of her daddy first. Except that he was the one who had protected and comforted her when she was a little girl. He had always put her first and had been on her side then. But that, of course, was before his marriage to Laura. Laura was his first love now. Jennifer hurried across the road and along to the end terrace house. Her granny didn't have anyone else to be loyal to or put first. Her granny would protect her and look after her.

'Jennifer!' Sophie stood aside to let her in. The hall was spotless as usual. There was always a strong smell of lavender wax polish and every surface had a hard gleam of reflected light. It was the same in the kitchen. Only, in the kitchen, the pungent smell was of pine disinfectant.

'What a nice surprise,' Sophie was saying as she plugged in the electric kettle. 'That's right, take off your haversack, or whatever you call it. I take it that means you're going to stay the night. I wasn't expecting you but of course I'm delighted. Absolutely delighted! You know you're welcome at any time, Jennifer. You're just in time for morning coffee and I've got – '

'Oh, Granny, it was terrible and I was so frightened.' Jennifer burst into sobs punctuated by loud moaning sounds as if she was in a panic of pain.

'Jennifer!' Sophie hastened towards her, caught her by the arm and led her to one of the kitchen chairs. Sophie had never been a demonstrative woman, never had cuddled her grandchild, had never given anything but the most fleeting kisses. She was a taut, held-in woman who was incapable of showing love and affection. But Jennifer knew she loved her in her own way. It was the one thing she'd always been certain of. Her granny was the one sure, safe rock in Jennifer's life.

'Now just you sit there and try to calm yourself,' Sophie said. 'As you know I'd normally never give someone as young as you any strong drink. But I do believe at the moment a little whisky might be the best thing to strengthen you and calm you down. All right?'

Jennifer nodded, still sobbing and making little animal noises.

The whisky made her cough and burned her lips and throat but it gave her a warm feeling that brought a comfort of sorts.

'Now,' Sophie sat opposite her at the table, 'tell me what all this is about. What was terrible? What were you so frightened about?'

Jennifer hesitated. She had been so shaken by her mother's disbelief she was now afraid that her granny might not believe her.

'It was that man.'

Colour began to drain from Sophie's face.

'What man?'

'Mr Fisher. He did awful things to me. Dirty things, and Mummy didn't care.' Her sobs grew louder at the sight of her granny's grey, horrified expression. 'I'm sorry, Granny, don't be angry with me, oh please don't. It wasn't my fault. And I'm not telling lies. I would never tell lies to you. Please believe me.'

'I'm not angry with you, child. How could I be angry with you? It's that filthy pair of perverts I'm angry with. I've always been afraid of this happening again. It's been a recurring nightmare all my life . . .'

Jennifer's sobbing hiccupped to a stop. She started in perplexity at the older woman.

'Again?' She wiped at her eyes with the back of her sleeve. 'It didn't happen to me before, Granny. I've never felt safe since he's been around but it never . . .'

Her granny was no longer listening. There was a haunted faraway look in her eyes.

'I hated them, the dirty perverts. I was glad when they died. After what they'd put me through. They committed suicide, you know. Older than I am now, they were. And they'd long since ruined me and my whole life . . .'

The words were babbling out as if the older woman had completely taken leave of her senses.

'Granny, please, I don't understand . . .'

'No, nor did I at first. I was only a child. Younger than you. Much younger. When they died they left a note saying "Sophie, we're sorry." Sorry? Not as sorry as I am that they'd just taken sleeping pills. I'd wanted them to die a painful death. I wanted to watch them die in agony. That's what I wanted . . .'

'Granny, please don't. You're frightening me.'

'Everyone thought I was grieving but I was secretly rejoicing . . .'

Jennifer couldn't cope with this new horror. The shock of hearing what Paul Fisher had done had obviously been too much for the old woman. She had taken ill. She looked demented. Her talk as well as her appearance were becoming wilder and wilder. Then suddenly it stopped. Her face twisted, drooped down at one side. There was tragic appeal in her eyes. Jennifer began to weep.

'I'm so sorry, Granny. Oh, I'm so sorry . . .'

XII

HIS WIFE. HIS *wife*? Bessie couldn't believe it. Gregory had actually brought his wife with him to the college. It defied understanding. She knew he was a cool customer, but this was ridiculous.

'Pleased to meet you,' she said, smiling uncertainly at the woman with the tired-looking skin, a mole on her left cheek and a short uneven haircut. Her hair looked as if it had been chewed by the dog.

'Nice to meet you too, Bessie,' Isa said. 'So you're the new genius of a painter Gregory has discovered.'

'Yes. I mean, no. I'm no genius.' Her laughter sounded false. 'For goodness sake!'

'Gregory says you have a very original and striking talent. He's very proud of you.'

They were chatting while Gregory stood calmly by, his head tilted slightly back, for all the world looking proud of both of them. He must be mad. Or was a situation like this normal in the outside world? She had been dreaming, and worrying, about a secret love affair. Later at the college, when she'd managed to get speaking to him alone, she said, 'You brought your wife?'

'Oh yes, she always comes with me when I have a lecture engagement.'

'But . . . I thought . . . You did ask me to sleep with you, didn't you?'

'To have sex with me, yes.'

'Not to sleep with you?' She was confused and had to get things straight in her head.

He smiled patiently. He looked like some Sultan from one

of the books of fairy tales from her childhood with his noble head, warm eyes and great bush of a beard.

'We'll arrange that for a later date. There will be plenty of opportunities for us to enjoy each other here. Isa doesn't attend the lectures or the painting sessions. She's just come for her own kind of holiday. She'll be perfectly happy exploring York.'

'I see.' She didn't really. *Enjoy* each other? Did people enjoy quick sex as a change of entertainment from going to the theatre or a concert nowadays? Was she so out of touch with modern trends? Had she spent too long in the Co-op, cloistered in the aisles of fruit and veg, soap powder and detergents?

To add to her confusion, she *liked* Isa. They sat beside each other at mealtimes and chatted happily. She discovered that Isa was going to the theatre with a couple of American ladies she'd met in York. Isa was a very friendly easy-to-get-on-with person in her Jesus sandals and shapeless cotton dress. Bessie couldn't understand how Gregory could contemplate cheating on her. Or even why he'd *want* to. Isa Seymour wasn't catwalk material. But then, neither was Bessie Alexander. Even after knowing Isa a couple of days, *Bessie* couldn't contemplate cheating on her. That evening, the evening Isa was going off with her American tourists, Bessie avoided Gregory, avoided everybody in fact by shutting herself away in her room directly after dinner. She decided to go to bed early and read the book she'd started on the train. Abandoning now all thoughts of a Mills and Boon romance in real life, she gave only a passing regretful glance at the black see-through nightie. With a sigh, she donned the cotton pyjamas she'd bought in a sale at a cut-price store. How low can you get? Peter had been with her and suggested the purchase. He loved a bargain, especially if it meant saving money on her. She propped herself up in bed and had just got to a romantic part of her book when she was startled by a gentle tapping on the bedroom door. Before she could call out, 'Who is it?', the door opened and Gregory entered, closing it quietly behind him. For a moment, Bessie's mouth literally hung open in shock. Then, panic coming to her rescue, she clutched the blankets up to her chin – a quite unnecessary act of modesty as her pyjamas were nearly throttling her.

'You can't come in here,' she said. But of course he already was in. His big body dwarfed the narrow room. He was towering over her, his bulk casting a giant shadow.

'It's all right,' he said gently. 'Isa is away to York.'

'It's not all right.' Her voice sounded high and strident. 'She might come back at any minute and your room is just across the corridor.'

'What are you getting into such a panic about?'

To hear him speak it was as if he'd just dropped by for an innocent cup of tea. His voice had a slightly puzzled, faintly injured tone.

'Go away!' She aimed a whispered shout at him. 'I want you to go away.'

He sighed.

'Very well.'

He looked really huffed. Her distress of course had been partly due to the shame and embarrassment of the thick winceyette pyjamas. At least she hadn't been caught wearing rollers.

She watched him leave and shut the door behind him. Only then did relief set in. It was wonderful to think she had nothing to worry about now, no guilt to torment herself with. She could relax with a clear conscience and appreciate the holiday. No anxiety about what she was going to give the family for their next meal, no cooking, no shopping, no hoovering, no washing, no scrubbing. *No Granda!*

What ecstasy! She cuddled down in bed, hardly able to wait until next day when she would be able to paint to her heart's content.

It only took another couple of days to send her into raptures of happiness. The freedom to sit at her easel out of doors was indescribable. It was a freedom of spirit Bessie had never experienced before. So happy was she, and so full of gratitude, that her heart overflowed with the need to share everything with Peter and Daisy – and even Granda if he wanted to listen. She longed to tell them all about the college with its big bright art department and the campus with the colourful flowerbeds and the lake and the way the pale green leaves of the trees glistened like silver in the sunshine. And how when she was painting outdoors she'd heard, through the open windows of the music room, someone playing Mozart. She had been, still was, on a high of happiness.

Her fingers fumbled impatiently as she dialled her home number.

'Peter!' she shouted with excitement. 'Peter, is that you?'

'Who did you think it was – Prince Philip?'

The sound of the sneering voice immediately chipped the keen edge off her blissful state. She had forgotten what it sounded like. But she still had an eagerness to tell him about the college and some of the friends she'd made. Before she could launch into all the details, however, his voice pushed on:

'You never left enough milk and we'd to take our tea black. It made Granda feel sick. Everything takes far too long to defrost and I had to go out for fish suppers last night and they were nearly the death of me. I've been suffering purgatory with indigestion ever since.' He belched to prove the point. 'You know how greasy stuff gives me the bile.'

All her enthusiasm, all her happiness, seeped down and down until it trickled out of her toes and disappeared. After she replaced the receiver, it took a minute or two before she could rouse herself to move away. She suddenly saw, with frightening clarity, what her life was like at home. It was too terrible for tears. She felt dazed with the thought of it. But after a good night's sleep, and waking up in the college bedroom with the sun beaming in, Bessie's gratitude rushed back. She bounced from the bed and sang as she dressed. She could hardly wait to get to her easel.

First there was the delight of joining all the others in the canteen where the noise of enthusiastic chatter filled the room. Bessie enjoyed a good breakfast – she never had much of an appetite at home – and added to the racket of talk and laughter.

Gregory still looked huffed. She detected it in the increase of dignity about him, the slight tilt of his head, and the accusatory note of his cool politeness. She felt a pang of guilt, but was able to distance herself from him by sitting at the far end of the table between two women from London. She successfully avoided him for the rest of the week by sticking like a limpet to whoever she could. Including Isa. She didn't feel a bit jealous, nor it seemed did Isa when it became obvious that two of the younger students were trying their best to flirt with Gregory.

She didn't risk phoning home again. Didn't have time, really. There was a last-night party which was great fun. She hadn't laughed so much in years. Gregory didn't attend. Probably he was away somewhere with one of the admiring girls who had been in the audience when he'd given his last lecture. Bessie didn't care. She was as free as fresh air to enjoy herself.

On the way home she could hardly wait to tell Peter and the family all about her adventure. A born optimist, she always forgot the bad. The moment she entered the house, it all came back to her. It was like stepping into a funeral parlour. Or a tomb. She'd even forgotten that the flat – especially the kitchen at the back – was so dark and oppressive. The sun didn't seem able to penetrate the gloom. The only place it reached was her studio. Granda and Peter were sitting side by side waiting for her like judge and jury. Their sour faces proclaimed an unmistakable verdict of guilty.

Beside Alexander, you are found guilty of cruelly neglecting your poor old husband and his poor old dad and you are sentenced to long-drawn-out reminders of your selfish behaviour ad infinitum.

She dumped her case down and went over to the sink to fill the kettle. Four rheumy eyes, full of bitterness, bored into her back.

Now she wished that she *had* enjoyed a bit of loving from Gregory. She began thinking about him again, in the romantic terms she'd done before she'd gone to York. She needed any straw to hang on to, any vestige of hope. Oh, how stupid she'd been. She'd spoiled the one chance she had of loving and being loved. Could she never do anything right?

She put cups and saucers on the kitchen table. Peter and Granda still sat like two accusations set in stone. Shadows gathered around them. Through the bitter silence, the kitchen clock slowly tick-tocked her life away.

XIII

'MRS PEMBERTON?' ANDRINA repeated into the phone. 'Mrs Pemberton, did you say?'

'Yes, dear, your mother's neighbour. Poor Sophie is in hospital. Jennifer was in a dreadful state when she came to my door. The poor child didn't know what to do. I could see at a glance that poor Sophie had taken a stroke and so I immediately returned to my own house and told Mr Pemberton to phone for the doctor. There was really nothing else I could do.'

'A stroke?'

'She's always been so highly strung. It came as no surprise to me, really. It's only a wonder she didn't take a stroke or a heart attack years ago. I said at the time when her poor husband died – and everyone in the terrace agreed with me – that I'd always thought – '

'What hospital?' Andrina interrupted, and when Mrs Pemberton replied, she asked, 'Did Jennifer go with her?'

'No, the doctor gave her a tranquilliser or a sedative or something, and told her to rest. There was nothing she could do either. She'd just be in the way, the doctor said. She could visit her grandmother later. The poor child was in such a state. Quite hysterical – but of course she's always adored her grandmother. Sophie has been so good to her. I always said – '

'I'd better go to the hospital right away,' Andrina interrupted again. 'Will you excuse me?'

'Of course, my dear . . .'

Andrina hung up.

'What's wrong,' Fisher asked, strolling into the hall.

'My mother's taken a stroke. I'll have to go to the hospital.'

'She's getting her just desserts at last, is she?'

'Paul! That's a terrible thing to say.'

'Be honest, darling. You hate her guts!'

Andrina avoided his eyes. 'She's always been a difficult woman,' she said. 'But she's still my mother. I can't just ignore her when she needs my help.'

'She ignored you when you needed her help.'

Andrina lit a cigarette. It occurred to her as she did so how horrified her mother would be if she saw her smoking. Anyone would think, to hear her mother talk, that 'Thou shalt not smoke if thou art a woman' was one of the Ten Commandments. For a long time now Andrina had taken perverse pleasure in smoking, even at times using a long, fancy holder. She enjoyed imagining each cigarette as cocking a rebellious snook at her mother. Even though her mother didn't know it. For so many years she had been intimidated by Sophie, dominated by her, been fearful of her. Not any more.

'I'm her only child.'

'She still treated you like a child, and a wicked child at that, even after you were married and a mother yourself. Bullying you, spying on you, you told me.'

'I know, I know. But apart from anything else – what would people think if I didn't go?'

'Ah!'

'Don't "ah" me! It's not only how it would look. I do have some feelings for her, despite all she's done. You don't need to come with me. I can phone for a taxi.'

'No, I'll drive you there if that's what you really want to do.'

'I'll just fetch my handbag.'

They didn't talk on the journey to the hospital. Andrina's mind was in turmoil. One minute she had slipped back to when she had been a baby and had been neglected and abandoned by Sophie. The next minute she remembered how, after her mother had been 'saved', she had gone to the opposite extreme and tried to stamp out every natural expression of Andrina's passionate personality, her taste in clothes, in jewellery, in make-up, in men. Her mother had forced her into a life of deceit for years.

Did she really want to see her mother? They had successfully avoided each other for years. She'd almost forgotten in her busy, happy life how her mother used to make her feel. Now, it was all tumbling back to her: the fear, the self-consciousness. She became aware of her low-necked emerald dress. Green, according to her mother, was a Catholic colour as well as an unlucky one. Her expensive gold choker and earrings would not meet with approval either. Nor would her high-heeled shoes. Her make-up, of course, had always been a bone of contention. Now the black mascara and eyeliner that dramatically framed her eyes would shock her mother. As would her full lips, their sensual pout accentuated by lipstick. Another thought struck her. Maybe her mother would be unable to say anything because of her stroke.

Andrina felt bitter laughter swell up like a lump in her throat. Her nagging, neurotic mother, who never stopped talking, being struck silent by God. She liked that idea.

She would see of course that her mother received every medical care and attention. *She* would not disown or neglect her. She was a true Christian as well as a good daughter.

She liked that idea too.

Paul sat at one side of her mother's bed and she sat at the other. Strange how shrunken and grey Sophie looked. Not frightening at all. And she really couldn't speak. Andrina felt a surge of elation and self-confidence.

'Now, don't worry, Mummy,' she told the tragic-eyed figure in the bed, 'you're going to be all right. I'll see to everything.' If there was any fear present, it was in her mother's eyes. 'You're not going to stay in a public ward like this. I'll have you transferred to a little private room on your own. We don't care what it costs.' She fluttered her dark screen of lashes across the bed at Fisher. 'Do we, darling?'

'Whatever you say, sweetheart.'

'After we leave here today, I'll go over to your house, Mummy, and see what Jennifer is up to. She just disappeared from home, you know. We were terribly upset, weren't we, darling?'

'Appalled, more like.'

'At the lies she was telling, Mummy. She really is a very difficult child.'

Her mother was struggling to move her head.

'Forgive me for saying so, Mummy, but the trouble is you've always spoiled Jennifer. It's time she learned not to keep running to you every time she takes a tantrum.'

She was enjoying herself. Never before had she been able to express herself like this. She fancied a cigarette but automatically suppressed the craving. Then she thought: why should I deny myself the pleasure? There never had been any pleasure she denied herself – except, that is, in her mother's presence. She had always been far too afraid to be her natural self with her mother. But now, right now, the fear had gone. She made quite a sensual performance of taking her gold cigarette case from her handbag, selecting a cigarette, tapping it on the case, then lighting up with the gold lighter. She inhaled deeply, pleasurably, like she did after enjoying sex. Then, blowing a leisurely stream of smoke across the still figure in the bed, she observed the horror in the dark sunken eyes, and was glad she had come.

'I know you love her, Mummy, and you mean well, but she's got to realise that her home is with me.'

XIV

BERNARD WAS GLAD that the Boeing 747 was steadily piling up the miles between him and Andrina. It had shaken him to discover how strong the chemistry was between them. No way was he going to dance to her tune again, but it took all his self-discipline to banish her from his mind and concentrate on the job in hand. He had already been over to LA to make sure that the arrangements were right for the arrival of the principal. His priority was the female singer. He had detailed his men to bodyguard the three Page Boys. Although the Page Boys shared in Eve's worldwide popularity, it was Eve who was the main focus of the fans.

He'd walked the route. He'd also met the owner of the company who was going to provide the stretch limos, talked with the drivers, and had a look around the cars. Right now, Rod McGowan, his number two, would be going through the whole checking process yet again. He'd made sure the cars were fully equipped, that the drivers were competent and the company had back-up should one of the cars suddenly break down.

He'd met the hotel manager of the Beverly Wilshire and the hotel security manager had gone over all the plans. He'd arranged for his security people to protect the floor where the principal's room was situated – day and night. He'd also cleared it with the police that he and his men should carry guns.

The plane swooped downwards. There was a judder as the undercarriage hit the tarmac. Then the race along the runway until the speed was brought under control and the plane stopped. Eve was stretching and yawning, catlike, Andrina-like. He wanted to avert his eyes, to blot Andrina from his mind.

But Eve's life might depend on him doing no such thing. He must keep his attention riveted on her.

He'd warned the twins, Sean and Sally, to stay clear of him. He didn't want to see them or speak to them if it could be avoided until the job was over and they were all off duty and back home in Scotland. They were working on the crowd control side with some of his best and most experienced men. He could now only trust that they would be all right and put any worries about them out of his mind as determinedly as he was trying to banish Andrina.

He got Eve into the limo and he sat in front with the chauffeur. In front was another limo carrying three of his security men. Behind was a back-up car, another limousine with the band's manager and the three Page Boy musicians, Joe, Billy and Dave.

Later, alone in this hotel room, Bernard sank once more into sensual dreams of Andrina. He felt himself drowning. He closed his eyes and smelled her perfume.

XV

'COME IN.' BESSIE stood aside to let Andrina enter the lobby. 'I'm afraid Jennifer isn't here but maybe Daisy will know where she is.'

Bessie led Andrina into the kitchen where Daisy was doing her homework at the table.

'Darling, do you know where Jennifer is? Here's her mum looking for her. Do sit down, Andrina. I've a pot of tea made. I'll pour you a cup.'

Andrina smiled.

'Thank you.'

Bessie thought – what a beautiful woman! If only I looked like that the world would be my oyster. She had a sudden vision of herself in a slinky dress with a low-cut top and a slit skirt with a shapely leg teasing out, and men whistling at her. It only lasted a second.

Andrina was about the same age as herself but with full upturned breasts and straight back. No rounded shoulders there.

Daisy said, 'I thought Jennifer was at her granny's.'

'She was. Then her granny took ill. My fiancé and I have been at the hospital. But when we went out to Bearsden to collect Jennifer, she'd gone.'

Bessie poured the tea. 'She probably went home to Monteith Row.'

'No. Paul and I have been home. I've left him there in case she turns up. He said he'd phone here immediately to let me know. Can you think of anywhere else she might be, Daisy?'

Daisy shook her head. Andrina continued: 'It's really too bad of her, worrying Paul and me like this. She's always been difficult, of course. Her father's away on holiday so he can't be of any help. Not that he ever was. He was never there when I needed him.'

Bessie had a sudden urge to paint her. It was something about the full pouting lips and the unusual coloured eyes. Those eyes could be wide and childlike one minute and dark with emotion the next. She could see the smouldering background to the painting – ominous clouds with streaks of fiery red building up.

She pulled herself together and said, 'Daisy, are you sure you don't know of any place or any other friends she might be with?'

Daisy flashed her a dark look. She was still clinging to the sulk she was using to punish Bessie for going away to York and neglecting her.

'She hasn't got any other friends.'

'Has she done anything like this before?' Bessie asked Andrina.

'Oh yes. She's always disappearing off without as much as a by-your-leave. But it's usually to her granny's. What worries me is that Mrs Pemberton, my mother's neighbour, told me the last she'd seen of Jennifer was walking down Drymen Road wearing a backpack. When she wasn't home, I was sure she must be here. Apart from my mother's, this is the only place she's ever stayed overnight.'

'Oh dear.' Bessie was now worried as well. She liked Jennifer and had tried to mother the child because she always looked so lost and vulnerable and in need of a reassuring cuddle.

'Maybe you should contact the police.'

Daisy cast her a look of disgust.

'For goodness sake, Mum.'

'Well, if she's been missing all night.'

'And all day,' Andrina added.

'Oh dear. Yes, definitely, phone the police, Andrina. Poor wee Jennifer!'

'For goodness sake, Mum. She's sixteen. If she wants to go off on her own, why not?'

Bessie nearly said, 'I'm forty and you don't think I should go off on my own', but she was too distracted by visions of

Jennifer's pale unhappy face to get into an argument with Daisy. She addressed Andrina instead.

'I'll go with you to the police station.'

'I don't like to bother you.'

'It's no bother, Andrina. Honestly.'

Just then Granda came shuffling into the kitchen.

'Is my tea not ready yet? I'm sitting through there starving. I could be dead for all you care. No wonder I'm down to skin and bone . . .'

'Oh, I'd better go,' Andrina said, already backing towards the door. 'You've enough to do without me bothering you.'

'No, really, it's no — '

'I'll get Paul to take me. I should have thought of that in the first place. He'd want to go with me.'

Bessie saw her to the front door nursing murderous thoughts of Granda. There were times when she really hated the selfish old sod and this was one of them.

'I'm sorry, Andrina. If there's anything I can do to help, please don't hesitate to ask.'

Impulsively she gave Andrina a hug and she was rewarded by a smile and a wide-eyed gaze shimmering like a rainbow. Bessie felt moved by such beauty. One day, she determined, I'm going to paint her.

She'd hardly had time to return to the kitchen when Peter arrived. Peter of the sallow skin with the deep lines down each cheek into which the corners of his eyes and mouth sank down. She was sure he had ulcers because he really did suffer with his stomach at times. But would he eat the special light dishes she tried to make for him? Once in a blue moon, if she was lucky. She was so fed up trying to coax him to eat a poached egg or milky porridge for breakfast instead of the big fry-up he favoured.

'Your tea won't be a minute,' she told him. They still did things the old-fashioned Scottish way with dinner in the middle of the day and 'high tea' in the late afternoon. Usually it was a fry-up. Or fish and chips. Scones and cakes, too, and plenty of butter and jam. Occasionally during the summer she tried to get away with cold meat and salad but it always meant a hue and cry of 'Where's my chips?'

'You must have passed Andrina, Jennifer's mum, on the stairs. She was up here looking for Jennifer. The child seems to have gone missing. Isn't it awful?'

'Where's my chips?' Peter had got his eye on the cold meat and salad.

'I haven't had time to make chips. I just told you – Andrina was here. I had to stop to talk to her.'

'Your tongue never stops. And when you're not wasting your time gossiping, you're acting like a schoolkid splashing colour on bits of paper.'

She took a deep breath. Memories of the happy hours at the college flooded over her and nearly brought tears to her eyes. Only she'd never been a crying kind of person. At the college there had been such stimulating, intelligent conversation. She had never been used to such talk. Indeed she had long since had any suspicion of it mocked out of her. For years, she'd never visited an art gallery, never been caught reading anything serious. Her mind had atrophied. Her capacity for loving had shrunk back, given up, lost hope.

No, not quite. There was a stubborn bit about her. She never gave up hope altogether. As she chewed absently at her salad and chips, as Granda's and Peter's and Daisy's voices moaned on like a Greek chorus, she remembered York. She remembered Gregory, who could talk about so many interesting things with such authority. More than that he listened to her as if what she was saying was of riveting interest. Gregory looked at her with such serious concentration, it was as if she was the only person in the world.

She determined to phone him.

XVI

JENNIFER TOOK THE train to London. No one knew her there. The tannoy at Euston Station had a ghostly ring. She couldn't make out what it was saying. Allowing herself to be carried along with the people from the train, she found herself in the vast forecourt. Sound echoed hollowly round her head in a meaningless buzz. For a few minutes, she stood wondering what she'd do next, where she'd go. People brushed by, two-dimensional images flowing round her. Panic made her heart pound in her ears as the enormity of all that had happened and what she had done became a reality.

The attack by Fisher was horrific enough. Her granny's illness was horrific enough. But then her granny had been taken to hospital and Mrs Pemberton had said, 'I've phoned your mother, dear. She and her fiancé are going straight to the hospital. Then after they see your granny, they'll come and collect you and take you home.'

She couldn't go home. Not with Fisher there. She just couldn't. Sweat broke out all down her spine and she shuddered involuntarily. She had no choice but to run away. But how could she with no money? That was when the most awful thing happened. At least the thing that was causing her most anguish and guilt. She had stolen all granny's money. Granny's handbag had been lying on the kitchen chair. She'd opened it and taken all the notes from the wallet, and all the coins from the purse. About fifty pounds in all. It was like stealing from the dead. No, worse than that, because her granny had been the one person who'd loved her and been good to her for as far back as she could remember. Then, another even worse anguish made her bend forward and screw up her face with the physical pain of it.

She had been the cause of her granny taking ill. It was because her granny loved her so much that she had been shocked and distressed at what Fisher had done. Over and over again, Jennifer flayed herself for telling her granny. It had been so selfish and thoughtless. After all, Granny was an old woman. How could she have done this to her? She might even die. Mrs Pemberton had warned her to prepare for the worst. There was no doubt in Jennifer's mind that this awful stroke had been her fault. Granny had been perfectly healthy and happy until she'd arrived.

'Are you all right?'

Jennifer looked up. A man was bending over her.

Like a startled fawn she took to her heels and didn't stop running until she reached Euston Road. Heart pounding and gasping for breath, her throat raw and painful with the undue exertion, she leaned against the wall of a building across the road from the station. After a minute she glanced back and was relieved to see no sign of the man. She tried to be sensible. The fact that Fisher had attacked her didn't mean that every man was a potential attacker. Her mind told her that. Her emotions, however, were no longer governed by logical thought. She now found she was afraid of men. There was no use denying it. But then, she told herself, it had only been a day or two since the attack. Given time, she'd get over it. Yet despite how she struggled to reassure herself, she believed the fear had gone too deep. No matter how she might appear to recover, she could not imagine deep down ever being free of such terror. Even her trust in Uncle Bernard had been spoiled. He had been the first person she'd thought of going to for help. He was clever and strong and it was his job to look after people, and to protect them. She'd even got as far as his office. Then she'd begun to tremble so much she had to retreat out to the street again. She had remembered his maleness and his dark sexual eyes, and she'd become afraid. Safely away from the office, she told herself not to be so stupid and melodramatic. But it was no use.

At least she had money and could get away, pay for somewhere to stay, buy something to eat. How she got the money smashed in her skull again and she wanted to die. She found herself hitching up her backpack and starting to walk along Euston Road. She hadn't gone very far when she saw a building with a noticeboard on the wall. The word QUAKER caught her eye and she stopped to read it. Daisy's mother was a Quaker. She'd wanted to go to Daisy's house but that would be the first place her mother and Fisher would look for her. She read: 'Once we have said "Our Father" in the morning, we can treat no one as a stranger for the rest of the day.'

Jennifer felt like weeping, it meant so little to her. Behind her on the pavement hurried innumerable strangers. On the road, endless traffic thundered past. At the side of the building which proclaimed itself 'Friends House' there was a garden: on the gate it indicated that any members of the public were welcome to rest there. Jennifer went in. There were a few seats among the greenery and thankfully she took off her backpack and sat down. The garden was an oasis of peace. She must have dozed off, because all at once, it seemed, it was dark. Her wristwatch told her it wasn't all that late but she remembered her daddy telling her that it got dark quicker down south in England. The traffic had thinned out and there weren't as many people around. She wished there were more: the noise and bustle seemed safer. Despite having rested, she still felt tired. The air had a chill in it and she shivered. It occurred to her that she'd had nothing to eat for a long time so she put on her backpack and returned to the station. She bought a sandwich and a paper cup filled to the brim with boiling hot tea. It was so hot it was difficult to hold the cup. It tasted good, though. She enjoyed the sandwich too and began to feel better.

Now she needed somewhere to stay until she found a job. Fifty pounds wouldn't last for ever. She felt reluctant to leave the station. At least she could find her way around there and wouldn't get lost. Everything was signposted. It wasn't so cold as outside either, and it was dry. It had begun to rain just before she'd come in. She couldn't bring herself to venture back out into the darkness to look for a hotel or some sort of lodgings. It seemed a much more sensible idea to wait until morning. Nothing seemed so scary when it was light and there were ordinary, normal people going to their work in offices and shops. She hunkered down with her backpack clutched in front of her. At least she wouldn't look suspicious if any policeman saw her. She could be waiting for a train. Nevertheless, a policeman did eventually move her out of the station. 'Come on, you can't stay here all night,' he'd said but in quite a kindly tone. She sat outside then, in the covered area where the buses stopped during the day.

Sleep didn't come easily. She kept dozing off and waking with either a police siren screaming past, or an ambulance, or the shouts and laughter of drunken revellers. Finally there were the early deliveries to the station shops and restaurants. English accents echoed all around her, emphasising the fact that she was alone in a strange country, among strangers. Half the time she didn't understand what anyone was saying.

She floated in and out of a world in which the border between nightmare and reality had become blurred. Her physical discomfort became so acute that she was forced to move. Her thigh bones felt bruised as if the flesh had been rubbed away and there was nothing left to cushion them. Every part of her had stiffened and she cried out with the pain of straightening up. The station had come to life again. The first place she made for was the Ladies, where she relieved her bladder and washed her face and neck. As she tugged a comb through her hair, then secured it with an elastic band, she stared at herself in the mirror. Her fringe was plastered wetly to her forehead. Her eyes were dark-rimmed and brimming with apprehension. She hoped her appearance wouldn't make it difficult for her to find a job. Her unmade-up face and dusting of freckles had the look of a ten-year-old. She decided that she must buy make-up. That would make her look older.

The first thing, though, was to find a place to stay. Still reluctant to leave the station, she lingered over a cup of tea, a bowl of cornflakes and a slice of toast in the buffet. But at last she had to venture outside. The throng was even greater than the day before. She stood helplessly watching, completely overwhelmed by it, sometimes jostled by hurrying passers-by. Not long ago she'd thought Glasgow was a busy metropolis. It had been the centre of her earth, but it could not compare with this. The mere thought of Glasgow made her homesick. Only now did she begin to realise that she loved the place. She prayed that she would be able to return there one day.

Too nervous now to cross the traffic-crowded road, Jennifer kept to the side she was on. She began walking away past the station frontage and then round a corner. It didn't take her long to spot a B&B sign on a run-down-looking building. The windows were dirt-stained and covered by drooping lace curtains. Above the door it said 'Guest House'. Obviously the bin men hadn't yet been round. Boxes overflowing with refuse and piled on either side with black bin bags waited to be cleared.

Jennifer would have preferred a decent hotel in a nicer area but she suspected that a single night in a decent hotel in London could swallow up what money she had left in one go.

She rang the bell and a hard-faced woman appeared. Her blonde hair had an orangy tint and was dark and greasy at the roots. Her make-up ended in a brown line under her jaw and her neck was a mouse grey.

'I am looking for a room.' Jennifer controlled the urge to turn and run.

'Got any money?'

'Yes.'

The woman gave a jerk of her head and stood aside to allow Jennifer to enter.

Inside the shoebox of a hall there was a smell of cats and stale sweat. There were a couple of doors on the right side. On one door, a piece of cardboard indicated that it was the dining room. The other had a bell on the tinted glass and a notice that said 'Private. Ring for proprietor. In an emergency out of hours ring . . .' with a telephone number. It wasn't until later that Jennifer realised that Mrs Phillpot, the landlady, did not live on the premises. Payment was asked in advance before Jennifer was even shown the room. Not knowing if this was normal practice or not, she didn't argue. Her heart sank when she saw where the woman led her. It was a tiny attic, three flights up with a sloping ceiling. The floor was covered with brown linoleum, much worn and holed in places. The only other articles in the room apart from the bed were a small chest of drawers and one spar-backed chair. Still, it was a roof over her head and the bed looked clean.

The problem that really worried her was that she did not have enough money for more than perhaps a couple of nights. It was now a matter of urgency that she find a job. She asked Mrs Phillpot if it would be all right to leave her backpack in the room while she went to look for a job and Mrs Phillpot agreed. Despite her hard eyes, she seemed a very easygoing sort of person.

Back outside Jennifer took special note of the street so that she would be able to find it again. Its proximity to the station would help, of course. There could be no better landmark. She began wandering from street to street. Every time she came across a café or restaurant she plucked up the courage to go in and ask for work. Waitressing, washing dishes, scrubbing floors. Anything. They just took one look at her and shook their heads. One woman said, 'Run away from home, have you?'

Jennifer blushed guiltily and the woman said, 'Take my advice, love. Get on the next train back to Scotland.'

But apart from anything else she no longer had enough money to get back to Scotland. It was frightening how quickly money disappeared. All she'd had was a couple of cups of tea and a pizza all day, and she had taken a bus at one point. Her feet were killing her. In Oxford Street she asked for work in innumerable shops, again without any luck. One of the problems was that she had neither training nor experience. She spent money on some cheap make-up in an effort to make herself look older. All to no avail. By the time she returned to the guest-house, she was exhausted and sick with worry.

'No luck?' Mrs Phillpot asked.

Miserably Jennifer shook her head.

'Have you been to the DHSS?'

'No.'

'You'd better.' The landlady scribbled an address on a piece of paper and handed it to Jennifer.

Jennifer was profuse in her thanks. It really was very kind of the woman. She felt cheered and went to bed thinking that tomorrow was another day. Everything would be OK tomorrow. Before she could get to sleep, however, she lay listening to the night noises of the house, the creaks and groans, the muttered voices, the padding feet.

Outside distant traffic rumbled and every now and again the siren of a police car or an ambulance wailed louder and louder, then receded. She was just dropping off to sleep when she heard footsteps outside her door. Suddenly remembering that there was no lock, she sprang out of bed, grabbed the chair and wedged it underneath the door handle. She could hardly breathe, her heart was beating so fast in her chest and throat. She remained standing, tightly gripping the chair, shivering in her pyjamas, bare feet sticking to the linoleum. She could hear breathing at the other side of the door.

No more sleep.

XVII

HISTORICALLY, BETWEEN LOS Angeles law enforcement and private security, there existed a snob element. Police officers looked down their noses at security people. They regarded them as not very bright, people who couldn't do anything in life. John Hudson, chief of security at Paramount Studios, had more of an open mind although he was an ex-police officer. A calm, intelligent-looking man, with sandy brown hair and thoughtful grey eyes, he could sit perfectly relaxed behind his desk, hands loosely clasped in front of him, and make you feel he was listening with keen interest to every word you uttered. He gave the impression of a man who had all the time in the world to devote to you. He was, as it happened, extremely busy but he was well organised. Everybody from outside the studios, and often inside too, who came to see him was given the length of time for the interview beforehand from his secretary. After the allocated time span had passed, one of his security men or his secretary would come and remind him of another appointment. Or he would glance at his watch, rise, stick out his big hand and say, with what anyone would swear to be totally sincerity, how he'd enjoyed the meeting.

Like most men in his profession he was fit and had a good physique, although he was not young. He had been with the LA police department for twenty-seven years and retired as captain in charge of training for the department.

The boss at Paramount Pictures liked his police connection, especially as Paramount was in the middle of LA police department. This was why the president of Paramount had offered Hudson the job. There had been no regrets on either side.

'I make all private security people check their guns,' he told

Bernard. 'The exception was when we had the President here. Secret Service came then and I allowed one or two of their guys to carry a gun.'

Bernard wasn't thrilled with the idea of him and his men being unarmed and he said so. 'Look, I don't need to tell you that there's some crazy people around, John. Miss Page has already had a couple of phone calls and letters from some nutcase.'

'I don't want guns on the lot,' Hudson repeated patiently. 'My people are not armed. Look, Bernard, I want her safety as much as you. I don't want anything to happen at Paramount. But if I didn't lay down ground rules here, there would be bodyguards coming in with Uzis. Some guys tend to see an assassin behind every bush and they get trigger happy.'

Bernard grinned.

'No Uzis. I promise.'

'OK, OK. You can carry a gun, but only you. Not any of your men.'

'Fair enough.'

'And don't worry. I'll have plenty of my uniformed guys around. As I said – I don't want anything to happen any more than you do.'

Afterwards they went to the cafeteria, where Bernard met some of Hudson's men. One of them, with a neck like a tree trunk and shoulders a couple of monkeys could have perched on, came swaggering up to Bernard and said, 'I hear you're *the* karate expert in your country.'

Bernard laughed.

'I wouldn't go as far as that.'

'That's what I heard. And you're *the* expert in Atemi.'

There was a challenge in the man's tone and Bernard thought, You're thick in the head as well as on the neck. But he kept a smile on his face and said, 'So?'

'So try me.'

'Try you?'

'Try to put me down with a pressure point. Any one of them. You won't be able to. I've had a Japanese master try with me and fail.'

'Great,' Bernard said, 'but I'd rather just get on with my beefburger.'

'Leave it, Earl,' Hudson told the man. 'You don't need to prove yourself. We all know how good you are. Let the guy get on with his meal.'

'I just want him to try me. It won't take a second.'

'Forget it,' Bernard said, already eating the beefburger. Earl seemed to take his enjoyment as a personal slight.

'So you're not so tough, eh?'

'That's right,' Bernard said, helping himself to more tomato sauce.

'All I'm asking you to do is try one pressure point, for Christ's sake.'

Bernard looked over at Hudson, who gave him a barely perceptible nod and a wink.

'OK.' Bernard rose. 'Grab my right wrist as hard as you can.'

Earl got a grip of Bernard's wrist.

'Hard as you can,' Bernard repeated and Earl grimaced with concentration.

'OK now,' Bernard said. 'Shut your eyes.'

Earl squeezed his eyes shut and no sooner had he done so than Bernard's left fist belted round and smashed into the side of Earl's chin. Earl went down like a log and lay prostrate beside the table.

Hudson laughed.

'Yeah, there's nothing to beat that pressure point on the chin. I've used it many a time myself.'

In a moment or two Earl regained consciousness and struggled to his feet.

'Christ, that was great,' he said. 'How did you do that? I don't know what happened, but I've got to give it to you.' He stuck out his hand. 'Put it there, buddy.'

They gave each other a hearty handshake.

'Great,' Earl repeated before swaggering off.

'Sorry about that,' Hudson said. 'Earl's a good guy. One hundred per cent conscientious. He lives for the job and keeping himself one hundred per cent fit for it. If he's around the movie lot where your principal's working, you can rest easy.'

Bernard didn't feel so sure.

XVIII

'I KNOW WHAT she's like and yes, I know the trouble and worry she's caused us but she's still my child.' Andrina gazed appealingly across at Paul Fisher, who was intent on donning his tailored jacket, straightening his bow-tie and smoothing back his hair. 'Try to understand, darling. Something terrible might have happened to her.'

'There's people go missing every day. They usually turn up sooner or later.'

'Usually, but not always. If I just knew where she was. If I just could be sure she was all right. My mother keeps asking. Every time I go in to see her she goes on and on. It's beginning to get me down. It's not easy to look at Mummy's face all twisted like that either.'

Fisher made a close-up check of his moustache in the mirror.

'It would have been better if the stroke had killed her.'

'Don't say that, Paul. Sometimes you can be so cruel.'

'Not cruel, just honest. You've thought that yourself, I'm sure. Especially the state she's in now.'

'She's my mother.'

Satisfied with his appearance, he turned to Andrina.

'I know she's your mother but as far as I've heard – from you, don't forget – she's the one who's been cruel.'

'Oh, that was long ago. When I was a child. Before she was "saved". Now, poor soul, she's like a child herself and it's not doing her any good pining for Jennifer. My first loyalty is to you, darling. But you of all people should understand.'

'I do understand.'

'I'm talking about your loyalty and devotion to your wife.'

'Andrina, I'm here living with you now, three or four days out of every seven.'

'Have you told her yet?'

'She must know. She's not stupid.'

'But have you *told* her, Paul?'

'Not in so many words.'

'What on earth does she think you are doing through in Glasgow so much?'

'The casino. She knows I work till all hours. It's more sensible that I stay here. I used to try to persuade her to come to live in Glasgow. I offered to buy her the best house I could find in the best district. I've never spared her anything. But she's Edinburgh born and bred and all her relatives are through there. The climate's not so damp on the east coast. Glasgow makes her arthritis a hundred times worse, she says.'

'I don't know why you worry so. If the pair of you were divorced, she wouldn't be on her own. She'd have her children and all her relatives to comfort and help her. In my mother's case, I'm all she's got.'

'And she's damn lucky she's got you after the way she's treated you.'

She rewarded him with another kiss. She loved to see him in the casino. Someone obviously in charge, in his smart dinner suit, his expensive haircut, his neatly manicured hands. Once they were married she would be sure of his devotion and loyalty.

She would make sure too that he never strayed again. He swore that he had never been unfaithful to his wife before he'd met Andrina, and Andrina believed him. That was the kind of man she wanted for a husband. Robert had been so unglamorous and such a bore. Bernard was far too randy to be trusted. Any glamour that had surrounded Bernard had been dangerous, even life-threatening. It had never been the kind of life she'd wanted anything to do with. He'd mixed in a terrifying world of gangsters and criminals in the clubs and pubs of the city.

No, she was far better with Paul. At her age especially. She wasn't a teenager any more. She slid on to Paul's knee and kissed him more deeply. She felt him begin to tremble. But as he caressed her, and they had sex, she kept thinking of Bernard.

Then she remembered Jennifer again. Her mind strained, trying to imagine where she might have gone. Then, with images and sensations of Bernard still fresh in her mind, she recalled that he'd had contact with Jennifer not that long ago. Hadn't he been getting her involved with some pop group or another?

Her heart began to race with anger and concern. She'd kill him if she discovered that he was the cause of all this upset and worry. Or if he'd done the child any harm. Her first impulse was to tell Paul. Then she thought better of it. Paul had only met Bernard for a few fleeting seconds but he hadn't liked him.

He'd better not have had anything to do with Jennifer's disappearance. How dare he upset me and worry me like this? she thought angrily.

As soon as Paul had gone she dressed, hurried from the house and took a taxi to Bernard's office. It was only after she'd climbed the stairs and opened the door marked CPS – Close Protection & Security – that her courage began to desert her.

One man was perched on the edge of the nearest desk. Big and broad-shouldered, he had a cropped head and wore a black patch over one eye. The way he was staring at her made Andrina feel nervous.

The bespectacled young woman at the desk said, 'Can I help you?'

'I'd like to speak to Mr O'Maley, please.'

'Bernard O'Maley?'

How many O'Maleys were there? Andrina thought irritably. Bernard had three brothers, but as far as she knew, none of them were in the security business.

'Yes, Bernard O'Maley.'

'I'm afraid he's in America at the moment. He won't be back in Glasgow for another few weeks. But perhaps I can help . . .'

'No, I don't think so.' On second thoughts – just in case – she said, 'Actually it's about my daughter, Jennifer. I'm terribly worried about her. She's gone missing. I know Bernard saw her not that long ago . . .'

'Oh yes, it was me who arranged for her to meet the

Who Dunnits. Jennifer and her friend Daisy. Nice girls. Daisy especially was in seventh heaven about meeting the group.'

'Have you seen her since? Jennifer, I mean?'

'No. I'm sorry. Have you reported her missing to the police?'

'Yes, of course, but they haven't been very helpful. Oh, I suppose they do their best but apparently there's so many missing persons on their books.'

'I could give you the name and number of a good detective agency. We don't do that kind of work as a rule. Although if Bernard was here he might do something because Jennifer's a relation. She called him uncle, I remember.'

'No, he's not a relation. He was a friend of Robert, my ex-husband . . .'

The man with the eye-patch spoke up.

'You must be Andrina Anderson.'

'Yes.' Andrina gave him a puzzled look. He put out a hand.

'I'm Michael, Bernard's twin brother.'

'Gosh.' Andrina couldn't contain her astonishment. He looked so unlike Bernard, except perhaps for the build.

He laughed.

'I know. I know. He's the one with all the good looks. I'm the ugly one.'

'No, I . . .' Andrina flushed with embarrassment. 'You'll have to forgive me, Michael. I'm so worried about my daughter I hardly know what I'm saying or doing.'

'I know exactly how you feel.' His broken-nosed face became serious.

'What do you mean?'

'My son and daughter have joined Bernard's firm. They're only eighteen, just kids, and they're over in America just now getting into all sorts of dangerous situations for all I know. I came up here to find out if there was any news of them. The wife and I have had no letters, nothing, not even a postcard to let us know if they arrived safely. The twins didn't leave us an address. You'd think it was the secret service they'd joined.'

The woman said, 'Trust me, Michael. Bernard and the twins are OK.'

'I know Bernard'll be OK. He's got the luck of the Irish

and he's an old hand at this. But my children . . . Bernard's my brother and I love him but I feel like killing him at times.'

Andrina's attention had returned to the girl at the desk.

'He didn't take Jennifer with him, did he? Surely he couldn't have . . .'

'Of course not,' the girl said. 'Bernard was reluctant enough to allow the twins to go. He thought *they* were too young. No, no, Mrs Anderson. You can definitely put that out of your mind.'

Andrina sighed.

'I'm sorry to have troubled you.'

'As I said earlier, I could . . .' the girl began but Andrina was already opening the door on her way out.

Michael followed her.

'Can I give you a lift home?' he asked. 'My car's outside.'

Andrina smiled and fluttered her eyelashes at him.

'Thank you. That would be very kind. My own car's out of commission at the moment.'

XIX

'HERE, YOU'LL NEVER guess who I've been with!' Michael burst into the cottage. Caroline and Big Martha were sitting in front of a crackling log fire. A shaggy red rug accentuated the warmth and the firelight flickered across the varnished wood floor and cast dancing shadows up to the beamed ceiling. It was still September but the weather had turned chilly and Big Martha's blood had become thin.

'The twins?' Caroline and her mother cried out eagerly. He hated to disappoint them. Some of his excitement siphoned off.

'No, of course not. They're miles away, worse luck.'

Caroline's attention returned to her knitting. 'So they couldn't help at the office?' she asked.

'It's maddening. Because neither Bernard nor the twins gave us an address or phone number, the office are afraid to give one. I told them what harm could it do knowing where they were, for God's sake. But at least they've promised to get in touch and tell the twins to phone us.'

'Thank goodness for small mercies. Now maybe I'll get the chance to ask them about everything, including exactly when they'll get back.'

'Yes, they're fine. The girl assured me of that. We've to stop worrying, she said.'

Martha was dozing in her rocking chair but listening at the same time. At seventy-three she wasn't nearly such a thorn in Michael's flesh as she used to be. He had grown quite fond of her despite the fact that she was like a mountain to push around in her wheelchair and she still had an awful tongue in her head. He called her his sparring partner and she called him a flat-faced, one-eyed monster. 'Well, who have you been with?' the old woman asked. Trust her not to miss a thing.

'Andrina Anderson.'

Caroline looked puzzled.

'Who's Andrina Anderson?'

'Does Robert Anderson ring a bell?' Michael asked.

Silence for a long moment. Then Martha said, 'Is he the one who used to be Bernard's teacher?' She turned to Caroline: 'Bernard's talked about him. Remember when the twins asked him how he learned karate, he told them about his old teacher who ran a karate club. You don't, do you? You're only a girl and your mind's like a sieve.'

Caroline laughed and rested her knitting on her lap.

'Hardly a girl, Mammy.'

'Anyway,' Michael pressed on, 'Andrina is – or rather was – Robert's wife.'

'So?' Martha asked.

'Remember Bernard was married to Doris, then Jane.' Suddenly it came back to him. Years ago he'd made the mistake of mentioning to Caroline he'd seen Bernard with a woman, first in a car, then going into a cottage. This very cottage had been their love nest. Caroline had told Jane. The result was that Jane had thrown Bernard out and eventually divorced him. He'd regretted telling Caroline and already he was regretting saying anything now. The trouble was that he and Caroline were so close they just naturally told each other everything. But still . . .

'Well then . . .' both Martha and Caroline urged impatiently, 'what about it?'

'Listen, Caroline, and you too, Ma' – although he realised that old Martha wasn't that daft – 'you must promise to keep this strictly between ourselves.'

'What, for Christ's sake?' Martha shouted at him. 'Will you spit it out?'

'Mammy! What have I always told you about using bad language!'

'Oh, shut up,' her mother said.

Michael raised a conciliatory hand.

'OK. OK. Remember why both Doris and Jane got a divorce?'

'Now look, Michael,' Caroline said gently, 'I know Bernard has his faults. I know he's a bit too popular with women at times but he can't help being such a good-looking man. It's not his fault that women chase after him.'

'My God!' Michael groaned, 'if Bernard committed murder, you'd try and make out it was the bloody victim's fault.'

'Now, don't you start . . .'

'Well, you'd make anybody swear the way you go on about him.'

Martha hooted derisively.

'He's jealous, and no wonder when he's stuck with an ugly mug like that.'

'You're no raving beauty yourself, Ma.'

Caroline tutted.

'Stop it, you two. And just you remember, Michael. Bernard has been good to us.'

'How could I ever forget it?'

'All right,' Martha said, 'we remember how Bernard had a fancy woman. Here . . .' A light dawned in Martha's rheumy eyes. She never missed a trick, that ould woman. 'Are you trying to tell us it was that Andrina Anderson?'

'The very one,' Michael said. 'She came into the office while I was there. I knew right away she looked familiar.'

'It must be more than ten years ago.' Caroline sounded doubtful.

'Listen, pet, if you'd seen her, you'd know why I remembered. She's an absolute stunner.'

'Here,' Martha was wide awake now, 'she was friendly with his second wife. Don't tell me she was pals with his first as well.'

'Must have been. He and Doris used to visit her and Robert. Then, after he married Jane, he and Jane used to visit them. Best of buddies they all were.'

'And neither of the two wives ever twigged?'

'Oh!' Caroline gasped, 'what a wicked, deceitful woman. I've never heard the like of it!'

'I could hardly credit it myself. He must have known Andrina for years – off and on. More on than off, I'd say.'

'That woman must have cast a spell on Bernard. There's a soft bit about him.'

'What?' Michael's voice screeched up two octaves. 'Bernard? Caroline, now you're being ridiculous.'

'With women, I mean. He must be, to get himself entangled like that.'

Michael remembered how, long before Bernard had got himself married, his brother had been indifferent to girls who tried their damnedest to entangle him. He had some sort of charisma – probably sexual – that females went for. If he knew Bernard, it would have been him that took the initiative with Andrina. If Bernard wanted something he never gave up until he got it, and Andrina Anderson was a very desirable woman.

Caroline said: 'Fancy causing all that unhappiness, breaking up two marriages. It's really wicked. A woman like that ought to be punished. She shouldn't be allowed to get away with it.'

'Now, Caroline, I warned you. All that's in the past and it's none of our business. It never does any good to meddle in other people's affairs.'

He hoped she'd take the hint and remember her part in causing Bernard's divorce. Admittedly she'd had a couple of glasses of whisky at his other sister-in-law's funeral at the time. He accepted Caroline's story that it had been the whisky and the upset at poor Theresa's death that had loosened her tongue. But telling Jane, for whatever reason, had certainly not done Bernard's marriage any good.

'I'm only saying . . .'

'As long as you don't say it to either Doris or Jane.'

Martha piped up then.

'What are you blethering about? Do you think either of them are likely to drop in here while they're passing on their way to a climb up the Campsies?'

'Aye, OK, Ma. I'm just saying.'

What he didn't say was that Bernard had become friendly with Jane again over the years. Perhaps he'd already told Caroline that, or Bernard had. He couldn't remember. But surely even Bernard would never have the gall, the brass neck, to bring Jane to the cottage where he'd had his fling with Andrina. No, definitely not, Michael assured himself. And there was no other way that either Doris or Jane was likely to meet up with Caroline. Not that Caroline would purposely . . .

'They'd batter the shit out of her if they found out, and serve her right,' Martha said.

'Mammy!'

'Well, wouldn't they?'

'Yes, they would,' Michael agreed. 'I wouldn't be surprised if they resorted to murder. That's why I hope to God they never do find out.'

'Are they still friendly with her?' Caroline was obviously intrigued.

'Yes. Bernard's said that Jane was still the best of friends with Robert's ex-wife. It was one of the times he was telling me how sorry he was that he'd lost touch with Robert. I'm not sure about Doris but I wouldn't be a bit surprised if she's still pals with Andrina as well. Could you beat it?'

They couldn't.

XX

To Bessie the quiet backwater of the small gallery in Parnie Street had the hushed atmosphere of a church with its deep pile carpet and oak panelling half-way up the walls. Only a few minutes' walk away and parallel to the street was the busy Glasgow Cross, the oldest part of Glasgow. In Parnie Street, more traditional paintings were exhibited. In Gregory's equally small but brighter West Campbell Street gallery, modern works had pride of place. Here the walls were painted a stark white and the floors were uncovered wood that made feet clang and echo. Bessie had gone to West Campbell Street in the hope of seeing Gregory. She regularly dreamed of him now, as the only water in the desert of her life. Even if the water was only a mirage, it was better than nothing. A sparkle of hope.

He had been his usual charming self since the York débâcle, yet she detected a subtle coolness about him. Well, not so subtle really. Before York, he'd flirted with her at every opportunity. He'd come up behind her while she was admiring a picture and slip an arm around her waist. Or he'd tickle her ribs and make her giggle and squirm away. Sometimes he touched her hair and told her how pretty it looked, so soft, so honey-coloured. She giggled and blushed as if she was sweet sixteen.

Now he was polite. He even offered her a cup of coffee. But he was not in the least flirtatious. He seemed shut into himself, although he still paid her the compliment of listening intently to every word she uttered. She thought him a true gentleman in every sense of the word, and with such an impressive appearance. Gregory would always stand out in a crowd and have admiring glances from every woman, married or unmarried, stealing towards him. He said it was nice to see her again and invited her to call in any time.

She starting taking the flirting initiative. Only in the mildest, most tentative way. An occasional flutter of the old lashes, a gazing up with widened eyes, a sidling nearer than was necessary when she spoke to Gregory. Anyone seeing her would think either he'd gone deaf, or she'd gone daft. The latter, of course, she was forever telling herself, was the truth. What on earth did she think she was doing? Alone in her saner moments she'd try to think things through. If he responded, then what? Could she – as the saying went – go the whole hog? And him a married man to boot. To boot? In the middle of her other wonderings, she wondered what these expressions actually meant. Where and how had they originated? Anyway, she knew what she meant.

Every time she imagined going the whole hog she took fright. In one way she wanted to. In another – well, actually, in two other ways – she didn't know how she could. One of the two negatives – three actually, when she counted Isa – was how she would look to Gregory, stripped of her Wonderbra and her panties that concealed the stretch marks. She lived through and suffered this scenario a thousand humiliating times, as she bent over the sink peeling potatoes or washing dishes. Or while she cooked the meals, or did the ironing, or scrubbed the kitchen floor. Scrubbing the floor made her knees dark red, not a pretty sight either. Even struggling along the street weighed down with bags of shopping she could still see Gregory's disgusted expression at the sight of her naked body. In the middle of Sauchiehall Street she would groan, sometimes out loud, at the shame of him turning away from her. She couldn't imagine herself ever being able to face such a dreadful situation. She'd had to face so many humiliations in reality, she'd run right out of courage.

The other stumbling block was her membership of the Society of Friends. That didn't cover being *too* friendly. She went through every word of the *Advices and Queries*, and even the *Christian Faith and Practice*, searching for a loophole.

'. . . are you sufficiently conversant with our Christian discipline,' she read, 'to be able, when difficult questions arise, to consider them with an informed mind as well as a loving and tender spirit?'

Well, she was considering the question all right, and trying her best to do so with an informed mind. And she was loving. The trouble, she decided, came from the fact that she was loving in the wrong kind of way.

But there it was. There *she* was. In her desert and with such a thirst in her. It was fortunate in a way that she had other even more urgent matters to take up her time and attention. Granda was really going beyond the score. There was another one. Beyond the score? Life was full of questions. Granda was worrying her to death. Sometimes he acted so crazy she had quite a struggle to hang on to her own sanity.

He would keep speaking to people who weren't there. Weren't alive. She'd hear him chatting away, or shouting angrily, at his long-dead mother or father. He was a bit deaf and always shouted even when he was just asking what time it was. He'd talk to a customer about his account. At times she could swear there really *was* somebody in the bedroom with him. She'd knock on the door and go in, and there Granda would be, propped up in bed or sitting on his saggy armchair by the bedroom fire talking to himself. It could be quite eerie, especially in the middle of the night when the rest of the house, the rest of the world it seemed, was dark and silent. Sometimes it was as if she and Granda were alone in the universe. She was so tired at times she too became disorientated. She would go into the kitchen for something, and for the life of her couldn't think what she'd come for. She'd find herself in the kitchen, or any place for that matter, and have no memory of *how* she got there, never mind why. She was getting depressed more often too. After a terrible night with Granda, and only an hour or two's sleep, she'd stagger from bed and just stand in the middle of the room – like an idiot, Peter said – with a completely blank mind. She's stand for ages like that unable to puzzle out what to wear, even *how* to get dressed. It took all her willpower and determination – and she'd decided she had an incredible amount of willpower and determination – to get started, and to plod her way through another day.

Peter insisted that, as far as Granda was concerned, it was just old age. Peter of course slept the whole night through without moving a muscle. So deeply still and peaceful did he look that sometimes she thought he was dead. Occasionally she shook him awake to make sure he was all right. A couple of times it was because she was so desperate for help with Granda. He'd been furious. Admittedly by the time he'd stomped through to Granda's bedroom, Granda was sound asleep and snoring. It wasn't the only time she'd wished them both dead. Only for a second, and she didn't really mean it. That's what she told God anyway.

Peter said it was her that was going off her head. Even though he'd seen Granda behaving very strangely during the day. Only occasionally though, and at weekends. Peter was at the office every day during the week.

'You'll be old yourself some day, don't forget,' Peter told her.

She felt ancient already.

It had become too much of an effort to go to the gallery. Still, tired or not, she always managed to climb up to the loft and cling to the altar of her easel.

Life was funny. Funny meaning queer, odd, contrary. Just when she'd given up all thoughts, even dreams about Gregory, he contacted her. Phoned her out of the blue. And not with his cool, dignified, huffy voice either. He sounded sad, rather pathetic really. He had missed her. Dreadfully.

They were on the phone for a long time. At last he persuaded her to come to the West Campbell Street gallery next morning for a cup of coffee.

'It would do my heart good to see you again,' he said.

It didn't do her heart any good. She suddenly realised she'd been letting herself go. She'd never shampooed her hair for nearly a fortnight. Her make-up purse was empty. Not that she ever wore much make-up at the best of times. She used to think she'd quite a good skin until Peter said a ghost would look brighter. She did have a somewhat drained appearance. With an effort she stirred herself and plodded out to the shops again. This time to buy an expensive Estée Lauder face powder, lipstick, rouge and even mascara. She felt she'd 'gone the whole hog'. Excitement gave a bounce to her step.

XXI

NO LUCK AT the DHSS. For a start they asked too many questions and that made Jennifer nervous. She couldn't give the address of the guest-house. She was too frightened to stay there another night. She told the DHSS woman that she had just arrived and hadn't booked into any place yet. The woman asked where she came from. She said Glasgow but gave no specific area. Even having mentioned Glasgow was worrying. What if her mother had reported her missing and the police traced her? Then Fisher would come for her. The DHSS woman asked why she'd left home. She couldn't bring herself to tell the truth. Who would believe her? Her mother hadn't. Already the DHSS woman's eyes were hard with suspicion and disbelief. She looked that way at everybody but Jennifer didn't know that. She made up a story about her mother not wanting her at home any more. Which was true up to a point. Since Fisher had come on the scene she was just in the way.

The woman said to come back with her address so that the DHSS could get in touch to let her know if she was entitled to anything. It could take several weeks, she warned, before any decision was made.

Jennifer left the DHSS office without hope. She trailed the streets again looking for work, again without the slightest success. There were too many people after too few jobs, and she didn't look nearly as clean and as well turned out as most other applicants. She longed for a hot bath and a change of clothes, especially underwear. This morning she'd changed into the spare panties and bra she'd been carrying in her backpack. Now they felt sticky and dusty.

Utterly worn out, she decided she'd simply have to book in

at one of the many small hotels she'd seen, even if it took her last penny. She ended up in one near the British Museum, in a street of Georgian terraced houses. Nearly all of them had been converted into hotels, mostly of two houses made into one while preserving the elegant outside façade. It was sheer bliss to get into a decent room with a bathroom attached. There were even tea-making facilities, including sachets not only of tea, but of coffee and drinking chocolate and sugar and miniature tubs of milk, and even some biscuits. After washing her hair and soaking for ages in a hot bath, she drank two cups of chocolate and ate all the biscuits. Her feet still throbbed but apart from that she felt wonderful. At the back of her mind, though, and at the pit of her stomach, fear and apprehension still wisped about. She tried not to think of what would happen next day. She'd seen the hotel tariff and calculated that bed and breakfast would take all but fifty-six pence of her money.

Fifty-six pence would probably not even buy her a fish supper. A couple of cups of coffee if she was lucky and that would be it. And nowhere to sleep. Her heart fluttered at the thought. She must banish it from her mind, she told herself. She must concentrate on appreciating this blissful night in this beautiful warm room. It even had a television set. She undressed, washed her underwear and her T-shirt, and hung everything over the radiator to dry. Then she lay in bed feeling clean and cosy and safe. She enjoyed watching television programmes as if she'd never watched them before. She could have stayed in that room for ever.

Morning came too soon. She had another bath. She dressed slowly, then sat at the dressing-table mirror combing her hair and trimming her fringe with her nail scissors. She was ravenously hungry and looked forward to eating a good breakfast downstairs in the dining room. But she wanted to delay the time when she would have to leave the sanctuary of the hotel. It seemed incredible that she would have to walk the streets again.

She ate as much as she could at breakfast and lingered as long as possible over a cup of tea. Eventually there was nothing for it but to pay her bill and leave. Once outside she berated herself for spending so much money. It had been a crazy thing to do. Now what? She no longer believed there was any chance of finding a job. Oh, she tried. And kept trying. For several long hours, she wandered this way and that. It had already dawned on her how enormous London was. She'd never given the capital city much thought in the past. If she had, she'd vaguely taken for granted it was something like Glasgow. Bigger, of course, but not *that* much bigger. There seemed no end to it. And no one seemed in the least friendly. No one smiled at you. No one chatted at bus stops and exchanged comments about the weather or the latest news. No one launched into their life's history. No one cared.

She'd tried to ask a woman for directions to the nearest railway station and all she got was a dirty look.

She'd been hoping to go to the toilet there, and shelter from the rain. If you'd asked a woman in Glasgow to direct you to any place at all, she would have directed you. The chances were she might have *taken* you to the place,

If Jennifer had never known homesickness before, she knew it now. She could have wept. London was too big for her. Far too big. It was getting dark and it had begun to rain. Water straggled her hair and trickled down her face and neck. She didn't know where she was. Too weary now to go any further, she sat down in a shop doorway and hugged her backpack in front of her. She laid her head down on it and allowed the tears to flow. Completely drained, she sank into sleep.

'Shove along, hen!'

Jennifer awoke in confusion. She thought she heard a Glasgow voice. Sure enough, a woman was bending over her.

'This is ma skipper, hen, but ah don't mind sharing. Just shove along a bit.'

'You're from Glasgow.' Jennifer uttered the words like a hallelujah.

'Aye. You as well?'

'Yes.'

'A posher bit, ah'll bet.'

'Not really. Monteith Row.'

'Oh aye. At the Green. It used to be posh but it's gone right downhill. What's your name, hen?'

'Jennifer.' She was wide awake now and wondering if it had been wise to give her address. But the woman was obviously homeless like herself. What harm could she do?

'I'm from Anderson, the other side of the Clyde,' the woman said. 'Here, that sounds like the line of a song.' She burst into a parody of a drunk's slurred singing, 'the other side of the Clyde.'

Jennifer began to feel nervous, wondering if she was drunk.

'Bev's the name,' the woman said. 'Short for Beverley but I've never been called that. Just Bev.'

Bev had two plastic carrier bags and from one of them she was pulling a ragged blanket, a pair of men's socks and a headsquare. She tugged the socks on over her shoes. Then she produced a piece of cardboard and slid it underneath her bottom.

'Aren't you going to take your shoes off?' Jennifer asked.

'Not on your nelly. I've had a good pair of shoes pinched off my feet as I slept. Pinched off my bloody feet. Now I make it as difficult as I can for the thieving bastards. I tie a piece of string round my feet as well.' This she proceeded to do.

'The place is hotching with thieves. Present company excepted, of course. You look a decent wee lassie. Run away from home, have you?'

Jennifer nodded.

'Let me guess,' Bev said, settling down beside Jennifer and tucking the blanket around her thin legs. 'What they call a broken home. Meaning your mammy's got a new man and he's a fucker? Could be the other way around, of course. I've known folk that their daddy's brought a girlfriend and she's made him choose. Her or me. Sometimes it's young lads who've been chucked out. There's plenty of young lads around who've been abused. Lads or lassies, the problem's usually a fucker.'

'He tried to have sex with me and my mother didn't believe it.'

'What did I tell you? Even if your mammy did believe you, she'd think it was your fault. Funny that, isn't it.'

'I'm frightened to go back home. But I wish I was back in Glasgow all the same.'

'That makes two of us, hen.'

'Why did you leave?'

Bev fished a packet of cigarettes and a box of matches from her other carrier bag and offered Jennifer a cigarette. Jennifer shook her head.

'Huh! You'll be glad of a smoke yet, hen. It takes the edge off of your hunger. You'll see. Anyway . . .' Bev lit up and inhaled deeply. 'I came here to escape a man – more than one. I'm hell of an unlucky with boyfriends. One after the other, they just take one look at me and think I'm a punchbag. Maybe it's my big boobs.'

'They hit you?' Jennifer sounded incredulous.

'Battered the living daylights out of me, hen.'

'That's terrible!'

'Usually when they were drunk, right enough. But what the hell, drunk or sober, it doesn't hurt any less. By God, when I think of it . . .' She took another long drag at her cigarette.

'I couldn't stay with anyone like that. Once would be enough for me.'

'All very well to talk, hen, but where do you go with a black eye and a burst mouth? No cash either. And you're loath to give up your nice wee house. It was rented but it was in his name, you see. You talk about being frightened? Well, I was frightened all right. Frightened for him coming in drunk. That was Jimmy Rossy, the one before last. I started taking a drink myself to try and give myself a wee bit courage.'

'Had you no family to help you?'

'Naw. They're dead and gone donkey's years ago.' She laughed. 'I might not look it, but I'm a year or two older than you, hen.'

In fact she looked old enough to be Jennifer's mother. In her late thirties, Jennifer guessed, but still a good-looking woman with her corn-coloured hair and blue eyes. Despite her too big sweater and faded denims it was obvious that she had a shapely figure.

'The trouble was,' she went on, 'that wee drink grew into quite a few wee drinks. Then one day he threw me down the stairs and I broke my arm and after I came out of hospital I was far too terrified to go back so I slept in the park.'

'Glasgow Green?'

'Hell, no. I haven't sunk that low yet. No, I always slept under the bushes in Kelvingrove Park in the West End. You met a really good crowd there.'

'Under the bushes?' Jennifer echoed incredulously.

'There was a bit of the park called Skid Row. OK, we were all drunks but we helped one another.'

'But why did you leave Glasgow?'

'I'm telling you. I thought Jimmy Rossy was bad. But that was before I met Gus McCabe. I'd pulled myself together, got a job as a waitress, hadn't touched a drink for months and then I met Gus. The perfect gent he was. Or so daftie here thought. He'd come to my table and order a meal, nice as you like, and leave me a great tip. Eventually he asked me out and soon I'd moved in with him. I'm telling you, hen, I thought my ship had come in. He came from a good family, that man, and he'd this lovely flat in Byres Road.'

'Don't tell me he started hitting you?' Jennifer was so horrified and fascinated with Bev's life story that she had forgotten how soaked she was and how miserable and shivery she felt.

'Hen, you couldn't imagine what this guy was like. He was evil. Do you know what finished me off with him?'

'What?'

'He poured hot oil down me.'

'Oh no!' Jennifer screwed up her face in sympathy.

'Aye. All down my chest. I was in agony. There I was in the hospital again. I was on first-name terms with all the doctors and nurses in Casualty by this time. I'm telling you, I had to get *right* away, *far* away from that nutcase. I'd started drinking again, of course, and I knew I'd never get off the bottle if I stayed with him. He had me crying, hen, and I don't cry easily. Oh, see that man. A real nutcase, so he was.'

They were both silent for a few minutes. Then Jennifer said, 'How do you manage to live down here? Even just to get enough money to eat? I've spent all my money already. I've been to the DHSS. They said they'd let me know what they decide about my case.'

Bev laughed.

'Want to know what they'll decide? They'll decide you're not entitled to a penny because you've made yourself homeless. You left your home voluntarily. That's what they told me. Of course, I gave them a false name and address. I was that scared of Gus McCabe finding me. I'm still scared of that. He'll never give up trying to find me. Once he gets an idea into that twisted brain of his . . .'

'He'll probably have forgotten all about you and be living with somebody else.'

'I keep trying to tell myself that and oh, I'd love to believe it. For my own peace of mind. Anyway, I tried to get work just like I bet you have. But nobody wanted to know.'

'But how are we supposed to live?'

'We beg, hen. All day and every day. Even then most folk don't want to know. They hurry past you looking the other way. Sometimes I only make enough for a sandwich. And that's my lot.'

Jennifer shrank inside. She felt herself growing smaller.

'I couldn't beg. Oh, no, I just *couldn't*.'

'Listen,' Bev confided, 'if you're hungry enough, you'll stoop to anything. If begging's the worst you have to do, you'll be lucky.'

XXII

'HOW DO YOU find this job compares with your work as a police officer?' Bernard asked. He and Hudson were walking towards one of the many gates.

Hudson said, 'Well, mostly as a police officer, I was dealing with strangers, out in the city of LA. Here, most of the people I deal with are known to me. And it's not a democracy in a studio like out in the streets.'

'How·come?'

'It's how much money you're making and did your last picture do well. You don't treat every case the same in here. There's a lot of politicking. You have to be a public relations person, hold people's hands, make them feel safe, make them feel loved.'

Bernard grinned.

'That doesn't sound like such a bad deal. There's some beautiful women around here.'

'Oh, I don't mind looking after the women, but when it comes to holding hands with the men . . .'

Bernard was still laughing after they'd said goodbye. He hailed a cab to take him back to the hotel. Eve Page was sleeping until lunchtime after partying most of the night. He had been at the party with her and had been bored out of his skull with all the chattering and false laughter and even false 'kiss, kiss' bonhomie. All the 'look at me' posers, ready and willing to do anything to get a decent part in a picture. He had left a security woman in the suite with Eve, a man outside the door and one at each end of the corridor. The Page Boys were staying with a songwriter friend at one of the Beverly Hills hotel bungalows. Their friend had pretty good security arrangements there already. It was Eve Page he was worried about. Some guy kept phoning and writing and trying to bring her gifts.

On one occasion, Sally and Sean had stopped him in the hotel foyer. That worried Bernard too. He could hardly say, 'You shouldn't have done that. You're only supposed to be on crowd control.' However, the man could have pulled a gun on them. It made him sweat to think about it. He wished to God he'd never allowed the twins to get into the business and he determined to find a way of getting them out of it. The trouble was, not only did they love the job, they were damn good at it.

He'd no sooner entered the hotel suite than the bedroom door opened, and Eve Page appeared. Every time he saw her, Andrina came to him like a tug at his gut. He would be glad when this job was over.

'Ready?' he asked.

'The last thing I feel like doing is playing a love scene, far less singing right now. Hours and hours of filming.' She rolled her eyes. 'It wouldn't be so bad if it was only one take. It's going over the same thing again and again that gets me.'

'Just keep thinking of the money,' Bernard said, going to the door and checking outside before ushering her from the room.

They went down in the lift and he preceded her into the foyer, his big bulk all but hiding her from view. Everything seemed OK and they continued side by side, not talking any more. One of his men joined them, as hard-eyed and as watchful as Bernard. There were a few hopeful fans outside. Eve Page stopped to sign some autographs, then it was into the limo and away. As usual, Bernard sat in the front beside the driver. Able to relax a little now, his thoughts returned to Andrina. What was it about the damned woman? He'd known many other beautiful women in the ten years or more since he had been with Andrina. He'd even been tempted to marry again. Third time lucky, he'd thought. There was a lovely woman he'd met in Edinburgh. He and Helen had been seeing each other for nearly a year now. Not all that often because he was away so much. Helen was a widow in her thirties with three children, a girl almost Jennifer's age and a younger boy and girl. All of them were still at school. Helen was in no hurry to get married again and neither was he. They understood each other. He felt wonderfully relaxed in her company. She had a peaceful, calming effect on him.

Andrina always had exactly the opposite effect: she had excited him to the point of madness. God, he didn't want that any more.

The limo was stopped at the gate of Paramount and their credentials were checked. The guards already knew each of them in the limo but Bernard admired their conscientiousness. John Hudson had trained his men well. Several of his uniformed guards were on the movie lot.

'You'll stay here?' Eve Page asked. She was nervous and jumpy.

'Relax.' He smiled at her. 'Everything's going to be OK.'

'That man phoned again.'

'Don't let a nutter like that spoil your performance. Trust me. You're perfectly safe.'

She smiled in return.

'I should, shouldn't I? You've a very good reputation.'

He winked at her.

'The best.'

'And modest with it?'

'If you've got it, flaunt it!'

She walked on to the set, laughing now.

He watched her sashaying along in her skin-tight dress. She had a figure like Marilyn Monroe. So had Andrina. And they could flaunt it, all right.

He longed for a cold shower.

XXIII

SHE AND GREGORY had been flirting again. Bessie bowed her head at Meeting for Worship. She knew perfectly well where her behaviour was leading and so would God. God wasn't daft, any more than she was. She'd got into the habit of speaking to God in her head, trying to explain to Him, trying to justify herself.

I've been having such a terrible time with Granda. He's getting worse. He soiled his bed the other night. I could have died. I know he can't help anything any more and I don't get angry with him, I mean, what good does getting angry do? Anyway I haven't the energy nowadays. But, oh, it's terrible. I feel I'm sinking deeper and deeper into a black pit. The times I'm with Gregory are the only bright moments of my life. They're like stars shining in my darkness.

Her conversation with God was interrupted by a man getting up and talking about international responsibilities, reconciliation and cooperation.

'We call upon people everywhere . . . to behave as nations with the same decency as they would behave as men and brothers . . .'

It didn't 'speak to her condition' at all. Except of course that she was teetering once more on the verge of behaving indecently.

Did You really mean that commandment – Thou shalt not commit adultery? Was it really You who wrote it? Or was it just Moses who made it up to get a bit of publicity for himself? Maybe he fancied himself as a creative writer. There's a lot of them around. Tell me, please. Give me a sign.

She closed her eyes tightly and waited. But there was nothing but an occasional shuffle of Quaker feet and a creaking of hard benches.

God obviously didn't believe in making it easier for anybody. Why should He send her a sign? Her, of all people. A mere speck in His universe. Why should He listen to her?

I'm sorry for 'the stars shining in my darkness' bit. I must try not to be hypocritical and hide from the truth. The truth is Gregory Seymour – that's him who owns the two art galleries – wants me to meet him in London and share a hotel bedroom with him there. In other words, commit adultery. He'd made up a whole tale about organising an exhibition of my work in London and I must be there with him to meet the gallery owner and sort out what paintings will be most appropriate to include in the exhibition. There's no exhibition, of course. I only wish there was. Gregory plans to take me to a couple of theatre shows. It sounds so wonderful, like a beautiful dream. Just to get away from home and Peter and Granda. Even Daisy is a trial at times.

She waited, but God didn't answer. At the same time the peace of the Meeting did help. Maybe that was God speaking to her. In the lovely soothing silence. Thankfully she relaxed into it, and felt better. After Meeting she enjoyed the warm handshake with everyone and the usual cup of tea and biscuits. She hung around, eager to join in the chat.

But, eventually, she had to leave. The other Friends at Meeting weren't any help to her although she admired them enormously and loved them dearly. But they all seemed so clever and so strong – mentally and spiritually, if not physically.

They didn't fuss, or boast, or talk about what they did at all unless in an official and practical way. They never tried to tell anyone what they should do, or criticise or condemn or try to convert anybody. You could turn up at Meeting for years and even take part in the business side and never be asked to join the Society. There were all sorts of folk really, some with very strong views and sometimes opposing opinions. But most of them tried to live up to the *Advices and Queries*, especially when it said 'In your relations with others, exercise imagination, understanding and sympathy. Listen patiently, and seek whatever truth other people's opinions may contain for you. Think it possible that you may be mistaken . . .'

Mistaken or not, she went to London. Gregory was arriving on a later train. She slunk into the hotel like a Russian spy. It was as if everyone in the city knew what she was up to. Gregory had booked her in as Mrs Seymour. Trembling, she accepted the key from reception and took her overnight bag up to the room. She'd already had several dry Martinis on the train and bought two miniatures for her handbag. She'd swallowed more than one Valium. Yet she was still in an anguish of nerves. She was in physical agony as well, because she wasn't used to wearing a suspender belt, and the silly wisp of a thing she'd bought in Glasgow was sawing into her belly like a razor blade. The suspenders weren't what she'd call comfy either. In fact, she discovered that she was allergic to nickel. A furtive inspection revealed strawberry red patches, one on the front and back of each thigh. She gave the patches a quick scratch. But scratching only made them more itchy than ever.

She decided to go down to the bar for another drink. It wouldn't look so eager if she met Gregory in the lounge rather than the bedroom. In truth, she was not in the least eager. She simply could not believe she was doing this. She had another drink. She took another Valium. Her head began to whirl. She became so light she seemed to be bouncing, unable to keep her feet on terra firma and not in the least caring. When Gregory arrived, she grabbed his hand and dragged him into the lift. Before he could recover his surprise, she hustled him into the bedroom and cried out, 'Alone at last.' Gregory's eyes bulged and his mouth gaped like a goldfish. He watched aghast as she started to fling off her clothes and dance around the room.

'Don't you want a drink or something first?' he managed. He was normally a dignified, well-organised man who did things properly. In reply Bessie startled him by belting out a striptease tune as she whipped off her cardigan (the pink cardy her good-living Christian mother had knitted for her last year).

'Da-da-da-de, da-da-da . . .'

Off came her skirt and was kicked high into the air. Then her blouse and her bra.

Gregory was plastered against the door somehow looking astonished, stunned and dignified at the same time. Gregory never lost his dignity. However, as she was happily rolling off her stockings and twirling them over her head, he came to life and began to divest himself of his jacket and trousers. In the unaccustomed haste, his feet became entangled and he stumbled wildly about for a few seconds until he managed to steady himself against the bed. As he was tearing off his Y-fronts, he tripped and fell but scrambled quickly to his feet again. Bessie had already removed every stitch. She bounced on to the bed and lay on her back, still being musical. He lay on top of her and began talking incessantly as he plunged in and out of her. Somehow he still kept his dignity and his head held high. It was her turn to be astonished. He twittered on like a bearded budgie.

'You're nice and moist for me. Yes, grip your legs around me. Yes, that's nice. Yes, that's right. Yes . . .'

They bounced up and down and sideways and rolled about until, before either of them realised it, they had tumbled off the bed and landed on the floor. Gregory hardly lost his bouncy rhythm but as he'd landed his elbow jabbed into her ribcage. It was then she heard (and felt) one of her ribs crack. She tried to keep a stiff upper lip but he was a heavy man and she had never been robust.

From then on it was downhill all the way.

God had spoken.

Go to Hell, He'd said, and when God said Hell, He meant it.

XXIV

'HOW LIKE YOU to suggest it was my fault,' Andrina complained. 'You've always been the same. Always blaming me. It was one of the happiest days of my life when our divorce came through.'

'That makes two of us,' Robert said. 'But if you can tear your thoughts away from yourself for a moment to think about our daughter and try to answer my questions about her . . .'

'I don't need to talk to you at all. Why should I have to put up with you grilling me like a criminal?'

'I'm not grilling you like a criminal. I just want as much information as possible so that I can try to find Jennifer.'

'The police are trying to find her.'

'Her and a million others. I must do something. I can't just sit around wondering what might have happened to her.'

'What can you do? You're at work every day.'

'I can search for her after school and at weekends.'

'Anyway, Paul and I have already searched everywhere.'

'I must do something,' he repeated.

He felt guilty as well as distressed. He wondered, in his heart of hearts, if he'd failed the child, shut her out since his marriage to Laura. Not consciously. He'd told Jennifer she was always welcome to visit. Both he and Laura had genuinely tried to make her welcome when she did arrive at the door. Laura made a special meal. He always slipped Jennifer a generous amount of pocket money. But now he remembered the times he'd gone into the kitchen to give Laura a hand and left Jennifer sitting alone in the lounge. Perhaps she'd wanted and needed to talk to him.

Scenes rolled before his mind's eye. He laughed and chatted happily with Laura as she stood at the cooker while he set the kitchen table. They missed each other with being out all day teaching at different schools. There was always so much to tell each other after work. Funny stories to share about the children's antics. He remembered returning to the lounge and being stopped in his tracks by the sight of Jennifer's drooping, tragic figure.

'Jennifer, are you all right, dear?' he'd asked.

She straightened up and a mask of brightness clamped over her face.

'Fine, Daddy. I'm fine, thank you.'

'Are you sure?'

'Perfectly.'

He was about to say that he was sorry to have left her sitting on her own but just then Laura called:

'Come on now, before it gets cold.'

He put his arm around Jennifer as they went through to the kitchen. He was extra attentive to her, or so he thought at the time, urging her to eat plenty. He also made a point of asking her how she was getting on at school. All the same, now, when his tortured mind picked over that and other scenes, he realised that his admiring glances at Laura, their secret loving smiles, could have made his child feel lonely and shut out.

'Had there been a quarrel or anything?' he asked Andrina now. 'There must have been some specific trigger, surely.'

'Nothing at all.' Andrina's eyes slid away from him. She went over to the sink to fill the kettle. 'Would you like a cup of coffee?'

He knew she was lying. He'd experienced her evasive tactics so often in the past.

'I'd prefer if you told me the truth.'

She turned to stare at him, eyes round, childish, brimming with innocence.

'But I have told you the truth.'

Once he would never have doubted her. Now he knew there was no limit to the deviousness of which she was capable.

'Not any more, Andrina.'

'What do you mean?'

'I know you too well. There's something you're not telling

me. Has it anything to do with that tailor's dummy you're sleeping with at the moment?'

'How dare you insult me and my fiancé . . .'

'Fiancé is it, this time? Well, that's a new one for you. What does his wife say to that? Of course, he's an Edinburgh man, isn't he? So at least there's a few miles between you and the present Mrs Fisher?' His voice acquired a threatening tone. 'But you listen to me, Andrina. If it *has* something to do with that creep, he won't know what hit him . . .'

She gave a burst of sarcastic laughter, spiced with triumph.

'Oh, I think if it's the person I suspect who has had something to do with Jennifer's disappearance, you'll not find him so easy to deal with.'

Robert was taken aback.

'What are you getting at now?'

'I came home here one day and Bernard O'Maley was here with Jennifer. I nearly fainted from shock.' Her beautiful face contorted with bitterness. 'I'd never seen him for years and didn't want to after the wicked way he treated me. But there he was, cool as a cucumber, and with Jennifer.'

'It must have been you he came to see.'

'Oh no, it wasn't. Apparently he'd met Jennifer at one of these pop concerts and then he'd arranged for her to meet the stars and get their autographs. Naturally, she was thrilled and I remember him saying that he'd arrange for her to meet somebody even better.'

Robert felt sick.

'I don't believe you.'

'A lot of good you'll be at finding her. A lot of good you've ever been to her. At least I went to his office and tried to find out. He's away in America just now bodyguarding Eve Page and the Page Boys. They're in Hollywood making a film. They admitted at the office that Jennifer and her friend Daisy had been to a hotel to meet a group of men. They swore blind though that Bernard hadn't taken Jennifer to America. But I don't know. How can I be sure?'

Robert sank down on to a chair.

'But . . . he's old enough to be her father.'

'Bernard pursued me since I was fifteen – younger than Jennifer is now.'

'He would have been nineteen then. Only a few years older than you were. Nobody knows better than me that he's no angel but I still can't believe what you're suggesting . . . not with a child . . . and certainly not with Jennifer.'

'Trust you to defend him. Your long-lost buddy.'

Andrina sat down opposite him. 'I went to see Daisy too. Daisy Alexander. But she said she didn't know anything.'

'The artist woman's daughter?'

'Yes. Bessie Alexander was very nice and wanted to help but there was nothing she could do. Despite what you obviously think of me, Robert, I've been extremely worried. If I just knew for certain where she was and that she was all right . . .'

There was a tense silence for a moment. Then Robert said, 'I'm sorry. Of course you must be worried. Could you give me Daisy Alexander's address? I'll have a word with her and her mother. I've met them a couple of times at Sophie's and I know they come from the south side, but . . . By the way, I was very sorry to hear about Sophie's illness. I must try to get in to the hospital to see her.'

'I've got the address and phone number here.' Andrina reached for her handbag and found her address book. She opened it and handed it across to Robert.

'Thank you.' He jotted the address down and passed the book back to her. 'I might be more successful than you. I don't mean that as a criticism,' he added. 'It's just I've had some experience of this sort of thing at the school. Young girls confiding in their best friend and swearing them to secrecy. That's probably what's happened.'

He sounded so matter of fact. So formal. So calm. Inside he felt ill with worry and confusion. He believed, as he'd always done, that Andrina had neglected Jennifer. She'd put her lover first when Jennifer had been a baby and he'd no doubt that she still put her lover and her own gratification first. Nor would she, he suspected, be capable of experiencing any guilty conscience about her behaviour. She'd certainly never showed any conscience in the past. Hatred of her surged up inside him when he remembered some of the things she'd done. He controlled the emotion and continued to speak calmly.

'It could be that she's persuaded Bernard to take her with him to meet the stars. The chance to go to Hollywood would be every young girl's dream and to her, he was always Uncle Bernard, remember.'

'What difference would that make?' Andrina asked.

None to you, he thought bitterly. You would sleep with anyone if they took your fancy.

'Bernard mixes with all these glamorous women. Why should he want to seduce a little freckly-faced girl?' A sudden picture of Jennifer nearly brought tears to his eyes. The hair she used to wear in pigtails now held tightly back with an elastic band except for a fringe covering her brow. Her face with its vulnerable expression, its dusting of freckles across her nose and cheeks, and her wide, sensitive mouth. He couldn't bear the thought that someone, anyone, might have hurt her. Or that she could be in danger.

Andrina said, 'I'd believe anything of him, after the way he treated me and the wicked lies he told about me.'

She really was incredible. A masterpiece of self-deception. If anyone deserved first prize for lying, it was her.

'I'll pursue that line of enquiry, of course,' he said. She laughed. She actually laughed.

'Oh Robert, you haven't changed. You were always so terribly *serious*.'

His daughter was missing, for Christ's sake. How was he supposed to be? He felt like slapping the stupid laugh from her face. He had better things to do with his time and energy, however. He rose.

'I'd better go. I'll be in touch if I make any progress.'

She rose gracefully from her chair. There was an awareness in every movement, every sensual curve, as she preceded him to the front door. There she favoured him with one of her pseudo-shy sideways glances and provocative smiles.

He went down the stairs and out on to the street thanking God for Laura.

XXV

THEY WERE HUNCHED in a deep bowl of blackness. The only light was from the fire in the centre which was fed with old cardboard boxes, bits of wood, newspapers, anything anyone could find. The rank odour of stale sweat, rotting food and cats' urine hung like a fetid blanket over everything. Against the inky blackness, the silhouette of derelict buildings quivered through the flames. A motley crew hunkered and squatted and sprawled around the fire. Most were men; they looked old but could have been any age. Most were glassy-eyed and loose-mouthed with drunkenness. Bev had made extra at the begging and had bought a bottle of William & Humbert Walnut Brown sherry. Jennifer had pleaded with her to stay off the drink but Bev had been in a strange, reckless kind of mood and wouldn't listen.

'Listen, hen, we deserve a wee bit of comfort now and again. And after the day I've had . . .'

They had separated earlier and agreed to meet up outside the National Gallery at five o'clock. Bev was going to work Trafalgar Square. If they were lucky and had made enough, they would go for something to eat at five.

'The National is usually a good pitch. You try working that today,' Bev advised. 'Although of course it's well past the height of the tourist season now. Tourists would have been your best bet.'

'What do I do?' Jennifer felt really miserable but she was ravenously hungry and neither she nor Bev had any money, not even for a cup of tea between them or to get past the turnstile in the station lavatory. They'd had to find a bit of wall to hide behind and each took a turn as a lookout while the other squatted down for a quick pee. Then they hadn't been able to have a wash. There was nothing for it but to beg.

'You just hold out your hand if you haven't a hat or a box or anything else. And you say something like, "could you spare some change so that I can get a cup of tea, please?" Or if you can find a bit of cardboard and a pencil or a pen, you could write on it, "I'm homeless and hungry. Please help me".'

'Must we separate?' Jennifer was terrified to be alone again.

'There's no chance at all of making anything if two of us are hanging about the same spot,' Bev told her.

Jennifer thought she'd never felt more ashamed in her life when she'd had to relieve herself in a public place. However, hanging about in front of the National Gallery with her hand held out and murmuring, 'Could you help me please? Have you any spare change please?' came a close second. She couldn't raise her head to look people in the eye. Most didn't look at her either. One or two who did were rude and made her feel a thousand times worse. 'Why don't you get a job and do a decent day's work,' one woman said in disgust. Another said, 'I'm not giving you any money to go and spend on drugs.' Some people were embarrassed and apologetic. They dropped a few coins into her hand and said, 'Sorry, that's all I've got' before hurrying away. At the end of a long stint, when she counted what she had, it only amounted to a few pence over two pounds. She'd had nothing but a cup of tea and a bun all day because she didn't begin to get decent money until later in the afternoon. Now she was frozen stiff, as well as famished. Bev hadn't arrived by five o'clock. Or even by half-past. By a quarter to six Jennifer was nearly fainting with a heady mixture of thirst, hunger and panic. More panic than anything else. She could see Trafalgar Square from the steps of the Gallery but it was dark now and she realised with mounting panic that, despite the glittering array of lights, it wasn't going to be easy to find Bev. She would have stood her ground – she had to sit eventually – for longer at the Gallery but a couple of youths began to pester her. She suspected they were drunk but that did not make them any less frightening. She ran into the square, then stopped abruptly. The place was milling with people. Jennifer's throat tightened with fear. To her immense relief, she spotted Bev sitting near the foot of Nelson's column.

'Bev!' She flew over to her. 'Oh, I'm so glad I've found you. I thought you said you'd meet me at five o'clock. I waited and waited.'

'Did you, hen?' Bev laughed. 'I must have taken longer than I meant to at my ablutions. Ah wis havin' a wee paddle in them fountains.' It was when she lapsed into the Glasgow vernacular that Jennifer realised Bev was very drunk.

'You've been drinking.'

'I just had a wee drop of sherry to heat me up and now I'm going to buy another bottle of my favourite Walnut Brown.'

'Oh Bev, don't drink any more. Please don't. Especially on an empty stomach. Let's go for something to eat. You promised we would. I've got two pounds.'

'See him up therr.' Bev staggered to her feet and pointed upwards: 'he's cawed Nelson. An' this squerr is cawed after him. Some victory or other he hud. See me, ah'm no ignorant. Ah know a thing or three.'

'Yes, but come on and get something to eat. It'll make you feel better.'

'Better? Better?' Her drunken good cheer suddenly drained away. 'I'll never feel better.'

'You must have made some money if you're able to buy drink.'

'My mammy was a decent respectable woman,' Bev sighed. 'She hadn't any money but she had her pride. What have I got, hen?'

With an effort, she brightened up.

'Come on. We'll find a chippy and treat ourselves.'

And so they did. Bev still insisted on buying her bottle. They ate their fish and chip suppers sitting in a deep doorway in Shaftesbury Avenue. They hoped to stay there all night. However, an unshaven man wearing a long coat tied with string arrived to claim the doorway just as they were settling down. He gave them both such a kick to shift them that Jennifer gasped with pain. She struggled up clutching her back-pack. Bev jumped up too but shouted at the man – once they were both at a safe distance,

'We might have knew it was your skipper. It still has your putrid stink about it.'

There was certainly the most vile stench off the man, a mixture of urine and faeces. He made a rude sign at them before skippering down.

They must have walked for miles after that. Jennifer felt like fainting from fatigue. Conversation had long since become too exhausting and they were trudging along the dark streets in silence when suddenly Bev spotted the derelict site.

'That'll do us,' she said, dragging Jennifer along by the arm. 'Hallelujah, there's even a fire.' Jennifer had begun to lag behind. She felt as if she was moving in a dream and was ready to sink down anywhere. Still, she murmured apprehensively, 'There's a whole lot of men there.'

'They're alkies and winos by the look of them. They won't do us any harm.'

'How do you know that?'

'Listen, hen, I've been there myself. See if Marlon Brando had come to me and said, "You can have me or a bottle", so help me, I would have taken the bottle.'

Jennifer managed a weak smile.

'You're kidding me.'

'No, honestly, hen. There's no romances among alkies. They're just a crowd of drunks sharing a bottle. The bottle's the be-all and end-all of your life when you're like that. I'm telling you the bottle I've got is our passport to a warm skipper and an even warmer welcome.'

And so it was. Bev shared her bottle generously around. As a result they were given a place nearest the fire and treated, and toasted, as if they were a cross between friends and members of the royal family.

Jennifer sank into a deep sleep to the slurred sounds of 'It's a long way to Tipperary, it's a long way to go . . .'

She awoke chilled and shivering. It was as if her hip-bones had broken out of her skin. Every bone in her body ached and she could hardly move. It took her ages, moaning out loud, to ease herself into a sitting position.

The fire had disintegrated into a heap of ash. Bodies were

bulky shadows in the cold, grey light. Jennifer's luminous watch told her it was in the early hours of the morning.

Somebody groaned. 'Anybody got a bottle?'

A few grunts and mumbles indicated by their tone that there were no bottles. Jennifer had never seen such pathetic dregs of humanity. Unshaven, unwashed, poorly clad, some of them weren't wearing enough to protect them against the weather. Others were bulky with layers of assorted clothes. There was something frightening too about the dark sunken eyes and the way hands like claws violently trembled once the bodies attached to them began to stir.

Jennifer shook Bev awake.

'Christ,' Bev groaned, 'I could kill for a drink. Got any money left?'

'No. Not a penny.'

'Shit. I'll have to find some cash pretty quick or I'll die of thirst.'

'Haven't you any money left yourself?'

Bev began searching through her trouser pockets and then her plastic bags. In one of the bags she found fifty pence.

'That won't get me a bottle.'

'I was thinking of tea. A hot cup of tea will make us both feel better. Come on, Bev. Let's see if we can find a place. Anyway,' she lowered her voice, 'I'm bursting to go to the lavatory.'

'Och, OK. Give me a hand up. At least a cup of tea'll keep us going until the punters start appearing. Although they're usually in such a hurry to catch the bus or the train or the underground to their work, we'll be lucky if we make anything for hours.'

They reached Euston Station eventually. No other place was open as far as they could see. They went to the Ladies first, used the lavatory, had a wash and brushed their hair. It was a worry having to part with money at the turnstile but it was worth it. They re-emerged feeling almost human again. Then the cup of tea they shared thawed them out and made Jennifer feel at least a bit more able to face another day.

Just as she and Bev were wandering across the concourse, Jennifer caught sight of a familiar figure. There was no mistaking that curly head, that odd mixture of clothes. It was Bessie Alexander, Daisy's mum.

'Oh my God,' Jennifer wailed.

'What's up?'

'That woman over there. She mustn't see me.'

'Come on.' Bev grabbed her hand and pulled her towards the nearest platform.

'What if she comes down here? There's nowhere to hide.'

There were no trains waiting. Not even many people. They would stick out like the proverbial sore thumb.

'If she's going for the Glasgow train, she won't get it on this platform.'

They stood for a while until they heard the tannoy announce the train to Glasgow. Jennifer began to cry.

XXVI

BESSIE WAS KEPT waiting so long at the hospital she thought she'd never see Glasgow again. Gregory was already on his way back to Scotland, so she was on her own. She doubted if she'd ever see Gregory again.

At first when she'd felt her ribs crack, she'd gritted her teeth. It wasn't easy when Gregory was bouncing up and down on top of her, not to mention distracting her with conversation. But then there came one bounce too many and she just opened her mouth wide and screamed. The scream reverberated, ricocheted, filled to bursting point, it seemed, every corner of the hotel. One thing was certain: there was nothing wrong with her lungs.

That was when Gregory really lost his dignity. He fell off her, scrambled to his feet, grabbed at his trousers and did such a funny dance in his haste to get into them that she would have laughed had she not been in such pain.

'What the hell . . .?' he was gasping.

She was gasping too. But it was with the struggle to try to sit up. She couldn't do it.

'My chest. I can't move. Gregory, help me up.'

He did so but she felt his help was only to hasten his flight. At the same time as hauling her up, he was struggling into his shirt.

'My God,' he wailed, 'a heart attack!'

If it had been Peter, he would have complained, 'Trust you to take a heart attack at a time like this.' She suspected Gregory was thinking the same thing.

'No. It's my ribs. I think they're broken.' She stood up, clutching at her naked bosom and peering down as if expecting the dreadful sight of a rib-bone sticking out.

'Get your clothes on before somebody comes,' Gregory hissed at her. 'The whole place must have heard you.'

'I can hardly breathe, never mind move. How can I get my clothes on?'

'Here, I'll help you.'

He tried to fasten her into her bra and just in time caught another scream in the palm of his hand. 'It's all right,' he said. 'If we just get out of here, I'll take you for medical attention.' He abandoned the bra and managed to ease her into her loose top and trousers before there was an urgent knocking.

'Are you all right, Mrs Seymour?' a muffled voice asked through the door.

'Yes.' Her voice sounded pathetic.

'I'll open the dor,' Gregory whispered. 'You show yourself.'

Yelping with every move, she reached the door. Gregory swung it open and stood stiffly out of sight behind it, as if he was glued to the wall.

She tried to smile at the security man and members of the hotel staff who were congregated outside.

'I'm sorry to have caused any alarm. I fell and hurt my chest. I think I'll need to go to hospital. Would you please phone for a taxi?'

Gregory packed up there and then and carried his overnight bag with great dignity to the taxi along with her own. He said he would never forget the humiliation of settling the bill at the desk and having to suffer the barely concealed hilarity in the staff's eyes on the way out.

He could not, he assured Bessie, go back there that night, or ever again. They all knew how she must have come by her injury. He could see it in their faces. And they thought it was his fault.

'Damn it,' she managed. 'It *was* your fault.'

He looked pained but he did say, 'I'm sorry, Bessie. Are you all right?'

'All right?' She meant to laugh sarcastically but it was as much as she could do to try to hold herself together while she struggled to breathe. Even talking became out of the question.

Gallantly he waited with her in Casualty, but after two long hours she managed to say, 'You go on home, Gregory. They're obviously going to keep me in overnight. There's nothing more you can do.'

'I don't like leaving you like this.'

'I'll be fine. Honestly. On you go. There's no point in you hanging around all night.'

'Well, if you're absolutely sure.'

'Yes, I'm absolutely sure.'

'Very well.' He gave her one of the rail tickets, dropped a kiss on her brow and repeated, 'I feel awful leaving you like this. I'm so sorry.'

She nodded in recognition of the fact. Then he backed away and disappeared.

Well, she thought, so much for romance. That's the last I'll see of him. At least in the capacity of a lover. She didn't feel sad. On the contrary, she had a hysterical urge to laugh but daren't. At the same time she was embarrassed. Guilty too, of course. Actually she didn't know why she wanted to laugh because it wasn't in the least funny. It was terrible. Disastrous. A complete humiliation.

As it turned out she was in the hospital the whole night. Most of the night anyway. But not in a bed. On a stretcher. She was, after an absolute *age*, examined and gave another of her award-winning screams. Then she was X-rayed, after another lifetime of waiting. Then they bound her up. Or kind of half bound her up with a stretch bandage which flattened one boob and allowed the other complete freedom. She looked very odd once they got her top back on. Another taxi took her to Euston Station in order to catch the early morning train. She had to carry her overnight bag awkwardly under one arm before she managed to plead with a railway worker to put her out of her agony and he kindly carried her bag the rest of the way to the train. She would never forget that journey home as long as she lived. Every movement of the train nearly made her faint, and to manoeuvre out of her seat to go to the toilet was an impossibility. It was amazing how one needed to use chest muscles to get up and down. She'd never realised that before.

The painkillers she'd been given helped, but not much. Back in the Central Station in Glasgow, another railwayman helped her with her bag and half lifted her into a taxi. Then there were the stairs to the flat to negotiate. The taxi man was kind too. As well as carrying her bag, he took hold of her arm and supported her as she slowly eased her way upwards, one step at a time. He even rang the doorbell to save her raking through her handbag for the keys.

'What's up with your face?' Peter asked as soon as she shuffled into the sitting room. 'I thought you weren't coming back until tomorrow morning.' He and Granda were watching television and Peter had only half an eye on her.

'I fell,' she said, 'and broke my ribs.'

'Trust you,' Peter said, 'to do a stupid thing like that.'

'I'm going to bed.'

'Put the kettle on first. We haven't had our tea yet.' His whole attention had returned to the television.

The bloody selfishness of them. Sod them and their tea! Oh, if only she could be shot of them. If only she had some money and somewhere to go – she'd go.

'Make your own tea,' she said and wept cautiously, for fear of hurting her chest, all the way to the bathroom. In bed she had to sit propped up with pillows the whole night. She couldn't get up in the morning other than to make an excruciating journey to the bathroom and back. Peter gave her a cup of tea in bed before he went to work and Daisy promised to make the meal when she came home from school. Bessie sat listening in a mixture of mental and physical agonies as Granda shuffled and crashed about the house having a terrible argument with President Nixon.

This is your life, Bessie thought. This is your life. Anger blew up to her head and she escaped in spirit to the loft where she slashed colour on to canvas. Peter was quite indulgent – for a couple of days. It was almost as if he enjoyed being in charge, having her helpless. Daisy didn't make the meal, when it came to it.

'I'm sorry, Mum,' she said, 'I just haven't time. Nigel is coming for me an hour earlier than we'd arranged . . .'

There was a long story then about Nigel and why there had been a change of plan.

'Well, if you could just make me a cup of tea, Daisy.'

Daisy had very quickly done so. Practically flung it at her in her rush to get on with the urgent business of putting on the glamour for Nigel. She'd favoured Bessie with a quick kiss though before she'd disappeared.

Silence again. In the silence, Bessie tried to think how she could escape. What could she do? Where could she go? How could she get the money to live? How could she find the courage? Granda was now chatting with his brother Bert who'd died five years ago. He was telling Bert he was going to get married to Mary McLellan. They were arranging a stag night now. After a while Granda opened the bedroom door.

'Oh there you are,' he said. 'All ready and waiting.'

'Go away, Granda,' she managed. 'And shut the door. I'm not well.'

'My bonny wee bride.'

He came hirpling gleefully towards her bed.

Oh my God! He was trying to get in beside her. She let out a belter of a scream. Really let it rip. It was quite amazing. Lungs like drums she had. Nothing else about her was powerful. On the contrary, she was worryingly weak, physically and morally.

Granda got the fright of his life. He jerked about like something out of a silent film.

'Eh? What? What's up, Bessie? What's all the racket? Was that you?'

'Just get out, Granda. Get out. Go back to your room. I'm not well, can't you see?'

'All right. There's no need to bring the house down. I only wanted to know when I was going to get my tea. I've been sitting through there for days without a bite to eat.'

'Peter'll be in soon. He'll make you something to eat. Now will you please *go*.'

He went away muttering to himself. The scream had hurt her ribcage and she took another painkiller. It made her feel sleepy and she was glad.

After a couple of days of unusual care and attention, the novelty for Peter wore off. It was about time she was up and around, he said. She'd be going as stiff as a poker, and that wouldn't do her any good. Then it was, 'Are you still in bed?'

The tea and scrambled eggs on toast was reduced to tea and toast. Then the toast disappeared and she only received a cup of tea. Even this was handed over with a grudge. Eventually she had to get up and creep about the house doing what she could. Slowly she healed. At least her ribs did. However, her period came heavier than ever. This time it never stopped. From one month to the next it just went on drawing her life's blood from her. The doctor gave her more Valium. He had always said everything was 'just her nerves', and this was no exception. He never even examined her. Somehow she still managed to hang on to her painting, shutting herself up in the loft long after everyone was in bed, the spotlights illuminating the cam-ceiled cave.

At one point she phoned the Samaritans and had to hang up because she recognised a Quaker voice on the line. She leaned her head helplessly down on the phone. She was beyond weeping. Then one day she returned to the doctor's house – he had a room in his house he used as a surgery – feeling as if she was going to die and ready to go down on her knees and plead with him to do something, anything, to help her. She discovered he'd gone on holiday. As soon as she returned home, she checked how much money she had, then phoned another doctor and made a private appointment. This doctor told her she had a tumour and must be admitted immediately to hospital for a hysterectomy. Peter took the news quietly. She didn't care what he or anybody was thinking, but she could imagine he wouldn't be feeling very pleased. She seemed to be making a habit of neglecting him. Although he did appear worried. He helped her to pack, carried her case and drove her to the hospital.

In the hospital they had to 'build her up' for a couple of days before she was fit enough to be operated on.

Peter came to visit every day and sat anxiously watching her. She even began to feel sorry for him. Only she had more important things to think about.

Out came not only her womb but her ovaries. She had been a right mess, the surgeon said. But she would be all right now.

All right? Her hormones, her nerves, her mind, her emotions were in absolute turmoil and chaos. She felt no longer a woman. She felt she had lost her femininity. She felt . . . oh, she felt . . . so utterly bereft. The last dregs of her self-esteem had gone.

XXVII

Bernard saw the woman come on to the lot and hover in the wings, watching Eve and the boys performing. He thought she must be one of the make-up artists or one of the females from the costume department. None of Hudson's men approached her and this seemed to confirm she was legit. Nevertheless, he kept his eye on her.

The scene finished and Eve and the boys were walking across towards the exit when the woman suddenly shot forward and flung herself around Dave's neck.

Bernard, who was nearest, beat the other security guys to it. He hauled the woman off and, with a jerk of the head, indicated that the boys should continue on their way.

The woman was struggling and babbling out a whole lot of nonsense.

'Calm down,' Bernard snapped. 'Dave's gone and you'd better be on your way too.'

'Let go of me, you big ape!' the woman spat at him. 'Who are you to come between those who are joined in holy matrimony? Let no man put asunder, the Good Lord said.'

Christ, Bernard thought, another nutter. This time a religious one. Always the worst.

He propelled her outside.

'Dave isn't married. And the next time you come anywhere near him, I'll have you arrested.'

'The Good Book says . . .'

'Or better still, I'll have you chucked into a madhouse where you belong. Now bugger off and don't come back.'

He shoved her towards one of Hudson's uniformed guards who dragged her, yelling and protesting, towards the nearest gate.

Later he was glad that Eve had arranged to join the boys and their friend for a drink at the bungalow. He wanted to check the layout of the Beverly Hills Hotel and the bungalow where the boys were staying.

The Pink Palace, as the hotel was nicknamed, was an unusually shaped place with its stucco walls painted salmon pink. Flanked by tall palm trees and other lush greenery, it looked more striking than the hills rearing up behind it. In the Beverly Hills garden there were ten luxurious bungalows, long buildings with low tiled roofs, large windows and rooms big enough to hold a grand piano.

He walked around the place and had a word with the security men already there. Then the hung about for a while, outside in the garden and inside the house. All the time, in the background, was the tinkling sound of laughter and talk rising to endless crescendos. This was the boring part of the job, waiting, and for hours on end. It gave him too much opportunity to think.

At last he heard Eve calling goodnight to the boys and he escorted her out of the bungalow and into the waiting limo. All was quiet and still, except for a gentle rustle in the bushes and slight nodding of the high palms. When they arrived back at the Beverly Wilshire, it was to discover that the man who had been pestering Eve had got himself arrested. Not knowing that Eve wasn't there, he'd turned up with a gun and tried to shoot a path to her room. Sean had eventually managed to disarm him.

Bernard froze at the thought, yet he couldn't help being proud of his nephew. Sean was proving to be a first-class operator despite being the youngest in the firm. He had a good physique, hard and muscular without being hefty. No doubt he would attract many a pretty girl before long. Probably already had. He had been worried at first about Sean perhaps being more vulnerable than Sally. But not a bit of it. Even now after only a few weeks, Sean was as tough as they come. Those soulful brown eyes were deceptive.

'Good work,' he told Sean. 'Disarming anyone isn't an easy thing to do.'

Sean grinned.

'Praise, Bernard?' The twins had dropped the 'Uncle' since joining the firm. 'Are you sure you're feeling all right?'

Cheeky young devil.

After that night they had peace from the male nutter but the woman was reported to be hanging about the bungalow. She was the one who gave all the headaches for the rest of the stay in Hollywood. Dave was inundated with phone calls, letters and gifts. This woman lived in fantasy land and really believed she was married to the musician. It was really beginning to get to Dave, who was obviously relieved when they boarded the plane for home. They left busy LA with its skyscrapers that looked as if they were made of glass. They flashed in the sun during the day. At night they sparkled like huge beacons crowding together and vying with each other in height.

'I'll be glad to see my girlfriend again – somebody sane and normal,' Dave told Bernard. 'We plan a quiet wedding soon after I get back.'

'Quiet?' Bernard said. 'You'll be lucky.'

'It's all arranged. The minister's going to marry us in Mary's flat. There'll be just the two of us and a couple of witnesses. We didn't want a lot of fuss and publicity. Mary's six months pregnant.'

'Right. Congratulations then, I hope it all goes well.'

He was glad to be back in Britain himself. He liked America, especially New York. He'd been to the Big Apple several times and found it more vibrantly alive than Hollywood. But it was always good to come home. Glasgow was still his number one favourite city. More for the people than for anything else. And of course having been born and brought up in the place, that's where his roots were.

If and when he married, Helen would, he hoped, sell her flat and come to live in Glasgow. He'd buy a nice place for her with a big garden for the children and an indoor gym where they could all work out. Helen wasn't enthusiastic about anything as strenuous as karate. Yoga was more her line. But the children were keen. He'd already bought them karate suits and taken them to the local karate club. Many a laugh they'd had sparring together. Helen would feign anger and say,

'Bernard, will you behave yourself. You're getting them too excited.' Or, 'Bernard, stop it, somebody's going to get hurt.'

The children would complain that she was being a spoilsport. 'We're enjoying ourselves, Mum,' they'd say.

He'd bought each of the kids a couple of T-shirts: one that sported an American football logo and one with Beverly Hills emblazoned across it.

He'd bought Helen a more expensive gift from one of the posh shops on Hollywood's famous Rodeo Drive. She always said he shouldn't bring anything back but he enjoyed giving presents to her and the kids. Usually he bought something for Sean and Sally too but now of course they could buy things for themselves. He still bought a present for their young sister, Maureen, and for their mother and father and grandmother. He hoped his gifts to Caroline, Michael and Martha would act as peace offerings. They had not been happy, to say the least, about Sean and Sally coming to the States with him.

As a last-minute impulse he bought Jennifer a couple of T-shirts as well. Before he got a chance to deliver them to her, however, before he'd even had the chance to go out to the cottage, Michael phoned him at the office.

'Bernard?'

'Michael! I was meaning to go out to the cottage tonight after I tie up a few loose ends here. Did the twins not tell you?'

'Yes, but I thought you'd better know about this straight away.'

'About what?'

'Robert Anderson has been here.'

'Robert Anderson?' Bernard echoed in surprise. 'I haven't heard from Robert in years.'

'Did you see his daughter before you left?'

'Jennifer? Yes, why?'

'She's gone missing.'

Bernard absorbed this information in silence for a moment. Then he said, 'Surely he doesn't believe . . .'

'His ex-wife does, I think. At least it was her who told him that you'd been with Jennifer. Had her up at some hotel . . .'

'That woman's a bloody menace. I bumped into Jennifer at

the Who Dunnits concert. She and her friend – Daisy Alexander – are fans and I arranged for them to meet the boys and get their autographs. I wasn't even there in the hotel when they met the group. I got a girl in the office to fix it.'

'I just thought I'd better warn you, Bernard. The poor guy has been all over the place. I know how he must feel.'

'I do as well,' Bernard said. 'Jennifer's a nice kid. I'll do what I can to help. Robert moved to Bearsden after he remarried, didn't he?'

'Yes, he left me his address and phone number in case I heard anything.'

'I think I must have it somewhere but give it to me just in case.'

Bernard jotted down the number.

'OK. Thanks, Michael. I'll get in touch with him right away.'

After he replaced the receiver, Bernard sat staring at it for a few minutes. Concern for Jennifer fought with fury at Andrina. He battled for control of his feelings until he was able to dial Robert's number and speak with a calm voice.

'Robert? Bernard O'Maley here. I've just heard about Jennifer. Michael phoned. First of all, let me assure you that I have had nothing whatsoever to do with her disappearance. I'm as fond of Jennifer as I am of my own niece. I'm shocked and concerned and I want to help as much as I can.'

There was a pause. Then Robert said quietly, 'Thanks, Bernard. I didn't believe that her disappearance was anything to do with you. I'll be grateful for any help you can give me.'

'When did she go missing?'

'Just after you left for the States, apparently. I was abroad on holiday and didn't find out until I returned. God, Bernard, it's been well over a month now. Anything could have happened to her. I'm worried out of my skull.'

'Can we meet? I'll need a list of everyone she knows – friends at school, at any clubs, people who live around her home area, etcetera. I'll get on to it immediately. I'm not a detective, of course, but my work experience and contacts should help.'

'Andrina would know more about her friends.' Robert was

fighting for control. 'I haven't been keeping in touch with her as much as I should. I feel as guilty as hell.' He cleared his throat. 'I lost touch with the neighbours in Monteith Row years ago. Would you go and speak to Andrina?'

'Leave it with me. Leave everything with me, Robert. I'll make it my first priority, I promise you.'

'Anything could have happened to her,' Robert repeated. 'It doesn't bear thinking about.'

'I've got your address,' Bernard said. 'I'll be in touch.'

XXVIII

Bessie felt so weak after the operation she had to lie down for a rest every afternoon. Or every afternoon that she got the chance. She began to seriously wonder if it would be possible to slip something into Granda's tea. She'd mentioned this to Daisy once and added – 'Something lethal!' Daisy had giggled, knowing that she didn't mean it. It was true that she was only joking when she said the lethal bit. However, if she thought she could have successfully managed it, she would have slipped him one of her tranquillisers. Granda always refused any medication. 'Strong as a horse,' he was fond of boasting. And she'd say, 'Aye well, one of these days, I'm going to call in the vet and have you put down, Granda.'

Granda laughed, knowing she didn't meant that either. 'I'll see you out,' he said.

She was beginning to believe him. Some days she felt she was floating away. Almost 'beyond the veil'. She'd once heard that expression at a Catholic funeral and thought it very appropriate.

One day, after a terrible night with Granda when he'd nearly set his room on fire, she'd meant to make herself a cup of tea but found herself hanging on to the kitchen table, unable to reach, far less fill, the kettle. She crumpled to the floor. She didn't faint. She just lay there, stretched out on the linoleum, absolutely at the end of her tether. It was then she said to God – and meant it with all her heart, mind and soul – *I can't cope any more. I'm just going to leave everything to You.*

Then the strangest, most wonderful thing happened. It only lasted a few seconds but she experienced the most exquisite sensation. At the same time she was suffused with light. She lay on the cold kitchen linoleum for a minute or two afterwards absorbing the miracle of it. She still felt weak. Nothing in her life had changed. Peter was snoring in one bedroom. Even his snoring had a resentful, grumbling tone. Daisy was sleeping in youthful contentment in another. She daren't think what Granda was up to in his room. But a jewel of happiness was now tucked away in her secret heart and it was giving her hope. She had not been having a one-way conversation with God. He had been listening.

Oh, many a time after that, she tried to explain the experience in other ways. It had been caused by her suddenly relaxing. Then of course she often thought, 'Why would God want to get in touch with me anyway?' Yet, all the time, she clung to the memory of how she'd felt and especially the sensation of being suffused with light. Quaker writings often referred to 'the light'. *Advices and Queries* ended with something that one of the northern Friends had written in 1656:

'Dearly beloved Friends, these things we do not lay upon you as a rule or form to walk by, but that all, with the measure of light which is pure and holy, may be guided; and so in the light walking and abiding, these things may be fulfilled in the spirit, not from the letter, for the letter killeth, but the spirit giveth life.'

Why me? she kept thinking in genuine humility. Even when she read in *Christian Faith and Practice*: 'In the Light, everyone should have something to offer', she couldn't imagine what she could have of the slightest value to offer, in or out of the Light.

After a while she thought of her painting, then blushed at her temerity. Where had that got her, or anybody? Except a disastrous trip to London to break the Seventh Commandment.

She hadn't been back to the gallery since then. Nor had Gregory been in touch with her. She hadn't been fit enough to climb the stairs to the attic to work but as soon as she regained enough energy, she hauled herself up the rickety ladder to savour the smell of paint and feel in touch with herself again. But now there were even more distractions than usual.

There was the distress about Jennifer's disappearance and first

Jennifer's daddy coming asking about her and then that Bernard O'Maley person. They still hadn't found her.

Then her own father died. He and her mother had been very close. Her poor mother was inconsolable. There was a big funeral in the Church of Jesus in Bearsden. Her sister Moira had seen to all the arrangements. It was a sad Christmas. Usually it was her mother who had the family for a jolly Christmas dinner in Bearsden, but this year a very subdued Mrs McVinney and Moira had come to her. Nevertheless, her mother had gone to the trouble of cooking and bringing along a turkey. It just needed to be heated up. Granda had been comparatively *compos mentis*, so all in all it hadn't been too bad. She'd managed.

Then Granda had taken ill. Peter had tried his usual blinkered trick of dismissing the true situation with, 'It's only his age,' but she knew Granda better than he did, and Granda was in pain.

'Peter, I'm getting the doctor whether you like it or not,' she told him.

It turned out to be a strangulated bowel and Granda was carted off on a stretcher to the hospital. As the ambulancemen were carrying him out, he turned to her and said in one of his few lucid moments, 'You'll be glad to see the back of me, Bessie.'

'No, no, Granda.' She put a big effort into trying to sound genuine. 'And I'll be in to visit you in the hospital just as soon as I can. Take care now.'

Peter of course, better late than never, was making a great fuss of Granda. He insisted he was the one to go with the old man in the ambulance. 'You stay and make the tea,' he told her.

Granda died the next day. Bessie had arrived at the afternoon visiting hour and was told that he'd just 'slipped quietly away'. She reckoned it was the only quiet thing Granda had ever done since she'd known him.

Peter sobbed broken-heartedly at the funeral. She really felt sorry for him. But he refused to be consoled. Instead he turned bitterly on her because she was unable to shed a tear.

'Even Daisy wept for Granda – but you? Oh, not you. I've never been able to understand you.'

Well, that was true anyway. She felt sad. Sad for Peter and sad for Granda. Sad because she had no tears left. In her secret heart though a spark of gladness burned. She would have more free time to paint. She could go up to her studio now with no interfering cries of 'Bessie, Bessie, where's my tea?' Or 'Bessie, I couldn't get to the bathroom in time.' 'Bessie . . . Bessie . . .'

The day after the funeral, when she was alone in the house and actually, unbelievably, free from any worries or interruptions, she went up to the loft. She sat in front of her easel and allowed the sweet joy of freedom to course through her veins. She was still sitting there hours later when Peter and Daisy returned home. As if in a dream she heard them moving about downstairs. Eventually Peter's head appeared through the open trapdoor.

'What do you think you're playing at? What about our tea?'

'Just coming,' she replied automatically.

Later her mother arrived. Her mother had never been one to visit her. Perhaps once or twice a year at the most.

'You know you're always welcome to come out to see us in Bearsden,' she always used to say. Now, feeling lost and lonely without her partner, she began popping in to see Bessie more and more often. Morning, noon and night, in fact.

'Moira works shifts,' she explained, 'and then she has her own life to lead.'

Why is it that no one thinks I should have a life of my own? Bessie thought, but she didn't say anything. Her mother was so obviously lonely and missing her father. And it was true that Moira worked shifts at the library and was out a lot.

'Since your father died,' her mother explained, 'I can't bear to be alone. I just can't bear it.'

Then, who would have thought it, Moira of the prim manner and horn-rimmed spectacles, met a man, no oil painting himself, became engaged to him within a few months, and announced they were planning to emigrate to Canada.

'We want to take Mother with us, of course,' she assured Bessie. But Bessie knew (and she suspected that Moira also knew) that her mother was far too old to tear up her roots and travel thousands of miles to live in Canada. Even though everyone kept assuring her that Vancouver was a beautiful city.

'No, no,' her mother said. 'I was born here and I'll die here and be laid to rest beside my husband.'

Peter then suggested – *Peter* of all people – that she should sell her house in Bearsden and come and live with them in the flat.

'You could have Granda's old room. We would do it up for you and make it any way you fancied.'

Bessie could hardly believe her ears. He had just come out with this plan to her mother without ever discussing it with her. He'd never once hinted . . . She was so overwhelmed with hatred for him she could have died of it.

Later he'd told her in private, 'Your mother'll pay her way and the extra will help you with the housekeeping.' He meant help *him* financially, Bessie thought. He knew. He must have known that she was just beginning to feel the benefit of being without Granda in the house. She was beginning to regain some energy. The anxiety and fear that had so often taken away her ability to sleep, or to relax, had gone. It was so wonderful. It was a kind of happiness. She thanked God for it. She'd been getting on so well with her painting. There was such peace and quiet while Peter was at work during the day and Daisy was at school.

'Oh Peter,' her mother had put her arm around him and kissed him. 'How kind of you, dear. You'll never know how I appreciate this. I'd feel so happy and safe with you and Bessie. And of course it would be wonderful seeing my lovely granddaughter every day.' Then she'd turned to Bessie and added, 'But wouldn't it be a bit much for you, dear? I wouldn't want to be a worry or a burden to you.'

What could she say except 'Of course you wouldn't be a burden, Mother.' This was, after all, her mother, who was more entitled to be looked after by her than Granda.

It's not that I mind. I know it's right that after giving birth to me and bringing me up, she should be looked after in her old age by one of her daughters. And if she won't go with Moira and Moira won't stay here, then it's up to me. It's only fair. I see that. But oh, I've used up so much energy and patience and everything else on Granda. I don't think I've anything left for her.

But what could she say? Her mother was so grateful, so excited, so happy at the prospect of moving in.

So, there you are. OK, God. Che sarà sarà.

XXIX

'PLEASE TRY TO stop drinking, Bev. You're ruining your looks and your health.'

'Aw, shut up.'

'Maybe if we saved up enough, we could get train tickets and go home. We'd be all right if we stuck together. Think of it, Bev. We could go back to Glasgow if we could get enough money together.'

'Then what? Eh? Do you think Glasgow DHSS is going to be any different than down here? So what do you fancy, eh? Sleeping in Kelvington Park or Glasgow Green? Oops! Couldn't do either, could we? Glasgow Green is too near your fuckin' Fisher. And Kelvingrove Park is too near Gus the Gunman. You look surprised, hen. Didn't I tell you Gus had a gun?'

'But why would he want to harm you now? It's ages since you've been away.'

'He used to frighten me with it. He was evil, that man. He tormented me with that gun. Just for a change from knocking me about. Just for laughs. It depended on the mood he happened to be in. I never knew. Sometimes he could even be Mr Charming. I never could find out where he kept the gun. If I had, I would have shot him with it.'

'Oh Bev . . .'

'Think I'm kidding, hen? Well, I'm not. I used to dream of shooting that man while he slept. To be free of fear, that's what I prayed for. Oh aye, I used to pray. Please God help me, I used to pray. But He never did, hen. I had to bloody well help myself. Anyway, you that's suddenly got the idea of going home. Where's home for us? Have you asked yourself that? Where's home? *What's* home?'

There was silence for a long minute. Then Jennifer said, 'Home for me was with my granny. I didn't actually live with her but I always felt more at home at her place when I went to visit her. She's in hospital.'

Jennifer had an overwhelming longing to find out how her granny was keeping.

'I think I'll phone.'

'Home?'

'No, the hospital. They seemed to think she'd be kept there for ages. So Granny's neighbour told me.'

Bev shrugged, then took a swig from her bottle.

'You do what you like, hen, and I'll do what I like. OK?'

'They couldn't trace the call, could they?'

'Shouldn't think so.'

'Anyway, I was thinking, Bev. We're both old enough now by law – well Scottish law anyway, I don't know about English – to get married. That surely means we must be legally entitled to leave home.'

Bev laughed.

'I've been over the age of consent for a long time. So we haven't broken any laws? That's a relief!'

'What I mean is, no one can force us to go back to live at home. Can they?'

'I don't know. You're the clever dick.'

'So if we stick together and protect one another – just as we've done here – we'll be all right.'

'Well, hen, you might be all right. You can tell old Fisher to fuck off. What do you plan to do with Gus if he turns up? Frighten him away by wagging your finger at him?'

'We could report him to the police if he came near you but I honestly can't see him turning up, Bev. Not after all this time. A man like that. He's sure to have found someone else to bully by now. Oh Bev, just think – to be back in Glasgow again.'

'You're dreaming. Even if we managed the fare – look at us. We're a couple of dirty tramps. Bag ladies. Not even ladies. I'm an alkie.'

'No, you're not,' Jennifer protested. 'Oh Bev, you're not.'

'You keep telling me I've a drink problem. That's just a polite way of putting it.'

'You're not an alcoholic. I didn't mean that.'

Bev sighed. 'You're not *just* a dreamer any more. You're a restless dreamer. While I'm in such an honest mood – you could make it. But not me. I've got nobody. You've got your daddy and your granny. Oh, I know you've told me your daddy puts his precious Laura first. But Laura or no Laura what do you bet your daddy would still help you. And your granny's probably OK by now.'

'Bev, you've got me.'

'We're not joined at the hip, hen.' She lit a cigarette. 'Aye. It's time you went back. You're a lot tougher now than you were when I first met you. You could tell that guy to fuck off, all right. And your daddy would help you to get cleaned up and get a job. And once you had a job, you could maybe get a wee house of your own.'

'Now *you're* dreaming.'

'Aye, but it's a dream that could come true for you. I was just being selfish before. You wouldn't need to sleep rough back home. You go for it. I'll help you with your fare.'

'I couldn't leave you.'

She looked at Bev's pinched face, and the dark shadows under eyes that were still as blue as the sky. Her good bone structure proved that she had once been a really fine-looking woman. Once she had fair hair. Now her hair, like her skin, had dulled. But she wasn't really a tramp, or a bag lady. She tried to keep herself clean. They both did. They tried to have a wash every day. Either in a station lavatory or in a fountain or a pond in one of the parks, or in Trafalgar Square. It wasn't easy to wash and dry clothes but they usually managed that too. At least they tried to keep their panties clean.

To wash and dry their jerseys and trousers wasn't possible. Neither of them had a change of trousers and Bev's jersey was big and long and a terrible problem to dry. She did try to wash it once but even when she held it in front of the hand dryer in the lavatory for ages, it was no use. They were both thrown out and Bev had to put the jersey back on, soaking wet. She hadn't a shirt to wear underneath. At least Jennifer had that.

Scottish reticence and an inborn shyness prevented Jennifer from displaying much outward affection for Bev. Certainly she could never have said out loud that she loved her. But she did. Now she said, 'You're my best friend. I'm not going to leave you here on your own.'

'I'm touched,' Bev said sarcastically, but Jennifer could tell by the way Bev averted her eyes and the nervous tic on one side of her face that she really was moved. They were sitting in the small park area in the middle of Russell Square. The trees were bare and they could see the huge Russell Hotel across the road. In there would be comfortable beds, wonderful bathrooms, dining rooms with everything you could wish to eat and drink. They liked to sit and imagine what it would be like to stay there. It was another world. There were so many places like it in the vast metropolis of London. Hotels, restaurants, theatres all mobbed with well-dressed, well-fed people, enjoying the good things in life. Especially at night, the whole place lit up and sparkled with lights and life.

A different world.

The world that she and Bev belonged to was dark and cold, hard and dangerous. Back streets, derelict buildings, shop doorways. The police moved them on, of course, long before the shops were due to open. They were forced to keep constantly trudging about, as much to prevent seizing up with the cold as anything else. Sometimes Jennifer was sure she'd die of it. Now, at Christmas, all they needed was snow to finish them off. Maybe it was the time of year that was making her feel especially homesick. She imagined George Square in Glasgow all lit up with fairy lights, and people singing Christmas carols in front of the City Chambers. Then at New Year it would be such a happy, friendly crowd milling about, singing and dancing and wishing each other a Happy New Year.

Her granny always made a spicy Christmas pudding at Christmas and fruit cake and shortbread at New Year.

Jennifer sighed.

'I tell you what,' Bev said, 'you phone your granny. If you haven't enough for the phone, I can help you out. I've nearly a pound . . .'

'But we haven't had anything to eat yet . . .'

'Never mind that just now. We'll be OK. The Salvation Army won't let us starve at Christmas. We'll find out where they dole out their Christmas grub. No, you phone the hospital and see how your gran is. They can do wonderful things with stroke patients now. She'll maybe be able to speak to you herself. If you can't speak to her, phone your daddy.'

'We won't have enough for both calls.'

'Well then, why don't you ask for a reversed charge call. When you phone your daddy's number, I bet he'll be so glad to hear from you he'll be delighted to pay.'

Jennifer felt apprehensive as she and Bev started searching for the nearest phone. And worried.

'But Bev, I told you. I can't leave you. If I go back to Glasgow, you'll have to come with me.'

'OK. OK. We'll work something out. But first, just make the phone call, will you?'

They sorted out enough coins between them to phone the hospital. No chance of a reverse charge call there. Eventually Jennifer got through and asked, first of all, if they would tell her which ward Mrs Sophie McPherson was in. She was asked to wait.

'She'll have been discharged by this time. She'll be back home,' Jennifer said to Bev. 'I should have tried her house first.'

Then a woman's voice on the phone asked, 'Are you a relative?'

'Yes, I'm Jennifer Anderson, her granddaughter.'

'I'm sorry, Miss Anderson. Your grandmother died three days ago.'

Jennifer replaced the receiver, then stood staring at it. Her eyes slowly filled with tears that spilled fitfully down her cheeks.

Bev said, 'What's up?'

'She's dead.'

'I'm sorry, hen. Och never mind.' She put her arm round Jennifer and pulled her to her. 'Have a wee swig out of my bottle.'

XXX

ANDRINA LIT UP a cigarette and blew smoke towards Bernard. She hated him for coming back into her life, disrupting it. It couldn't just be a coincidence that he had turned up and immediately afterwards Jennifer had suddenly disappeared. He must have had something to do with it. Even if it was just to unsettle Jennifer. Like he's unsettling me now, she thought.

She wished Paul was there. She tried to avoid Bernard's eyes because when she looked at him, she wanted him right there and then. He knew it too. His eyes had that deep dark sexual awareness. She could drown in it.

He was remembering, as she was remembering, and his eyes were telling her that he wanted her too. But he kept asking questions about Jennifer.

'I told you, she didn't know any of the neighbours,' she repeated, unable to resist sliding him a smouldering sidelong glance. 'Any more than just to say hello or good evening. She always kept herself to herself. You shouldn't have been pestering them.'

'Pestering them? They were only too pleased to help.'

'But they couldn't help, could they?'

'You never know. Little things mount up and begin to make a picture. I've been to the school as well.'

She tutted.

'What on earth will everybody think?'

'Does it matter?'

'Well, you know what people are like.'

'I know what you're like.'

She inhaled deeply on her cigarette.

'Oh?'

'Still worried about protecting your respectable scandal-free image. Still as randy as a bitch on heat.'

'How dare you speak to me like that! You who seduced me when I was only a girl.'

'Come off it, Andrina.' He continued coolly: 'can you give me the address of that friend of hers – Daisy somebody. I'd like to talk to her next.'

Andrina was visibly trembling as she got up, went over to the writing bureau and scribbled something on to a piece of paper.

He took his time reading it. It was only a few words. She knew he was lingering near to her just to torment her. No other man she'd ever known exuded the powerful sexuality that he did. Before she could do or say anything, he had left the sitting room and was strolling across the hall towards the front door with that subtle self-confident swagger of his. Then, without even turning to say goodbye, he was gone.

Oh, how she hated him for what he could do to her. Her whole body throbbed with passion. She went over to the drinks cabinet and poured herself a large vodka. Alcohol was something she was normally careful about. It was too easy to put on weight at her age. In the days when she'd known Bernard she'd thoughtlessly indulged in everything that aroused the senses. He had fed her with Belgian chocolates, champagne, caviare, strawberries and cream. She'd been carried away by dreamy, sensuous music.

He hadn't changed. She had known him so well years ago, and she knew him still. As she sat drinking the vodka, and inhaling deeply at her cigarette, her mind drifted back over the passionate hours she'd spent with him. She recalled his big, tanned, muscular body. Oh, how beautiful he had been.

She leaned back in her chair and stretched luxuriously passion melting away the hatred. How lucky she was to have had such an experience. It was something beautiful and special, a God-given gift to be treasured in secret between them. And he had promised to come back, to keep her informed about how his investigations were progressing. She would be ready for him next time, dressed in the erotic way she knew he liked.

Andrina awoke the Sunday after Bernard's visit, her blood

still hot with need. As soon as Paul awakened, she caressed him into arousal and they had the best sex they'd ever enjoyed together.

Now she felt sated with pleasure, fulfilled, satisfied with her world. Even thoughts of Jennifer lost their anxious edge. Jennifer would be all right. She would be enjoying herself somewhere on her own. She always had been a loner, always hanging back, never wanting to join her and Paul in anything. Jennifer *must* be all right. Even the hospitals had been checked. She was not ill. She'd been involved in no accident. She *knew* Jennifer was perfectly all right.

When Paul got up and made a pot of tea and brought a tray back to the bed Andrina murmured, 'Darling, put on our Gregorian chant tape. I feel so wonderful. I feel our love this Sunday morning has almost been a religious experience.'

Paul enthusiastically agreed. 'Yes, if we'd had time I would have loved to go to morning service. I really feel in the right mood.'

She smiled and walked her fingers up his arm.

'So do I, darling.'

They lay in each other's arms and listened to the spiritual music and felt uplifted. Andrina thought it wonderful. She felt their relationship blessed, purified. Soon, they would be married. Paul had, at last, asked his wife for a divorce. He hoped to get a 'quickie' as he called it and they'd be married as soon as possible after the final papers came through.

It hadn't been easy for him these last few days. His wife hadn't taken it at all well and his children had been difficult too. Young people could be so selfish. Poor Paul. She was sorry for him and glad that she had been able, this morning, to soothe away any doubts or anxieties.

They lay listening to the music and felt in complete harmony.

She was sorry when they had to get up and get dressed but she tried to make the rest of the day a really memorable and happy one for him. She wished he hadn't to go back to Edinburgh later that evening but he still had many things to attend to, loose ends to tie up at home. Soon, however, they would start looking around for a house in Glasgow so that they would have a home of their very own to move into as soon as they were married.

Everything was working out perfectly. She sang in the choir and gazed at Paul as she sang. She could see the admiration and pride in his eyes as he gazed back at her.

She wasn't even afraid of Bernard coming back. People like Bernard had their uses. There was a wicked side to them but from such wickedness could come good. She knew this now, and the knowledge gave her a deep satisfaction.

She sang going about her household chores. She'd long since given up her job and was content to look after the house and concentrate on making tasty dishes for Paul to enjoy.

'You're a wonderful cook,' he told her with an appreciative sigh after relishing one of her meals. 'And a perfect housewife. You keep this flat like a new pin. You're even good at sex. How lucky can any man get?'

She blew him a kiss, wondering dreamily as she did so when Bernard O'Maley would return.

XXXI

'BUT . . . I SAW her only yesterday. She was perfectly all right.' Andrina's stricken gaze clung to the nursing sister in disbelief.

'Your mother was never perfectly all right, dear,' Sister Gilchrist gently corrected. 'She'd suffered a serious stroke.'

'But I thought . . .'

'Drink your tea. Is there anyone I can phone to come and collect you? You shouldn't be driving when you're in such a state.'

Dazedly Andrina shook her head.

'There's no one.'

The words had an ominous ring. They brought fear. Paul was in Edinburgh with his wife and family. He'd warned her never to phone or in any way contact him when he was there. Things were at a very delicate stage in his divorce negotiations. It would take very little to make his wife turn nasty. She could withdraw her cooperation just out of spite. Paul had so many anxieties at work as well as at home they always overwhelmed any problems of her own.

'Your fiancé?' Sister suggested. She'd met Paul on a few occasions when he'd accompanied her to the hospital.

'He's away at the moment.'

'A friend, then?'

With a gust of thankfulness, Andrina remembered Bessie.

'Oh yes, my friend Mrs Alexander. She'll come.'

'Give me her number. I'll phone her while you drink your tea. Then I must do my rounds. Will you be all right waiting here?'

'Of course. You've been very kind.'

Left alone in the Sister's office, Andrina sat with a mercifully blank mind. Automatically she sipped at the hot sweet liquid. Her usually straight-backed graceful figure had shrunk. She was like a rubber doll from which most of the air had seeped away. That was how Bessie found her.

'Andrina, I'm so sorry.' Bessie hurried over and put her arms around her. 'Come on, I'll take you home.'

'I don't know if I could drive . . .'

'Of course not. I've got a taxi waiting outside.'

Firmly supporting her, Bessie led her friend away.

Once in the Monteith Row flat, despite Andrina's protests of not being hungry, she made an omelette, some toast and a pot of tea.

'You'll feel better if you eat something. And don't worry, I'll stay with you tonight.'

Andrina's lips trembled.

'Thank you, Bessie.'

'You'd do the same for me.'

'You knew Mummy, didn't you?'

Bessie nodded.

'A most unusual and interesting woman.'

'Yes, she was very highly thought of in Bearsden. She worked hard for the church. Even before she went to live in Bearsden she was always busy helping somebody.' Andrina cast a tragic gaze across at Bessie. 'I'm afraid I let her down. I wish I hadn't.'

Bessie tutted.

'Now, don't you go blaming yourself for anything. I admired your mother very much but she had impossibly high standards. Nobody could have lived up to them.'

'I did try.'

'Of course you did. She ought to have been very proud of you.'

Andrina gave a half-heartbroken, half-sarcastic laugh.

'Proud of me? If only you knew.'

'I know you're not only a beautiful, talented woman, you've a good, kind heart as well.'

'Oh, Bessie.' Andrina stretched out her arms like a child. 'What would I do without you?'

Bessie gave her a comforting hug, then said, 'Come on, drink your tea. We've a lot to arrange. Everybody will have to be notified for a start. Sophie was a very popular and respected woman in her community and in the church. A great many people will want to attend her funeral.'

'Oh dear, I don't even want to think of such a thing. It's too awful.'

'It's best to keep busy. I'll help you.'

There had been a time – a lifetime ago, it seemed now – when she and Bernard had actually looked forward to her mother's funeral. Surely they must have been joking? She had been perfectly serious when she'd told Bernard that she'd never marry him while her mother was still alive. She had been far too terrified of the scandal. She knew her mother would disown her if she discovered her daughter having anything to do with Bernard O'Maley. And that, of course, was eventually what happened.

But long before Sophie had found out about her affair with Bernard, they'd discussed what Andrina would wear at the funeral. Bernard promised to buy her the best and most expensive outfit in town. She saw herself in a glamorous wide-brimmed hat – of shining Italian straw perhaps. And high-heeled shoes.

'Have you anything black to wear?' Bessie asked as if reading her mind. 'I personally don't think it's important but your mother was a stickler for doing the conventional thing, wasn't she? I think you should wear it as a mark of respect.'

'Poor Mother,' Andrina said, 'she'd never rest peacefully if I turned up in scarlet or white. I'll buy something tomorrow.'

Sophie McPherson, she put in the newspaper notice. Dearly beloved mother of Andrina Anderson.

'I did love her, you know,' she told Bessie.

'Of course you did,' Bessie assured her. 'And she loved you in her own way.'

Andrina felt a terrible anxiety to believe the words.

'She loved my father but I never once saw her kiss him or even take his arm. She didn't seem able to show love or affection.'

'Poor Sophie. All shut into herself like that. I once tried to kiss her goodbye after an especially enjoyable visit. She was so hospitable. But she shrank back as if she was terrified of any display of affection. I think she must have been hurt and betrayed in the past so much that she was never able to get over it and trust anyone again.'

'You're probably right. She was painfully neurotic. Never at peace for a moment.'

'Well, she's at peace now, Andrina.'

Andrina nodded.

'I must give her a funeral that she'd be proud of. She was terribly proud as well, you know. Yes, I'll do the funeral tea. I won't let her down in that.'

'Oh, Andrina, that's far too much for you to do at such a time. Get a caterer to come in. Or better still, book a meal at a hotel.'

'No, you said it was best to keep busy, Bessie, and you're right. I want to do this for my mother.'

Bessie hesitated then reluctantly gave in.

'If you feel you must.'

It was the saving of Andrina. Plans for the funeral filled her mind to the exclusion of everything else. She was determined that every detail of the service and of the funeral tea afterwards should be perfect. It was as if it was her last chance to please her mother.

Everything was indeed perfect. The coffin was the best that money could buy. There never had been such a profusion of flowers. The undertakers were suitably dignified. The line of cars slowly following the hearse were gleaming black Daimlers. A host of solemn, well-dressed mourners paid their last respects.

Andrina looked lovely standing beside the coffin in the church as she sang her mother's favourite hymn. Then in a clear voice she gave a moving eulogy.

Sounds of sobbing echoed through the church.

'Your mother was always so proud of you, Andrina,' people said afterwards. 'And rightly so.'

They complimented her on the meal too. Throughout the whole day she kept her head held high. She was gracious and attentive to everyone. It was only after the mourners had left and she was alone with Bessie again that cracks showed in her dignified composure.

'Did I do all right, Bessie?'

'You were wonderful.'

'She always liked me to sing in the church.'

'You sang beautifully, Andrina. You really did. It was extremely moving. What you said too. No wonder so many people couldn't hold back their tears. You were so very genuine in your praise of her. And so loving.'

'I tried my very best,' Andrina said. Then added wistfully, 'I always did.'

XXXII

JENNIFER DIDN'T KNOW what she would have done without Bev. Her grief would have been too much to bear on her own. Bev made her talk about her feelings. They shared their memories – Jennifer's memories and love for her granny and Bev's memories and love for her ma, as she called her mother. Huddled together in shop doorways they'd stare out at the dark night and talk, half to each other and half to themselves.

Bev said,

'My ma was battered as well, you know. Funny that, eh? Me shacking up with the same kind of bastard as she did. You'd have thought I'd have had more sense after seeing what happened to her. Living through it with her. But it's not a matter of sense, is it? I mean you believe the bastards, you trust them, you fall for them and once they've got you . . .' She shook her head. 'Then, after every time it happens, they tell you how sorry they are. Oh, they can be so bloody convincing. They swear it'll never happen again . . .' She lit a cigarette and puffed at it for a few seconds before she was able to go on.

'I'd heard it all before. My da was the very same with my ma. My poor ma. I wish I'd been able to help her. But you get hell of a mixed up inside. I mean, I loved my da as well, you see. And I kept believing him just like my ma did. But oh, my poor ma.'

Jennifer didn't say anything. Didn't even look round. They both stared ahead, the bond of sympathy so strong between them it was almost tangible.

Eventually Jennifer managed to speak.

'You and your ma loved each other, despite everything. All right, you both had weaknesses and made mistakes but they were only in trusting and loving too much. Or maybe in trusting and loving the wrong people too much. But you and your ma loved each other, that's something to be happy and glad about. When I was a very young child, I loved my mother but I don't think I ever really trusted her. Then the love withered away. My granny became the only person I could depend on. She always wanted me. Always took my side. Was always there for me.' Jennifer struggled to control her voice. 'I loved her for that. For her loyalty. For the feeling of security she gave me. She could be quite fierce, you know. She once fought off a murderer. It was in all the papers at the time. I always felt she'd protect me against anything. Even my mother. Yet, my mother is so beautiful, so charming, that everyone likes her, especially the people in the church . . .'

Her voice acquired a bitter, sarcastic note.

'She sings in the choir, would you believe. Sometimes, when I watched her and listened to her, I used to think – maybe it's me. Maybe I'm just jealous of her because she's so beautiful and likeable and I'm neither of those things. But then I'd remember that my granny knew her better than anybody. My granny could see through her and that made an extra strong bond between my granny and me. It was like a secret we shared. Now she's gone and there's only me and I feel so vulnerable, so unsafe, so outnumbered. Who is there to believe me now?

'There's me,' Bev said.

'Oh, but if you met her, you'd think I was just being stupid, Bev. You'd be on her side. Once you saw her . . .'

'Aw, shut up. Don't insult me. You accuse me of being too trusting. Well, it's time some of that rubbed off on you. Surely to God you can have a wee bit of faith in me. And I could say much the same to you as far as your granny is concerned. You loved her and she loved you. That's something you should be glad about and grateful for. And to hell with your selfish, randy sod of a mother.'

'I suppose you're right.'

'You still want to go back to Glasgow, don't you?'

'I suppose so.'

'Never mind "suppose so". Do you or don't you?'

'Yes, I do.'

'OK. We'll both go back.'

'And to hell with Gus McCabe?'

'To hell with Gus McCabe. From tomorrow we work everywhere from morning till night – bus queues, theatre queues, everything that moves, we ask for money. Then we'll sit outside Euston Station with a bit of cardboard saying "Please help us to get home to Scotland". That should do the trick.'

For the first time Jennifer turned round.

'Oh Bev, I hope so. Oh, wouldn't it be wonderful to see Glasgow again? London's all right for Londoners and tourists with plenty of money. But Glasgow's home.'

Bev burst into song,

'We belong to Glasgow, dear old Glasgow town . . .'

Jennifer giggled.

'You always manage to cheer me up.'

'Aye. Right. That's my good deed done for today. Now, belt up and let me get some sleep.'

Jennifer settled down as best she could on the piece of cardboard she now carried around under her arm. It did very little to cushion her bones against the hard ground but at least it absorbed some of the cold. She still felt chilled to the marrow, though. They would only sleep, if they slept at all, for a short time. Then, to prevent themselves dying of hypothermia like so many other homeless people, they would get up and start walking about. Only the other day they'd stumbled across the dead body of an old man. He'd literally frozen to death. That night Jennifer felt she was going to freeze to death too. The only thing that kept her hanging on was the thought of returning to her native city. Bev had once said, 'Where's home? *What's* home?' but they both knew in their hearts that 'home' was Glasgow.

Eventually, near to tears with the misery of her blood turning to ice, Jennifer groaned out loud, 'Bev, I can't bear another minute of this. I'll have to get up.'

'Aye, OK hen.' Bev struggled into a sitting position. 'Here, do you remember in front of the Central Station – you know, in Gordon Street?'

'What about it?'

'There's gratings – something to do with the Central Hotel

– hot air belts up from there all the time – all night long, I've heard.'

'Gosh, what a marvellous skipper.'

'Aye, that's where we'll be able to thaw out.'

Jennifer laughed.

'Not tonight we won't.'

'Soon though. Now that we've made up our mind.'

They staggered stiffly to their feet.

'My God, I could kill for a drink.'

Jennifer tutted, 'You're always saying that.'

'Well, it's true.'

'Something's just occurred to me.'

'What?'

Shoulders hunched forward, they slowly began to plod along the dark, deserted street.

'We don't need to worry about being recognised in Glasgow. My skin looks a different colour. I'm not sure if it's weather-beaten or ingrained dirt. A bit of both, I suppose. And my hair's like rat's tails. Cutting it, especially my fringe, with nail scissors hasn't improved how I look.'

'You're not actually dressed like a Paris model either, hen.'

'You needn't talk. Bev, the bag lady.'

'Aye, OK, OK. Our nearest and dearest won't recognise us.'

'Nearest and dearest – that's a laugh!'

By the time the city came to life and they could start begging, Jennifer wanted to sink down on to the pavement, hard or not, and just huddle there, not doing anything. She felt exhausted and ill. Bev looked as if she felt the same.

Rain swirled around the two friends as they stood outside the tube station entrance at Tottenham Court Road. Soaked to the skin they trailed along to Oxford Street and hung around Oxford Circus for a while. After that they made their way back to Great Russell Street and stood outside the British Museum. From there they found themselves wandering through Russell Square, then Gordon Square, automatically drawn towards Euston. There they sat huddled together on the pavement outside the station with the piece of cardboard propped up in front of them. They had tried begging within the shelter of the station but the police had chucked them out.

They sat with heads sunk into their chests, Bev too exhausted to hold her head up, Jennifer too ashamed.

'Please help us to get home to Scotland' was written on the cardboard and Jennifer repeated the words in her head for hours like a mantra.

At last, grudgingly, they used some of the money they'd collected to buy a cup of tea and a pizza which they shared between them. Jennifer hadn't wanted to touch a penny but Bev said, 'Look, hen, we're going to pass out if we don't get something. Then some rotten sod'll steal our dosh. And I don't know about you but I'm dying for a pee.'

'I've been in agony for hours. I wouldn't be surprised if I've wet my pants,' Jennifer confessed.

'Well, come on, you silly cow. Let's treat ourselves to a pee.'

Afterwards, when they were washing their face and hands in the gloriously hot water in the station Ladies, Bev said, 'I've seen the day when I'd try to be quiet and dainty having a pee. All worried in case anyone heard me, if I was out visiting somebody and using their lavvy. Now I sound like a horse and I don't care a damn. It's just such a bloody relief.'

Jennifer laughed despite the misery of the rain-sodden clothes sticking to her body and making her teeth chatter.

'I know what you mean.'

The tea and the pizza helped and they were able to face returning outside.

'Tea's OK,' Bev sighed, 'but, oh, I . . .'

'Don't say it,' Jennifer interrupted fiercely. 'Don't even think about it. We need every penny to get back home. Just keep thinking about Glasgow.'

'Aye, OK, OK.'

After dark they worked theatre land. From Shaftesbury Avenue to St Martin's Lane. From Haymarket to the Strand. Among the glamour and the glitter, the beautiful expensively dressed people and the sparkling lights, Jennifer and Bev looked and felt like waifs from another planet. Often they separated and met up again at pre-arranged times and places. Each time Jennifer was in an agony of suspense in case Bev had spent any money.

'Think of the Central Hotel,' she kept saying to a dripping Bev. 'Think of that grating, that lovely hot skipper.'

'Aye, OK hen.' Bev wiped away the rivers of rain from her face with the end of her jersey. The jersey was half hidden by a black bin bag stolen from a stationer's shop piled up with rubbish that had been left out for the refuse collectors. After emptying out the rubbish, Bev had torn a hole in the plastic bag and stuck her head through it and she'd fixed Jennifer up with the same makeshift rain cape. The only trouble was they had been soaked to the skin before they'd managed to find this protection.

'Better late than never,' Bev said. 'And it suits you no end. Now if we can just get a couple of smaller white bags for our heads, that'll complete the outfit. Black and white – very smart, eh?'

Jennifer managed a chittering laugh but she was almost weeping. They still hadn't enough money. As they trudged about looking for a safe skipper, Glasgow faded far away and became no more than a dream.

XXXIII

WHEN BESSIE'S MOTHER had said she couldn't bear to be alone, she'd meant it. She followed Bessie about, was at her heels the whole day, brown eyes anxious, sparse dry frizz of hair neglected. Bessie wondered if grief had gone to the old woman's head, knocked her completely off balance emotionally. Mrs McVinney was full of fear. Bessie discovered she not only locked her bedroom door but jammed a chair under the door handle every night.

She delayed going to her bedroom for as long as possible. The television was kept on until all hours. Then, through the bedroom wall, Bessie could hear her mother's radio. It went on the whole night. Talks, music, game shows, quizzes, news from everywhere from Moscow to Timbuktu, America to China, Africa to the Netherlands, Scandinavian countries to the Holy Land. Bessie didn't know about her mother but felt she was becoming an expert in world affairs. She'd tackled her mother about it.

'Mother, why on earth do you keep your radio on all night?'

'It's company for me, dear. I hope you don't mind. I'll try and turn it down a bit if it bothers you but I'm getting a bit deaf, you see . . .'

'But you've got Peter and Daisy and me for company. We're here all night just through the wall.'

'I know, dear, but your father was always with me in our bedroom. It was where we were closest . . .' Her cheeks, dried and wrinkled like old parchment, suffused with colour. 'Not that I mean in a – you know – that kind of way. We were soul mates, your daddy and I. God joined us and I look forward to the day when He'll join us together again.'

Bessie tried to tell herself that it wouldn't last for ever. It didn't last for ever with Granda. It had only felt like it.

And it felt like it again.

The only time she could escape from her mother was on Sunday mornings at Meeting for Worship. Her mother had always been shocked at Bessie having anything to do with Quakers.

Bessie didn't bother explaining or defending any more. She was too grateful to get away on her own from the flat and enjoy a bit of peace and quiet.

Please help me to be patient and loving with my mother. You know she's a good, kind woman and a good Christian. She deserves to be cherished and looked after in her old age. I want to look after her and make her feel happy and secure and cherished. I don't mind You looking into my heart, because that's truly what's there. Nevertheless there are times when I feel I could kill her. Remember I felt like that about Granda too? I'm getting depressed with myself but what can I do? That's what I feel.

She tried to believe that somehow God would work everything out for the best. But it wasn't easy. Her mother would reprimand Bessie for her choice of women's magazines. The old-established *People's Friend* became the only magazine that met with approval. Arts publications with their nude or modern paintings were definitely out.

'You ought to be ashamed of yourself, Bessie,' was the sad murmur. Pictures were taken down off walls; Peter helped with much gleeful enthusiasm.

'I've never liked these monstrosities.'

Peter and her mother became like the terrible twins, ganging up against her.

Bessie began to catch them whispering together in corners. They would stop when she entered the room. She believed they were speaking about her, hatching some plot against her, even. Then she worried about becoming paranoid. A couple of times, she'd lost her temper with her mother. A dreadful, undreamed-of occurrence that brought tears to her mother's eyes and outrage from Peter.

She hadn't shouted or anything. It was just that she had allowed her irritation to get the better of her. But then, her mother managed to climb up to the loft one day when Bessie was out at the shops. She'd tidied the place. More than that – to use her own words – 'I've given it a really good spring clean, dear.'

It was too much.

'Hells bells!' Bessie yelled. 'Is there no place on earth I can call my own? No place where I can have my privacy? You'd no bloody right to set foot in my studio, far less interfere with anything.'

Her mother had drooped away, quietly weeping, to her room, which was even more terrible. Bessie had to apologise, of course, but it was through clenched teeth. She was genuinely sorry to have hurt the old woman, who had obviously thought she was doing a good turn. But Bessie still fumed in secret. There was a fire raging inside her.

'How could you do that to a poor old woman?' Peter sounded truly shocked. 'It's you who are selfish. *And* cruel into the bargain. And to your own mother!'

'All right. All right. I've said I'm sorry,' she told him.

In the end she not only couldn't say anything, she couldn't do anything.

When she did get herself moving, she got into such muddles. The house began to look like a tip. Her mother tried to do things to help but somehow only made everything worse, and when she spoke helpfully over Bessie's shoulder in the supermarket she nearly blew what was left of her mind.

I'm sorry. I'm not having any more of this. Hell or no hell, I've had enough.

After that, she either didn't get up in the morning, or she sat in a corner of the kitchen, withdrawn into a silent world of her own. What was the use? was the most frequent echo in a mind gone dull and totally lethargic. What was the use?

Her mother eventually called in the doctor. Surprise, surprise. Anti-depressant tablets. Drugs. The simple answer to unasked questions.

But there you are.

'Take your medicine, dear,' her mother urged. 'And that will make everything all right.'

'No, it won't, Mother.'

'But the doctor said . . .'

'What does he know or care about me?'

'Oh, now, Bessie, don't be silly, dear. The doctor knows best.'

'I'm exhausted. I'm tired out of my mind. I've nursed my father-in-law for years. For years, Mother. You don't know what that means, do you? You've never had to do it, you see. Your mother and father died in a nursing home. Father died in a hospital.'

Her mother withdrew from her, hurt, worried, frightened.

She's reading my mind. She's getting the message. I'm sorry but I just cannot help it.

No more was said that day but the next day her mother quietly announced, 'I've decided that I'll go into a retirement home. There's a very nice one in Bearsden and all my friends are in the district. They'll be able to visit me.'

Bessie brightened with hope.

'And you'll be able to visit them, Mother. And of course you won't be on your own. There'll be plenty of company for you there.'

Then she felt guilty and struggled to douse the light in her eyes.

'Of course, we'll miss you, Mother.'

'What are you talking about?' Peter recovered from his first wave of shock. 'Your mother's not going into any old folks' home. What a disgrace. What a showing-up that would be. There's plenty of room for your mother here. There's no reason for her to leave, and as far as I'm concerned, she's perfectly welcome to stay.'

Bessie stared at him, his tight mean mouth, his bulging eyes, his white bald head.

'Do you know something, Peter? I hate you. I really do hate you.'

Her mother became agitated to the point of tears.

'Oh dear, I don't want to cause any trouble or ill-feeling between you. I'm really sorry I came, Bessie. I didn't mean any harm.'

'I know, Mother, and I'm sorry too. It's just as I said. I'm so tired.'

Her mother got up and came over and kissed her.

'I can see that now, dear. Now, don't you worry. Everything's going to be all right.'

Then she disappeared to her room.

Within a few days she'd arranged to go into a private nursing home owned by the Church of Jesus. Bessie went with her and could sense, even see, the nervous beating of her mother's heart. She's afraid, but she's doing this for me, Bessie thought. And she remembered with anguish the thankfulness in her mother's eyes when she'd first been shown into the bedroom in the flat: 'I'll be safe and happy here for the rest of my life. Thank you for taking me in, Bessie. It's very kind of you, dear.'

The old woman lasted barely two months in the home. Bessie visited her every afternoon until one day – one beautiful sunny day – she'd gone to Bearsden in the morning instead. That afternoon she'd been invited to tea by Andrina McPherson. She'd bumped into Andrina in town and been struck again by the woman's beauty.

'I'd love to paint you,' she'd said and Andrina had been flattered and intrigued. She had taken her sketchpad to the house in Monteith Row and after a delicious tea, Andrina had posed for her. How happy they'd both been. Bessie had never felt so happy in years.

Then she'd had a phone message from Daisy.

'Mummy, the matron of the home says you're to go there immediately.'

Andrina had kindly driven her to Bearsden in her car.

She had run down the corridor towards her mother's room only to be stopped by a sad-faced nurse outside the door. The expression on the nurse's face said enough.

'No, no.' Bessie shook her head.

'I'm afraid so,' the nurse murmured. 'We found that she'd passed away when we went to see why she didn't come through to the dining room for her normal cup of tea.'

'No. Oh no.' Her mother had died alone. 'Oh, poor Mother.'

She had gone straight back home and shut herself up in the loft. Not even bothering with a brush, she smeared paint over the canvas with her hands, smacking it on. Mixing it with her tears.

XXXIV

BERNARD STARED AT the photograph of Jennifer that Robert had given him. Straight, nut-brown hair, a fringe reaching her eyebrows, earnest grey eyes, a wide sensitive mouth, a faint freckling over the bridge of her nose and cheeks. She was fifteen when the photo had been taken and she looked twelve. When he'd last seen her in the flesh, she must have been sixteen, nearly seventeen, and she still had a vulnerable, childlike appearance. He tried to imagine what she'd look like now at seventeen, going on eighteen. That is, if she was still alive. He hadn't said to Robert but he knew that many youngsters, especially women, either ended up in prostitution or as victims of malnutrition, hypothermia or murder. London was the place most runaways made for. He'd thought this from the start but he'd made a thorough check of Glasgow's homeless and down-and-outs just in case. The irony was Jennifer didn't need to be short of a few pounds – at least after she was twenty-one. Sophie had ordered in her will that the Bearsden house had to be sold and the proceeds and any other money put into a trust fund for Jennifer.

The girl could of course have found a job and a place to live, but he doubted it. He'd checked every agency in London. Nobody had her name on their books. He felt sorry for Robert. Guilty too for the way he'd betrayed him in the past by sleeping with his wife. How Robert had managed to forgive him, he didn't know. He would have committed murder in the same circumstances. Of course, when Robert found out, it had killed their friendship. Now they were slowly picking up the old threads again. They'd met for a drink several times and he'd been out to Robert's home in Bearsden. He also dropped into the karate club now and again to give Robert a hand with the lads, and to do a bit of sparring. A new PE teacher had joined the club and was more or less taking over from Robert. Guy Nolan was young, keen and aggressively fit.

It was true that Robert had visibly aged in the past few months.

'The chances are she's perfectly OK,' Bernard said. 'She'll have used a different name, got herself a job and a place to stay and be living the kind of life she wants to live.'

'But surely you would have come across her by now.'

'Not if she's using a false name, and London's a big place, remember. But I haven't given up hope. I'll find her. I promise you. It makes it more difficult if she's using a false name, that's all.'

'Bernard, I appreciate all the trouble you've gone to. You've enough to do seeing to your own work. You can't have much time to yourself, much of a life for yourself, with all this and the security jobs you've been doing.'

Bernard shrugged.

'I suppose you could say my job is my life. Funnily enough, I've had to do another bit of detective work.'

'Oh yes, I think you told me. That woman who's been pestering one of the Page Boys. You would have thought she'd have given up long ago.'

'Nutters like that never give up. They're obsessive, and their obsessions get worse, not better. She got worse of course when she discovered that Dave was married and had a child.'

'Oh well, I suppose she can't do much harm from America.'

'She's kept in touch by sending him filthy, disgusting packages.' Bernard shook his head. 'She's a good looking woman too. You'd never think that her head was full of worms. Anyway, the last stuff had English postmarks so she's over here. And now she's sending death threats to Dave's wife and child.'

'The quicker she's found then, the better.'

'Aye. The police are on to it and I've been doubling up enquiries with those I'm making about Jennifer. I've also had to put twenty-four-hour guards on Dave and his family. They've been going through hell because of this crazy female. Dave wants me to be with his wife and kid and I occasionally take a turn with them but I can't be there all the time.'

Robert supported his head in his hands for a moment or two.

'I feel terrible imposing on you so much, Bernard. Even if you'd accept payment . . .'

'Forget it. As I told you, while I'm on the phone or out and about trying to trace this crazy woman, I'm doubling up with enquiries about Jennifer. I think I've got a good lead on the woman so I'm off to London again tomorrow. Dave has to be there in a couple of days for a concert. This woman is in London so while Dave's there, I'll be stepping up security all round.'

'The more I think of London, Bernard, any hope I have seeps away. I can't see how anyone can be found there.'

'Missing people are being found all the time, Robert. Especially homeless kids. They've favourite haunts – railway stations during the day, shop doorways at night . . .'

'Oh God.'

'There's also agencies and religious groups and hostels, remember.'

'Jennifer hasn't turned up at any of these places so far.'

'I'm just as obsessional as that crazy woman. When I put my mind to something, I never give up. I'll find that woman, and I'll find Jennifer, believe me. And it's not just me on the job. You've met my nephew, Sean, haven't you?'

Robert nodded.

'Good looks obviously run in your family, Bernard. He'll break a few hearts, that one.'

'He's not just a pretty face. He's a first-class operator and he's on the forefront of both cases. He's travelling with me to London tomorrow.'

Bernard was glad that his brother Michael had become more relaxed in his attitude to Sean being part of the firm. Indeed he showed pride in his son when Bernard praised the lad's expertise at the job. He tried to be fair and give Sally equal praise. There was no doubt in his mind though that of the two, Sean was the one in whom he had the most faith. Sally was good, but more impulsive and aggressive. Sean was an operator after his own heart. Without needing to be told, he put into practice Bernard's own ethics and beliefs. Sean gave everybody he had to deal with – even the worst drunks or gangsters – a certain modicum of calm respect. The priority of his security firm was to avoid trouble, so he and Sean spoke to the gangsters as if they were businessmen because that was how they regarded themselves. All of his men kept the peace in pubs and clubs, prevented punters or fans from getting hurt at gatherings, indoors or out of doors, and prevented harm to any individual principal.

Sean could keep that peace in exactly the way Bernard did himself. There was an aura of strength about him, an air of quiet authority. He, like Bernard, gave respect, and was respected in return.

Bernard had already decided to give him a few more years, and then make him a partner in the firm. He would have perfect confidence in Sean as a partner right now. The lad was still so young, however, only twenty years of age. Perhaps on his twenty-first birthday: a partnership because, despite his youth, he was one of the best in the business.

Robert asked, 'Have you kept in touch with Bessie Alexander? Her daughter might still get a letter or some sort of communication.'

'She seems to be having her own problems at the moment. I called up there the other day. Her daughter's getting married – a shotgun affair. Apparently the father's none too pleased about it. But don't worry. Either Sean or I will keep checking with them.'

'I feel I should be doing more.'

'You're a teacher, Robert. You've got enough responsibility with that. I keep telling you,' he grinned at the older man, 'leave everything to the experts.'

Robert smiled wanly in return.

Bernard rose, hitching his shoulders and buttoning the jacket of his Giorgio Armani suit.

'I've another call to make. I'd better get going.'

They had been having a drink in a pub in West Nile Street. Now Robert got to his feet, shabby in comparison in his old tweed jacket with its leather elbow patches.

'I'd better make a move and get home. Laura will have dinner waiting for me.'

'Can I give you a lift?'

'No, I've parked the car round the corner.'

'Still that old banger?'

'Not the old banger you remember.'

'Another old banger?'

'How did you guess?'

They parted laughing. Bernard drove off in his Porsche and gave Robert a wave as the teacher was easing his lanky body into an ancient Cortina.

The 'other call' he'd to make was to Robert's ex-wife. Andrina had phoned the office and left a message for him to come to Monteith Row that evening. He hadn't mentioned this to Robert in case Robert thought it was good news about Jennifer. Bernard didn't believe that it was. He had still to make up his mind what to do about Andrina. He knew she had wanted him from that first visit he'd made to the house enquiring about Jennifer.

He could bet his last dollar that this was the reason she'd asked him to call tonight. She really was begging for it.

XXXV

What is it about this place? Are there people-magnets stuck to it or something? First Granda comes to live here. Then Mother. Now Daisy's husband has moved in. Soon there'll be a baby as well.

Peter's been telling me I'm useless, hopeless and helpless for so long, it's got to me. I keep telling myself that it's not true but I can't quite convince myself any more.

I've painted so much – the loft is stacked with canvases but I've only ever sold a few and they were mostly to friends and relatives just doing me a kindness, I'm sure.

I haven't a penny in the bank. So how could I buy a place of my own? Or pay a rent if there was a place to rent? Peter wouldn't part with a penny to help me to survive. So how could I even get anything to eat? What if I was lonely? What if I became fearful like Mother? I hope the fact that Mother left what money she had to the Church of Jesus secured her a place in heaven. But it didn't help me much, did it?

But I keep thinking – damn it, I am going to get out of here! I am going to survive.

Then the other day, I went into a café. There were newspapers on a shelf near the table where I was sitting. I picked one up and began leafing through it just to waste some time. Anything to delay going back to old sour face and the awful grind of my life. It was while I was sipping my tea and trying not to weep and turning the pages of this newspaper that my eye caught a 'flats to let' column. It consisted mostly of furnished flats at ridiculously high rents. Then I noticed an unfurnished place at an astonishingly reasonable rent.

Now, maybe I'm wrong, but I took this as a sign from You. You were throwing me a lifeline. If that's true, I thank You most sincerely. Oh, I thank You from the bottom of my heart.

I went straight to the factor. I got a viewing time. Oh, it's such a lovely place. I had to supply references and I managed to get a couple of really good ones.

You'll probably know this already. I'm sure You must have organised the whole thing. But anyway, I got the flat.

I've got a place to go to. Imagine*!*

I haven't told a soul except You.

I'm so excited, so happy, so sad, so afraid. But thank You. Thank You. Oh, thank You, God.

XXXVI

IT WAS JUST as he thought. She was waiting for him, posing for him exactly as she'd done long ago. The outside door was ajar. That was the first confirmation. He knew she would be waiting in the bedroom. He entered the hall and shut the door behind him. Sure enough, there she sat on the edge of the bed, dressed in a low-cut black top that displayed generous cleavage. Her skirt was slashed up to her thigh. Her black-stockinged legs were crossed and he could see the lace tops of her stockings and above them, the soft white flesh.

She was even wearing, as she so often used to, a wide-brimmed hat and she was gazing at him, smouldering-eyed, from underneath its brim.

He went over to her and slid his hand up her leg and into her groin, at the same time pushing her back on to the bed. He caught her look of surprise. In the past they had played so many leisurely games. He had enjoyed her with his eyes as she had paraded about the room for him. She had performed a slow striptease like a professional. He had kissed her from the soles of her feet to the top of her head. He had covered her in rose petals. He had licked champagne from her most intimate parts. He had been both gentle and passionate.

This time it was fast. Afterwards she sounded dazed, confused.

'I suppose . . . it's been so long, Bernard darling. I don't blame you for being impatient. But remember how wonderful it used to be? We took our time. We were real gourmets . . .'

'Yes,' he said. 'But I loved you then.'

There was silence for a long minute as the words sank in. Then she said in a small, tight voice,

'Get out.'

'Sure.' He got up from the bed and zipped up his fly. 'I'm off to London tomorrow. I don't suppose you're interested or you would have asked me, but as well as other business, I'm following up a few leads I hope might help me track down Jennifer. I'm as certain as I can be she's in London.'

'You always were a bastard. Time has obviously done nothing to improve you.'

'That's my Andrina. You never could see past your fanny.'

'Get out. And don't ever come back here again.'

'I'm on my way.' He turned at the door, winked at her and said, 'Thanks.'

The bedside clock she flung at him bounced noisily off the door. He left the flat smiling to himself. Yet he couldn't deny the deep sadness in him. He had loved her, and for so many years. No way though was he going to allow her to use him again and not only that, but to ruin his relationships with other women.

She was a witch, and a bitch, and he had been a fool to have loved her so much and for so long.

It was for Robert's sake and for Jennifer's, not Andrina's, that he would continue to look for the girl. God knows what would have happened to her by now, if she was still alive. Prostitution, probably. Some pimp would have his claws in her. One problem Robert hadn't thought of – Jennifer was of a legal age to do what she wanted. Even if Bernard did find her, he couldn't force her to return with him to Glasgow. It would have to be done by persuasion.

Eve Page and the Page Boys were booked into the Hilton but weren't due to arrive for a couple of days. Meantime he and Sean checked the hotel's security and then both went out to do their first day's foot-slogging detective work.

Bernard opted for the railway stations, the underground stations and outside theatres and cinemas and main tourist areas like Trafalgar Square.

Sean was to explore the streets along by the river. They both had a picture of Jennifer and they planned to show it to every prostitute, dosser, wino and homeless person they came across.

By late afternoon, Bernard was beginning to feel it was a hopeless task. He hadn't even stopped for anything to eat since breakfast and, despite his physical fitness, he was feeling tired. It was a hot summer's day and he was wearing a suit. It was part of his policy that he and his men always looked smart and well turned out at all times.

He longed for a beer and wished now he had stopped for one at Euston. He'd already been to all the other stations and the surrounding streets without success. Now he cut through Russell Square on his way to Oxford Street and Shaftesbury Avenue via the British Museum. Begging was one way homeless people survived and he reckoned where there were lots of tourists, there would be beggars. He decided to give his feet a few minutes to cool off on one of the seats in the tree-lined grassy area of the square. It was then that his heart took an unexpected leap of joy. There, on one of the benches, sat two females. One was a disreputable-looking blonde. The other, hardly recognisable in her neglected state, was Jennifer. He had an excellent, well-trained memory for detail and there was no mistaking that waif-like figure and that way she had of gazing apprehensively upwards. At the moment, she was blinking up through the too-long straggly ends of her fringe. She wasn't looking in his direction. Neither of them had noticed him. They were both gazing as if in a dream at the huge Russell Hotel towering up over the trees.

He approached them carefully and soundlessly. Then once in front of them, blocking their view, he said gently,

'Hello, Jennifer.'

Silence. Then the blonde turned to Jennifer and asked incredulously, 'Is that your daddy?'

Jennifer shook her head.

'The fucker then?'

Another shake of the head.

'It's Bernard. He's a bodyguard.'

'Wow!' the blonde gasped. 'He can guard my body any time.'

Bernard sat down on the bench beside Jennifer.

'Your daddy's sick with worry about you.'

'He's got Laura. I find it hard to believe he's all that bothered about me. Especially after all this time.'

'He's never stopped looking for you and worrying about

you. I volunteered to help. One of my men and I have been searching everywhere for you.'

'I notice you've never mentioned my mother.'

'I'm sure she's been worried too. But I can tell you this, Jennifer, your father's a broken man. He's aged before my eyes with worry about you.'

'I'm sorry,' Jennifer said in a small voice. 'I didn't mean to hurt him.'

'All he wants is for you to come home.'

'I can't.'

'How do you mean, you can't?'

Bev interrupted then.

'We haven't any dosh for the fare for a start.'

'Oh, don't worry about that.' Bernard still addressed Jennifer. 'I'll pay for your ticket back to Glasgow.'

Jennifer said,

'It's not just the money.'

'What then?'

'No way am I ever going back to Monteith Row or anywhere near my mother and that creep of a man she sleeps with.'

'OK. We'll find you somewhere else.'

'Not at Daddy's love nest either.'

'OK. We'll find you someplace else, I said. *I'll* find you someplace else.'

'And another thing,' Jennifer said, 'I don't go anywhere without Bev. I don't know what I would have done without her. She's from Glasgow as well and she wants to go home. Don't you, Bev?'

She turned to the other woman, who nodded enthusiastically. Bernard hesitated, groaning inside. There were limits. However, he managed in the end, for Robert's sake – he owed him, after all – to capitulate.

'Aye, OK. Bev as well. Now, I'm on another job down here, so I can't get back to Glasgow for a few days.' He brought out his wallet. 'I'll give you enough money to get cleaned up first of all. For God's sake, get your hair done. You don't want to give Robert another shock seeing you in this state. I'll also give you the fare home. No, on second thoughts, I'll go and get your tickets. Will you promise to stay here until I get back? I'll pick up a taxi. I won't be long.'

He replaced the wallet without giving them any money. 'When I get back, I'll give you the tickets and the money to get yourselves a make-over. OK?'

Both women nodded, flushed now, obviously excited. It was pathetic. They stank to high heavens.

He winked at them before leaving.

'Stay cool.'

XXXVII

'WHAT DO YOU mean – you've got a flat?' Peter was outraged.

She hadn't dared tell him until everything was signed, sealed and delivered. She'd received a generous cheque from a couple for whom she'd painted a picture of their son. With that cheque she'd paid a couple of months' rent in advance. She'd already secretly moved a suitcase and all her canvases out of the house. She hadn't meant to tell Peter in front of Daisy and Nigel, but there never seemed to be the opportunity to be on their own. Even in their bedroom, by the time she'd cleared up and got through every night, he was snoring.

'Will I make you a cup of tea, Mummy?' Daisy sounded apprehensive and childish.

Nigel said nothing, just stared owl-like at her through his thick spectacles, obviously dumbfounded.

'I've got a flat and I'm leaving here and going to start a new life on my own.'

'Don't be stupid.' Peter dismissed the mere idea.

She struggled to keep calm.

'I mean I'm leaving you, Peter.'

'What do you mean – you're leaving me?'

'Our marriage has been over for years.'

'You're mad,' Peter said. 'You've gone right off your head.'

Certainly she had developed one hell of a headache.

'I've already taken one suitcase over to the flat, and everything from the loft. I've a holdall ready for me to collect from the hall cupboard. And that's it.'

Peter had gone a sickly grey.

'You're not taking one item out of my house. Everything in

this house belongs to me. I've worked hard all my life for everything in this house.'

'I don't want anything from this house, Peter. Apart from my paints and canvases which I'm quite sure you don't want anything to do with, all I'm taking is my clothes and some personal gifts. Things that my mother and father gave me, for instance.'

Her mother had once given her a lovely patchwork quilt that she'd sewn herself. Her and Father had decided to buy one of these electric overblankets and they didn't need the quilt any more. Then there was the mug nine-year-old Daisy had given her on her birthday. On it were painted the words 'To the best mum in the world'. She had always treasured that.

She'd called to see the bank manager, and what a traumatic experience that had been. However, she had managed to convince him that she had earned a fair sum at her painting and her prospects of earning much more were very good indeed. She felt guilty about that. She hadn't felt in the least confident about her earning capacity. So desperate was she, however, to get a loan to buy a bed to sleep on and a chair to sit on and perhaps even a table for the new flat, she put on a performance of a confident, professional woman that deserved an Oscar.

She was given just enough to buy the bare essentials including a kettle, a couple of pots and pans, and enough linoleum with which to cover the floors.

'But Mummy, you can't,' Daisy wailed, tearful now. 'What's going to happen to us? What's going to happen to me?'

'Darling, I'm not moving to another planet. And you're a married woman now, don't forget. I wasn't much older than you when I was expecting and I had Granda and Peter to look after, as well as seeing to myself.'

'But you can't,' Daisy repeated. 'What about my career? I can't look after a baby when I'm at university. I'll have to have an abortion.'

'Of course you won't. Find out if they have a crèche or nursery facilities. I'm sure lots of other students have had to cope with the same problem. Ask around. Get professional advice. Now, I really must go. I've written my address down on this piece of paper. I'm not on the phone yet but I hope to get one put in as soon as possible.'

There was a stunned silence as she walked from the room out to the hall to collect her bag. There would be plenty of taxis cruising around and she planned to hail one as soon as she got downstairs and out of the building.

'Mummy!' Daisy ran after her and caught her at the outside door. Daisy, such a sweet baby with a downy head, suckling at her breast. Daisy, toddling, then bumping down and holding out plump outstretched hands to be picked up.

'Don't leave me, Mummy. I'm sorry if I've upset you in any way. I didn't mean to.'

Nigel and Peter appeared behind her.

Peter said, 'How can you be so selfish?'

That did it! She shouted at them.

'Selfish? *Me?* I've kept this house spotless. I've made your meals. I've been a bloody cleaner, laundry maid, nurse, every damned thing. *And* I've managed to paint as well. What the hell have any of you done?'

Peter was the first to recover from the initial shock.

'You've gone off your head. I always knew . . .'

'You know nothing, especially about me. You've been too wrapped up in your mean-minded, whining self.'

'You shouldn't talk to Daddy like that,' Daisy sobbed.

Bessie turned on her.

'I'll talk any fuckin' way I like!'

'Oh!' they all cried out in shocked unison.

'And as for you,' Bessie went on, 'you've done nothing with your life. You expect life to do everything for you. And me to be your skivvy into the bargain. You're completely irresponsible. You thought nothing about having this baby except I'd take it off your hands. Well, tough luck. This time you'll have to take responsibility for your own actions. I've had it up to here with the lot of you.'

She got out, struggling breathlessly with the heavy bag, down the stairs, and out on to the street. A taxi came by, and she clambered into it.

Her heart and head were still thumping with anger as the

taxi weaved its way through the traffic from the south side of the city to the West End.

It was the side of town where the university and the BBC were situated and it was peopled with lots of young students and television people. The flat was in a red sandstone building in Botanic Crescent.

A low road ran off Queen Margaret Drive, where the BBC was situated, and alongside the leavy, tree-lined Botanic Gardens. Arching up to the right of this road, and separated by a grassy belt and more trees, was the Crescent. First of all there were large three-storeyed terrace houses, one of which housed the BBC Club. Then there were four-storeyed red sandstone buildings with big bay windows and gardens in front. Her flat was one up. She paid off the taxi and lugged her bag through the tiled close and up the stairs.

Key in the door, door opened, step inside, shut door behind her.

She'd done it!

She dumped the case down and began wandering through the flat. It was far too big for anyone on their own. A hall big enough to have a party in. A huge kitchen. A bathroom big enough to live in. A large bay-windowed sitting room of ballroom proportions, looking on to the trees of the Crescent and the Botanic Gardens beyond. Two bedrooms. A large dining room. The dining room, facing the front and bright with sunlight, could be her studio.

Everything was so big, so empty, so quiet. She felt faint.

'Courage, Bessie,' she told herself firmly.

Her voice echoed through the cavern of silence.

XXXVIII

WHAT BLISS! AT Bernard's expense they'd had a shower at the station and a shampoo and blow-dry at the hairdresser's. Then Bernard booked them into a small but comfortable hotel. They'd washed their clothes and luxuriously soaked themselves in a hot bath. He had told them he'd contact them again in a couple of days. Meantime they were just to relax and enjoy a rest and some good grub.

'He's a gentleman and a scholar,' Bev said. 'Sexy with it as well, eh?'

'I suppose he is,' Jennifer giggled.

'No suppose about it, hen.'

'He's old enough to be our father.'

'Not mine, hen. Anyway I wouldn't care if he was old enough to be my grandfather. I'd still say he was gorgeous.'

'I've always like him. Not in that way,' Jennifer added hastily. 'I used to call him "Uncle".'

'Oh aye. Was he another of your mammy's boyfriends?'

'Oh no, I don't think so. Bernard was a friend of my father. He must still be, judging by the way he was talking about him.'

'I suppose you're right. Anyway, what a bit of luck! I was beginning to think we'd never make it.'

Jennifer could have said – what with you drinking the money each time we managed to gather some together. But she held her tongue. She couldn't blame Bev for drowning her sorrows. Now though, they had a real chance to make a fresh start. It was wonderful.

'Do you know,' Jennifer admitted, 'I'd begun to feel I wasn't part of the human race. Just some garbage for people either to ignore or push out of their way.'

'How do you think I've felt? I've been on the streets for

longer than you. And I was alone at first. God, that was no joke. Terrified out of my wits, I was.'

'I don't know how you survived.'

'Och we're all tougher than we think, hen.'

They enjoyed a delicious dinner, then stretched luxuriously out on the two single beds in the room and watched television.

'This is the life,' Bev said. 'Our sexy pal can take as long as he likes. I'd be perfectly happy to stay here for a week or two, never mind a day or two.'

Jennifer snuggled further into the duvet.

'Me too. Still, I suppose it'll be good to see Glasgow again.'

'It's not going anywhere.'

'I'll feel safer there. It's not so big and I know my way around. And Fisher had better not try to come near me again. I'll tell him where to go.'

Bev laughed.

'That's my girl. You tell him to fuck off.'

'No way am I going back to live with my mother ever again.' Jennifer's voice grew loud with emotion.

'OK. OK. Nobody's saying you have to go back to her.'

'I don't want to live with my father and Laura either.'

'Don't worry. You won't.'

'As long as we stick together. Even if it means sleeping rough in Glasgow, I don't care.'

'Well, I do, hen. I'm getting too old for skippering. It's not too bad in summer. But with another winter coming up . . .'

'Right enough. It doesn't bear thinking about. But surely in Glasgow, somebody will help us.'

'When are you going to phone your da? You promised Bernard.'

'Tomorrow, when I feel better.'

'You should have let him phone like he wanted to.'

'I just want to get myself together first.'

'Aye, aye, OK. Now will you shut up. I'm trying to watch the telly.'

Jennifer was quiet after that, drifting in and out of warm and comfortable sleep. On the edge of her consciousness, however, tiny worries and apprehensions still niggled. Bernard wasn't going to keep them in this hotel or any other hotel for ever. Once they got back to Glasgow, he'd deliver her to her father and that would be that as far as he was concerned. He had enough to do even now without bothering about her. A crisis had arisen with one of the Page Boys. Or rather, with his child. Some mad woman had kidnapped Dave's baby. Bernard had left immediately he'd had the call on his mobile phone. But he'd reminded her once again by calling over his shoulder:

'Phone Robert right now, Jennifer. Tell him you're OK. Tell him you'll be home in a couple of days.'

'Yes, all right,' she'd replied.

But she hadn't been able to bring herself to phone. In trying to analyse why she was putting off contacting her father, she came to the conclusion that the tough shell she'd grown around her in order to survive these past months would suddenly shatter at the sound of his voice. She'd be a little girl again and the horror of all she'd gone through since she'd last seen him would completely overcome her.

But perhaps tomorrow, after a decent sleep – she felt as if she'd never had a decent sleep for years – she would feel better, stronger, able to cope. It was one thing being able to cope physically, of course. She'd discovered, like Bev, that she was tougher than she looked or what she'd always thought she was. If someone had told her that she'd survive icy winter nights in draughty shop doorways, or desolate days trudging, chittering ankle deep in snow, or being soaked to the skin with no hope of getting dry, she wouldn't have believed them.

Emotionally it was a different matter. She'd toughened up a bit. At least on the surface. She didn't believe she'd go into such a panic if faced with Paul Fisher again. To some degree, however, she was still at the mercy of her emotions. Strangely enough, even more so now that there was a chance of getting back to a more comfortable and civilised way of life. She wanted to take that chance, longed for it. No way did she want to go back on the streets again, in London or in Glasgow or anywhere else.

Neither she nor Bev wanted even to put a foot out of the hotel. It was as if it might disappear if they left it and their food and shelter there evaporate into a dream like all their other dreams. They wandered about inside, admiring every corner of the place. They sank into the comfortable chairs in the lounge. They felt like queens being served in the dining room with its pristine white table cover and sparkling cutlery.

They appreciated, savoured, every moment and every moment was sheer joy. The second night when they settled down in bed to watch television, Jennifer said, 'Just think of all the poor folk out there just now trying to find a decent skipper.'

'Aw shut up. Don't spoil things.'

'I wasn't trying to spoil things. I was just being thankful that we're not one of them any more.'

'Aye, well, don't count your chickens, as they say. Don't tempt fate.'

'How do you mean?'

'You know what I mean, hen.'

Jennifer fell silent. Eventually she said,

'Daddy'll see us all right.'

'Oh aye? Your daddy's a man of money and influence, is he? He can buy us a flat? Or get the council to give us one? I thought you told me he was just a poorly paid teacher in some rough school.'

'Well, yes, but . . .'

'Stop kidding yourself.'

'Do you know anybody?'

'Oh aye, Gus McCabe. A very influential man. Owns a big flat in Byres Road. Plenty room for us there. Two punchbags. He would just love that.'

'I meant on the council.' Jennifer sighed. 'I wish my grandfather was alive – as well as my granny. Grandfather was a senior magistrate at one time. He would have been Lord Provost if his health hadn't failed.'

'Too bad.'

Suddenly they were both diverted by a news item on the television. It was about the Page Boy kidnapping, as it was called. The police had arrested a woman and the baby was safely back with its parents.

'That means our sexy pal's off the hook. What do you bet

he'll be here at the crack of dawn to pick us up and shove us on the first train going up north.'

'Isn't he coming with us?' Jennifer queried anxiously. 'I thought he was.'

Bev shrugged.

'Don't know, hen. We'll just have to wait and see.'

As it turned out, Bernard couldn't come with them. He saw them on to the train and waved them off with the promise he'd see them as soon as he could in Glasgow. He thought Jennifer had contacted Robert and took it for granted they'd be met by him in Glasgow.

Once the train sped off, Bev said, 'You're crazy, lying to him like that. What's the idea?'

'I didn't actually lie to him.'

'You let him think that you'd phoned your da and everything was OK. Why, for God's sake?'

Jennifer's face screwed up with anxiety.

'I just want to take one step at a time. I just want to get back to Glasgow first.'

'OK. OK. It's your funeral.'

XXXIX

When Bessie shut the sitting-room door, the outside door reverberated as if someone was trying to get in. Often there was a creaking of floorboards, probably from the flat above but it sounded as if someone was walking into Bessie's hall. The bedroom at the back was near the well of the stairs and voices or footsteps of anyone going up or down the stairs made sudden, hollow sounds that startled her. The bathroom door squeaked. So did the kitchen door. A rushing, hissing sound seemed to go on for ever before dying away into the walls. She couldn't fathom or trace it. Eventually she realised it was one of the neighbours who'd flushed the toilet. She peered timidly out from behind her curtains and tried to assess whether or not she was in friendly territory.

She longed for a friend, someone to speak to. She went to Meeting on Sunday morning, but kept her head down except when it came to the time to smile and shake hands with everyone. She escaped before the tea and biscuits and chat, however. What could she say to these good people?

'Oh by the way, I've changed my address. I've walked out on my husband and pregnant daughter.'

She couldn't be bothered cooking. It seemed such a waste of time just for herself. She opened a tin of soup for lunch and ate a packet of crisps. She had several cups of tea during the afternoon and then for what she had begun to call dinner at home, she had a slice of bread and jam, and a cup of coffee.

Back in the Shawlands Cross flat, they'd changed from the old Scottish custom of 'high tea' and now had 'dinner' each evening. This had been Daisy's idea. Daisy was all for 'moving with the times'. And having 'proper civilised eating habits'.

Bessie wondered how civilised the family eating habits were

since she'd left. She somehow couldn't imagine Daisy, or Peter or Nigel making the three-course family meals plus coffee that she had been cooking every night. And of course they wouldn't go out for a meal. Peter was so mean he'd always refused to even buy her a cup of tea outside.

'We've plenty of tea at home,' he'd say. It wouldn't matter if she was collapsing with fatigue or her tongue was hanging out with thirst. No tea or food in a restaurant and that was that.

Her anxiety about Daisy not getting enough nourishment grew to panic proportions. She'd never forgive herself if Daisy became malnourished and the baby suffered. She didn't really believe that Daisy would get an abortion. Several times she'd gone out and hung about outside a phone box. At last she'd dialled the flat. There was no reply. She worried about that as well. It was dinner time. They were always in at dinner time. She couldn't bear the worry and suspense a moment longer. She jumped on a bus to take her over to Shawlands Cross. Once she tracked Daisy down, she would stress to her the importance of eating well. After all, the poor girl was still very young and it was her first pregnancy. She could be upset about her mother deserting her in her time of need, could be pining and unhappy and generally neglecting herself. By the time Bessie had reached Shawlands Cross, she was in a state of near collapse with worry and agitation. She hurried from the bus but before she had a chance to run across the road to the flat, she had to stop at the lights because they'd changed to red. As she stood along with a crowd of other people waiting for the return of the 'green man' Bessie's eye was caught by a group of people tucking into fish suppers at the window table in Jaconalli's chippy. Obviously, Daisy, Nigel and Peter were not being starved of nourishment after all. It didn't look as if Daisy was pregnant either. She was wearing her skin-tight dress, the one she said she could not get into only a few weeks ago.

Bessie caught a bus back to the West End.

Botanic Crescent was still and quiet except for a faint babble of voices as she passed the BBC Club. The cool tiled close and stone stairs leading to her flat were empty and alien. The hollow sound of the door opening and shutting echoed in her heart as well as every room. She hurried into the kitchen to switch on her transistor. She was truly glad of the radio. It was company. She wasn't used to being on her own in such silence. She had never been on her own in her life. There had been her mother and father and Moira in her first home. Even old Towzer had been company. Then after her marriage, there had been constant company from the word go. To think she'd always longed to be on her own for a bit of peace and quiet. Freedom! she'd always thought. Oh, for freedom.

Now, look at her. With an effort she pulled herself together. Anger helped. Bloody hell! *Fancy them wolfing away at fish and chips!*

Her fingers itched to paint. She felt feverish with the need to work. Tomorrow she would start another painting of Andrina Anderson. This time she would do the painting for herself. The first one had been a present for Andrina. The poor woman's daughter had disappeared and she was being very brave about it. She had also been kind and sympathetic when Bessie's mother had died. It was because of that that Bessie had not only given her the painting as a present but had made the portrait less than completely honest. In a way it was the same as she'd done for the couple whose son she'd painted. She had been trying to be kind and please the recipient. That was why of course neither painting had pleased herself. The one of Andrina had especially niggled at her and left her feeling frustrated and unfulfilled.

She had made a good copy of Andrina's beauty. But a photograph could have done that. There were other things about the woman that intrigued her as an artist. She liked Andrina. She was charming and talented. Her mother had obviously passed on her cookery and baking skills to her daughter: Bessie had enjoyed more than one delicious tea at Andrina's flat and it cheered her up to think of visiting there again. She resolved to phone Andrina the very next day and arrange a visit. She was sure Andrina would agree to more sittings. She had enjoyed posing. Not only that, but she happily chatted all the time while Bessie painted. She didn't expect any verbal response, didn't even seem to notice the one-sidedness of the conversation. Bessie was sure she did notice the untidiness and, by Andrina's standards, lack of material comforts when she visited Bessie's flat. However, Andrina was too polite to say anything about that. Instead, she pressed invitations on Bessie to come to the Monteith Row flat.

Bessie found her a complex kind of person and she had become quite obsessed about how she could convey this on canvas. She wanted to be with Andrina again, to study her again. The more she thought along work lines, the less lonely and afraid she felt. She began to recognise and become familiar with the sounds of the place. Indeed, instead of being fearful in the house, she began to feel safe.

Much of the echoing noise, especially of her own footsteps, was caused by the bare linoleum or bare floorboards. But she had another worry. Her money was fast running out. She would enjoy having tea at Andrina's for more reasons than the quality of the home baking. Bessie was fast becoming just plain hungry.

The date with Andrina was for a few days hence. Meantime, the problem of the lack of money loomed large. Bessie was forced to seek out the nearest office of the Department of Health and Social Security. She had never set foot in such a place before and found it a painfully humiliating experience. The only thing that saved it from being a total disaster was her artist's eye. She had a small sketchpad in her handbag – something she never moved without – and she passed the time by surreptitiously sketching the different characters around her.

There were lantern-jawed men with hunched shoulders and loose, shabby clothes. There were harassed women, old before their time, nursing babies and shouting at older children who were racing about and causing a disturbance.

'Do you want me to get flung out, you wee bastards?' was one woman's desperate cry. Another woman, miserably hunched and weeping, was explaining to another woman how she'd acquired her terrible black eye. Her companion's face was creased with sympathy and she kept shaking her head and tutting.

The air was heavy with hopelessness, anxiety and despair, the décor a seedy and depressing dark brown. Everyone had been dehumanised by being given a number. When your number was called, you went over to the counter where you were forced to answer the most intimate questions and discuss your most private business in full hearing of the person on either side of you at the counter. Not to mention the waiting folk sitting behind you.

Bessie tried to hang on to some pride and dignity. She was honest about her circumstances. She also told them that she was an artist, and was just having a temporary lull in her earnings. Perhaps this was slightly more hopeful than honest. However, the word 'artist' seemed to have a bit of magic attached to it. At least for the lady behind the counter who was dealing with Bessie's case. After filling in a few forms, Bessie was told that she would receive a cheque, and a book for future payments that she could collect every week at the local post office. She was even treated with a modicum of respect and quite a nice smile.

The cheque, or indeed the payments, didn't amount to much as far as electricity, gas and any other bills were concerned but at least she had been given time to get herself organised, to try to establish an income. The DHSS had thrown her a lifeline, God bless them.

Jubilant, she hurried straight from the DHSS office to the nearest fish and chip shop and bought a fish supper. Then she returned to the flat and sat cross-legged on the floor of her studio, eating the fish and chips out of their newspaper wrapping.

The room was large and square. Two long windows framed the empty fireplace, flooding the room with cool, clear light. The floorboards were already taking on the traditional studio look with flecks of paint splashed here and there. A particularly large yellow smear showed where Bessie had inadvertently stood on a tube of cadmium yellow. On the far wall stacks of canvases awaited her attention. Her easel took pride of place in the centre of the room like some primitive altar. A stool beside it held her palette and jars of oil and turps. Discarded brushes were scattered among the paint-soaked rags around the base of the easel.

The huge canvas on the easel dominated the room. Stark images of industrial might, wheels and cogs, crushing humanity, alleviated only by the central images of rebellious figures locked in mortal combat with the nightmare of rampant industrialisation.

She felt great satisfaction gazing at those rebellious figures.

And the fish and chips were absolutely delicious.

XL

OH GLASGOW! THE train clanking over the bridge. The River Clyde sparkling underneath. Central Station. Not too big like Euston. Familiar. Manageable. Scottish accents all around. Bouncy bustle and friendly smiles.

Oh Glasgow!

Jennifer and Bev stood dazed and smiling at nothing in particular and everything in general. They couldn't believe they'd actually made it.

Finally Bev said, 'Now what, hen?'

The smile faded from Jennifer's face.

'I suppose I'd better phone Daddy.'

'About time too. If you'd phoned in London when you were supposed to, he would have been here meeting you.'

'I know. I know. I just wanted to be safely here first. I suppose I didn't want to risk anything going wrong.'

'Aye, OK daftie. You're here now.'

They found a phone box and crowded close together into it, fussing about getting the right money between them. Jennifer dialled the Bearsden number. As soon as she heard Robert's voice she began to weep as she'd known she would. Impossible to contain her grief.

'Daddy.'

'Oh Jennifer, darling. Where are you?'

'The Central Station. Uncle Bernard bought our tickets.'

'Don't move from there,' Robert said. 'I'll be with you as fast as my car can take me.'

'Thanks, Daddy.'

She hung up and let the sobs racket out.

'Will you shut up?' Bev shouted. 'What the hell are you

bawling about? The time for that was when we were nearly freezing to death in some rotten skipper, not now.'

'I know.'

They squeezed out of the phone box and Jennifer wiped her eyes as best she could on the back of her sleeve.

'Now look at you,' Bev groaned. 'You were like a tramp before in those old rags. Now your face is a mess as well.'

'At least we're a lot cleaner now,' Jennifer managed.

After a minute or two's silence Bev said, 'Look, hen, this is your chance. Don't mess it up with trying to tag me along. I'll be OK.'

'You shut up. Do you really think I'm going to walk away from you now?'

'You don't owe me anything.'

'What?' Jennifer shouted incredulously. 'I owe you everything. I'd be dead or worse if it hadn't been for you. I'll never desert you, Bev. Never.'

'Don't talk rot. A thousand things could change between now and never.'

'I won't change.'

'Aye, OK, OK.'

They stood in silence after that, Bev clutching her two plastic bags and Jennifer clinging on to her backpack.

'There he is,' said Jennifer at last. And she began to weep again.

'What's up with you, you silly wee cow?' Bev muttered irritably. 'Smile for the man. Look pleased to see him, for Christ's sake.'

The sight of the thin, gaunt-faced anxious-eyed man with hair more grey than brown running towards her about broke Jennifer's heart. She loved him and regretted, more than words could ever express, having caused him pain. She fell into his arms and she could feel his tears mingling with her own. Eventually he let her go and dried both their faces with his handkerchief. He was leading her away when she suddenly remembered Bev. The tragic look in the older woman's eyes when she turned back made Jennifer feel ashamed.

'Wait a minute, Daddy. I want you to meet my best friend,

Bev. I wouldn't have survived this past year if it hadn't been for her.'

Robert put out his hand.

'Bev, I'm very pleased to meet you and I thank you for anything you've done to help my daughter.'

'Think nothing of it, pal.' Bev had quickly recovered her usual cheeky manner.

'Can I give you a lift anywhere?' Robert asked politely.

Jennifer said, 'Daddy, she's nowhere to go. Nor have I, for that matter. I'm sorry but I don't want to stay either with you or with Mummy. All I know at the moment is that Bev and I must stick together.'

Robert studied them both for a moment. Jennifer remembered that serious, thoughtful look so well. Then he said, 'We've obviously a lot to talk about and things to sort out. Meantime Bev is very welcome to come with you to Bearsden. You look as if you both need a good meal. Let's start with that.'

'Thanks, Daddy.'

They didn't speak much in the car. Except Robert said, 'It's maybe not the right time to tell you this, darling, but because we're going to Bearsden and we'll be passing her house and you might want to . . .'

'It's all right,' Jennifer said quietly. 'I know. I phoned the hospital.'

'Right.'

Another silence. Then:

'What part of Glasgow do you come from, Bev?'

'Anderson originally. But I've been around a bit.'

'Any family?'

'Not a bleeding one.'

Jennifer nudged her. She didn't want her friend to make a bad impression. The sight of Bearsden, however, overawed them into silence. Even Jennifer had become so used to the rough and seedy side of existence that she had forgotten what suburban good life could look like.

Along the wide, undulating street known as the Switchback with its leafy trees and pretty bungalows. Then on to Canniesburn Toll and Drymen Road. More mature trees. Big villas now set back in large, well-clipped lawns. Past 'the village', the row of shops, and the terrace where Sophie had lived. Then along a bit and across the road, Laura's bungalow. Jennifer saw Laura watching for them from the sitting-room window.

The car stopped. Laura disappeared then reappeared at the front door.

'Do come in. Are you all right, Jennifer?'

'Yes, thank you.'

'And who is this?'

'Bev, my best friend.'

'Hello, Bev.'

Bev nodded but kept unusually quiet.

'I've some nice homemade soup heating up and I've a steak pie in the oven. I'm just seeing to some chips. You go into this bedroom and dump your belongings, girls, and tidy up if you like. There's a bathroom *en suite.* Then come through to the kitchen and we'll eat. Robert, you open a can of peas while I see to the chips.'

Left alone in the bedroom, Bev whispered, 'Very posh. Bathroom *en suite*! Do you think it'll be OK if I have a pee?'

'Of course. Don't be silly, Bev!'

Jennifer was tidying her hair at the dressing-table mirror when Bev reappeared, tugging up her jeans.

'Have you seen it in there? A coloured suite and all sorts of bottles of God knows all what perfumery stuff. And, would you believe it, there's a doll with a knitted dress and underneath the dress is a spare toilet roll. The place is carpeted as well. This is the life, eh?'

'I'm not staying here.'

'You're daft.'

'You don't understand. I've nothing against Daddy or Laura but they're so happy together, I've always felt I don't belong. An intruder. I found you can feel more lonely being a gooseberry than you can on your own.'

'Oh, aren't you the sensitive one! Well hen, I'm not that fussy. As far as I'm concerned, this is a lot better than what we've been used to. And they're welcome to their lovey-dovey bit.'

'It's not just for my own sake. I don't want to spoil things for them. And this is their bedroom, by the way. The spare room hasn't got an *en suite*.'

'Oh, is that not terrible. I'm going to complain about that, so I am.'

They went through to the kitchen, giggling secretly together but once in the room, they were once more quiet and uncertain.

Robert said, 'Come on now, don't be shy. Sit down at the table. Make yourselves at home.'

They sat, heads lowered, only tentatively glancing up now and again when they were spoken to.

'Is Bernard still down there?' Robert asked.

Jennifer nodded in between taking mouthfuls of soup. 'I think he's coming back to Glasgow tomorrow.'

'I'll never be able to thank him enough for finding you.'

'He's been very kind to us,' Jennifer said. 'Saw us on to the train and everything.'

'After you have your meal, you must phone your mother. She'll be so glad to hear from you.'

'I'm not staying with her either. Has she got married to that Fisher man?'

'As far as I know, the divorce isn't through yet. Anyway, she's still at Monteith Row.'

'Nothing's changed then.'

'Surely you can at least phone her, Jennifer, and let her know you're all right.'

Jennifer shrugged.

'If you say so.'

He was trying to palm her off on to her mother. Just as he'd always done from the day he'd married Laura. But her mother wouldn't want her either. Especially not with Bev.

No, nothing had changed. Suddenly she felt as if the soup was choking her.

XLI

BESSIE HAD SOME difficulty in trying to explain to Andrina that this painting was going to be different from the original one that Andrina had prominently and proudly displayed on her sitting-room wall.

'It's not really meant to be you,' she lied. 'It's more like how a writer uses a model from real life as a trigger for a fictional character he wants to create.'

She hadn't wanted Andrina to see it and did succeed in preventing her from having even a glimpse while she was working on the picture. It would have seriously inhibited her if Andrina had made any comments, good or bad.

Once it was done, it was done. She didn't care what Andrina said then. At the same time, she had no desire to hurt or upset the woman. To paint this picture was something she felt she just had to do. And she'd done it. That was all. She did feel the better for having done it, though. Indeed she gazed on the finished product with a kind of reverence. In a way, she felt like this about all her paintings. She never really believed she could do it and when she did manage it, she always thanked God most sincerely for the miracle.

Andrina had stolen a peek at it before she could remove the canvas.

She'd stared at the barely recognisable picture with its red and green tones instead of flesh colours. Bessie quailed inside, expecting an outburst of fury and insulted as well as hurt feelings. But not a bit of it.

'Gosh!' Andrina laughed. 'I see what you mean now about just needing a trigger like writers do in creating fictional characters. That's not me at all.'

Side by side with Andrina, Bessie gazed at the picture. It

showed passion. Yet there were other layers, like shadows, overlapping each other, cooling into a blank distance. What the critics were later to call 'chiaroscuro'.

'You're not angry?'

'Of course not.' Andrina shrugged. 'As I said, it's nothing like me. You've made something up. To be honest though, Bessie, I can't say I like it. It's not very *nice*, is it?'

'I don't think of my paintings as being nice or not nice.'

'Anyway, I'm glad you're not expecting me to hang that on my wall.'

Bessie wrapped the canvas and packed it away. Her visit to Andrina's house finished with a delicious lunch and Andrina chatting away quite the thing. The painting was never mentioned again. Andrina seemed to have quite a talent for not thinking about anything she didn't want to, or that she sensed to be unpleasant. She hadn't mentioned her daughter for ages. Although to give credit where credit was due, when Bessie asked if there was any news of Jennifer, Andrina said, 'I pray every night that she is safe and well and that one day she'll return.'

It made Bessie feel guilty and ashamed.

More often than not, she completely forgot to say her prayers. Actually she never knew what to say. Or, as often as not, she said so much she fell asleep in the middle of her long list:

Please, have mercy on everyone who is in pain either at home or in hospitals. Be with them. Comfort them.

Please have mercy on anyone who has suffered a bereavement. Comfort them and give them strength.

Please be company to the lonely.

Please stop men fighting and warring with one another. Help them to have patience and to understand each other's point of view. Help them to feel for each other.

Please help and protect little children. Keep them safe from harm.

Even when she hadn't fallen fast asleep before she came to her more personal requests, she seldom had the temerity to request anything. She preferred to keep reminding herself of how lucky she was. Now she really was experiencing freedom. Sometimes she danced around the house hugging herself in thankfulness and joy at the extent of her good fortune. This was her space. She could be alone if she wished. She could sketch and paint for as often and for as long as she liked. She could go out and come in whenever she liked. There was no one to question or criticise her. She could even invite whoever she liked to the house. Andrina had been several times but only after a formal invitation. Andrina liked everything to be correct and well organised. There could be no squatting on the floor by the fire with a mug of tea and a sandwich when she came to call.

'I always like to behave properly, Bessie.'

Most of her neighbours, Bessie had discovered, were out at work during the day and were usually too busy catching up with tasks in the house, or too tired, to socialise. They were very pleasant people, though. At least the ones she'd met so far. And what a bit of a luck! She'd got chatting to an awfully nice woman in the Botanic Gardens. Bridie O'Maley. She was there with her family. Innumerable children were running wild all over the place while Bridie sat plump and bespectacled, calm as you like, enjoying an ice-cream cone.

'O'Maley?' Bessie echoed. 'You're not by any chance related to Bernard O'Maley?'

'My brother-in-law. I'm married to Frank, the youngest of the family.'

'The one that writes the television plays?'

'That's him.'

'Gosh, they're great. I always used to enjoy them. I haven't a television set at the moment but I hope to get one again soon.'

'You know Bernard then?'

'He called up at my old house over in the south side a few times asking about Jennifer. Did you know Jennifer?'

Bridie shook her head.

'I don't think so.'

'She's the daughter of a friend of mine. She ran away from home. She's been missing for ages and Bernard was trying to help find her.'

'You hear about an awful lot of folk going missing these days. Especially young folk. It's a worry.'

Bridie had invited her back for a cup of tea. She lived just two closes along the Crescent. Bessie had a lovely time and invited Bridie to come to her place.

Then, as if she hadn't been lucky enough to have found a new friend, Bessie sold the Andrina picture for an enormous sum. She'd taken it to Gregory's gallery in the hope he might raise some much-needed cash for it. She hadn't seen him for ages although he had phoned after she'd returned from London to check that she had got home safely. He'd been impressed with the painting. Or so he said. Anyway, he told her to leave it with him. Next thing she knew, some American millionaire who had a famous art gallery in the States had commissioned six paintings. It had made the newspapers and Bessie had become a bit of a celebrity overnight. It wouldn't last, of course, but it was exciting. Especially when the millionaire had started asking to see all of her work.

Now unexpectedly she had enough money to buy the flat. Once that had been done, she'd paid the gas and electricity bills, and had the phone put in. She carpeted the bedroom and bought some furniture, curtains, and a television. Then she stocked up on paints and canvases and a new easel. In the end she'd spent practically every penny on the strength of the American's cheque. But oh, what fun she had. What joy! She kept walking round and round the flat with hands clasped under her chin hardly daring to believe her good fortune. She had everything, every room exactly as she liked it now. The colours, the textures – a delight to the eye. Back at the Shawlands Cross flat, most things, she realised now, had been to Peter's taste.

Bessie looked into the hallway and thought of the stark contrast to her previous lifestyle. Gone were the swirling brown and orange carpets and beige walls with their minute flower patterns. She sighed with mingled relief and pleasure as she cast her eyes again around the varnished floorboards that gave the hall a clean, open look. The only furniture was an old kitchen table with two drawers that she'd placed at the end wall. She'd painted the table a pale Mediterranean blue. On it, apart from the phone, was a tall, narrow purple ceramic vase that she had turned into a light. Beside it was a large white plaster bust she had rescued from a skip outside the art school and subsequently repaired.

The walls were a very pale bluish lilac and instead of paintings or prints, she had hung a couple of outrageously bright ethnic rugs.

The whole flat was like heaven on earth and in it she had precious freedom, freedom of mind, freedom of spirit. No responsibilities.

She relaxed in the sitting room in a soft pool of light, reading. The large room was warmly dark with only a few of the variety of lamps illuminated. They cast orange glows and huge shadows across the walls and on to the high ceiling. The wall opposite the old Victorian fireplace was covered in a disparate collection of paintings, some of which she'd worked on even before her marriage. Huge landscapes, small sombre etchings, bright splashes of colour, all depending on the mood she'd been in at the time. Above the fireplace she had placed a huge antique wooden-framed mirror so that the paintings seemed to surround her, encompass her with their colour and textures. Her shadow mingled with the rest making her feel part of her room, her home.

No sooner had she begun to appreciate her peace, her freedom, than on to her doorstep arrived unexpected visitors.

One of them she recognised immediately as Jennifer. The child had obviously suffered something terrible. Her face was so drawn, so pinched and unhappy. An older woman, equally pathetic, stood close to Jennifer on the doormat. Behind them was a worried-looking man that Bessie remembered as Jennifer's father.

'Oh Jennifer.' Bessie clutched the girl to her and gave her an affectionate hug. 'Come away in, dear. It's so wonderful to see you're all right.'

As it turned out, Jennifer couldn't stay either with her father or her mother. They'd been given Bessie's new address by Daisy, and they'd come to appeal to Bessie to give Jennifer and her friend shelter.

'I'd pay for their keep until they get fixed up with a job,' Robert said. 'And find a place of their own. It would only be a temporary arrangement.'

Bessie closed her eyes. But she could still see the tragic appeal in the faces of Jennifer and her friend. How could she turn them away?

So there you are.

You're doing it again, God.

XLII

'FORGET IT,' BERNARD said. 'I was working down in London anyway.'

'No, I'll never be able to do that, Bernard. By the looks of her, you got her just in time. She looked half-dead.'

'You should have seen the state she was in when I first found her. At least she'd had a clean-up and been fed and rested before she arrived back here.'

'You must at least allow me to pay you for the hotel and train tickets.'

'Listen, Robert, I employ a hundred or more men now. I get business from all over the world. I'm not short of a bob or two, believe me.'

'But that doesn't mean . . .'

'Forget it, I said.'

'At least let me buy you another drink.'

'OK. OK.'

Robert went over to the bar and in a few minutes came back carrying two pints of beer. He knew that Bernard seldom drank spirits, didn't drink much at all in fact. Bernard liked to keep his wits about him. It was part of his job.

'What do you make of that Bev woman?' Robert asked after he'd settled down at the corner table opposite Bernard. It was early evening and the pub was as dim and hushed as a church. Only another couple of men stood over at the bar drinking and talking confidentially. The seats and benches at the few other tables by the wall where Bernard and Robert sat were unoccupied.

'A right wee hairy.'

Anxiety tightened over Robert's eyes.

'A prostitute, do you think?'

Bernard shrugged.

'Maybe not. Anyway, don't worry. I don't think Jennifer has been on the streets in that sense. In fact, I'm sure she hasn't.' He firmed his voice in an effort to banish Robert's anxiety. 'On the contrary, I believe Bev's been protecting Jennifer. The tart with the heart.' He tried to keep the sarcasm from his voice but didn't succeed. Bev was obviously on to a good thing sticking to Jennifer. Not only had she had a free ride to Glasgow, she now had a good billet. Robert had been telling him about fixing both females up in a flat in the West End.

'How did Bessie take it?' He went back to the subject now. 'Surely she didn't welcome Bev with open arms. Let's face it, Robert, that female doesn't exactly look as if she belongs there. She looks like a wee alkie to me. I'm not complaining – as I told you, the money means nothing to me – but the drink bill at the hotel suggested she'd downed enough to sink an Irish navvy. Jennifer doesn't drink, does she?'

'No. She wouldn't even take a sherry or a glass of wine with the meal when I took her home that first day.'

'So what's happening with Bev?'

'I don't know. There's bound to be problems and it's not fair on Bessie. The first problem is that Jennifer is sticking to Bev like glue. She won't move a step without her. How is she going to get a job or any place else decent to live or make any friends of her own age with somebody like that as a hanger-on?'

'Big problem,' Bernard said.

Robert sighed.

'Enough about my problems. How did that business with Dave work out?'

'Oh, I had a few leads that paid off. I tracked the woman down to a restaurant where she was working as a waitress. I'd picked up some clues from her letters about the place – a nickname it had and something she mentioned about some other famous guys who went there. This was supposed to make Dave jealous. A right nutter she was.' Bernard shook his head. 'Beautiful, though. You'd never guess to look at her. Anyway, I told the police about the letters and where she was and they picked her up. Belongs to a wealthy and influential family in the States, would you believe. She'll probably be deported back to LA. She knew me from that time I was over in Hollywood with Eve and the boys. I had a letter from her the other day threatening to kill me.'

'My God, Bernard.'

Bernard grinned.

'I can live with that. It's not the first death threat I've had. In my job you get used to it.'

'And I've always believed teaching was the most stressful of jobs.'

'Well, put it this way, Robert, I wouldn't change places with you. I couldn't cope with your kind of stress. I'd murder some of the ungrateful wee bastards you have to deal with, day in day out.'

'I haven't regretted a moment of teaching. But I must confess recently I've been feeling more like sixty-six than fifty-six.'

'Now that you know Jennifer's OK, you'll be fine.'

'But is she? That's what's worrying me.'

'Bessie seems a decent motherly kind of woman. She'll look after her and make sure she's OK.'

'She's a bit odd though, don't you think?'

'You mean with all this art business? I wouldn't hold that against her. From what I've heard she's heading for the big time. They're planning an exhibition of all her latest work and because there's been a hype of publicity and that old American guy is paying such a high price for the paintings, she's a bit worried about security. She phoned my office. I probably won't be there but I've promised to send one of my men. Sean can go along.'

'That's your nephew?'

'Yeah. A great kid. He'll take over once I give up and I'll be sure of the business being in capable hands.'

Robert hesitated, then said, 'By the way, you know that Andrina's been friendly with Bessie?'

'I knew Andrina was the model for one of the paintings the American bought. It's a real corker. Makes you think, doesn't it? You'll have seen it, I suppose.'

'Yes. Amazing, isn't it? I see something different in it every time I look at it. You mentioned earlier that nobody would guess by looking at that nutter what she was like inside. The same applies to Bessie, don't you think? That's one of the reasons I said about her being a bit odd.'

'But the thing that's inside Bessie is talent, Robert. There's nothing sinister, nothing to worry about in that.'

'Oh I know. I've just got into the habit of worrying about everything these days.'

'You must be neglecting your karate.'

'Too true.'

'Well, there's your answer. Get back to a good training routine. Do regular work-outs. Get the old deep breathing going. But who am I to tell you? You're the guy who taught me everything I know.'

Robert laughed.

'Not quite, Bernard. But you're right about getting back to my old routine. That's the answer.'

Bernard glanced at his watch.

'I'm going through to Edinburgh tonight. I think I've mentioned Helen and the kids.'

Robert smiled.

'A few times. It sounds serious.'

'Yeah. There's only one thing wrong with her.'

'And what's that?'

'She's from Edinburgh.'

Robert laughed.

'The Far East? Terrible!'

'I've told her – she'll have to forget that and become a Glaswegian.'

'Quite right.'

'She's thinking about it. I'm going to insist on an answer tonight.'

'Good for you. I wish you luck.'

'She's got great kids.'

'You a family man? It takes a bit of imagination, that one, Bernard.'

'I'm going to give it my best shot.'

'Seriously, Bernard, if how you've been to Jennifer is anything to go by, you'll do all right.'

'Thanks.' He rose to his feet. 'I'll let you know how it goes.'

'I'll stay and finish my beer. Here's to you!' Robert raised his glass in Bernard's direction before the big man strolled away and disappeared out on to West Nile Street.

XLIII

IT WAS DRIVING Bessie mad the way Jennifer kept trying to keep the place clean and tidy. Bev didn't seem to care. But, damn it, *she* cared when Jennifer even came into the room she used as a studio and began trying to tidy and clean it up. She knew that Jennifer didn't mean any harm and was truly trying to be helpful. Nevertheless, if Jennifer came into the studio once more, especially while she was working on a painting, and started picking things up, she'd scream.

'I *like* everything covered in paint,' Bessie insisted. '*I* like to be covered in paint.'

'Oh, Bessie.' Jennifer laughed and gave her an affectionate hug. Bessie hadn't so far dared to say so, but as far as being houseproud was concerned, Jennifer was a bit like Andrina. Bessie could see the pained expression on Andrina's face at the sight of Bessie's chaotic living conditions. She also noticed the fastidious way Andrina had removed newspapers, bits of paint rag, pairs of tights and other sundries from any chair before sitting down on it. But Andrina never said anything, never complained or criticised. Jennifer never complained either but she had tutted a bit when Bev spilled face powder on the spare room carpet.

'Damn it all,' Bessie said, 'it's *my* carpet.'

The drink stains were a different matter, however. That indicated a different kind of problem. A problem suffered by Bev.

'Bev, you've been drinking all my booze,' Bessie accused.

'OK, OK,' Bev admitted. 'I had a wee refreshment. Is that such a big crime?'

'It was more than a wee refreshment, as you so euphemistically call it.'

'Oh my,' Bev turned to Jennifer, 'she's blinding us with the big words now.'

Jennifer said, 'She shouldn't have spilled any of the stuff on the carpet, Bessie, but don't worry, I'll clean it up.'

'You've got a drink problem, Bev,' Bessie repeated.

Bev rolled her eyes.

'Here we go again.'

'Well, haven't you?'

Jennifer answer for her friend.

'Maybe she has a wee problem, Bessie. It started, you see, when her boyfriends battered her about and now she can't seem to stop. At least not for any length of time.'

'All right,' Bessie said, 'now that we know what's up, we can try to do something about it. For a start I'll make sure I don't have any drink in the house. It wouldn't be right of me to put temptation in your way.'

'Gee, thanks a bunch.' Bev's mouth twisted with sarcasm, but Bessie said, 'No thanks needed, Bev. We all have our problems and weaknesses. Now, let's think. What else could we do? Counselling? A doctor could maybe advise about that. Or how about Alcoholics Anonymous? They're supposed to be really supportive and understanding.'

'Forget it!' Bev began to look panicky. 'You're not going to put me into any strait-jacket.'

'Strait-jacket? Of course nobody's going to put you into any strait-jacket, Bev.'

Jennifer was also beginning to appear tense.

'I think it was more just a figure of speech, Bessie. She's been battered about and in and out of hospitals so much, and all sorts of people there kept doing all sorts of things to her. She just can't cope any more. She's had enough of people trying to help her.'

Bessie's heart melted towards Bev. She knew how it felt not to be able to cope.

'I'm sorry, Bev, if I've blundered in with two left feet and said all the wrong things. I seem to have a knack for it.'

Bev shrugged.

'I shouldn't have nicked your booze.'

'Oh, you didn't *nick* it. You and Jennifer are my guests here and very welcome to share everything I have. It's more just a case of manners, I suppose, of asking first. I sound like a schoolmarm now,' she groaned. 'Just ignore me, girls. Or, I tell you what, let's make a bargain. I'll put up with your faults, if you'll put up with mine. That way we can all stay good friends. OK?'

'Aye OK. But I feel you've got the worst of the bargain, hen.'

Jennifer said, 'Once Bev starts work she'll be all right. It's been a worry not being able to get a job.'

'Back to the old waitressing,' Bev said. 'I'm quite looking forward to it. We used to get some good laughs.'

'Hard work though – on your feet all the time,' Bessie said, secretly glad that after tomorrow, because Bev had found a job at last, she would be out of the house all day.

No harm to the poor woman. But it's awful difficult for me even to think about work while she's forever hovering about me with a fag in her mouth, peering over my shoulder, laughing and making rude comments about my painting. She's a poor soul, I know that. But she's keeping me back from my work.

Jennifer was having more difficulty in finding a job although she had the better education of the two. Eventually, her father suggested she go to Jordanhill College and take a teacher training course. Jennifer hadn't been very sure at first. She'd asked Bessie.

'Do you think I'd be any good with children?'

'You've been good with Bev.'

'Bev isn't a child.'

'Surely it's the qualities of kindness and understanding that matter. That's what you've shown with Bev. And look how good you've been babysitting for Bridie O'Maley's lot.'

'I suppose you're right.' Jennifer laughed. 'If I can survive the O'Maley crowd, I can survive anything. But little did I ever think I'd follow in my father's footsteps.'

'You couldn't have a better role model as far as I can see. He's a good man.'

'I know. I'm glad he's so happy with Laura.' Anxiety tightened over her face.

'I hope you understand why I didn't want to go and live

with them, Bessie. I know it would have been so much easier for you if I had.'

Too true, Bessie thought, and immediately felt guilty. 'I told you right from the beginning that you were welcome and I meant it,' she said.

'I couldn't go to Monteith Row either. I'd rather have died than gone back to live with my mother.'

Bessie kept silent. Andrina wasn't perfect – who was? But surely she wasn't *that* bad. The way Jennifer talked, anyone would think her mother was a monster.

Jennifer went on in a slightly bitter tone, 'I know you like my mother. She can be so charming.'

'Well, we've just got to take people as we find them, Jennifer, and Andrina's never done me any harm. In fact, if anything, she's been kind to me. You always sound so bitter about her. Don't you believe she was really pleased to see you again and to know you were safe and well? I do.'

Jennifer shrugged.

'I suppose so.'

'And she is your mother.'

'She gave birth to me – yes.'

'And brought you up.'

'That's what you think.' The bitterness had returned. 'In between her fancy men, maybe.'

Bessie sighed.

'I see. Your mother is so beautiful, and so sexy. I suppose men have always pursued her. Maybe that puts her in much the same category as Bev.'

'What?' Jennifer screeched in disbelief.

'Not in looks,' Bessie hastily tried to explain. 'But I was just wondering if your mother had an addiction like Bev has an addiction and she has to struggle with temptation just as much as Bev has. Only it's a different addiction and a different temptation, that's all. If you see what I mean.'

She wasn't sure what she meant herself. She hadn't had time to think it through.

Jennifer was silent. She too seemed to be trying to think things through. Eventually she murmured, 'I never thought of it like that.'

Another silence. Then, 'Have you met her latest?'
'Paul Fisher?' Bessie said.
'What did you think of him? Be honest, Bessie.'
Bessie hesitated, then said, 'I wouldn't trust him as far as I could throw him. But your mother thinks the world of him and she's the one who's going to marry him.'
'He can be very charming. Especially to my mother.'
'But . . .?' Bessie prompted.
'In confidence?'
'Of course.'
'He was always trying to come on to me. You know, things he'd say, touching me accidentally on purpose, just generally being a pest. At the same time, I knew he hated me. He believed I was trying to put my mother off him and I suppose he was right about that. Then he tried to have sex with me. That's why I ran away. That's what he wanted all the time, I suppose – to get rid of me. Frighten me completely out of the picture. And he succeeded.'
'Oh dear . . .' Bessie, lost for words, pulled Jennifer to her and cradled her in her arms. Jennifer began to weep against Bessie's chest.
'She didn't believe me.'
'There, there,' Bessie repeated, as she patted and nursed Jennifer. 'There, there.'

XLIV

JENNIFER HAD STIFFENED away from her mother's embrace the first time she'd come to see her at Bessie's. Bessie had done her best to keep the conversation going during the visit. Even Bev had kept trying to break the ice, but Jennifer had remained sullen and silent. At least she had been spared having to face Paul Fisher, because her mother had come on her own. Andrina and Bessie had become friends. Bessie seemed to be able to make friends with all sorts of unlikely folk. Bessie liked people. She'd recently even tried to make excuses for Fisher. Although Bessie had denied this.

'I thought you said you wouldn't trust him as far as you could throw him.'

'I wouldn't. And I'm a bit worried about how much your mother trusts him. There's an immature, naïve bit about Andrina.'

'Oh, that'll be right,' Jennifer scoffed. 'She's the most self-centred, selfish woman imaginable. She cares about no one but herself and her own gratification. It's just her nature, Bessie.'

'It's strange,' Bessie looked thoughtful, 'how patterns can repeat themselves. Your mother had an awful childhood. She felt neglected and unloved, just like you do. Maybe that explains why she seems to love herself so much. It's her way of compensating, and feeling more secure. Maybe the sex thing has something of that in it too. I know she's physically a very sexy person. There's no denying that. All the same . . .'

'Bessie,' Jennifer interrupted, 'will you leave the psychology to the psychologists. You know nothing about it. You especially haven't a clue about my mother.'

'Oh, I don't know. We've had some long talks, Andrina and I.'

'*She's* talked a lot, you mean.'

'Well, even so. I did learn about what kind of childhood she had.'

'My granny was one of the kindest, most loving people in the world. I wouldn't believe a word against her. If my mother has told you my granny was cruel and unloving to her, she's a liar.'

'No, no, dear. Your mother was terribly upset when Sophie died. But none of us are perfect, Jennifer. You'll have to learn to stop seeing things in black and white. I'm sure your granny was one of the kindest and most loving people in the world just as you say. She certainly was kind and loving to you. But you mustn't close your eyes to the fact that she disowned Andrina, didn't speak to her own daughter for years.'

'With good reason. I loved my granny and I'm not going to sit here and allow you to try to stop me loving her.'

'God forbid!' Bessie cried out. 'There isn't enough love in the world. No, no, real love is surely being able to love people *despite* their faults. Knowing their faults, understanding them, and *still* loving them. Loving the *person*, not the faults. I think we should always try to separate the two. Oh, please don't think I'm trying to *stop* you loving anybody, Jennifer. Especially Sophie, who was always so good to you. I'm putting my two big feet in it again. I'm sorry. It's just that I keep thinking how we all seem to be victims of victims.'

'My mother a victim? That's a laugh. As far as I can see, she's always done all right for herself, thank you very much.'

Bessie sighed.

'Maybe you're right. Anyway, who am I to dole out advice? A right old mess I've made of any relationships I've ever had.'

Jennifer couldn't help laughing at that, but her conversations with Bessie made her think. Thoughts kept hovering about the edges of her mind, making her feel – not exactly worried – but uncomfortable.

The next time Andrina came to tea she at least spoke to her and was somewhat taken aback by the eager gratitude in Andrina's manner as a result. Of course, it probably stemmed from guilt. Her mother had felt guilty and now she imagined she was being let off the hook. All was forgiven, the beautiful

Andrina was thinking. Well, it wasn't. At the same time, Jennifer was surprised at the idea of her mother feeling guilty. She'd never thought her mother had ever felt anything at all. At least as far as she was concerned.

Andrina began to include her in her confidences with Bessie and her appeals for advice and, it seemed for reassurance.

'We've been going together for ages now – Paul and I – and I know he's doing his best to get a divorce but honestly, sometimes I think all this legal business is going to go on for ever. Now he tells me his wife is contesting it and that means the divorce will take years before it can go through. We've had to postpone buying a house. I've never wanted him to set me up in a house in his name. Not until we were safely married. I mean, what if something went wrong and he walked out on me? At least I've got a place of my own at the moment.'

'Have you met his wife?' Jennifer asked.

Andrina shook her head.

'I've wanted us all to talk things over face to face but Paul would never hear of it. His wife suffers from arthritis, poor soul, and it's understandable that he doesn't want to upset her. But as I keep telling him, I've no intention of upsetting her. We might even get on very well together. We might become good friends.'

'I hardly think so,' Jennifer said.

'It can happen,' her mother said in such a knowing manner that Jennifer took it that it actually had happened to her mother before.

After Andrina had gone, she said to Bessie, 'Would you believe it?'

'What?' Bessie had begun to wash the dishes. Bev would soon be home with her feet killing her and much in need of a cup of tea and something to eat.

'Imagining she could be best friends with his wife.'

Bessie shook her head over the soapsuds.

'That's what I meant about her being a bit naïve. Poor Andrina. She sounded worried, didn't she? I can't help wondering what that man's up to.'

'I wouldn't be a bit surprised if she's done it before.'

'What?'

'Managed to be friendly with the wife of her current lover.'

'More like wishful thinking. She wants what she wants without any bad feeling. Could you dry, dear, and put the dishes back on the table. Bev'll be in soon.'

'All right. It's a bit pathetic in a way.'

'What is?'

'Being so conceited and so blinkered.'

'She has something to be conceited about. If I looked like that, I'd be awful pleased with myself.'

'There's not a thing wrong with your looks, Bessie.'

Bessie laughed as she dried her hands on her apron. 'You must be joking.'

'For a woman your age,' Jennifer said, gazing at her earnestly, 'you haven't any wrinkles worth speaking about . . .'

'No, don't let's speak about my wrinkles.'

'. . . And you've such thick curly hair. But best of all, you've got a *caring* face . . .'

'Careworn, you mean. Hurry up with these dishes, Jennifer. You accuse Andrina of talking too much! Now, what did I tell you – there's Bev at the door. And this is her pay day so we'd better keep our fingers crossed.'

'I'll answer it.'

The moment she opened the door, Jennifer's heart sank along with her spirits. She'd been so caught up with thoughts about Andrina, she'd forgotten it was Bev's pay day. Usually she went to meet her and managed to prevent her going to the nearest pub. Today, she had put her mother first and now, seeing Bev, smelling the reek of alcohol from her, she was overcome with regret.

'Sorry hen,' Bev said, walking unsteadily into the hall. 'I just went in for a wee refreshment because we'd been run off our feet all day. Just a wee pick-me-up, you understand . . .'

'If you could just keep it to one or even two drinks, Bev.'

'Aye, aye. That's all I meant it to be.'

'Well then . . .' Jennifer followed the small, skinny, busty figure into the kitchen.

'You've got us now and this nice home. You don't have any sorrows to drown now and nothing to escape from.'

'OK. OK.' Bev addressed Bessie. 'Your turn.'

'I never said a word.' Bessie was putting cutlery on to the kitchen table. 'Sit yourself down. You've had a long day. You must be tired.'

'Saint Bessie,' Bev sneered. 'Always ready with a helping hand.'

Jennifer tutted and cast an anxious, apologetic glance towards Bessie. 'Now, Bev, there's no cause to take anything out on Bessie,' she said. And then to Bessie: 'She didn't mean anything. It's the drink. It always makes her a bit sarky.'

'I don't care what she calls me. I've more urgent and important things to worry about. Like the exhibition.'

'Oh yes, when is it?'

'It opens a week today. There's been a whole lot about it in the papers already. All that publicity makes me nervous. And Lester Morgan commissioning all my work like that. Did I tell you he's got a huge gallery in the States? It all seems like a dream. Or a miracle or something. I can't believe it. Can't take it in yet.'

'What are you going to wear, hen?' Bev asked. 'You'll be the celebrity. You'll have to look special.'

'Oh, don't start that again. I'd a hard enough time with Andrina. She wants to take me shopping on Monday.'

'Wear a skirt, for God's sake. Or a dress. You can't slop into the limelight in your old trousers. Especially stained ones like those you've got on.'

'It's not that I don't like skirts and dresses. I do and I've nice long ones, but they always make me look like a walking wigwam.'

Bev and Jennifer laughed at this image, and Jennifer said, 'You always put yourself down, Bessie. There's nothing wrong with your figure. You just don't make the most of yourself.'

'Aye, hen, this might be your big chance in more ways than one.'

Bev made an unsteady path to the nearest chair and thumped down on to it.

'There'll be a few handsome men there, as well as your old millionaire. I'll bet one of them's bound to fall for you if you put on the glamour. Jennifer, hen, give us a pull off with these shoes. They're stuck to my bloody feet.'

'Me put on the glamour?' Bessie laughed. 'I'm no Andrina. Anyway, she'll be the belle of the ball, not me.'

'You haven't invited her!' Bev and Jennifer cried out in unison.

'Well, I couldn't very well say she couldn't come, could I?'

'Oh, Bessie,' Jennifer groaned, 'she'll spoil your big day.'

'Oh well,' Bev said, 'I wasn't going to come in case *I* spoiled it. But if she's going to be there – what the hell!'

XLV

After trying on everything she had in her wardrobe including the new outfit she'd been persuaded to buy in Frasers, Bessie ended up in a pair of denim trousers and a loose denim shirt.

Jennifer and Bev had capitulated in good grace, saying, 'Och well, I suppose she might as well be herself. And at least the trousers aren't covered in paint.'

They dressed themselves down, instinctively not wanting in any way to outshine Bessie at the 'big do'. They had both been looking forward to 'dolling themselves up', as Bev had put it, and it was a terrible wrench to abandon their smart outfits. Jennifer opted instead for a pair of denims and a open-necked checked shirt. With a sigh, Bev donned the plain black skirt and white blouse she wore at work, only indulging in a strand of pearls and a pair of high-heeled shoes. She sprayed perfume all over herself to cover any smell of food that might have clung to her waitressing clothes.

On the way to the gallery in the taxi, Bessie seemed to shrink smaller and smaller.

'This is terrible. I need to go to the bathroom again.'

'Bessie, forget it,' Bev told her. 'It's just nerves. Enjoy yourself. This is your big day. You've done it, hen. You've made it.'

'I haven't done anything different from what I've always done.'

'You've never hit the headlines like this before, have you?' Jennifer said.

'It's that Lester Morgan.' Bessie fidgeted with agitation. 'Americans have to do everything in such a big way. He couldn't just buy one painting, take it back to the States and quietly hang it in his gallery. Now he's gone and taken pneumonia or bronchitis or something and won't be there tonight. That sounds awful. Of course I'm sorry for the poor man but what with one thing and another, I just know the night's going to be a total disaster.'

'Come on, hen,' Bev scoffed. 'You were tickled pink before.'

'And pleased and excited,' Jennifer added.

'Of course you were, hen. I'm telling you, it's just last-minute nerves. Like brides have before their wedding.'

'For pity's sake don't remind me of my wedding,' Bessie wailed. 'That's liable to make me suicidal.'

Bev and Jennifer giggled.

'Never mind, hen, once you're there you'll be OK. You'll have a great time. Just think of all the different kinds of folk that'll be there and the ideas you'll get for more pictures.'

That cheered Bessie. But not altogether.

'It's just I'm terrified about people not liking my pictures. It's like being naked, you see. My paintings are such an intimate part of me somehow. People can feel, or think, or say, what they like about them. But not when I'm *there!*'

She became agitated again.

'I'm dying to go to the bathroom. I'm going to disgrace myself, I know it!'

'There'll be a toilet in the gallery,' Jennifer put an arm around Bessie's shoulders. 'You'll be able to go there, don't worry.'

Bessie nodded, tense and white-faced.

'Anyway,' Bev scoffed, 'what are you blethering about folk not liking your pictures? Why do you think there's been all this fuss? Why do you think the American guy wants to show off your pictures here, there and everywhere? Especially that one you did of Andrina. Why do you think everyone wanted this exhibition?'

'It's the stand-up one that's worrying me more than any of the others.'

Bev and Jennifer had christened the Andrina portrait 'Stand up the real Andrina!' And even Bessie now referred to it by that name.

'They'll love them, all of them.' Jennifer gave Bessie's shoulders a reassuring squeeze. 'And they'll love you.'

The gallery in Sauchiehall Street was huge and spacious. A chrome and wooden stairway led the eye up to the mezzanine floor where some of the smaller exhibits were on display. The full-length windows at street level were draped with swaths of natural muslin, giving a soft light without shadow. The uncluttered floor of polished pine stretched from wall to wall with only one or two chrome and leather chairs to break the surface. Small track spotlights focused on Bessie's progressively larger canvases. It was as if, with her freedom, her canvases mirrored her spiritual development and confidence. Cameramen and reporters were crowding round someone over near the 'stand-up' painting.

'What the . . .?' Bev said. The three of them had entered the gallery unnoticed. Everyone's back was to them. All eyes were straining to see the centre of attention.

'It's her.' Jennifer could hardly speak for fury. 'I knew it! She just has to be in the limelight.'

Bev was also enraged.

'The fuckin' cow – look at her as well – dressed to kill. By God, I'll kill her when I get my hands on her.'

'Oh please,' Bessie whispered, 'don't cause any trouble, girls. I'd rather keep in the background, honestly.'

'Don't be daft. Who's she to steal your thunder?'

'Well, she was the model for the painting.'

'She's so . . . so stupid, so egotistical.' Jennifer was stuttering with anger. 'She doesn't see what the picture's saying about her. She doesn't see what everyone else sees. She's just making a fool of herself.'

'Oh dear, poor thing. I hope the papers don't print anything that'll hurt or upset her. She doesn't mean any harm?'

'What?' Bev spluttered. 'Look at her. She's not caring a fig about you. She's evil.'

'Oh no.' Bessie was appalled. 'Oh no, you mustn't even think such a thing. Andrina is *not* evil. She's more like a thoughtless child. A child needing constant attention.'

Bev and Jennifer groaned, then Bev said, 'Well, hen, you may be daft but I'm not. She's not going to get away with this. You're not going to stand here like an accident looking for somewhere to happen and nobody paying a blind bit of notice.'

Suddenly, and to Bessie's horror, Bev loudened her voice into an absolute roar, 'Here she is at last, folks! The star of the show you've all been waiting for. The Glasgow girl – the genius that everyone in this city is rightly proud of.'

'Oh God!' Bessie groaned.

Bev and Jennifer began to clap and cheer and the crowd of people, including the reporters and photographers, moved towards them.

Then Andrina came sashaying towards Bessie, but Bev and Jennifer were too quick for her. They wriggled through the crowd and caught her, linked arms with her and turned her in the opposite direction.

'What are you doing?' Andrina's expression seesawed between astonishment and annoyance.

They let go of her in front of a waitress carrying a tray of glasses full of champagne.

Jennifer said, 'We just wanted to make sure you got a drink. We wanted to be the first to toast you.'

'Oh, I had a drink, darling. I must have put it down somewhere. I love champagne, don't you?'

Bev said, 'Never drink anything else. Oops!' She had lifted a glass from the tray and bumped into Andrina, splashing the champagne all down Andrina's glamorous outfit.

'Oh sorry, hen. Here, let me mop it up for you . . .'

'Leave it alone. You'll only make it worse. Oh, I'm absolutely soaked.' Andrina's voice broke. 'I don't know why, but I'm sure you did that on purpose.'

'What?' Bev's eyes widened. 'Now what reason could I possibly have for doing such a thing? No, no, hen, it was just a wee accident and I'm really sorry, so I am.'

'I'll have to go home and change now.'

'Oh, is that not a terrible shame,' Bev sympathised.

'Do you want me to come with you, Mummy?' Jennifer asked.

'No thank you, dear. That's kind of you but I'll just get a taxi. I'll be all right.'

'I'd slip out of the back door if I were you,' Bev advised. 'You don't want anyone to see you like that. You look as if you'd peed yourself.'

'Oh!' Andrina gasped in distress.

'Are you sure you don't need me to come with you?' Jennifer repeated.

'No, no, dear. You stay and enjoy yourself. Give me a ring tomorrow and let me know how things went.'

When she'd hurried away, Jennifer said, 'I feel awful.'

'Why? It got rid of her, didn't it?'

'I know but I can't help feeling sorry for her.'

'What? A few minutes ago you were furious.'

'I know. She is terrible, right enough.'

'And she had to go.'

'Yes, you're right. She would have completely spoiled everything for Bessie.'

'I know how you feel, though,' said Bev. 'She's that bloody likeable with it!'

They began to giggle and the champagne they swooped on and began to drink did nothing to quell their hilarity.

'Here, would you look at that,' Bev nudged Jennifer.

'What?'

'That gorgeous man over there.'

'He looks like security. Remember Bernard told Bessie that he couldn't come tonight but he would be sending his nephew, Sean.'

'He looks as if he's more interested in guarding Bessie then the pictures. Look at the way he's staring at her.'

'Maybe Bernard has told him to act as Bessie's bodyguard.'

'Och away, this is Glasgow, hen, not Chicago. Here, look at her looking at him now.'

Jennifer rolled her eyes.

'For goodness sake, Bev. You've a one-track mind. Bessie's old enough to be his mother.'

'Maybe so. But I detect some of the old animal attraction there.'

'That's just you. There's no maybes about it. She *is* old enough to be his mother.'

'OK. OK.' Bev held up her hands. 'It's all in my dirty one-track mind.'

XLVI

FOR A FEW minutes Andrina was distraught. She couldn't get away from the gallery quick enough. She couldn't bear anyone to see her in any way less than perfect. Perfectly demure when she attended church. Perfectly glamorous when she went anywhere else. Perfectly sexy when she was having a sexual encounter. She had always been as meticulous about her clothes and her personal appearance as she was about her house.

After she had arrived safely home from the gallery, she was tempted to change and go to the casino to see Paul. Then she thought it might look a bit odd. He knew how much she had been looking forward to spending the evening at the exhibition. She could go back to the gallery but it might look strange turning up wearing a different outfit. She calmed down once she was safely back at Monteith Row and had taken off the stained garment. She slipped into a frilly satin négligé and stared at herself in the long mirror in the bedroom. Suddenly she felt lonely. Unhappiness that seemed out of all proportion to the evening's events frightened her. She struggled to quell her foolish fears. Apart from the accident, she had enjoyed the evening. It had been absolutely lovely being photographed and admired by everyone. It made her think that she ought to have been an actress or a model. One of the photographers had, in fact, asked if she had ever been a model. She'd laughingly replied, 'No, never' and he's said, 'You pose like a professional.'

The whole episode had been delightful. Indeed, she couldn't remember ever having enjoyed herself so much in her whole life. Not only did she feel famous, she *was* famous. She had only come to realise this as she posed beneath Bessie's painting.

It had been a pity that Bev had spoiled such a gloriously happy time. Thinking of Bev brought back the unhappiness.

She was sure the woman had spilled the drink over her on purpose. Yet why should Bev do such a thing? She had never done anything nasty to Bev. Even though she secretly thought the woman was not a proper friend and companion for Jennifer, she'd still been as kind and as charming as she could to her. She hadn't once interfered with the friendship, never said one word against Bev. She hardly dared face the thought, because it was so bewildering, so hurtful – but Bev didn't seem to like her.

She tried to tell herself that it didn't matter whether Bev liked her or not. Why should she care? But she did. She couldn't bear anyone not to like her. Standing in front of the mirror in her bedroom, she faced this indisputable fact. She blamed it on her mother. All these years, from babyhood up until the day her mother died, she'd suffered from her mother's dislike. First, Sophie's downright, cruel neglect. Then her active dislike. She'd never been able to please her mother, no matter how hard she'd tried.

And oh, how she'd tried. A lump of regret and sadness swelled up in her throat. She'd never understood her mother's behaviour any more than she understood Bev's. For years her mother, her own mother, had refused even to speak to her. She'd hated Sophie for that and all the other cruelties and neglect. Yet at the same time, she had loved her. In this vulnerable moment, gazing helplessly at herself, she realised this. And she deeply regretted never being able to please her, no matter how she tried.

Her mother had never recognised any good about her at all. Never. She never saw that Andrina was a loving and demonstrative person. Or that she was a good cook and housewife. Or that she looked good. Nothing. Often she still longed to appeal to her mother. Why were you like that to me? What harm did I ever do to you?

It took a terrible effort to pull herself together. She was just being silly. She was making a mountain out of a molehill. Bev was such a clumsy person and the way she tottered about on those ridiculously high heels, it wasn't surprising that she'd stumbled and spilled the drink. Of course it was an accident.

She decided to have a leisurely bath. She had face pack as

well and tried out the new eye-pads that she'd treated herself to. Her eyes were her best feature, everyone said so, and she took great care of them.

Afterwards, she put on fresh make-up in readiness for Paul's arrival. During the few days – or rather nights – he stayed with her, she kept her make-up on in bed. She was always eager to look her best for him. This night she took particular care, perfuming her body, painting her toenails, applying several coats of mascara to her long lashes. They didn't always have sex because working so late as he did, he was sometimes too tired. Tonight, she not only wanted but needed him to make love to her, to hold her in his arms, to tell her how beautiful and desirable she was. Unfortunately, as it turned out, Paul had had such a stressful time at the casino, he wasn't even interested in hearing about the lovely evening she'd had at the gallery. He was full of talk, as he undressed and came to bed, of someone who had been cheating the system and losing him a terrible amount of money. She listened dutifully and sympathetically. Tomorrow, over 'brunch' – Paul always slept late – he would feel better and she would get the chance to tell him about her triumph.

In the morning she slipped out of bed, put on fresh make-up and dressed. Then, as usual, she went out for the morning papers before cooking Paul's favourite mixed grill. He enjoyed relaxing at the kitchen table reading the papers, while she busied herself at the cooker. He looked very handsome in his pale blue shirt and navy suit. The dark colour of the suit made his slicked-back fair hair all the more striking. Like her, Paul took a pride in his appearance. As he always said, 'I've a reputation to keep up. And of course I'm in a glamorous occupation. Appearances are important.'

'One or two eggs, darling?' she asked, smiling round at him. To her surprise, he glowered angrily back at her.

'Have you read this?'

'What?'

'What they've written about you in all the papers.'

Her heart began to flutter apprehensively.

'No, I thought I'd enjoy a good read after breakfast.'

'You'll not enjoy this. If you do, you're an even bigger fool than they're making you out to be.'

'What?' Her heart was pounding now and she felt faint. 'I don't know what you're talking about. The journalists and photographers were all terribly nice. One of them even said – '

'For God's sake, Andrina. Why didn't you tell me you were the model for the picture in the exhibition?'

'But . . . but it wasn't really me, you see. Bessie said it was an act of creativity like writers create fiction characters. They often get inspiration, an idea from real life, but . . .'

'She got an idea of you all right. Christ, I don't know how I'll be able to face them in the casino, or my wife and family.' His voice grew louder and he crashed up from the table. 'Why the hell did you need to blabber about me? You stupid cow, you had no right to mention my name.'

She put her hand on the cooker to steady herself.

'All I said was that you were my fiancé and you had the best casino in Scotland. Darling, I said nothing but good about you. I'm proud of you and I wanted them all to know . . .'

'Well, I'm bloody well not proud of you. And you're not my fuckin' fiancée. I'm a married man. I'll have to go through to Edinburgh right now and see if I can't straighten out this mess. I'll probably have to contact the press as well. I'll have to think what's best to do.'

What mess? I don't understand.'

'You've made a right fool of yourself, you idiot. But you're not going to get away with making me look a fool as well. You're not going to drop me in it.'

Andrina had begun to weep.

'In what? I don't understand.'

'Oh, stop saying that. Just read the bloody papers. I don't suppose you'll even understand what they're saying, but I'm not waiting to find out.'

She watched in disbelief as he stormed from the kitchen. After a few minutes, she heard the front door bang. It was a long time before she could move. Only the smell of burning brought her back to life and she hastily switched off the cooker and rescued the burning frying pan. By the time she had doused the flames and got the crisis under control, it was as much as she could do to stumble over to the table and collapse on to a chair. Too terrified now to look at the papers, she waited until she had enough strength in her legs, then she got up and made herself a strong pot of tea. Her hand trembled so much as she poured out a cupful that some of it splashed into the saucer. Heedlessly, she drank from the cup, keeping her eyes averted from the papers.

They lay on the table, lethal bullets waiting to pierce her heart.

XLVII

BESSIE GROANED.

'This is terrible, absolutely terrible. How could they?'

Bev lit a cigarette and relaxed back on one of the kitchen chairs. 'It wasn't the journalists. It was her, the silly cow. Serves her right.'

'Even if she's read the papers,' Jennifer said, 'she might not understand what they're getting at.'

'Come on, Hen,' Bev scoffed, 'she can't be that daft.'

Bessie rubbed at her hair in distress, giving it an even wilder appearance than usual.

'I lied. I more or less told her it wasn't her. I said an artist often works like a writer. You get an idea or a stimulus from real life, then create something new out of it.'

'Well, that's perfectly true,' Jennifer soothed her.

'Don't let's kid ourselves,' Bessie said. 'That painting was my interpretation of Andrina.'

'What about the other one she's got on her wall? That was your interpretation too.'

Bev said, 'You just told the truth as you saw it, hen. And the guys from the papers have obviously seen it as well – helped by the blind conceit of the woman posing under the picture and rabbiting on about herself and her precious fiancé.' She flicked at one of the papers. 'According to this, a happily married guy with three of a family.'

'I wish I'd never painted the awful thing now. I feel really terrible. Poor Andrina!'

'I suppose I'd better phone,' Jennifer said. 'I did promise.'

'I don't know how I'll ever be able to face her again,' Bessie said, making Bev cry out, 'Will you shut up and stop being so daft. You've done nothing wrong. All you've done is paint a bloody picture.'

Jennifer agreed.

'Yes, Bessie, if artists had to worry all the time about what people thought and what effect their work might have, they'd never do anything, would they!'

Jennifer rang Andrina's number.

'Is that you, Mummy?' she said. She was taken aback by the quavery, fearful voice at the other end of the phone. After a moment or two she replaced the receiver and turned to the others.

'She burst into tears and then hung up.'

'I should go and see her.' Bessie nursed her head in her hands. 'Apologise. I don't know.'

Bev stubbed out her cigarette. 'Well, I do. You're not moving from here. You go if you like,' she added to Jennifer.

Jennifer nodded.

'I suppose I'd better.'

Bessie burst into tears. 'Some Quaker I am.'

'God!' Bev groaned. 'Now she's bringing religion into it!'

'Well, it says in *Advices and Queries* that we should value that of God in everybody and we should not make use of another person "through selfish desire".'

'OK. OK.' Bev turned to Jennifer. 'While you are out, hen, get some sackcloth and ashes for Bessie.'

That brought a faint smile to Bessie's face and she dried her eyes. 'Sorry,' she said. 'On you go, Jennifer.'

On the way to Monteith Row in the taxi, Jennifer felt tense and emotionally confused. She was completely on Bessie's side and agreed with Bev that what had happened with the newspapers was all Andrina's silly fault. She had called the tune and now she was paying the piper. At the same time she couldn't help feeling sorry for her mother. Especially when she remembered the bewildered voice on the phone. Andrina had sounded like a frightened child.

Once at Monteith Row, Jennifer hurried up the stairs and rang the bell of the flat. There was no reply. She knocked loudly on the door, still no response. She tried calling through the letterbox.

'Mummy, it's me. Open the door. It's all right. I'm on my own.'

Eventually the door opened a crack and Andrina's face, swollen and blotchy with tears, peered apprehensively out.

'It's all right,' Jennifer repeated. 'It's only me.'

The door opened wide and Andrina stretched out her arms. 'Oh Jennifer . . .'

Jennifer patted her mother as she led her back into the kitchen.

'How could they do that?' Andrina sobbed. 'How could Bessie do that? I love Bessie.'

'And she loves you. She's terribly upset at all that nonsense in the papers. But you know what journalists are like.'

'No. No, I don't. I don't know what anyone's like any more.'

'It's a nine-days' wonder. No, not even that. Mummy. What's news today is history tomorrow. You'll see, by tomorrow, they'll be on to something else and somebody else.'

'Bessie told me that that picture . . .'

'I know what Bessie told you and it was the truth. The trouble is, once something is in the public domain, everybody's free to find their own truth in it. Their own interpretation, or whatever.'

As Andrina accepted Jennifer's handkerchief and mopped at her face Jennifer added, 'I'll make us both a good strong cup of tea, will I?'

'Thank you, dear. You're very kind. Forgive me for being so upset. It's not just the newspapers. Paul's left me.' Tears welled up again and she hastily wiped at them with the handkerchief. 'He called me such awful names. I didn't think . . . I mean, how could he speak to me like that? And how could he desert me just when . . .' She stuffed the handkerchief against her mouth and fought for control.

Jennifer plugged in the kettle and set out two cups and saucers. Both women were silent until the tea was made and poured.

'Nothing would surprise me about him. Not after the way he treated me. But you didn't believe me, did you?'

'Oh Jennifer, I'm so sorry. I honestly didn't think . . . I mean, I loved him, you see . . .'

'But you didn't love me.'

'Oh darling, I did. I do. Oh please forgive me.' She began to sob uncontrollably and Jennifer said,

'I can't do that, Mummy. Not when I think of all I suffered after I left here. And I couldn't stay. I was too afraid.'

'I tried to find you. I really did try.'

'What good would it have done – if you had found me?'

'And then I thought you must be all right. I really convinced myself that you must be all right.'

'I can believe that.'

'I never meant you to suffer. I can't bear to think I made you suffer.' Andrina's voice had acquired a note of hysteria and her eyes stretched wide with distress. 'I'd rather die. I wish I was dead.'

'For goodness sake,' Jennifer groaned. And then, realising that Andrina might be in danger of actually doing something reckless or foolish, she asked, 'Would you like me to come and stay with you for a few days?'

'Oh darling, would you?'

'Just for a few days.'

'Oh, Jennifer, thank you. I feel so devastated.'

'You'll be all right. Drink your tea. Then wash your face and put on fresh make-up. I'll have to go and tell Bessie and Bev, and collect some things.'

She worried all the way back to Botanic Crescent. Part of her pitied her mother and wanted to be with her to look after her. Another part of her wanted no such thing. Far better, and happier, to continue living with Bessie and Bev, without taking on more responsibilities. She had enough to cope with trying to keep Bessie's place clean and tidy and Bev on the straight and narrow. For a few minutes in Andrina's kitchen, she'd wrestled with the idea of bringing Bev over to Monteith Row. However, she couldn't, try as she did, see such an arrangement working out. Bev would be far too much for Andrina. Anyway, no way would Bev be persuaded to live under the same roof as her.

'What?' Bev screeched when she heard the news. 'Have you gone out of your tiny mind? You can't stand the woman any more than I can.'

'I wouldn't have considered moving in even for a few days if Fisher had been there. But he's left her, apparently.'

'There'll be another Fisher in no time, what do you bet?'

Jennifer sighed.

'Oh, I suppose so. That's why I made it clear it was only a temporary arrangement.'

'And don't think for a minute,' Bev said, 'that I'm going with you – temporary or not. But it won't be temporary. Wait till you see. Once she's got you there – that'll be it. And then what'll I do?'

'You can stay on here. Can't she, Bessie?'

Bessie had been sitting listening.

'Of course!' She made an effort to look sincere. 'Of course you can, Bev.'

'Aye. OK hen. Thanks.'

'When are you going?' Bessie asked Jennifer.

'As soon as I pack my things. I promised I'd be right back.' Then, seeing the expression on Bev's face, she hastily added, 'It won't make any difference to us. I'll still see you every day, Bev. After all, it's only twenty minutes or so from here.'

Bev shrugged. 'As I've told you before, we're not joined at the hip.'

'I know. But I don't want anything to come between us or spoil our friendship. I couldn't bear that.'

'You're breaking my heart. Away back to Monteith Row, for God's sake. I've got my work to go to.'

When Bessie saw Jennifer to the door Jennifer said, 'I hope I'm doing the right thing, Bessie.'

'She is your mother.'

'Today it felt as if it was the other way around.'

'You've had to learn to survive in very hard and dangerous circumstances, Jennifer. She hasn't.'

'Maybe it's time she did learn to fend for herself.'

'She needs you, Jennifer. I think you're doing the right thing.'

Jennifer kissed Bessie.

'You will keep an eye on Bev, won't you?'

'Don't worry.'

Jennifer raised her voice.

'That's me away, Bev.'

'Aye. OK. What do you want me to do? Tell the Provost to put all the flags at half mast?'

'Cheerio, then.'

Bev bawled back, 'Just go, for God's sake!'

XLVIII

SOMETIMES THINGS HAPPENED all at once – good and bad – and Bessie's life became confused. It was good that Jennifer had been reconciled with her mother. Bad that she had now to cope with Bev on her own. Well, not bad exactly. Bev wasn't bad. She just had a drink problem. It got worse after Jennifer left. She came in drunk and it wasn't even pay night. And when Bev was drunk, she could be very difficult indeed. If Jennifer could see that beige carpet in the spare room now!

And added to the confusion was what had happened in connection with the young security man who'd been at the exhibition. Sean O'Maley was Bernard's nephew. At the exhibition, despite all the people crowding around her asking questions and taking photographs and praising her pictures, she became aware of Sean's eyes on her. He had such a steady, thoughtful gaze. She'd thought – what a nice-looking young man. His stare had made her feel somewhat uncomfortable but she'd told herself that security men were like that. It was their job to be observant. Bernard had watchful eyes but his were different – hard, suspicious. Sean's eyes were a deep liquid brown that seemed to melt into every secret corner of her being. She felt herself begin to blush and become flustered. It was a struggle to bring her wayward feelings under control. He had come up to her afterwards and asked how she was getting home.

'I don't know. A taxi, I suppose. I came in a taxi.'

Her heart was swelling and interfering with her breathing. Especially when he smiled at her and offered to give her a lift home in his car. It wasn't a soft smile. His lips drew tightly back to show strong white teeth. She was tempted to abandon

Jennifer and Bev to their own devices. Steady on, Bessie, she chided herself. What on earth are you thinking about?'

'Thank you, Sean. But there's my two friends who lodge with me. Jennifer and Bev.'

'There's room for them too.'

'Fine, then.'

He had told her to sit in the front beside him while Bev and Jennifer chattered together in the back seat. They were both drunk. All that champagne! That must be why I'm feeling so strange, Bessie thought. She'd had a few glasses of champagne herself. The thought relaxed her and she was able to smile at Sean in the darkness of the car and talk naturally to him. He was such a nice boy and with such startling good looks. He wasn't as big and brawny as his uncle. Maybe just over six feet tall, long-legged, broad-shouldered and narrow-hipped, and obviously very fit. She could imagine his rock-hard muscles. Even the muscles on his face were hard and taut, so that when he smiled, his cheeks tightened back into an indentation on each side, harder than dimples. Only his eyes seemed different. If the eyes were the window of the soul, there seemed strange enigmatic depths to Sean. His dark stare haunted her long after she'd gone to bed that night. She tossed restlessly about, desperately trying to banish him from her mind. But his stare refused to go away, penetrated deep inside her.

The next day she got up early, made herself a strong cup of tea, told herself not to be daft, and busied herself preparing breakfast for Bev and Jennifer. Then, of course, they'd read the morning papers and everything was banished from her mind, except thoughts of Andrina. Helped by Jennifer and by her own capacity for self-deception, Andrina had to all intents and purposes completely recovered from her original distress. Despite the fact that she could be selfish and egotistical, she was also an affectionate woman and readily forgave Bessie for any pain and embarrassment she might have caused.

'I know it wasn't your fault, Bessie,' she said after they'd warmly embraced. 'It was these awful newspapermen. Anything for a lurid or sensational story. They're so ignorant too.

They got it all wrong. They obviously know nothing about art.'

By this time Sean had called at the house several times. The exhibition was to go on tour and as well as keeping her up to date on how things were going while it was still in Glasgow, he discussed arrangements for moving the paintings during the tour and exactly where each venue would be. She knew in her secret heart that he didn't need to do this. She had been kept informed of everything by Lester Morgan's lawyer. Lester had been flown home in his private plane. His doctors thought he'd stand a better chance of a complete recovery back in Williamsburgh.

However, Sean was such a nice young man and just trying to be helpful. It would be unkind to put him off. So she kept telling herself. But she couldn't help wondering if there was more to it than that. Just in case, by some unlikely chance, there *was* more to it, she tried to do the right thing and discourage him. She dropped her age laughingly into the conversation whenever she could although it felt like plunging a dagger into her heart. She knew he was barely twenty and she was double that age. She also managed to divulge that she was a Quaker. That was usually a right turn-off.

However, Sean said, 'Bessie, I don't care a damn what age you are. Or if you're a bloody Hottentot. So will you forget it!'

'How can I forget it? It's a fact. And it's important.'

'Not to me.'

She felt on dangerous unknown territory. Surely it *couldn't* be that he was romantically interested in her? No. Of course not. Silly woman.

Bev and Jennifer had begun to tease her about him and Andrina was becoming intrigued.

'He seems to have a crush on you, Bessie,' she said.

Bev gloated. 'Didn't I tell you, Jennifer? And she feels the same about him, you mark my words.'

'I'm dying to meet him,' Andrina said. 'You must introduce me to him, Bessie.'

Bev blew smoke from her cigarette in Andrina's direction. 'Over my dead body,' she said.

'Why not?' Andrina's eyes widened innocently.

'Because I'm not going to allow you to spoil Bessie's fun.'

Bessie tutted and fussed about, pouring more tea for everybody.

'You're daft, the lot of you. I'm old enough to be his mother.'

'So?' Bev raised a brow. 'Grab the chance with both hands, hen. It might be your last chance of having a wee fling.'

'Do you like him, Bessie?' Andrina asked.

Bessie cursed herself for blushing, and the hot tea didn't help.

'Of course I like him. He's a nice boy.'

Bev laughed.

'He looks all man to me, hen.'

'Be sensible, Bev. Even if I did fancy him – *which I don't* – I'm too old.'

Andrina cried out: 'Old? You're not old, Bessie. You're two years younger than me!'

Jennifer had begun to look anxious and uncertain.

'You don't really . . . I mean, even if he did . . . you wouldn't . . .'

Bessie sighed.

'Don't worry, Jennifer. Apart from anything else, I'd never have the self-confidence to have a love affair with anyone, far less a handsome young man. Sean could get anyone and I'm sure in his job he meets lots of glamorous young women. Why should he feel in any way romantic about me?'

'Yes, it'll be your painting,' Jennifer said. 'Some people go overboard for any kind of talent. Guys go overboard for women like Eve Page and she's no chicken. If she couldn't sing and was just an ordinary housewife, they wouldn't even look at her.'

'Thanks, Jennifer,' Bessie said with an unusual note of sarcasm in her voice.

'I'm only thinking of your own good. What you need, Bessie, is a nice older man who loves you for yourself and will look after you in your old age.'

'You're cheering me up no end.'

'I just don't want you to get hurt, Bessie. You're not very sophisticated or streetwise, are you?'

'No, I suppose not.'

Andrina looked dreamy.

'I wouldn't mind a younger man.'

'Oh, shut up, Mummy.'

'Really, Jennifer, your manners have deteriorated terribly since you've been away.'

Bev laughed.

'She wasn't away at a finishing school in Switzerland, hen. She was living rough.'

'Well,' Andrina looked huffy now, 'you'll never get any man to admire you for any reason unless you smarten yourself up and learn how to behave properly.'

Jennifer rolled her eyes. She didn't say anything then but as soon as her mother had swanned off to the bathroom, she remarked to Bev and Bessie, 'Could you beat that? I'll certainly never learn how to behave properly from her.'

'I don't like to hear you talk like that about your mother,' Bessie said. 'It means a lot to her to do everything properly. Look at the way she sets her tea-table when Bev and I go over there. I know you enjoy all her wonderful cooking. And I'm sure you appreciate her beautifully folded napkins and the fine bone china and silver tea service. I always marvel at the trouble she goes to cutting all the crusts off every sandwich . . .'

'For goodness sake, Bessie, you know fine what I meant. Anyway, I *have* somebody who admires me. At least I think he does. I hope he does. I certainly admire him.'

Bessie was happily surprised.

'Really? Who is he? When did this happen?'

Bev also leaned forward with interest.

'Here, you're a dark horse. I'm supposed to be your best pal. I thought we didn't have any secrets from each other.'

'I haven't seen either you or Bessie for over two weeks, remember. I've had so much to do with getting everything organised for Jordanhill. It was through that I met him, in a way. I'd gone over to see Daddy and get his advice about a couple of things and Freddie was there.'

'Freddie?' Bev and Bessie exchanged glances. Then Bev said, 'And who is this Freddie when he's at home?'

'He's a teacher, like Daddy. He started his teaching career in fact at Daddy's school. But now he's in Bearsden Academy. He teaches French and German. He's terribly clever.'

'What the hell does he see in you then?' Bev asked. Jennifer knew Bev didn't mean to be offensive, so she just shrugged.

'I don't know. But he insisted on taking me home that first night and then he asked me to go to the opera with him. He got tickets. It was great. I'd never been to an opera before. We've been out several times now and we've chatted on the phone. I really do like him.'

'Like who?' Andrina wanted to know as she returned to the kitchen.

Jennifer blushed.

'Oh, just somebody I've met.'

You've got a boyfriend?'

'You don't need to sound so astonished, Mummy. I'm not a freak or anything.'

'You're a lovely girl, Jennifer,' Bessie said.

'No, I'm not that either, Bessie. Anybody with a freckly face and hair like mine is no raving beauty.'

Andrina said, 'If you hadn't that awful fringe, dear. And there are creams and things to cover up freckles – even to get rid of them, I've heard. I'll take you tomorrow to my hairdresser and beautician – don't worry, I'll pay for everything . . .'

'No thanks, Mummy. If Freddie doesn't like me for myself, than I don't want him. It wouldn't be me all tarted up. Anyway, I'd feel naked without my fringe.'

Bessie sighed.

'You're quite right, Jennifer. For better or for worse, it's always best to be yourself.'

She was thinking of Bessie Alexander, not Jennifer Anderson, and accepting that as far as she was concerned. It would be for worse.

XLIX

'TELL ME, DARLING, what's he like? Why have you never brought him home to meet me?'

'Actually, you have met him, Mummy.'

'I don't think so, dear.'

'Yes, years ago. Freddie told me. He remembers. At his cousin's house. His cousin Jane. Uncle Bernard's ex-wife. You know Jane.'

'Of course I know Jane.' She thought for a minute. 'I vaguely remember a Freddie. But that's ages ago. You'd only be a child then. He was a grown man.'

'I wasn't going out with him then.'

Andrina's eyes went vague as she tried to work things out.

'He had just started as a teacher at Robert's school, I think. That would make him at least a man in his twenties. So he must be in his thirties now.'

'So?'

Andrina lit a cigarette.

'I think he was the one your daddy had problems with. Now, what was it again . . . I wish I'd paid more attention at the time. Your daddy went on so much about his school and his colleagues and his pupils – honestly, he could talk about nothing else. I stopped listening eventually. It became so boring. He just lived for that school. I expect he's still the same but the woman he's married to now is a teacher, so I suppose that'll be her pet subject too.'

'I guess I'd better not talk shop then once I get a job.'

'Oh, I'm sure you'll not be like that, dear.' She didn't look at all sure and she added. 'I hope you won't. All the same, you seem to be following in your father's footsteps. First the profession and now the partner.'

Jennifer laughed.

'Mummy, Freddie and I aren't married. We're just good friends.'

'I don't understand that.'

'What?'

'Going out with a man so much and still being just good friends.'

'Mummy, you're hopeless. Sex isn't the be-all and end-all of life. Or relationships.'

'It's a very powerful physical and emotional need.'

'Not for me.'

'Now you're getting me worried. It's not natural to be like that.'

Jennifer felt a pang of bitterness and was tempted to bring up her experience with Fisher. Although she'd got over the trauma of his attack, deep down it still affected her, made her shrink within herself for protection. She felt angry too, angry that her mother had let her down so badly. But Andrina had been pathetically eager to make up for that. With difficulty Jennifer pushed Fisher to the back of her mind.

'There's no need to worry,' she told Andrina coolly. 'I'm in no hurry, that's all. I want to concentrate on my career for a while before getting serious with anyone.'

'Yes, of course, you've plenty of time. And I don't want to lose you just yet. You're happy here with me, aren't you?'

'I suppose so,' Jennifer admitted. 'But I must try to visit Bessie and Bev more often. I feel guilty about Bev.'

'Darling, you're not her keeper and she is a mature woman.'

'Well, she's older than me. I don't know so much about being mature.'

'You often talk about being streetwise, Jennifer. Don't you think she is as well? More so even than you?'

'All the same, underneath that tough exterior, there's another Bev. I suppose all of us have different layers. We're not all what we seem on the surface.'

'Anyway, to get back to Freddie. Whether I've already met him or not, why don't you bring him here for dinner one evening?'

'I'll see. I'll maybe mention it to him when I see him tonight.'

'I hope he cooks you a decent meal and doesn't just open lots of tins.'

Jennifer didn't care if he bought fish suppers from the local chippy, she just enjoyed Freddie's company, talking to him, listening to him. She was also looking forward to seeing his flat.

It turned out to be a very respectable place up a tiled close in Roxburgh Street in the West End. He ushered her eagerly into a spacious hall and then through to a large kitchen where he poured her a sherry while he added the final touches to the meal.

In the dining room, romantically lit by candles, she smiled across the table at him.

'You make me feel ashamed.'

'Ashamed? How do I manage to do that? It's certainly not my intention.'

'You're such a good cook. I can't cook at all. My mother's the one in our house for producing wonderful meals.'

'It just needs a bit of practice, that's all. And a helping hand from Marks & Spencer's food department.'

'Ah, so that's your secret.'

'I worry about you, Jennifer.'

'Because I can't cook?'

'No. Because you're training to be a teacher.'

'What's wrong with that?'

He sighed.

'When I remember how I was when I was at your stage . . .'

'You were at university before you started teaching, weren't you?'

'Yes and so full of airy-fairy notions and high ideals. I soon got that knocked out of me, I can tell you. Teaching is for the tough.'

'Oh, come now . . .'

'No, I mean it.'

'Not every teacher is a karate black belt like Daddy, surely.'

'No, but it helps. Apart from being able to defend yourself, it gives you self-confidence and that gives you an aura of strength and authority. If you're not tough physically, you've got to be strong in spirit.'

'Defend yourself?' she laughed. 'Against what?'

'Seriously, Jennifer, you must try to get into some place like Bearsden Academy.'

'So that you can keep an eye on me?'

'I mean any school in a respectable neighbourhood. As compared with where Robert teaches.'

'As far as I can gather, Daddy likes his school and he has a good relationship with his pupils.'

'You're not your father, Jennifer. You look so fragile and waif-like. They'll make mincemeat out of you.'

Jennifer laughed.

'Oh Freddie, you can't always judge by appearances. I'm tougher than I look. If I can survive on the streets of London, I can survive in a Glasgow school. As a matter of fact, I think I'd like the challenge of a tougher school. I'd feel I was doing something worthwhile if I managed to help some of the more deprived children. Daddy tells me a lot of them have slept rough so I'd be off to a good start understanding how they feel.'

'OK, maybe because of your experience you'll be better able to cope than I was when I began teaching. I certainly hope so. But another thing, just because I teach in Bearsden doesn't mean I'm not doing a worthwhile job. I believe I am, and I believe the children in respectable districts are just as much entitled to attention and consideration as anyone else. Their schools should be given just as much funding as the schools in tougher districts.'

'Sounds fair enough to me.' Jennifer cocked her head to one side and studied Freddie's earnest, bespectacled face. 'Do you like teaching?'

Freddie took a long time in answering.

'I still get discouraged and frustrated, but more by the powers above than by the children.'

'I take it you don't mean God.'

'Just the gods in the Education Department and the government.' He shook his head. 'All the red tape and paperwork. I see the day coming when we'll be so snowed under by all that, we won't have time to teach at all. But as far as the actual teaching is concerned – yes, I do like it. And I don't regret going into it, despite my horrific experience at Sinnieglen. Robert deserves a medal for sticking it out there for all these years.' He smiled. 'Maybe where I went wrong was in not taking up karate.'

'You seem to have done all right without it.'

'I work out in the gym for an hour or two each week and I have the occasional swim. But there's so much paperwork to do at home I don't get much time for sport. Or any kind of leisure activity . . .'

His smile always warmed her. It was so kind and shy and boyish.

'I'm glad you came, Jennifer. I enjoy your company so much.'

'Come on,' Jennifer said, 'I'll help you with the dishes.' She got up and started gathering up the dirty plates. Freddie came across to her and said, 'Leave that just now.' He sounded quite masterful, not a bit shy. 'I can't kiss you if you hold a stack of plates between us.'

She felt a flutter of nerves that edged near claustrophobia.

'I don't want to leave you with all the debris. It wouldn't be fair,' she said.

He took the plates from her and put them back on the table. Then he took off his glasses. His eyes looked loving, and tender, if a bit short-sighted. He didn't seem to notice her shrinking back. Then he kissed her so gently and held her so comfortably, she managed to relax a little.

'Of course,' he said, 'if you do go to Sinnieglen, Robert could always keep an eye on you. But I'd still feel better if you were safely beside me in Bearsden Academy.'

She couldn't help laughing then. In fact, she felt so relaxed and so safe in his arms, she even told him about Andrina's dinner invitation.

L

BESSIE KEPT LOOKING at her watch, then at the clock. Then she went to peer anxiously out of the front room window. It was now two o'clock in the morning and Bev hadn't come home. She was on one of her drinking bouts but even so, she usually came staggering and falling up the stairs by midnight. Once the pubs were shut, she made straight for Botanic Crescent. Well, straight wasn't too apt a word. She took the whole width of the pavement and often the road as well. Sometimes she slurred out a song coming up the stairs and this had caused a complaint to be raised by one of the neighbours. Bessie had apologised on Bev's behalf and promised it wouldn't happen again. The noise, she meant. She knew it was no use promising that Bev wouldn't get drunk and incapable again. She spoke to Bev about it of course. Many times. Bev was always very reasonable when she was sober.

'Aye, OK hen. I'll not do it again. I've no right to cause you so much trouble and worry. You're a good soul, so you are. I don't know how you put up with me. If you'd any sense in your head, hen, you'd chuck me out.'

That was true. They both knew it. They also both knew that Bessie, being Bessie, couldn't throw her out on to the street. Especially now that Bev had lost her job.

'I wasn't drunk,' Bev had assured Bessie. 'I'd just had a couple but the boss smelt it on my breath. I was that upset, hen, I went right out and had a bucketful – right there and then.'

Bessie didn't know what to do for the best. She had commissions for work and wanted peace and quiet to get on with it. She'd had several phone calls from Lester Morgan, who planned to return to Britain soon and had been thinking of renting a separate studio and hiding there from Bev so that she could get on with her painting. At the same time, she couldn't help asking herself what was most important in the end – a human being and a good friend, or some tubes of paint and a piece of canvas. Bev was a good friend. To mention but one friendly act out of many, when Bessie had gone down with the flu, Bev had nursed her, couldn't do enough for her. During that time, she'd never touched one drop of alcohol.

'Oh Bev,' Bessie had said afterwards, 'you're so good to your friends. Why are you so bad to yourself?'

'The booze, you mean?' Bev shrugged. 'I don't know, hen. Sometimes I think I was born with this weakness in me.'

'It's half the battle if you can admit it's a weakness, a problem. That's what I've heard. The next step is to get help, Bev. Professional help.'

'I'm past believing that anyone can give me a magic cure.'

'I'm not saying there's a magic cure, but surely you'd get advice . . .'

'Once when they put me in hospital, I was in for a month. They told me I was a compulsive drinker. They gave me loads of vitamins. I felt the better of having that rest and all them vitamins. But, the first day I got out, I bought a bottle of sherry and that was me again. Nothing's any use, hen, believe me. You see, I don't take the drink. It takes me.'

'But you can keep off it. You've proved that. You can keep off it for weeks, sometimes a couple of months at a time. If you could just resist that first drink, Bev.'

'I know, I know. And I will try.'

Bessie wasn't sure if it was the right thing to do but she had started meeting Bev at her work on pay night, as Jennifer used to. That worked for a while but then Bev started drinking on other nights. To prevent the stair-singing being repeated, Bessie usually watched for her coming home and immediately she saw her staggering up the Crescent, she raced down and linked arms with her and whispered to her to keep quiet. Bev always whispered back in a giggly sort of way and, supported by Bessie, tiptoed as best she could up the stairs and into the flat.

But tonight there had been no sign of her. Bessie couldn't understand it. As far as she knew, Bev hadn't any money. Worry and anxiety gave her a splitting headache but she couldn't relax to sleep even after she'd taken a tablet. She wondered about telephoning the police but hesitated in case it might get Bev into trouble. On the other hand, the police might think it was none of their business if a grown woman was a few hours late in coming home. Exhausted, Bessie had fallen asleep in an armchair near the window. She awoke stiff and unrested. After checking her watch she got up and hurried to Bev's room. Bev wasn't there and her bed had not been slept in.

Now what am I supposed to do?

A small secret voice deep inside her whispered that she was glad to be free of the problem of Bev. She had gone, hopefully for good. She would, if her previous history was anything to go by, be sleeping rough. With any luck, Bev had returned to the other world of the homeless.

Bessie felt ashamed of the voice.

OK. OK. I know perfectly well what I'm supposed to do.

At last she left the house to go and look for Bev. She had put off the task for as long as she could by having a hot bath to loosen her aching bones. She was too old to be sleeping in chairs. Then she had three cups of tea and a bowl of cornflakes. She had to force the cornflakes down because she wasn't really hungry.

She wandered about the West End first of all. She combed every inch of the Botanic Gardens. Once she'd found Bev dead to the world in one of the glasshouses. Bev had said later, 'I just went in to have a wee look at all the tropical plants and trees and the heat in there knocked me out. It was like a bloody oven.'

This time there was no sign of her in the Gardens or the glasshouses. No sign of her in any of the streets or doorways of the west side of the city. At the end of the afternoon, Bessie returned to the house to have something to eat and a rest. She'd only had a cup of tea and a cheese sandwich in a café at lunchtime. After sitting with her feet up for half an hour, she heated the remains of a steak pie and forced herself to eat it along with some tinned peas. Now she felt sick with worry. She tried to watch *Coronation Street* on television, but that didn't help. It was now pitch dark outside. Bessie debated with herself whether or not she should postpone a further search until morning. After all, it was a very cold night. It was the cold that reminded her. Jennifer and Bev had once spoken about the gratings outside the Central Hotel in Gordon Street.

'If ever we're needing another skipper,' they had joked – or so Bessie had thought at the time – 'it's over these gratings in Gordon Street.'

Bessie flung on a warm cape and hurried from the house. She was rather fond of capes and had treated herself to two. One was actually a poncho and it had been the primitive colours that had attracted her. She now wore the other, a dramatic red cape with a long stole that she flung over her shoulder to make the warm nest over her ears and chin. She felt glad of its protection. An icy wind was hissing through the trees in the Crescent and Bessie was thankful that she was wearing her high boots over her trousers.

There was a long queue for the taxis outside the Central. A London train must have come in. Bessie skirted the queue and saw over beside the wall, the group of winos and down-and-outs crouched over the gratings. Much to her disappointment, there was no sign of Bev. Plucking up courage, she approached the group and, addressing the only female present, asked if she knew somebody called Bev and described her friend. The woman looked like the absolute dregs of humanity. Her skin was as coarse as old leather, her eyes sunken and inflamed, her teeth brown stumps. Her head and body were covered in a hotchpotch of shawls and scarves and a man's long raincoat tied in the middle with string. She stank with a mixture of alcohol and Bessie daren't think what else.

'I might have seen her. I've an awful memory, hen. It's the cold that does it. If I had the price of a bottle of whisky to warm me up, it might help.'

Bessie hesitated, then took the plunge.

'Here.' She gave the woman some money. 'Now tell me about Bev. Where is she?'

The woman looked positively gleeful. Bessie thought she was going to do a dance.

'The wee blondie? Skippered down in London? Then came back to do a bit of waitressing? Aye, she was here and we had a rare chat. Nice lassie. She shared a bottle with me. A real stoater, it was. By Christ, it was a lot better than the jake I'd been drinking before she came.'

'Where is she?' Bessie was getting desperate.

'I think you might find her by the Anderson bus station, hen.'

'Thank you.'

Rather than wait in the queue at the taxi rank, Bessie began to half walk, half run in the direction of the Anderson bus station. By the time she was nearing it, she was out of puff and had to slow down. Every now and again, in fact, she'd to stop to get her breath back. It was during one of these times that she noticed a car slowing down alongside her. The driver rolled down his window and beckoned her over. For an eager, hopeful, crazy moment, she thought the word had got around about her search for Bev and this was someone who had information to help her. She hurried, smiling gratefully, over to the man. But before she could ask him anything about Bev, he said, 'How much?'

She'd always had a slow-working mind, especially when it came to thinking the worst. So she just stared at the man in bewilderment for a few moments.

'Look,' the man said, 'you're not getting into the car until you name your price.'

The penny dropped, as the saying goes. And Bessie went. She ran as fast as her legs could carry her until, seeing a cruising taxi, she hailed it and sat shivering in the darkness as the cab skimmed through the city streets.

It was only when she was safely in her own home that she burst into tears of distress. Even there, she jerked with fright when she heard the doorbell ring. So upset was she, she nearly didn't answer it. The ring was repeated several times and finally she went to the door and close to it in an anxious voice asked 'Who is it?'

'It's me, Sean. I said I'd try to call up tonight, remember?'

She hadn't, with all the worry about Bev. Hastily trying to dry her eyes on the sleeve of her blouse, she opened the door.

'Bessie, what's wrong?' Sean came in and immediately took her into his arms. That set her off into another paroxysm of sobbing. Being in his arms, held tightly against his hard body, completely unnerved her.

She babbled out what had happened.

'Bessie, darling,' he said, 'what am I going to do with you?'

LI

WHAT ARE YOU trying to do? Test me or something? I keep failing, so what's the point? Humiliation? All right, You're really going for the jackpot now. Sean loves me. And I love him. Oh, I do, You know I do. I love everything about him. I love his perfect body. It's so beautiful. I love to watch him. He has the grace of a tiger, smooth, effortless, powerful. I love his deep rich voice, his dark eyes. I love his hard, tight smile.

He held me in his arms and I felt I belonged there. Oh, you don't need to tell me. I know only too well that I don't. He kissed my tears away and I became breathless with a mixture of passion and panic.

He kissed my mouth and I felt hungry for him yet oh so ashamed of myself.

The awful thing is, you see, the outward shell of me is getting older but inside, I'm as young as I ever was. I'm still the wee girl I was at home in Bearsden. As well as being that wee girl from Bearsden, I'm still the same foolish teenager. I was always concerned about the small size of my boobs. Well, here I am in my forties and still worried about my bust measurement. Granted I have more around there than I used to, but still not enough to give me as sexy a cleavage as Andrina. Except when I wear my new Wonderbra. What a find! When I look at myself in the mirror, I'm full of admiration. And yes, I'm looking at myself an awful lot these days. I know that there's no future in any relationship with Sean. At the same time, I'm nearly killing myself in my efforts to try to look as attractive as possible for him. After these ghastly aerobics classes, I literally stagger home. I'll have to give them up. Talk about murder!

I bought myself one of these electric things that are attached to the wall and from it goes a band round your waist or your hips and vibrates like mad. I staggered away from that as well. I felt every part of me, including my head, vibrating for hours afterwards.

Talking of heads reminds me of my yoga classes. I stood on my head there. Murder that was as well. And oh, the torture of not eating chocolates. I seem to be a chocaholic. I never realised it before. If I take one I have to guzzle the lot. Now I really know the struggle Bev has and how she must feel. I suppose it's the same with any addiction.

I still don't know what to do about Bev, by the way. I think she's into prostitution. She denies it. Although she admits she doesn't know any more what she does when she's drunk. She told me she woke up and found herself lying in bed beside this strange man in a filthy room in some slum or other. She was so ashamed she vowed she'd never touch a drop of booze again. That's when she came back to me. She was in an awful state, poor soul. She'd escaped in such a hurry she hadn't even stopped to look for her bra and knickers. Horrible, she said the man on the bed looked and still snoring like a pig when she left.

So Bev and I are both struggling with our addictions. Absolute torture, it is. I'm getting now that, apart from Sean, I think about nothing else except chocolates. I know it sounds ridiculous. But there you are.

And what's it all for? To make myself look younger and slimmer and more desirable. Remember how I worried about Gregory seeing me naked? Now I'm agonising about Sean seeing me.

But wait a minute, what is all this? What am I thinking of?

No, it must stop. To be perfectly accurate, it hasn't started. Not the sex part anyway. Although Sean wants it to. Bev says he's besotted with me. I can hardly credit it but he does act like somebody who is very much in love. He sends me red roses. That's never happened to me in my life before. He tells me I'm beautiful. That's a first as well. He says I'm so different from anyone else he's ever known. I'm so talented, he says. Jennifer keeps saying that's what's at the root of it. Poor Jennifer is obviously afraid that I'll turn out like her mother and start having a string of affairs. Apparently Andrina even tried to flirt with Freddie Hancock, Jennifer's boyfriend. There was a big bust-up over that. Not that Freddie had responded or encouraged Andrina or anything, Jennifer said. She blamed everything on her mother.

So why do I go on with all this charade of exercising and dieting and spending a fortune on beauty parlours? I've become a sucker for creams and potions and pills that claim to cure wrinkles and bags under the eyes and generally reverse the ageing process.

Sean tells me he loves me just as I am. I want to believe him. I do believe him.

He says I'm every inch a woman. He says I've such good bone structure and such a good clear smooth skin. He had me looking in the mirror the other day. He actually stood beside me and said, Look at yourself. Look at your lively hair. I had to laugh at that. Lively hair! Look at your sweet face. Look at your shapely, womanly body. Shapely, womanly body! I like that. And do you know, as I looked at myself, I began to think – well, I really don't look so bad for a woman of my age.

You glow, he said. I liked that too. I knew where the glow comes from, of course. It's the love I have for him lighting up my body, my skin, my eyes, my life.

Just now and again, only occasionally, very tentatively, I wonder if, after all, it could be possible for Sean and I to have an affair. Oh, I don't mean anything serious or permanent. Nothing will change the difference in our ages. But I'm a free agent and so is he. Would it be so bad to give physical expression to our love? Just for a little while?

LII

IN ONE WAY at least it had been a relief to leave Bessie's flat. Jennifer loved Bessie dearly and she realised that Bessie had the right to live how she liked. However, it was a source of some exasperation how untidy Bessie was and how she got paint over everything. Maybe it was because Jennifer had been brought up in Andrina's immaculate flat that made her yearn for cleanliness and order. She had certainly yearned for a home like that during her nightmare on the streets. She had also been accustomed to seeing her mother always so perfectly turned out and kept being shocked by Bessie's dishevelled state. Bessie often wiped her paint-stained hands on her clothes and it didn't make a bit of difference if she didn't happen to be wearing one of the smocks that Jennifer had persuaded her to buy. Bessie just wiped her hands on whatever she happened to be wearing. When she got paint on her hair, she looked like a human rainbow.

'Bessie!' Jennifer would repeat patiently, 'why don't you use your paint rag?'

But Bessie was always losing paint rags.

On the other hand, it had become increasingly difficult to be civil to Andrina after the dinner party for Freddie. She ought to have known, of course. Actually she had known. She'd said to Freddie days beforehand, 'My mother's a very attractive woman.'

'Yes, I remember,' Freddie said. 'Once seen, never forgotten.'

'She's sex mad as well.'

'Really?' Freddie laughed. 'Well, that's interesting. I'm beginning to look forward to this dinner.'

'It's not funny.'

'Why the worried face? You don't think . . . She's not really likely to make a play for me, surely?'

'Would you like to take a bet on it?'

'You can't mean it, Jennifer. Apart from anything else, she knows you and I are serious, doesn't she?'

'Oh yes. I've told her often enough. But believe me, that won't make one bit of difference to my mother.'

'Darling, forgive me for laughing but honestly, you've no need to worry. I'd prefer you to your mother any day. You're the one I love and want to marry, not your mother. I don't care if she does a striptease or goes down on her knees and pleads with me to go to bed with her – it's not on. I can't see it happening, though. I think maybe you're overestimating my charisma.'

As it turned out, her mother hadn't actually done a striptease but she'd done just about everything else. Jennifer had never been so embarrassed in her life. Andrina had worn a low-cut blouse and a long skirt with a slit up one side almost to her hip. She'd had her hair done and her face beautifully made up. She'd cooked a meal more fit for a king than a schoolteacher. She'd even produced a bottle of champagne. And an expensive box of Belgian chocolates. Freddie had been overcome with it all. Or so it seemed to Jennifer at the time. The intensity of his appreciation had been only too obvious. He not only praised the meal to the highest heavens, he praised Andrina.

She blossomed and thrived on every word. She fluttered her lashes and smiled her shy sideways smile at him. She leaned over him as she plied him with more champagne and showed far too much bosom. She gazed up at him with round starry eyes as he said goodbye and told him she'd enjoyed his company *so* much.

Jennifer had been furious.

'But . . . but . . . I don't understand, dear.' Andrina had looked genuinely taken aback. 'I thought everything went perfectly. I thought you'd be pleased. I tried so hard.'

'Yes, you did, didn't you?'

'Well, then, what's wrong? Why are you angry with me?'

Later Jennifer had to concede that what Bessie said was probably true. Andrina couldn't help it. It was just the way she was. All the same, it was very hard to bear. It was, in fact, bloody infuriating. The quicker she was married and living permanently in Freddie's flat the better. She was living more there than in Monteith Row as it was.

The flat needed redecorating and once they decided that the date for the wedding was to be sooner than later, they set to with a will to transform the place. She hardly took time to go and buy her white dress. Her mother was getting her outfit made and was always darting off to the dressmaker's and enthusing about the lovely material and the perfect fit.

Jennifer did see to the invitations. Her mother hadn't wanted her to invite Bernard but she'd insisted. Apart from the argument about Bernard, Andrina was in seventh heaven organising everything, although she did take a lot of persuading to accept Jennifer's wish that Bessie and Bev had to be her matrons of honour, and the O'Maley children bridesmaids and pages. However, she eventually got together with Bridie and they agreed that the girls should wear pale blue dresses with tartan sashes. The pages, Andrina enthused, would look wonderful in tartan trousers and waistcoats.

She had kept voicing her worries about the O'Maley young people.

'These O'Maley children are a bit wild, don't you think, dear? Do you think they'll be able to behave properly?'

She wasn't too concerned about Bessie. 'I'll see that she wears something pretty,' she said. And: 'Are you sure Bev will remain sober long enough to walk up the aisle with you?' she worried.

'They'll all be fine.' Impatiently Jennifer brushed aside all her mother's criticisms. She was looking forward to moving into a home of her very own far more than the wedding. Her home *and* Freddie's, of course. She could hardly wait. Freddie was her best friend as well as her lover. They went walking in Botanic Gardens arm in arm, chatting all the time. They went shopping together. He was looking forward to the actual wedding more than she was.

'All that lovely grub your mother's providing! I can't wait.'

'Oh, I see,' Jennifer said, half in fun. 'My mother is the big attraction of the wedding day, not me.'

'Oh sure.' Freddie gently pulled her into his arms. 'And why do you think I'm marrying you? Because you've a mother who's a good cook?'

She rested her head against his chest.

'You won't ever let her come between us, will you?'

'Darling, how could I? I admire you. I adore you. What's more, I'd trust you with my life. Forgive me for saying this, darling, but I wouldn't trust your mother one inch – not as far as any kind of relationship is concerned.'

'I suppose she's a bit pathetic, really,' Jennifer conceded.

'I've more mature pupils in Bearsden Academy.'

'What do you bet she'll try her best to outshine me on my wedding day?'

'Do you care?'

Jennifer thought for a moment.

'Not really. As long as we're happy. Oh Freddie, the flat's lovely now, isn't it?'

'I can't wait to carry you over the threshold.'

She laughed.

'I've been over the threshold on my own two feet a hundred times already.'

Although it was a white wedding, it was to be a quiet affair. There weren't many relations on either side. As far as friends were concerned, the O'Maley brothers, their wives and families were invited. A few schoolteacher friends of Freddie, and Bessie and Bev. That was about all. Except, of course, Daisy and her husband, Nigel. Jennifer had invited them for Bessie's sake in the hope it would result in a reconciliation.

Jennifer had hesitated about inviting Sean O'Maley because, as she said to Bev, 'I'm worried about Bessie becoming too fond of him and then getting hurt.'

'You can't invite all the other O'Maleys including his mum and dad and his Uncle Bernard, and not him. Don't be daft.'

Jennifer sighed.

'I think the world of Bessie – I hope she knows what she's doing.'

'If she wants to risk getting hurt, that's her decision. Anyway, I think she can handle it.'

'All right. I'll send him an invitation with the rest. Or at least my mother will. She's in her element just now. She's even doing all the catering, you know. She's already got her freezer and Bessie's stacked with goodies.'

'Of course I know it,' Bev groaned. 'I'm dying to get my teeth into some of that stuff she's cooked, but it's as much as my life's worth to touch it.'

'I'm pleasantly surprised at Bessie's interest in getting a new outfit for herself.'

'Oh yes?' Bev laughed. 'Let me tell you our Bessie is a reformed character. After every painting session, she has a bath and washes her hair and changes her clothes just in case . . .'

'Just in case what?'

'Just in case Sean arrives on the doorstep unexpectedly, of course.'

'Poor Bessie.'

'Poor Bessie nothing! She's got a gorgeous young boyfriend. What's poor about that?'

'It's terrible. I wonder if I should talk to her,' Jennifer murmured half to herself.

'Don't you dare!' Bev said. 'Just you concentrate on your own man. It's "poor Bev" you should be saying. I'm the only one who hasn't got a man.'

'If you could just keep off the drink, Bev. It's ruining your looks.'

'I'll do my best to keep sober at your wedding anyway, hen. I've treated myself to a dress and coat. I won't let you down, don't worry. I wonder what our Andrina is going to wear. She's promised to get a wee suit made. Have you seen it yet?'

'No, I haven't been over to Monteith Row for ages. I can hardly bear to leave Freddie for a minute. Oh Bev, he's so good to me. I enjoy his company so much. He makes me feel good about myself too. I know I'm not beautiful like Mummy but he makes me feel beautiful.'

'How is she, by the way?'

'Oh, she's busy getting everything ready for the reception and she's quite happy for me to keep out of her way. I'm going over to Daddy's place a couple of days before the wedding to relax and of course Daddy will bring me to the church and give me away.'

'I wonder what Bernard's new wife is like. That was a quiet affair. Bridie told me that even his brothers weren't there. It was just at a registry office and Sean and Sally as witnesses.'

'Oh well, the whole O'Maley family can have a get-together at my wedding. Except the Tony one. I've never met him. He's always away on tour with his band. I think Bridie said he's based in Liverpool now. Bridie says I'm better not knowing him. He's pretty awful, apparently. She says her husband, Frank, is definitely the best of the bunch.'

'Well, she would. I thought Sean's dad was very nice. But that old mother-in-law of Michael's spoiled Bridie's party, remember that night?'

Jennifer laughed.

'I know. I wasn't going to invite her but Bridie said Michael wouldn't leave her out there in the cottage by herself. He's awful good to her. So I thought – och, why not? So they're all coming. A good job the house at Monteith Row has big rooms.'

'Here,' Bev said, 'something's just occurred to me. I'd better warn Bessie.'

'About her and Sean, you mean? Oh, for goodness sake, yes. If his mother and father notice anything between them, they'll not be exactly pleased, will they?'

'No, not exactly. Not that it's any of their business. But we don't want any trouble or ill-feeling on your wedding day, hen.'

LIII

Bessie had to put her foot down when a drunken Bev brought a man to the house.

'Don't look so bloody shocked,' Bev sneered. 'You bring your man in so why shouldn't I?'

Bessie ignored Bev and addressed the man, who was perfectly sober and obviously just a punter Bev had picked up.

'This is my home. Bev only lodges here. Would you please leave.'

The man shrugged and left without saying anything. Bev was furious. She staggered after Bessie into the kitchen.

'What do you think you're playing at? Who do you think you are – Saint Bessie? You lost me a couple of tenners there.'

'So you *are* on the game?'

'Never you mind what I'm on. I pay my keep, don't I? I can't get a regular job. How am I supposed to live?'

'You've had several jobs and lost them through drink. And don't try to shift the blame on to me for charging you for your keep. You pay me a mere pittance, Bev, and you know it. Even if you were my sister and we were sharing a home, you'd have to pay your share.'

'OK. OK. I'm paying my share. But where I get the money is my business.'

'Not when you start bringing men home and using this place as a brothel. Apart from anything else, that man could have turned nasty.'

She made a pot of coffee and set out cups. 'Here, drink this and try to sober up.'

'I don't want your bloody coffee. That's all I ever get from you. Coffee and lectures. Lectures and coffee.'

'Just get it down, Bev. We'll talk some more when you're sober.'

'Get it down yourself.' Suddenly she grabbed the cup of coffee and flung it at Bessie. Bessie cried out as the boiling hot liquid splashed her neck and soaked into her jersey. Hastily she pulled the jersey off and tossed it aside before dashing to the sink and splashing herself with cold water.

'You're not my bloody sister, or my mother, or my anything,' Bev slurred. 'You're nothing but a pain in the arse. I'm going out for a drink.'

'The pubs are shut. Go through to your bed.'

'Who said anything about pubs?' She waggled a finger. 'I know places and I know people.

'I know places and I know people,' she mumbled again. She got up, knocking her chair over, and made for the door. Bessie watched helplessly as she disappeared out to the hall. Then there was a thud and when Bessie went out Bev was lying unconscious near the front door. It took all her strength to drag her into the bedroom and haul her up on to the bed. It wasn't that Bev was a big heavy woman. Far from it: she seemed to have been getting smaller and more emaciated-looking recently. Nevertheless, Bessie wasn't a big woman either and she certainly wasn't muscular or strong. After struggling to undress Bev, and covering her with the duvet, Bessie felt over-strained and exhausted. It wasn't the first time she'd had to put Bev to bed, but bringing the man to the house was really too much. Something had to be done. But what? She'd read somewhere that nobody can help alcoholics. They have to hit rock bottom before they can help themselves and that's the only thing that works. It was beginning to look as if by providing shelter and supportive friendship, she was only postponing the day when Bev would be forced to do something permanent to help herself. Bev couldn't be frogmarched to AA. Bev couldn't be forced to do anything.

Yet, how could she abandon Bev? How could she put her out on the streets? She couldn't be so cruel. Nor could she live with the guilt of such action. Then other thoughts began itching at her mind. Thoughts she didn't want to face.

Perhaps this was a case of having to be cruel to be kind.

Perhaps she was just too afraid of the guilt she would feel. For the rest of the night she struggled to try and think things through and find out what was right, and what was the best thing to do for Bev's sake. She knew in her heart that she should put Bev out to find her own salvation. She had tried everything else.

The next day, as usual, Bev didn't remember a thing about what happened. Sitting at breakfast together, Bev was chatting away quite the thing. She'd been a bit bleary-eyed and confused at first but after she'd had a couple of mugs of tea and she'd been persuaded to eat some cereal, she became her usual chirpy self. Eventually she said, 'What's that red mark on your neck, hen?'

'You threw a boiling hot cup of coffee at me last night. I was lucky I was wearing a thick jersey or it might have been worse.'

There was silence for a long minute. When she was sober, Bev never argued about what she'd done when she was drunk. She always took Bessie's word for it.

'I'm awful sorry, hen. You're the last person I'd want to hurt. You know that. I swear to you. I'll never touch another drop of alcohol as long as I live.'

'Oh, Bev, how many times have you said that?'

'This time I mean it. I definitely mean it.'

'Another thing – last night you brought a man back here.'

Bev looked evasive.

'I'd clicked, had I? About time I had a boyfriend.'

'This was a punter, Bev. Now, I must make this absolutely clear. I can't have you using this place for prostitution.'

'Oh God . . .' Bev put her hand to her eyes. 'I'm sorry, hen. It won't happen again. I promise you. That'll never happen again.'

It was then that Bessie knew she should have said – No, it won't happen again because I want you to pack up and leave here right now. But she couldn't. Instead she said,

'If you'd just avoid taking that first drink, Bev.'

'I told you, hen. I'll never touch another drop.'

'Not even at Jennifer's wedding?'

'Especially not at Jennifer's wedding. You and Jennifer are

my best mates. The last thing I want to do is spoil the wedding for either of you. I know how you're looking forward to it as well. Then she added half to herself, 'I'll just keep thinking it's for your sake and Jennifer's sake . . .'

'For your own sake, Bev. It's for your own sake.'

'Aye, OK, hen.'

'And never mind thinking it's for the rest of your life. Just concentrate on today. It's just one day you're to worry about. Every morning when you get up, tell yourself – I've only to make sure I don't take that first drink *today*.'

'All I have to do,' Bev sighed. 'If only it was as easy as that.'

'What's the alternative? Think of that. Think of what you're doing to yourself.'

'It's what I'm doing to you, hen, that's what worries me. I'm so sorry.'

'That was yesterday. Today is what we must concentrate on.'

Bev nodded. 'Is Sean coming today?' she asked.

'I'm not sure. It depends if he's working in Glasgow or further afield.'

'Don't worry. If he does come, I'll keep out of your way.'

'You don't need to do that. We don't go to bed or anything.'

Bev raised a brow.

'Why not? You're obviously crazy about each other.'

'You know why not.'

'Bessie, age doesn't matter these days.'

'Well, it should. He could get a young woman. Why should he lumber himself with me?'

'Because you're a lovely person and because he loves you.'

'Oh Bev, what am I going to do?'

'You're going to go to bed with him for a start and enjoy a bit of real loving. Don't you want to?'

'Of course I want to.'

'Well then. You talk to me about living just for the day. Why don't you take your own advice? Just think of today. Enjoy it and to hell with tomorrow.'

Bessie laughed as she got up and started clearing the table.

'That wasn't exactly the advice I gave you.'

Bev got up then.

'Leave these. I'll wash up. Along you go to your studio. I'll come through in a wee while and see how you're getting on.'

Bessie's smile still clung to her face but she was suddenly knotted with frustration and exasperation. This couldn't go on. She could stand everything else except interference and lack of freedom to work in peace. To have Bev filling the studio with cigarette smoke and cheeky chatter made it impossible to work.

No, something would definitely have to be done.

LIV

' "SHALL I COMPARE thee to a Summer's day?
Thou art more lovely and more temperate." '

'I didn't know you read Shakespeare.' Bessie struggled to appear casual as she made a pot of coffee.

Sean was lounging back in a chair watching her.

'I remember that sonnet from school.'

'You said the lines beautifully.'

'I meant them. You are lovely.'

'Oh Sean . . .'

'And I love you.'

'I keep telling you, you mustn't talk like that.'

'And you love me. You do, don't you?'

She couldn't lie to him.

'Yes, I do.'

'Well then . . .'

'It's because I love you that I don't think we should take our relationship any further. We're loving friends just now. That means you've no serious commitment to me. You're free to meet a younger woman, somebody a lot more suitable.'

'We've already gone over all this. I don't want a younger woman. I just want you. Bessie, Bessie, how many times must I tell you? There's nobody like you in the whole world. You're beautiful, you're gentle, you're talented, you're loving, you're caring and far too generous for your own good. I want to look after you.'

She stood helplessly gazing at him, the coffee pot forgotten in her hand. He came over to her, took it from her and put it on the table. Then he gathered her into his arms.

'Bessie, my dearest love. You mean more to me than anything or anyone else in the world.'

He had said all this before in letters. Everywhere he went he sent her the most beautiful love letters. She had them hidden away in her dressing-table drawer. Every night before she went to bed she read and re-read every one. Some of them started – 'Beloved'. Others 'Dearest' or 'My Dearest Love' or 'My Lovely Girl'.

Girl! She could have wept at that. Oh, to be a girl again for him. She remembered her girlhood and realised now that she had been lovely then. Fair haired, with grey-blue eyes, a clear, smooth skin and a slim figure. She'd told Sean this with sadness and regret in her voice and he'd said,

'But darling, you're still the same girl – in looks as well as in everything else.'

How kind he was. How she wished what he said was true. Perhaps she did look that lovely girl to him because looking at her through the eyes of love he was unable to see clearly or to think realistically. But oh, how wonderful it was to be in his arms, to be made to feel safe, and loved, and beautiful! As she surrendered to his kiss, she allowed herself to be transported to that other rose-tinted world. She allowed herself to believe in it, to savour it, to treasure it. Just for tonight.

He carried her through to the bedroom and, unable to face the harsh reality of the light, she pleaded with him not to switch it on. Even so, she clutched her arms across her body in case, by some grey shadow of the moon flitting through the window, he might see her scars and imperfections.

Gently he prised aside her arms and kissed every part of her until she relaxed and was able to stroke him and kiss him in return. He kept telling her how beautiful she was –

When all the time he was the beautiful one.

As she sank deeper and deeper into physical rapture, even as she allowed waves of it to completely engulf her, the certainty remained that what was happening was wrong. She was only enjoying a few moments of love. It was a self-indulgence; a selfish act from which no good could come.

Just this once, she kept telling herself. She told him how much she loved him. His smooth dark hair, his dark, thoughtful eyes, his hard taut features. The steely sinews of his neck, his powerful chest and arms. His firm, flat abdomen and narrow hips, his long strong legs. She kissed and caressed every part of him.

They were in a daze afterwards. Forgetting the coffee, forgetting that Bev had come in and was singing to herself in the kitchen, they said goodnight. They didn't even arrange when they'd see each other again.

'Well then,' Bev said when she joined her in the kitchen. 'So you've taken the plunge at last. How was it, eh? Wonderful, I'll bet. Your eyes are shining, hen.'

Bessie flopped down on to the nearest chair.

'Have I gone mad or something?' she asked.

'Mad with happiness, by the looks of you. I'm hell of a jealous. Fancy landing a gorgeous guy like that.'

'Why is my life always so complicated and difficult, I wonder.'

'Here, hen, I only wish my life could have a complication like him.'

'Nothing ever turns out as I expect.'

'Stop moaning, for God's sake. Just think yourself damned lucky.'

Bessie took a deep breath.

'Yes, I suppose things could be worse.'

'A lot worse. Well?'

'Well what?'

'Haven't you noticed anything about me?'

'Oh Bev, you haven't had a drink.' Bessie went over and hugged her friend. 'Good for you.'

'Do you know where I was earlier on?'

'Where?'

'The reading room of the Mitchell Library, of all places. I wanted peace and quiet to think but I couldn't go to the park in case I met some of my drinking pals and was tempted. So I sat in the Mitchell Library leafing through newspapers and magazines, and thinking. I'm forty and what have I done with my life? I haven't even any weans. You've been lucky, Bessie. You've been married and you've got a daughter and one of these days you'll have grandchildren.'

'I'm not so sure about the grandchildren,' Bessie sighed. 'Daisy's been pregnant to Nigel already and she had an abortion. She doesn't want any children, she says. As far as marriage is concerned, I wasted over twenty years of my life tied to the wrong man.'

'At least you've done something now. You've made your mark, hen. People know your name and respect it. And now you *have* got the right man.'

'Oh Bev, I love him.'

'I know you do, hen. And he loves you.'

'It's so wonderful. I still can't believe it. It's like something I've dreamed up.'

'Believe it, hen, and be happy.'

Bessie nodded.

'Yes, I should treasure every moment and be thankful, shouldn't I?'

'Well, I would if I were you. By God, just give me the chance of a decent, loving fella . . .'

'Your chance will come, Bev. Maybe you'll meet somebody nice at the wedding.'

'I doubt it. As far as I can gather, most of the guys invited to the do are married.'

'You never know, maybe some of Freddie's schoolteacher friends. Anyway, there'll be other times and other places.'

'Does Jennifer know you've turned veggie? Or Andrina? I suppose she's the one who'd better know.'

'I still eat fish. But yes, I did mention it to Andrina. And it'll be OK. She's going to make a broccoli quiche and a lentil dish. I can't remember what she called it.'

'Sounds horrible.'

'No, you'd be surprised. I really enjoy vegetarian dishes now and they make me feel so much better. I've lost a bit of weight as well.'

'That's not with what you eat, hen. That's all this mad exercising you do. A treadmill! What next?'

'It was in a sale at the sports shop.'

'You're getting to be a bloody masochist. That exercise bike was bad enough but weights, and that vibrating thing, and now this . . . I know why you're doing it, hen, but you've no need to be pushing yourself so much. He'd love you anyway. He loves you for yourself. I'm sure he'll have told you that.'

He had, of course. But the self-image that she'd held or been conditioned to hold for so many years couldn't be so easily ignored or changed. Her past was stirred up when Peter called unexpectedly. She had been enjoying Satchmo singing 'What a Wonderful World' on her record player and he'd really put a damper on it. He'd come to ask her, not to return 'home' exactly, but to get together again. On his terms, of course. All would be forgiven. He would sell his flat and come to live with her in the West End. She would be allowed to continue with her painting as long as she kept it to regular hours – say two hours a day while he was at work. She must forget about it though, switch off, the moment she stepped out of her studio.

He'd give her a little more housekeeping money, he assured her magnanimously. Things would be much easier for her than they used to be, he promised.

Of course, he said, the place would have to be kept a lot better than this. He wasn't used to living like a tramp or a gypsy. In disgust he looked round the untidy sitting room with its coloured bean bags and piles of magazines, books, records and tapes strewn around on the floor. Not to mention its trailing greenery. Somehow her plants always got out of hand and spread upwards, outwards and sideways in riotous profusion. She even had a large nude painting on the wall but Peter tried to avoid looking at that.

She stared at him. She thought of all the years he'd whittled away at her self-confidence and she could have wept.

'Peter,' she said as calmly as she could, 'I want a divorce.'

He stared at her in amazement.

'What do you mean, you want a divorce?'

'Ask my lawyer,' she said, getting up and beckoning him towards the door.

'You've showed yourself in your true colours here.' His voice betrayed a quiver of disappointment. 'This place is like a tip. I take a pride in myself and my home. You obviously have no idea what pride and decency mean.'

'Goodbye, Peter.'

'Divorce or not, you'll not get a penny out of me.'

She suddenly saw him as a pathetic old man, and felt sorry for him.

'I don't want anything from you. Nothing at all.'

They were in the hall now and she was praying to be free of him, never to see his sour, misery-laden face again. Yet, at the same time, sorry for his wasted years as well as her own. Maybe with someone more like himself, someone more conventional, he could have been a different and happier man. She wanted to say that she was sorry but knew it was no use.

'Goodbye,' she repeated firmly and closed the door.

LV

Seeing Peter again and talking to him – or rather listening to him – had made Bessie appreciate her new life all the more. Leaving Peter had been a rebirth. She had started to find her true self from the day she'd walked out of his house.

In galleries and museums she took pleasure in touching things, feeling the curves of statues, the texture of tapestries. She walked down Byres Road at midnight and soaked up the buzz of lights and cars going by, and the noise of people enjoying themselves. She often worked by spotlight until one in the morning. Then because she had been so absorbed, she'd forget what time it was. She'd go out to the shops and wonder why they were all shut. Then she'd laugh at herself. Life was good. She felt herself open up like a flower in the sun. Her life with Peter seemed like a bad dream now.

Peter had always made her out to be stupid but he had taken her for a right fool if he thought she didn't know the real reason he'd called at her flat. She had established herself as not only a good painter but a painter who could make money. It was the money that had attracted Peter, the money he wanted, not her.

Sean wanted her for herself. She knew that from the honest, the sensitive as well as the passionate way he treated her. She knew by the patient way he kept building up her self-confidence. She would become agitated and reluctant to allow him to keep the light on while they made love. She would try to cover herself up and hide her nakedness. She would plead with him, 'Don't look, please don't.' He would gently take the covers away and say, 'For goodness sake, you're fine. You're lovely. Why should you be so embarrassed? I like you for what you are. I find you attractive the way you are.'

'I just can't see myself as attractive.'

'What do I see, Bessie? I'll tell you. I see a person who is slim, has a good figure. A delightful person who has blonde bubbly hair. You're a bit older than me, but you look lovely. Yes, OK, if I want to be picky, you've got small flaws here and there. You're not perfect but who is? But Bessie, believe me, you are an attractive person.'

When he was away from Glasgow on a job, he wrote to her as often as he could. The first thing he did when he returned to the city was come and see her. Each time was like the first time. Seeing each other, speaking to each other, making love, was always an unbelievable delight, a magic journey of discovery. She was still shy but gradually she began to think – Yes, Sean is right, I don't look so bad. But more important than how she looked was how Sean made her believe she, as a person, was *worthwhile*. She *mattered*. She was worthwhile as a person *in her own right*.

It was incredible. Deep down she began to really believe it. 'You look great,' he enthused. And her shoulders went back. And her head balanced with easy dignity on a straight back.

She went to Meeting and just sat feeling grateful for being given the gift of love. Yet afraid to pray in case God would remind her that she was doing wrong. Yet could loving, and being loved, be wrong? She wanted to ask somebody's advice but didn't know who or how. After Meeting finished she wanted to cling on to someone's hand and say, Please help me and advise me. Instead she just shook hands and smiled around. And said nothing.

Then Sean asked her to marry him as soon as her divorce came through. He wanted to leave his parents' cottage and get a place of his own. He wanted her to sell the Botanic Crescent flat, and come to live with him as his wife.

Oh, if only she could. Oh, heaven on earth. She asked him if they couldn't just go on as they were – taking one day at a time, just living for the day. He said 'no'. He loved her and wanted her as his wife. He wanted to start planning for their future.

What future?

She timidly, apprehensively, turned an inward eye to God.

Please help me.

It was all she dared to say.

To Sean she pleaded, 'Let's leave any discussion about our future until after Jennifer's wedding. My mind's full of all the excitement and preparations for that just now.' Reluctantly he agreed. She discovered, however, that he'd been forced to say something to his family. They'd questioned him about his frequent visits to Botanic Crescent until eventually he'd admitted that he not only loved Bessie, but had asked her to marry him. They were horrified, as Bessie had known they would be. Bernard had promptly sent him on a job to London but Sean told her not to worry, he'd be back in plenty of time for Jennifer's wedding.

Then, of course, Bernard no doubt had been asked to visit her and sort things out, because he knew her better than Sean's parents and he'd been to her flat before.

She knew the moment she saw his big body framed in her doorway that he'd come about her relationship with Sean. She allowed him to push past her and stride through to the kitchen. Heart in mouth, she followed him. He turned on her with hard, angry eyes.

'What the hell do you think you're playing at?'

'If you're referring to my relationship with Sean, I think that's my business.'

'The hell it is! He's only a boy. His mother and father want something better for him than this. He deserves something better than this. They blame me, of course, for sending him on the job at your bloody exhibition. I blame myself. But it's the last thing any of us would have thought might happen.'

'We love each other.'

'Aw, don't give me that shit. He doesn't know what love is. He's had no experience of love, or life, or anything. OK, as an older woman, you can give him a bit of experience, but that's all. Even that has a touch of obscenity about it. You're the same as his mother – fair, fat and forty.'

She flushed and fought to hold back her tears.

'Would you please leave?'

'OK. I'll go but I'm warning you, Bessie. You're not going to be allowed to ruin Sean's life.'

After he'd gone and she was left standing in the empty silence of the kitchen, the tears came. She felt as if, unexpectedly, her life had collapsed about her like a pack of cards.

By the time Bev came back from visiting Freddie's flat where she'd been helping him and Jennifer to paper their hall, Bessie was quietly composed. She was sitting drinking a cup of tea when Bev entered the kitchen.

'Oh good, is that tea on the go, hen. I could do with a cup. The love-birds had me working like a slave over in Roxburgh Street. I was up and down that ladder like a bloody yo-yo.' She poured herself a cup of tea and sat down opposite Bessie at the table. It was then that she noticed Bessie's red-rimmed eyes.

'Have you been crying?'

'You could say that.'

'What's up, hen? What's happened?'

Bessie took a deep breath.

'Oh, nothing that I didn't expect.'

'How do you mean?'

'His family found out and are on the warpath.'

'Aw to hell with them!'

'Bernard arrived as their spokesman.'

'Christ, I know he can be a great guy but I've always said I wouldn't like to cross him. I can just imagine what it must have been like, but don't let him or any of them get you down and spoil things between you and Sean.'

Bessie nodded, then took another mouthful of tea.

'Sean and I are going to talk things over after the wedding.'

'God, they'll all be at the wedding!'

'I know. I wish they hadn't known until afterwards. It's going to be awkward. To put it mildly.'

'For God's sake, remember it's supposed to be Jennifer's happy day. Try not to cause any trouble and spoil things for her.'

That brought Bessie to life.

'What?' she cried out angrily. 'Me cause trouble for Jennifer? That's the last thing I want to do. If there's going to be any trouble, it certainly won't be caused by me.'

You're a fine one to talk, she thought, but managed, with great difficulty, to hold her tongue.

LVI

ANDRINA KEPT CHANGING her mind about what to wear at the wedding. She had shown a book of patterns and sample materials to Bessie, and Bessie had suggested one of the soft pastel florals. Bessie also suggested a suit or a long-sleeved jacket over a dress.

'For pity's sake, Andrina, whatever you do, don't go showing too much leg or bosom. You'll just embarrass Jennifer.'

'What does Jennifer know about style, Bessie? Anyway, she's so enamoured and completely carried away with that flat she's hardly taken any interest in what she's going to wear herself. Honestly, the way she goes on about that place!'

'Oh well, after being homeless and living in the awful conditions she did, I suppose it's sheer heaven having a place of her own. Let her enjoy it.'

'Of course! You know me, I'd never dream of interfering. No, I'm letting her go her own way. But honestly, Bessie, I shudder to think what kind of wedding she would have if it wasn't for me. Something like Bernard's latest, I suppose. Did you hear that he didn't even have his brothers there? And heaven knows what kind of meal they had.'

'Bernard was here the other day.'

Andrina looked intrigued.

'Really?'

'Trying to warn me off Sean.'

'What a cheek! It's none of his business. I hope you told him so.'

'Yes, I did. But of course, it's understandable in a way. Sean is his nephew.'

'That doesn't mean to say he can run Sean's life. Or yours. Fancy him, of all people, telling you or anyone who they should or shouldn't have sex with. He'd have sex with anything that moved.'

Bessie laughed.

'Oh Andrina . . .'

'It's true. My mother always said he was an animal and she was right.'

'Now, you don't mean that.'

'I do. I hate him.'

'You're just saying that. I can't imagine you hating anyone. But I appreciate your loyalty.'

'He probably fancies you himself and he's jealous of Sean having you.'

Bessie laughed again.

'Don't be daft.' Then she became serious again. 'No, I knew it would happen when any of Sean's family got to know about us. It's the age difference. Of course, I hadn't been prepared for a confrontation with Bernard. Sean will be furious when he finds out. I won't tell him, especially what Bernard said.'

'What did he say?'

'He suggested it was a kind of incestuous thing. He more or less said I was a carbon copy of Sean's mother. Fair, fat and forty, he said.'

'Oh, how awful.' She rushed over and hugged Bessie. 'How cruel and how untrue. You're nothing like Caroline O'Maley. And you're certainly not fat, Bessie. Oh, I do hate him. I do!'

'It's all right. I've got over it. Don't say anything about this to Jennifer. She thinks the world of him and we don't want to upset her when she's so happy just now. Promise me?'

'Yes, all right. But he makes me so mad. Arrogant bastard.'

'Andrina!' Bessie was amused rather than shocked.

'I know I'm not usually a swearing woman. But he'd make anyone forget their good manners.'

'Just calm down. I have. By the way, to change the subject, I hope that's the last lot of stuff you've brought today. My freezer can't take any more. And don't forget, everything in there has to be carted back to your place nearer the time. When, exactly?'

'The day before should do. I'll get Freddie or Robert to bring everything over in the car.'

'Are you sure you're going to manage everything, Andrina?'

'Of course, dear. I've catered for far bigger parties than this. My goodness, this is nothing – just a few people in comparison with the parties I used to have when I was married to Robert. You didn't know me then, of course. I remember our house-warming party. The place was absolutely packed and overflowing and I'd baked and prepared everything myself.' She smiled proudly. 'And that was without the help of your freezer. It's all down to being well organised. And enjoying it, of course. I enjoy cooking and baking and being a good hostess.'

Bessie studied her beautiful face with interest.

'Won't you feel any embarrassment with Robert and his wife being there?'

'Huh!' Andrina tossed her head. 'Why should I feel embarrassment? I feel nothing for him.'

'That's all right then.'

'I'm going to enjoy the whole occasion enormously.' She lowered her voice confidentially. 'She's a grumpy schoolmarm type, I believe.'

'Here, you'll never guess the other visitor I had.'

'Who, dear?'

'My millionaire. Well, he's not mine exactly. But you know who I mean. He's had a spell of convalescence back home in Williamsburgh and now he's come over again to arrange for the packing and shipping of my paintings. They've been exhibited all over Britain. And he wanted to see what I've been working on.'

'Absolutely everyone knows your name. I'm very proud to have you as my friend.'

'Oh, for goodness sake, don't be daft. I think *he* must be daft to spend so much money on my pictures. And to want to buy everything I paint doesn't strike me as being all that sensible either. I don't like being inhibited in any way and I told him – '

'What's he like?' Andrina interrupted.

'Tall. Almost as tall as Bernard, I'd say. And well made like him. But with a shock of snowy white hair and a white moustache.'

'Is he going to be around for a while?'

'A few weeks. I've invited him to dinner. I'm going to cook him a really nice meal. I feel I owe him. He's been so kind.'

'Why don't you ask him to the wedding?'

'He's never even met Jennifer. Or Freddie. He'd not know anyone there.'

'He'd know you. I expect, to a man like that, it would be quite a novelty – a homely Glasgow wedding. He'd jump at the chance.'

'But it's not up to me to invite people to Jennifer's wedding. It's up to Jennifer.'

'And to me, Bessie. I'll put an invitation card in the post for him today as soon as I get back home.'

Bessie shook her head.

'Andrina!'

'Oh, why not? He'll enjoy it. You know he will. And, as you say, he's been so good to you – paying you all that money . . .'

'Yes, all right, all right. But we'd better check with Jennifer first.'

When Bessie did mention it to Jennifer, Jennifer was delighted.

'What a wonderful idea, Bessie. Yes, definitely, you must invite him. Maybe something will come of it yet.'

'Come of what?'

Although she knew what.

'You and what's his name – Lester Morgan.'

Jennifer had always been worried about the idea of her and Sean.

'Jennifer, I've no romantic designs whatsoever on Lester Morgan.'

'I bet he fancies you. Think of it, Bessie. You'd be set up for life. No more money worries.'

'I haven't any money worries.'

'I wish I'd enough money to afford to stop working,' Andrina sighed. She'd had to go back to work part-time and vowed she'd give it up at the drop of a hat if she could.

'I'd never do that,' Bessie said. 'My painting is part of me. It *is* me. I'd die without it.'

Dreamily, Andrina closed her eyes.

'If I came into lots of money, I'd go on a world cruise. Wear lovely clothes. Dine at the captain's table. Meet handsome Italian lovers.'

'Yes, I'm sure you would,' Bessie said.

After Andrina left, Bev came in. She'd managed to get another waitressing job, this time in a small private club in a lane off Argyle Street.

Bessie noticed her friend was unusually subdued. 'Are you all right?' she asked.

Bev hesitated and then said, 'A man I used to know came into the club tonight.'

'An old flame?'

'I lived with him for a while. He used to batter me about. Threaten me with a gun sometimes.'

'Oh Bev! He didn't try anything tonight, did he?'

'Gus McCabe, his name is. He can be such a charmer when he likes, and he liked tonight. Apologised for how he'd been before. Made a whole lot of excuses. Complimented me too. Said how good I looked, etcetera. Offered to buy me a drink.'

'Oh, you didn't, Bev . . .'

'No, I didn't. But I felt like one, I can tell you.'

'Thank God you're all right.'

'Kept insisting on seeing me again. Taking me out for a meal. He wanted to be good to me to make up for everything, he said. You should have seen the smart suit he was wearing. And he'd one of those crombie coats. He always looked the gentleman, that man.'

'Oh Bev, don't listen to him. Don't go out with him. That kind never changes. He'd do the same to you again.'

'Don't worry, hen. I don't want anything to do with him. I hope to God he doesn't come back. I'm frightened of him, so I am.'

LVII

'I'D BE DELIGHTED to go to Jennifer's wedding,' Lester said. Bessie had served him a meal in the kitchen: Marks & Spencer's steak pie, potatoes and mixed veg. She'd made a Scotch trifle with lashings of sherry for pudding. He was obviously a man who relished his food. He sat with a big white napkin tucked into his collar and demolished every crumb she put before him. Afterwards he thumped his wide girth and said,

'By God, that was good!'

'I'm glad you enjoyed it,' Bessie said, rising. 'Come on through to the sitting room with your coffee.'

He rose too.

'I'll help you wash the dishes first.'

'Oh, let them wait.' Bessie dismissed the dishes with an airy wave of her hand. 'I sometimes let them pile up for a couple of days. I've far more interesting things to think about.'

'It's time you had a dishwasher, Bessie. I'll send you one for Christmas.'

She laughed.

'Don't you dare! You've done more than enough for me already.'

He followed her through to the other room, coughing loudly and thumping a fist against his chest.

'What have I done?' he asked. 'Except to have the good luck to discover a wonderfully original talent.'

'Are you all right?' Bessie asked. 'You've still got a terrible cough.'

'I'm fine. Fit as a fiddle.'

'Can you find a seat? Just put those books on to the floor.

I seem to collect so many books these days I can't find enough places to put them.'

'Why is that? Couldn't you afford books before?'

'Well, I suppose that was part of it. But even if I got books out of the library it caused a terrible fuss. Of course there was time, or rather the lack of it. I nursed my father-in-law for years. Day and night.'

'By the sound of it, it was a miracle you managed to paint.'

'I suppose it was. Looking back it certainly seems like that. I'd made a studio up in the loft and I used to shut myself up there whenever I could. Usually when my husband was in so that he could keep an eye on his father. I suppose it was a bit selfish of me.'

'Nonsense. Why shouldn't he take a turn with the old guy?'

'You're a widower, aren't you, Lester?'

'Yes. My wife died of cancer several years ago.'

'Oh, I'm sorry.'

'It was a blessed relief in the end. For her, I mean. I wanted to hang on to Alice as long as possible but she was in pain.' He shook his head. 'I miss her still. We had a good marriage.' He made an obvious effort to brighten. 'Now,' he said and took a deep swig of his coffee, 'I want to see the rest of your work. I can't wait a moment longer.'

'Oh, relax and have another cup of coffee. There's plenty of time to look at my paintings.'

'No, I insist.' He got up. 'Right now. Lead me to them.'

'You're an awful man,' she said. 'Where do you get all your energy?' He was seventy if he was a day but with a fresh complexion and a luxurious bush of hair.

'Enthusiasm, Bessie. Enthusiasm. And my love of all things beautiful. You must come out for a visit, Bessie. I've got a houseful of antiques and beautiful *objets d'art*. You'd love them too. And I could introduce you to so many interesting people. Painters, sculptors, writers.'

'Sounds wonderful.'

'Come back with me next month.'

'Can I take a rain check, as they say in your country. I've rather a lot on my mind just now, Lester. What with the wedding and everything. My friend Bev and I have to be Jennifer's matrons of honour.'

He looked puzzled and she laughed.

'That's the term used for a woman too old to be called a bridesmaid. That's what I think, anyway.'

'You're not too old for anything, Bessie,' he said gallantly.

His attention was caught by the canvases stacked around the studio and the large one propped on the easel. He went into mounting raptures of delight as he examined each one in turn.

'Bessie, Bessie, what a treasure trove. What a find! I'm going to have a wonderful exhibition of all your work over in the States. Oh, you must come. You must be there for the opening.'

Bessie felt overwhelmed, even slightly embarrassed by the extent of his excitement. She couldn't help thinking – surely they couldn't be *that* good. Her success in the art world still didn't seem quite real to her.

'I'll let you know nearer the time if I can manage.'

Lester was like a child with new toys. She could hardly drag him away from the studio. At first she said it was too cold and was making him cough, but he ignored that. It came to the point when she had to be almost rude.

'It's getting awful late, Lester, and my friend Bev will be in soon. She works nights in a club in town and she's so exhausted and footsore when she gets in, I usually run a hot bath for her and make her a cup of Horlicks.'

'Oh sure, sure. I've taken up far too much of your time. I'd better shoot off.'

'No, I've enjoyed your company. I really have, Lester. Do come again. You'll always be welcome. But I'll see you at the wedding anyway.'

'I'm really looking forward to that, Bessie. It's kind of your friend to include me.'

He gave her a bear hug before waving her goodbye and clattering down the stairs.

Bessie smiled to herself and shook her head as she shut the door and returned to the kitchen. Next time I see him, she thought, I must remember to ask what vitamins he takes. Surely there must be some magic potion he swallowed to give him such energy.

Yet he was probably right when he said his secret was enthusiasm. It was amazing what effect the power of the mind and the emotions could have on the body. Hadn't she been transformed by her love for Sean? She looked an entirely different person from the bent, careworn woman who had been married to Peter. Thinking of Sean and her love for him, she cleared the kitchen table and washed the dishes, singing happily.

Maybe Sean would like to come with her to the American exhibition. She began running Bev's bath, adding the herbal bath salts that always helped her friend's aching feet. She usually had the bath timed just right for Bev's arrival and Bev would immediately sink gratefully into it. Then they'd have a cup of Horlicks together. Horlicks helped Bev to sleep. These past few nights she had been unusually tense and anxious. Every night Bessie prayed that Bev would not be tempted to start drinking alcohol again to help her relax. Bessie knew all the excuses for Bev's bouts of drinking. This time of course there was the genuine fear of Gus McCabe.

She went to the front-room window and peered anxiously down the Crescent for Bev's small figure clipping along in her high-heeled shoes. The Crescent was deserted, the only sound the creak and rustle of the trees in the wind. Then she heard the throb-throb of a taxi as it approached the close. It stopped and Bev emerged and hurried inside the building. Bessie was waiting with the door open when she arrived.

'Are you all right?' Bessie asked as she locked up for the night.

'I'm all right now.'

Bev was trying to light a cigarette with a violently shaking hand. She dropped her handbag and its contents spilled noisily out on to the hall floor. At that Bev burst into tears.

'Don't worry,' Bessie said. 'Away through and get your bath. I'll see to this. Then we can talk.'

'Do you believe in fate, Bessie?'

'I believe in God. And I believe we should take responsibility for our own lives.'

'A lot of bloody good that is to me.' Bev's mouth twisted with bitterness. 'Or your – something of God or good in everyone. There's people that are just plain evil, Bessie, and I know better than you about that.'

LVIII

'Oh Sean.'

'Just until I find a place for us both.'

'Darling, I don't mind you staying here. You could stay here for ever as far as I'm concerned. I mean, if we were getting married, it would be silly to give up this lovely flat. Far more sensible for you to just move in here.'

'There's no "ifs" about it. We *are* going to get married.'

'It's just I didn't want to rush into things. We'd agreed to wait until after Jennifer's wedding to talk about us.'

'That was before Mother and Father and Bernard started trying to lay down the law. I'm not a child. How dare they try to interfere in my life. And worse, how dare they speak about you as they did? I couldn't stay there another minute, Bessie.'

He gave her one of his clinched smiles. 'Good job I didn't. I set upon Bernard and my father separated us just in time. Bernard's not your run-of-the-mill older guy. He'd probably have made mincemeat of me.'

'Oh Sean. I'm so sorry there's been all this trouble with your family.'

'Forget it. It's high time I left home for good anyway. Now, can I move in with you now or are you going to throw me out? It's make-up-your-mind time.'

'All right. But what we arranged still stands. There's nothing permanent until we talk everything through after the wedding's out of the way.'

'OK. OK. But if you ask me, it would be better if you gave this wedding a miss. Can you imagine what the atmosphere's going to be like? I don't care a damn but you seem so concerned about everything being perfect for Jennifer. I just can't see how it can be in the circumstances.'

'Oh dear.' Bessie's face creased with worry. 'But I can't just not go. Jennifer would be so hurt. She regards Bev and me as her best friends. We've to be her matrons of honour. And don't you dare laugh.'

'I'm not laughing, darling.' He pulled her into his arms and snuggled kisses into her neck. 'Of course, if you're a matron of honour, you must do your duty.'

'You *are* laughing!'

'Let's just be happy together and to hell with everybody else. We'll go and we'll enjoy ourselves. I hear the bride's mother is a wonderful cook.'

'Yes. That's another thing. I couldn't let Andrina down either. She's bound to need a helping hand. The reception's far too much for her to do all on her own.'

'OK. OK. I said we'll go. And we'll dance, shall we? Like this?' He grabbed her by the waist, lifted her off her feet and whisked her round and round. She screamed and laughed in protest.

'Stop it, you idiot! You're making me dizzy.'

As usual she was amazed at his easy strength. She often sensed a joy about him, a kind of celebration of his physical strength and fitness. Or maybe it was just a joyous celebration of youth. She felt saddened by the thought, but it was only a sadness for herself.

He had put her down when suddenly there was a noisy scrabbling at the front door. Somebody was in a panic to get the key in the lock. Then they recognised Bev's voice.

'Bessie!'

In a few rapid strides Sean made it to the door first. Bev fell into his arms and then reached for Bessie.

'I'm sorry, hen. I didn't mean to cause you any trouble but I was frightened he was following me. He tried to stop me in the lane when I came out the club, but I got away and then – '

'Who?' Sean interrupted as he took a quick look outside at the empty stairway. 'Describe him. I can have a word with him. I'll guarantee he won't bother you again.'

Bessie was already leading Bev through to the kitchen. Sean strode after them.

'Bev, did you hear me?'

'Yes, but he'll be well away now and anyway, I don't want to cause you any trouble, Sean. He's a right nutter, this guy.'

'I've dealt with nutters before.'

Bessie had gone pale with anxiety.

'Darling, let's just leave it to the police. Bev has told me about this man. He owns a gun.'

'I've dealt with gunmen before.'

'Oh darling, please. I couldn't bear to think of you in any danger.'

He smiled then.

'Bessie, it's my job.'

'I know, but I still can't bear to think about it.'

Bev dried her eyes and tried to sound calm.

'You can phone for the police if you like. Or I can call at the local station tomorrow morning. But it'll be his word against mine. I know this guy. I've been through this before. He's a respectable businessman from a good family and he can charm the birds off the trees. The police won't want anything to do with it. Anyway, they can't be there to protect me every night when I come out of my work, or anywhere else I am in the dark.'

'OK, Bev. We'll leave it for now,' Sean said, but he winked over at Bessie. 'Just you try to relax. Take a hot milky drink and a tablet to make you sleep.'

Bessie made her the drink and gave her the tablet before tucking her up in bed.

'You're going to be all right, Bev,' she soothed her.

'Aye, OK, hen.'

Back in the kitchen, Bessie looked at Sean.

'Do you not think I ought to have phoned the police?'

'She's probably right. It would be her word against his. What proof has she? She hasn't a mark on her.'

'It's awful to let him get away with frightening her like that and with what she's told me about what happened in the past with him, it won't stop at just frightening her.'

'He won't get away with it. I know that club. It's on

Bernard's books. Bernard's got most of the clubs and pubs in Glasgow sewn up. I'm going to work there tomorrow. Just for the one night, if I'm lucky.'

'Oh Sean.'

'Don't worry. You can come with me if you like. We can have a nice meal and relax and listen to the music. There'll be no problem. Just keep clear of Bev. Let her go out on her own.'

'But surely it would be better if I stuck close to Bev and came out arm in arm with her . . .'

'You can't be there to protect her every night, Bessie, any more than I or the police can. You just do as I tell you.'

He tried to make her laugh again. He danced with her. He tickled her. He tried to take all her clothes off in the kitchen. She did laugh and allow herself to be chased protesting through to the bedroom. But even as they made tender and passionate and dazzling love, her deep apprehension remained.

Bev was all apologies next day and made a determined effort to be cheery and brave.

'Sorry I went over the top last night. It was just he stirred up such awful memories. I don't think he'll try anything again. I could report him to the club and he'd lose his membership.'

'Is that the Hole in the Wall club?'

'Yes, do you know it, Sean?' Bev asked. 'It's very nice. Small and terribly select. No bouncers needed or anything like that.'

'Oh no,' Sean corrected, 'there's always a man checking the place and on call from the owner's other club along Argyle Street, the Clock Tower. I had to go from the Clock Tower to the Hole in the Wall once. It was just a member who'd downed one whisky too many. He was making a bit of a nuisance of himself and I persuaded him to leave in peace. Normally it's one of the quietest clubs in Glasgow.'

Bev sighed.

'I know. I was happy to get any job but especially happy to get one in that place. I felt so safe.'

Sean patted her hand.

'And you will be safe, love.'

'Oh aye,' Bev cheeked back, 'you going to turn into a fairy and wave your magic wand or something?'

'You'd be surprised what magic I can perform.'

Bessie felt so sick with worry she couldn't eat any breakfast.

'Sean wants to take me to the club for a meal tonight but you said it was a private members-only place, didn't you, Bev?'

'Oh yes, it's all these well-heeled businessmen and their wives who go. You'll not get in unless you've a special membership card. The door's always kept locked and it's only your card that can open it from the outside. It's one of these electronic things.'

Bessie felt relieved but only for a moment because Sean said, 'I know the manager. One phone call and we're in. Don't worry.'

'Are you doing this to try to nail Gus McCabe?' Bev asked him.

'Ah, so that's his name, is it?'

Sean was perfectly relaxed and smiling, lounging back on the kitchen chair, his long legs stretched out under the table.

'Oh here.' Bev looked worried now. 'Keep clear of him, for God's sake. I'd never forgive myself if you got hurt, Sean. I know how much you mean to Bessie. Oh please. I'd go back to that man rather than have anything bad happen to spoil things between you and Bessie.'

'My dear wee Bev,' Sean said, 'I'm not going to allow anything bad to happen to any of us.'

Bessie went over to the cooker, fetched the coffee pot and refilled their cups. She looked perfectly calm but inside she was repeating like a mantra,

Please, keep Sean safe. Oh please.

LIX

THE ENTRANCE HALL of the club had an air of money. It was in the crystal chandelier, the tall Chinese vase and Persian carpet. It was in the heavy oak-panelled walls of the entrance and the door of the 'Ladies Rest Room'. Inside the rest room was a crystal vase of fresh flowers. Padded coat hangers hung ready on the brass rod in the cupboard where ladies could safely leave their coats. Two deep-cushioned armchairs awaited any lady who wished to have a rest. Gold taps glistened at the washbasins, along with piles of soft hand-towels. No noisy hand dryers or rough paper towels here.

Bessie hung up her cloak then examined herself in the long mirror. It was on occasions like this, when she was out with Sean, that she worried most acutely about their age difference. She lived in fear of someone mistaking her for Sean's mother. Yet as she looked at herself, she was soothed by the memory of Sean's words: 'You're beautiful. You're a worthwhile, beautiful person.' She rubbed a powder puff over her face and added a little rouge to her cheeks. There was nothing she could do about her hair. After she rejoined Sean in the entrance hall, they went through to the restaurant bar area. In one corner a man was playing lazy, sentimental music on a baby grand piano. In another there was a bar with four high stools fronting it. A couple of men were drinking and quietly talking there. Sean led Bessie over to one of the half-dozen or so tables and settled her into a chair. It was late and only one other couple was eating a meal.

'Very nice,' Bessie said, indicating the pristine white linen table-cover and napkin, and the sparkling glasses and cutlery. She had another look at the gold-framed paintings that had caught her eye when they'd first come in. 'There must be a high membership subscription for this place.'

'There's three bedrooms upstairs and a room through there with comfortable chairs and plenty of magazines and newspapers.'

Just then Bev approached them, ordering-pad and pencil at the ready. She was looking very smart in her black dress, white lace collar and apron. Her blonde hair was tied back in a white lace ribbon. She smiled.

'What are you having, folks?'

Bessie studied the menu.

'It's a bit late for me to be eating dinner. I think I'd better skip the starter. I'll have the poached Highland salmon with the lemon and lime butter sauce.'

Sean ordered Aberdeen Angus braised steak with wild mushroom and forester sauce. Then they watched Bev trip away to the nether regions of the kitchen.

'She looks quite perky again,' Sean remarked. 'She's made a quick recovery.'

'You can never tell with Bev. But she is spunky, right enough. She always seems to bounce back. As long as she doesn't start drinking again. That's what worries me.'

The food was delicious and after the coffee, Sean said, 'Come on, let's have a dance before the pianist quits for the night.'

Bessie was embarrassed.

'This isn't a dance hall. Sit down, for goodness sake.'

Sean laughed and pulled her up from her chair.

'There's enough room over by the piano for a few turns. Come on. What are you afraid of?'

It occurred to her that if she'd been sweet seventeen she would have eagerly melted into his arms and danced all night, and not have cared who saw them. However, there was no one else left in the room but themselves and the pianist, so she smiled at Sean and allowed him to take her into his arms. The pianist was playing and singing softly, 'A kiss is just a kiss, a sigh is just a sigh . . . as time goes by'. It made her feel sad and she clung to Sean and pressed her cheek as well as her body against his. She wished she could merge completely with him

– become one with him so that time would never matter any more.

'I love you,' she told him.

'And I love you, darling.' After a few minutes, he said, 'It's nearly the time Bev said she would be leaving.'

'Oh Sean . . .'

'You go to the Ladies' Room and collect your cloak. I'll meet you in the entrance hall.'

He left her standing by the piano and before she could say anything, or call to him, he'd disappeared. She murmured a quick thank you to the pianist before hurrying out to the hall. Sean was nowhere to be seen. Hastily she collected her cloak but had only waited for a moment or two when she heard a cry from outside. She rushed to open the door and peer out into the gloom of the lane. In the amber light over the doorway of the club, she saw Bev struggling with a man. Before she could move, another figure shot out of the darkness and felled the man with one blow. Immediately Bessie recognised Sean's tall, sinewy figure. She rushed and put her arm around Bev as Sean hauled the man to his feet, then doubled him up with another punch to the lower abdomen. The man sank to his knees clutching himself and groaning in agony. Sean jerked him up again and pushed his face close to the man's.

'Listen! If you go anywhere near Bev again – anywhere near her – you'll have me to reckon with, and I won't let you off so lightly next time. I know your name, I know where you work. I know where you live. Remember that.'

He flung the man to the ground and turned to Bev and Bessie, who were still clutching each other, rigid with shock.

'Come on, girls. Time to go home.'

He linked arms with them and dragged them away to where he'd parked his car. Bessie marvelled at how calm and relaxed he looked as he drove home. His arms hung loose, his hands rested easily on the wheel. He joked with Bev.

Afterwards, Bessie said 'You amaze me.'

'I'm *that* good at making love?'

They were lying in bed together and she gave him a friendly punch.

'Don't be so conceited. I was talking about earlier. It didn't seem to bother you in the slightest.'

'Oh that!'

'I was so worried. I couldn't bear anything to happen to you.'

'Darling, my job is to prevent trouble and when I can't prevent it, deal with it as quickly as possible. I'm dealing with situations like that all the time. Well, not *all* the time. There's quite a lot of variety in the job. That's what makes it so interesting.'

'I admire you so much, Sean.'

He put a finger against her lips.

'I *will* begin to sound conceited if you keep going on like that.'

'I was only joking. You're far from being conceited. Not like Bernard. No doubt he's got plenty to be conceited about. But he's very arrogant and self-assured, isn't he?'

'Bernard's a great guy. OK, I was mad at him for how he tried to break us up but he meant well and he'll come round in the end when he sees how happy we are together. He's always been good to me and the rest of the family and wanted the best for us. He's a real cool operator. You should see him in action.'

'You obviously admire him.'

'Yes, I do. But I still would never allow him to say a word against you.'

She snuggled down gratefully but as usual his hard muscular body reminded her of his youth and vigour and she felt a pang of – she was not sure what – regret, fear, sadness. To soothe away her uncertain emotions and concentrate only on love, she began to stroke his body, and kiss it. He responded with loving caresses until they were both overcome by a wild torrent of passion.

'I love you.' The words were repeated over and over again to each other and Bessie felt the emotion so genuinely and so strongly, she believed that, if necessary, she would die for him. That was one belief she had not the slightest doubt about whatsoever.

What did she matter compared with this loving, courageous, beautiful man?

The next day he had to go to a job in Edinburgh and he was up and dressed before she was awake. Normally, anxiety awoke her first so that she could slip out of bed, put on some make-up, tidy her hair and be presentable for him. This morning, however, he wakened her with a kiss and her breakfast on a tray along with a single red rose in a small vase.

'Here's the morning paper as well. I'll have to go. I'll see you tomorrow.'

'You can't manage back tonight?'

'No, it's an overnight bodyguarding job. After I see the guy safely off tomorrow afternoon, I'll come straight back here.'

She nodded then raised her face for his kiss. She felt like weeping with anxiety for his safety but managed to smile and say, 'Take care.'

'Of course. Do you think I want to miss the wedding on Saturday?'

Then he had gone.

Courage, Bessie, she told herself firmly. Then she settled back to enjoy the luxury of breakfast in bed and to read the newspaper at her leisure. It was wonderful to be treated so well, to be loved and cherished and looked after. Oh how she savoured it.

Thank you. Thank you.

LX

SEAN CAME BACK early from Edinburgh and insisted on taking her shopping.

'Shopping?' Bessie laughed. 'What on earth for?'

'Something I want you to wear at the wedding.'

'But darling, I've already bought that velvet trouser suit.'

It was in a deep royal blue, almost navy, and she loved the richness of the colour and the soft feel of the velvet. She was always taking another admiring look at it in the wardrobe. There was also a white blouse to wear with it. It had a frill at the neck, and cuffs that frilled out from each sleeve. 'I thought you liked it.'

'I do, except for one thing. I think you should wear a skirt instead of trousers.'

'There was a skirt to go with the jacket but I thought the trousers would be more suitable for me.'

'Why?'

She shrugged.

'My legs aren't as good as I'd like them to be. Trousers hide them.'

'Bessie, there isn't a thing wrong with your legs.'

She saw the tightening of his mouth and the slight hardening of his eyes and she felt afraid. Not that he would strike her or anything so dramatic. But she feared a lessening of his love.

She forced a laugh.

'All right, a skirt it shall be.'

He insisted on buying her a dress as well. It had a nipped-in waist and softly flared skirt and she was amazed at her reflection when she tried it on. Sean stood beside her at the bedroom mirror.

'Now,' he said, 'what is wrong with that figure and those

legs? If you can't see how attractive you look, there's something wrong with your eyes.'

She had to admit, at least to herself, that she did look good. Indeed she didn't look much older than Sean – if at all. She realised that her flushed cheeks, her eyes that sparkled with a kind of wonder, were all due to love, but, yes – her figure did look neat and her legs shapely. Even her ankles appeared slim in the high-heeled shoes Sean had persuaded her to buy. She had promised to wear them at the wedding.

'Meantime,' Sean said, 'we're going to christen the dress. I'm taking you out tonight for dinner.'

They decided to go for a drink first and then eat in a hotel near the Campsie hills.

Once out of the city Sean stopped the car, and hand in hand they enjoyed a walk. She took off her shoes and carried them in her free hand. At one point she teased him by running away from him. He caught up with her and they fell laughing on to the velvety soft grass. She was breathless from running and the kisses he showered her with.

'How do you fancy making love al fresco?' he said.

'Don't you dare!' Secretly she felt panic-stricken. 'Just you contain yourself until tonight when we're in bed.'

He laughed at her. 'Contain myself? I haven't heard that one before.'

It was an expression her mother had used when she was extolling her to be patient.

'Well,' Bessie's voice held a note of apology as well as embarrassment, 'I can't help thinking how near we are to the cottage where your folks live. I'd die if any of them happened to pass by and see us.'

'I've just had a thought,' Sean said. 'Why don't we call in now on our way to the hotel. We've plenty of time before dinner. I've booked a table for half-past seven.'

'Call in?' Bessie's eyes widened with shock. 'Why?'

'Well, I think it would be better to break the ice by meeting them before the wedding, instead of at it. Don't you? If we weren't going to be at the wedding it would be different. You wouldn't need to meet them at all if you didn't want to. But as things stand . . .'

She was silent for a moment. She had been worried about a confrontation at the wedding. Although she was determined to be as inoffensive and as friendly as possible and not allow anything to spoil Jennifer's day. Nevertheless . . .

'All right, darling,' she murmured uncertainly. 'Maybe it would be for the best.'

He kissed her.

'They won't eat you. I won't let them.'

She nodded, too worried now to speak.

It turned out that only Sean's father, Michael, and Martha, Sean's grandmother, were at home. Michael was restrained but polite. He made them tea and set the table with cakes and scones and strawberry jam. He seemed a caring kind of man, judging by how kind he was to his mother-in-law. He helped her out of her cushioned easy chair by the fire to a seat at the table and tucked cushions at her back. Then he made sure she had what she wanted to eat before attending to Sean and herself. His conversation was limited to offering them more tea and cakes or commenting on the weather. Martha, however, was not so circumspect.

'Well,' she suddenly announced, staring in Bessie's direction. 'I can understand now what he sees in you. You don't look like a woman in her forties. All the same there's no getting away from the fact that that's what you are.'

Sean said, 'What does age matter?'

'It matters a hell of a lot to me,' Martha bawled at him indignantly. 'I used to be a fine-looking middle-aged woman once and now look at me!'

'A likely story,' Michael said. 'I've known you for years and you've never looked any better.'

'You shut your ugly face!' Martha said. 'One thing's for sure, you never won any beauty contests.'

Bessie felt quite upset at the way the conversation was going but Sean seemed used to it – indeed they all did. Both Michael and Sean laughed and Martha continued to tuck into her scone and strawberry jam with obvious enjoyment.

Back in the car, Sean said,

'They're always like that but in actual fact, although they'd never admit it, they're very fond of one another. It's a pity my mother and my sisters weren't in. I'm sure they would have loved you, Bessie. But of course I might have known they'd be in Glasgow shopping for things for the wedding. And they'll probably make a night of it and have a meal there as well. Mother's been back and forth several times trying to get something for Gran but Gran keeps giving the thumbs down. At the same time she refuses to go with Mother to the shops.'

'I don't suppose she's able. It's a wonder she's managing to the wedding.'

'Oh, my father takes her everywhere in a wheelchair. She'll be there all right. Especially when she knows there's going to be a good feed. The old girl enjoys her grub. Father liked you, by the way. I could tell.'

Bessie wasn't so certain but her heart warmed to Sean for trying to reassure her.

They were too early for dinner so they passed the time by having a drink at the bar. There was only a young couple there and they'd set the jukebox to play a Shirley Bassey number. They were dancing to it in the non-touching way that young people had, as if they were in a dream of their own, dancing on their own. Sean and Bessie got up to dance but Sean held Bessie close in his arms.

Afterwards, in a dream of love, Sean took her hand and led her into the small, dimly lit dining room.

'You look especially beautiful tonight,' he told her.

She nearly replied it was only because in the shady room with only the soft candlelight, he couldn't see her faults. But she managed to swallow back this comment. She knew Sean didn't like her to put herself down. He had shown her, made her keenly aware, that it was only a habit, something she must now learn to discard.

She felt good. She felt beautiful. And oh, she didn't want to leave him now.

LXI

IT WAS THURSDAY and Jennifer was on her way to Bearsden to stay until the wedding. She decided to call in at Bridie O'Maley's house and check that the bridesmaids and pages hadn't caught measles or chickenpox or anything awful, and also to make sure that their clothes were ready. A plump bespectacled Bridie happily assured her that all was well and every one of them, including Frank and herself, were looking forward to the wedding with great excitement.

The only worrying note had been when Frank appeared from his writing room to join them for a cup of coffee. He was a tall man like his brothers but in every other way except his height, he wasn't like them at all. Lanky and awkward-looking with long floppy hair and a thin sensitive face, he was dressed casually in faded denims and an open-necked denim shirt.

'All set for the wedding, Jennifer?'

Her face lit up.

'Oh yes. Wait till you see our flat. We've got it exactly as we want it now. You must come to our housewarming party.'

'Great.' Frank raised his coffee cup. 'Cheers. Here's wishing you every happiness in it. I hope first of all the wedding goes well. You've made a brave mix there.'

'How do you mean?' Jennifer was taken aback and Bridie hastily cut in:

'Frank, for goodness sake, get back to your room. What's the idea coming out at this time in the morning? You usually stay out of my way until lunchtime at the earliest.'

He rolled his eyes and said to Jennifer, 'She'd lock me in there all day if I let her. A right slave-driver she is these days.'

'Well, we need every penny he can earn,' Bridie explained.

'The price of children's clothes and shoes – especially shoes – it's just terrible.'

'But what did you mean,' Jennifer persisted, 'about a brave mix?'

Frank hesitated, then said, 'As far as I'm concerned, Bessie can spend the rest of her life with Sean and the best of luck to them. Unfortunately the rest of the family, especially Bernard, isn't so enthusiastic about the affair.'

'Oh that!' Jennifer said. 'I agree with Bernard and his family, as it happens. I think Bessie is being very foolish. Not that I've anything against Sean. He's very nice but far too young for Bessie. It can't last and I don't want her to get hurt.'

'As far as I can see,' Frank said, 'they love each other.'

'Yes, I know. Or at least they're in love. It's a different thing, don't you think? And it doesn't last.'

Frank looked thoughtful.

'Well, it's an interesting idea to pursue – the different kinds of love and whether or not . . .'

'You've set him off again!' Bridie interrupted, laughing and shaking her head. 'The next thing we know he'll have a play about a love affair between an older woman and a young man.'

'Well,' Frank said, 'it would make a good story. And especially with all the family conflict it triggers off.' He was beginning to look intrigued. His eyes were filling with a glow and a hint of a smile that betrayed anticipation hovered about his mouth. 'It could even lead to violence if . . .'

'For goodness sake,' Bridie shouted, 'would you shut up and get back to your room, Frank!'

'All right. All right.' Frank rose from his chair. 'I'm going.' Already he had a faraway look. He wandered off, cup in hand, and disappeared back into his writing room.

Jennifer said, 'I thought that if the family met Bessie and Bessie met them – Sean's mum and dad I mean – they'd get on famously together and Bessie would come round to their point of view and . . .' She began to look a bit concerned. 'Maybe I haven't thought about it enough. But Bessie gets on so well with everybody and everybody likes her, I just thought . . .'

'Of course,' Bridie patted her hand. 'It'll all work out fine, you'll see. I'm sorry about Frank. He's always putting his foot in it. He's away in another world half the time. You've seen what he's like. Don't let him worry you. I don't.'

Nevertheless Jennifer couldn't help feeling a niggle of anxiety. She decided she might as well pay Bessie a visit. After all, she was only a couple of closes along the Crescent and Bessie might be offended if she just passed by without calling in to at least say hello.

Bessie was delighted to see her and rushed to put the kettle on.

'No, honestly,' Jennifer stopped her, 'I couldn't drink any more coffee just now. I've just had a cup with Bridie.'

'Are you sure?'

'Yes. I just didn't want to pass your door.'

'I'm so pleased to see you. Have you been out to Bearsden?'

'I'm on my way. Daddy collected my case and dress and everything yesterday. He wanted to collect me and take me over then as well but I'd one or two things still to do to the house.'

'It must be like a wee palace by now. You're only five minutes or so down the road but you might as well have been miles away for all any of us have seen of you lately.'

'I know, but once the wedding's over and Freddie and I come back from our honeymoon, you must come to the housewarming party.'

'And Sean?' Bessie queried.

'Oh, is that still on?'

'Jennifer, you know perfectly well how Sean and I feel about each other. He's coming with me to the wedding.'

'I was just wondering . . .' Jennifer hesitated and avoided Bessie's eyes. 'I mean, do you think that's wise . . . In the circumstances, I mean . . .'

'You invited him.'

'Mummy invited him. It was Bernard I insisted who must have an invitation. I was just thinking about you, Bessie. Sean's mother and father are quite understandably concerned about your relationship with Sean. I mean, you told me yourself.'

'I promise you, Jennifer, I'll be as nice to them as I possibly can.'

'But it's how they might be to you . . .'

'Oh, don't worry about that. I'm just going to concentrate on being a matron of honour you'll be proud of. It'll be a happy day, you'll see. Everyone will *want* to make it a happy day for you.'

Jennifer kissed her. 'As long as you're going to be all right,' she said.

'Your mother has bullied me into getting a new outfit. But I dug my heels in and refused to buy the matronly dress and coat she picked out. I've bought a dark royal blue velvet suit and a white frilly blouse to go with it. Very feminine, Sean says. I'd got trousers at first but he made me get a skirt instead.'

'That sounds nice, Bessie . . .' Then she added, somewhat uncertainly, 'And not too young.'

'If you like I'll try it on now to make sure it meets with your approval.' Bessie's tone held amusement.

'No, no. I'm sure you'll look fine.'

'And I haven't been near a tube of paint recently so you've no need to worry on that score.'

'Where's Sean just now?'

'Through in Edinburgh.' She sighed. 'Bernard keeps sending him on jobs away from Glasgow. I'm just hoping Bernard doesn't find any work abroad for Sean to do. If there's any kind of security job comes up in Australia, you can be sure Sean will be the one Bernard will pick to go.'

Jennifer thought that would be a good idea and the best thing that could happen but she refrained from saying so. Instead she changed the subject.

'The buffet supper Mummy has planned sounds wonderful. Freddie's really looking forward to it.'

'I'm going over on Friday night to help her get things organised.'

'That's kind of you, Bessie. Now, I'd better get over to Bearsden. Both Daddy and Freddie have insisted that I stop working in the house and just pamper myself until the wedding. Laura's made appointments for me in the local hairdresser and beauty salon. She's really kind. I'm so glad Daddy's got somebody nice this time. Mummy's all right in her own way,' she added hastily, 'but you know what I mean.'

Bessie laughed.

'Yes, I know what you mean, dear.' She went to the door with Jennifer. 'I'll see you at the wedding then?'

Jennifer smiled and waved goodbye. Going down the stairs she thought – yes, her mother *was* all right. She had her faults and weaknesses but then, who hadn't? Bessie had proved she was far from perfect. It was really very foolish and self-indulgent of her to be taking over Sean's life the way she was. But knowing Bessie, it wouldn't be a conscious selfishness. Her love for Sean was blinding her to what she was doing.

Then she remembered Bernard. If anyone could sort people out, and avoid trouble, he could.

LXII

ANDRINA WAS BLISSFULLY happy. The buffet was all organised. She'd written out a menu for her own benefit. The house was sparkling. She'd polished every corner. Her kitchen was large and had a dining area which had once been a bed-recess. A table in there would hold all the puddings. The Scotch trifle made with lashings of sherry wine was decorated with cherries and looked beautiful in her large crystal bowl. Then there were *crèmes brûlées*, strawberry gâteaux, fresh fruit salad, lemon torte and a chocolate mountain of profiteroles. And of course jelly for the children. All around the kitchen she'd spread platters of roast beef, fresh salmon decorated with cucumber, broccoli quiche, lentil bake, prawn, apple and celery salad, cold poached supreme of chicken set in a Chablis sauce with a lattice of leek and aspic jelly, and of course, green salad. In the sitting room there would be coffee, *petits fours* and chocolate mints. Bottles of white wine would be suitably chilled in the fridge and red wine would await uncorked at room temperature.

Andrina was looking forward to the event. She imagined how she would swan around making sure everyone enjoyed themselves. The occasion would be not just a great success, but a triumph. But there was even more to it than that. It was a smack in the eye for Paul Fisher. Although of course he wouldn't be there to see it. He'd never set foot in the flat since the day he'd been so insulting to her and walked out of her life. It was for good in every sense, she realised now. Clearly he had never appreciated her. She was well rid of him. Now she was extremely excited about Lester Morgan being at the wedding. So far she hadn't met him. She had meant to pop over to Bessie's on the evening he had been there to dinner.

Bessie was not the world's best cook and she'd prepared a wonderful pudding to take over to help Bessie out. Unfortunately, Freddie had arrived to collect Jennifer's case. He had been so flattering about her cooking that she felt she had to offer him supper, and he just stayed and stayed. It would have been so interesting to meet Lester before the wedding, more or less on her own, and she was disappointed she didn't manage it. But she was too polite, too good a hostess, to hasten Freddie away. Lester sounded very nice, as well as being a millionaire. It was the millionaire part that thrilled Andrina the most. Already she had been transported in her dreams, whisked off to America to live a life of luxury and to be pampered and adored as Lester's wife. She dreamed of furnishing a huge house in elegant Williamsburgh, of lying out on the patio sunbathing and sipping tall glasses of iced tea. She dreamed of queening it as a hostess to all the important people of the district and in the art world. She saw herself arm in arm with Lester and him gazing proudly down at her as they strolled into the theatre or to other large houses where they had been invited to dinner. It was a bit difficult to see him clearly in her mind's eye because she had not yet met him. But the description Bessie had given her was enough to create a picture. It was just a little hazy, that's all. It was her enjoyment of being his wife that mattered, the thrill of all the luxury, the petting and pampering. The sex.

In bed at night she vividly imagined them making love. It seemed ages since she'd been with a man and she longed with every passionate fibre of her being for a man to love her, caress her, penetrate her. So intense and vivid were her imaginings and such was the fever of her need that she gave herself an orgasm. Even in sleep she dreamed of being happily married to Lester. By the next day she felt convinced that not only did she already know him, but their impending marriage was a fact. She was singing about the house in seventh heaven. She had always known that she was meant for better things. She could hardly believe that she'd once been tied to a boring, poverty-stricken schoolteacher. Or that she'd once been foolish enough to fall in love with a bully of a man who was still the same coarse, foul-mouthed bouncer in pubs and clubs that he'd always been.

When Bessie arrived with Sean and the food that had been stored in Bessie's freezer, she had become so carried away with thoughts of her happy future that she almost told them about it. But they were full of talk about Jennifer's wedding.

Now Bessie was saying,

'Bridie was telling me that Frank was putting his foot in it and worrying Jennifer.'

'Worry her? How could he worry her?'

'Apparently he thought you'd made a brave mix of guests.'

Andrina shrugged.

'If he meant Robert and Bernard, I couldn't care less. I'll be perfectly charming to both of them, I can assure you.'

Sean gave her one of his hard dimpled smiles. She noticed how strong and white his teeth were. When he smiled he'd almost a predatory look. It reminded her of Bernard in a way. Although it was Bernard's eyes that made him look wicked.

'I think,' he said, 'Frank was meaning how my family would act to Bessie. And that might cause an atmosphere.'

'Oh!' Andrina felt herself flush. She'd forgotten that neither Bessie nor Sean would know about her affair with Bernard. 'Of course. That's what I meant too. I'll see that everyone mixes well and there's a lovely friendly atmosphere. My parties have always been a great success and this one will be no exception, I assure you.'

'Do you want me to stay overnight?' Bessie asked. 'And give you a hand in the morning?'

'No, no, dear. Just help me unpack these things and lay one or two items out to defrost. That roll of meat, for instance, will take absolutely ages. It's as hard as a rock.'

'It's far too much work for you, Andrina. I'll come back for an hour or two tomorrow. Even if it's just to wash dishes and hoover the place.'

'Oh, all right, dear. That would be a help.'

She gave them tea and dainty sandwiches and fairy cakes after they'd unpacked everything and put some of the things in the fridge and others out on platters. She longed for them to go away again. Not because she didn't like them. Indeed she was very fond of them both. But the secret loving way they kept looking at each other and the way Sean often held Bessie's hand or put his arm around her shoulders made Andrina feel lonely. She needed to get back to Lester. Visions of him and their happy future together obsessed her the whole night, and the next morning.

'Are you all right?' Bessie asked eventually. They were having a cup of tea before Bessie went home to dress. 'You're awful quiet. You're not losing Jennifer, you know. You're not losing a daughter, as they say, you're gaining a son.'

'What? Oh yes. No, I'm fine.'

'Well,' Bessie finished her tea, 'I'd better be off. Sean will be back soon and we're picking Lester up at his hotel.'

'I must have a bath with my new bath salts. They have a gorgeous perfume. And I'll take my time and have my make-up and hair just perfect.'

Bessie laughed.

'I'm sure you will. I'd better rush. I'll pick up a taxi outside.'

'Oh, will I phone for one for you? Or do you want me to drive you home?'

'No, no, not at all. There's always plenty of taxis cruising about. You just relax now and enjoy your bath.'

They kissed, and when Bessie had gone, Andrina danced along the hall, round and round, making her skirt swirl out. She never wore trousers – she had such shapely legs, it would be a pity to hide them.

She sprinkled a generous amount of bath salts into the steaming water, undressed, climbed in and lay back with eyes closed.

It was while she was carefully applying her mascara that she remembered her mother. How shocked she would have been to see her now.

She sighed. It was surprising that Sophie had ever managed to conceive. Was it because of her unnatural attitude to sex that her mother hated the child that was the result of that conception?

Andrina leaned forward, chin cupped in hands, and gazed at herself in the mirror. Her mother had hated her. She could face that now. But still she could not understand why. She felt overwhelmingly sad about the coldness she could still feel emanating towards her from Sophie, even from beyond the grave. Probably the lack of love from her mother was the reason she'd turned to Bernard with such passion and appreciation. She could even face the fact of her love for Bernard now. If it hadn't been for her mother, she would have married him. Looking back she realised that Bernard had loved her too. She could have wept. It was only with a determined effort that she managed to banish her mother from her thoughts. She raised her chin and pulled back her shoulders.

She was a beautiful, loving and lovable woman. And this was her happy day. This was the first day of the rest of her life.

She donned her ivory satin underwear. Then the off-the-shoulder ivory two-piece slithered on. She perched the wide-brimmed ivory straw hat on to her glossy crown of auburn hair. Finally her high-heeled ivory shoes complemented her dainty feet and shapely legs. A choker of pearls, high against her creamy throat, made an elegant finishing touch. She stared with satisfaction at her shining reflection in the long mirror. She gave a happy twirl.

With adrenalin pulsing through her veins and almost making her float through the air, she set off to stun everyone in the company, especially Lester Morgan.

LXIII

JENNIFER WAS SO excited that she had become confused, uncertain, even apprehensive. Before, she'd been so busy with working in the house, she had not had any time to think. She hadn't realised how tired she'd become; it wasn't until she'd arrived at Laura's house in Bearsden that the exhaustion hit her. Far from making her feel better, loafing about with nothing to do made her lethargic and depressed. Laura and Robert were out at work during the day. At least on the Thursday and Friday, and it was then that Jennifer sat in the quiet bungalow with time to think.

It occurred to her for the first time that Freddie was quite a few years older than her. She was still only a young girl. She had all her life before her. She was about to start her teacher training course at Jordanhill College. She got on well with Freddie, of course. Who wouldn't? They were good friends. But was that a good enough reason to get married? Was she more in love with Freddie's house than with Freddie? Her mind shuddered back to the nightmare of being homeless and struggling to survive on the streets. No way could she ever risk going through such a scenario again. She longed for the permanent safety of the flat in Roxburgh Street. Did she long for the permanence of Freddie?

Laura had persuaded her to go and have her hair done, plus a manicure and a face make-up on the Saturday. Really nervous to the point of visible agitation by this time, she'd cried out, 'I like my hair long and straight, and I like my fringe. I don't want it changed. It wouldn't be me. I don't want a whole lot of make-up on to try and hide my freckles either. That's the way I am.'

'No one's wanting to change you, darling,' Laura said. 'It'll be a nice treat for you to have your hair shampooed and your make-up and nails done, that's all. You'll be able to relax in the salon and then just come back here and put on your dress and veil.'

It was a white cotton dress with a high Victorian-type stand-up collar edged with a little pleated frill and leg of mutton sleeves. A simple coronet of flowers topped her veil and she was to carry a posy of matching flowers.

She'd gone to the hairdressing and beauty salon, but with bad grace. She felt in what her mother would call 'one of her moods'. She stared with a mixture of gloom and despair at her reflection in the hairdresser's mirror. A freckly-faced wee girl, that's all she was. What on earth was she getting herself into? She didn't want to get tied down in marriage or anything else. She even began to think of her rootless time in London as a sort of freedom.

How could she cope with studying at college, cleaning and cooking and running a house, and looking after a man? Panic set in. She couldn't do it. She suddenly felt childish. She wanted her mother. She longed for her, and needed her as she had longed for her and needed her when she had been a small child. Then she remembered with terrible sadness that her mother had never been there for her when she was a small child. Andrina had always been obsessed with Andrina, and Andrina's needs and problems.

Jennifer could have wept then as she stared at her reflection, and later when she looked into the long mirror in Laura's house. Never before had she felt such desolation and loneliness. Her life stared back at her. Somehow she'd always been either at the mercy of other people or of circumstances.

'You look lovely,' her father said. 'I'm proud of you.'

He didn't know her any more than her mother did. He knew what he wanted, though. He wanted his safe, happy life with Laura. He *liked* being tied down. She doubted if he'd ever experienced true aloneness. Even as a small child she'd felt alone in spirit. Her father had been totally committed to caring about other children, children he called 'deprived'. He had been too busy to notice that she was being neglected and deprived. Oh, not of material things. Andrina had never failed to dress her like a little lady. But always, Jennifer felt, the priority of their love and understanding, as well as their time, had been for other people.

On her way back from the hairdresser's, she passed her granny's house and her sadness deepened a hundredfold. There was nothing for her here now. Once she was twenty-one, she would get the money her granny had left her and she could buy a flat, start a new life in Edinburgh or anywhere.

Yet here she was, doing nothing in her mounting agitation and confusion, as her father and Laura led her from the house. Her vision was blurred by her veil. Her hearing was all but blotted out by the panicky thumping of her heart. She didn't want to hurt Freddie. She didn't want to hurt or embarrass anybody, or to let them down – even her mother. Andrina had gone to so much trouble to organise a wonderful reception.

But oh, the whole thing made her feel sick at heart. She kept asking herself what she was doing and why. The only assurance and comfort she could find as the bridal car sped towards her mother's branch of the Church of Jesus in Rose Street in town was the fact that she could still say no. When the minister asked if she'd take this man to be her wedded husband, she'd say 'No!'

And she'd say no because when it came down to it, she was afraid that one day she'd suffer the same hurt from him that she'd suffered from her parents, especially her mother, the one person she'd once imagined most close to her, and whom she'd most trusted. No, she didn't want to be in that situation ever again. She'd rather be on her own. Safely withdrawn into herself, uncommunicative, uncommitted.

Before she realised it, she was at the church. The car had stopped and her father was helping her out. She was allowing him to arrange her veil and tuck her arm through his.

The organ music of 'Here Comes the Bride' was filling the church. Everyone was standing and looking round at her. Then she saw Freddie. He too was looking round at her. *Her* Freddie. The man in whose arms she'd already lain in the silent darkness of the bedroom in Roxburgh Street. The man who'd already promised to love and cherish and look after her and who had already kept that promise. She was not afraid of him. A smile came like a warm light to her face and with it, a glow of happiness. Freddie wasn't just her best friend. She loved him. And she knew, by the warm light in his eyes, he loved her too. The strength of that love gave her courage. She suddenly felt lucky. She would never need to be alone again. With Freddie by her side, she could cope with her mother, she could tackle anything.

The ceremony progressed and she said 'I do' with total conviction and great joy in her heart.

Then they were officially man and wife.

'This,' she told him as they left the church arm in arm, 'is the happiest day of my life.'

'Mine too,' Freddie said, squeezing her arm. 'Definitely mine too.'

Into the car now, she and Freddie with eyes only for each other. Eventually, however, Freddie said,

'I'm starving. I'm looking forward to the reception, aren't you?'

LXIV

'COULD YOU BEAT it?' Bev cried out. 'I could kill that woman! Cheerfully kill her.'

They were on the way to the reception in Monteith Row in Sean's car.

'It was a bit much, right enough,' Bessie agreed.

'A bit much? A bit *much*? The woman wore white at her daughter's wedding.'

'Ivory,' Bessie corrected mildly.

'White, ivory, what's the difference? Her and that big hat as well. She tried to outshine the bride, steal all Jennifer's limelight, spoil her own daughter's big day.'

Sean intervened.

'Oh, I doubt if it spoiled anything for Jennifer and Freddie. They're so wrapped up in each other they wouldn't even notice Andrina.'

'Everyone else did, though. You couldn't miss the woman. And Jennifer and Freddie certainly won't be able to miss her at the reception. She'll be swanning about showing off all the food she's made. I've a good mind to spill some more champagne.'

'Don't you dare,' Bessie warned.

'Never in my whole life have I ever known such a blindly selfish, egotistical woman.'

'Will you calm down and forget about Andrina. Just try to enjoy the rest of the day for Jennifer's sake.'

'Aye, OK, OK. But it's not going to be easy.'

It's not going to be easy for any of us, Bessie thought. She wasn't particularly looking forward to spending several hours in close proximity with Sean's family. Frank and Bridie were her neighbours and friends, but his parents, and his sister, his grandmother and Bernard were a different matter. She'd seen them in the church. She and Bev and Sean had been sitting in a different pew from the rest of the family and she didn't have the chance to speak to them. They had stared at her with undisguised hostility. Her heart quailed at being confined in the same room as them at Andrina's house.

Courage, Bessie, she kept thinking. The cars drew up one after the other in Monteith Row and everybody piled out and climbed the stairs. The children, noisy and jumping about with energy; the adults polite and restrained. Once in the house, and all crowded into the kitchen, she was introduced to Sean's mother and Bernard's wife, Helen. Helen was elegant in a honey-coloured two-piece and had some warmth in her manner, unlike Bernard, and his brother's wife. Old Martha was eagerly instructing Michael about what food to bring her from the mouth-watering spread. She was a mountain in brown silk topped with a hat decorated with artificial yellow roses.

Andrina, now without the cartwheel hat to hide the shining glory of her ruby-coloured hair, was bright-eyed and bushy-tailed and urging everyone to collect plates and napkins and enjoy the buffet. At one point, while Bessie was trying to ignore the black looks aimed towards her and was attempting to swallow down some salad, Sean's mother, resplendent in an apricot Crimplene dress and pearls, approached, plate in hand.

'I'd like a word with you – from one mother to another.'

In desperation, Bessie looked around for Sean, but his back was to her. He was laughing and talking with Jennifer and Freddie at the other side of the room. Jennifer looked like an excited little girl in her white cotton dress with its Victorian-style high frilled neckline. Freddie had a protective arm around her.

'You're a mother yourself,' Caroline went on, 'and as a mother you must know how I feel. Every mother wants the best for her children . . .'

She had obviously decided to hammer home the mother theme. Bessie groaned inside.

'As a mother, you must know what it's like to worry about your children's future. You want them to be happy and to have a family of their own one day. It's the natural way of things, don't you think?' She paused for a reaction but Bessie was already beginning to feel depressed and it took her a long minute to get up enough energy to speak.

'I understand how you must be feeling.'

'Well, why are you doing this to me? But most important of all, why are you trying to ruin Sean's life?'

'I'm not trying got ruin Sean's life. I love him.'

'Love him? You don't love him. You don't know what love is.'

'How can you say that? You know nothing about me.'

'I know you didn't stick with the man you promised to love and cherish until death do you part. You walked out on your husband.'

'You don't know the circumstances.'

'I know my circumstances. My husband's an alcoholic. I went through hell with him while he was drinking. There were times when he'd spent all his wages on drink and me and the children had nothing to eat. But I stuck by him. I did what I believed to be right for him. *That's* love.'

The Quaker William Penn had once said, 'Never marry but for love . . .' She had not loved Peter, that had been the problem. But oh, she truly loved Sean.

'What's between Sean and me is different altogether from the relationship I had with my husband.'

'Oh, that's quite obvious. Sean's only a boy, for a start. That's your daughter over there, isn't it?'

Bessie nodded.

'She's not much younger than Sean, is she?'

Bessie gazed helplessly over at her daughter. Daisy was even more like her Aunt Moira now than she'd been as a child. The same severe hairstyle, the same hornrimmed glasses. Her husband Nigel suited her perfectly. He was a right old-fashioned-looking berk as well. Bessie immediately felt ashamed of harbouring such uncharitable thoughts and, catching her daughter's eye at that moment, she smiled warmly across at her.

I'm glad, I really am, that Daisy and Nigel are well suited and happy together. And I'm glad, truly glad, that they both seem to get on so well with Peter.

Caroline said,

'She's married a man a few years older than her, hasn't she? And that's as it should be. And, God willing, she and her husband will be blessed with a family one day. And that's how it should be. That's right and natural. You're denying Sean the natural right to be a father as well as everything else.'

'I really don't think,' Bessie said in desperation, 'that all this is any of your business.'

'What?' Caroline gasped incredulously. 'I'm his mother. I carried him in my womb. I watched him grow up. I've loved him and taken care of him for all the years of his childhood. And you can stand there and say what happens to him is none of my business? My own flesh and blood?'

'Sean's not a child any longer. He's a man and how he lives his life is his own business. And how I live my life is my business.'

'Oh really?' Caroline raised a brow. 'I thought you were a religious woman.'

Bessie flushed.

'I'm a Quaker, if that's what you mean.'

'And how, tell me, can you square your present behaviour with your religious beliefs?'

She couldn't. All she could say was, 'We love each other. I can't see how, by loving someone, I'm doing anything wrong.'

'Oh, can't you? Well, if you profess to be a true Christian, I think you should look at the situation and your feelings for Sean again. No doubt it's most enjoyable and flattering to be having a romantic relationship with a handsome, virile man so much younger than yourself. But is it the right thing for Sean? He'll still be in his prime when you're an old woman. Is that the future you want for him? Looking after an old woman?'

Memories of the horrors of nursing Granda flooded Bessie's mind. She felt sick to her very soul.

'Will you excuse me?' she said very politely. 'There are other people I'd like to talk to.'

She moved away with as much dignity as she could draw around herself. She strolled across the room between the crush of children, eyes blurred, not knowing where to go. Bridie was intent on catching one of the children who was hugging a bowl of strawberry jelly to himself and dodging about. 'Frank,' she was crying out, 'get that bowl off him! Other folk want a share of that jelly.'

Bessie smiled at them in passing. *Please don't let me cry.*

Sean was still deep in conversation with Jennifer and Freddie. Three young people having a good time together. She couldn't see Bev anywhere, Andrina was over in the corner smiling and fluttering her eyelashes up at Lester Morgan. They were obviously having a good time too.

Bessie joined Andrina and Lester. Smiling, she said to Andrina, 'The food is delicious.'

Lester agreed enthusiastically.

'I was just telling Andrina what a talented woman she is. That's a talent too – creating such a wonderful meal, *and* being such a charming hostess.'

'Oh absolutely.' Bessie struggled to keep the bright smile on her face. 'I always enjoy coming to visit Andrina. The only thing is I eat so much I put on pounds of weight.'

Lester threw back his head and gave a resounding laugh.

'I was just telling the lady that I'd be as heavy as a prize bull if I came here very often.'

Andrina gazed starry-eyed up at him.

'You can come here as often as you wish, Lester. I admire a man who can appreciate good food.'

'I appreciate all the food and the beautiful things in life, honey. Good food, beautiful women. And believe me, I've seen a few beautiful women in my time, but none that can hold a candle to you.'

Andrina flushed and gave him one of her shy, sideways smiles. 'Oh Lester,' she said in her softest, sexiest, most inviting of voices.

Bessie felt extraneous. She moved away without either of them noticing. She slipped out of the ripple of noise in the kitchen into quietness of the hall. She tried the bathroom door, hoping to find solace in isolation. It was locked. Unexpectedly the tears spilled over as she turned away.

'Darling.' Sean strode towards her and pulled her into his arms. 'What has she been saying? When I asked Gran if she'd seen you, she said Mother had been talking to you.'

Bessie felt ashamed of her lack of control but she couldn't speak, couldn't stop the tears.

Sean's eyes glittered with anger.

'How dare anyone upset you like this. Wait there.'

He strode back into the kitchen before Bessie could put out a hand to stop him. She was in a panic of distress now. Hastily she tried to dry her tears. Her feet faltered towards the kitchen but she didn't feel composed enough to face anyone, far less intervene between Sean and his mother. She turned into the sitting room. At first she thought she was alone with her chaotic thoughts, then she noticed Bev sitting over in the corner, glass in hand.

'That's not alcohol, I hope.' Bessie was immediately jolted out of her own concerns.

'Don't start nagging at me and spoiling everything,' Bev said. 'I couldn't toast Jennifer's happiness in orange juice, for God's sake. I can't stomach the stuff anyway. Never could. What's up with your face? You look as if you need a drink.'

'Never mind about me. You're not just toasting Jennifer's happiness and you know it. You'd be through there beside her if you were, not sitting through here beside a bottle.'

'Aw shut up! Stop being such a wet blanket. Away through with your boyfriend where you belong, and think yourself lucky.'

'Don't try to kid me that you're happy, Bev. Drink doesn't make you happy.'

'Shut up, I said. What do you know about me? What do you know about anything?'

'Come on, Bev. I'll take you home.'

'Piss off. I've had enough of you. I'm going, but I'm going on my own. You stay with lover boy.'

'Bev, please . . .'

'Get your hands off me.' She grabbed the bottle and lurched for the door. Bessie hurried after her, and at the front door again tried to physically detain her friend. But suddenly Bev swung the bottle round and crashed it against Bessie's head. The bottle didn't break but Bessie, knocked back against the lintel of the door, felt as if her skull had been fractured. For a few minutes everything went black. When she came to she was sitting on the floor in a daze.

Blinking and taking a few deep breaths, she managed to pull herself back to her feet.

Far away, in the distance it seemed, were the happy sounds of a celebration. Clutching at the doorway, Bessie tried to steady herself.

LXV

THEY'D RETURNED HOME after the reception and been out again to cruise around in Sean's car searching for Bev.

'Look,' Sean said eventually. 'Enough's enough. Let it be, Bessie.' He swung the car towards home.

'Maybe if we had a walk through Glasgow Green. I was just thinking she might have gone straight from Andrina's into the Green.'

'We drove through there.'

'I know but maybe on foot we'd have a better chance . . .'

'No, Bessie. You've done all you could. It's time to call it a day. And I don't mean just for today either. It's time you left Bev to find her own salvation.'

'She wasn't even wearing her coat and it's a bitter, cold night.'

'Forget her, Bessie.'

'How can I forget her?'

'Try.' He stopped the car and helped her out. Then they climbed the stairs together arm in arm.

Once inside the flat, he helped her off with her cape.

'Cheer up, darling. It's supposed to be a happy day. Be happy for Jennifer. Be happy for us.'

'How can I be happy for us after causing a quarrel between you and your mother?'

'It wasn't a quarrel. I just told her quietly, but very firmly, that she must not interfere.'

He led her through to the sitting room and poured out a couple of glasses of whisky.

'Get this down you and you'll feel better. Remember you promised to set the date for our wedding after we'd been to Jennifer's.'

'I said we'd talk about us. But not tonight, Sean. Not with all this about Bev on my mind. Not to mention the bump on my head.'

'Don't remind me of that, Bessie. I could kill her for doing that to you. I wish you'd let me take you to a doctor.'

'No, I'll be OK after a good night's sleep. Tomorrow . . .'

'I'm off to London tomorrow.'

'But only for a couple of days. Sean, please, I just can't think about anything tonight.'

He put up his hands in good-humoured capitulation.

'OK. You win. We'll get everything fixed up as soon as I get back.'

She lay beside him in bed loving him for his consideration in not attempting to have sex with her when she was so tired and worried. Then loving him so much she wanted to give herself to him heart and soul and body. As if it were for the very last time. She turned to him and began kissing his dear face, his dark eyes, his strong taut features. Her lips moved into his neck and then lovingly over his firm body. He responded by showering her with tender kisses until their bodies and hearts and souls merged.

They fell asleep in each other's arms. In the morning, as usual, he gave her breakfast in bed.

'You spoil me,' she told him.

He dropped a kiss on her head.

'I love you.'

'I know. Being with you has been the happiest, most wonderful time in my life. I never knew before what it was like to be loved and cherished and looked after, as you've loved and cherished and looked after me. You've made me feel worthwhile.'

'You *are* worthwhile, darling.'

'Thank you, Sean.'

'Why the sad face then? We're only at the beginning of our relationship. We've years and years – the rest of our lives – to spend loving each other.'

She raised her face for his kiss.

'You'd better go, Sean. You'll miss your train.'

'OK. See you when I get back.'

'Yes. See you when you get back.'

His firm tread across the hall. The front door opened and shut. Then the empty silence of the house engulfed her. Absently she drank a cup of tea, then put the tray aside and lay back on the pillows. Her mind was lost in confusion. Her heart thumped with fear.

She got up eventually, dressed and went to Meeting. There she sat among Friends in the waiting silence. And gradually, in the peace, her spirit calmed. She waited for the tea and biscuits and friendly chat. She lingered, not wanting to leave the familiar sanctuary and not wanting to part with the others, longing to siphon off some of their courage and spiritual strength. Yet all the time knowing that it was not from them or from anyone that courage and strength must come. She slipped away on her own at last. She walked through the park, hoping yet without hope of finding Bev. *Please have mercy on Bev and keep her from harm*. She took the bus over to see Andrina but Andrina was not at home. She returned to Botanic Crescent and called in at Bridie's house rather than return to the solitude of her own.

Bridie's house was jolly and noisy and didn't give her any opportunity to think.

Frank called over the rabble, 'Sean's away until tomorrow then?'

'Yes, late tomorrow afternoon.'

'Why don't you come round to us for lunch, then? Come early. It'll pass your time and keep you from being lonely.'

'That's right,' Bridie agreed. 'I don't like to think of you in that big flat all by yourself. No word of Bev yet, I suppose?'

'No.' Bessie shook her head. 'Sean and I looked all over the place and no sign of her.'

'She's maybe gone back to London,' said Frank.

'I was wondering about that. There's a man here that she wants to keep clear of . . .' She sighed. 'But I don't know. Poor Bev. It doesn't bear thinking about. I wish I could have helped her.'

'Bessie,' Frank protested, 'nobody could have done more. I don't know anyone else who would have put up with her.'

'And after all,' Bridie cut in, 'she was nothing to you.' Then, seeing Bessie's look of surprise, she added, 'No relation, I mean. It wasn't as if she was your sister.'

Later that evening Andrina and Lester arrived at Bessie's flat. Andrina was bubbling over with happiness. Leaving Lester in the sitting room for a moment, she ran through to the kitchen on the pretext of helping Bessie to bring in the supper trolley. She wanted to have a private word.

'You'll never guess!' she whispered to Bessie.

'You slept with Lester last night and he was wonderful?'

'Yes, but not just that. He's asked me to go back to the States with him.'

'That was quick work.' She sounded sarcastic and she hadn't meant to be. She had slept with Peter the first time they'd been alone. She genuinely hoped Andrina would have better luck than she did afterwards.

'You've agreed?' she asked, but knowing that Andrina had jumped at the chance.

'Of course! We're crazy about each other. It was love at first sight, Bessie. Oh, I'm so happy.'

Bessie kissed her.

'I'm glad, Andrina. I really am.'

'You must come with us. You ought to be at the exhibition. Oh, think of all the fascinating people you'll meet, Bessie. Lester knows lots of artists and people you'd be interested in. Oh do come!'

Bessie smiled. 'Maybe I will. I'm very happy for you, Andrina.'

Next day Bridie wasn't so generous.

'Trust her,' she rolled her eyes, 'to get a rich old man with a bad cough. Next thing we know she'll be back, a wealthy widow queening over us all.'

Bessie shook her head.

'We don't even know if they're going to get married.'

'What do you bet?' Bridie said. 'She won't let him go, Bessie. She's landed him. Now all she has to do is haul him in.'

Bessie laughed.

'A willing victim, though.'

'Yes,' Frank agreed. 'Lester will go to the grave exhausted but after having enjoyed every last minute of his life.'

Bessie glanced at her watch.

'I'd better be going along and getting organised for Sean coming home. I haven't done a thing in the house, not even washed a dish, since before the wedding.'

Frank got up and saw her to the door along with Bridie. 'Oh, I'm sure Sean won't even notice the house. You're all he cares about,' he said.

The words echoed in Bessie's heart as she walked the short distance to her own flat.

Yes, he cares about me. And I care about him. I've been thinking and thinking about what is best for Sean. I know what would be best for me. It would be sheer joy for me to spend the rest of my life with him, to be loved and looked after by him.

That set me thinking. There is a purpose in everything. There was a purpose in me looking after Granda. I learned exactly what it was like.

I couldn't do that to Sean. He would look after me until the very end. I know that. But I couldn't submit him to such an ordeal.

I love him, you see. And I want him to have the very best in life. Not just for now but always.

I want him to fall in love again and with a young woman who can give him the love and loving children he deserves.

But oh, how can I find the courage?

But find it she must.

She'd never considered herself a religious woman. The bigotry of her mother's church upset her. She'd once gone to a service in a Baptist church and cringed with embarrassment when people kept sticking up their hands and yelling hallelujah. She'd more than once visited a Catholic church with Bridie and Frank and the ritual there had felt equally alien to her.

But she did believe in trying to understand the beliefs and the needs of others. To her the Quaker idea of 'that of God in everyone', whatever their God, was what she personally felt most at home with. Sometimes it was hard to find that small light in the darkness of herself or in others but it was something she felt was worth trying to find, and something always to be respected.

She struggled to find the light in her darkness now as she waited for Sean's return. By the time he arrived she had at least found enough strength to tell him that their relationship was over.

He was incredulous at first.

'Darling, you don't know what you're saying. We love each other.'

'Yes, I know. But one day you'll love someone else, Sean. You'll be happy again and you'll have a family and live a normal life.'

'A normal life? What are you talking about? The only normality I want is my life with you.'

'Sean, please try not to make it more difficult for me.'

'Are you trying to tell me you don't love me? Is that it?'

'Oh no. Oh no, Sean, never think that. I love you more than life itself and I'll always love you. It's because I love you that I'm letting you go.'

'Darling . . .'

He came towards her, arms outstretched, but she stopped him in his tracks by the sudden harshness of her tone.

'Just go! Take your overnight case. I'll pack and send the rest of your things out to the cottage tomorrow.'

'They've made you do this,' he cried out. 'They've been speaking to you again.' He was agitated now. His distress was twitching at his facial muscles, fevering his skin.

'Nobody has made me do anything, Sean. I have decided for myself. Now please walk out of here and don't come back.'

'Oh Bessie . . .'

She could see him fighting to contain his tears, struggling to be manly. But he was only a boy. She wanted to take him in her arms and comfort him, mingle her tears with his. Instead she turned away.

'Goodbye Sean.'

She went through to her studio and shut the door. She heard the silence in the rest of the house before the outside door clicked shut.

Only then did she allow the sound of her sobbing to escape.

She picked up her brushes. She didn't need a photograph of Sean in order to paint his portrait. The picture of him was etched for ever in her memory. Still weeping but with the greatest of care and concentration, she began putting paint on canvas. She had given him love. Now she was giving him a kind of immortality.